My Splendid Concubine

3rd edition
- a novel -
Lloyd Lofthouse

Publisher's Note

Certain characters in this work are historical figures, and certain events portrayed did take place. However, this is a work of fiction. All of the other characters, names and events as well as all places, incidents, organizations, and dialogue in this novel either are the products of the author's imagination or are used fictitiously.

This revised and edited 3rd edition combines all previous editions of this historical fiction novel.

3rd edition April 2013
2nd edition February 2009
1st edition December 2007
Copyright © 2013 by Lloyd Lofthouse
ISBN 978-0-9860328-4-4

Cover Art by Denise Killingsworth
The cover of this novel is a photo of the original quilt the artist was commissioned to create for *The Concubine Saga*.
www.denisequilts.com.

D0924564

- PRAISE FOR -

2nd edition of *My Splendid Concubine*

"A powerful novel whose beauty exceeds that of the book's cover."
– Commentary of a Writer's Digest judge, April 2009

Honorable Mentions in General Fiction
2009 San Francisco Book Festival
2009 Hollywood Book Festival

1st edition of *My Splendid Concubine*

2007 iUniverse Editor's Choice
2007 iUniverse Publisher's Choice
2008 iUniverse Reader's Choice

Honorable Mention in General Fiction
2008 London Book Festival

"Packed cover to cover with intriguing characters and plot, a must read for history fans and a fine addition to any collection on the genre." *– Midwest Book Review, May 8, 2008*

"A stunning work that enmeshes imperialism, modernity, miscegenation and plain old desire in a sweaty matrix of destruction and painful birth." *– City Weekend Magazine, May 8, 2008*

"Those who are interested in unconventional romances with an out-of-the ordinary setting will find plenty to enjoy." *– Historical Novel Society, May 2008*

Preface

Robert Hart (1835-1911), the 'Godfather of China's modernism', was the Inspector General of China's Customs Service. He was also the architect behind China's railroads, postal network, telegraph systems and schools. No Westerner, including Marco Polo, has ever achieved Hart's status and level of power in China.

How did this young Englishman achieve success in an alien empire?

What would become an academic and then personal treasure hunt started with Robert Hart's journals written over his fifty-four years in China, some of which had been published by the Council on East Asian Studies at Harvard.

However, a few of these diaries covering a critical period of Robert's early years in China were missing since Hart burned them shortly before his death. Enough information survived to reveal that he had an affair for about a decade with a Chinese concubine named Ayaou, who bore him three children.

My wife, who at the time was researching and writing her next novel, *Empress Orchid*, said there was an underground archive in Shanghai where old books, manuscripts and documents of all sorts had been stored for decades since the Cultural Revolution.

The problem was that the public wasn't allowed access. We went to China believing that if we kept trying we might be able to 'pry' the door open, and eventually a favor was granted.

At six one morning, the gatekeeper led us to a Russian military style brown building that looked as if it were in the middle of being renovated.

Cautiously we went down a crumbling concrete stairway into the underground and found what had once been a bomb shelter during the Cultural Revolution. A series of long damp tunnels led to more rooms.

The pungent odor of insecticide choked us the moment we passed through the vault-like door at the bottom.

Signs everywhere warned us: *"Xian-ren-muo-ru"*—"No Visitors—Officials Only."

Inside were makeshift shelves crowded with dust covered chests. Although searching for records that dealt with the topic of my wife's book, we also searched for Imperial records that detailed Robert Hart's time in China. We wanted information on his early years while still an interpreter for the British Consulate in Ningpo—his years with Ayaou.

We weren't allowed to take anything out, so we returned each morning and spent days in the claustrophobic, chemical laden, damp and dim archive that felt more like a tomb.

In time, we discovered a stack of boxes sealed with white banner shaped paper stamped with red ink that said *Red Guard Headquarters*. These boxes were filled with affidavits about the 'British Imperialist Robert Hart's intimate corrupted life' gathered from the provinces and cities including Canton, Zhejing and Ningpo.

The Red Guards had put Robert Hart on trial more than fifty years after his death to prove that what he had done for China was evil. People who knew of the Inspector General were 'ordered' to confess whatever stories or rumors had been passed to them.

The results were written on crumbling, aging documents in these boxes. What we discovered was a story that speaks to the heart. To do it justice it was decided to use a fictional narrative format and write a historical novel that would blend psychology, sociology, politics and art with the dynamic process of history and weave it into one seamless tapestry while attempting to stay as true as possible to the events of the time.

Part One: Chapter 1
October1854

A repulsive odor assaulted Robert Hart's sense of smell before the *Erin* sailed into sight of Ningpo, China. From the stench, it was obvious that the city'raw sewage from the city ran into the Yung River staining the water dark-brown.

It was more than he could stand. His trip to China from Ireland had not been the adventure he had imagined.

A month earlier, his ship had reached Hong Kong on July 25, where he had witnessed an American mercenary using dead infants for target practice. It didn't help that the infants were floating in Victoria Harbor.

Then there was Chen, the British consulate's ten-year-old Chinese messenger boy in Victoria City who tried to sell him a woman.

"Do all foreigners have different colored hair?" Chen had asked. "Yours look like wet sand. I seen red and yellow too. Does it come in green and blue? Look at my hair." The boy ran a hand through his thick dark hair. When he took his hand away, the hair fell back into place. It looked as if someone had put a bowl on his head to cut it.

Chen, a thin lad about four feet tall, was Robert Hart's first Mandarin teacher. He spoke enough English to correct Robert when his Chinese pronunciations were off.

His first weeks in China were spent on Hong Kong Island at the consulate in Victoria City practicing simple Chinese with this boy. The desk Robert used was by a window that revealed Victoria Harbor, and Chen was usually there when he arrived.

In prior conversations, Chen had asked questions about Ireland. This time he was attempting to earn a bit more than the consulate paid. "I know woman who love see your hair,"

Chen said. "Would you like meet her? She singsong girl and better than prostitute."

When he did not respond, Chen said, "If you want more than evening with prostitute, I arrange time with suitable singsong girl for lower price than decent girl from peasant family. You buy singsong girl as young as thirteen for mere two hundred yuan and make her your concubine. When you return to England, I sell her someone else. I not charge much and she keep you warm in winter. She also save money by not letting merchants cheat you as they do foreign devils."

The price Chen quoted was low. Two hundred yuan was about thirty-three pounds. It shocked Robert that a woman could be bought in China as if she were a piece of furniture.

It bothered him more that he found the idea tempting. "How much would it cost to buy a respectable village girl?" he asked, disgusted with his own curiosity.

Robert had not counted on the Chinese culture seducing him so soon after his arrival. His mind wasn't ready. He had been raised to respect women as equals—not property. He resolved to attend church services twice that Sabbath to atone for being tempted.

"Mr. Hart." A bold voice called.

Robert turned and saw the Governor of Hong Kong, Sir John Bowring, standing in the doorway. His appearance was striking. He had a wide forehead with a receding hairline. What gray hair he had was thick and curly. He wore small wire framed glasses, and his features were rugged as if they had been chiseled from weathered granite. Sir Bowring was also Her British Majesty's Minister to China and was soon to be on his way to Peking to negotiate with the Imperial government.

When Chen saw the governor, he bolted from the room.

Sir Bowring may have heard the conversation, so Robert again regretted his question about the price of a village girl. His face burned with embarrassment. The governor would think him a libertine. What a horrible first impression.

"Don't let the boy shock you," Sir John said. "You are no longer in England. I can see you are upset."

"Not as much as I was when my ship reached Hong Kong," Robert said, wanting to change the subject.

The governor said, "Are you talking about the smell of China?"

"No. There was this American shooting at targets in the water. I do not recall the man's name. I heard he was a mercenary on his way to Shanghai. When I looked closer, I saw he was shooting at little bodies."

"Did he have long, black hair?" the governor asked.

"Yes, I believe so."

"It sounds as if you met Frederick Townsend Ward. He's looking for employment in China to make a name for himself and a fortune." The governor crossed the room to the window and looked out at the harbor. "Look at the shipping," he said. "There are opportunities to be had in China."

"What I saw was horrible," Robert said, as he joined the governor at the window. "I almost lost my supper. He was shooting at three bloated infants."

"They were girls," the governor said. He turned from the view to face Robert. "The peasants living along the Hsi River throw them into the water to get rid of them soon after they're born. Girls are considered a burden in China. It's a common practice. Those who live in poverty don't have much to go around, and feeding a female child means less food for the rest of the family. It might help to know that the infants were dead before Ward shot them."

"How can anyone civilized do such things?"

"The Chinese don't see it that way," the governor said. "Just because it is shocking, don't turn away from such lessons in life."

He placed a hand on Robert's shoulder. His voice softened. "Study everything around you. Go out and walk in the streets and read the shop signs. Bend over the bookstalls and read the titles. Listen to the talk of the people. If you acquire these habits, you'll not only learn something new every time you leave your door, but you'll always carry with you an antidote for boredom."

"I didn't expect to see dead infants as if they were drift wood."

"Nevertheless," the governor said, "take everything that happens and learn from it. In the end, you will be a better, stronger person. Don't shy away from understanding such things even if you disagree with them."

The stench of Ningpo brought him back to the present. It had been weeks since his conversation with Sir John Bowring

3

in Hong Kong. However, that conversation had reminded him of the dead infants. He hoped he wouldn't see any floating in the Yung River.

When the medieval walls of Ningpo came into sight, Robert saw a large fleet of Chinese junks. The dense forest of masts hid most of the city, but a large pagoda in the center towered above everything.

"How can they stand it?" Robert said, trying not to breathe through his nose.

"That's China," Patridge replied. "But to be fair, London and most large European cities aren't much different. You must be from the countryside."

"Ireland, not far from Belfast." What Robert didn't share with Patridge was that he'd left like a runaway child escaping his sins, which he'd hoped to forget but had discovered were like sticky cobwebs trapped inside his head.

Originally, he intended to stay in college for a master's degree then follow his father's example to become a Wesleyan pastor.

That dream ended because Robert drank too much while at college and slept with too many women.

When his father discovered his transgressions, Robert felt he had no choice but to leave and discover a means of redemption.

Besides, the eighteen-hour days spent at college studying had worn him down to the point that he saw authors creeping through the keyhole.

"I thought I detected Irish in your accent," Patridge said.

The two men were standing on deck by the rail. The merchant was six-foot tall and had the shape of an upside-down pear with thin legs. Robert was shorter by several inches.

He had shared a cabin with Patridge, who was the principal agent of the English merchant Jardine, Matheson & Company, the most successful opium merchant in China.

Since Patridge had done most of the talking during the short voyage south from Shanghai, the conversation had been one sided and Robert had learned more of the merchant's life than he wanted to know.

"Compared to the openness of Shanghai, the older cities like Ningpo are worse," Patridge said, "They're rat warrens with narrow twisted streets going everywhere without apparent purpose."

Where Patridge saw rat warrens, Robert saw exotic beauty.

Questions lined up inside his head. Before he had a chance to ask, Patridge said, "Look over there." He was pointing at a flagstaff flying the British ensign. "That's our consulate with the blue tile roof."

His hand swiveled to point out an American flag farther up river. "And over there is the American consulate."

Then he pointed at a bend in the river. "That's the Portuguese where you see their flag."

Robert searched to see the places Patridge pointed out. The *Erin* soon reached the receiving ship-alongside of which she found her berth. There were no docks. All the ships were anchored in the river.

Before parting, Captain Patridge offered an invitation. "If you can't get used to the city, you're welcome to join me in July at the house I built on Zhoushan Island. I guarantee that with the arrival of the summer heat, the humidity, the sewage, the flies and the mosquitoes, you will find Ningpo unbearable. On the other hand, the sea breeze makes my summer home a refuge from refuse." He laughed—an obnoxious sound that grated on Robert's nerves. He was tired of hearing that laugh.

Robert glanced toward the city's ancient wall and wondered what it was like inside. "I appreciate the invitation," he replied, and hurried to climb down into a sampan summoned to take him ashore.

He glanced up at Patridge. "How do I find this Zhoushan Island if I decide to accept your offer?" Robert was being polite. He had no desire to spend a summer listening to Patridge's constant prattle.

"I can tell by the expression on your face that you aren't interested, but I'll bet you'll come." Patridge was smiling. "Just wait until the boredom sets in. When you change your mind, Payne Hollister will show you the way."

"Payne Hollister?" Robert asked.

A disgusted look flashed in the merchant's eyes then vanished. "I'm not surprised they didn't tell you who he was back in Hong Kong or Shanghai," Patridge said. "That's an example of the dammed government bureaucracy for you. They post a man and don't tell him anything about where he is going. Hollister is the British consul here. We shared a house once. He's cooperative. A good man."

Robert wondered what he meant by that.

Patridge shaded his eyes against the glare of the sun and leaned over the rail. "See, he's waiting." He pointed.

Robert turned and saw a man wearing white trousers and a snuff colored coat standing near the water's edge.

The British Consulate was known to the Chinese as the *Yin Kwei Yamen. Yamen* meant a place where a department of a government did business. As Robert was rowed ashore, he felt excitement foaming to the surface. Before reaching land, he was shocked at the sight of a woman rinsing rice in the water that carried sewage from the city.

The sampan ran up on the riverbank into the muck. The Chinese man jumped out and with an effort pulled the sampan closer to dry soil. Since Robert did not want to get his shoes wet, he added a tip to the agreed fare. The Chinese man handed back the extra money and left.

The man in the snuff colored coat walked up to him. "You must be Hart," he said, and offered a hand to shake. "I'm Payne Hollister, the British consul here." His hair was a dark sandy color mixed with a touch of gray, and he had blue eyes.

"How did you guess it was me?" Robert asked.

Hollister pointed toward the British Consulate as if he had not heard the question. "This way," he said, and started walking with sharp, crisp steps.

"After I sailed from Hong Kong to Shanghai on the *Iona*," Robert said, "we were chased by a pirate junk, a Cantonese Comanting with an eye painted on the bow."

He couldn't help himself. The words poured out as if they were lonely. Patridge hadn't been interested, and Robert wanted to share his ordeals with someone.

"That Cantonese pirate almost caught us," he said. "However, we gave the pirates the slip. Then we spent two weeks struggling against the monsoon and ran out of food. If the captain hadn't gone ashore and bought some peanuts and water buffalo meat, we might have starved."

Hollister stopped and closed one eye while studying Robert with the open one. "Every time a ship arrives," Hollister said, "I come to see. I've been working the consulate alone for more than a month since my last assistant quit."

Robert wanted to know why the man he was replacing had quit but felt it wasn't right to pry. Instead, he pointed toward the pagoda inside the city walls. "That looks interesting," he said.

"I'll show you around tomorrow, and I'll give you tips on how to survive here. One thing that helps is the Christian missionaries and a handful of merchants. If we didn't depend on one another for companionship, one could easily go crazy living among these heathens. You're invited to join a gathering of the missionaries and their families this Friday if you're so inclined."

"Of course," Robert said. "Is there a Wesleyan minister among them? If so, I want to attend his services."

"There are Protestants and such," Hollister replied, "but I don't know exactly what religions are here. I do not attend services. I've got better things to do. You can discover more from the ministers on Friday when we cross to the other side of the river where most of them live."

Hollister had some boys carry Robert's luggage to the walled British compound. Once inside, Hollister said, "This is your room. Take the rest of the morning off and settle in."

It was a small room with a fireplace opposite the bed. After Hollister left, Robert opened his trunk. There was a noise. He looked up to see two Chinese women peering through the room's one window, which faced an alley.

They were lovely. He wanted to turn away. He didn't think it right of him to ogle them but couldn't help himself. He'd been without a woman far too long but was determined to stay chaste this time.

They laughed and vanished. Again, Robert was reminded of what he'd learned from the messenger boy in Hong Kong, so he stepped to the window and closed the shutters to avoid other tempting sights that might come along.

It took only a short time for Robert to unpack and put his personal things away. Besides his clothing and a few other items, there were old letters from family and close friends at home in Portadown, in the county of Armagh.

He sat on the bed and read one letter after another. He'd read some so many times that he had memorized the passages.

The letters brought tears to his eyes.

7

One letter from his sister Mary, the oldest of his eleven siblings, described the walk down the hill and over the bridge and along the road with the high trees on both sides that led to the church the family attended.

He'd loved that walk each Sabbath. He missed his friends and family. He especially missed Mary. Since he was the oldest and she was the second, he was closer to her than the others. He compared her laugh to Patridge's. Her's sounded like chimes carried by the wind and was pleasant.

His mother had offered a daguerreotype of the family to take with him, but Robert had left it behind. He'd felt guilty every time he looked at it and lost sleep from imagining what thoughts must've lurked behind their eyes because of his behavior in Belfast.

It didn't take long for Robert to discover that Hollister kept a concubine. He called her his wife, but they had never officially married. She stood about five-foot and had a triangular face with a wide forehead and a small chin.

"This is Me-ta-tae," Hollister said, matter-of-fact, as if he were pointing out his hat or cane. He patted the top of her head as if she were a pet. "Don't mind her. She lives in the consulate with me. She makes life easier by doing the cooking and cleaning. She washes our clothes too."

Robert soon discovered the Christian ministers in Ningpo called her 'Hollister's whore' when Hollister wasn't around.

This kind of talk bothered Robert. He'd been raised to respect women, so he made it a point to treat Me-ta-tae with courtesy to make up for the cruel things some said of her.

The city of Ningpo had been built in the tenth century during the Tang Dynasty. The river protected it on one side, and it was encircled with medieval walls and a deep moat. There was a lake inside the walls with a canal leading through an open gate under the wall that allowed small boats in from the river.

When Hollister took Robert on the tour, he found the streets, houses, wood carved doorways and windows intricate—a hint of a culture he was eager to unwrap layer by layer.

"They live like rats," Hollister said. "The cities were planned without logic. The streets are like a twisted maze. It's easy to get lost."

Robert didn't find the city a rat warren. He found it fascinating.

Later, when he was alone, he explored the noisy business district along the main east-west street. It was a jumble of storefronts and noodle shops hung with glazed duck carcasses. Dry good shops, job printers, and bakeries were crowded together. Pharmacies sold roots and herbs, powdered deer antlers, withered frogs and snake glands. Each narrow alley was the center of a different industry—one creating things out of bamboo and another making lanterns. It was all packed into a ghetto about a mile and a half across.

A merchant from Shanghai, a friend of Hollister's, came to visit, and he wasn't alone. He arrived at the consulate with four Chinese concubines, and it was obvious he was proud of his acquisitions.

To his consternation, Robert found he was having trouble keeping his eyes off the girls. He didn't care for their painted faces, but they had beautiful black lacquer hair and a delicate bone structure.

"Where did you meet them?" Robert asked.

The American was lanky with narrow shoulders, long arms and legs. He had huge ears and large green eyes. He looked ungainly like a scarecrow that had escaped from a cornfield. He reminded Robert of Ichabod Crane, a character from *The Legend of Sleepy Hollow* by Washington Irving.

"I didn't meet them," the American replied. "Women are traded here like goods. If you want one, I'll introduce you to the matchmaker. She specializes in getting women for foreigners. You can pick from Korean girls or girls from Siam or Vietnam. If you are willing to pay a premium, she claims she can get you a Han Chinese from a respectable family.

"My girls come from Kansu province in the east where the peasants sell their daughters to avoid starvation. All four were virgins when I paid for them. I wouldn't have it any other way."

"Fascinating," Robert said. His education of China was continuing quickly. The messenger boy in Hong Kong was only the primer.

"I'll introduce you to the old hag, and she'll hook you up. What you get depends on how much you are willing to pay. That way, you will have a girl to keep your bed warm. It gets cold here in winter."

"Let me think on it," he replied, wondering why everyone considered Chinese girls marvelous bed warmers. Was that all a woman was good for in China? If that was true, it was a horrible fate.

"No problem," the American said. "Ningpo isn't that far from Shanghai. When you are ready, make a trip back. Meanwhile save enough so you can buy a pair of lovebirds. That way you will have one sleeping on either side of you. If my girls don't please me, they know I'll send them back to Kansu and starvation."

He was glad when the American turned toward Hollister. From the heat he felt spreading across his face, he must have been beet red to the tips of his ears. He wasn't sure if he was disgusted or embarrassed.

When Robert mentioned that he wanted to employ a Chinese man to teach him Mandarin, Hollister said, "Don't waste your money or time, Hart. They will cheat you and you'll learn nothing. When I first arrived here, I hired one. He confused me. Just follow my example. I make do. Besides, it is their place to understand us. We don't have to understand them."

Robert disagreed and hired a teacher anyway. He made a point of not telling Hollister. The cost was seven yuan a month, about one British pound.

However, the teacher wasn't that good. He didn't have much patience, but he told Robert the reason the Chinese built cities the way they did.

When Robert first asked, the teacher looked over his glasses and studied his student's face as if he were stupid. "The answer is simple," the teacher said. "The streets are narrow and crooked to keep evil spirits out and confuse them when they get inside."

This was Robert's first lesson that the Chinese were superstitious.

"It would help," his teacher said, "if you were to buy a concubine and study the language with her."

Learning Mandarin turned into a lonely and tedious task. It didn't help that his teacher snapped at him when he mispronounced words. He was also assigned to help the ship captains and European merchants do business with the local Chinese Maritime Customs House in Ningpo. This became a challenge as he hadn't mastered a rudimentary knowledge of the language, but he had no choice. It was his job. He was determined to make the best of it and didn't complain.

Somehow, he managed to translate between the English merchants and the Chinese officials, who spoke no English. It was as if he'd been tossed in the fire and had to avoid being burned. It didn't take long to guess why the last interpreter must have quit.

Two weeks after arriving in Ningpo, a Chinese servant named Guan-jiah was assigned to him.

Guan-jiah told Robert he'd been born near the end of 1836, which according to the Chinese calendar was the year of the Monkey.

He spoke clumsy English but understood more. He was a bony, short man with a turned-up nose and eyes set far apart. He kept his skull shaved except for a tail of hair called a *queue* growing from the back of his head. He had long ear lobes, which he was proud of because they resembled Buddha's ear lobes.

The Chinese believed this was a sign that a person was born to be kind-natured, and he was sometimes too agreeable. He demonstrated a deep desire for knowledge and proved to have an excellent memory.

"This servant of yours is an odd lot," Hollister said in a low voice when Guan-jiah was doing chores outside, "but maybe that's because he applied to become a servant inside the Forbidden City when he turned thirteen."

"What do you mean?" Robert asked. "How does applying for a job make you odd?"

Guan-jiah was hard working and seemed honest. His behavior had not marked him as strange. His voice sounded like a girl's, but what was strange about that? He was still young and hadn't grown into his man's voice yet.

Hollister smirked. "You have much to learn, Hart. You can't apply for a job inside the Forbidden City unless you're a eunuch."

"No!" he said, shocked. How could Hollister say something so vicious? "Do you mean Guan-jiah had his testicles removed?" Robert did not want to believe it was true.

Hollister nodded. "He lost more than that. They chopped off his member too. He's flat as a woman down there. He didn't get the job, so he came home and learned English instead and started working as a servant for foreign merchants. This job is a move up for him—more pay."

"Why would a man castrate himself to get a job? That's madness!"

"Live here long enough and you'll see many crazy things that make no sense. I have better things to do than talk about your servant. He is odd, because he chopped his member off before he turned thirteen. One thing to learn is that you should never trust the Chinese. What kind of person in his right mind would do something like that?"

Robert later learned that what Guan-jiah had done for his family was a sign of *piety* and respect for his elders. He'd sacrificed his manhood to help his family survive. When he failed to get the job in the Forbidden City, he'd gone to work for foreigners. What he was doing to help his grandparents, parents, uncles and aunts and siblings caused him to *gain face* for the sacrifice but *lose face*, because he worked for foreigners.

At first, he found this strange, but once he learned the true meaning behind *piety* and *gaining* or *losing face*, it was easier to accept. Guan-jiah was willing to sacrifice for his family. Robert respected that.

"Look, Master," Guan-jiah said, before Robert's first month in Ningpo ended, "if you want to go out and buy anything, I will help you save money. Tell me what it is you want and let me go to the shop and buy it for the Chinese price. If you try, they will charge you as much as ten times what I will pay." He smiled a pleasant smile that reminded Robert of one lass he had seduced in Belfast.

Robert stared at Guan-jiah thinking that he wasn't exactly a man but was closer to being like a woman without breasts. If Guan-jiah had let his hair grow long instead of shaving his head almost bald, he would have been cute.

The eunuch's skin was smooth like a woman's and his eyelashes appeared feminine. Robert found this thinking strange and made it a point to avoid his servant as much as possible for the next few days. Eventually, he forgot that for an instant he'd thought the young man oddly attractive.

He decided to test Guan-jiah to make sure he was honest. He went to the shop without telling his servant and found out what the asking price was for a foreigner. Then he sent Guan-jiah.

After the servant proved himself, he let the eunuch do the shopping. If Guan-jiah made a small profit for himself, that was acceptable.

As the years went by, Guan-jiah proved his loyalty and worth many times. He stayed with Robert to the end.

On rare occasions, when Hollister had someone in for dinner, usually one of the merchants such as the American that looked like Ichabod Crane, the visitor often arrived with a concubine.

This reminded Robert of the easy pleasures this alien land offered—thoughts that bothered him. It didn't help that his Mandarin teacher suggested several times that a concubine would help him learn the language faster.

This triggered wild, erotic dreams where he had two or more of the delicate, dark-haired women in his bed. Having such dreams made him think he was about to lose control and left him feeling as if he were a carpet that had the dirt beat out of it in Ireland only to be walked on and soiled once in China.

He didn't want others to see him as one who was into lasciviousness even in his youth's worst agony. He wanted others to see him as a God loving man who worked hard by day and treated others with respect and courtesy.

However, his nature, as he understood later, wanted to believe in love like Shakespeare's *Romeo and Juliet* but without the tragedy. To old China hands, such as Captain Patridge, such thinking made Robert into an old-fashioned nut, or to the Chinese a *cooked seed*, meaning someone who lived in a fantasy world.

In time, his perspective underwent a gradual change. Eventually, when he saw a pair of love-ducks idling in the waterweeds in spring, he admired them for what they had.

On one snowy night, he saw by the light of the moon the reflection of a white mountain sandwiched between clouds making it look transparent, and he was moved almost to tears believing it was God's way to show him love—nature was man's best mentor, as the Chinese said. It just took a practiced eye to see it.

Robert often walked alone in the evenings along the muddy boat-trackers' footpath beside the river. Western ships sat at anchor with lanterns glowing from aft windows.

Those lights floating above the water created a scene that was poetically beautiful—almost as if the world had turned into a setting full of quiet and passionate people and the boats into fairy tale castles.

Then at other times, he heard the pirates and the war junks in the river firing cannons at one another, and the violence shattered his tranquil mood.

Early in March 1855, Hollister moved from the consulate. "I built a thirty-eight-foot sloop for a price I could never get outside China," he said, "so I'm going to live on it."

Robert wondered what it was going to be like living alone in the consulate. Of course, he had Guan-jiah and Hollister during the days, but at night there was only silence. Robert grew up in a house full of people and even at college he had his fellow students as company.

"Have you christened your boat?" Robert asked.

"And waste a good bottle of wine." Hollister laughed. "There's no need for that. It's called *The Dawn*. I will keep my sloop anchored in the river with the rest of them. It's the only way to escape Ningpo—its stench, its smothering walls and prying eyes."

It was the way Hollister said those last two words that caused Robert to suspect he knew what the missionaries were saying about him behind his back.

"He's going to hell living with that whore." Robert heard one pastor say.

"If he gives her up and asks Christ for forgiveness, he still has a chance for redemption," another replied. "But nothing can save her. She's doomed."

"I disagree," a third pastor said. "If she takes Christ into her life, she will be forgiven."

Robert's father was a pastor, so he wasn't sure what he should think. He believed that Christ was not as judgmental as some of the ministers thought. After all, He'd said, *'Let him who is without sin cast the first stone'* when he'd defended a woman accused of adultery.

14

Robert had trouble sleeping. During the long nights, every sound in the empty consulate woke him. Even the silence bothered him. He lay on his bed staring at the ceiling for hours. Noisy crickets would have been better than this.

At times, he saw things in the dark. When he got up to confront the phantoms, they evaporated. He wondered if he were going insane.

In desperation, he convinced Hollister to play chess with him in the early evenings and attempted to lead their conversations away from China and the topics the missionaries usually brought up. His goal was to keep Hollister there so the nights wouldn't seem so long.

"Have you read any Dickens?" Robert asked one rainy night. "*Oliver Twist* is an interesting story about the workhouse and child labor and the recruitment of children as criminals. I was wondering what you think of the hypocrisy it reveals through Dickens' sarcasm and dark humor?"

"Do you find it wrong that the children should be used as criminals?" Hollister asked in a challenging tone.

Robert didn't understand why Hollister was so upset. "Isn't it obvious?" he replied. "Children should be raised properly and be taught the virtues and the word of God. They shouldn't be slaves risking their lives for the betterment of some rogue."

"Well, I haven't read *Oliver Twist,* but I believe it's better to be working for thieves than driven to an honest death in the workhouse where you never get enough to eat. I should know. My mother died soon after my birth, and my father died when I was six. I spent several months in a workhouse before I found my auntie."

"You were in the workhouse?" Robert replied, shocked. "You're fortunate you had a loving aunt to rescue you from such a horror."

"She didn't rescue me. I escaped and found her. She was my father's sister. Until I knocked on her door, I'd never seen her before. My father didn't approve of her. He believed in God, and she didn't. She was kind enough to take me in. After I finished my education, she arranged this position in the British consulate through an acquaintance. She was good to me—better than my father was. He taught me nothing but verses from the Bible and when I didn't learn fast enough, I'd feel the back of his boney hand."

Robert attempted getting the conversation back to books. "You should read *Oliver Twist*, but since you haven't, what books have you read?"

Hollister snorted. "I read *The North China Herald* and the *London Times* when it comes in," he replied. "I don't have time for books. However, I do have time for a good game of cards or chess, and our games would be more entertaining if we wagered money. I'll match you five yuan for each game."

"Five!" Robert said. He'd never gambled before. "Let's start with one yuan." He was willing to risk that small amount. After all, he beat Hollister three out of four games.

After they started gambling, Hollister paid more attention to what he was doing, and he won half the games. Once money was involved, the conversation dried up but Hollister stayed later.

When he won, Hollister scraped the money off the table with a cackle of glee. "I'm going to take all your money," he said. "That last move of yours was stupid. Now I've got you."

Hollister had a few traits in common with one of Dickens' other characters, Mr. Ebenezer Scrooge from the *Christmas Carol*. When he lost, he cast dark glances at Robert as if he were cheating. That made Robert feel uncomfortable, but it didn't stop him from playing his best. Besides, he found the man's disagreeable character better than being alone.

Several times over the next few months, Hollister sailed away for days at a time. When he did this, Robert had conflicting emotions. On one hand, he envied Hollister for living as he wanted—something he was sure he'd never copy.

However, it bothered him when Hollister left without letting him know, and the empty nights grew longer.

When mornings arrived, it was a treat to have Guan-jiah walk through the gate to start his workday. Robert taught him how to play chess and occasionally managed to get him to stay late for a game.

Since all but one of the missionaries lived across the river and seldom came into Ningpo, days passed where he didn't see one English soul. He spent his evenings reading the old letters, which turned into a dull ache that took away his energy and enthusiasm for the next day's work.

He didn't think he could have felt lonelier if he'd been the last penguin in Antarctica. He reconsidered Patridge's invitation to spend the summer on Zhoushan Island. The opium merchant's noxious laugh and endless chatter would be better than this.

One Wednesday before sundown, Me-ta-tae visited looking unhappy. She wore black silk pants and a deep-red, patterned blouse with five bats flying above several lotus blossoms. Her hair was tied back into a bun with a silver metal pin that had dangling crystals hanging from it holding the bun together. This exposed her appealing pixie ears, slender neck and delicate bone structure. Her skin looked pale and as smooth as creamy porcelain.

Robert couldn't help himself. His fingers tingled with the desire to explore her body.

Intending to cheer her up, he hurried to the consulate garden and cut a dozen dark-red roses.

Her eyes fluttered and she attempted to hide a smile when he presented them to her.

"The weather is perfect for the roses," he said, seeing this as an opportunity to practice his Mandarin. He also wanted to keep her longer. She was better company than Guan-jiah. "The color contrasts well with your skin."

She touched one petal. "The dew still clings to it," she said, and smiled. One drop clung to a fingertip, and she examined it as if it were a precious jewel.

The sight of her doing this reminded Robert of his sister Mary when something made her exceptionally happy such as seeing interesting shapes in the clouds.

"This season brings out the best vegetables they sell in the market," she said. Her eyes met his. The way she looked at him made his stomach ache. He hid his hands behind his back before he reached for her. He stared at her lips imagining what they would feel like against his, and his thoughts tangled into knots.

"I have seen you walking alone beside the river in the late afternoons," she said.

"I enjoy those walks." He managed to get out, knowing exactly why he was feeling nervous. "I miss your cooking."

He couldn't think of anything else to say, and his Mandarin was improving but wasn't good enough for a conversation with depth to it.

He didn't want her to leave.

"The prices are better this time of year," she said. Her eyes avoided his. He watched her struggle to keep her shy smile under control. It was obvious she was enjoying this as much as he was.

"The vegetables further south are of a better quality than here," she said. "Tell me what you want, and I will cook for you. Maybe you do not like walking alone beside the river. Maybe you would like me to join you."

Robert imagined Me-ta-tae walking beside him and cooking in the kitchen. When she had lived in the consulate with Hollister, she'd done all the cooking. When Hollister had moved out, the good food went with him.

"I'm pleased that you came for a visit," he said. "How is it on *The Dawn* with Mr. Hollister?"

Her expression turned sour. Robert regretted driving her smile away.

"I hate it!" she said. "I don't like living on a boat."

Robert shifted from foot to foot. "Is there anything the consulate can do for you?" he asked.

She stamped a foot. "I'm bored and lonely."

"I understand," he replied, and allowed one hand to escape from behind his back and touched Me-ta-tae's bare arm above her wrist with his fingertips. Her skin was soft and inviting. He imagined her living in the consulate with him and saw her walking naked through the empty rooms. He blushed at his thoughts and jerked his hand back as if burned.

"Mr. Hollister won't allow me to entertain my friends on his boat. And when he loses at horses or cards, he yells and hits me. He scares me when he does that." She pulled up a sleeve to reveal a bruise on her upper arm.

It was difficult for Robert to believe that Hollister had hit her. He was supposed to be a gentleman. Robert was sure that the government did not tolerate such behavior. The bruise must have been from an accident.

When she left, he bitterly felt the isolation and realized that he'd come to China without much thought. That night was full of lusty dreams. In the morning when he awoke, he discovered the blankets twisted around his legs, and he had an enormous erection.

The next day, Robert spent most of the time thinking of his passion, which overpowered reason and conscience. He saw his life as a Christian full of constant warfare, because he had to struggle just to deny lust. However, it was a necessary fight to live soberly, righteously and godly.

That Saturday, Guan-jiah said that Me-ta-tae was back and wanted to see him.

He invited her inside. As night arrived, they sat before the fire in his room and he served jasmine tea. The look on her face told him that something was bothering her. "Is something wrong?" he asked.

"I'm worried that Mr. Hollister is going to abandon me," she said, as tears filler her eyes.

William Lay, who Robert had stayed with while in Shanghai on the way to Ningpo was the assistant to the British Vice-Counsel. Lay had told Robert what happened to women who lived with foreigners.

Hart couldn't stand the thought of Me-ta-tae becoming a whore for sailors. "Hollister would be stupid to abandon you," he said. "I'd never do that."

He regretted his words immediately but said nothing to change their meaning. Instead, he imagined that Hollister would sail away, and she'd be his woman. After all, she wasn't Hollister's wife in the Christian way. She was his concubine. He paid for her like buying a hen. It wasn't like adultery.

"I'd treat you better," he added, and felt the heat in his face as it turned red. He wondered if he had enough to buy her.

Me-ta-tae's lower lip trembled.

Without thinking of the consequences, Robert took her into his arms. She looked at him with eyes full of tears.

Hot blood rushed into his head and he kissed her neck. The warm scent of her skin was intoxicating. His hands found their way under her blouse, and he caressed her breasts.

They moved to his bed and their clothing ended on the floor. Robert sensed movement outside his half-open door but ignored it. Touching her naked body excited him beyond his self-control and his resolve to stay abstinent evaporated.

Soon after he entered her, it was over.

Avoiding his eyes, she slipped off the bed and dressed.

"Don't go." There was a scratchy, pitiful sound in his voice as if he were begging. He couldn't stand it. "Tell Hollister I'll buy you if he doesn't want you."

He heard a scuffling noise outside his door as if someone was hurrying away. Then Me-ta-tae left.

He felt confused and empty. It wasn't as if she were the first woman he'd been with, but that thought didn't stop him from feeling cheap. With her abrupt departure, he discovered that he had a yearning for something more, but he couldn't put words to it.

The next morning Guan-jiah came to tell Robert that Hollister was outside asking for him. "He's angry, Master. I don't recommend speaking to him. Not after last night."

He felt terrible. She must have told Hollister what happened. He despised himself. Me-ta-tae had come to him for comfort. He couldn't deny that she was desirable, and he was a bull in heat. It was a mutual act, but it was still a defeat.

He didn't want to face Hollister, so he said, "Make excuses for me, Guan-jiah. Send him away."

Robert felt as if he were a coward but what other choice did he have if he wanted to avoid a fight. Jealousy was unpredictable and dangerous, and Hollister had every right.

Guan-jiah nodded and left the room.

"What do you mean he isn't here?" Hollister yelled. Robert heard every word from where he was hiding behind the door. "Not only does he cheat at chess, but he's trying to steal my woman too. You tell him I'll be back."

Robert was mortified. He never cheated at chess. How could Hollister say such a horrible thing? And he wasn't stealing his woman. She had come to him willingly, and he wanted to buy her.

Hollister didn't return to work for a week. Then he quit his job with the consulate and sailed away.

When Me-ta-tae went with him, Robert felt more despondent. The affair left him feeling guilty. The fact that Hollister quit surprised him. The man never had enough money because of his gambling, and he lived beyond his means.

Maybe his reason for leaving was to avoid his creditors. Maybe it had nothing to do with Robert seducing his concubine.

Later, Guan-jiah said, "Master, do not think of that woman. Me-ta-tae is not good. She seduced the previous interpreter, and Master Hollister was angry with him too. They had a big fight. The next day that foreigner was gone. I

20

followed her once and discovered she was having sex with one of the merchants too."

Robert looked at him sharply and remembered the noise in the hallway. He'd been watching. He started to scold Guan-jiah but fought back his anger. Could it be that his servant was living vicariously through watching others have intercourse, because he couldn't?

He kept silent out of pity. Despite such depravity, Guan-jiah had a good heart. Robert refused to judge him. What would he have done?

"Master," Guan-jiah said, "it is best to take life easy and to find your way across the river by searching out stepping-stones hidden just below the surface. Nothing is wrong with falling and getting soaked sometimes."

By mid-June, Robert could scarcely breathe because of the sultry heat. He spent twelve hours a day studying Chinese, several more hours working at the consulate and a few attempting to sleep. The mosquitoes made it impossible. He recalled Captain Patridge's invitation and felt it was a good way to escape.

On July fourth in 1855, he received a letter from his friend William Lay in Shanghai informing Robert that he had been nominated to the position of provisional assistant in the consulate with a salary of 270 pounds a year, about twelve hundred Chinese yuan.

Robert determined that whatever his income, one-tenth would go to charitable and religious purposes. It was his way to atone for what had happened between him and Me-ta-tae.

He had now spent enough time in China to earn some vacation time, so he left Ningpo during the hottest part of summer to stay with Captain Patridge not realizing how much that decision was going to change his life.

Chapter 2

When some of the men around the table laughed, it reminded Robert that Patridge's stories had gone on for what felt like hours.

"We were scared for our lives," Patridge said. "In 1842, I worked on a ship carrying opium along the coast of China. A monsoon struck, and my ship and another were wrecked on the island of Formosa. The crews consisted of 180 Bengalis and 13 white men. The natives captured us and immediately beheaded the Bengalis. I was terrified watching all those heads hit the ground with my hands tied behind my back.

"The thirteen of us that remained alive felt we were doomed until the ship's carpenter had a great idea. He said we should kowtow to the governor of Formosa by standing on our heads." He paused and looked around the table. "And we did."

"Gentlemen, it worked. This governor was so impressed that he spared our lives and kept us in prison instead. Eventually we gained our freedom. I'm sitting here today telling you about the time I came a chop away from the grave." He put his hands around his neck, stretched it and crossed his eyes.

Robert had trouble believing the tale, so he allowed his mind to drift to other thoughts. He didn't enjoy the stories.

However, if he had to put up with this to escape the isolation and stifling heat of Ningpo, he would. It was a small price to pay. On the other hand, if the story was true, he might be able to learn something. It wasn't that important to listen though. Robert did not expect to be shipwrecked anytime soon.

Patridge's house was on the western end of Zhoushan Island with the mainland about five miles away. It squatted on a hill close to a hundred feet above sea level. Robert wasn't the only houseguest. The *Maryann's* captain, a man named Roundtree, had come ashore too and was staying in the house with three of his officers.

At dinner the night, Patridge, Captain Roundtree, his officers and Robert sat at a table on the veranda while concubines served food. The first course was a delicious soup made from lily flowers, black mushrooms and sea delicacies. Robert sipped from a glass of red wine and listened to the conversation instead of taking part.

From the veranda, Robert saw the track they had used to reach the house. It looked like a brown string winding its way through thick stands of trees and checkered green farmlands toward the top of the hill. When typhoons roared in from the Pacific, raced across the East China Sea and slammed into the island, the twenty miles of hills slowed the storm's impact.

Ningpo was about fifty miles to the south. Shanghai was a bit farther to the north. If you sailed west into the bay, you eventually reached the city of Hangzhou. Robert recalled a conversation he and Guan-jiah had. It took place during the trek to the house that morning with the others from the *Maryann.*

"Guan-jiah," Robert said, "before I came to China I read *The Travels of Marco Polo.* Do you know of him?"

"No, Master," Guan-jiah replied.

"He came to China from Europe more than six hundred years ago and served under Kublai Khan during the Yuan Dynasty. Polo wrote that Hangzhou was the finest and noblest city in the world."

"Hangzhou was the capital of the Southern Sung Dynasty, Master," Guan-jiah said. "I've heard it is beautiful. Sung philosophy says that we have the power in our minds to overcome our emotions."

"Marco Polo believed it was God's will that he came back from China so others in the West might know what he'd seen." Robert turned to his servant, who was the last in line. "Do you believe in this Sung philosophy, Guan-jiah?"

"The Sung said that if you know yourself and others, you would be able to adjust to the most unfavorable circumstances and prevail over them."

"That's admirable, Guan-jiah. You never mentioned you were a scholar. If the Sung Dynasty was that wise, I want to see Hangzhou one day."

"I am no scholar, Master, but I must believe in the Sung philosophy to survive. I have read and contemplated much literature. However, I am like a peasant and have never mastered calligraphy. It is a skill that has eluded me."

"How old were you when you studied this philosophy?"

"I was eleven, Master, two years after I was sent to Peking."

That meant Guan-jiah had been neutered at nine. How unfortunate. Robert didn't want to offend the eunuch, but he was curious. "Why were you sent to Peking?" he asked.

"To work, Master. My family was starving. It was the only way I could help, but I failed." He stared at his feet in shame.

"How can you say you failed?" Robert said. "After all, you are paid well compared to most Chinese peasants. Your family does not go hungry, and they have shelter."

"But they suffered for many years," Guan-jiah said, "and that is my burden. After I failed in Peking, I went into a Buddhist monastery. One of the older monks spoke English, and he became my teacher. When I was fourteen, I returned to Ningpo and went to work for foreign merchants. Now I work in the consulate for you."

Roundtree's voice intruded on Robert's thoughts and brought his focus back to the dinner table. "I heard that you spelled your name differently with another 'r' in front of the 't'. If that's true, why did you change it?"

"What?" Robert asked, thinking the question was directed at him. Then he realized that the question had been directed at Patridge. No one noticed he'd spoken.

"I never changed my name," Patridge responded. "Why would I?"

"I've heard it said a man named Partridge caused some mischief about 1841 back in London. He dropped that first 'r' so his name would become Patridge making it harder to be tracked down."

Patridge shook his head with a look of feigned innocence. "Nothing happened to cause me to change my name. It's always been Patridge."

Robert wondered what this was about. Right then the main course arrived, and he was distracted. He was so hungry

24

that he forgot what he'd been thinking. Dinner consisted mainly of a leg of boiled mutton, several roast pheasants, roasted goose and a juicy piece of bacon.

"Here's another story," Patridge said, pounding the table for emphasis while laughing.

This was like the food Robert ate at home in Ireland. Until that moment, he hadn't realized how much he had missed the taste of food like this. Saliva filled Robert's mouth. He reached for the platter of meat. As he was spearing the meat with his fork, his eyes searched the table taking in the mashed potatoes and the bowl of brown gravy. His stomach grumbled in anticipation.

After Patridge regained his composure, he said, "We were halfway between Hong Kong and Shanghai becalmed in a small cove. Just a mile from us, but closer to the beach, were the pirates who'd been chasing us."

"Are you talking about the *Iona*?" Robert asked.

"Of course," Patridge said. His eyes opened wider. "You were there too."

Robert vaguely remembered seeing him on board the schooner, but he had not seen him once during the pirate episode.

"Chinese pirates are devils," Roundtree complained. "You'd think the blasted Imperial navy would do something about them."

"If Sir John Bowring wasn't handing out licenses to fly the British flag to every smuggler and pirate along the coast, maybe the Chinese navy might be able to do something about it," Robert said.

A stunned silence settled around the table until one man cleared his throat. Robert squirmed in his seat. He wondered what he had said to cause this response. Maybe it was best to keep his mouth shut and listen.

"It doesn't matter what Sir John is doing," Patridge said, breaking the uneasy silence. "We didn't need the Chinese Imperial navy on the *Iona*. A little adventure adds flavor to life if it doesn't hurt profits. Don't you remember me telling the captain to lower the ship's boats so we could row over and give those pirates a fight?"

"I must have been below deck when that happened," Robert replied. He decided to say nothing more on the subject. He didn't care much for braggarts. After all, Patridge wasn't a bad sort. The meal was a feast, and Robert was stuffing himself. No need to embarrass his host.

"That blasted captain said the water was too choppy," Patridge continued, "and when that calm ended, we set sail. Very disappointing. I was looking forward to a good fight."

If Patridge was changing the facts to suit his storytelling, what else was he embellishing? Robert shrugged it off. If the man wanted to make himself sound like a lion, who was Robert to complain?

The warm but fresh air, the conversation, the bounty of good food and the lovely concubines made for a satisfying evening. Patridge treated his concubines like servants. Robert was confused. He wasn't sure what the status of a concubine was yet. Maybe it was a combination of things besides keeping a bed warm at night.

After a while, Robert noticed that each of the six men had a concubine serving him—one standing behind each man.

Patridge started another story about a merchant at a port in China. "This merchant was lonely, so he bought a Chinese woman for seventy-two yuan. The girl was warranted sound, virgin, and respectably connected. However, the merchant heard her speak English and Bengali. It turned out she'd been a common whore for the commonest sailors, and the merchant ended with syphilis!" Patridge laughed.

All the men joined in except Robert. He didn't see the humor. The merchant had been cheated, and syphilis wasn't fun. Hart knew all about it. While in college, he came down with an illness the doctor identified as syphilis. He was first prescribed Guajacum and then mercury. They were administered to the infection in a paste, which Robert had to rub on.

"He paid too much," Roundtree said, after the laughter died. "He should've had a virgin princess for that much. Since you can buy most girls for much less, it sounds like he was a fool."

More like a victim, Robert thought, but anyone who trafficked in flesh deserved whatever he got. He sipped slowly on his second glass of wine. Everyone else was starting on a fourth or fifth.

The concubine serving Robert was called Willow, and she brought him plum pudding, mince pie and tarts. Robert wondered how he was going to eat it all. He decided to take it slow, one bite at a time. He was not going to pass up eating any of this food.

When Willow wasn't getting food or drink, she stood close behind Robert, and he felt the heat from her body. She was petite with a small mouth and a set of leaf shaped eyes. Her nose was almost a blade it was so thin. Her long black hair was tied in a bun on the back of her head. A wooden pin with bright colored hanging glass decorations held the bun together. When her head tilted this way or that, the glass tinkled like a wind chime. Her skin was the color of pure ivory, and she glided gracefully when she moved. She reminded Robert of a fragile porcelain statuette he'd seen in a museum.

After coffee, the six men took a walk along the top of the hill. Captain Patridge had a string of fruit trees bordering a trail along the ridge leading from his hill to the next. They walked in the shade of the trees as the sun set in a blaze of orange and purple fire along the western horizon. Fruit hung heavy in the trees. Robert smelled the sweet, ripening scent of peaches, plums and apricots. If he hadn't been so full, he would have picked one to eat.

Willow walked behind him. She did not speak a word of English and kept her gaze on the ground. When she answered his questions, he had to strain to hear her whisper. Her village dialect confused him. She never asked a question and at times could not answer some of Robert's. His tongue still found the Mandarin he was learning cumbersome. Though she didn't say she couldn't understand him, he saw her nodding at the wrong times. Was it possible she didn't understand the Ningpo and Shanghai style of Mandarin Robert was learning? This bothered him. He was curious to know more about her. China was a strange land with one written language and many spoken ones.

After the walk, they gathered on the veranda to enjoy the soothing breeze. The temperature, though humid and warm, was cooler than Ningpo. The greatest blessing was there were no mosquitoes. Robert didn't miss Ningpo in the slightest. He was glad he'd come even if he had to listen to Patridge's outrageous stories.

Patridge's summerhouse was built in a Mediterranean style with a wide, covered veranda overlooking the ocean. From the veranda, streams were visible running down from the hills. The walls were made of thick, plastered stone, which kept the house cool on the hottest days. Blue glazed tiles covered the roof. An open garden in the Roman style was located at the center of the rectangular house. All the outside doors were made of thick sturdy timbers and the windows had shutters that could be barred from the inside.

A natural spring fed into a storage tank, which took up half the kitchen. The water was refreshing and worth the trip since the water in Ningpo tasted bad.

When Patridge had guests, which was often, he entertained in a large room that faced west. He slept with his concubine of the moment in a large bedroom office combination on the north side of the courtyard. The guest bedrooms were on the south side. All the rooms, except the servant and concubine quarters, had doors that opened on the enclosed garden. The Chinese servants and about a dozen concubines lived in a separate building behind the kitchen. That's where Patridge had sent Guan-jiah.

The stables were built against the servants' quarters, and those rooms smelled of manure and horse piss. This building was taller than the house and offered a windbreak when storms came howling across the island from the east.

Robert thought if he ever had a house like this, he would build the stables so no one had to smell the animals. He had to admit Patridge had done well for himself in China. He wondered if he would match the man's success.

Captain Patridge passed around a box of gold tipped Egyptian Shah cigarettes for an after dinner smoke. Robert searched his pockets for a match, but Willow appeared with a candle. He took hold of her hand to steady the flame. Her skin was warm and smooth. He didn't want to let go.

With the sun gone, the sounds of frogs and crickets filled the night with their mating calls. One of the other concubines lit a half-dozen lanterns along the veranda. The dim, flickering lights drew in some moths and a few beetles.

"It's been a good day, gentlemen," Captain Roundtree said, as he stubbed out his cigarette and stood. "There were no pirates. We have women to keep us warm and none of us is hungry or broke. I'm going to turn in. It was a long, hard trip from Hong Kong. The weather was a beast." Captain Roundtree left with the concubine who'd been serving him through dinner. His third officer and the two midshipmen also excused themselves and left with their concubines.

"Where can I find a supply of these?" Robert asked, holding up the cigarette.

"I'll connect you with the man I buy them from," Captain Patridge replied. He put a hand over his mouth to cover a yawn before continuing. "He lives in Shanghai but will have no problem getting some to you in Ningpo."

There was one lantern left glowing. The concubine who'd lit them had extinguished the others. Captain Patridge's concubine had already gone inside.

Patridge stood and looked at Robert. "How does this compare to Ningpo?"

"You were right about everything. I'm grateful for your invitation."

"Take advantage of Willow," Patridge said. "Although she doesn't play musical instruments or dance, she'll make your night pleasant. After you've finished with her, I'm sure you will sleep soundly." He squeezed Robert's shoulder. "Let me know at breakfast if you're happy with her. I have others if she isn't satisfactory."

"Thank you, Captain," Robert said. He couldn't look Patridge in the eye, and his ears burned from embarrassment. He was glad when Patridge went inside.

Willow's presence in the darkness behind Robert worked like a magnet arousing his sexual cravings. What was he to do? When the Sabbath came, there was no church and no minister to bolster his resolve not to stray from the path he had chosen. His heightened desire reminded him that he'd failed once with Me-ta-tae. He didn't want to fail again. Every time he strayed, he paid a price. With Me-ta-tae, he'd made an enemy of Hollister. In Ireland, he'd embarrassed himself and his family. Why didn't he have the strength to wait until he found a proper wife?

The lone glowing lantern hung from a rafter to his left. The breeze buffeted it about causing it to make creaking sounds and to cast strange shifting shadows over the table. The chair Robert sat on felt hard, and he squirmed about attempting to find a comfortable position. Due to the silence, he heard Willow's shallow breathing. He wanted to look at her but didn't allow it. He cursed his libido.

The food and wine made him feel lazy. His eyes drifted shut. He thought of the large corner room that Captain Patridge had made available for him. The room at the consulate had been smothering and cramped. The room here had a wide-open window facing the ocean and mosquito netting around the bed to keep him safe from the bloodsuckers. He wondered if that net protected him from Willow.

Patridge said there were other women implying that if Willow did not please him, another would take her place. Just the idea caused his heart to palpitate as if it had a life of its own. The constant struggle was exhausting.

In an attempt to get his mind off the woman standing behind him, Robert focused on the brig sitting at its anchorage in the small cove. Lights glowed from the aft windows. He heard a bell ringing from the ship marking the time. He counted eleven. It was late. He was tired, but he couldn't move. Willow's presence was like an anchor holding him in the chair. He wanted to take her with him, but his conscience said it was wrong. It was as if he were part of a painting. He didn't know why, but it reminded him of Rembrandt's *The Night Watch*. It was all so dark except for two people dressed in white and glowing as if they were lit from within like Willow and Robert on that veranda.

"Do you need anything, Master?" It was Guan-jiah, who must have been in the shadows watching.

"No." Robert was drowsy and his tongue felt thick and heavy.

"Master, in China we believe that we have found the true meaning of life and understand it. For us, the end of life lies not in life after death, for the idea that we live to die, as taught by Christianity, is baffling and makes no sense. The true end, as we Chinese believe it, is the enjoyment of a simple life and in harmonious social relationships while we are alive."

"Are you a philosopher too?" Robert asked, impressed. He knew what Guan-jiah was doing. He was telling Robert it was all right to spend the night with Willow. Was Guan-jiah reading his mind? Robert narrowed his eyes and studied his servant wondering if the eunuch was up to something.

"No Master, but I have had much time to contemplate life and its mysteries. I have sought answers to my questions for many years."

"And this contemplation must have started when you were in that Buddhist monastery?"

He nodded. "Have I offended you, Master?"

"No. I value your advice. Thank you. You may go now." Guan-jiah turned and walked into the darkness. With a sluggish effort, Robert stood to go inside. Willow blew out the last lantern and quietly followed.

Once in his room, Willow came to take off his shirt. Kneeling, she slipped off his shoes, unbuckled his belt and pulled down his trousers. He stepped out of his pants and stood watching her undress. The sight of her naked body thrilled him. He found that he had trouble drawing in a full breath. Then she blew out the candles plunging the room into gloom. He listened to her climb onto the bed.

Robert was glad that the darkness hid his guilt and his erection. A long moment passed while he listened to the only sounds in the room—the pounding of his heart and the breathing of two people. He decided to accept what Willow offered. After all, he was a traveler on a lonely journey, who occasionally embraced human affections the same way he took the sun and water.

It was as if there were two people inside him. The first person was the man that arrived from Ireland running from his sins. The second man was the one from Ningpo. The Ningpo man felt lonely and tired, but there was no despair as there had been in the first man when he had reached Hong Kong a year ago. If Guan-jiah hadn't stepped out of the darkness and talked to him, Robert was sure he would have slept alone. His servant had awakened the Ningpo man.

He was still nervous, so Robert turned away from the bed to the washbasin sitting on top the small three-legged table in the corner. After rinsing his hands several times more than he needed, he searched in the darkness for a towel.

He sensed her presence before she took his hands in hers. She hadn't made a sound. She led him to the bed where the starlight coming through the window lit the sheets. When Willow stepped closer, the light reflected from her face and her bare shoulders.

The sight of her naked skin caused his breath to catch in his throat. He had trouble swallowing. There was no warmth in her eyes, but they were not cold either. Robert took her face between his hands and bent to kiss her lips.

She slipped away, crawled under the thin sheet. He followed. She twisted around snuggling her face against his neck. Her thin chest pressed against him, and she molded her body to his. Her breasts were small and soft. Any doubts that this was something he shouldn't be doing fled. He rolled over on top of her. She was wet inside and received him easily.

The sex act was over in a few strokes.

Willow quietly cleaned him with a damp cloth then left the room. He waited for her to return, but she didn't. She hadn't said one word. Robert wished she had spoken—like where she was from, what was her favorite food, or if she'd had a good time. He wanted to make her smile or laugh. It disappointed him that there wasn't more to it.

Then he heard the sound of breathing at the open window. Robert saw the figure of a man there—about Guan-jiah's size. When the shape left, Robert hurried to the window and watched his servant merge with the night.

Robert returned to the bed and struggled with the discomfort of Guan-jiah watching him have intercourse with Willow. He was sure his servant had also spied on him when he'd made love to Me-ta-tae in Ningpo.

He had been with several women since going off to college at fifteen. The idea of going through life and never knowing such pleasure was horrible to contemplate. He had no idea how Catholic priests survived and was glad he wasn't one.

Maybe the only way Guan-jiah came close to experience what it was like to be with a woman was to stand in the shadows and watch. Robert decided that if he could somehow make up for Guan-jiah's loss by not complaining, he would keep quiet. However, that was not going to be easy.

His encounter with Willow was an extension of the meal as if Patridge had planned for her to be the dessert. He no longer made an effort to kill the guilt, although it was lurking nearby. It was like a sleeping monster waiting to pounce on him as if it were a lion if he stumbled.

He was beginning to understand that, unlike Victorian England, China with its Buddhist, Confucian and Taoist influences fit who he'd been while in College. Here he knew that if he took up his old Belfast ways, he'd not be condemned. Here, if Robert so desired, he could follow where his nature led instead of fighting it. However, he hadn't sailed halfway around the world to indulge in women.

The concubines were not there for breakfast. Two male servants put the food and drinks on the table.

"How was your night, gentlemen?" Patridge asked, as Robert leaned back in his chair with a full belly. "I hope it was satisfactory."

Roundtree belched. "You have splendid concubines, Patridge. Why do you think we didn't sail straight to Shanghai to unload our cargo and take on a new one? It's a long voyage to England, and your women are better than prostitutes."

"I want to keep my employees happy," Patridge replied.

Robert wondered if he would return next summer if the captain invited him again. After a night with Willow, Robert was not sure this was what he was looking for. He wanted to know the woman first. He considered taking his vacation next summer in Shanghai. He could stay with William Lay and his opinionated, grumpy brother Horatio. Shanghai held more people from England and Europe. If Robert spent his month there, he might meet someone.

By midmorning, a dozen men arrived from the *Sampson,* a schooner that dropped anchor near the brig sometime during the night. They arrived on the veranda armed with cutlasses and muskets. One man had a healing scab running down the right side of his face. The scab started above his eye and stopped at his jaw line. What with his tousled hair and leathery skin, he looked like a true pirate. Robert shuddered, because the sight reminded him of the narrow escape with the pirates while sailing on the *Iona.* It was shocking to be reminded that life was so fragile.

"Why come here armed like this, Captain Bainbridge?" Patridge asked. "Has something happened?"

"Aye," Captain Bainbridge of the *Sampson* said in a rush. "Taiping rebels took the *Nancy* on the Woosung River about twenty miles above Shanghai. My ship had moved farther from shore after unloading our opium when they struck."

"Slow down, man," Patridge said. He beckoned a servant to pour wine for Bainbridge and his men. "Take a drink to calm yourself before you continue. This is serious. I want to hear every word."

Bainbridge gulped his wine. "The rebels hit us by surprise early in the morning swarming from the shore in sampans. They overwhelmed the small boats surrounding the *Nancy* and captured the unarmed Chinese boat people that work for us.

"Most of the brig's crew managed to dive into the river and swim to the *Sampson*. If we hadn't put up a hard fight, we would have fallen too. Though we managed to escape, the boat people, the brig and the opium were taken."

Robert wondered when the man was going to find time to breathe.

"We saw old captain Tingle and a few of his crew that didn't get overboard in time," Bainbridge said. "They put up a stiff fight. I am sure he's dead by now. The Taipings don't take kindly to opium and want to see all foreigners beheaded anyway."

Bainbridge held out a Chinese placard. "I took this off a rebel I killed."

Captain Patridge interpreted it into English. "The Taipings are calling on the people to rise up and exterminate the Imps and Monkeys, which of course refers to us."

"The boat people may live a few more days," Captain Bainbridge said. "If they can't produce a ransom, they'll be beheaded."

Robert remembered what had happened to the Bengalis in Patridge's story. He questioned his decision to come to China. He wanted his family to be proud of him and forgive him for his sins, but to do that he had to become a success. However, if he did not survive, he would never achieve his goals.

"We can't allow the Taipings to get away with this," Patridge said.

"I agree," Robert said, without thinking. "These Taipings sound like cowards. They are nothing but common thugs and thieves. I want to be part of whatever you do." He felt himself wilting under the combined glare of everyone and regretted his outburst. He then remembered the moment he had spoken out during dinner last night. Everyone had stared at him then too. Why hadn't he learned from that mistake and kept his mouth shut? He hated acting the fool.

"It'll be my pleasure to have you with us," Patridge said, breaking the silence. Robert relaxed at the reprieve and started to breathe again. He was glad Patridge had agreed to take him along.

"We'll take both ships to the Lookong receiving station and pick up more men and weapons," Patridge said. "We should reach the Taiping camp along the Woosung River in two days and hit them before the sun rises. If luck is with us, we'll reclaim the opium before the Taipings burn it, and we will free the boat people."

Before leaving for the Lookong receiving station, Robert instructed Guan-jiah to return to Ningpo. "But, Master, my place is beside you. If you are going into danger, I should be there too."

"And if you die, Guan-jiah, who will take care of your father and mother? Has anyone else in your family sacrificed as you have?"

Guan-jiah's expression was unreadable. "You are right, Master. I will return to Ningpo and await your return." He nodded and left to pack his meager belongings. As he walked off, Robert followed his servant's frail slender frame with his eyes. He looked too young to think so old.

Chapter 3

The Yangtze had a metallic smell like blood mixed with manure. There was no breeze and it was hot and humid. The creak of the rigging and the sounds of oars dipping into the muddy yellow colored water were the only noises. The men in the small boats strained and sweated to tow the armed merchant ships into position to destroy an enemy.

The schooner had eight cannons; the brig, the *Maryann*, had twelve. Although the merchant ships could bring ten of those cannons to bear on the shore, those eight and six pounders didn't offer much firepower, so every gun was loaded with sections of chain and iron balls the size of grapes.

Robert imagined the carnage—the yard long pieces of chain twirling through the air ripping flesh and bone rending men like swine being slaughtered. He stared past the boats strung out along the twin cables and studied the multitude of campfires flickering along the far shoreline. There were too many. He feared death. It was warm and humid. When he shivered, it had nothing to do with the temperature. It was as if he were shaking fear off as a dog shakes water from its coat. He turned from the sight and went below deck to the main cabin of the *Maryann* where Captain Patridge was meeting with the officers.

As Robert entered the cabin, he saw Patridge spreading a map on the table and putting lead weights on the corners, so the map wouldn't curl up. Captains Bainbridge and Roundtree stood on either side of him. The junior officers crowded the rest of the table. Robert found a spot behind two of the men and watched over their shoulders.

Patridge pointed a stick at the map. "At the north end of the camp is a crude stockade," he said. "This is where our boat people are held. I have heard that tomorrow before the Taipings break camp, the boat people will be executed. Usually the Taipings allow their prisoners the choice of joining the rebellion or losing their heads, but because they were involved with us and the cargo was opium, it was decided they are all to die."

Robert knew next to nothing about the Taiping rebellion. He had heard that the leader of the rebels was a man named Hung Hsiu-chuan, a Christian convert, who claimed he was the new Messiah and the younger brother of Jesus Christ. Robert learned this from the Ningpo missionaries, who said that Hung did not comprehend the importance of the Trinity and had taken it on himself to add a third book to the Old and New Testament—this third book was the Taiping Bible.

"Excuse me," Robert said. All eyes turned on him. He hated being the focus of attention. It made his stomach queasy.

"Yes, Robert," Patridge replied.

"Will the Taiping leader, Hung Hsiu-chuan, be there? Will we get a chance to capture or kill him and end this rebellion?" Robert had no idea how large the rebellion was.

There was nervous laughter around the table. "No, Robert," Patridge replied in a condescending tone that caused Robert to burn with embarrassment. "Hung is in his capital city of Nanking surrounded by tens of thousands of his soldiers. His generals do his killing for him. He set himself up as an emperor, and he lives in a palace with hundreds of concubines. To make Nanking his capital, he slaughtered an Imperial army of thirty thousand in 1853. Today he has an army estimated to be more than a million strong. We will be going against a thousand of them—a trifling number considering the whole. Does that answer your question?"

"Yes, thank you." A few of the officers chuckled, and Robert was sure they were laughing at him. His question had revealed how ignorant he was. He should have kept quiet.

Patridge turned back to the map and tapped a spot north of the stockade. "The cargo of opium is piled here close to the river. After the beheadings, the opium will be set on fire. Once it is burning the Taipings will break camp and leave."

"Where did you hear this?" A junior officer asked.

"Money buys spies," Patridge replied. "That's all anyone needs to know." He glared at the junior officer until the man squirmed. "No, you aren't the one. You haven't worked for me long enough to be who I'm looking for, or I'd suspect you gave the Taipings the information about this opium shipment."

"Surely, you don't suspect one of us," Captain Bainbridge said.

"I suspect everyone who works for me and has been in China long enough. Thefts and losses like this have plagued us in this region for two years now. That means someone is selling information about our opium shipments to the Taipings."

Patridge looked at the faces in the crowded cabin, as if he were attempting to discover the guilty party. "Know this," he said. "There is a traitor working for me. Anyone who turns that man in will receive a comfortable reward."

Robert wondered who the traitor was. He jumped at the sound of a sharp crack and saw that Patridge had slapped the table with his stick. "Enough!" He leaned over the map. His hand moved south, below the stockade, where he marked out a wide oval—most of it inland away from the river. "The majority of Taipings are camped here around the prisoner stockade. The situation does not offer us a good range of fire for our cannons.

"The camp extends inland and the Taipings have dug shallow trenches for protection and filled them with spikes. However, they have no defensive positions facing the river. This is where we'll bring to bear all the firepower of the canons." He tapped the map below the stockade along the shoreline.

"We want panic among the Taipings, and we do not want to hit our boat people. The landing will take place near the opium. We'll recover the cargo first then free the prisoners."

Robert had been in China a year, and the suffering and poverty he had witnessed were the reasons he'd volunteered for this fight. He hadn't come to recover opium. The boat people were looked down on by almost everyone. He felt it was his duty to do what he could for them. It was wrong to make opium more important than human life.

On impulse, he said, "Captain." All eyes shifted to Robert. He felt a hot flush spreading up his neck and over his face, and he had second thoughts about speaking. However, since he'd committed himself, he wasn't going to back down. "Would it be possible for at least one of our boats to land closer to the boat people? If we free them, we'll have more hands to load opium and fight."

"Hmm," Patridge replied. Robert watched the captain's expression change. His face said he did not like being interrupted. Then his face became thoughtful. "Yes, you are right," he said slowly, as if he were still weighing his response. "The boat people could help us get in and out faster."

Patridge pointed his stick at one of the junior officers standing to Robert's right. "Unwyn Fiske," he said, "you will take your boatload of men and make for the shore below the stockade. Get in there and get the boat people out and rejoin the main column over by the opium where I'll be."

"Bloody hell," Unwyn said. "How am I supposed to do that? I don't speak Chinese and none of my men does either. The original plan was better." He cast a dark glance at Robert.

Patridge's eyes swiveled back to Robert, who felt the heat in his face again. "You speak some Mandarin don't you, Hart?" he asked. "After all, you do work in the British consulate in Ningpo."

"That's right, Captain," Robert replied.

"Then Unwyn will make room in his boat for you. You will be the one to tell these boat people what they are to do. Am I clear?"

Robert nodded and wondered what kind of mess he'd gotten himself into. Instead of being with more than a hundred armed men, he was going to be with a score. He stared at the map and saw that where he was going was closer to what the cannons would be shooting at.

Earlier, Robert had seen an undermanned gun crew clumsily practicing with an eight pounder. The man carrying the bucket full of chain and grape had slipped and dropped the heavy load spilling its contents. When they fired the practice shot, they missed the floating target by several yards. It occurred to him that one of the cannons could miss the Taipings and hit his group. He should have kept his mouth shut.

Robert considered mentioning his concerns about the cannons, but this time he refrained from speaking. He wished that even one small sloop from the British navy had been with them.

"That's settled," Patridge said.

With the attention off Robert, he glanced around and looked at Unwyn, who was glaring at him. They locked eyes for a moment, but Robert broke first and focused his attention on Patridge. He felt his face heating again. What kind of man was this Fiske fellow? Robert squirmed uncomfortably while not looking at the man.

Captain Patridge waited for everyone's attention before speaking again. "If we lose the initiative of surprise, I don't have to tell you what these thousand maniacs will do to us.

"We are only two hundred, but we may not be alone in this fight. There is an American in Shanghai, a man called Frederick Townsend Ward. He's a soldier of fortune, a mercenary. The Chinese government commissioned this Ward to build an army to take the city of Sungkiang back from the Taipings. Before we left the Lookong receiving station, I sent a note to Ward letting him know what we're up to in the hope he might want to get in on the action as a first move to take Sungkiang.

"To lure him here to help us, I offered part of the opium as a reward. It is the reason we are here. This was a major shipment, and we are not going to lose it. I want you to tell your men I will pay a bonus to all involved if we recover all the opium."

Does that offer include me? Robert thought. *After all, I don't work for him or his company.* Then Robert felt ashamed. After all, he hadn't volunteered to join Patridge in this venture out of greed. If any of that bonus came his way, he'd have a little more to send home to his family. He wouldn't turn it down, but he wouldn't ask for it either.

Patridge rubbed his chin while his eyes examined the faces in the room. Then he said, "I've met Ward several times. He is recruiting his army in Shanghai from the waterfront scum, deserters and Filipino cutthroats. The money to finance this army is being squeezed out of the Chinese government and the merchant associations. They want to be rid of the Taipings, because they are bad for business. My company paid too. That's enough. Dismissed."

On the way out, Unwyn put a hand on Robert shoulder and pulled him aside. "What were you doing in there?" he asked.

Robert felt his back stiffen, and he stood a bit straighter. "Stating my opinion." He didn't like the tone of Unwyn's voice and this time he kept contact with the man's eyes.

"Well, next time you decide to open your mouth, keep it shut. How much combat experience do you have?"

"Aside from a few fistfights in Belfast when I was drunk, none," Robert replied.

Unwyn pushed his face closer to Robert. The man's sour breath spit at him, as he said, "When we reach that prisoner stockade, Hart, you are going in alone. Unlike you, I have been in combat. I joined the Royal Navy when I was thirteen and served fifteen years before I went to work for Captain Patridge. The reason I left is that I saw too many men wanting to be heroes blown to bits." Without saying another word, Unwyn stepped away and climbed the ladder to the deck. Robert used his sleeve to wipe the spittle from his face.

He discovered he was holding his breath, so he forced himself to breathe. Robert didn't doubt what Fiske had said, but he was more afraid of looking like a coward than of dying. His greatest fear was that he'd not perform properly. He had no desire to be a hero.

The small merchant army climbed down the boarding nets and crowded into the boats. The way they were armed and dressed made them look like a band of rowdy pirates. There were just enough men left behind to work the cannons.

A young ship's boy sat crowded against Robert in the stern of the boat. He felt the boy trembling and noticed a dazed look on his face. "How old are you, son?" he asked.

"Eleven," the boy replied in a small, quivering voice. His frightened eyes rotated to Robert.

"And your name?" Robert asked.

"Brian," he replied.

Robert nodded and slipped an arm across the boy's shoulders. "Brian, I'm afraid too," he said. "Let me share something with you that will help bolster your courage. Have you ever heard of the Battle of Agincourt, which took place on October twenty-fifth in 1415?"

Brian shook his head. "But I know that October twenty-fifth is St. Crispin's Day. My dad was a cobbler." He paused, and then asked, "What happened at Agincourt?"

"Well, King Henry the V, the British King, gave a speech to his troops. He only had six thousand and the French numbered twenty-five thousand. Do you want to hear what King Henry said to his army?"

The boy nodded. He swallowed and Robert watched his Adam's apple bob up and down. Brian was thin as a tadpole.

"Shakespeare wrote this but it's still the King's words. Listen close. 'If we are marked to die, we are enow to do our country loss; and if to live, the fewer men the greater share of honor. O do not wish one more? But he, which hath no stomach to this fight, let him depart. His passport shall be made and crowns for convoy put into his purse. We would not die in that man's company that fears his fellowship to die with us.' " Robert paused and gave the boy a chance to think and saw that he didn't understand what King Henry meant.

"Look, Brian," he said. "In that speech King Henry said he forgave any man afraid to fight because the odds were so overwhelming against the English army. The king even paid for passage back to England for any man who did not want to fight.

"If you want to leave, I'll speak up for you. If a king can offer a way out, I don't see why you can't have the same choice."

Brian shook his head. "No sir," he said in a heavy cockney accent. "I'm going to stay with my mates. They'd think I was a coward if I left now. Besides, I am not in this for the honor like that king talked about. You heard. There is going to be a bonus. That means more money I can send home to my mum. You see my dad died before I learned the trade."

"That's my boy," Robert said, and gave Brian's arm a squeeze. "Look, Aristotle, a famous Greek philosopher, thought that a courageous person is not one who has no fear, and not one who is overcome by fear, but one who can control fear and act according to a sense of duty. I can see that you know your duty to your mum and your family and are determined not to disappoint. I feel the same way. Stay near me when we get into this fight. I'll watch out for you."

"I have seven brothers and three sisters," Brian said. "This will be one tale I'll be telling in front of the fire when I get home." He smiled showing that he had some missing teeth and a few half-rotten ones.

"Who's talking?" Unwyn said. He stood in the bow of the boat and Robert sat in the stern, wedged in so tightly that he had no room to move. Unwyn's eyes darted from man to man and stopped on Robert the longest. When his gaze shifted to Brian, Robert felt the boy tremble.

"If anyone gives us away so we lose our surprise, I'll shoot the bastard between the eyes myself. Keep silent!"

Robert squeezed the boy to reassure him that all was well. There must have been twenty men crammed in that boat. His heart pounded in panic when he couldn't free the four double-barreled pistols tucked under his belt. Even the twenty-seven-inch cutlass was pinned against a leg. The only weapon he could free was a twelve-inch double-edged dagger in a leather scabbard between his shoulder blades.

Brian's weapon was a pike. He had no pistol or cutlass.

Looking over his shoulder, Robert saw the masts of the ships outlined by the half-moon and a sky full of stars. If he saw them, so could the Taipings. That was a chilling thought. The sky had cleared, and there was twice as much light compared to when they left the ships. If they were discovered before reaching shore, they would sink to the bottom of the river and drowned. It would be a slaughter. If the Taiping campfires indicated the numbers waiting onshore, the odds were horrible. It looked as if the rebels numbered more than a thousand.

His thoughts were interrupted when the boats swung toward the far side of the river away from the rebel camp. When they reached a position opposite the designated landing place, the boats turned. The banks of oars rose and dipped and the boats shot forward one behind the other.

The orange glow of campfires revealed the moving figures of men. Most wore red jackets and blue trousers. Someone laughed sounding like a hyena. Luck was with them at least for the moment. It looked like Patridge had been correct. Most of the Taiping defenses faced away from the river. Their sentries stood watching for Imperials or Ward's army expecting an attack from land.

Unwyn gestured to the man at the tiller to guide the boat away from the others. Robert stared at a shore littered with empty sampans. He saw the outline of the prison stockade where the boat people were supposed to be. Inside that area, it was dark like spilled ink. What if they had been moved or what if they were already dead? He shivered at the thought, and Brian looked at him. Robert forced himself to smile to reassure the boy that all was well. He ran his fingers like a comb through the boy's shaggy brown hair. Brian smiled but his eyes were filled with fear.

Campfires flickered around the stockade. Someone among the boat people in that darkness cried out in misery, and Robert ached for them in their predicament. He thought that at least one was alive to save.

Before the boat ran aground, the men with Patridge let off a ragged volley. Shortly after that, the *Maryann* and the *Sampson* fired their cannons. The combined blasts deafened Robert, and the bright flash of light left dancing spots in his blinded vision. Then the boat jerked as it slid into land. When his vision cleared, he saw that the chain and grape had hit this side of the Taiping camp turning men into pieces of raw, bloody meat-missing arms, legs and sometimes heads.

The men in the bow piled out and ran toward the stockade, where Robert heard voices screaming in panic. He followed, but before jumping out of the boat, he fired a pistol at shadowy figures wearing the Taiping red and blue. As he crawled over the side and into the water, Robert sunk up to his knees in sticky mud and lost sight of Brian.

The ships fired another ragged and pitiful salvo into the camp below the stockade. A rattle of pistols and rifles roared again from the men with Captain Patridge. The guns from the ships began a constant barrage—their muzzles sporadically spitting jagged orange death flames.

A figure appeared before Robert with what looked like red eyes and a black gash for a mouth. The wild creature, looking like a demon from hell, jabbed a spear at him. Robert's cutlass knocked the spear aside while his pistol fired a bullet into the man.

It was as if Hart's weapons had taken charge, and his body was taking commands from them. He had just killed someone. The thought numbed him for a moment.

His boots made sucking sounds as he freed himself from the sticky mud. Just as he reached shore, he slipped and fell. When he looked up, his eyes met a man's leg. The rest of the man was nowhere to be seen. The leg was naked. The muscles were twitching. Swallowing the bile that rushed into his throat, Robert regained his feet and staggered away in a daze.

He stumbled again but this time when he looked down he saw Brian, the eleven-year-old boy from the ship—the one that sat beside him in the boat. The boy was on his knees with both of his hands gripping the shaft of a spear embedded in his stomach. His discarded pike was beside him. He vomited blood and folded forward over the spear—his body going limp.

Oh, dear God, Robert thought. He saw the Taiping that speared Brian attempting to pull his weapon free. It appeared stuck in the boy's guts, and Brian's body was flopping like a fish on a hook.

"Bastard!" Robert yelled. His fear fled as anger raged through him. He fired the other barrel of his first pistol into the rebel who had impaled Brian and yanked another pistol free. The rebel he shot dropped to the ground holding his hands over the hole in his abdomen. Robert stepped forward, put his boot on the wound and ran the rebel through the heart with the cutlass.

Robert spotted Unwyn, who stood with a furious expression at an open gate in the stockade. Unwyn lifted one of his pistols, aimed and shot a man running toward him. The other sailors took up kneeling positions beside Unwyn and fired into the panicked rebels.

Three older sailors knelt behind the small knot of firing men and quickly loaded empty pistols and rifles as fast as they were handed back.

"Hart," Unwyn yelled, "use your Chinese and get those wretches moving this way so we can join Patridge." He lifted a pistol and fired at a Taiping with a sword swirling above his head. That Taiping's chest exploded, and the man toppled in a mist of blood.

"You'd better move fast!" Unwyn roared. "They're swarming like hornets. It won't take long before they get organized."

"We should all go in," Robert said, as he joined the group. "Why stay here?"

"I'm not getting any closer to the Taipings," Unwyn replied. "Going inside that stockade could turn into a trap. I did not come here to die saving these people. I came to get my share of the reward by regaining the company's cargo."

His words angered Robert and he glared at Unwyn.

"Get moving, Hart, so we can get this over. This fool's errand was your idea so the risk is yours."

Robert stared at the man, then turned and forced his legs to take one step after another. Once inside the stockade, he yelled in Mandarin as best he could. "*Ni men huo jiu. Zou kuai.* You to be rescued. Run fast." He pointed.

Startled people stared at him. Some of them were whimpering but most were mute with shock. Robert managed to get those closest to pay attention and thirty or forty started to move. One old grandma, stooped and bent, hobbled by Hart holding the hand of a naked toddler.

One of the boat people, a young man, ran past just as Unwyn's group fired a volley. The boatman came between Unwyn's people and Robert. He jerked as if hit and stumbled sideways knocking Robert down. Hart pushed the man off and discovered he was covered in blood. He saw more than one bullet wound. Unwyn's men had shot him. If that boat person hadn't been there, the bullets would've hit him and he'd be dead.

Part of the stockade on the far side opened. Taipings poured in. A pregnant woman tried to escape, but a Taiping sword slashed into her back. It happened so fast that she had not seen the man who'd stabbed her. Robert watched in horror as she tumbled forward with a stunned expression to pitch face down in the dirt, twitched, then stopped moving.

Robert turned and stared at Unwyn and the others. He waved to get their attention. "Here," he yelled. "I need you here to help save these people. You can't help them from there."

Unwyn saw Robert and shook his head. He made an insulting gesture with one of his hands and said something Robert couldn't hear. His mouth looked as if he'd told Hart to go to hell.

Twisting around to face the Taipings, Robert emptied the pistol in his hand and pulled another free after tucking the empty one under his belt. Any fear or doubts he harbored when this battle started were gone. He couldn't stop thinking of Brian dying and now this innocent pregnant woman.

Their deaths filled Robert with a level of anger and revulsion he'd never felt before. His eyes searched for the rebel who killed the pregnant woman. When he recognized the man, he ran forward and shot him in the stomach. A gut wound was a horrible way to die, and Robert wanted this man to die slowly with much pain.

More boat people ran past Robert toward Unwyn and the others.

The second barrel of his third pistol emptied. Robert threw it at the nearest Taiping. It bounced off the man's head and knocked him flat. Robert hacked at the man's neck opening it to the spine.

With his last pistol held against his side, he watched a screaming man charging toward him. The man swung a sword at his head. Robert's cutlass blocked it. The force of the blow numbed his hand. He barely held onto the blade. His other hand, the one holding the last pistol, thrust it into the rebel's face and Robert pulled the trigger. The man's lower jaw vanished in a pink mist. The rebel staggered back with his arms flailing. Robert swung the cutlass at what was left.

Robert had one shot left and there was no time to reload.

The stockade looked almost empty. A last knot of boat people, mostly young girls, was gathered off to one side. They hovered over someone on the ground as if their long dresses offered protection. Robert ran toward them. "Hurry, run!" he shouted in Mandarin, not wanting to see these innocents die.

Obviously paralyzed by fear, the girls just stared at him. "Hurry!" He pushed one of them to get her moving. After that, one by one, they started to run.

Once the young girls were gone, Robert saw what looked like an adolescent boy in baggy clothes holding a long stick with both hands. He stood with his legs straddling the figure of an old man. This boy stood with his back to Robert facing the Taipings. The remaining children, who hadn't run, huddled at the feet of this defiant boy.

Three Taiping rebels rushed them with lowered spears. Thinking that this stupid boy was going to get him killed, Robert fired his last shot. One of the Taipings stumbled but managed to regain his balance and kept coming. Robert refused to desert this bunch. He hurried to stand next to the boy and held the cutlass ready.

The boy's face was covered with dirt. He reached behind Robert and tugged at the dagger freeing it from its scabbard. The rebels arrived and with an effort, Robert held them at bay. He knocked aside a spear with the flat of his cutlass. Then he slashed across another man's chest cutting him open to the bone. A third man jumped on him. They tumbled to the ground in a tangle of arms and legs. Robert felt the man's hands around his throat cutting off the air. Then he saw the boy stick the dagger through that rebel's neck. Robert butted the man with his forehead. Blood sprayed in Hart's face from the knife wound to the man's neck.

He pushed the body away and scrambled to his feet to discover that for the moment no more Taipings were close enough to threaten them. The boy had killed the third Taiping. Robert's face was covered with blood. He used a coat sleeve to clear it from his eyes.

"Let's move!" Robert said, and grabbed the boy. "We have to get out of here!"

"No! Not without my father!" The boy tried to free himself from Robert.

The voice stunned him. It wasn't a boy as he'd thought. More Taipings gathered. They shouted. "Death to the foreign devils!"

Robert knelt beside the old man, lifted him and draped him over his shoulders. His legs stumbled with each step. Unwyn and the others fired at the Taipings entering the stockade. He glanced back and saw that the girl and the other children were following him. He'd failed Brian. He was not going to fail this family.

Once he reached Unwyn and the others, he put the old man down. Unwyn turned to Robert in a fury and said, "You are a fool, Hart! I've seen a lot of idiots like you die trying to be heroes."

"You're a coward, Unwyn!" Robert shouted, as blood rushed into his head overwhelming reason. "If you had entered the stockade with me, we could've saved more lives." Robert slapped Unwyn across the face. The officer reeled back and started to lift his pistol. In response, Robert lifted his cutlass to deliver a killing blow.

"Save that for later!" One of the others yelled, as he stepped between them. "We have to save ourselves first."

The breaking dawn sent blood-red cords of pale, washed-out light over the earth along the eastern horizon. Behind them, orange flames from the cannons still flashed from the smoke filled river. Robert saw bodies and parts of bodies everywhere but there were still hundreds to fight.

The small group Robert was with ran toward Patridge and his men thirty yards away. Robert picked up the old man and followed.

Patridge's merchant troops fired steadily into the Taipings, who were now gathering to attack. What Robert had done to save lives had nothing to do with wanting to be a hero. He still felt responsible for Brian's death. After all, he told Brian he would look after him. He had failed.

When they reached Patridge, the boat people started to load opium into the boats that lined the shore. The first time the boats returned to the ships, they went with full loads of opium. There wasn't enough room to carry the children to safety. Robert thought such logic insane. He didn't like it.

With the old man off his back beside the piles of opium, Robert stepped away and fumbled at his belt for his empty pistols. His fingers trembled and it took an effort for him to load them one at a time. Once loaded, he fired rapidly into the gathering mass of Taipings then started to reload again. The girl in the baggy clothing came up beside him with his bloody dagger clutched in her hand.

"Get to a safer place!" Robert yelled.

Her eyes begged for an opportunity to fight. She didn't want to leave.

Robert watched a man, who must have been the leader of the Taipings, wave a double bladed ax over his head. In his other hand, he held a spear. He pointed it at Patridge's men and yelled something, which sent hundreds of howling, crazed Taipings toward them.

Robert knew they were doomed. He firmly pointed a finger beyond the firing line. "Leave the opium and get your family in a boat. Do it now! If I am to die, I want to know that you and your family escaped. Do not let this end in vain."

A fire lit inside her eyes. She stared at him as if she were memorizing his features. She gently caressed the back of his hand with her fingertips. Then she nodded. She must have sensed that she couldn't fight his will for she retreated.

Robert knew that he might not survive long. He decided to save the last shot for himself. He'd stick the barrel of the pistol in his mouth and blow his head off. If the Taipings caught him, they would give him a *chi-lin*, which meant death from a thousand cuts. They'd work him over for days. It was a sure fate for any foreigner who fell into their hands. He'd cheat the crazy bastards of that pleasure, but first he would kill as many as possible.

He regretted the decision he'd made to volunteer. Now he would never marry and have a family. He would miss all the laughter and pain of watching his children, who would never be born, grow. He heard himself try to laugh, but the sound he made was raspy. His throat was so dry it hurt. A glass of cool water would have been refreshing before death.

He hadn't realized how much he wanted children and to watch them grow. He had never given it a thought before. He shook his head. His body felt heavier. Something worse occurred to him. He would never get a chance to redeem himself in his family's thoughts for the sins of lust committed in Ireland. His father and mother would go to their graves remembering the worst about him. His oldest sister, Mary, would forgive him. He was sure of that. He held that thought as if it were precious.

Robert loaded his pistols and looked out over the battlefield. It appeared like a scene out of Dante's Inferno. The howling Taipings backlit by their fires were a dark forest of demons right out of hell and behind Robert was Dante's infernal river, the Acheron. Could it be that, like Dante, this was another step in Robert's journey toward redemption? If so, if he survived, what other tests would he have to face?

Then, without warning, a solid body of men numbering in the hundreds poured across the shallow trenches at the south end of the camp. A short man with thick raven hair hanging to his shoulders urged these men along. He wore a Prince Albert frock coat and held a walking stick in one hand. Robert recognized him. It was the same man from Hong Kong that used the infant corpses in the water for target practice. It was Ward. His men were dressed in green turbines and knickerbockers. Robert beheld an impressive sight—every man was armed with a rifle or a Colt revolver. The firepower they put out was enormous.

The remaining Taipings retreated northeast out of the camp. The strength went out of Robert's legs. He sat on a bale of opium gasping for breath. He couldn't believe he was going to live to see another day.

Ward's force quickly secured the place. Robert joined the line of boat people and sailors loading opium. Thick clouds of dark gunpowder drifted west with the sluggish breeze.

Ward came into their lines while his soldiers looted the camp and slit the throats of the dead and wounded. Robert shuddered when he watched one of Ward's men pry a dead man's mouth open and cut out the gold teeth.

"Captain Patridge." Ward boomed with a deep, resonant voice that sounded as if it belonged to the devil. He had a smooth, pale complexion with a crooked nose like the beak of an owl. There was a thick, shaggy mustache under his nose and a square patch of hair centered under his lower lip. His nose looked like it had been broken several times. "Where's that promised opium?" he asked. A crooked smile creased his thin lips.

Captain Patridge bowed courteously and pointed at the pile remaining on the beach. "That's the half I promised if you arrived in time to join the fight."

Ward had been a hired gun in the California goldfields involved in the illegal coolie trade between China and Mexico. When he arrived in China, he first offered his services to the Taipings, but he somehow ended leading an army against them and working for the Ch'ing Dynasty.

Robert glanced at the boats that were returning empty. Patridge had managed to move more than three-quarters of the opium onto his ships before Ward arrived. However, what remained was a respectable amount.

After Robert shoved his empty pistols under his belt, he climbed into one of the boats that was already half full with the family of children, the old man and the girl he thought was a boy. Glancing up, Robert noticed Unwyn ordering people into the waiting boats. He regretted the words they had exchanged earlier. Unwyn's eyes met Robert's in a fleeting glance and in that moment Robert knew that Unwyn hated him. It was in his eyes. Robert glanced away first. He didn't want anything more to do with that man.

Exhaustion overcame Robert but it didn't matter. He was alive and so was the family he'd helped save. His ears buzzed so every sound was muted. His throat was parched. The girl sat opposite him in the middle of the boat beside the sick looking old man. Somehow, she had washed the dirt from her face. She held one of the old man's hands helping him drink water from a cup.

The cap she'd been wearing when Robert first saw her inside the stockade was gone, and her black hair had fallen loose about her shoulders framing her face. She had a darker complexion than most Chinese women Robert had seen. Her high cheekbones showed off wide set, single lidded, almond shaped eyes and a voluptuous mouth with what the Chinese called *petal lips.* Surely, the angels from heaven looked like this girl. Robert was convinced she had saved his life when she'd thrust that dagger into the Taiping's neck.

As they moved away from shore and the sailors rowed toward the ships, the family with Robert relaxed. Everyone was waking from the same nightmare feeling fortunate to be alive.

The opposite shore was covered with green fields and rice paddies. A cooling breeze ruffled the trees and bushes. A bird chirped in song. A sudden thrill rushed through Robert as if he had just stolen back his life. Everything became more beautiful. A drowsy weight crawled over him adding pounds to his limbs and eyelids and he briefly dozed.

A moment later, when he awoke, Robert saw the girl with the *petal lips* staring at him. She blushed and smiled. Her smile reminded Robert of a *hong-mian*, a leafless tree that grew in southern China in the spring. After a longer winter's sleep, its large red flowers bloomed all in one night.

Her pure smile, unintentionally affectionate and out of place, belonged to this moment. "My name is Robert Hart," he said in clumsy Mandarin and offered his hand in greeting.

She ignored the hand and pointed to the old man. "My father, Chou Luk. These are my younger sisters and brothers." She stopped and a moment of silence hung between them. Then she added, "I'm Ayaou, Precious Jade. I thank you for saving my family."

Chapter 4

It was a mystery to Robert. He was a twenty-year-old nobody, and the last place he wanted to be was inside Ward's house in Shanghai. The mercenary general had decided to hold a victory celebration and invited Captain Patridge, who brought Robert, who had no idea why Patridge was paying so much attention to him. Maybe it was part of the captain's nature to be friendly, which probably explained why he loved telling bad stories to a captive audience.

Like the French and English, the Americans had added on to Shanghai, but the American concession was closer to the old walled city where the fighting had taken place between the Imperial army and the Taipings. Most of Shanghai outside the old walls was a foreign city, not Chinese, and each country had put its cultural stamp on the architecture.

Ward's house differed from the buildings Robert had seen in the American concession. It was one story with a Cape Code style roof, but it had round-edged, thick concrete walls with deep windows and doors. The house looked odd.

"Strange, isn't it," Patridge said. "Ward calls it his adobe Cape Cod hacienda. Because of the rainfall, a steep pitched roof was needed. The Pueblo Indians invented adobe houses, but it is supposed to have a flat roof. Ward says that adobe houses are made of mud and can be found in the American Southwest. Don't engage him in a conversation on that topic. If you do, you will have to listen to his story about some American named William Walker, who invaded Mexico a few years back. Ward was an officer in this Walker's army. From there Ward went to the Crimea to fight but resigned after a short time. The rumor is that he was insubordinate to a superior officer."

After having seen Ward in action, it was easy for Robert to believe the rumor. In fact, he wanted to believe it because he did not like the mercenary.

Inside the house, the rooms were long and deep with low, opened beam ceilings. There was an endless supply of food, whiskey and wine. The Chinese servants never stopped scurrying about with loaded trays. There were boxes with cigars and cigarettes, and the stench of thick tobacco smoke filled the place. Robert walked from room to room and saw the guests getting drunk. He listened to one conversation after another.

"The Asian whores in the French sector are of the highest quality," one of Ward's army officers said.

"I earned a thousand percent profit on the last cargo of silk I bought and shipped to Paris," a merchant said in another conversation. "The Chinese have no idea what the European market will pay."

"I had a similar experience with spices," his companion replied. "And I know of a German who made a fortune selling Chinese antiques in America."

The talk Robert heard soured his stomach. and he lost his appetite. He didn't belong here. They had no common interests—one example was the Chinese culture, which he found fascinating like the Greek and Roman cultures had fascinated him when he had studied them at college.

Chinese art, literature, philosophy and history set his curiosity on fire. It differed from any culture he'd known. The Chinese had been a literate society when the Greeks and Romans and all the rest of Europe were still running around wearing animal skins, and the Chinese kept their culture alive while the Roman Empire collapsed sending Europe through a thousand years of darkness. The oldest known dynasty in China was the *Santai* also called the *Three Dynasties* from two thousand years before Christ. To think that China had an unbroken civilization that went that far back inspired Robert to understand how they managed to hold things together.

Robert wanted to slip inside the skin of one of their famous scholars and know what he knew and experience what he'd felt. He wanted to do the same with one of their great generals now that he had tasted battle. After the fear and shock had bled away, it was an exhilarating experience to savor.

In this room were opium merchants and mercenaries that looked down on the Chinese and laughed as they cheated them at every opportunity. They had no sense of the beauty here. Robert was disgusted and thought of them as the spoilers of the earth—the filth of life. They were not people he wanted to know. It was as if he were a book of good literature floating in a sea of decay.

He found a corner and stood in the shadows wanting to return to Captain Patridge's house and idle away the rest of the summer.

Captain Patridge walked up to him, and said, "What are you doing, Robert? This is your chance to meet the rulers of Shanghai. Do not waste your time."

Patridge nodded toward two Chinese men talking loudly with each other on the far side of the room. "The one with the droopy mustache is Hsueh Huan, the governor of Shanghai. The dark, swarthy man standing next to him that looks like a Filipino pirate is Boss Takee. The governor works for Takee and his partner, Wu Hsu. When I see Wu, I will point him out. Takee, by the way, also works for me." He paused to study Robert, who wondered what the captain wanted from him. Robert wasn't sure if the man wanted friendship or something else. Patridge knew many important people so why add a low ranking interpreter to his group.

Robert had already overheard a conversation between Takee and another man, a Henry Burgevine from North Carolina. Burgevine was Ward's second-in-command. He was a big man with a swollen, red face. Takee sounded like one of the pimps Robert had seen in Ulster.

"How much do you know about Jardine, Matheson & Company?" Patridge asked.

"I've heard how they managed to establish their business on the East India Company's preserves by obtaining an appointment from the King of Prussia."

"But you don't know the details, do you?"

Robert shook his head.

"I'm going to tell you."

Robert mentally groaned but didn't reveal how he felt. He reminded himself that he knew what he had been getting into when he left Ningpo. Patridge's prattle was preferable to roasting in a steam bath in Ningpo where the mosquitoes had been sucking him dry.

"In 1834, Dr. William Jardine sailed his ship, the *Sarah*, to London with a cargo of tea. Because of his appointment from the King of Prussia, the East India Company couldn't do anything to stop him. With that bold move, he demonstrated the East India Company was no longer a power in the East, and others copied him. It was too late for the copycats though. Jardine, on the other hand, was the first to do it successfully. He built a fortune shipping tea to England. On the return trips he smuggled opium into China."

"I heard he died in 1843," Robert said in an attempt to make conversation. "Did you meet him?"

"In 1840. By then he was one of the richest and most powerful men in Britain, and his company is still growing and prospering. For that reason, I want you to meet Boss Takee. Your position in Ningpo may benefit him somehow."

Robert didn't know exactly what Patridge meant, but his curiosity got the better of him. He managed to keep his mouth shut and ears open. He understood that one should also learn from bad or distasteful experiences. This was another reason he'd joined Patridge's fight against the Taipings—to experience something new even if it were dangerous.

Ward walked into the room. Concubines in bright colored silk dresses surrounded him. They were all taller than he was. He was dressed in a red silk vest open at the front, which exposed his dark, hairy, muscular chest. His baggy trousers ballooned around his hips and legs like a cloud of black satin. A thick cigar bobbed in his mouth and smoke billowed from his nostrils like some western dragon looking for prey. In this image, Robert saw differences between Chinese culture and Western. In China, the dragon was protective, friendly, a sign of good luck.

"Quiet!" Ward's voice boomed. "I want everyone's attention. Clear the center of the room. It's time for some singsong girls to dance for us." One of his concubines slipped both of her hands inside his vest and whispered in his ear. Ward listened with a growing smile and burst out laughing. Robert did not approve of the man's behavior.

The men crowding the room drifted toward the sides, where servants and concubines with painted faces waited.

Captain Patridge walked into the middle of the room. "I'm presenting you with a special entertainment. The three dancers are Ayaou, Precious-Jade; Shao-mei, Little Plum Flower, and Lan, Orchid."

Hearing the name *Ayaou* grabbed Robert's attention. Was this the same boat girl he'd saved? It surprised him to hear she was a singsong girl. He thought she was part of a family. Did singsong girls have families? He didn't know what to think, because he did not know exactly what a singsong girl was. However, he did recall that she had looked like a boy when he first saw her. She probably wouldn't be that attractive. Then he remembered her smile in the boat right after the battle with the Taipings. When she had smiled, his first impression had changed.

Patridge nodded toward a bearded, older man in a knee length gray cotton dress holding a stringed instrument called an *Erhu*. It was the Chinese version of a violin. With him was a boy who was playing an instrument called a *Yang-Chin*, the equivalent of a Chinese piano except it was played with a pair of chopsticks that had cushioned tips.

Robert recognized the old man as Ayaou's father, the sick-looking boatman Ayaou had defended so fiercely inside the stockade. He was the same man Robert had carried to safety.

"This is Chou Luk," Patridge said. "The dancers are his daughters."

"Dance called Great Gobi Goddesses," Chou Luk said in heavily accented English. "It traditional folk dance created in Ming Dynasty. My daughters are proper age. I am open to offers." He smiled and all the lines on his face twisted. It was a nasty expression.

Offers. What kind of offers? Robert was shocked and disgusted at what he suspected.

"Chou Luk is a valuable employee," Patridge said. "These three beautiful young women will make excellent concubines. Chou Luk assures me they've been taught how to pleasure a man and are certified virgins."

Robert couldn't believe what he'd just heard—that a father would do this to his daughters. What an evil man! It was beyond comprehension. What must the daughters feel? Maybe it was something to do with this culture. Though it appalled him, Robert wanted to understand.

At the time, Robert didn't realize that if Chou Luk sold his girls and they became concubines, even to foreign devils, that was a move up from a boat girl or a singsong girl. Most boat girls had little choice. The chance for a boat girl to become a concubine in a respectable family was almost nonexistent. Another way to escape the life of a boat person was to become a prostitute. Chou Luk was doing his best to make life better for his girls and possibly for himself too. If he gained a son-in-law, who respected him and took care of him in his old age, he improved his life.

Chou Luk began to play the *Erhu*. All the men in the room leaned forward—the lust and greed hot in their eyes. Robert was ashamed to feel the same, so he suppressed his desires.

Three women drifted sensually into the room. It was impossible not to lust after them. Robert's eyes fastened on the tallest, Ayaou. It was the same face he'd seen in battle but everything else had changed. What shocked him the most was that the girls didn't look offended. The way they looked at their father said they loved him.

All three girls were dressed in scanty midriff blouses of the same color with black silk pants. The dancers' narrow waists showed off their developing hips. The two younger girls were still without breasts, but Ayaou had developed a full set. Her nipples under the red silk blouse were almost visible. Ayaou and her sisters glided through the intricate dance. Their hands expressed meaning while exotic movements advertised their bodies.

Chou Luk and his partner played beautiful and heavenly music, while the dancers told their story with graceful arm movements. Robert was sure that the sisters had been instructed to smile because their smiles were stiff. As they moved, the room full of aroused men observed without shame.

He thought Ayaou recognized him, but she went on dancing without hesitation. She was naturally graceful. Her sisters were not. Robert thought that he detected a look of obvious dislike for what she was doing. This attracted him to her more. He wondered if she had danced for men like this before. He didn't know why, but he hoped this was the first time.

He couldn't take his eyes off Ayaou's nut-brown skin. The music grew louder. The dreamy look in Ayaou's eyes changed. It was as if she had been caught in a spell. Her bosom bounced as she performed the motions of rising and falling to illustrate ocean waves. To Robert she was transformed into a goddess free of the men drooling over her. He imagined her moving gracefully and innocently through a world of wild passion while avoiding the dangers.

As the dance ended, the sisters joined hands. The two younger sisters hummed as Ayaou sang. Robert was surprised that her voice wasn't scratchy like other Chinese singers he'd heard. It was soft and melodious. The tone of her voice put feeling into the words that built images in his mind of lovers walking through a grove of trees that swayed rhythmically with the wind. He struggled to understand the words but barely succeeded. It was something like *life is like dew on a leaf.*

The song ended. Shao-mei and Lan ran from the room like mice chased by a cat. Robert noticed Ward staring at Ayaou. He didn't like what he saw in the American's eyes. Ayaou looked in Robert's direction. Their eyes met. She gave him a dirty look as if she could have spit on his face. He stopped breathing and felt dizzy. Why? He'd saved her family. He thought it couldn't be him, so he turned to see who was behind him. There was no one. Confused, he turned back and saw she was smiling as if taking pleasure in tricking him. His heart beat faster, and he breathed again.

"One more song!" Ward called, and Chou Luk complied. Without hesitation, when the music played, Ayaou started to dance. Robert's mind ordered him to talk to Ayaou. He moved toward the door where the younger sisters had escaped. Slipping through the opening, he stepped into another room. He hoped that she'd exit this way toward the walled garden, which occupied several acres planted with flowering plants and trees.

The air was thick with foul odors from vomit, spilled liquor and cigar smoke. It was difficult to breathe. Robert was dripping with sweat. Wanting to stay sober, he poured the rest of his wine into a crack in the tiled floor.

For a moment, he thought of leaving without attempting to talk to her. Then he remembered Ayaou's defiance in the face of death. Her contrasting smile full of life and energy kept sneaking back into his head. So he stayed and continued to watch. He wanted to meet the girl that fought beside him. He was afraid it might not happen.

About a third of the men had already left the room with some of the painted whores. Robert looked around at those that remained and saw Ward, Patridge and Boss Takee. They were all looking at the same girl, Ayaou. Robert wondered what price her father was asking. The greed in Chou Luk's eyes warned Robert that the old man was going to squeeze every yuan he could out of the winner. This wasn't going to be easy, and that frightened Robert. He had to have her. It didn't matter what he had to do.

When Ayaou started to leave, Robert stepped into the shadows. The soft scent of exotic spices signaled her passing. He followed. When she went through the door and entered the garden, he made his presence known by clearing his throat.

She reacted as if she'd been expecting him. They stared into each other's eyes—both nervous. Robert touched her arm with his fingertips. When his fingers made contact, she looked away and examined the garden as if seeing it for the first time.

Was she here to meet her lover? Robert thought. After all, she was every man's dream.

Without warning, she led the way deeper into the garden. He followed. Soon they were lost in the darkness.

"What are you doing here?" she asked.

"I wanted to see you." He stammered and was relieved that the words found their way out of the prison that his mouth had become. She made him feel so alive that he wanted to climb the nearest building and fly off the roof. Thank heaven the moon was full and bright so he could see her clearly. Her dark eyes with their long lashes studied him. He could not fill his lungs. It was as if someone had tied a rope around his chest constricting his ability to breathe. He found it difficult to believe this girl had stood without fear by his side in battle.

"How old are you?" he asked, wanting to start a conversation.

"How old are you?" She shot back.

"Twenty," he said, and waited for her answer.

"Old enough," she said.

"By the way, I haven't told you my last name. It is Hart— Robert Hart. I'm Irish."

"That still makes you a foreign devil!"

"Sure, you're right," he said, gathering his courage to continue. "But does that mean I can't talk to you?"

"Meet me in the root cellar," she said quickly.

His insides fluttered and jumped.

"You haven't had much to drink," she said, as if she had to let Robert know her feelings. "I also saw that you were staying away from the others. Don't you like them?"

"No," he replied, and was glad she had noticed.

"That's good," she said. "Wait a moment after I leave, and then go through the kitchen. You will find a wood hatch that blends with the floor beside the back door. It is dark there. You will have to feel for the recessed iron ring that will allow you to pull it open. The stairs are narrow and steep so be careful. Make sure no one sees you."

When she pulled away, their arms touched. A sweet electric shock raced throughout his body. She hesitated like a startled doe and glanced back at him, which told him she too had felt the electricity pass between them. She disappeared.

It took an effort to walk back inside the house and glance into the main room. Ward, Patridge, Takee and two others were standing close to Chou Luk. Ward said something to Chou Luk. Takee scowled, shook his head, reached behind him, grabbed the hand of one of the painted whores, and dragged her from the room.

They had to be talking about Ayaou's price. This alarmed Robert. He moved closer to eavesdrop.

Chou Luk said, "I am open to offers until noon tomorrow. The man that offers the most will have Ayaou for his concubine."

"And she is a virgin?" Ward said.

"Yes," Chou Luk replied.

"She better be." Ward left with his woman.

Robert was glad that he still had time to find enough money to win. If he entered the bidding now, he would not beat the others. These men did not like to lose. Robert decided to wait until noon the next day to top the highest bidder. If he did that, he felt he had a chance. To get Ayaou he had to be tricky. Robert turned and walked through the kitchen thinking that if he'd never met Patridge, he wouldn't have seen Ayaou dance or hear her sing.

Once Robert was by the back door, he searched the floor for the wooden hatch, but the light was too gloomy. He had to get down on his hands and knees and feel for the iron pull ring with trembling hands. When he couldn't find it, he worried that it wasn't there—that she had lied to him and wasn't waiting. Then his fingers touched the ring. He pulled.

Chapter 5

How well did he know this girl he'd exchanged a few words with in a foreign tongue? Since he did not understand much Mandarin, he didn't know exactly what she had said to him. Was he a fool? What was waiting for him down there?

Robert's imagination conjured up her smile, the shape of her lips and the look in her eyes. She was an angel. Ayaou wouldn't hurt him. No woman with her eyes could do injury to another person. After all, she stood beside him and killed Taipings. She was loyal and had courage.

He lowered the hatch into the open position and stared at the narrow steps leading into what looked like a black, sinister abyss. With both hands on the walls on either side of him, he descended.

Once his head dropped below the level of the floor, he closed the hatch behind him. All light vanished. He was blind. The air was cool and dry. He smelled ripe peaches and pears and the musty sweet smell of grain. He fumbled in his pocket for a match but couldn't find one.

After his eyes adjusted, the room wasn't as dark. There were baskets of yams and bags of rice. Manure clung to the produce. The low ceiling sloped down toward the far end of the cellar where a dim light leaked around a stack of burlap bags filled with rice. Robert gasped and jumped when a rat the size of a small cat ran across his boots. While he waited for the shocked pounding of his heart to subside, he questioned his reasons for coming down here.

With reluctant legs that grew heavier with each step, he walked the length of that narrow root cellar and had to get down on all fours to squeeze around the fifty-pound bags of rice and into the narrow space beyond. He stopped. What if she wasn't there? What if this was a trap? What if there was someone else waiting on the other side to chop his head off?

One of his younger sisters had crawled into a hollow tree once when she was four. That dead space in the tree had extended into one of the larger branches. She jammed herself in there. Robert and his father heard her screams and used saws to cut away the end of that dead branch, so they could pluck her like a tooth from a jaw. He now knew what she must have felt, but unlike her, he still had time to escape. Shaking off his doubts, Robert moved forward.

Once he crawled beyond the bags of rice, light brushed away the gloom. He saw Ayaou sitting against a wall with her knees pulled to her chest. He breathed with relief. The top of her head was inches from the close ceiling. She turned the lantern at her feet to its softest illumination and put the light on top of a small barrel of wine nestled in the corner behind her.

"Robert Hart," she said, chewing the syllables, "I know why you're here."

Guilt burned his face. He didn't know what to say. If she were reading his mind, she knew how much he wanted her. He shifted uncomfortably in the tight space until he faced her.

"I believe you are here to make me your concubine," she said.

"Are you playing games?" Robert asked. He had no idea what she was up to. "I'm not here to cause you unhappiness." Defensiveness crept into his voice.

"My father is up there negotiating my price and the price of my two sisters," she said. "I will be seventeen soon. My sisters are fourteen and thirteen. How do you think this makes me feel?" She looked sad.

"I'd hate it if I were you." He reached for her hand, and there was no resistance.

"I do not hate those men," she said, shaking her head. "My father hates what he does to feed his family. He has to sell us. He is not the only man in the village who does that. He has to treat us like hens and fish in the market. He cannot afford to be soft hearted." Tears glittered in her eyes.

"But he's selling you to a stranger." Robert stammered.

"That is my fate." She lowered her head to stare at the ground.

"No, it's not!" He burned with anger.

She looked up. "I do not know what it is like where you come from, but in China a girl is born to be a foot warmer for a man."

"Any man?"

"It makes no difference. You cannot understand. After all, you are not Chinese." Her chin came up as if challenging him.

"I'd like to try," he said. "How much will your price be?" Her hand felt lifeless like cold, dead rubber.

"I do not know. My father said I am no beauty. My skin is too dark. I am too thin. My chest is a washboard." She lifted a foot. "My feet were never bound. I do not have a pale moon face, and that is the requirement for selling at a high price to a Chinese man." She extracted her hand from his grasp. "My father has done what he can. My sisters and I are healthy as sows. My family needs the money, so he can see a doctor for his intestine problem. If he has any money left, he will provide educations for my brothers and buy them wives. That way they can carry on the family name."

A rice bag touched Robert's left knee. The stone wall touched his right. She changed position, folded her legs under her and their knees kissed.

"There is an empty rice bag in the corner behind you," she said. "Hang it in the opening so no light leaks out."

He twisted around to do it.

"Do you think," as if having difficulty expressing her thoughts, she paused and bit her lower lip, "that you would like to be my master? I mean, would you buy me?"

Robert reached for her hand again and held it between both of his. Her flesh was alive now, because she was trembling. "I want to talk about this another time?" Getting to know her was more important.

"I do not have time," she replied, and a tear escaped onto her cheek. "My father will decide soon to which man I will be sold. Do you work for Patridge?"

Robert shook his head. "No, I'm an interpreter, a provisional assistant at the British Consulate in Ningpo. Captain Patridge invited me to his home during the summer."

"You do not sell opium," Ayaou said. "I like that. My father says opium is not good for people but times are bad. We have to survive. My father says Captain Patridge is interested in nothing but money." She took her hand back and crossed her arms over her chest. "Did you know that he keeps eight concubines in Shanghai and another four at the Lookong receiving station? I heard that when foreigners leave China, they sell their concubines to be whores."

"I'll never abandon you," he said.

Her tears started to flow, and Robert's heart went out to her. It took an effort for him not to make more promises he might not be able to keep.

"You are a good man," she said. "You risked your life to save us. No Chinese man or any other foreign devil would have done that. Boat people are unworthy. I want you to be my master. Have you got money?"

"Not enough to compete with men like Ward and Patridge." He sounded frustrated.

"That is too bad." She started to cry in earnest now, and she sobbed.

He felt desire spreading through him. He pulled her closer. "But I want you to be mine. I'll do anything."

"Then you must hurry," she said, throwing her arms around his neck. Robert felt her hot tears against his face. The floor creaked above them and dust drifted down. Startled, they looked up and listened to the heavy footsteps.

Once it was quiet again, he turned back to her. "You must forgive me, because I'm going to kiss you," he replied. They talked in whispers afraid someone might hear them.

She leaned away from him. "I am not sure I will like that." She pouted, and her lips looked inviting. "My father had me practice kissing by sucking a carrot."

"A carrot."

"Yes, he said barbarians liked it."

"What did he mean?" Robert was having trouble swallowing. His heart was pounding like a drum ready to burst.

"He said the carrot is the barbarian's tongue."

"I see. So, you didn't like it." It was a struggle not to smile.

"No, my father ruined my appetite for carrots for good."

"That's a pity." He almost laughed.

"How are you going to kiss me?"

"I'll show you."

"Do I have to suck?"

"You don't have to do anything." Her obvious innocence captivated him. He hoped she was the woman he'd always dreamed of.

"That will be nice," she said.

She jerked as Robert moved toward her. Her head ended in an awkward angle, and he kissed the side of her nose. Robert took her face between both hands, held her still, and kissed her again. Her lips were stiff and dry at first. After she relaxed, they were soft, warm, and moist. The moment turned serious. When Robert slipped his tongue into her mouth, she gasped, and said, "I like it, Robert Hart."

"Kiss me back," he whispered.

She was cautious like a chick ready to leave its nest for the first time but once their lips met, she became the aggressor and her tongue the invader. His hands moved to her clothes. He peeled off the thin layers of silk. There was no resistance as he stripped her.

She unbuttoned his shirt and slipped her hands inside to explore his chest and back. Her eyes opened wide with surprise. She pushed away from him and stared at his chest. "So much hair," she said. She ran her fingers through it. "It feels strange to touch and looks like dark grass." She laughed and threw herself on top of him pushing him onto his back. She pressed her lips against his. Their tongues danced.

His hands explored her muscular, naked legs and ended on her bottom. There wasn't much room, but he managed to pull off his shirt and crawl out of his pants and for an instant, their lips parted.

"Do not stop," she said, and fear flared in her eyes. Her voice sounded frantic and demanding. "Touch me everywhere."

They rolled over, and their naked bodies mingled. He kissed her neck and ran his tongue along her smooth flesh. She tasted like the ocean.

"Make me yours before my father sells me," she said, whispering.

Her words brought back reality. Her father was taking bids on her virginity. In a moment, Robert was going to steal it. His conscience screamed no, but it could not fight his desire.

"Take me." She begged and pulled him toward her.

"But your father—"

"I want you, Robert Hart! Pity me! It is my last wish before I'm sold. I will never forget how you carried my father to safety." She sobbed and tears wet her face. "You are making me a happy woman. My life is worth this moment."

Heat flooded him. He held her with both hands while he grunted like a stag in rut. He thrust into her for a long time. After she gasped and her body convulsed, his orgasm quickly followed.

Once it was over, sweaty and exhausted, they slept in each other's arms.

When Robert awoke, she was gone. He felt lost. For a moment, he wondered if he had imagined it all, but the sexual scent of their encounter filled the space. He was glad that Guan-jiah had not been there watching from the shadows. It wouldn't have been the same. He cradled the back of his head in his hands and stared at the ceiling basking in the memories of his time with Ayaou. His mood suddenly shifted to one of regret, and he was confused. Both Me-ta-tae and Willow had left him soon after making love too.

A deep stabbing pain blossomed in the center of his sternum. It hurt and he rubbed at it. He wanted to wake just once with the woman he'd made love to next to him. He wanted to sit up and study her sleeping face. He wanted to kiss her lips and light the fire again. Every sexual encounter since his first time at fifteen had ended the same way. Robert was sick of these brief interludes.

Chapter 6

"Is there something bothering you?" Unwyn asked. He was the *Maryann's* duty officer. "You've been pacing and watching the shore all morning. It's too hot to be out here. The deck is like a frying pan. I'm about to have tea. You're welcome to join me."

Robert didn't look at him. "No, I'm fine." What he said wasn't true. He hadn't slept. He had no appetite.

"I shouldn't have been so hard on you during the fight, but it was for your own good. It was foolish taking a risk for those boat people."

"It was no bother," Robert replied. He still didn't look at Unwyn. He couldn't take his eyes off the shoreline and the city. Where was Chou Luk? It was almost noon and the deadline for bidding on Ayaou was ending.

"Patridge was wrong about you." Unwyn snapped. "You are a prig. I detest people like you. Rot in hell!" He spat over the side.

"What?" Robert turned to Unwyn, whose face was red and swollen from anger. "Don't take that tone with me!" Robert said. "I've done nothing to deserve it."

"People like us come to places like China for one thing—to become rich or powerful or both." Unwyn leaned closer until Robert smelled his sour breath. "You won't achieve that by risking your life to save peasants."

"What I did was the right thing to do," Robert replied. "Get out of my face."

"You are a fool and fools deserve what they get. Patridge was wrong taking you to Ward's celebration. He will gain nothing from it." Unwyn walked away with stiff, angry steps.

Robert didn't understand why Unwyn was so upset. Later he realized that by ignoring the man, Unwyn must have felt slighted, but Robert could think of only one thing then, Ayaou.

When Captain Patridge finished his business in Shanghai, he expected to sail back to his summerhouse on Zhoushan Island. Robert wanted to pay Chou Luk and take Ayaou with him. If needed, he'd use the money in his Hong Kong bank account. He was ready to sell everything he owned and ask for an advance on his pay. He was willing to offer as much as four hundred yuan to beat the others. However, if Chou Luk had changed his plans and didn't come to the ship, what was he to do?

Robert had a tin flask with whiskey in it. He took a swallow to calm his nerves. The whiskey burned as it went down. It started a fire in his empty stomach. He should've taken Unwyn up on his offer and mended the rift between them. He regretted not doing so but made no attempt to go after Unwyn and explain himself.

Captain Patridge walked up. "Since I have business to finish, I'm going ashore for a short time. Would you care to join me?"

"I can't for I have to talk to Chou Luk when he comes on board." Robert stood by the ship's side as Patridge went down the ladder to his waiting boat. At the bottom, the captain gave Robert an odd look before the boat left.

Robert's heart beat faster when he saw a small junk with a central cabin covered in bamboo matting moving toward the *Maryann*. After it came alongside, the first face to appear on deck was Ayaou's father, Chou Luk. His younger daughters, Lan and Shao-mei, were close behind him.

Unwyn appeared. "All right, Hart," he said in a tone full of malice, "you tell Chou Luk that Captain Patridge went ashore to finish some business with Boss Takee. He's to wait for the Captain's return. After you have done that, take these two girls below to the main cabin and see they don't leave it. They are the Captain's new concubines. The Captain does not take kindly to anyone spoiling the goods but a little touchy feely never hurts." With a lecherous look on his face, he winked at Robert, as if he were considering it for himself.

Robert didn't like the way Unwyn was talking to him but didn't want any trouble. He just wanted him to leave.

He didn't see Ayaou, which made him wonder where she was. He started to worry. He told the girls to follow him below. Once they were in the captain's cabin, Robert said, "You will stay here for your master." He looked around the cramped space. When his eyes returned to the girls, he asked, "How is your sister, Ayaou?"

The sisters, who were standing close together, didn't move and kept staring at the floor. Shao-mei, the older one, looked terrified.

"I'm Hart," he said. "Robert Hart. Do you remember me?"

Shao-mei's eyes came up. She shook her head.

"I'm Ayaou's friend. I carried your father to safety during the fight against the Taipings."

"We don't know what happened to Ayaou," Shao-mei said. "Our father doesn't share with us his business. He said that we have been bought. We haven't seen Ayaou since last night. Maybe you'll be able to find her. Will you?" She stepped closer to Robert and looked boldly into his eyes. Her fear had vanished.

"What kind of man is Captain Patridge?" Lan asked. "Will he beat us?"

"He won't beat you if you do what you're told. You'll not go hungry and will always have a comfortable place to live." Robert thought of Willow and the other concubines staying at Patridge's summerhouse and the life they lived entertaining his guests. He hated lying to these girls.

Clearly, Shao-mei still had a young girl's dreams, where Willow's dreams were dead. Shao-mei and Lan's innocence struck pain inside him as if an ice pick had pierced him. Soon Shao-mei's eyes would be dull like Willow's. He wanted to save Willow but didn't know how. No, Robert could not tell them the truth. What purpose was served by scaring them?

The cabin was oppressively hot, so Robert went to the windows running across the stern and opened them letting in the sluggish breeze. It improved the situation a bit. The sun wasn't beating on them in here.

Back on deck, he waited and hoped for Ayaou to arrive. The minutes dragged like hours. He couldn't wait any longer. There was another Chinese girl beside Chou Luk. She couldn't have been much older than Ayaou.

Robert bowed to the old man, and said, "The weather is hot this time of year, and the air is thick with moisture." He dreaded asking about Ayaou. It also didn't help that his conscience was berating him for wanting to buy a woman. To think such a thing was foreign to the way his father and mother raised him.

"I have seen years where it is worse and some where it is better," Chou Luk replied.

"Have you noticed the prices in the market since the Taipings have been here?" Robert hated himself for not getting to the point.

Chou Luk nodded. "The farmers are afraid. If they pick their crops and attempt taking them to the cities, the Taipings steal the food."

Robert found it difficult to swallow. He ran a finger around the inside of his tight collar to loosen it, but that didn't help. It was blasted hot. He was streaming with sweat. "Over here is some shade," he said. "We can sit and talk in comfort."

Sitting was a relief as his legs had turned to water and were trembling from nervousness. He ordered a deck boy to bring tea and biscuits.

"Is this young lady your daughter too?" Robert asked, and nodded toward the new girl sitting behind and to Chou Luk's right.

"No." Chou Luk smiled. "This ugly girl is my new daughter-in-law."

"I'm sure she'll provide many healthy grandchildren for you."

"Sons, many sons." Chou Luk smiled revealing a mouth filled with rotting, blackened teeth. "She'll also help take care of me in my old age. What about you, young man? Got a wife yet?"

Now was the time. "I have been thinking." He tried to smile, but his jaw felt locked. "If I may, I'd like to purchase your daughter, Ayaou. I'm willing to pay whatever price you ask." He knew it was stupid to say such a thing. What if her father asked for too much, and Robert didn't have the yuan.

"You want Ayaou!" The old man looked surprised.

"What is a suitable price?" His hands started to shake. He hid them in his pockets.

Chou Luk gestured for his new daughter-in-law to pour more tea in his cup. He then spent a long moment sipping as his eyes avoided Robert. A boat bumped the side of the brig. Robert heard Captain Patridge's voice. Ayaou's father handed the cup to the girl and looked toward the opening in the rail. His leather-skinned, narrow face was blotched with age reminding Robert of a picture from the Dark Ages of starving people. Chou Luk's hollow eyes had dark fleshy bags under them. A large half-inch mole sat securely on the left side of his jaw between his mouth and ear. He had stringy, dark hair with strands of white showing through.

"Ayaou," Robert said in an insistent voice. "I want to buy Ayaou."

"Ayaou is no longer available," the old man said. He didn't look at Robert.

"What did you say?"

"Frederick Ward bought her last night for three hundred yuan, much more than I expected," Chou Luk said. "She's not my property any longer. Frederick Ward is a wealthy, powerful man. He'll make a suitable son-in-law."

"But you said the bidding would last until noon," Robert said. "I heard you say that."

Chou Luk ignored him. The anger simmered and thickened in Robert's belly. Chou Luk walked to the rail to greet Captain Patridge.

Robert stared into the two empty teacups wanting to smash them. What was he going to do now? He didn't move while he listened to the drone of their voices. Money exchanged hands. Chou Luk left.

"Why are you sitting there, Robert, looking so forlorn?" It was Patridge.

Robert scrambled to his feet holding back tears of disappointment and suddenly realized how much Ayaou meant to him. She had been his first virgin. She had picked him. That thought alone caused his guts to knot up in pain like a wet, twisted dishrag. He grimaced.

"What is it?" Captain Patridge put a hand on his shoulder. "My god, you look like you were tortured. Maybe I can help."

How could he? How could anyone do anything for him? He had allowed himself to blunder into a situation that he couldn't control. Robert wanted to escape this horrible place but at the same time, he didn't want to go. If he left Shanghai, he might never see Ayaou again. Feeling lost, he sat on the deck and stared into nothingness.

"We'll be leaving tomorrow morning." Captain Patridge squatted beside Robert. "I've negotiated for a cargo of silk that'll go to England after the brig drops us off at the Lookong receiving station. With the silk already at the station and the lot I just bought, we'll have a full load and a profit."

Robert couldn't bear the idea that what he'd started with Ayaou wouldn't continue. His expression must've given him away, because Patridge looked at him with compassion.

"It's Ayaou," Robert said. "I wanted to make her my concubine, but Ward bought her. Chou Luk didn't keep his word. I miscalculated. I'm a fool."

"No, Ward is the fool," Captain Patridge replied. "He has a dozen whores as concubines, and he paid more for Ayaou than I paid for both of her sisters. He's drunk from power and wealth. Did you know that they call Ward the *Devil Soldier* behind his back? By the way, where are my two concubines?"

"In your cabin."

"Chou Luk should have waited," Patridge said. "Though you don't have the wealth Ward has, you're a dependable man. It probably has not crossed Chou Luk's mind that we think differently from the Chinese. He sold three of his daughters to men he believes are going to help take care of him. You think that I will. He'll get no help from Ward either. Ward is a lunatic bent on self-destruction. He's taking his army to Sungkiang before the week is out. I wouldn't take that rabble to the latrine. They're worthless. Did you see how they acted at the Taiping camp?" Patridge shook his head.

Robert's mind was stuck on Ayaou. Patridge's voice droned on. "And as for me," Patridge said, "I expect to return to England a wealthy man. None of my concubines will go with me. I will sell them to someone else. I plan to get my capital back and make a profit." He laughed. "After all, I taught them how to please properly. How about you, Robert? When the time comes, I'll sell Willow to you at a reduced price just because you are a friend."

Robert coughed up some mucus and spit it over the side. Women in China were treated like furniture. No, they were treated worse. He was disgusted.

A few years later Robert learned how wrong he was. Family was more important than the individual in China. It was explained by the simple fact that the last name came first. After he learned Chinese ways and mastered the language, Robert introduced himself to a Chinese person as 'Hart, Robert' instead of the other way around.

It was unthinkable for a daughter or a son, no matter what his or her circumstances, not to take care of a parent. To the Chinese, *piety* was more important than one's comfort or situation.

Emperors of the Han Dynasty were known to have sold their daughters but the price was different—it was peace instead of silver. One day Robert heard a singer storyteller present the story about Princess Wen-cheng, who lived about sixteen hundred years in the past. The singer sat with an audience around him. He had a *pipa* propped on his lap. The *pipa* was a four stringed instrument similar to a guitar but the strings ran the width instead of the length. He'd sing the story and pause while he strummed the *pipa* for a dramatic touch.

Princess Wen-cheng was sold to a warlord in Tibet, and she was the only Han living there. Before she left her father's court, there was a parting between the emperor and the princess full of tears and sobs. The Chinese had a term for this type of purchase. It was called *ho-phan*, which in English translated to *barbarian harmony*.

Robert eventually learned that Chou Luk, like the Han Emperor, also suffered. He had two choices. He could sell his daughters and gain the money to take care of his medical needs and buy a wife for his son or die and possibly leave his family to starve. He could have earned more if he'd sold his son, but without a son no one would carry on the family name.

Patridge squeezed Robert's shoulder. "Cheer up, Robert. You'll get over that Chinese siren. I predict that in a few weeks you won't remember her. I suggest you find an experienced whore. One who is beautiful too. I'm going ashore soon to conduct more business. Come along. I'll show you around. After I'm finished, we can have some fun. After all, everything is for sale in Shanghai."

"I'm tired." His despair was like a ball and chain.

"You have my permission to use my cabin to sleep. I won't be back for several hours."

"Lan and Shao-mei are in there!" Robert said swiftly.

"That's right," Patridge said. His face brightened. "Come with me. I know what will free you from the doldrums."

Robert followed the captain below to the cabin where the two sisters huddled side-by-side on the window seat holding hands. Their eyes, both frightened and confused, studied Captain Patridge. They'd worn cloaks when they'd come aboard, but the cloaks were off. They were dressed in the skimpy outfits they'd danced in the night before.

"I paid eighty yuan for the pair. The father did me a favor, because he works for me. That's why they were such a bargain. Shao-mei is fourteen and she's just blossoming. Lan is thirteen." Patridge put an arm across Robert's shoulders and pulled him closer. "I like you, Robert." He whispered like a conspirator. "Listen, I'll sell you Shao-mei for the same price I paid. She looks like her older sister anyway and because she's younger, she's tastier, more desirable—fresher meat. I've always liked the younger ones. That's why I'm keeping Lan."

Robert wanted to say how disgusted he was but didn't.

Patridge stepped toward the sisters and leaned over Shao-mei. He took her chin and tilted her face toward his. "I'm selling you to Mr. Hart here." Her frightened eyes shifted to Robert. The captain squeezed her chin and shook her head a bit as if to scold her. She strained to stand on her tiptoes. Her shoulders tightened from pain. Robert was tempted to say something but decided she was in no danger. He saw no need to intervene. What Patridge did with his property was none of Robert's business. It didn't matter that the property was human. It still didn't feel right though.

"He's going to be your master," Patridge said. "Make him happy. If he isn't happy, he might not want you." A lecherous grin spread across his face. "I'll keep you if that happens." He released her, and Shao-mei lost her balance and staggered back. There were red spots where his fingers had squeezed her chin.

"You'll go with me," Patridge said to Lan. "Get your cloak." He grabbed her hand and pulled her off balance, so she stumbled. A startled look flashed across her face.

"Shao-mei," she cried in desperation. "Don't leave me alone."

After they left, Robert was alone with Shao-mei. He saw the shock on her face as she stared at the closed door. Robert was amazed at how much she resembled Ayaou. She had a round face with full cheeks and a lovely pair of dimples, but her shoulder length hair wasn't as dark and shiny as Ayaou's. The only blemishes were two pimples on her forehead. Though Shao-mei still hadn't filled out completely as a woman, her developing breasts were small. Her hips were shapely and she had a slender waist and muscular legs.

She came to kneel at his feet and touched his ankles with her fingers. She looked timid but with a twinkle in her eyes. "I'll do whatever you want, Master." There was relief in her voice. Robert was struck speechless and stared.

After an empty moment, she asked nervously, "Why have you no words? You don't like me?" Doubt appeared on her face.

A shiver rushed through him as her fingers gently crept up his legs. He stumbled back to get away from her and sat abruptly on the window seat. He buried his face in his hands.

Robert jerked as Shao-mei rested her head on his lap and circled his waist with her arms. "I do a good massage," she said in a small voice. "I've practiced on cabbages daily. My fingers will relax you. I also do pressure-acupuncture. It'll make you feel as if you just ate a chicken full of vitality."

"No." He pushed her away. Robert thought of the carrots Ayaou practiced sucking and kissing. He felt guilt from the fact that he had an erection.

"You are unhappy with me?" she said, while tears filled her eyes.

He made no reply.

"You don't find me pleasing." Her lower lip trembled.

"It isn't that. You're lovely, Shao-mei. It's just that I'm tired and want to sleep." He stood and walked to the bunk nestled against the starboard side of the cabin. He slipped onto the bunk and closed his eyes.

"I'll keep you company." Shao-mei joined him. Her slender, young body molded to his. She buried her face against his chest.

He pushed her away.

Shao-mei propped herself up on one elbow and wiped the tears from her eyes. "You're sweating, and your face has turned red. Is it too hot? Let me take off your jacket and pants."

Robert felt as if he were dreaming when Shao-mei pulled off his boots and took hold of the cuffs of his pants. Ignoring his protests, she undressed him leaving his legs and feet naked. A tug of war raged inside him. His mind was in shock although his body was stimulated and delighted. His erection swelled toward the bursting point. He was glad that he had on baggy underpants to hide it.

Her fingers unbuttoned his shirt. He was like a helpless baby in its crib. She pulled the shirt off, and when her fingers went to his underpants, panic threatened to castrate him.

"Stop!" He was desperate, grabbed her hands, and locked them in his. Touching her excited him. "Look, Shao-mei, you don't know what you're doing." His heart thundered inside his chest. He was having trouble breathing. Good Lord, this was the sister of the woman he had deflowered. It wasn't right.

"I know what I'm doing," she said in a frustrated tone. "If I can't make you like me, you won't keep me. You're thinking about returning me to Captain Patridge. I don't like him. He already hit me once last night after he bought me. I made him angry. He threatened to pull the nerves out of my body and make them into a rope to hang his clothes on. You can't give me back to him!"

"This is making me crazy." Robert let her hands go. He stared at the crisscrossing timbers of the cabin's ceiling. "Stop bothering me," he said, controlling the expression on his face. "I'm going to sleep." He shut his eyes.

It was quiet. The only sounds were his heart and his ragged breathing. Then he heard the soft sound silk makes when it slides across smooth skin. He cracked open an eye and saw that Shao-mei was naked. He stopped breathing. His stealthy eye traveled the length of her taking in the smooth, tanned skin and the gentle curves.

"Don't worry, Master," Shao-mei said, trying to sound confident and brave. "I'm not a finished woman, but I am a woman." She slid her hands down the length of her nude torso to her vulva. "Two months ago, I had the hot tide for the first time. I'm ready to have babies."

This dazzled Robert. He was in complete disarray. It took an effort to breathe.

"If you aren't pleased because I don't have full breasts yet," she said with determination, "I promise that they'll grow to the size of tomatoes in a few months. I'm not lying. See, these nipples were not like this a few weeks ago." She fondled a nipple. It hardened and stood at attention. "The captain wasn't bothered. He liked them."

Robert shook his head in disbelief. He couldn't take his eyes off her.

"You will discover that I'm good. I'll keep your bed warm. I'll cook for you. I'll clean your clothes and keep your house in order. I'll make sure that none of your servants cheat you."

It would have been a lie to say that he wasn't tempted. He didn't know if he had the strength to resist his lust.

This desirable young virgin was offering herself to him, and Ayaou belonged to another man. Robert had promised to make Ayaou his concubine. He'd followed through with that promise when he made the offer to her father. He had no control over what Chou Luk had done with Ayaou.

Robert resented what had happened, but what could he do to change the circumstances? Ward had an army. An image of Ward devouring Ayaou entered his mind, which put his heart through the torture of *chi-lin*, the thousand cuts.

On the other hand, it wasn't as if he was going to lose Ayaou completely. Having Shao-mei in his life was God's way to make up for his loss. In this younger sister, there was a shadow of Ayaou. They were like twin trees in the forest—both unique but still alike.

His eyes drifted back up to Shao-mei's face. She smiled and lovely dimples appeared on her cheeks. However, her eyes looked puffy because of her recent tears. What had Patridge done to her? Groaning, Robert closed his eyes and rolled over to face the bulkhead. There were two images in his mind now—Ayaou and Shao-mei.

He tried to convince himself that Ayaou had given herself to him last night for a reason. She knew that they might not be together. He'd been her first choice. Robert shouldn't consider it a betrayal by taking her sister as his concubine. In fact, he'd be doing her family a service. Shao-mei would be protected instead of exploited and abandoned. He'd never share her with another man. However, as good as these reasons sounded, his conscience refused to buy them.

The bunk creaked as Shao-mei slipped into the narrow space between the outer edge and Robert. Her arms snaked around his body. She pulled herself as close to him as she could. Her naked skin touched his, which aroused him further. He listened to the sound of her breathing.

Robert's erection was so hard that the skin on the end of his member felt as if it were going to split like a ripe plum while his heart drummed wildly inside his chest.

"Let's sleep now," Robert said, turning toward the wall.

She squeezed closer to him. Her naked body was like a spoon pressed against his body. Oh, Dear God, help me, he prayed. Give me the strength to resist this desire.

Shao-mei sighed and physically relaxed. Soon her breathing developed a steady, slow rhythm. She'd fallen asleep. Robert was relieved.

His left side was turning numb. He wanted to roll over but feared waking her. Carefully, slowly, he moved until his weight was off his left arm. When he finished, he was on his right side facing her. Without a sound, she threw an arm across his torso. He gasped and held his breath for a few heartbeats. The arm was slender and long and ended in a delicate hand with lovely fingers. Each nail on each finger was perfectly shaped. It was a hand meant to be held by a lover. He had an urge to lift the hand to his lips and kiss each fingertip, but he resisted. He traced the blue line of a vein back toward her shoulder.

Next, he studied her face. It was a smaller version of Ayaou's with orchid-leaf eyebrows and water chestnut shaped lips. She slept so soundly that she didn't stir when he accidentally touched her chin. Since his touch didn't wake her, he ran a finger along her cheek where her skin was smooth like warm glass. When he felt the beast stirring in his loins, he yanked his hand away from her as if he'd burned himself.

Robert closed his eyes and concentrated on something mundane like a long day at work poring over paperwork checking manifests from outbound and inbound cargoes. It didn't work. He couldn't get the image of her arm and her face out of his mind. He wanted so much to touch her.

He opened his eyes and looked at her again. This reminded him of a Chinese story he'd read. It was about a large family with eight sisters all married to one master. The story portrayed harmony, which was the key for the family's survival. Robert thought the story was fake—especially the part where the master was attracted to every one of the girls and took turns to *spread* his affection evenly. The master had written poems to praise each of his women. To Chinese scholars his most famous poem was the one he wrote for his fifth lady, who died of a sickness. The tragedy brought on by her death must have been the reason it was famous. Robert mentally recited the poem to get his mind off Shao-mei. This time the distraction worked.

'The maid gently closes the gate
I watch the river from above
Many sails pass
I see no sign of my love
The slanting sunrays cast a lingering glow
The broad water in it continues to flow
The islet with its plots of white flowers in bloom
Each and all contribute to my utter gloom.'

Robert wished Ayaou were here. He was tempted to tell Shao-mei that he loved her sister. He wouldn't send Shao-mei back to Patridge, but she had to know that Robert's love belonged to Ayaou. Tomorrow he'd talk to Shao-mei. He'd make her understand.

What a strange land China was. His mind calmed; his desire faded, and his beast slept.

Chapter 7

It's amazing how deep you can sleep when trying to avoid a quandary.

"Wake up, Robert! I believe you owe me fifty yuan."

Robert's eyes opened. It took a moment to focus. Then Captain Patridge's fuzzy face appeared.

"I see that Shao-mei achieved what I intended," Patridge said.

"What's this about fifty yuan?" Robert said, struggling to think. "Half of eighty is forty." He sat up and rubbed his eyes. Somehow, while he slept, Shao-mei, still nude, had moved inside against the bulkhead with her back turned toward him. The curve of her naked back was a magnet.

She stirred, rolled over and their eyes met. She giggled. Robert smiled and pinched her cheek. "Put your clothes on," he said. Having her get dressed was for him—not Patridge. Robert couldn't recall having seen anything so lovely in his life. His fingers tingled to explore.

"But you haven't made me your concubine," she said in a whisper, eyeing Captain Patridge with fear over Robert's shoulder.

"He doesn't need to know. Once I pay for you, you're mine." She was going to be his property. The idea shocked him. The possibilities were endless. Lewd visions flickered across his mind. He blushed. Clearing his throat, he picked up her clothes and thrust them at her. "Get dressed!" His voice sounded scratchy with emotion. His stomach was queasy again. Robert wondered if this would make him happy. He'd made promises. Memories of what happened in the root cellar with Ayaou were still fresh. He turned to Captain Patridge. "How did half of eighty become fifty?"

The captain shrugged. "Can you blame a man for wanting to make a profit?" Robert waited in silence. "All right," Patridge said. "Forty-five."

"Forty-two and I don't have it on me. You will have to accept a note drawn on my Hong Kong account."

There had been a moment when Robert considered letting him keep Shao-mei. Now he didn't want Patridge touching her, and he didn't like the way he was looking at her. There was something filthy about it.

"A note will be sufficient," Patridge replied.

"Then let's complete the transaction. I'm sure you have paper and ink."

Patridge appraised Shao-mei, who was standing beside Robert with her naked back exposed to him while she dressed. The captain's eyes shifted back to Robert. "You should work for me," he said. "You know how to bargain. I pay better than the government."

Robert glanced at Shao-mei, and his breath stuck in his throat. What was taking her so long to dress? He couldn't stop his beastly thoughts from going where they wanted. "Hurry and get dressed!" He lashed out as if his tongue were a whip. She turned timidly and looked as if she were about to burst into tears.

He leaned toward her and whispered so Patridge couldn't hear. "I'm not angry with you, child. I'm angry with myself." She looked confused. Robert hoped that his Mandarin was understandable—that he hadn't botched the translation.

"She was that good, huh," Patridge said. His eyes were glued on her. "We should renegotiate the price."

"Not a chance, Captain," Robert replied, stiffness creeping into his voice. "Give me the paper, and I'll write the note to my bank."

Patridge looked doubtful. "You know what, Robert, I regret selling her to you. Her sister Lan was stiff as a chopstick."

"If you're unhappy with Lan," Robert said, wanting to save both sisters, "how about selling her to me at a discount? I'll pay thirty-eight for her. After all, having intercourse with a chopstick can't be enjoyable." It was difficult keeping the scorn out of his voice.

The captain's eyebrows lifted, and he studied Robert. "Greedy aren't you," he replied. "No, I'll save Lan as an investment. After I train her, her value will increase."

"Keep my offer in mind if you have second thoughts."

"Are you interested in all my concubines?"

"No, just the two."

Patridge laughed. "I suspect you've come out on top on this one, and I mean that literally."

"You've no idea." He felt his face turn hot. The desire he felt for the girl had to be obvious. It was better that Patridge saw it as lust instead of contempt for the captain's way of life. Robert had already made an enemy with Unwyn; he didn't need two men hating him.

"Damn, I sold her too cheap," Patridge said.

"The paper please."

Patridge went to the desk and pulled out a sheet of paper, a pen and a bottle of ink. "Tell me what it was like."

"What are you talking about?" Robert replied.

"Did you have a good time? Did you enjoy making love to her?"

"A gentleman doesn't tell stories," Robert said, but he didn't feel like one. He felt like a cad. He remembered how close he had come to taking her virginity as he had already taken Ayaou's. He wasn't any better than a thief was.

He took the paper and with a shaking hand wrote a note directing his bank in Hong Kong to pay Captain Dan Patridge seven pounds. "Correct me if I'm wrong, but I believe that is equal to forty-two yuan." With the pen poised above the paper, Robert looked up. "My offer for Lan is still good. I can write fourteen pounds as easily as seven."

"No," Patridge said. "I'm keeping her."

Robert wondered if he were trying to be a Don Quixote. A book he read in its original Spanish. Had he fallen into the trap Miguel de Cervantes had written about in 1605? Was he chasing windmills trying to save Shao-mei and her younger sister? Was he acting the fool? Was Shao-mei his Dulcinea? Was he that blind? Well, he wasn't crazy, or at least he hoped not. He didn't think he was a Don Quixote.

Then Robert remembered something William Lay had said during a conversation in Shanghai a year before. "*Robert, my father believed that we Westerners have a great ability for getting and making more things, but we don't get much enjoyment from them. The Chinese, on the other hand, focus on enjoying the few things they have, and one of those things is women. China is a man-centered universe where the women have one primary purpose—to provide happiness for men in ways we could never imagine."*

William had described a savage ordeal of how Han women had their feet bound as children to please men. It was an agonizing procedure because the bones had to be broken during the process. Some of the girls died.

Robert glanced at Shao-mei. He stared at her normal sized feet. Seeing them boosted his mood. In fact, she had graceful feet. He was glad she hadn't suffered from the pain of foot binding. Then he looked at her face and was reminded of how lovely she was. He didn't like what he was starting to think. It bothered him that his flesh was so weak. He forced his eyes back to the paper. He blew it dry and handed it to Patridge. They shook hands to seal the bargain. Robert decided he would do what was right for Shao-mei and save Ayaou if a chance presented itself. He'd not give up easily. Not like Quixote had. Besides, Don Quixote would have been lost in China. The dragons here were supposed to be friendly creatures.

"All right, let's complete our business," Patridge said. A look of lust and envy appeared in his eyes. He glanced at the bunk bed where Robert and Shao-mei had slept. Robert felt his face twisting itself into a mask of disgust, which he struggled to control. He wanted to tell Patridge to keep his eyes off her.

"I came to get you. Tonight General Ward is having a dinner and a strategy session at his house with the officers of his army. Tomorrow he'll march out of the city to take back Sungkiang from the rebels. If he pulls this off, he will be in favor with the Imperial court in Peking. I want to take advantage of this moment to start a business relationship with the rascal."

"I understand." Robert reached for his boots. Shao-mei, who was now dressed, knelt and slipped them onto his feet. Although she was putting his boots on him, her eyes were fastened on his face as if he were a book that she wanted to read.

Having her dressed didn't help him. Her outfit was so skimpy and sexy, that he was mad with desire to get her clothes back off and run his tongue over her naked body. His expression must have given his thoughts away, because she looked startled and quickly finished lacing the boots with fumbling fingers. Forgive me, Lord, Robert thought. He was a starving beast trapped with a delicious meal that he dare not eat. Robert stood and allowed her to finish dressing him.

It occurred to him that if he had dinner at Ward's house, he might see Ayaou again. He found five yuan in his pocket and gave it to Shao-mei. "Buy something else to wear that covers better and keep any money you have left for emergencies."

Remembering that Patridge was still there, Robert decided to stage a show. He leaned forward and kissed Shao-mei on the mouth. He made sure it was a long kiss, and he couldn't resist slipping his tongue between her sweet lips. She stiffened, and her body twisted to the side like a chicken on a market scale being weighed with its wings and feet tied together. He steadied her by putting both hands on her hips, but touching her aroused him again.

Captain Patridge burst out laughing. "Now I know I was cheated."

Chapter 8

Had Robert heard Patridge right when the captain said they were on their way to see the Son of Heaven?

"Before we go to Ward's," Patridge said, "you will meet this man. He is looking for a first-class interpreter."

Didn't they call the Emperor of China the Son of Heaven? Robert thought. "I'm not exactly fluent," he said. "Who am I to talk to the Son of Heaven? Even Sir John Bowring, the governor of Hong Kong, hasn't met him yet."

"You're not listening, Robert. It's not the Son of Heaven. It's Prince Kung, the brother of the Emperor, the true manager of the Imperial court. He has come from Peking to deal with the problems caused by the foreign powers. He wants someone that knows several languages fluently to interpret for him. We are on our way to a house near the waterfront."

"That doesn't tell me about the location," Robert said. "Where exactly is this house we are going to?"

"It is in the walled section of the Chinese City where he's interviewing people for the position."

He wasn't happy that Captain Patridge had arranged this audience with Prince Kung without warning him. "How did you manage it?" he asked.

"I asked the governor of Shanghai, Robert," Patridge replied, "When you see the prince, don't be shocked. He looks young. Do you know how old the Emperor is?"

"No, but I suspect he's an old man with a long white beard."

"Wrong. The Emperor is twenty-four." Robert couldn't help thinking of Guan-jiah and how young the eunuch was. Could the Emperor of China and his servant, who recited Confucian philosophy, be so close in age?

When they reached the house, Robert was ushered into Prince Kung's office and guided to a chair. The ink strokes of a Chinese calligraphy hanging on the wall were thick like the trunk of an old dead tree. The massive rosewood desk had intricately carved legs that looked like dragons. The dragon tails touched the floor and the heads supported the thick slab top. The serpents' eyes stared at Robert as if he were something to eat. A huge ceramic pot sat in a corner with a thick clot of yellowing bamboo growing from it.

A servant brought tea. The prince was slim with a pair of penetrating eyes and a scrawny mustache. His head was shaved bald except for his *queue*, a strand of braided hair that fell from the back of his skull to his waist. He wore a gold-laced robe embroidered with stars and blue-green ocean waves. Long strands of beads made of jewels and jade and other colorful ornaments hung from his neck. He was dressed like an emperor, but he looked so young—almost like a boy. Even Guan-jiah looked older.

After tea, Prince Kung leaned forward and stared into Robert's eyes. "Do you know the difference between the verses of the Tang Dynasty and Sung Dynasty and the style of ruling between Han-ti, the Emperor of the Han Dynasty and Nurhachi, his ancestor, the founding Emperor of the Ch'ing Dynasty?"

Robert fumbled for answers—his Chinese pronunciations clumsy. The room felt small. The blood color of the walls was dark and menacing. It was as if the walls were a vise closing on him. This was more difficult than a simple conversation in the vegetable market. It took an effort not to run from the house.

After a few more questions were tossed at Robert like rocks that he couldn't catch, Prince Kung turned to Captain Patridge. "This one does not grasp the complexities of Mandarin or Chinese history enough to serve us. We want someone who understands how the Chinese think and is capable of explaining that to the representatives of the foreign powers. If he is the best you can bring us, you are not useful." A bored expression clouded the prince's face. They had been dismissed.

Outside, Robert said, "Why in blazes did you arrange that meeting?" He was fuming with anger. He hated being embarrassed.

"Don't let it worry you," Patridge replied. "The Prince has seen you. That's what's important. In China, introductions like this turn priceless later. One day, maybe years from now, he'll remember this meeting and see the growth of your knowledge and skills." The captain put a hand on Robert's arm in a conciliatory gesture. "Look, Robert, I didn't do this embarrass you. Believe me when I say that I did this with your future in mind."

With an effort, Robert suppressed his temper. "I don't see how. That prince looked like he was still a youth."

"He's older," Patridge replied. "The Chinese don't show their age as we do. He's twenty-two."

Robert was now motivated to master the Chinese language. He didn't want to be embarrassed again. He wondered what he could do to learn how the Chinese think. For that to happen, he'd have to live in a Chinese house with Chinese people. He did have Shao-mei. Maybe living with her would help.

The dinner at Ward's was a repeat of the victory celebration over the Taipings. It was lavish and grand to show off the man's wealth and power. Robert resolved that if he were in a similar position, his parties would be sedate with people in conversations about art, literature and politics. Men like Ward would never be invited.

Robert sat on one side of Ward while Patridge sat on his other side of the long table. He wanted to be as far from Ward as possible. The room was oppressive with its low, open timbered, and smoke stained ceiling. The only person between Ward and Robert was one of the mercenary's concubines. Another concubine sat between Ward and Patridge.

Ward, sweating profusely, tossed down another glass of brandy. Robert doubted he tasted it. The man's body gave off a rancid odor like spoiled milk.

"So, Patridge," Ward said in his loud, obnoxious voice, "are you joining me on my way to victory at Sungkiang? Here's a chance to make a name on the battlefield."

"Unfortunately, I can't," Captain Patridge replied. He lifted his glass of wine and held it out. "I have business to attend to, but I'll drink to your success."

Ward waved a finger at one of the concubines. She stepped forward to pour more brandy into his glass. He lifted the glass and clinked it against Patridge's. Some of the brandy and wine slopped onto the table. "To gold and silver and the women it buys," he said, and Patridge echoed him. Ward drank half the glass in one gulp.

"What about you, Hart?" Ward said, slurring his words. "Unwyn said you fight like a gladiator. He said you took on a dozen Taipings."

"He flatters me," Robert replied. "I had help."

Ward laughed. "That's not the way I heard it."

"I understand you bought a new concubine last night named Ayaou," Robert said, shocked at his boldness. He had to be careful. He had said that without thinking.

"That bitch." Ward jerked his jaw to the side signaling for his glass to be refilled. A concubine leaped to obey.

"She wasn't to your liking?" Robert asked. He hid his trembling hands under the table and kept them on his lap.

"I bought her when she was dirty with her cycle, but she paid for it. I showed her who the master was." Ward lifted the glass to his mouth and spilled half its contents down his bare chest before he slammed it back on the table. "When this battle is won, she is one virgin I'm going to enjoy. She's too damn delicious! I love breaking a bitch that's never been ridden."

Robert clenched his hands into fists. He had always prided himself at controlling his temper. This was a test he wasn't sure he could win. "Her music was lovely," he said, choosing his words to lure Ward in while keeping the tone of his voice calm. "Do we hear some tonight? What do you say, Captain Patridge?"

"That would be pleasant," Patridge echoed. He watched Robert with narrow eyes.

He's wondering what I'm up to, Robert thought. *Why should he care?* Then he remembered confiding his feelings for Ayaou to Patridge. That had been a mistake. He shouldn't have told Patridge anything, because the captain might reveal what Robert really wanted.

Anxiety invaded his stomach, and he lost his appetite. He had felt like this in Belfast when his sister Mary warned him the family knew he was ruining his life with liquor and women. Because of his big mouth, he could lose this opportunity to get Ayaou.

He considered walking away. After all, he did have Shao-mei. He wouldn't be alone. She was a willing, sweet girl. And with Shao-mei, there was no crazy Ward to complicate the situation.

"Ayaou," Ward said as if he were a bull, "bring that damned Chinese stringed piano out here and play for my guests."

She glided through the door that led to the kitchen. Robert wanted to look at her. With an effort, he denied the desire. He blushed when he remembered the root cellar where he had made love to Ayaou. He realized he could not stop now. He had to have her. He knew it would take every bit of cunning he could muster for a chance at success. He stared at the tabletop afraid that Ward might notice his expression of anxiety. He couldn't allow anything to give away how he felt and worried about Patridge doing just that.

Ayaou stood behind Ward. She glared at the painted concubine next to the general and did not look at Robert. He knew that this was probably best, but he had hoped for a smile.

"Move," Ward ordered. He didn't say who should move.

Robert brought one of his hands out from beneath the table and picked up the wineglass. He needed a drink. Food was put in front of him, but he had no appetite. He paid no attention to what it was though he hadn't eaten all day. Another platter loaded with beef and pork arrived. The guests speared pieces for their plates. Robert sipped wine.

"Didn't you hear me?" Ward shouted. He used the back of his arm to sweep the painted concubine out of her seat. She lost her balance, fell over and cracked her head against the wall. She doubled over in silence and didn't move for a moment. Then she stood and stumbled from the room. At the door, she hesitated and glanced at Ward with a look that reminded Robert of a puppy that lavished attention on its abusive master. He saw tears in her eyes, but she wasn't sobbing. Looking as if she had been abandoned, she left.

Robert understood why Patridge did not like this man. He didn't like him either. Ward was a disgusting creature. However, Ward was a dangerous man to dislike.

Ayaou slipped into the vacated chair. She placed the *pipa* next to her face and started to play. There was a bruise on her forehead. Seeing it brought Robert's blood to a boil. *The bastard*, he thought. Robert struggled to stay seated and not smash in the man's smug expression. It would be stupid to lose control.

Instead, Robert diverted his anger into the wineglass. He squeezed it so hard it shattered. He cut himself in the process. A servant cleaned up the mess. Robert wrapped his hand with a cloth napkin to stop the bleeding, and the pain subdued his anger. He decided to do something risky and dangerous. If it didn't work, it might cost his life.

Ayaou finished the first song and started another. Robert leaned forward and placed his good hand on her arm to stop her. "General Ward," he asked, "is that invitation to join you in the attack on Sungkiang still good?"

"Of course," Ward replied. "I can use every white man possible. These Orientals can't think. They botch every battle they get into. It is the primary reason the Taipings have been winning the war. I am going to change that."

"I want to join you but on one condition."

"What's that?" Ward swayed in his seat struggling to overcome the alcoholic fog clouding his brain.

"I'm still mastering Mandarin," Robert said. "This trip to Shanghai has interrupted my studies."

"Why is this important?" Ward slurred his words. He took another swallow of liquor. His forehead and upper lip were beaded with sweat.

"My career depends on it."

"Bring your teacher."

"He's not available."

"Come on," Ward said. "Anyone that speaks Chinese will do."

"Anyone? Like whom?"

"Like one of my concubines," Ward said. "I'm sure any of them can speak the damned language with you."

"How about Ayaou?"

"That's possible, but why her?"

"I know her father, Chou Luk. I know her family." Robert didn't say what he thought—that she was supposed to be his woman, not Ward's.

Ward stared at Robert, who worried that the American might guess the truth. Ward turned to Captain Patridge. "Is Hart after his lesson, or should I suspect he's after my virgin?"

"Oh, he's after his lesson." Patridge lied. "The British government pays him to learn Chinese. He isn't interested in your concubine. Why should he be? He has his pick of them at my summerhouse."

Patridge wasn't watching Ward. He was looking at Robert. His eyes said that Robert owed him, which made Robert uncomfortable.

Maybe Ayaou had been right. Maybe Patridge was in it for the money. This confused Robert. How could he benefit this man financially? Patridge was a man who liked telling exaggerated stories and doling out concubines as bed warmers. Who was he to question Patridge's motives? After all, he had accepted Willow. He had no right to judge Patridge or be suspicious of him.

"All right," Ward said. He turned to Ayaou. "Get ready. Do a good job teaching Hart his Chinese. If you don't, I'll give you a twin to that bruise you already earned."

Chapter 9

An eerie silence ruled the night. It hadn't always been like that. Soon after Ward's army surrounded Sungkiang, out came the whiskey, and a wild boisterous celebration followed. Robert saw no reason for it. There had been no battle—no victory.

He had been outfitted with a Dreyse needle gun. The weapon was slung across his back. It was the first breech loading, bolt-action rifle he'd handled. Ward said the Prussian and German armies used it, and it could fire up to a dozen rounds a minute. Robert also had a Colt revolver. He felt more like a bandit than a soldier.

Ward assigned a hundred of his roughs to be under Robert's command. In his crude and clumsy Chinese, Robert talked to the noncommissioned officers in charge of the men under him. "I want to set a guard for tonight and have the men dig a trench between the city and us and fill it with wooden stakes."

The swarthy men with pockmarked faces stared at him as if he were some apparition that had sprouted from the ground. They started talking among themselves in a language Robert didn't understand. It wasn't Chinese—at least any dialect he'd heard. The group stopped talking. Then they laughed and turned their backs on him and walked away.

He burned with anger and frustration. Soldiers should not act like this. In a real army, he'd be justified to shoot them. If he attempted to punish them now for their insubordination, some of them might shoot back. Robert's Colt held six rounds, but there were at least a dozen heavily armed men in the group. He felt helpless.

After most of Ward's army was dead drunk, Ayaou was escorted to Robert. "It's about time you came," he said in a scolding tone. "I've wanted to practice my Chinese." He turned to her guards. "Thank General Ward for me. You may go. I'll escort her back to his tent later." He watched the men leave. They were probably going to get drunk.

Ayaou stood shrouded like a dark, cloaked ghost with her face hidden. From where they stood, Sungkiang was below them. A moat and a wall surrounded the city, and a few lights flickered inside. On Ward's side of the moat, the Taipings had planted a host of sharp, wooden spikes in the ground to slow the attack planned for morning.

"We may be the only two sober people here," Robert said. "Ward is a fool. This army deserves a better leader or the officers a better army."

Ayaou put a finger to his lips. "Shush," she said. "The night has ears. I'd better go back to his tent soon, so he will not suspect us."

"You can't leave," he said. "I found a spot in a stand of trees where we can be alone." Taking her hand, he led her through the snoring camp. Touching her excited him, but he had no choice but to contain his passion. Men were sprawled everywhere sleeping in drunken stupors. There were no sentries.

When they reached the trees, he stopped outside the grove. "If things go wrong, we'll meet in there. It will be a good place to make an escape to the countryside."

She stepped back and folded her arms across her chest.

"Are you worried about him?" he asked, but didn't add that he was worried too. Ward was unpredictable. "He will be drunk like most of his men," he said. "We'll be safe until morning." He was willing to say anything to get her to relax and stay.

She shook her head. "Not good. He is a demon."

"Nonsense," he said. He pulled her against him and wrapped his arms around her holding her close. She didn't struggle. "I don't want you out of my sight. I don't like what's happening." He waved a hand at the silent camp. "This is an invitation for disaster."

"Show me how to use that." She pointed at the pistol.

"Not here," he said. He led her into the grove of trees to a small clearing where they had some privacy. "We'll stay here tonight and part in the morning before the battle. If the fight turns against us, there's a dry gully on the other side of these trees. We'll follow it into the countryside." He sat and directed Ayaou to sit by him. Robert taught her how to work the Colt. He made her repeat everything and show him by unloading and reloading the revolver several times.

She struggled to hold the weapon steady. "It's heavy. What if I drop it?"

"Don't worry. If you have to fight, you'll find the strength, and they will be too close to miss. When you see the man you're shooting at fall, shift to another target right away. Always pick the closest one. Keep firing until every cylinder is empty then sit and reload. I'll be right beside you. Don't forget what I told you about turning the barrel of the pistol into a pointing finger. Just point that dangerous metal finger at the target and squeeze the trigger. Don't jerk it."

She put the Colt on her lap.

"Here," Robert said, "wear this?" He unbuckled the holster and belt. It was too big for her waist. He used his dagger to dig another hole in the leather to get the belt to fit. When he buckled it on her, she leaned toward him. His hands found her naked body under her clothing. He kissed her neck and the soft skin behind an ear. Their lovemaking turned frantic. It was as if the world was going to end, and this was their last chance. When she peaked and had her orgasm, he thought the noise was going to wake the camp.

"I had a hard time after you were gone the night after we ..." She stopped talking as if searching for words. "My father told me that I'd be Ward's woman, and I didn't want to go on breathing. He said Ward would kill him and the rest of the family if I took my life."

She leaned her head on Robert's shoulder. He smelled the familiar scent of the ocean in her hair. He wanted to see her face. The campfires had died, and there was no moon to light the night. He explored her face with his fingertips. Soon they were kissing and made love again. After they finished, he wrapped a blanket around her. "I want you to sleep," he said.

"What about you?"

"I'm not tired." He scooted back, leaned against the nearest tree, and patted his lap. "Put your head here. Let me be your pillow." He watched her fall asleep wrapped inside the blanket like a caterpillar inside its cocoon—to wake at dawn a butterfly. He didn't want a butterfly. He wanted a Mute Swan, Ireland's largest bird. They mated for life.

Ayaou cried out Shao-mei's name in her sleep. She didn't know that Shao-mei was Robert's concubine. When she found out, would she be angry and accuse him of betraying their love? He felt as if he were a coward for not telling her. It seemed impossible that so much had happened so fast.

He thought about the Chinese people he'd met since arriving on the mainland a year ago. Most had been friendly, and they were always respectful. China, with its many spoken languages, had found one common bond with one written language, something that did not exist in Europe. However, the Chinese were not all the same. He'd met a few from the north and discovered that up there the Chinese looked more like Mongols than the people living around Shanghai or Hong Kong. They were hard living and stood taller. They were also conservative in their beliefs.

In Hong Kong, on the other hand, he'd met a different type from a more sophisticated culture living an easier life. The southeastern Chinese were not as physically strong as those from the north were. The northern Chinese were wheat eaters, and those living farther south primarily ate rice. He wondered if eating wheat was the reason for the taller, more robust physique of the northern Chinese.

Stars appeared in the sky. It took a few minutes to adjust to the darkness. Ayaou was sound asleep and didn't move when he ran his fingers through her long hair, which felt soft and silky. He lifted a strand. When he let go, he watched it flow like water back into place. He loved this woman, but he didn't know her that well. He knew that she had courage. During that battle with the Taipings, she'd stood by his side, fought hard, and saved his life as he had saved hers. That wasn't such a bad beginning.

Then he wondered what his next move was going to be. How was he going to keep her? He had to admit that it had been foolish to rush into this without a plan. It wasn't like him. All the way through college, he'd never approached anything without a plan except where women were concerned. When he was around attractive women, he lost control. He hated losing control. He tried to think of something that he could do to keep her. He was exhausted from the long day. Maybe that was it. Maybe he just needed to sleep. It was frustrating. Here she was in his arms. They had made love twice. He questioned his purpose. It sickened him to think that he might have been motivated to have intercourse with her again. If true, he was a hypocrite.

It was late and clouds obscured the stars. A chill crept into the camp. He buttoned his jacket and pulled the collar around his neck and ears. He yawned. His eyes started to close. It was a struggle to stay awake. He wanted to watch over Ayaou but decided to rest his eyes. How could that hurt?

The first sounds Robert heard were the cocks crowing from the surrounding farms. He awoke to the washed-out blue light of dawn.

Then the enemy came.

With the morning sun behind them, the Taipings charged from the city. They came with muskets, crossbows, swords, spears, axes and clubs. They hacked their way into the camp killing many of the drunken men of Ward's small army where they slept.

The crackling sound of musket fire on the outskirts of Ward's camp woke everyone deeper inside. The army panicked. Those that survived dropped their rifles and ran.

Robert started searching for targets and fired his weapon as quickly as possible—pulling the trigger and reloading. He checked Ayaou often. The last time he saw her, she was calmly sitting there reloading the pistol. That was when Taipings, like locusts, swarmed over them in the grove of birch trees.

When Robert's rifle emptied, he reversed it and used it as a club. A young Taiping overcame him. The man obviously had been trained in a hand-to-hand form of combat. After a few kicks and blows, he took Robert's rifle.

Several other Taipings surrounded Robert shouting and cursing. He was determined not to cry for mercy or die like a coward. Then one man pounded on the back of his head. He felt a stabbing pain run down his side as a sword scored his ribs. Before he lost consciousness, he heard several loud, rapid gunshots.

Chapter 10

Robert awoke choking. His rib cage ached. He thought he might have lost a limb in the fight. He made an effort to lift his arms and discovered with relief that he still had them. He stared at his hands and wiggled his fingers to see if they worked. Then he saw his bare feet and wondered where his boots were.

"Ayaou," he said, but heard no answer. Was she dead? A crushing depression threatened to sink him. It was his fault. If it hadn't been for him, she would have been safe in Shanghai. How could he live with himself? Maybe he should find a way to take his life and end it now.

"Don't be stupid," he said, talking to himself. "Wait until you know the facts."

The underside of a dry, straw roof greeted him. A narrow, low opening appeared to his right and moonlight leaked into the place. It looked as if he were in a peasant's hut.

Was he a prisoner?

There were dry rustling sounds of mice and rats inside the straw walls of the hut. From outside came the noise of frogs and crickets, which told Robert there were no people close by, or the insects would have been quiet.

He rolled onto his side and gasped. A burning pain raced the length of his ribs. He then managed to prop himself up on one elbow. His right arm was strapped to his body, so he used his left to explore. He touched a rag that was wrapped around the top of his head. There were several bowls filled with water in reach. He picked one up, sipped the water, and relished it as it trickled down his parched throat. He coughed and closed his eyes. He felt weak. His flesh burned. To quench the fever he poured a bowl of water over his head.

The next time he opened his eyes Ayaou was sitting beside him.

"Oh, merciful Buddha," she said, and smiled with happy tears in her eyes. She held out an egg. "You've lost weight. I'm going to open this raw egg and pour it into you. I've also got apples, some peaches and tomatoes, and a few squash I took from the fields."

"Are the Taipings letting you cook? They didn't strike me as the type."

"We can't cook because the Taipings might see the smoke and discover us."

"So, we're not prisoners." That was a relief. "How close to Sungkiang are we?" he asked.

"Several miles."

Robert opened his mouth. She poured the raw, slimy egg in. He gagged but swallowed anyway. She used his dagger to cut an apple into slices and fed them to him one at a time. Energy started to trickle back. "How long have we been here?" he asked.

"Several days," she said in a rush of words, "and you were unconscious with a fever. You talked in your sleep. I couldn't understand what you said, and I'm worried that Ward will find us."

"Not to worry," Robert replied. "Ward will think we're dead. He might be dead, and if he isn't, the Tapings are more dangerous right now."

She lifted the Colt. "It's loaded. If any Taipings find us, I'll shoot them." She pointed toward a dark corner. "And I saved your rifle."

He saw it in the corner next to his boots.

"You fought like a demon," she smiled, "until one Taiping jumped on your back and hit you on the side of your head with a rock. I thought he killed you. There was so much blood. I emptied the pistol into them. The ones I didn't shoot ran. Then I dragged you away before they returned. I remembered what you said about the gully. Later I paid a peasant to let me use his donkey. We were fortunate the owner of this hut had fled. We have no money left."

Robert felt his pockets and discovered they were empty. She could've robbed him and saved herself. Instead, she risked her life for him. A lump of gratitude mixed with love gathered in his throat. Ayaou's loyalty touched him deeply. He valued loyalty and hard work above all else.

Her eyes filled with tears. "Buddha has been with us," she said. There was a moment of stunned silence when they saw the tears on both their faces. Then they laughed. It felt good to be alive.

"Are you a Buddhist?" Robert asked.

"Why would you ask that?"

"Because that's the second time I've heard you mention his name."

"Oh." She laughed. "I don't think I'm a Buddhist. It's just something we say when there is trouble. We are always willing to be helped by Buddha when we need him. My father took us on pilgrimage to the Pootoo Islands off the coast of Ningpo. Once we went on the annual pilgrimage to Miaofengshan in the north. I remember thousands of pilgrims, old and young, men and women, on the trail carrying sticks and yellow bags. We traveled day and night to reach the sacred temple. What I remember most was the vegetarian meals the monks served. After my mother died, we stopped going."

It was quiet for a moment, as they felt sad for the loss of her mother. Robert spoke first. "I want you to discover what happened to Ward and his army."

She hesitated. "But I don't want to leave."

"Go early in the morning while it is still dark. Before we return to Shanghai, I have to know what happened."

After Ayaou left, the days dragged. Robert rested the revolver on his stomach and dozed. It was hot and stuffy inside that hut. It was difficult to sleep. A jar of water sat on his right side, and the food was on his left. Flies crawled on the leaves Ayaou had used to cover the food.

He pried back the makeshift bandages to discover the sword wound down his side had not been deep. She'd packed the wound with what looked like spider webs and ground pepper. There was no sign of infection. He was healing.

Idle thoughts led him to realize he hadn't attended a church service since leaving Ningpo. The minister from the Church of England, who Robert had trusted with his Belfast sins, would ask questions. Since Robert had confided in the man, what was he to say about his life now? Was he to tell this minister that he'd fallen overboard and was drowning in adulterous sin with a woman the minister considered a savage because she wasn't a Christian? No, Robert couldn't imagine himself sharing intimate information like that with any man of his kind.

Ayaou returned early in the night. She knelt beside Robert and felt his head and the back of his neck. Her touch woke him. She said, "You aren't eating enough. That worries me."

She went to the rice paddies where she caught several frogs. Back in the hut, she pulled off their heads and skinned them. After sprinkling salt on the raw meat, she told him to eat.

"I don't eat raw meat," he said, "and not a bloody frog that looks like a small human with four limbs."

"But I insist. You have to get well by eating, because I can't carry you to Shanghai. I've caught mice too. Mice are a Chinese delicacy—delicious."

Oh god, Robert thought, *I'm going to retch.* She couldn't seriously expect him to eat raw mice. "Tell me what you heard about Ward." Robert tried to avoid watching Ayaou spitting out mice bones. He wondered if he could still kiss her after seeing her do that.

"It was easy," she said. "Everyone in Shanghai was talking about it. When the survivors from Ward's army reached Shanghai, they collected their pay and deserted. Ward survived without a wound. He vowed revenge against the Taipings and is recruiting a second army. His posters are everywhere."

This wasn't what Robert wanted to hear. "Help me get outside," he said, and struggled to stand. "I have to do something to get my strength back. When we reach Shanghai, I want to confront Ward." He didn't have much hope of defeating the mercenary general. Now that Robert had Ayaou, he wasn't going to let her go. He'd die first.

It was cool and shadowy in the straw hut the next day, and Ayaou slept beside him. Robert couldn't sleep, so he watched the peasants working the rice paddies like others had done for centuries—maybe for millennia. In the distance he saw a waterwheel moving water from a stream or canal into the fields.

A man wearing a high, cone-shaped bamboo hat was turning the wheel with his legs. He sat high on top of the water wheel as if it were a unicycle. The wheel was made of rectangular buckets, which scooped the water out of the stream to lift over the dike and dump into the rice paddy. Robert watched the way the light reflected off the man's muscular, bare legs as he turned the pedals.

China had been preserved like one of those thousand-year-old eggs he'd refused to eat soon after arriving in Hong Kong. The printing press, the compass, the crossbow and gunpowder had been invented centuries before they appeared in Europe, but China had never used them as Europe had.

Robert had always thought of farmers as honest, hardworking people that lived simple lives. Because of the simplicity of what he was watching take place outside the hut, he wanted to capture the scene in a painting so he could preserve it.

Robert pondered the possibility of Ayaou and him taking up such a life but of course, life wasn't that easy. However poor or powerful you were, tragedy and hardships had a way of finding you.

A poem he'd read by the eighteenth century Chinese poet Yuan Mei came to mind:

On the Road to T'ien-T-Ai
Wrapped, surrounded by ten thousand mountains
Cut off, no place to go—
Until you're here, there is no way to get here.
Once you're here, there is no way to go.

Robert wondered if he had any place to go—if his life was about to end before it had a chance to begin.

At night, Ayaou started to help Robert take short walks. It was slow progress at first. By the middle of August, the pain left and his appetite returned. As the long days progressed, he resolved that whatever it took to keep Ayaou from Ward, he'd do it. If there were a way, he was determined to find it. Maybe they could flee to India, but how would he earn a living there? If he returned to Ireland, his parents would never understand a Chinese girl like Ayaou. Besides, Ayaou wouldn't be able to adjust. She would be lost outside China. This was her country. It would be selfish to take her away from her people.

After one long, exhausting walk, he propped himself against the inside wall of the hut. Ayaou sat beside him. "Move closer so I can put my arm around you," he said. "I like holding you. It reminds me of why I want to stay alive."

She leaned over and fed sweet, pale-yellow pieces of baked yam into his mouth. He didn't question how she got the yams. She must've stolen them from someone's kitchen. After all, they couldn't risk a fire, and they didn't have money. What other way did she have to get cooked food?

She touched his hair. "I love your funny accent. You are everything an ordinary Chinese man thinks ugly—big nose, hairy body, and pink skin, but I can't have enough of you. In China it's stupid for a woman to dream, but I dared to dream of belonging to you. I wouldn't mind being your foot warmer in the winter and a cool breeze for you in summer." She cast her eyes downward. "I miss my sister, Shao-mei. It was bad luck she had to be sold to a man like Captain Patridge."

Robert stiffened. He'd forgotten Shao-mei. He felt heat filling his face and knew it was turning red. Why couldn't he hide such a response when he felt guilt or shame?

"Are you all right?" Ayaou asked, concern showing in her eyes.

"We have to leave for Shanghai," he said.

"You're not ready."

"We have no choice. We must go."

"What's the hurry?"

"It's for Shao-mei. I must speak with Captain Patridge."

She shook her head. "My sister's fate has already been decided with Lan's. They belong to Captain Patridge now."

"No, not Shao-mei. Not anymore."

Ayaou blinked. "What do you mean *not anymore*?"

"Stick that roll of cloth behind me, Ayaou." She did as he requested. "I'm going to tell you a story." He had no choice. He had to tell her about Shao-mei even if it meant losing her.

After she helped prop him up, he took a deep breath against the dread growing in his stomach and started. "After I failed in buying you from your father, I was crushed and fell into a depression. Captain Patridge wanted to cheer me up. He offered Shao-mei to me for the price he paid."

"Did you accept?" Her voice was calm.

He couldn't read her expression. It frightened him. For a moment, his tongue didn't want to work. He glanced away from her not wanting to see the hurt in her eyes.

"So, you bought Shao-mei to replace me." She stared at him. Her face stayed unreadable. Robert's heart constricted with fear and felt as if it were attached to a heavy anchor that had just been dropped into the sea.

He grabbed her right hand and held it in both of his. "I offered three times as much for you. I was willing to pay your father more. However, you were already Ward's property. I would never have accepted Captain Patridge's offer if you had been available."

"I understand," she said. She took her hand back. Her eyes avoided his.

Robert thought she was collapsing and was desperate to pull her back. He didn't want to lose her. "I have not had Shao-mei," he said. "You are thinking I did."

With tears rolling down her cheeks, she said, "Look what you've done to me. You've spoiled me with pleasure to have me discover that I don't deserve it."

"Ayaou, Ayaou—" He found himself unable to respond.

"I lied to Ward about my monthly cycle," she said. "And then you were there at the house asking for me. I couldn't believe it. I thought you were planning to steal me from him."

"Are you telling me that Ward hasn't touched you yet?" he asked, feeling thrilled that no other man had been with her but him. As quickly as the words left his mouth, he felt terrible. He had always hated people who lived a double standard. It wasn't right to have such thoughts. Hadn't he been with many women? Hadn't he had syphilis? Not that he wanted her to contract a disease from having intercourse with other men. That wasn't what he meant. If Ward had already used her, Robert would still have forced himself to make every effort to take her away from that monster. If he could've stuffed his spoken words back onto his mouth, he would have.

"Not yet," she said. "But he'll soon learn that I've already been *kai-bao*, peeled like a corncob. He'll toss me to his men. He'll demand his money back from my father. He'll beat me to death himself." She moved a few inches from Robert. Her eyes glowed like a cat's at night. "I am not sorry. I could've lived and died like a hen. I'm glad that you have Shao-mei."

"Shao-mei now has a chance to avoid life with Captain Patridge," Robert said, grasping at slippery strands of straw.

"Yes." She turned to him. "Keep her. She'll be good for you. I'm happy for Shao-mei. Fate will tear us apart, because Ward will not let me go. He is a powerful man. How can anyone stand alone against him?"

"I'll hide you from him." His thoughts were stubborn and unyielding. Robert knew he'd do anything to keep her.

"That will not work," Ayaou said. "Once Ward knows you are alive, he will send someone to ask for me."

"I'll handle that when the time comes. Right now I'm concerned about Shao-mei. If Captain Patridge thinks I'm dead, he will take her back." He had doubts about handling Ward, but he wasn't going to let her know that he was worried.

She looked at Robert with gentle eyes. "You care about my sister?"

"Why not? Unless you have a problem."

"No, you don't understand. My sister and I are like a hand and a foot of the same body. When sisters are sold or married off, they seldom see each other again. It is common for a man in China to take sisters of the same family to be his wives or concubines. If you—"

"No, Ayaou, you do not understand. We will save Shao-mei and find her a good man to marry." Her words gave him hope. He didn't want to lose her. If he didn't succeed, he'd tear his tongue out.

"No man is going to be more decent than you, Robert," she said. "Shao-mei is a prize. She is more beautiful than I am. All my relatives wanted to adopt her." Ayaou put her hand over Robert's mouth to prevent him from arguing. "If I am your happiness, by having her you will achieve double happiness."

"Ayaou, you are thinking crazy."

Ayaou got down on her knees. "Robert, if you love me the way you say you do, take my sister as proof. I want her to belong to you."

"I don't want Shao-mei as my concubine."

"But you aren't going to give her back to Captain Patridge are you?"

"No!"

"I can't give you enough, Robert," she said, pressing her lips to his, which aroused him to the bursting point. She gently pushed him down, pulled his trousers off, stripped, straddled him and took his erection inside her. She stretched her arms above her head pulling all the muscles in her body taut and remained still as if to preserve the moment. The sight of her naked body in that pose excited him. His hungry hands reached for her breasts.

Chapter 11

A few days later Ayaou and Robert started the journey to Shanghai and the ill-fated confrontation with Ward. When the lovers reached the banks of Soochow Creek, Ayaou saw two old women in a flat-bottomed riverboat tied to a bush.

"I think it would be better for you to ride into Shanghai, Robert. You don't look good. I'm worried. You should have rested longer before we left."

"I'm fine," he said. "Just tired. That's all."

"We shouldn't have mated so many times," she said. "You were like a wild beast."

"If you can get them to carry us down stream to the city, it would help," he said. "You talk to them, Ayaou. I'll stand under that Mulberry tree and look old."

She smiled. "That shouldn't be hard. You look like you have aged a dozen years since the battle. Here, tie this cloth over the lower part of your face. I'll say that you are my sick uncle." She tilted the conical bamboo hat Robert was wearing so it covered his forehead and eyes.

Robert bent over, stared at the ground, and took a few hesitant steps. "Does this help?" he asked.

"Good, you look like a crippled old man in pain. Since no one can see your face, they won't know you are a foreigner. I'll tell them I'm taking you to see a doctor."

She walked over to the women. Robert strained to listen, but she talked too fast. He couldn't understand a word. When she returned, she put her mouth next to his ear and whispered. "They are boat people like me. We are distant cousins, so they are going to give us a ride."

It wasn't easy finding room in the boat. It was loaded with vegetables and rice on the way to Shanghai. The women stood

107

in the stern sculling the one large rudder-like oar to move the boat. Robert sat in the bow and faked a sickness. He bent over with his back to them so they couldn't get a good look at him. Ayaou positioned herself in the center.

Willows grew along the banks and beyond were groves of pomegranate, plums and apricots. Soochow creek emptied into the Huangpu River, which writhed like a muddy dragon to the mouth of the Yangtze River in Wusong and then to the East China Sea. During Robert's language lessons, he'd learned that when translated from Mandarin into English, Shanghai meant, *go onto the sea.*

After the first Opium War, which lasted from 1839 to 1842, treaties had turned Shanghai into an international trading city. Then the English, French, Germans and Americans had built their concessions outside the old city. The British settlement was along the western bank of the Huangpu south of the creek. When Robert walked down a street in the British sector, it was as if he were in Belfast or London instead of China. The French had settled to the west of the international settlement. The French sector was the most picturesque with its wide tree-lined avenues.

Until the Taipings arrived to slaughter people by the tens of thousands, no Chinese were allowed to live inside the foreign enclaves that resembled Western cities. The Taipings soon learned to stay away from the superior military forces of the Western powers. Now Chinese from some of the wealthier and more powerful families were allowed in. In addition, servants, who worked for foreigners, lived there too.

Once inside the city, the masts of ships anchored in the Huangpu River were visible. The buildings in Shanghai were mostly two or three stories tall, and the masts towered above everything. The American settlement, where Ward lived, was on the western bank of the Huangpu and north of the creek.

The two boat women weren't going to the river. Their produce was bound for the French. They put Robert and Ayaou ashore near the American sector. People crowded the cobblestone streets and flowed into the city.

Robert continued his charade as a sick old man. He walked bent over staring at the ground and shuffled along. They found themselves stuck behind a large two-wheeled trucking cart. Six coolies strained at the ends of the pull ropes. The cart held at least a dozen huge pigs. Each pig was locked inside a loose weave basket. The baskets were stacked on the cart like firewood.

Once in the American sector, they found a pawnshop. Robert wanted to sell the rifle so they could eat. He took off the hat inside the store and pulled the cloth down that covered the lower part of his face. There was a long counter near the front with the shelves and second-hand goods behind it. Some of the shelves had locked glass doors. Robert saw pistols, swords, knives and rifles inside the cases. On the closest shelves were dusty banjos, guitars, woodcarvings and a chess set with a hand carved set of Chinese characters.

A short, thin man stood behind the counter. His skin was a pale, sickly yellow color the texture of tanned leather. He had a nose like a hatchet and small eyes set close together. A corncob pipe protruded from a corner of his mouth. He sucked from it and blew smoke through his nose. "Can I help you?" he asked in an unfamiliar English accent, which Robert guessed was American.

"Are you from the colonies?" Robert asked, curious. There were no other customers in the store. Ayaou moved behind Robert so he was between her and the man. She stared submissively at the floor. Robert didn't like that. This wasn't the girl who had stood beside him in battle.

"You don't have to do that," he said. "You aren't my servant. Stand beside me."

She didn't move. When Robert attempted to take her by the arm and pull her forward, she jerked free and continued to stare at the floor.

The man behind the counter studied Robert for a moment before he replied, "I'm from Maine." He looked Robert in the eye and with a wry smile said, "You need to be corrected, son. We aren't the colonies any longer. We kicked your English Lobster asses out of our country decades ago."

Robert smiled. "I'm not from England. I'm from Ireland."

"Is that so?" the man replied. His smile exploded revealing a mouth full of crooked, tobacco stained teeth. "My great-granddaddy came from Ireland. We may be kin. Too bad you Irish couldn't kick the English out of your country as we did."

"How many Irish fought on your side in the rebellion?" Robert asked.

"Many," the man replied and chuckled. "After all, my great-granddaddy was one. He shot a few of them red coated bastards."

"Look, I could use a little pocket money. I have this rifle to sell." Before they had entered the city, Robert had wrapped the rifle in a blanket. He unrolled the blanket and put the rifle on the scratched wood counter.

"Hmm." The man inspected the weapon. "It's been fired a few times and hasn't been cleaned."

"That was less than a month ago. Before that it was right out of the crate."

The man offered a quarter of what Robert expected. He countered by tripling the amount. They spent several minutes haggling. Eventually, when a price was agreed on, the man reached for the rifle. Robert put his hand on it. "Who do you plan to sell this to?" he asked.

"That's none of your business. We made a deal."

"I don't want to see this rifle in the hands of a Taiping."

The man from Maine made a face. He turned his head to spit on the floor behind the counter. "We don't see none of them on our streets. Most likely this rifle will go to some American that just arrived to make his fortune in China or to an officer in General Ward's army." He spit on the floor again. "Mostly that's who I sell to or buy from when they go broke in the gambling houses or get hooked on opium and whores." His eyes swiveled to inspect Ayaou. "She your slave? We got slaves down in the southern states. I don't much like that business. I'm an abolitionist. The good Lord didn't mean for any man or woman to belong to another. Maybe I shouldn't buy this weapon from you if that's the case."

"You a friend of Ward's?" Robert countered.

The man shook his head and spit again. Robert noticed that every time the man spit, he hit the same spot on the floor. It was stained darker than the rest of the wood planks. "I don't have no use for anyone like him." The man shifted his gaze to Ayaou again. "How much did she cost?"

"Nothing," Robert lied. "She's my wife." There was some truth to it. Robert hadn't paid for her—yet. The man raised his eyebrows in a gesture of doubt. Feeling a bit guilty at his small deception, Robert took the money and left. He hadn't exactly lied. Robert believed that what he'd paid for Shao-mei and what he was willing to pay for Ayaou was like a dowry. He

110

didn't think of Shao-mei or Ayaou as property to be bought. He saw them as individuals allowing him to pay for their freedom.

They found a street vender carrying his portable stove and wok on the ends of a shoulder pole. They bought sticky rice and fried vegetables and consumed them like hungry wolves. Robert didn't care much for sticky rice, but that day it tasted like a lump of heaven after what Ayaou had been feeding him.

After eating, Robert pulled Ayaou from the flow of foot traffic into a recessed doorway. "Ward's house is around the corner. Before I go, I want you to hear a poem that has been on my mind all day. An English poet wrote it. I'll translate the best I can. It is called *Break of Day* by John Donne. What he wrote is how I feel."

He didn't know any other way to tell her to stay behind. The thought of her in Ward's house was more than Robert could handle. He could have told her how he felt, but he was learning that the Chinese preferred explanations that came around to the meaning in a circle instead of a straight line. Once understood, the meaning was more powerful. The poem he'd selected was his first feeble attempt to think like the Chinese.

"John Donne," she said mangling the poet's name. "What does it mean? In Chinese there is meaning in everything."

"We are different. The meaning is in our poems and not so much with the names given at birth. Listen carefully. When I'm done, I want you to think about what I'm saying." Robert translated the poem awkwardly into Chinese.

'Stay, O Sweet, and do not rise;
The light that shines comes from thine eyes,
The day breaks not, it is my heart,
Because that you and I might part.
Stay, or else my joys will die,
And perish in their infancy.'

"What am I telling you with that poem?" he asked. Robert had deliberately changed a word in the fourth line from 'must' to 'might'.

She cocked her head at a slight angle in a thinking pose. Her eyes flirted with him. He was tempted to take her face between his hands and kiss her. It took an effort not to. Showing affection in public was something Robert was uncomfortable with. Her lips started to move. He realized she was repeating the poem in a whisper. He could barely hear her.

"It's beautiful, Robert Hart," she said. "You are telling me I must wait for you, so your heart will not break." He saw tears gathering in her eyes.

"Good. Don't forget. I want you to stay here until I come back. It will be dangerous for you to go to Ward's house."

Her body stiffened. Fear flooded her eyes. "You are going to confront him alone, and I have to wait here!" She started to cry. "You might not come back. He will kill you." She shook her head. "No, I cannot stay here. I have fought by your side twice. When you were wounded, I saved you and stayed by you until you were healed and safe. If you are to die at Ward's hands, I will die with you."

Robert didn't know how to respond. "I understand," he finally said. He could tell from the tone of her voice and her body language that she wouldn't stay behind. "After we arrive, I want you to pay close attention to my actions. If my face looks wild and full of anger, it isn't because of you."

"I understand," she said. "If you look like a tiger, he will think you are one."

"Yes, Ward must know the danger he's in if he tries to touch one hair on your head. Trust me that we'll walk into his house together and walk out. He'll not keep you. Say nothing and let me do the talking."

"I will die if I can't be with you," she said.

"It won't come to that," he replied. The truth was Robert felt better that she was going with him. Just thinking of leaving her alone on that street made his stomach churn with worry. What if he returned to find her gone? Anything could happen.

They reached Ward's house in the afternoon. It was on a side street where there wasn't much foot traffic. The house sat on more than an acre and was surrounded by a high wall. The gate leading through the wall was not latched. They slipped through, and Robert guided Ayaou to the side where they stood in the shadows watching. There was a hedge of sweet olive osmanthus ten feet high growing inside the wall and another hedge of the same evergreen shrub closer to the house. The osmanthus was loaded with orange flowers giving off a scent similar to ripe apricots.

Robert didn't like it inside the walls. They were isolated here. Taking the Colt revolver from its holster, he checked the loads and put a bullet in the chamber he left empty for safety. Once Robert was sure they were alone, he holstered the Colt and went to the door and knocked.

Ward's second-in-command, a man named Henry Burgevine, opened the door. He was a bear of a man from America's North Carolina. His face was covered with freckles. He had red hair and a thick beard with dried food stuck in it. Between the freckles and red hair, his face had an orange cast to the skin. The front of his filthy shirt was covered with wine and dirt stains. The man looked like riffraff.

"I want to see Ward," Robert said.

"What do you want to see him about?" Burgevine asked. He examined them as if their skin were blue. He filled the entire doorway. There was no way to squeeze by him without shoving him aside.

"We have business," Robert replied. He nodded past Burgevine toward the room. "I want to wait in there."

Burgevine stepped aside and watched Robert and Ayaou walk into the house. He closed the door and took a seat at a nearby table. Bowls filled with food sat in front of him. He took up a spoon and started to stuff himself. He glanced at Ayaou and said through a mouthful of food, "I can imagine what that business is going to be. Don't expect Ward to be happy. We're going to leave tomorrow to stage a surprise attack on Sungkiang. We're going to take it this time."

"That's what Ward said last time." Robert couldn't keep the anger out of his voice.

"We won't have any liquor with us. That will make the difference." Burgevine picked up a chicken leg and shoved it in his mouth. After the bone was pulled out, he kept chewing, and said, "If you're a smart man, conduct your business with him after we've taken Sungkiang. He'll be in better spirits then."

A noise came from the hallway. "Better spirits for what?" It was Ward. He entered the room holding a walking stick. He stopped when he saw Robert and Ayaou. His eyebrows lowered into a solid dark, angry line.

Robert sensed Ayaou's fear. He put an arm around her and pulled her close. He realized right away he'd made a mistake, but he couldn't help himself. He was afraid too, but he wasn't going to allow Ward to see it. He had to be strong.

Ward's expression changed. "What're you up to, Hart?"

"I want to buy Ayaou," Robert said. His voice was firm and confident.

Shades of gray filled Ward's face. "If you took my virgin, I'll see you flogged and her dead." He took a step toward Ayaou.

Robert freed the Colt from its holster.

Ward stopped. "What did you do when the Taipings attacked?" he asked. "Did you run away with the other cowards?"

"I fought until I went down," Robert replied. "I was wounded." He pulled up his shirt to reveal the pink scar running down his ribs. "Ayaou saved my life." Then Robert sneered. "I can see that you are still alive. What does that make you?"

"Why, you insolent dog," Ward replied. His voice started to grow louder. "I'll bet she did more than just save your life. That is still no excuse to steal my property." Ward was shouting now. He pointed his stick at Robert's chest. "You'll leave the bitch here. I might have my dogs eat her. I'll not sell her to you."

"No one is leaving until we make a deal," Robert said.

Burgevine started to stand. There was a menacing look on his face.

Robert pointed the Colt at the man from North Carolina. "Sit and finish eating. This is between Ward and me."

At Ward's gesture, Burgevine backed off. Without coming any closer to Robert or Ayaou, Ward pulled over a chair and sat.

"Name a price, Ward," Robert said. "I know how much you paid. I'll do my best to make you a profit."

Ward put his head back and roared with laughter. His thick, dirty raven hair brushed his shoulders as he shook his head. "It's not the money." Ward's smile looked evil. He stroked his mustache then the patch of hair on his chin below his lower lip. "How about this? I let you take her after I have at her for one night."

Robert grinned back and swiveled the barrel of the Colt in Ward's direction. "You're making me angry, Ward," he said. He cocked the pistol's hammer with an ominous click. Ward tensed as if he were going to leap.

"I wouldn't do that," Robert said. "I'll have no problem shooting you before you can leave that chair."

"Don't be ridiculous, Hart. I don't owe you!"

"Yes you do. I left Shanghai with your army to take Sungkiang, and they got drunk. The troopers you gave me to command laughed at me when I wanted to take precautions. When attacked, those fools dropped their fancy rifles and ran to Shanghai where they took your money and deserted. I was the one who stood, fought, and almost died. For that sacrifice, I demand nothing from you but Ayaou."

"That's enough!" Ward yelled with his face bloated in anger. He bolted from the chair and spread his legs for the blow he expected.

"It doesn't take much to pull a trigger," Robert said. "How big of a hole do you think this .44 caliber ball will make in you? I understand the sixty grains of black powder behind each ball makes a big kick.

"State a price." Robert glared at Ward. "Or name the time, place and choice of weapons. I'll fight for her. You know I can fight."

"You're desperate, Hart, aren't you?" Ward started to pace the room but kept his distance. After a moment, he made an outrageous offer. "Five hundred pounds!"

"Done!" Robert said. He cursed himself for being stupid. He should've negotiated the price down. He'd just agreed to pay more than three thousand yuan for Ayaou. Shao-mei had cost him forty-two.

Ward was stunned. Then he smiled. "You have thirty days to get the money while she stays here."

"No, she comes with me."

Ward sat. "You're a fool paying that amount. I'll bet she's not a virgin now. Besides, she's a boat girl. She's scum not worth the black shine on your boots. You can get three dozen virgins for five hundred pounds. You could open a whorehouse and make a fortune."

"You'll get the money before the thirty days are up." Taking Ayaou by the arm, Robert backed toward the door.

Ward grinned. His chest and shoulders jiggled as his eyes watered. He laughed in silence. It was intimidating. Robert watched Ward's hands and was aware of every movement Burgevine was making. Then Ward slapped a knee and broke out in loud guffaws.

115

"What?" Robert said. They were at the door and in one or two steps would be outside.

"This is my city," Ward said, suddenly sober. "Do you expect to talk to me like that and leave Shanghai alive? You had better shoot me, because I might come looking for you."

Robert couldn't move for a few heartbeats. He just stared at Ward. Then he turned and rushed from the house.

"Are you out of your mind?" Ayaou said, once they were in the street.

"Yes, I am." Glancing back to make sure they weren't being followed, Robert hustled Ayaou to the nearest corner. He wanted to get out of Shanghai as quickly as possible. He hid the pistol under his clothing before they merged with the foot traffic on a busy street.

"But I'm not worth that," she said.

"You are to me," he replied. Robert hurried from the American section of the city. When they entered the French concession, the wide, straight streets were lined with firmiana trees. Each stem looked as if it could be cut and carried away like a parasol. The trees were full of upright clusters of greenish white flowers. There were cafes with tables outside on the wide sidewalks where patrons were drinking coffee. There was hardly a Chinese face in sight. Now Ayaou stood out as if she were the foreigner. They walked past French women dressed in fancy European dresses. Couples walked arm and arm. A nanny scurried by with three children. There were also armed French gendarmes at almost every intersection. Every time they turned into another street, Robert looked back to see if they were being followed.

They left the French concession by passing through an opening in the thirty-foot high battlements that surrounded the old Chinese portion of the city. The streets became narrow twisting about like serpents while the upper levels of the two-story buildings protruded over the street with a thin strip of sky showing. The narrow streets were not only built like this to confuse ghosts but were also designed to allow one ox cart passage. Robert realized that the same twisted streets that hindered a ghost's passage through the city also made it difficult for anyone following them. He took Ayaou by an arm and started to pull her along faster.

"Robert, why are we walking so fast?" Ayaou asked breathlessly.

He didn't want to alarm her with his suspicions that Ward might have someone following them, so he said, "There was a ghost chasing us. I wanted to lose it."

"You saw a ghost," she said, shocked. She looked around. "I've never seen one, but I know they are there. I sometimes feel them waiting outside the gate to the city. When you walk through one, it is like a cold wind chilling your heart."

He studied her face and saw the fear in her eyes. Telling that lie had been a mistake. He hadn't realized that Ayaou was so superstitious. He should have known. It was obvious that most Chinese believed in ghosts. If they had not, they wouldn't have made the effort to build their cities like labyrinths. He resolved not to frighten her again.

They reached a corner and turned into a wider, busier street where it was easy to get lost in the surging Chinese crowd.

They had reached the Chinese merchant district. Large white banners printed with inked Chinese characters hung above shop windows. The signs read 'low price for sale'. There were only a few foreigners on this street.

"How can you possibly get five hundred pounds?" Ayaou asked. "It is many times what Ward paid my father. I'm not worth it."

"Don't worry about the money," Robert said. "You've already told me where I can get it. What we need to do right now is to find a boat and go to Captain Patridge's summerhouse."

As they moved through the crowds, a thought occurred to Robert that his parents would be shocked if they discovered he'd bought one concubine and was going for her older sister. His womanizing and drinking at college had scandalized his family. What he was doing now would probably kill his father, who seldom cracked a smile and spent most of every waking moment with a Bible. When he talked, the conversation was usually about scripture and what it meant. There was a ritual before every meal where Robert's father asked his sons and daughters what each had done for God that day. Maybe Robert could say he'd been thinking of God when he'd risked his life to save the two sisters from a horrible fate. Robert doubted his father would accept that.

Robert decided not to mention Ayaou or Shao-mei to any of his friends in the letters he wrote home. No one would understand anyway. Besides, someone might tell his parents. Robert looked around to make sure no one was watching. A shock raced through him when he saw a familiar face from Sungkiang. It was one of the men that laughed at him the night before the battle. The man was staring back with surprise. With heart pounding, Robert reached for his revolver.

Chapter 12

The man turned and ran. Robert had no way to know whether the man was running because he was a deserter or on his way to report to Ward.

"We have to find a ship now, Ayaou!" he said.

"We have been looking," she replied. "None of the foreign ships are going that way."

"What about a Chinese junk? There are more of them. We might stand a better chance."

It took an hour to find a Chinese boat leaving Shanghai to Zhoushan Island. Robert used the last of the money to purchase passage. It was a heavy Ningpo junk with a painting of a Phoenix on its high stern. It must have been painted recently as the vivid paint looked fresh. The fiery image of the bird's plumage contrasted with the dull gray brown of the hull—especially the tail of the magical bird.

Ayaou stood close to Robert as they hired a sampan to take them to the junk. "I've been in China a year, and I've never seen anything like it," Robert said. "Among my people the Phoenix is a symbol of rebirth, and it isn't as colorful as this."

"The reason you haven't seen it before is because the *Feng Huang* is the Emperor of birds. He hides when trouble is near. We see him during peaceful and prosperous times. Since the Taiping uprising, the *Feng Huang* has been in hiding.

"However, I heard one of the crew members say the son of the family patriarch married recently. The father had two of these birds painted on the hull. On this side we see the male. On the other side is the female. The tail of the bird is painted in the five sacred colors: red, blue, yellow, white and black."

"And what does that have to do with his son marrying?" Robert asked.

"Because having both the male and female birds together represents immortal love." She looked at Robert with adoration. "You said your Phoenix is the symbol of rebirth. In China when the male bird is painted on a house, it symbolizes loyalty and honesty exists in the people who live in that house."

"Immortal love," Robert said. He liked the idea. If what she said were true, he'd have paintings of the *Feng Huang* painted on the bedroom walls wherever they lived.

When the junk set sail and drifted down river toward the sea, Robert studied the shore looking for Ward. He also watched to see if any boats were following them. There was too much traffic on the river to tell. What if Ward didn't honor the agreement and put a price on their heads? After all, Robert had forced Ward to agree under duress. If that happened, could Robert trust anyone?

The junk left them on the eastern end of Zhoushan Island and sailed on to Ningpo. From where they went ashore, it was a long walk to Captain Patridge's summerhouse on the other end of the island. It was morning when they started walking. They didn't arrive until dark.

There were no ships anchored in the cove when they reached the foot of the hill Patridge's house was built on. Light glowed from the veranda. The scene reminded Robert of the candle that draws the moth to its flames. He also saw the light as a beacon—a lighthouse sending out its beam to keep the traveler safe on his path.

Coming closer, Robert heard people talking. He recognized Captain Patridge's voice. The other voice sounded like Hollister. Hearing the raspy sound of Hollister's intimidating voice tempted him to leave. He didn't relish a confrontation with the man, and he expected there'd be one. After all, he had seduced Hollister's woman, Me-ta-tae.

"Curses!" he said.

"What is wrong?" Ayaou asked, sensing from the tone of his voice he wasn't pleased.

"Nothing," Robert replied. He had no choice. There was no turning back now. If he were right about Patridge, this was the only place he had a chance to borrow the money he owed Ward for Ayaou.

"Hello." Robert called out.

"What? Who's there?" Patridge said. He came to the edge of the veranda and squinted into the darkness. "By the gods, it's Bob Hart!" he said. "We thought the Taipings caught you."

"It was close," Robert replied. "I did go to the Chinese death god. He kicked me back and said it wasn't my turn."

"Come and have a seat." Patridge pulled Robert into his arms and hugged him.

"Hello, Hollister," Robert said, when he saw the man sitting at the table. Robert forced himself to keep his voice as friendly as possible. "I didn't see your sloop, *The Dawn*, in the anchorage."

"My boat is anchored in another cove," Hollister replied. "I came on horseback to say goodbye to an old friend and take advantage of his hospitality one last time." Hollister took a cigarette from a box on the table. The girl standing behind him stepped forward to light it.

He inhaled deeply and blew the smoke out through his nose. He studied Robert through the tobacco cloud with half-closed eyes. "Played any interesting games recently?" Hollister asked in a lazy voice. "I'm up for a game if you are, but the stakes must be higher."

Robert was about to ask Hollister what he meant when there was a rush of feet. A slight figure dashed out of the house and flew into his arms. It was Shao-mei. She wrapped her arms around him and held tight. She was trembling when she buried her face against his chest.

"And yes, you have nothing to worry about," Patridge said. "I've taken good care of your property. It will stay untouched, although some of my guests expressed interest in her." He laughed.

"Shao-mei!" Ayaou called.

Looking confused, Shao-mei stepped back and glanced from Robert to Ayaou.

"I can see Shao-mei is as confused as I am," Patridge said. "How did you come by Ayaou?"

"That's something I want to discuss in private."

"All right, but where did you come from? I don't see a ship in the anchorage."

"A Chinese junk dropped us at the other end of the island," Robert said.

"You walked that far! Good Lord! You must be famished. I'll have food brought immediately."

"First I want to talk business," Robert said. "There will be time to eat later." He turned to Shao-mei. "Take your sister to the room and get her food."

The younger sister took Ayaou by the hand and started to leave.

"Wait," Robert said. The sisters stopped and looked at him. "Ayaou, tell what happened and our arrangement." Ayaou nodded, and Shao-mei led her into the house.

Hollister's eyes followed the sisters departure until they went through the door and out of sight. Robert didn't like that. He wanted to slap the man. *Keep your eyes off my girls*, he thought.

Once the girls were gone, Hollister looked at Robert. He said, "You've lost weight since I last saw you. I want to hear what you've been up to, but first I want to play that game of chess. If you win, I'll give you Me-ta-tae. If I win, I get Shao-mei."

"How is Me-ta-tae?" Robert asked, ignoring the request for a game of chess. He'd not gamble over women. He would not lower himself to this bastard's level.

"She got herself pregnant. I'm selling her. What else can I do? I'm not willing to support a family that isn't of my kind. Besides, I'm leaving for home soon. I'll find a proper bride there. I'm going to sail my sloop around the world with a few friends who want to return home too. I've had enough of China."

"If you're leaving, why do you want to gamble for Shao-mei?"

"That's easy. Since you were with my woman, I thought it would be sporting of you to give me a chance to get even."

"To risk losing Shao-mei?" Robert said.

Hollister shrugged. "Taking risks comes with life," he replied. "No matter what happens, you still have the other one. Her name is Ayaou, isn't it? I heard about you and her. And if you win, you'll have three girls to keep you company. Me-ta-tae will be happy to have you instead of me. She might not like competing with the others you've picked up, but she will have no choice. Getting greedy, aren't you?"

Angry blood rushed into Robert's head. His hands curled into fists. He forced himself to relax and keep his face composed. He glanced at Patridge. The captain was lighting a cigarette and acting like he hadn't heard a word.

Hearing that Me-ta-tae was pregnant shocked Robert. What if the child were his? If so, he had a responsibility as the father. On the other hand, there was no way to know who the father was since Robert had intercourse with her only once, but Hollister had her daily. Robert still couldn't help thinking that he was letting her down somehow. The truth was that there was nothing Robert could do to save her. It was a depressing thought. "And if you win, what happens to Shao-mei?" he asked.

Hollister shrugged. "That's up to me, isn't it?" he replied.

Robert shook his head. "There will be no game."

"Look at you." Hollister went on in a spiteful tone. "You're quite the dog. That Shao-mei reminds me of Me-ta-tae. When I bought her, she was always cheerful too. She was about the same age. What do you plan to do with them once you return to England?"

"Who said I'm going back? I'm beginning to like China." Robert glowered at him but put a brake on his tongue before he said something he'd regret. With no one talking, the silence turned thick and tense. Robert considered challenging Hollister to a duel, but that was a choice he could not risk. If he lost, all three girls would suffer, and he'd be dead. He had a reason to live now. He had Ayaou.

"Excuse us, Hollister," Patridge said, breaking the impasse. "Robert and I have business to discuss."

Patridge led Robert to his study. The coast was visible from one of the open windows. The captain lit a lantern and pointed to a chair. Robert shook his head. "I want to stand," he said.

"Is there something going on between you two?" Patridge asked. "I thought you and Hollister were friends. And what is this about his woman and you?"

"It's nothing," Robert replied. The trip from Shanghai had given him time to consider many possibilities, and Payne Hollister was one. "Seeing him here answers some of my questions. It tells me how he built a boat, kept a separate house, gambled away more than he earned and quit his job at the consulate. I imagine his services have saved you money in taxes and of course there is moving the opium past the Imperials. You can't depend on the boat people for everything. I think you are looking for a replacement."

Patridge went behind the desk and sat. "I've considered that."

"That explains why you invited me here," Robert said. "You knew Hollister was leaving. You wanted to find someone else in the consulate to help you save money and get your opium past the Chinese. If I am correct, I'm ready to hear your offer."

"What do you have in mind?" Patridge asked. He became impatient and started to tap his fingers on the desktop.

"Simple. I want five hundred pounds and for that you will gain my help to speed the movement of cargo including opium through Ningpo. I will save you time and money. The term for this arrangement will last one full year from the day I return to the consulate in Ningpo. At the end of that year our partnership ends."

"Do you mind explaining why you're making this offer? To tell you the truth, I'd written you off. You appeared to have too many scruples to do something like this."

"Let it suffice to say that every man has his price."

"It has something to do with Ayaou, doesn't it?"

Robert nodded.

"Nothing like a woman to turn a man's head," Patridge said. A big smile spread across his face. "It's a deal." He offered his hand across the desk.

Robert stared at it for a long moment before reaching out to shake and seal the bargain. "One year," he said. "And I want the money now."

"I'll have it for you in the morning."

"What will our arrangements be?" Robert asked.

"I'll send word to you about the shipments we want you to handle. You do the rest. If we are both pleased, we'll both prosper."

"I don't want to deal with strangers," Robert said.

"I'm a busy man, Robert. I may not always be free to come to Ningpo to instruct you. You've already met Unwyn Fiske. I could arrange to keep him working here for me. It's time for him to be promoted anyway. He would like a ship but will be satisfied as my assistant."

"No, not Fiske."

"What do you mean? He's a good man."

Robert told Patridge about his run in with Fiske during the fight to regain the opium and free the boat people.

"He treated you like that?" Patridge said. "I'll have a word with him. He won't do it again."

"I don't think you understand. I don't want anything to do with that man."

"I do understand. Let's not waste another word on this. I'll take care of him."

"Good," Robert said.

"Did you know that he was the bastard of an earl? He is the man's only son but can't inherit the title or the family estate. After Unwyn left the navy, his father set him up for a career in China with the idea that he would make a fortune here. The earl used his connections to gain Unwyn his position with me. However, if he is going to continue to behave as he did with you, he won't prosper with us. After all, he is a bastard. Don't worry about him, Robert. You are more valuable to me in your position with the consulate. Fiske is only a first mate on one of our ships."

"But I will worry while he's in China," Robert said, remembering how close he came to dying from friendly fire. "Maybe you can give him that promotion he wants and send him to India. I don't fancy running into him after you two have talked. He's a disagreeable man with an unpredictable temper."

"Don't worry about Unwyn. I'll handle him," Patridge said. "How about sealed letters? I could send you instructions in envelopes sealed with wax."

"If you are going to do that, we need a code of some kind," Robert said. "What if someone reads one of your letters instructing me to lie about a cargo? If a letter like that reached an official in the consulate, I could lose my position."

Patridge chuckled. "I doubt it, but if it's a code you want, we'll devise something. After all, we're not here for our health. It's making money that brought us to China. Foolish missionaries are the exception. They came to convert these heathens and possibly lose their heads in the process. The Chinese don't want to be converted. They resent anyone who wants to change them."

Robert wanted to protest but restrained himself. Though he'd had fantasies for success like most, he had not come to China just to profit at the expense of others. He also had not come to convert the Chinese to Christianity. So far, he had seen nothing wrong with Chinese beliefs. They weren't perfect, but the Christians weren't either.

"You surprise me, Robert," Patridge said. "What brought about these drastic changes? It can't all be because of Ayaou."

"Coming so close to death gave me something to think about," Robert replied. His eyes went to a carved ivory opium pipe sitting on a side table. Stepping over to the table, Robert picked it up. The scenes etched in its sides were from the Kamasutra. "Many people spend their lives craving what this pipe represents. I'm searching for something else."

"You have gone through some remarkable changes." Patridge left his chair to stand beside Robert. "I bought that pipe in India where Britain has had more success."

"If you'll excuse me, I'm going to my room."

"By all means. I'll send a servant with food."

"Thank you. Oh, one more thing. Would you take care of Ayaou and Shao-mei for a few days after I'm gone?"

"You can count on me. We're partners now." A rustling noise at the open window drew Patridge's attention. He went to the window, looked out and then closed the shutters. Once he dropped the locking bar into place, he turned to Robert.

"Continue to see that my women go untouched," Robert said, "or it'll end our business agreement. And keep an eye on Hollister. I don't trust him." His eyes went to the opium pipe still in his hand. He put it on the table. He didn't like what it stood for.

"That's two men you've had problems with," Patridge said. "I know what happened between you and Fiske, but what happened with Hollister? He's not a bad sort."

"I don't want to talk about that," Robert said. "Ask Hollister if you must. I'm more concerned about my girls. I want your assurances they will be safe while I'm gone."

"Nothing will happen to them," Patridge said. "You have my word on it."

"After I'm done with Ward, I'm going to arrange for a house in Ningpo. I'll return for them when I'm done." Robert walked to the door and paused. "Is there a place where Shao-mei can sleep?"

"Isn't she sleeping with you and Ayaou?" Patridge replied.

"No."

Patridge shook his head. "I've seen it before," he said. "Dull old England still has a hold on you. Eventually, you will adapt and sleep with both girls. You've already had Shao-mei, so she'll probably think you're a master who sleeps with one woman at a time. Keep them happy, Robert. These Chinese women are like dogs. If you don't spread the affection, the bitches will fight each other."

He didn't care for the analogy, but Robert didn't want to argue. He was determined Ayaou was going to be his only woman. He had no idea what he was going to do with Shao-mei. "China will not change me that much," he said. "I won't sleep with two women at the same time."

"Have it your way," Patridge said. "Shao-mei will sleep with Willow in her room."

"Willow!" Robert said. His face became hot. He didn't like the idea that Shao-mei was sharing a room with a girl he'd had intercourse with.

Patridge laughed. "You worry too much, Robert. If you didn't figure it out the night you spent with her, Willow is not the talkative sort. I doubt Shao-mei will learn her name. If Shao-mei did find out, she'd think nothing of it. Wake up, man. This is China. You're not in England any longer. Send Shao-mei to the servants' quarters when you're ready. Willow will be waiting."

Robert walked into the inner garden and stood among the bamboo and flowers. He wondered if he should take the girls with him. If he did, there was a risk they'd be seen together and word would spread through the small European community in and around Ningpo. Ayaou and Shao-mei would be called whores like Me-ta-tae. After that, it wouldn't take long before word of Robert's behavior reached Ireland and possibly his family would hear of it. This was something he wanted to avoid.

The sound of a shoe grinding against gravel alerted Robert. He turned to see Hollister stepping out of the shadows. Robert's hand went to the revolver in his pocket. "You startled me," he said.

Hollister's eyes went to the pocket and then to Robert's face. His lips twisted into a smile that was almost a grimace. "Pardon me," he said. He took a step back. He had one hand behind his back. Robert kept an eye on that arm. If Hollister made a sudden move, Robert meant to shoot first. "I didn't mean to surprise you," Hollister said. "I was just out here taking the fresh air."

Hollister's hidden hand came into sight. Robert almost pulled the pistol from his pocket. He watched as Hollister lifted a cigarette to his mouth and took a puff. The man lifted his head toward the sky and let out a stream of smoke.

"Fine," Robert said. He went to find his girls. Hollister made him uneasy. He reconsidered taking the girls with him. They would be better off if they weren't around Hollister. Robert regretted he had to leave them here until he found a place to live in Ningpo. If Ward's men were looking for him, they would be watching for a foreigner with a Chinese girl. It was risky taking them with him, and he could move faster alone. He thought of Hollister, who reminded him of Unwyn Fiske. Robert should have shot Hollister when he had the chance. He doubted Captain Patridge would have done anything about it.

Robert reached the bedroom and found his women sitting on the bed talking and holding hands. When he entered the room, Shao-mei stood and bowed. "My sister has explained everything," she said. "I envy Ayaou's good luck and consider myself fortunate you are letting me stay with you. I'd like to be your second concubine, but Ayaou said you have your own beliefs and customs. I must learn to respect them. I'll do whatever you say." She turned to Ayaou. "Did I forget anything?" It could've been Robert's imagination, but he believed Shao-mei was watching him from the corner of one eye.

Ayaou smiled. "No, everything was clear." She turned to him. "Robert?"

He didn't know how to respond. He opened his arms and the two girls threw themselves on him. It was while he was holding them they had their first spat. "You're taking advantage of me, Ayaou," Shao-mei said, knocking a fist on Ayaou's shoulder. "I wish I were the older sister. I never get to choose."

"You wrong me!" Ayaou replied. "I told you I didn't choose Robert. He chose me."

"Well, you never taught me enough to be attractive. Have you forgotten it was your responsibility as the oldest to guide me?"

"All right. I will improve."

"That is a promise, sister! You can't take your words back or a bad omen will come to curse you."

It was a challenge to keep up with their rapid fire Chinese. Robert understood about a third of what they said and had to guess at the rest. He found it was impossible not to adore and want to keep them. His feelings for them shocked him when he considered the reasons he'd fled to China.

Shao-mei yawned, turned to the bed and pulled one corner of the blanket back.

"No, Shao-mei," Robert said in a panic. "You'll be sleeping with one of Captain Patridge's concubines. Her name is Willow. She will be waiting for you in the servants' quarters."

Shao-mei's eyes widened. They started to fill with tears. Her lower lip quivered.

"You heard our master, Shao-mei," Ayaou said. "You have to do what you're told." Shao-mei dragged herself to the door with a despondent look on her face. It made Robert feel as if he'd beaten her.

"Shao-mei," Ayaou said. The younger sister stopped and looked. "Remember that peacefulness brings good luck; patience is the best family heritage." Shao-mei nodded as if she had received a lesson in life and left the room.

Robert was baffled. He hated not understanding what was going on.

Guan-jiah eventually explained what Ayaou meant. "Once there was an Imperial minister named Chang Kung," he said. "He served under the emperor Tang Koachung. This emperor ruled China during the early part of the Tang Dynasty during the seventh century. The minister was envied because he had nine generations living together under the same roof. When the emperor asked the minister for the secret of his success, the minister called for a brush and paper and wrote a hundred times the Chinese character for *An*. It means patience or endurance. In other words, Ayaou was telling Shao-mei to be patient. They would win you over."

Ayaou and Robert slept together in a bed for the first time. After they made love and Ayaou fell asleep, he worried that Willow would talk to Shao-mei. If she found out he'd been with Willow, what would Shao-mei think?

His only hope was that Willow had already forgotten him. After all, he was probably just another faceless man—one in a long line of men that Patridge had ordered her to service. It was a pitiful thought. Robert had trouble imagining how Willow survived. She was a prostitute who was not paid. No, not a prostitute. She was a slave. He could never do that to his girls. He would never have intercourse with someone like Willow again. Since Ayaou and Shao-mei belonged to him, he would do everything to protect them from such a fate. They were his responsibility. He still hoped Shao-mei would not find out. He hated looking bad to other people, because he had done something without thinking it through.

Chapter 13

Death was whispering to him.

Since Robert planned to meet Ward alone, he knew there was a possibility his remaining days were few. He didn't want to worry the girls, so he was leaving without telling them his plans.

It was three in the morning. He stood in the doorway to the bedroom and watched Ayaou sleeping. They'd made love in that bed for five nights and four mornings.

Leaving without saying goodbye was digging an empty hole in his stomach.

His next stop was Willow's room in the servants' quarters where he stood in the doorway watching Shao-mei and Willow sleeping together in the same bed. The younger sister was a sweet girl. Robert was going to miss her too. When he turned to go, something crunched under one of his boots. He froze and held his breath.

"Huh?" Shao-mei said, her voice thick with cobwebs. Robert looked back and saw her staring at him. Willow, on the other hand, did not move.

"Master," Shao-mei said in a breathy whisper. She slipped off the bed and came to wrap her arms around his waist. She was naked. Her body radiated warmth. She pressed her face against his chest. His hands jerked like a fish on a hook, while his heart beat furiously from desire.

"Go back to bed," he said, while a lump formed in his throat.

She stepped back. Her face was full of love and innocence. If his heart could have melted, it would have.

"*Wu Hei Nee*," she said.

He didn't know what the words meant. He still didn't have a full working knowledge of Mandarin, and this was something he hadn't heard before.

"Don't say another word," he said. "Don't ask any questions. Just get into that bed and go to sleep." Disappointment swept across her face. When she returned to the bed, he felt as if he were being torn apart. What a rotten way to start a day that might end in his death.

Robert arrived in Shanghai late in the afternoon and went straight to the British consulate. He found a desk and sat to write a note telling Ward that he had the money for Ayaou and would turn it over to him at the consulate. Robert had changed his mind and decided that after the earlier confrontation at Ward's house, the consulate would be a safer place to complete the transaction. Besides, he wanted a witness. He didn't trust Ward.

Once he finished the note, he went looking for William Lay. He was going to ask to have the official consulate messenger take the note to Ward's house. He found William at his desk.

"This is a surprise," William said. "I thought you were on holiday."

"I returned briefly to take care of business with Ward," Robert replied. "I want the consulate messenger to deliver a note to Ward's house directing him to come here to collect the money I owe him. I'd like you to be a witness to the transaction when it takes place."

William looked surprised. "You haven't heard!" he said. "Patridge's summerhouse must be isolated. Most of China has heard by now."

"What are you talking about?"

William held up a hand. "Wait here. I'll be right back. There's something you must read." William left the room and returned with a copy of the *North China Herald*, Shanghai's English-language newspaper.

"Read this," he said, handing Robert the newspaper. "There's no way Ward can come to you even if our messenger delivers your note to his house."

The top headline jumped off the page. It read, *WARD DEFEATED AGAIN!*

"By the way," William said, "what kind of business are you involved in with Ward? I wouldn't think he was the sort you'd want to be seen with. From what I've heard of him, he's a rascal with a history."

"Let me finish reading then I'll explain," Robert replied, as he scanned the columns of type.

While he'd been gone, Ward had taken Sungkiang then attacked the Taiping stronghold of Tsingpu. That was where he lost his artillery, gunboats and his provision train. For a moment, Robert thought Ward was dead and felt a rush of excitement. Then he skipped a few paragraphs looking for what he wanted and discovered that Ward had only been wounded. The anticipation he'd felt a moment before died a quick death leaving depression in its wake.

The *Herald* did not take kindly to Ward either. The paper's correspondent had written, *"The first and best item is the utter defeat of Ward and his men before Tsingpu. This notorious man has been brought down to Shanghai, not as was hoped, dead, but severely wounded in the mouth, one side and one leg."*

Ward was only wounded, Robert thought. *Hell and damnation!* "It's too bad he didn't die," he said. He saw questions in his friend's eyes. It took a moment to explain what had happened starting with the battle to regain the opium from the Taipings. Robert did not mention Shao-mei.

When Robert finished, William said, "That is horrible. I'd want to get that man off my back too if I were you. I'll gladly be your witness, but don't be too hard on Ward. He's had bad luck. The Taipings know what he's going to do before he does it. They were ready for him."

Patridge had talked about a traitor feeding the Taipings information. Robert wondered if there was a connection. He dismissed that idea. It was too far-fetched. How could one man sell the Taipings information about opium shipments and the movement of Ward's army at the same time?

It wasn't right for Robert to wish death on anyone. He hoped that his Maker would understand and forgive him for his depravity—for he'd finally found love. With Ward out of the way, Ayaou would have been his without a challenge. He could have paid Patridge back the five hundred pounds and freed himself from their odious agreement. Robert patted the spot where the money belt was hidden. He'd probably checked that money a hundred times since leaving Patridge's house. He worried that it might vanish and wouldn't be there when he needed it.

"What are you going to do now?" William asked.

"What choices have I? You were right in saying I needed to complete this transaction quickly. I have to find the man."

"Do you want me to go with you?"

"Yes." He was relieved he didn't have to go alone. "How long will it take you to get ready?"

"Only a moment," William replied. "I'm going to my quarters for my pistol. I don't think it's wise for us to go without weapons."

"You're right." Robert patted his coat pocket. "I also have my pistol. I'll wait outside the consulate." When Robert left the building, he saw some Chinese men on the sidewalk across from the consulate. They were sitting on stools while barbers shaved their skulls and faces without the benefit of soap.

A street vender was selling battered, deep fried radish cakes on the corner. The smell caused Robert's stomach to grumble. He hadn't eaten since Patridge's house. He bought three of the cakes. If he were going to complete Ayaou's purchase, he needed the food to keep his strength up. There was no telling what was going to happen next.

The vender dipped the shredded radish in the batter mixed with flour then into the pan of oil simmering over a bed of hot coals kept inside a ceramic pot like stove. He sang while he cooked. "Radishes, a delicious taste to meet everyone's wishes; radishes caked with baby shrimp for a nice touch!"

William arrived, and Robert offered him a radish cake. William made a face and shook his head. "I don't trust the food from street venders," he said. "It's made me sick before. There have been days that I've spent most of my time squatting over the chamber pot instead of working."

Robert had eaten from street venders before, and nothing had happened to him aside from some indigestion. Maybe he had a stronger stomach than William did. Robert finished the food during the walk to the American sector. When they arrived at Ward's house, no one answered their repeated knocking.

"Here," William said. He grabbed the doorknob and pulled, but the door refused to yield. They went to the back looking for another entrance but found nothing open. Night was settling in and there were no lights in the house. It was obvious no one was there.

What was he to do? Ayaou belonged to Ward until he paid for her. This debt was not going to disappear. Unless Ward was dead, Robert had no choice but to keep hunting.

"This isn't doing us any good," William said. "Come back to the consulate. Maybe the bastard will die in a day or two, and your problems will be solved."

"But what if he doesn't die, and I don't pay him as he expects?" Robert shook his head. "No, I must keep looking. I won't rest until I've found him."

"Then I will stick with you until the task is done," William said. This show of loyalty had an impact on Robert. His eyes watered. He fought back the threatening tears. "My friend," William said, and put a hand on Robert's shoulder, "if you want to find Ward, we should be looking for the man he answers to—that's Boss Takee. He's responsible for recruiting Ward and making him a general in the pay of the Chinese. If Ward survives, it will be Takee who decides whether he gets another chance."

"Do you know where we can find Takee?"

"If we find him, it will be at one of his businesses in the Chinese sector of Shanghai. That isn't a place you want to go alone day or night. I suggest we try his opium parlor first. If he is not there, we'll go to the warehouses where the opium is stored. Since he is in charge of the native workers in those warehouses, he might be there. If we cannot find him at either of those locations, I suggest we give up. I don't think it wise to let others know we are looking for Takee. He has one of the largest and most dangerous gangs in Shanghai. Ward recruited most of his army from those gangs?"

A jolt of electricity raced through Robert. "Is Ward, Captain Patridge and this criminal Boss Takee connected?"

William's eyebrows arched in surprise. "You didn't know? I thought when you went to Patridge's summerhouse for your holiday you were joining him. After all, Hollister did soon after arriving to China."

"They're in this together." Robert was shocked. It hurt to realize how trusting and naive he'd been. Like a stupid, blind fool, he'd allowed himself to be manipulated. He was sure that Willow had been part of the plan too. What would Patridge have done next to steal his soul?

When circumstances changed, Robert resolved to extricate himself from Patridge and end the agreement between them.

What other choice did he have? To keep Ayaou, Robert needed Patridge, who could exert influence on Boss Takee to keep Ward in line and away from them. It made sense that while Robert did what Patridge wanted, he wouldn't have to worry about Ward. It would be like living in an invisible cage waiting for his first chance to escape.

"Are you okay, Robert? I've never seen you look like this before."

Robert snapped out of his black mood. "I'm fine," he said, although he didn't feel it. Night arrived and it was dark by the time William led Robert to a gambling establishment and whorehouse that also operated a back-room opium den owned by Boss Takee.

"Stiffen your resolve," William said, "because you are going to be sorely tested. I should know. I was tempted the first time I came here with my brother Horatio, who visits places like this all the time."

"What?" Robert said, thrown off balance. It was impossible to imagine Horatio Lay in a place such as this with the attitude he had of the Chinese.

"Don't be shocked, Robert," William said. "Horatio doesn't come here for the gambling or the opium. He comes for the women. My older brother is not one of the men that Boss Takee or Captain Patridge owns. Horatio visits other whorehouses too. I've told him to buy a woman, but he won't do it." William opened the door. They stepped into a gloomy interior where it took a moment for Robert's vision to adjust to the darkness.

"Gentlemen," a voice said in English with a thick Russian accent. An old woman appeared from the shadows. She had doughy skin and eyes like steel marbles. Her henna dyed hair was curly and brittle. She held a cigarette in one hand that was stuck in a long ivory holder. She put the holder in her mouth and sucked. He saw four burly men sitting like menacing gargoyles on stools in the murky corners. Robert recoiled and took a step back toward the door.

"Don't be alarmed." William whispered. "Those are the devils that protect this place of sin. This woman is the mamasan. She oversees the prostitutes. If we wanted a woman, she'd be the one to supply her."

"What can we do for you tonight?" She stepped closer to Robert. Her breath reeked of tobacco and the sour stench of liquor. When she smiled, she revealed a mouth full of stained teeth.

"What kind of women are you looking for, sir?" she said, staring into Robert's eyes as if she saw something that he didn't know was there. "We have women to fit all tastes. If you want a child, boy or girl, we can provide that too."

Panic raced through Robert, and he wanted to flee. It was as if she'd read his mind. He did want a woman—two in fact, Ayaou and Shao-mei. Her hand was like a claw when it closed on his arm. "Come this way. Maybe it is both opium and a girl that you desire. We offer many pleasures here. Would you like to start with a card game?"

William forced her to let go of Robert and almost had to push her to do it. "We are not here for women, gambling or opium," he said.

The four guards stepped out of the shadows with menacing looks on their faces. One held what looked like a wooden club at least two feet long. Robert reached in his pocket for the revolver.

"We are here on business to see Boss Takee," William said. "My friend knows Captain Patridge and fought with Ward as an officer in his army."

A change of expression flowed across the woman's face. Was it fear that Robert saw leap into her eyes? She stepped back and held a hand up toward the guards. They hesitated for an instant then retreated into their gloomy corners.

"You want to see Boss Takee?" The tone in her voice had changed too. The voice that greeted them sounded as if it had been coated with honey. This voice sounded as if it had been scraped with a rusty metal file. "I do not know where he is."

"Who does?" William demanded. "This is urgent. Captain Patridge and General Ward will be angry if we don't find Takee. Take us to someone who knows where he is." Robert stared at his friend, surprised at what he was discovering. William had an iron core.

"Come with me," she said, and led them through another set of doors into the smoke filled gambling den beyond. As they followed her, Robert saw card tables crowded with men. Women from all races in slinky Chinese silk dresses stood behind the men as they gambled. One man was stroking a woman's leg and running his hand up under her dress. She was licking one of his ears. The same man pushed out several hundred yuan and took two cards from the dealer.

They went through a door where Robert came to a stop as he hit a wall of smoke that wasn't tobacco. His eyes watered and started to swell shut. His lungs wheezed. "I can't stay here," he gasped. "What is that?"

"Opium," William said.

The woman was staring at them with hostility and fear.

"Go back out front," William said. "If Boss Takee is here, I'll bring him to you." Robert hurried past the card tables to the entrance hall. The four guards stared at him from their shadowy perches, and he kept a hand in his jacket pocket on the grip of the revolver.

"Rotten luck," William said, as he walked through the door. "Boss Takee left to Macao this morning and won't be back for a month."

They left the building, and Robert breathed the outside air as if it were nectar.

"At least we know you won't become addicted to opium," William said. They returned to the British consulate where Robert found an empty bed.

The next morning Robert was up early. After eating, he went looking for William. "What do I do now?" he said, after finding his friend at his desk.

William knew Shanghai, and Robert wanted advice.

"I asked around, and Ward's second-in-command, Henry Burgevine, is on board an American ship that's bound for California. He's sailing tomorrow morning, so you had better see him today. He may know where Ward is?"

William took a piece of paper and handed it to Robert. "That's the name of the ship. I regret I cannot come with you today. I can't afford to take more time away from my work."

"I am grateful for your help, and I'm sorry if I caused you any difficulties."

"It was nothing," William replied. "What are friends for? I'm sure you would do the same for me if I were in your shoes." He put a hand on Robert's shoulder. There was genuine concern in his eyes. "Robert, if you can't find Ward today, leave Shanghai and forget him. Ward and his kind are the wrong sort to deal with. You have your girl now."

Robert asked, "What about the Chinese? How do they look at Westerner's that own their women?"

"The Chinese do not judge a man's physical needs as in Victorian England. Here a man can have as many women as he can afford, which is a sign of his status.

"It's a Chinese tradition that a wealthy man has both wives and concubines, and they live under one roof. Even after a wealthy man has both wives and concubines, he'll still visit courtesans. There is no religious sexual repression in China. In fact, it's impossible for an official in the government to avoid dinners with female entertainers."

He tapped the desk for emphasis. "However, any girl bought by a foreigner *loses face* with other Chinese women and will never be able to live a normal life again. You see, most of us leave China eventually, and the women stay behind. It isn't an appealing fate."

"What do you mean by *losing face*?"

"That's complicated," William replied. "As I see it, *gaining* or *losing face* has something to do with your influence and power but even a penniless monk can have *more face* than a powerful general or governor depending on his reputation. I think it means to take a risk to achieve something. If you succeed, even if it means breaking a few laws and hurting or killing innocent people along the way, you *gain face* but if you take the risk and lose, you end with *no face*. With *no face*, a respectable Chinese man will probably hang himself."

Robert shook his head. "A difficult concept."

"In China, *face* is everything, because what one man does can destroy an entire family or clan."

"You mentioned most foreign men leave their women when they return home. What happens to the women?"

"After the foreigner leaves, the Chinese woman does not live a normal life. Most become dockside prostitutes. And if the woman had children by the man, the children suffer a worse fate.

"I've seen beautiful half-breed girls as young as eight or nine hooked on opium selling their bodies to any man that pays. They do it to survive. When most of these half-breeds get old enough to have babies, the baby usually ends in the river."

"It sounds like Chinese women have no value," Robert said, shocked.

"Not so." William shook his head. "If you are the dowager of a large, respectable family, you have power in the home."

William laughed at the confusion on Robert's face. "Let me explain further," he said. "The man could be a peasant farmer or the governor of a province appointed by the Emperor, and that governor commands an army and collects hundreds of thousands of taels in taxes each year. He married because of an arrangement made soon after his birth. Besides that first wife, he could have married two or three others and maybe has a few concubines. He also plays around with a singsong girl now and then, who is of course hoping he buys them and makes them his concubines so their status improves.

"However, once that first wife gives him a son, she has the power inside the home. She can make life wonderful or miserable for the entire family, including the husband. There is nothing the man can do about it. It's the Chinese way.

"When a son marries, he hasn't gained a wife—he's given a daughter-in-law to his mother. The horrible part is that the daughter-in-law can be treated like a slave, and the son can do nothing about it. The son won't cross his mother.

"Then the daughter-in-law gives birth to a son. One-day her husband's mother dies and suddenly the wife, who was the daughter-in-law, is now the dowager and has the power inside the home. Now she can make life miserable or wonderful for the family. When her sons marry, she has daughters-in-law to boss around until she dies, and the power inside the home passes to someone else. It can be a vicious cycle."

Everything Robert heard confused and bothered him at the same time.

William put a hand on Robert's shoulder. "Welcome to China, Robert," he said, with a big grin.

"What will I learn next?"

"From all the questions you were asking about the women here, I think that's what you were looking for. Go back to Ningpo and enjoy your concubine. I suspect you worry about what your family and friends back in Ireland might think of you, but this is China. No one will condemn you here. I will not."

William knew Robert better than he knew himself. What would William have thought if he knew the truth—that Robert had two women instead of one? Would William have condemned him and seen him for the depraved man he was?

For the truth was that before Ayaou had fought her way into his heart, Robert's desire for women kept him awake nights and filled his thoughts during the days. Every time he saw a woman with a beautiful neck or delicate hands or pixie ears, the temptations that had ruled him in Belfast returned. All he wanted was to touch his lips to the lips of every appealing woman he saw and send his exploring hands over their naked bodies. Those demands had made him a slave to his libido and had driven him into the arms of Me-ta-tae and Willow. If Ayaou hadn't come along, there would have been others. Robert was sure of that.

On the other hand, he was fooling himself thinking that Ayaou was going to suffice, because Shao-mei was there too. Robert couldn't deny that he also wanted the younger sister. It was against everything he'd been raised to believe. He hated himself for it. This constant battle with the flesh was exhausting.

He wondered again what Shao-mei had meant by the Chinese phrase *Wu Hei Nee*. He couldn't get those words and the inviting tone of her voice or that adoring look in her eyes out of his head. And every time he closed his eyes, he saw her naked body getting out of the bed.

Robert kept a straight face and hid the turmoil boiling inside. He thanked his friend again and went on his way. It felt good knowing he had William on his side. Only a friend would have done what William had done last night.

At the same time, it hurt to think he'd fooled himself into thinking that Patridge was a friend. Robert would be doubly cautious in the future before he let anyone else get close to him. Now he trusted two people—Ayaou and William. He wasn't as lonely as he had been.

Shanghai was different in the day. It wasn't as threatening. With the ship's name in his hand, he walked to the far side of Shanghai and found it anchored in the river. He paid a man to take him out in a sampan. Before he went up the ship's ladder to the deck, the unwashed bodies of hundreds of men assaulted his sense of smell.

"You taking coolies to America too?" a ship's officer asked Robert as he set foot on deck. "Well, we're full. Find another ship."

"I'm here to see Burgevine," Robert said. "I don't know anything about these coolies. Why are you taking them to America?"

"To build railroads," the man said. "They work harder than slaves and cost less. Feed them a bowl of rice and they'll work all day and half the night for next to nothing." The officer nodded toward an open hatch in the deck. "Take that ladder down to the first deck and walk aft. Burgevine's cabin is there."

The space between decks was cramped. Robert walked stooped over. There were bales of cargo but no coolies. They must have been crowded into the lower decks below the waterline. The foulness of unwashed, sweaty bodies was stronger here. There was also the sharp stench of urine. It was all Robert could do to refrain from retching.

Burgevine was alone when Robert entered the cabin. The man's big form was crammed into a small bunk. He was picking at his bare feet. The room smelled of sour, spoiled milk. With this stink and the reek of hundreds of unwashed bodies, Robert's skin was crawling as if he were covered with flies, fleas and lice.

"What are you doing here, Hart?" Burgevine said. He didn't look at Robert when he passed a loud fart.

The stench was worse than the flatulence from a full-grown swine. Robert had to step back so he wouldn't gag. "Good god, Burgevine," Robert said. "Did you have to do that?"

Burgevine let out a belly laugh, and said, "State your business or get out."

"I'm looking for Ward, so I can pay him for Ayaou," Robert said, struggling to ignore the man's repugnant, rough manner.

"You won't find him here," Burgevine replied. "He's out in the countryside with his favorite concubine and a Chinese doctor to help with the healing. Give me the money. I'll see Ward gets it." He pulled one of his filthy feet closer to his eyes, tore off part of a toenail, and tossed it on the floor. "Damn things won't stop growing," he said.

Robert was disgusted at the sight of the accumulated black grime beneath the man's toenails. "May I ask how you intend getting the money to him if you're going to California?"

142

"I'm making this one voyage to deliver these coolies for the railroad. It's good money. Once that's done, I will be back. By then, Ward will be ready to build another army. Trust me. I'll get the money to him." Burgevine sat up and held out a hand.

"I won't leave the money with you. I must put it in Ward's hands myself."

Burgevine's face turned scarlet. He stood fast and banged his head hard on the low ceiling timbers then dropped to his bunk with a stunned look on his face.

Robert was tempted to use the Colt revolver to pry Ward's location out of this louse that called himself a man. Instead, he backed from the cabin. In the hall, he looked both ways to make sure no one was sneaking up on him. Robert left feeling frustrated, angry and relieved at the same time. Once off the ship, he took William's advice and booked passage to Ningpo, where he planned to find a house and fetch Ayaou and Shao-mei from Patridge.

Leaving Shanghai without completing his purchase of Ayaou left him feeling empty and threatened. His goal was to build a safe nest with Ayaou and Shao-mei in it. However, with Ward out there like a vulture waiting to swoop and eat them, how could he relax? Life was turning into a nightmare—one Robert couldn't escape.

Robert arrived at Ningpo late in the evening. He went straight to Guan-jiah's house. Until he had his two girls with him, Robert wanted to avoid the consulate. If he went there, the missionaries and the European merchants would know he had returned. There would be questions. He didn't want anyone prying into his private life. Since there were no hotels in Ningpo for foreign devils, he'd ask Guan-jiah to put him up for the night. The only places available for a night's rent were for Chinese. It was stupid to attempt to stay in a place like that. Someone would slit his throat while he was sleeping. His body would end in the river as fish food.

The house Guan-jiah and his family lived in was a two-room space shared by a crowd of people, which included his grandparents, parents, sisters, brothers, and their wives, husbands and children.

Robert arrived in the middle of dinner. When he knocked, Guan-jiah was the one who answered. His eyes expanded. "Master, what are you doing here?"

"I came from Shanghai. I'm exhausted, and I want a safe place to sleep, Guan-jiah. Put me in a corner, and I won't be a bother. I'll pay. I couldn't think of any other place to go."

"But you have a room at the consulate. Are you in trouble, Master?" He was genuinely concerned.

"I'll explain later, Guan-jiah. Right now, I'm tired. How much for me to rent a space to sleep?"

Guan-jiah said, "No, Master. You will not pay to sleep here. You will sleep on my mat. I know it is clean. Right now you must join us and have something to eat."

"I don't want to be a bother," Robert replied.

"Master, I wouldn't be a good host if I let you sleep on an empty stomach. You must be hungry."

When Robert hesitated, Guan-jiah took him by the hand. Before he led Robert into the house, he had him take his shoes off and put them beside all the other shoes just inside the door. He then led Robert to where the family sat on the floor in a large circle eating. He went to a clay ceramic stove in a corner and filled a soup bowl for Robert from a large pot. Robert reluctantly sat on the floor with the rest of the family.

"I'm embarrassed, Master," Guan-jiah said. "If I had known you were coming, we would have added meat and an egg."

"Don't bother on my account," Robert replied. "I'm not that hungry. What you have is sufficient." Guan-jiah looked uncomfortable, but Robert had nowhere else to go. Besides, if he left now, he was sure that Guan-jiah would be doubly embarrassed.

The adults avoided staring at him. One little girl, looking like a doll to Robert, kept stealing looks and giggling. "Stop staring at my master, Sparrow," Guan-jiah said in a scolding tone.

Sparrow's face fell. She stared at the floor with her lower lip sticking out in a pouting gesture.

"It's all right, Guan-jiah," Robert said. "She's only fascinated with my strangeness."

Guan-jiah deftly used his chopsticks to snare a ball of sticky rice and dropped it into Robert's soup. A large porcelain bowl in the center of the mat had plenty of rice balls in it. Everyone was using chopsticks to pick up the rice balls and stuff them into their mouths.

Each family member held a small bowl in one hand and the chopsticks in the other. The bowl stayed close to the mouth the entire time they ate. The chopsticks moved in a blur carrying food from bowl to mouth. Robert had no idea how such a feat could be achieved with just two sticks.

Rice was the only food in abundance. There was no meat and few vegetables to feed at least two dozen people. Robert resolved to raise Guan-jiah's meager pay. Since Robert had received a rank advancement and his pay had increased, it was fitting that he pass on some to his faithful servant.

Sparrow handed Robert a set of chopsticks. He stared at what was in his bowl. It smelled wonderful. Saliva filled his mouth. He'd lied. He was hungry, but he'd never used chopsticks before. Robert took them and attempted to pick up a ball of rice to put in his mouth. The chopsticks kept popping out of his hand and crossing each other.

Sparrow tapped his arm and held up her chopsticks to show him how she braced one on her thumb where it stayed put. The second chopstick rested between the index and middle finger, so she could move it and catch the food between the stationary stick and the movable one. After several tries, Robert was successful and started eating. The soup was spicy. The peppers caused him to sweat and his nose to run. It was mostly water, but there were a few pieces of tofu and yam floating around.

Since his bowl was empty, Sparrow poured hers into his. Then she hopped up and ran to the clay stove to fill her bowl again.

"Thank you," Robert said to Sparrow in her language. She rewarded him with a large, toothy grin and scooted over to sit against him. She was so close he felt the heat radiating from her small body.

Robert had gained another friend. It felt good to be accepted—even by this little girl. At the same time, he was glad she wasn't a woman. He already had two. Three would have been too much. He wanted to laugh at his worries but restrained himself lest he somehow offend the others. They might think he was laughing at them.

After the bowls were cleared away, the family unrolled their woven reed mats and spread them out to sleep on. The family was getting ready to go to bed. What had been their kitchen and dining room now became a bedroom where the entire family was going to sleep side-by-side on the floor. Although the two-room house was crowded, it was spotless. There was no dust on the tile floor.

"Since everyone is going to bed, I don't want to bother anyone, Guan-jiah. Let's step outside for a moment. I want to talk to you."

"It is okay to talk here, Master. No one knows English but me."

"I'm not alone any longer," Robert said. "I have two concubines and plan to move out of the consulate and find a house." He stopped and stared at Guan-jiah thinking of Shao-mei. "Have you a woman, Guan-jiah?"

Guan-jiah looked startled by the question, and Robert cursed himself. He'd forgotten that his servant was a eunuch. On the other hand, if he found Shao-mei a good husband, it would solve one of his problems. Then it would just be Ayaou and him. Guan-jiah would make a good husband. He was considerate. He worked hard. He was thoughtful. He was courageous. Sure, he was a eunuch, but Robert would talk to Shao-mei and make her accept him. What choice did she have? After all, he was her master. She was his property.

Guan-jiah looked away from Robert, who took this gesture to mean *no*. He wasn't giving up that easily. He wanted to find a way to put Shao-mei and Guan-jiah together. If Shao-mei had a man to care for, even a eunuch, Robert wouldn't feel tempted. "What are your roots, Guan-jiah? Are you Han Chinese or are you Manchu?" If they were of the same ethnic group, it would be an easier match. Shao-mei could be his companion. He wouldn't have to be alone.

"My great-grandmother was from the boat people. Great-grandfather was Han Chinese. He was a village farmer far from here. He owned an acre and couldn't afford a better woman."

"Did you know your great-grandmother? She must have been a wonderful woman to leave behind such a large and happy family."

"She was trouble like all boat people," Guan-jiah said with bitterness. "My great-grandfather was fortunate when she died in childbirth without giving him the curse of a daughter. She left him four sons. That was good. He raised them as respectable Han Chinese. They went into the silk business and became wealthy."

"Is your family still in the silk business?" Robert asked.

Guan-jiah's eyes darted away. He looked uncomfortable. Robert returned to his original intent. One thing he had learned was the Chinese didn't like to talk about anything embarrassing. Something unfortunate must have taken the family fortune away.

To put it simply, a Chinese family didn't like to share problems with others. They preferred to keep all the bad history and news locked up even from one another. Robert admired Guan-jiah's honesty. His servant could have lied to him. Most Chinese always wanted to put a sunny face on for the world to see no matter what the truth was. This was one way they avoided *losing face*, which could bring dishonor to the family.

He was learning.

"My purpose for coming here was to ask you to find a house for me to rent," he said. "You are the only person I can rely on. Can you do this?"

"Yes, Master."

"That's good. I don't want a house near any major streets. Pick one of those narrow back alleys that twists about. Make sure the house is suitable to provide room and comfort for three people, and I don't want any missionaries or foreigners living nearby."

"Tonight is late. Not good. Not safe to be walking in the dark in Ningpo," Guan-jiah replied. "Tomorrow I look."

"I've heard about Imperial Commissioner Yeh's proclamation offering thirty yuan for the head of a dead Englishman," Robert said. "Is that true?"

"Very true," Guan-jiah replied. "That's exactly my worry."

Robert nodded and patted the revolver to check that it was still in the largest jacket pocket. Knowing it was there calmed him.

"You must stay in my house tonight," Guan-jiah said. "You will not have to go back to the British consulate. It is safer that you stay here anyway. Being a foreigner and walking the Ningpo streets in the dark is not good right now."

"I feel guilty for disturbing your family," Robert said.

"Stay, Master. I insist."

Robert was touched by Guan-jiah's loyalty. His life was in his servant's hands. Thirty yuan for his head might not sound like much to an Englishman but to a Chinese it was. Thinking of the reward for his head, Robert had doubts. He'd known

Guan-jiah for a little over a year. Was that enough time to trust the servant with his life? Possibly the eunuch's motive was to keep him in the house and wait until he fell asleep.

Then the knives would come out. He imagined Sparrow waiting her turn to carve on him. Then he was angry with himself for thinking such horrible thoughts. She was an innocent child and incapable of such guile. If there was anyone he could trust not to be tempted to collect that thirty yuan, it was her.

He was making himself sick with worry. There wasn't much Robert could do but put his life in Guan-jiah's hands. He did have his pistol to defend himself, but if he fell into a deep sleep, that weapon was useless. He would have to struggle not to sleep deeply that night. He didn't know whether he could succeed, because he was so tired that his bones wanted to take a break from holding his body together. It was going to be a difficult night.

"I would like to go house hunting with you tomorrow," Robert said.

"No, Master. If you come with me before I bargain for the price, it will cost you more. It is because you are a foreigner. Foreigners never pay the Chinese price. I'll get you a good house with a good price." He smiled.

"Guan-jiah," Robert said, "I want you to translate something into English for me. What does *Wu Hei Nee* mean?" He made sure to pronounce the phase exactly like Shao-mei had done with the same tones.

"It means, *I hate you*," he said.

Robert jerked. "But that wasn't what was in her eyes," he said. "There was nothing but love in her eyes."

"Master, that's how a woman tells you she loves you. She says, *Wu Hei Nee.*"

"She tells me she loves me by saying she hates me?" Robert said.

"It depends on the moment, Master. You said she was looking at you with love in her eyes."

"At least that's what I thought the look was," Robert said. "Maybe I'm wrong. This makes no sense. I'm confused. I've only known her for a short time. I haven't even been intimate with her, and she isn't the one I'm in love with."

How could he live in the same house with her knowing she loved him? He would have trouble sleeping. He had not bargained for two women loving him at the same time. He had no idea what he was going to do to make this work.

"Master, women in China have a surer *instinct* about life than men, and the Chinese have that *instinct* more than others in the world. We depend largely on our *intuition* for solving all nature's mysteries, and the same *intuition* makes many women believe a thing is so, because it is so. If she told you *Wu Hei Nee*, she believes that you love her too. This means you did something that caused her to think that way."

"Thank you, Guan-jiah," Robert said, feeling more confused. He understood what Guan-jiah had told him, but how could Shao-mei believe he loved her? He hadn't done anything to earn it.

Guan-jiah gave up his sleeping mat for Robert. After turning and tossing all night, Robert didn't see much difference between the mat and the floor. Besides, the slightest noise, a snort or a settling sound from the house, brought him to full alert. He was tempted to keep a hand on the pistol but was afraid he might accidentally shoot a member of the family. This situation was making him a nervous wreck. About five in the morning his resistance collapsed, and he fell into a deep sleep.

The next day Guan-jiah found a two-story house with access to the roof. After he closed the deal, he took Robert to see. The rooms were small and the stairs steep with narrow, slippery steps from being worn down for probably centuries until the surfaces were canted and the outside edges rounded. On the bottom floor was a kitchen and a sitting room. On the second floor were two small rooms with a narrow hallway. A door at the end of the hallway opened on a balcony where there was bamboo poles attached from wall to wall to hang wet clothes to dry. A metal ladder fastened to the wall went up to the steep tiled roof. The place was stuffy and smelled stale.

Guan-jiah had negotiated a great price and appeared pleased with himself. After they arrived at the house, the landlord became upset when he saw that his tenant was a foreigner. He turned to Guan-jiah and though Robert couldn't tell much of what he was saying in his rapid fire Chinese, he did know the man was demanding more money.

Guan-jiah stood firm. "You are a thief," he said. "Who else but a foreigner would consider renting this horrible house? It is old, cold and damp. It smells. Besides, everyone knows it is full of evil spirits and only a foreigner could live here. The evil spirits will fear him. In his country, my master lives in a house the size of Ningpo. Imagine how he will feel if you demanded that he pay more than we agreed on. No, if you do not stick to our deal, I will find another house for him. As it is, he is paying twice what he should pay. Maybe the price should be lower."

This went on for several minutes. Robert had to admit he was glad to have Guan-jiah on his side. His servant was tough. Guan-jiah prevailed, and the landlord agreed.

The price was three yuan a month. Robert signed the lease. He wasn't happy with the house. It wasn't what he had imagined, but when he compared it to where Guan-jiah lived with his large family, it was a mansion. Robert resolved to never let his servant know how he felt about the house. If the Chinese could put on a sunny face, so could he. Maybe Robert could get Guan-jiah to live with them. He dismissed that idea immediately. He didn't want the eunuch lurking in the hallway upstairs watching him and Ayaou make love.

"See that the house is thoroughly cleaned, Guan-jiah, and purchase a few pieces of furniture—a table, chairs, beds and three chamber pots. No, make that four. There will be times I'll want you to sleep over when we've work to do from the consulate."

Again, Robert thought of Shao-mei and how he could put them together. Possibly, he could produce a dowry for Shao-mei to make her more attractive as a potential wife. There had to be a way to overcome Guan-jiah's evident dislike of boat people. Another thought occurred to him. How would Shao-mei react when she discovered that he had married her off to a eunuch? Maybe it was a bad idea.

"Not to worry, Master. I'll take care of everything."

The front door looked like it was full of dry rot. That was regrettable because the carvings were interesting. Around the sides were carvings of scholars sitting inside pavilions studying scrolls. At the top, there were two painted concubines serving tea to a master sitting at a table writing something. On either side of this setting were carvings of bamboo swaying in the wind. Robert traced the crude figures carved in the wood. "Does this mean anything?" he asked.

"A poet once lived here years ago," Guan-jiah said. "He killed himself when no one liked his poetry. If he hadn't come from a wealthy family, he would have starved."

Robert took a small knife out of his pocket and opened the blade. When he poked the pointed end into the wood, the tip sunk in as if the wood were soft clay. "This door is rotten, Guan-jiah, see that it is replaced with one made of thick solid timbers that can be soundly locked from the inside."

"Yes, Master," he said, "I will see that it is done."

Robert decided that Guan-jiah would make a good, dependable and trustworthy husband for some girl like Shao-mei. It didn't matter to Robert if Guan-jiah couldn't have intercourse with her. He wondered if people adopted children in China. He'd find out.

Before departing Ningpo, Robert stood inside the doorway and imagined what the place was going to look like once he returned with his new family. It was difficult seeing this old, stuffy place as something inviting and warm.

Making it come alive would be up to the sisters. If they could impose their bubbly personalities on these drab walls, it would happen. Robert envisioned Guan-jiah moving in and living with Shao-mei. He hadn't given up on the idea yet. He liked Guan-jiah. His loyalty was admirable. He imagined Guan-jiah and Shao-mei as if they were adopted children, who would develop a platonic relationship. Why, he could be the father and Ayaou the mother.

Lord, what an idiot he was, he thought. Shao-mei was a curious and sensual girl. She'd probably kill herself if Robert married her off to a eunuch.

Guan-jiah's family reminded him of his family back home in Portadown, in county Armagh where he'd been born. Thinking of home caused a sorrow born of loneliness to spread throughout his body like a disease that made him ache.

His father was a Wesleyan preacher and for a living he sold food and liquor from the family store. He'd also managed to raise a family of twelve and Robert was the oldest. He had once hoped to join his father's business, and if God found him worthy, to become a Wesleyan preacher too.

However, his drinking and womanizing while in College had ruined that dream. Instead of joining his father, he'd run to China to escape what his family and friends thought of him.

Soon after arriving in China, he'd resurrected that dream with plans to return to Northern Ireland after becoming a success.

It looked like that wasn't going to happen. Robert had found something with Ayaou and Shao-mei he did not want to lose. He was like a child cut off from candy that couldn't live without it. Now he was in a place where he could have as much as he wanted unless someone like Ward came to take it from him.

Chapter 14

It didn't take Ayaou and Shao-mei long to turn the four rooms into a home. Before they arrived, Guan-jiah had completed all the repairs Robert requested. Soon after moving in, Ayaou and Shao-mei went out during the day and found items that added Chinese touches to the house—crafted objects, carvings and ink paintings. Everything they did to decorate the house pleased Robert.

When he arrived home each evening, the first thing he saw was an inked wall hanging two feet wide and five feet long. It read *harmony and tranquility* in Chinese. It was printed on white rice paper. The calligraphy was in black ink, and a thin red border ran around the perimeter about three inches from the edge. There were several red ink stamps in the lower right-hand corner showing the name of the artist.

The girls also got rid of the stale, sour odor and replaced it with the smell of garlic, ginger and hot spices sautéing in the wok. Almost every dish they ate came with these flavors until Robert grew so use to it that food tasted bland without them. Somehow, the rooms didn't feel as small as they had the first day he inspected the place. The girls had breathed life into the small house.

"Guan-jiah," Robert said, "the evil spirits that lived here must have gone into hiding."

Guan-jiah stood in the entrance to the house and looked around. "Yes, Master, the evil is gone, or your girls caused the spirits to act agreeable."

What they didn't know was that the evil had just gone into hiding and was waiting for the right moment to return.

The girls were cooking dinner, and Robert had invited his servant to join them. "It could be the garlic," Guan-jiah said.

"That will also drive away evil spirits." He walked over to the *tranquility and harmony* inked wall hanging and stood before it.

"If I could only learn to paint calligraphy like this," he said in a subdued, yearning tone, "but my hands are clumsy. They refuse to cooperate. Everything I paint looks like a cripple."

"It can't be that difficult, Guan-jiah. It's just Chinese writing but big."

"Oh no, Master. The horizontal lines in this painting are like a horsetail blowing in the wind. Can't you see the force of it? The artist has watched horses running, and he has spent time studying oak trees. He has gone into the countryside many times until he discovered what works for him. He spent years developing these strokes.

"There is swiftness in each horizontal stroke, but the vertical strokes are like the trunks of mighty oak trees that are anchored to the earth. See here where they look fat but solid. There is more to this than just the meanings of the words themselves. No artist is the same, Master. Some have no strength in their strokes. They are blind to what nature teaches us, but this artist is skillful in giving strength to his characters so they are fleshy. This is divine. Your concubines know what to look for."

Robert had to step back to see what Guan-jiah was excited about, and he started to understand. It must have been expensive. Robert wondered how much the girls had spent.

It was because of Guan-jiah, Ayaou and Shao-mei that Robert discovered the true meaning of Chinese art, and a new door opened for him. In his later years he developed a further love for Chinese art, crafts, antiques and calligraphy. Although he dressed in Western style clothing in public, his taste in things gradually changed to Chinese.

Guan-jiah questioned Ayaou and Shao-mei about the wall hanging. He discovered that the artist was seventy-four and had sold them the painting for five yuan, because they had flirted with him. And the reason they bought this one over hundreds of others was exactly what Guan-jiah had said.

"It may have taken minutes for the artist to paint," Guan-jiah said, "but it took a lifetime to harmonize with nature and develop the talent—the ability to make the brush do what he wants.

"You see, Master, the artist cannot erase mistakes. He has to have control of the brush and know what he is doing. Once the brush touches paper and the ink flows, it is over. The artist cannot fix mistakes. He has to throw out the paper and start again."

Robert bought several books and started to devour the Chinese classics. His skills in reading Chinese had developed faster than speaking the language. He'd caught onto the writing because of the way it was divided into subjects. One example was trees. There was a basic symbol for a tree and anything to do with trees had that symbol in it with more ink strokes for a variety of meanings. There was a family of symbols for rain and another for house and on it went.

Robert suggested that the girls join him in the evenings, so they could read together. "But we do not know how to read," Ayaou confessed.

He was shocked and turned to the wall hanging that Guan-jiah had praised. "If you can't read, how did you select that?"

"The artist told us what it said, and we loved the brushstrokes. He painted it for us as we watched."

"He wanted more from us than just the five yuan," Shao-mei added, "but you do not have to worry, Robert. He is too old and there is no danger he will steal us from you."

"And what about the lyrics you both sing. They are sophisticated. Do you realize what you are singing? How did you learn the lyrics to the songs if you can't read?"

"Our father made us memorize them," Shao-mei replied. She stood at the washbasin where she was cleaning the wok and bowls from the evening meal. "We go by the sound. We have good memories. Sometimes our father forgot we could not read, because we spoke so elegantly. We even mimicked court manners."

"What are you thinking, Robert?" Ayaou asked. "Are you disappointed that we do not read?"

"No." He put the book down and waved for them to sit with him. "I was wondering, Ayaou. Have you ever been curious about books? I mean did you ever want to read?"

Ayaou lowered her head as a trace of sadness crossed her face. "Women do not read except a few daughters from rich families whose parents can afford private tutors."

"Not us. Not boat-girls," Shao-mei said.

"Boys go to school though," Ayaou said, staring at the flickering candle flame, "and I envied them. I dreamed many times of being one of the ink-boys."

"What's an ink-boy?"

"Haven't you seen the opera *The Butterfly-Lovers*?" Shao-mei said. "The ink-boys were the servants hired to carry the boys' books and grind ink."

"Didn't your father know your wish?"

"She was punished for it," Shao-mei said, before Ayaou could answer.

Robert studied the girls and was sure they weren't joking. "What kind of punishment?"

"Father beat her when he discovered she was secretly teaching herself to read, but Ayaou did not quit," Shao-mei said. "She went to the teahouse trying to learn a few words there. My father found out and was furious. He said, *Not willing to stay in her lot is a girl's worse curse*. Father was ready to beat Ayaou to death to make her quit. And he almost did. He beat her until his stick broke, and she passed out."

"Then what happened?" Robert asked.

"I was sent to the Bark Lee Tong, the herb shop, to buy Ayaou a bowl of ginseng soup to wake her. It took the last yuan father had."

Robert looked at Ayaou. His respect for her deepened. She sat quietly in the shadows of the flickering candlelight with her expression serene. Her youth was glowing. Her black eyebrows looked as if they'd been waxed.

"Father cried when he saw me awake," Ayaou said softly. "He said he missed my mother and was sure she would have found a way to persuade me to quit what I was doing if she were alive. Father beat me because he wanted me to have a good future. To be ignorant and stupid is a woman's blessing. It took me many years to understand my father was right. Our family's condition could never support my dreams. Learning to read and write beautiful poems would make me feel miserable about my life. My father was trying to protect me."

"Did you decide to give up on your dream?" Robert carefully selected his Chinese words, so the question was not an insult. He couldn't imagine what it would be like not to be able to read. Reading was a large part of his life. He loved books.

"I killed it." She smiled bitterly. "I promised father I would never upset him again, but my desire never truly died."

"What did you do?"

"Nothing. What could I do? Knowing my father is at peace is the reason I stay in my lot."

"Me too," Shao-mei said, moving closer to her sister.

"What if," Robert said, "there was an opportunity? I mean there was someone willing to teach you. Would you learn?"

"Do not take the misery of other people and play with it," Ayaou said. She stood. "Let's finish washing the dishes, Shao-mei."

"I'm serious!" Robert pulled on Ayaou's arm and dragged her back to sit beside him.

The girls stared at him in disbelief.

"I want to teach you the verses and poems you sing every day. The lessons start now," he said, and wanted to find his brush pen, ink-stone and rice paper. "But for this to work, you will have to be my ink-boy."

Ayaou was excited and grateful. She threw herself at him to squeeze and hug him. Turning to her sister, she said, "Shao-mei, let's compete to see who will be a better student. Our master has spoken. We cannot say no."

"I do not want to learn." Shao-mei formed her lips forward into the shape of a teapot spout. "Father said it is a waste of time for a woman to learn to read. It is not reading that makes a man happy. Isn't that true, Master?"

"Well, I'm different. I'd like to see you read a book. That will make me happy."

"You are lying." Shao-mei made her hands into fists and hammered at Robert's shoulders. "You can't make me read if I don't want to."

"Ayaou will make you."

"She and I are almost the same size. She can't win."

"Then I will," Robert said. "Ayaou, take me to a cane seller next time we go to the market. I'll buy a cane to use on Shao-mei." He struck a pose as if to strike.

"You are not a master. You are a monster!" Shao-mei screamed happily and ran from him. Her behavior delighted him, so he joined in her game and chased her around the table.

It was difficult for Robert to accept that he was now the head of a family. What they had was like a fantasy, and he wondered when it would dissolve. He knew a weakness was hidden inside his relationship with the sisters that could turn into a nightmare, and it was called lust and jealousy. Thoughts of seducing Shao-mei were rearing their ugly boiled faces again invading his head like a swarm of unwanted demons.

Robert recalled his idea of matching Shao-mei with Guan-jiah. There had to be a way. However, if Robert taught her to read, what would Guan-jiah think? Maybe he wouldn't like it. Maybe in this culture ignorant women were more desired than intelligent ones.

"It is getting late," Ayaou said after the lesson. "Let's go to bed." The sisters went to clean up. Then Ayaou sent Shao-mei to her room, the smaller bedroom that wasn't much more than a closet. It was across the hall from the room Robert shared with Ayaou. It was easy for him to imagine her standing there in her room taking her clothing off before getting into bed.

Robert followed Ayaou up the narrow stairs built for smaller feet. He was constantly concerned he'd miss a step and tumble to the bottom. Breaking his neck wasn't a pretty picture to carry around.

Once they were in the bedroom and behind a closed door, Robert turned to Ayaou and reached for her like a hungry stallion running toward fertile grassy fields. He had an endless thirst for her lips. Ayaou had an equal desire. It was as if she had to restrain herself during the day to keep her hands off him, but once in the privacy of their bedroom, she unleashed her appetite. She loved to stand by the bed and undress him one item of clothing at a time. He did the same to her until they were both naked.

Since he had rescued her from Ward, her desire for him had increased. Robert wondered how she'd feel if she discovered he hadn't paid Ward yet. It was something he'd deliberately hidden from everyone. Even Patridge didn't know.

It used to be that she had to exhaust herself to be completely happy, but tonight Robert found Ayaou wasn't concentrating. In the middle of their bodily explorations, she suddenly stopped.

"What's wrong, Ayaou?"

"Robert," she said, "I must talk to you about something serious. Let us sit on the bed."

Robert sat and realized he was holding his breath. He had to force himself to breathe. Had she discovered she still belonged to Ward? He felt a stab of guilt for keeping that information from her. "What is it?" He dreaded what she might say.

"I must tell you Shao-mei feels ugly."

"Nonsense." He relaxed. She still didn't know about Ward. He wanted to make love again. If he smothered her with kisses, she would have to stop talking. After all, she was sitting there naked. She looked so tempting.

He reached for her. She scooted out of reach. "You do not understand," she said. "Robert, this is important. Listen to me."

"I do understand, and she's being ridiculous," he replied. "She's an intelligent, energetic and lovely child."

"She is not a child." Ayaou turned serious. "She is a woman ten months younger than I am. We can both produce children."

"What's this? What's going on?" Feeling odd, he left the bed and pulled a bathrobe over his naked body.

Ayaou motioned for him to return to the bed. When he did, she took his hands in hers. "While we were at Captain Patridge's house waiting for you to return, she told me about your first time together. She was heartbroken when you would not take her."

Robert stared at the woman in front of him with wide-open eyes. He moved his lips as if he was speaking but nothing came out. She talked as if it were normal that he should have her younger sister. Did she mean it or was this a test?

"You should have respect for my culture," she said. "China is a society where a common man can purchase as many concubines as he can afford. You must respect my wishes and consider my happiness. I believe that you are not sincere when you tell me you are a one-woman man. I believe that eventually you will get another concubine and why not now, why not Shao-mei, my sister, whom I love."

Robert had no choice but to make her see things his way, because what she had just revealed was his horrible fantasy. The nightmare he feared was rearing its ugly, lusty ghoulish head. Robert couldn't allow that to happen. He wanted to throw ice water on this and kill it before it started.

"It's just that I'm in love with you." He grasped at words that would save him while another part of him craved to open this new door and see what was on the other side. A battle raged inside him, but he continued to deny that he wanted Shao-mei. He knew he was falling in love with her. "You're the only woman I want." The lie slipped easily out of his mouth and into the room. "Besides, it would be a betrayal of our love if I took your sister."

It was also a betrayal of an oath he'd taken when he left Ireland. Robert had sworn to allow only one woman into his life—the one he would eventually marry. In Belfast, while he was attending college, he'd allowed himself to have as many women as possible. It had been wrong—something that he was sure he would answer for in the next life. The Chinese were fortunate they didn't believe in life after death. It was probably why Ayaou and Shao-mei were acting the way they were. They saw nothing wrong with one man having many women.

Loving and sleeping with Ayaou had been the first step in betraying his oath. Adding Shao-mei to the equation would take him to a level of sin he'd never imagined possible. Robert would be right back where he'd started with the same type of lascivious behavior that had led him to banish himself from home except this time it would be worse. Instead of one woman at a time, he would be in bed with two.

His words didn't register with Ayaou, who said. "I know that in your country good men take only one wife, but how do you explain the fact that most foreigners who come to China like Ward and Patridge buy as many women as they can afford?"

"I'm different! I have no respect for what they do! Besides, I cannot guarantee I can afford the responsibility of our relationship. How could I add on Shao-mei? I don't want to ruin her future. I care about her."

Again, Robert thought of Guan-jiah as a choice. It wasn't going to be easy because his servant was a eunuch. It also didn't help that he didn't have kind things to say about boat people.

For a moment, Robert considered selling more of himself to Patridge to raise a dowry for Shao-mei. There'd have to be so much money involved Guan-jiah couldn't say no. He had to admit there was a possibility a bribe in the form of a dowry wouldn't be enough for Guan-jiah to want Shao-mei as his platonic soul mate. If Guan-jiah wouldn't take her off his hands, Robert would have to consider the unthinkable. He would have to sell Shao-mei to a stranger and remove her from his life.

"You are making little sense to me and no sense to Shao-mei, Robert. She won't understand." Ayaou leaned over and kissed his neck, which caused him to break out in goosebumps. "She worships and desires you. While she was at Patridge's house, she saw what life was like for his concubines. She saw how Captain Patridge gave them to his friends as nightly gifts. She knows you saved her from that life. Now she only wants to know that you are pleased with her. If you take her, she will stop feeling insecure. She will know she belongs."

"What does she expect of me? I mean, what does she want?" His hands were clammy. He was covered with nervous sweat.

"You know how much I enjoy what you do with me. Shao-mei wants to know the same pleasure."

He choked. His heart started to race. It felt as if there were a peach pit stuck in his throat, and he couldn't swallow it. It was a trap he couldn't escape. His nature was driving him to betray his family, his friends and his religion.

"Would you spare a little of your love for her? A little. For me." Ayaou's words were gentle and soft, but in his ears the words amplified themselves and sounded as loud as thunder.

"But it would be wrong!" He heard his voice yell, which wasn't what his thoughts were urging him to do. His thoughts were screaming to agree with her. "I can't do it! You'd lose respect for me."

"I would not lose respect for you, Robert. Shao-mei is not only my sister, but she is also your second concubine. You bought her. You should take care of her and to do this you must make her feel worthy."

"How will you take it, Ayaou? I'm sure you'll be jealous." He stopped and stared at her incredulous. "Wouldn't you?" He was pleading for her to agree with him.

"Not really. Since I know that I am number one, the superior one, I will be happy. Let me put it this way—I will be worse off if you take another concubine, which you will like every other man in China who can afford it. You will find a stranger with a spoiled character. She might hate me and do nasty things to me. It happens often in households. There are even murders. I am safe with Shao-mei. She will be satisfied as your number two concubine. We both will feel fortunate to make a family out of this. Shao-mei and I are close like a tea mug and its lid."

"But I'm only capable of loving one woman," he said, doubting his words. He already knew he loved Shao-mei, but he wanted to think of her as a sister. "It'll be impossible for me to become intimate with Shao-mei. Ayaou, you'll tell her that I cannot be involved with two women at the same time. I just can't. You are the only woman I will share my bed with. We'll just have to find someone else for Shao-mei. What about Guan-jiah?"

He could tell that this upset Ayaou, because her voice went up an octave. "You don't love me enough. If you find a Chinese man for her, he will beat her, have other women, gamble, and make her life miserable. If you find another foreigner, he would be like Ward or Patridge and use her until he didn't find her attractive anymore. After that, he'd sell her to be a whore for sailors. Is that what you desire for my sister, who is like my other half? Besides, Guan-jiah is a eunuch. Shao-mei could never have children by him."

"How did you know he's a eunuch?" Robert said, stunned. "I never told you that."

"He smells like one," she replied. "Can't you tell? They all smell the same. They leak urine and wear a thick cotton pad to absorb it."

"I can't believe this is happening. You're saying this because I refuse to seduce your sister. You two are crazy!"

"You are selfish, Robert. Your passion is like an ocean. Why not spare a little for my sister? It is all she is asking for. Would you acknowledge that I sometimes cannot keep up with you? You want me three times a night, and sometimes that is not enough. Why can't you let Shao-mei take some pressure off me?"

"Ayaou, please understand I wouldn't care to be loyal to you if I didn't love you!"

"Shao-mei does not care if you love her, Robert." Ayaou shot back. "She only wants to make you happy. What you give her she will treasure for the rest of her life. I am sure she can never get this kind of love from any other man. I pity my sister and me too."

Robert rolled over on his side away from her. "Go away," he said in English, so she wouldn't understand. "You don't know what you're talking about, Ayaou. You've no idea what it has taken for me to forsake my God and what I was raised to believe, so I could live here and be in love with you. I'm sure that your naiveté and kindness hasn't prepared you to deal with your nature as a human. You don't know what jealousy is and what it can do to destroy you. It is easy for you to push me into this, but it'll be hard for you to deal with afterwards. It'll be too late and one can never undo a pot of tea that's already been brewed."

After Robert's tirade fizzled, silence filled the room like a whiteout after a snowstorm. Ayaou fell quiet and eventually went to sleep. What a strange night, a strange place and strange girls.

The next day a letter arrived from Ireland. It was from Robert's sister Mary. The seal on the letter appeared to have been broken. All his mail came through Hong Kong and then through Shanghai. Robert wondered if someone was reading his letters. This wasn't the first letter he'd found with the seal undone.

Was someone spying on him and if so, why? He shrugged. He was being paranoid again. Who would want to read his mail? After all, he was a nobody—just a lowly paid interpreter. He only had one enemy he could think of, and that was Ward. By now, Ward had probably forgotten Robert was alive. After all, the man was struggling to heal his battle wounds in some isolated house in the countryside.

What could Ward learn by opening Robert's letters from Ireland? The answer was nothing. Then it occurred to Robert that maybe the letters he was writing home were getting the same treatment. He stopped reading Mary's letter in an attempt to remember if he'd ever mentioned where he was living in Ningpo. He was sure he'd never written home about renting a house. As far as his family and friends knew, he still lived at the Ningpo consulate, and Robert wanted to keep it that way.

He started to read Mary's letter again. She had always been his favorite. She was the calmest and always level headed. She knew who she was and what she wanted from life. She set goals and worked toward them. As far as Robert could see, Mary didn't have his weaknesses. She took after father but in a better, less judgmental way. She enjoyed sewing, cooking and cleaning house. In the evenings after the dinner dishes were washed and put away, Mary always played piano and sang. She had a great voice, and Robert missed it. To bad he couldn't have found a woman like her for a wife before he'd left Ireland. With a proper woman by his side, he wouldn't be in this predicament with Ayaou and Shao-mei. There had been a time when he'd wished Mary wasn't his sister. Robert thought of her as the perfect woman.

Robert realized he had inherited some of their mother's wildness, which might have been the foundation of his problems.

In the letter, Mary wrote that a wonderful man, a linen merchant, was courting her. He worked long days like their father. They saw each other only on Sundays after church. She said she admired him for his industriousness and could only hope that he'd ask father for her hand in marriage. She wanted to move to Lisburn, where the man lived, and give him children to work in his family's business.

Reading the letter triggered guilty thoughts for the life he was living. He had to tame his wild streak. He should have been working endless hours toward his future instead of spending so much time with Ayaou and Shao-mei enjoying pleasure for its own sake. He couldn't ignore the temptation that was offered to him through Shao-mei. It was more than Robert could handle. He could lie to Ayaou, but he couldn't lie to himself. He was attracted to Shao-mei. She was a beautiful young woman. He ached to have her.

The conversation with Ayaou and the letter from Mary triggered a change in Robert. He started spending more hours at the consulate. He knew that he was doing it to avoid Shao-mei. It was a continuing struggle to keep her out of his head. He even started to work a few hours each Sunday. He was also taking care writing the letters that went to Ireland. He avoided mentioning anything that provided clues to where he lived in Ningpo. His letters became shorter and more cryptic. He stopped writing about Chinese culture and art for fear that one small incident or description might provide a clue to someone like Ward.

Chapter 15

God's servants did not know Patridge. Robert envied the man for that. He, on the other hand, was not an invisible person who could sin at will. He had crossed the river and eaten with the missionaries. He had also gone to church services on the Sabbath. They didn't know Patridge, but they knew Robert. They knew that he cared about his ultimate salvation.

The fact that Robert hadn't been to a sermon since leaving Ningpo for Patridge's summerhouse bothered him. If any of the missionaries knew the depth of sin he'd allowed himself to sink into, they would have been struck speechless. They'd pity him and pray for his eternal soul. Patridge, on the other hand, came from a different world—one that Robert was fascinated with but uncomfortable in. The captain didn't care what the missionaries thought.

Ayaou slipped from the bed, tiptoed from the bedroom, and closed the door gently behind her. The moment the door closed, he sat up. He knew she was going to Shao-mei's room to console her, because he refused to have intercourse with the younger sister.

His mind filled with a blizzard of conflicting thoughts and emotions. To escape his confusion, he lit a lantern and checked his pocket watch. It was a little past midnight. In desperation, he turned to a book of poems from the Southern Song Dynasty. He had escaped into poems and literature before. Maybe it would help this time too. As he leafed through the pages, one poem caught his attention. It fit his situation. He prayed that the poem offered a solution to his dilemma. The poet's name was Lu You—dead for six hundred years.

"Pink hands so fine,
Gold-branded wine,
Spring paints green willows palace walls cannot confine.
East wind unfair,
Happy times rare.
In my heart sad thoughts throng.
We've severed for years long
Wrong, wrong, wrong!"

Robert could have added lines of his own to make it fit his life. As he understood Lu You's history, the poet had to divorce a wife that he deeply loved. The man had written the poem to fit that occasion. Robert's predicament was different but similar since he was in love with two women. What was he to do? Get rid of one, so he could find happiness with the other. He couldn't bring himself to do that. He hated admitting he wanted both girls.

He got up, dressed and paced the room. He opened the shutters overlooking the alley and leaned out. He smelled the stench from the open sewer. He had a strong desire to take a walk where the air was fresh despite the hour and the dangers for a foreigner. He froze as he spied the hulking shape of what looked like a large man standing below his window.

"Who's there?" he said in Mandarin. The man held up an arm to cover his face and hurried away. Why would someone be lurking outside his house at this hour? Could it be a thief? Feeling nervous, Robert closed the shutters. Taking a walk to clear his mind was out of the question. There was no telling what was waiting.

What would Patridge think if Robert turned to him for more money to solve this problem? The captain would be glad of binding Robert's services to him longer. He'd also want to know why. He'd laugh at the answer. He'd think Robert a fool for not taking both of these fabulous girls. Maybe he was a fool. He felt like one.

Robert snuffed out the lantern light, undressed and slipped back into the cold, empty bed. When Ayaou returned more than an hour later, she put a hand on his shoulder. "Robert," she said in a whisper.

He pretended to be asleep and was relieved when her hand went away. In a short time her breathing told him she was sleeping. The silence was so complete that Robert heard Shao-mei crying in her room.

Depression sucked at him like a giant leech. He knew exactly how Lu You the poet felt when he had to give up a woman he loved. He must have paced in his garden or walked the streets to avoid madness. He must have missed the sound of her voice. He must have imagined kissing her lips and stroking the smooth warm skin of her naked body. Just thinking about how much he wanted her must have haunted him.

The next morning Ayaou and Shao-mei were quiet during the morning meal. Shao-mei ate slowly. She spent most of her time staring at the tips of her chopsticks. Robert noticed she had red, swollen eyes. She must have cried all night. He felt guilty for not making love to her. At the same time, he felt guilty for wanting to. It was a terrible conundrum. Guilt was tugging him in two directions. He hated it.

With his appetite gone, he pushed the bowl of food away and stood. "I'm going for a walk," he said, moving toward the door.

They stood as if to join him.

"No, I'd like to go alone." He left the house and walked the narrow, twisting streets. The city was wrapped in a blanket of soft, mushy fog—a perfect place to hide. He shivered. It was an odd chilly morning for August. He decided to go back and get his jacket.

Just as he turned to go to the house, Robert sensed he wasn't alone. He spun around and saw an arm appear from the fog with a club gripped in its hand. Robert sensed the body behind the arm. Without thinking, he ducked and stepped forward under the swing and punched out hitting something soft like a stomach. The club glanced off his shoulder. The assailant dropped the weapon. It clattered on the ground.

Robert dug his fist into the soft flesh again. There was a grunt. Then the assailant was running away gasping for air. For an instant, Robert was tempted to give chase, but his revolver was still in the jacket pocket inside the house. It was stupid to attempt catching the thug without his pistol. Robert could be killed. He wondered if this was the man he'd seen in the alley. He didn't think so. The other man was larger. Could there be two working together?

167

He stepped against the house and waited for the wild beating of his heart to subside. He listened to the receding patter of the assailant's running feet. If there was a second man, he could be waiting for a chance to have a go at him. Robert slid along the wall toward the door. He took stock of his situation. He rotated the shoulder the club had hit and was satisfied it wasn't damaged. There was no pain. There probably wouldn't be a bruise. He'd been lucky.

His quick reflexes had saved him again as they had in the battle with the Taipings. There had been other incidents in his life like this one where he had reacted with thoughtless speed.

He remembered one of the girls he'd been seeing in Belfast. She had stepped in front of a galloping horse pulling a wagon. At the same instant, without thinking, Robert yanked her back. Everything had slowed around him during that incident. It was as if a part of his mind had taken charge and acted. There had been no time to think. It happened faster than a breath or the blink of an eye. Then the girl had been clinging to him with her trembling body pressed to his. His reward that night had been a passionate one.

Once Robert was satisfied the assailant was gone, he quietly entered the house. He didn't want the girls to know he had returned. His jacket hung on a peg protruding from the wall just inside the door. He hesitated when he heard the girls talking in the kitchen.

"Ayaou," Shao-mei said, "you must admit you did a terrible job when you tried to persuade Robert to make me his concubine and treat me as he does you!"

"No," Ayaou said in a defensive tone. "I did exactly what I promised. I tried to teach him what is expected of a master who has more than one concubine. I cannot help it if he is a foreigner."

"You promised to share! You said you'd talk him into it. You never were as good a convincer as I was. It's either you are not trying hard enough, or you want to keep him like you always tried to get all the moon cakes during the moon festival."

"You always throw that at me when you want something!" Ayaou replied. "It isn't fair."

"You do not think I am good enough for Robert. You always think I am silly and stupid."

"That is not true, Shao-mei!"

"You are selfish," Shao-mei retorted. "You are not doing your best or he'd also be warming my bed at night. Then I would also know what it is like to be a woman fulfilled. I want Robert to be the man I give myself to. I do not want a stranger. I do not want Patridge. I do not want Hollister. Robert is not like the rooster that jumps on the hen and has his way with her against her will. He does not treat me like a hen. He is the only man I want. You have to share him with me."

There was a moment of silence before Ayaou said, "Why are you holding your head? Do not act so dramatic. It isn't my fault. I have done the best I can."

"I have a headache." Shao-mei said.

"Then eat. You haven't been eating. Have a bowl of rice porridge. I put sweet yams in it. Your favorite."

"No, I am not hungry. Just talking about food makes my stomach flip-flop. Leave me alone, sister. I don't want to talk anymore. I am tired. I'm going back to bed."

"Wash the wok and bowls before you go. You agreed that I would cook and you would clean up. What is the matter with you? You have never acted like this before. The sister I grew up with has always been cheerful."

"You are mean to me," Shao-mei said. "You won't share Robert. I also do not feel good, and you want to make me work."

Confused and with his ears burning, Robert almost forgot about his narrow escape with the assailant. When he lifted his jacket off the hook, he checked the pocket to see if the revolver was there. He was satisfied when his fingers closed around its walnut grip. He resolved to never leave the house without this weapon again. He decided to be cautious in the future when moving about the city. He'd talk to the girls about the man in the alley below the bedroom window. Maybe the girls were in danger too. It was possible because Robert was a foreigner that a thug thought there was something worth stealing from this house. It bothered him that so many unknown dangers were out there. He now realized that anything could happen at any time. It made him feel helpless.

At work, Robert lost his concentration and wasted his morning study time. By noon, he noticed a subtle change in his mood. He started to hum one of the songs that Ayaou liked to sing while cooking. Feeling better, Robert went home for lunch. He didn't know what had come over him, but he wanted to see his girls.

"Ayaou," he said, once he was home, "I want you to find me a new Chinese teacher. I want to learn to think like a Chinese man." Maybe, Robert thought, if he learned to think like one, he'd find a way to solve this problem with his two girls.

With hands covering their mouths, both Ayaou and Shao-mei burst out laughing. "How can you think like a Chinese man when you do not act like one?"

The new teacher's name was Tee Lee Ping. He was in his late twenties and wore a knee length summer robe made of linen. He had a round face with busy eyebrows. His features reminded Robert of a cartoon frog with a mouth that looked like it stretched from ear to ear even when he wasn't smiling. Once the greetings were over, Robert explained what he wanted.

"So, you want to think like a Chinese man," Tee Lee Ping said after a long silence. His eyebrows hadn't been still. They had done this strange dance above his eyes while Ping glanced back and forth from the girls to Robert. "And how exactly do you see me doing that for you?"

"By guiding me through great Chinese literature that shows how the Chinese people think, live and act. Literature is the eyes and ears of the past and present."

"Hmm," was Tee Lee Ping's answer. "Then I suggest you purchase a copy of the *Outlaws of the Marsh* by Shi Nai and Luo Guanzhong. It was written in what you would call the twelfth century."

"And it is about?" Robert asked.

"You will read it to learn. Then we will discuss it. After that, you will read *Journey to the West*."

"Wait." Robert held up a hand. "This *Outlaws of the Marsh* was written about six hundred years ago. How is that going to help me understand the Chinese today?"

"People don't change as the dynasties do. One example would be how clothing styles changed after the Ch'ing dynasty came to power. The clothing we Han Chinese wear today was not our traditional way of dressing when the Manchu came to rule China. Another example is the pigtail I wear. Before the Manchu, we Han did not shave our heads and grow a pigtail.

Han Chinese tradition dictated that removing hair was against *filial piety*, because hair comes from the parents. Therefore, I feel it is best to go back before the Manchu to see how we Han think. Changing the way a man cuts his hair or the clothing he wears does not change the way he thinks."

It was all so bewildering to Robert. "I can see that I have much to learn. When was the *Journey to the West* written?"

"According to your Christian calendar, the time would be in the 1590s during the Ming Dynasty. You may want to buy that book at the same time that you buy the other one. The *Journey to the West* has a hundred chapters. We will have a lot to discuss."

After that, Tee Lee Ping came every evening and worked with Robert. As they started to discuss the books, it was obvious Robert wasn't going to learn much about his women. Maybe if he had told Ping his real motive, the teacher would've suggested something else to read. Robert wanted to understand more about the ways of his two women instead of the challenges of one hundred and eight brigands in the *Outlaws of the Marsh.*

The *Journey to the West* was even less enlightening. It was about a journey by a Buddhist monk and his three guardians as they traveled from China to India to obtain a copy of a religious text called the Sutras.

Robert was learning about Chinese religion and mythology and the value systems of the people. He didn't see anything useful regarding his girls. He kept telling himself to be patient. He'd already learned that the Chinese were not direct in communicating what they meant. He was starting a journey where one must first travel north to arrive at a destination in the south. At some point, Robert hoped to discover what he wanted. He feared it might take years.

Robert read the books Ping recommended twice. In the afternoons and evenings, he spent time with Ayaou and Shao-mei teaching them to read and write the same thing but a simpler version. In this way, his progress in learning Chinese improved. He was becoming fluent and was erasing any accent. No matter how fast his girls talked, he understood every word.

The only thing missing was the harmony that should have been in the house. Too many days had passed since Ayaou and Robert had shared sexual intimacy. Ayaou had withdrawn. The more time that slipped by with the passion missing, the quieter the house became. Shao-mei, besides being tired all the time and having headaches, looked so sad that a worn-out dishcloth appeared happier.

Ayaou went about her daily business of shopping for food, preparing meals and washing. Robert knew what was on her mind, but he couldn't figure out a way to solve the problem. A victory for them was a defeat for him—a sweet defeat that he lost sleep over every night and ached for.

Robert's only hope was to learn how to think like a Chinese man. He wanted to sweep away his British upbringing into the alley where it would be carried into the river with the rest of the city's waste. If one speck of that other Robert Hart survived, he'd be doomed as if the hounds of hell were after him.

Tee Lee Ping continued to arrive every evening for several hours of instruction. One day before the end of September he handed Robert a gift. "You're an able student," he said. "From the start I realized you wanted to know more about your two concubines and why they act the way they do. I felt it best to start with the first two books you have read and discussed with me. In time, I believe you will see the reason I selected this path to the knowledge and understanding you seek.

"This gift is another Chinese classic titled *The Dream of the Red Chamber.* It was written about one hundred years ago. I recommend you read it to develop an understanding of Chinese women. There will be an opera in Ningpo in December that is based on this classic. Finish the book by then. Also share this book with your two concubines, and take them to the opera with you."

"An opera," Robert said. "I've never been to an opera—not even in Ireland." To think that his first opera would be in Chinese. "Is there anything I should know about this opera to understand it better?" he asked.

Tee Lee Ping held up a hand. "Be patient," he said. "Read the book first. Then we will discuss it. That way when you sit in an audience watching the opera, you will understand the reaction of the Chinese, who will be watching it too. Their reactions will teach you more about how they think. This, I feel, is the best road to take for your enlightenment.

"Mr. Hart," he said. "You are a rare individual for a foreigner. I have taught other foreigners before you. Usually they are missionaries or merchants and none ever wanted to know how the Chinese think. I have talked to my colleagues about you, and none have ever met a man like you."

The next morning, when Robert left the house on his way to the consulate, he remembered Tee Lee Ping's words. Robert might be rare, but that didn't matter if he got himself killed in the streets. Thinking that he might have forgotten the pistol, he reached in his pocket and was relieved to find it there. The freak fog that had almost been his undoing was gone. The sun was back, and it was already baking the clear air. He looked around searching the street and relaxed when he did not see anyone who looked menacing.

Chapter 16

Robert was in constant fear that Ward would come for Ayaou.

Usually only Ayaou and Robert were up early in the mornings for breakfast, but Shao-mei was getting up earlier. Her mood was gloomy. She complained often of headaches and feeling sick to her stomach. She didn't eat much but just sat staring at her food as if it were the enemy.

Robert thought she was depressed, because he wouldn't cross the hall to her room and sleep with her. It wasn't as if he didn't want to. He wondered if God were testing him to see if he was sincere in wanting to change from the man that left Ireland. Shao-mei and the forbidden apple from the Garden of Eden were similar, and, like Adam, Robert wanted to pluck the apple and have his way with it.

As the end of autumn drew near, the plants and pots of poet's jasmine the girls carefully tended were still in full bloom, and the sweet scent of jasmine filled the house. The wisteria was also in bloom. Dramatic clusters of blue, pink, purple and white flowers dangled from the vines. The girls always left the window open to encourage the wisteria to grow around the window frame and into the kitchen where they were training it to climb the walls. He didn't like the window open but said nothing. He didn't want to reveal his fear of Ward showing up to reclaim Ayaou.

It was a relief to set off for the consulate where he spent several hours a day dealing with shipping and doing his job as an interpreter. When one of Captain Patridge's ships arrived, Robert did the paperwork while counting the days until the deal he'd made with the devil ended. He did not like helping Patridge smuggle opium into China.

Robert was not alone at the consulate anymore. A Dr. Winchester had arrived on the *Styx* to take Hollister's place as acting Vice-Counsel in Ningpo. Dr. Winchester had been with the Consular service since 1843, and had come from Amoy where he'd been Vice-Consul. His wife was a large woman who astounded the Chinese with her huge size. She was not only tall but also wide. Her bosom alone would have concealed Shao-mei.

In mid-November, a small flotilla of Cantonese pirates chased several Portuguese lorchas up the coast and into the river to Ningpo. Both groups were pirates, and they blasted away at one another out in the river. Bullets and cannonballs smacked into the city's walls. The consulate was outside the city wall, so Dr. Winchester closed and barred the gates. He then retreated behind the thick walls of the consulate with his wife. Robert climbed a ladder to the roof where he hid behind a chimney to watch what was happening.

The Portuguese pirates left their ships and retreated into the city. They scattered in small groups and headed toward the foreign consulates looking for asylum. One group came toward the British consulate. When they started pounding on the gate, Robert climbed down from the roof, crossed the courtyard and reached for the bar to remove it and let them in.

"Don't open that gate, Hart," Dr. Winchester said. He stood in the consulate's doorway. "We don't want to risk those Cantonese pirates breaking in here to get the Portuguese." Robert, feeling helpless, stepped away from the gate.

The Portuguese continued to beat their fists raw while pleading for sanctuary.

"Sir, we can't stand here and do nothing," Robert protested. "We have weapons. We can fight."

"Why do you want to help these people, Hart? They are Portuguese pirates. They brought this on themselves, and there are only two of us to fight the Cantonese. There are hundreds of them, and the Cantonese pirates have cannons. They could blow the gate down. What would happen to us then? I have my wife to think of. Besides, they're all pirates and should hang."

Robert bit his tongue and kept silent. After all, he also had Ayaou and Shao-mei to care for. What would happen to them if he were killed? The Portuguese were still on the other side of the gate begging to be let in.

"In fact, it is probably better if the Cantonese didn't know who's inside these walls," Dr. Winchester said. He went to the flagpole and brought down the British ensign. Robert returned to his concealed place on the roof and flattened himself on the tiles behind the chimney.

The Cantonese pirates hunted the Portuguese through the day and beheaded those they found. The survivors eventually surrendered. The Cantonese loaded their prisoners onto one of the lorchas, towed it into the middle of the river and set fire to it with the Portuguese on board. From where Robert was hidden, he witnessed everything. The screams of the Portuguese roasting inside that ship were hideous. When the wind shifted toward the city, it carried the stench of burning bodies with it. Sometimes in his dreams, Robert still heard the pounding on the gate and the desperate voices of the Portuguese.

Dr. Winchester's wife called for Robert to come in for supper. He left the roof.

"Set one thief to get rid of another," Dr. Winchester said, as they gathered around the table to eat. "It is only fitting."

Guan-jiah came into the compound through a small side gate that opened to an alley behind the consulate. He kowtowed to Dr. Winchester, and said, "Masters, the Cantonese pirates have come ashore and are hunting for other foreigners to behead or burn. I came to warn you, so you will keep the gates locked. Load all your weapons and be ready."

Dr. Winchester hurried to get his double-barreled shotgun. When Guan-jiah didn't move, Robert urged him to leave and return to his family. "Surely, Guan-jiah, if they come in here to harm us, you will also suffer our fate."

"Master," he said, "if you have an extra weapon, I will stand and fight beside you."

"No, you have to go. You have a family to consider."

A stricken look filled Guan-jiah's face. He threw himself to the ground and kowtowed. "I am your slave, Master. I will not abandon you. Your fate is my fate."

Blood rushed into Robert's head. "Get up, Guan-jiah!" He knelt, took his servant by the shoulders, and made him stand. He was so overwhelmed by the eunuch's show of loyalty he couldn't respond. Instead, he went for his pistol and came back with a sword for Guan-jiah. They gathered around the dining table and listened to the shooting and screams outside the walls.

Mrs. Winchester sat at the table with a loaded single shot blunderbuss. She kept a burning candle nearby to light the fuse. The blunderbuss was loaded with small iron balls. "It was my father's," she said, "and I know how to use it."

"If they break down the gate and get into the courtyard, I will use my shotgun first," Dr. Winchester said. "My wife will shoot them with the blunderbuss when they reach the door to this room. Hart, while my wife and I reload, you use that pistol to hold them at bay. If they get inside, Guan-jiah, use that sword to hack at them. With any luck, we'll kill more than a score before any set foot inside this room." He turned to Robert. "If you are willing to go back up on that roof so we have a warning, that would be good of you."

Robert returned to the roof and crawled across the tiles to his former position behind the chimney. From his hiding place, he watched an American merchant crawl through a window across the street in an attempt to escape. Two Cantonese pirates saw him and gave chase. Robert wanted to shoot at them and give the American a chance. Then he realized he would be putting everyone in the consulate at risk if he did.

The sails of a large ship appeared out at sea. Robert squinted to see better. It looked like a naval ship. He scrambled down. "Telescope," he said, with excitement coursing through his veins. "There's a big ship coming in. It has the look of a man-of-war."

"Good God, could it be British?" Dr. Winchester said. "Maybe they discovered we were in danger and came from Shanghai." His hands were shaking as he pulled open a drawer in a cabinet and handed Robert a collapsing telescope. Dr. Winchester stood at the foot of the ladder as Robert climbed.

Once Robert trained the telescope on the ship, he saw it was a French warship. He started shouting in his best Mandarin that a foreign warship was arriving. "Run, run, return to our ships," he shouted, hoping the pirates thought his voice belonged to one of them. "It is a French warship coming to sink us. If they catch us, we will hang."

His ruse worked for the pirates rushed to the beach. Some of them pointed at the warship and looked frantic. They piled into their boats, rowed out to the pirate ships, and fled up river. Robert searched the streets with the telescope and was relieved when he saw the American merchant had survived.

The French warship, the *Capricieuse,* hadn't come to rescue them. It was ending a long voyage from South American, and Ningpo was its first port of call. Fate had been kind.

Dr. Winchester hurried back to the flagpole and ran the British ensign to the top. He called Robert over and pulled a crumpled letter from his pocket. He handed it to Robert. "This came the other day," he said. "It is an unsigned letter accusing you of theft from the consulate."

Robert was stunned. He opened the letter and read that he was taking bribes and stealing money from the consulate cash box. It also revealed he was living with two Chinese women, and he was pimping them as whores. By the time he finished reading, his ears burned and the strength in his legs had leaked out. He handed the letter back. "I don't know what to say." He stammered. "It's all lies. Why did you wait until now to show me this? Does this mean I'm going to lose my job? Am I to be sent to Australia and the penal colony for something I didn't do?"

"Rubbish," Dr. Winchester replied. "Think nothing of it. Since that letter came, I watched you carefully, and I saw your compassion for your servant earlier. No thief acts that way. I'm sure you will understand that I had no choice. I have concluded that whoever wrote that letter is someone who holds ill will for you. Your actions today prove that you are an honorable, God-fearing man. You are not the type to do what that letter accuses you of. Take care, Robert. Someone wants to ruin you. That man is a coward or he would have stood as a witness against you. I want you to know that I haven't shared this letter with my wife because rumors can damage a person's reputation. We wouldn't want that."

"Thank you for your trust, Dr. Winchester. You will not regret it." Robert thought of Ward. Who else could it be? It couldn't be Hollister. He had sailed to England long ago.

"Can you think of anyone who would want to do you damage?" Dr. Winchester asked.

"One man," Robert replied, and he told about his close encounter with death at Sungkiang and the heated confrontation with Ward days later. He did not mention Ayaou.

Dr. Winchester looked irritated. He said, "I've heard of this Ward, and none of it was good. If you have made an enemy of him because of his ineptness, you must be careful. Although I can't blame you for confronting him out of anger because he almost got you killed, it would have been wiser to avoid him after escaping the Taipings. You should have returned to Ningpo straightaway. The odds are he would have never discovered what happened to you or taken the time to find out. Men like him have colossal egos. He cannot take the blame for his actions. When something goes wrong, it is always someone else who is at fault. It isn't wise to make an enemy of a man like that."

"I agree," Robert replied. He now realized he had made a mistake. It had never occurred to him he should have just slipped away with Ayaou. The chances were that Ward would never have found out. He had been a fool to confront the man as he had.

Dr. Winchester folded the letter and handed it to Robert. "The letter is yours now. Maybe you will recognize the handwriting one-day and be able to put a name to the man who has accused you. If it is someone powerful like Ward, I suggest you forget it."

Robert took the letter and put it in his top left, breast pocket. He decided to carry it with him as a reminder to stop and think first.

Before Guan-jiah left the consulate to return to his family, Robert pulled him aside, "Guan-jiah, you are not my slave. You are my employee. We do not own slaves in Ireland."

Guan-jiah stared at his feet and shuffled them. "Master, an astrologer told me that we were tied together. Wherever you go, I will follow. In that way I am your slave even if you do not own me like an animal."

What could Robert say? After all, this was China. He could not force his beliefs on these people. They had their culture. "Guan-jiah, I'm going to raise your pay and give you a few days off a month to do as you please. What is your favorite leisure activity?"

"Eating," he replied.

"That's all you will do is eat?" Robert was surprised, because Guan-jiah was thin like a twig.

The eunuch eagerly nodded. "With money and time, I will eat more. I will eat crabs, drink tea, sing operas, fly kites, stew ginseng, hold conversations, take afternoon naps, have three meals in one, practice calligraphy, chew on duck-gizzards, eat carrots, walnuts, melon seeds, gamble for moon cakes, eat noodles, solve literary riddles, and sleep. It's what any good Chinese man does when he has free time. If I become tired of that, I can always find a second job."

Eventually the Taotai, the Chinese governor of Ningpo, hired another band of local pirates to control the Cantonese pirates.

In addition, the foreign powers, Britain included, were continuing to force China to swallow more opium trade. This made for hard feelings against people like Robert, so he started to keep a wary eye out for threats—not that he wasn't already alert because of the attack on him. Maybe such hard feelings for foreign devils was the reason for that assault in the fog. Maybe Ward had nothing to do with it. The thought that Robert could make some Chinese peasant rich by losing his head was something not to take lightly.

Robert didn't tell the girls about the unsigned letter or what had happened at the consulate with the Portuguese. He didn't want to worry them.

In the afternoons, Robert went home dreading what mood the girls might greet him with. Tee Lee Ping arrived about the same time to spend the next four hours in instruction and discussion. Sometimes it was funny to Robert when he heard gibberish coming out of Master Ping's mouth that made no sense to him. He put a serious look on his face and pretended to understand. Tee Lee Ping forgot that Robert wasn't a native speaker and that he had to do a lot of guesswork. Nevertheless, Robert didn't mind his teacher being difficult, which meant speaking and dropping idioms and slants like crazy. He felt the opposite. He appreciated it.

During break time, Ayaou hovered about the room. She'd ask Master Ping questions. They often ended in hot debates. It was to Robert's benefit as he practiced his listening comprehension along with his cultural education by seeing them negotiate and manipulate each other.

"You should give my master a discount in his tuition, because your Mandarin is not as pure as the Mandarin spoken by Peking opera actors," Ayaou said one night, and Robert was alarmed. He thought he was about to lose his teacher.

Ayaou believed Robert should learn the Imperial accent instead of the Ningpo accent. She demonstrated Master Tee Lee Ping's flaws. The look on his face said he was taking her criticism as an insult, but he did not say one word to her. The reason he swallowed Ayaou's insults was because she was a Chinese woman. This was the woman's role, to be the critic so one's head did not swell. Tee Lee Ping yielded to Ayaou when it came to proper pronunciation.

"You should split your pay with me," she said in a joking tone. He answered her with silence while he continued the lesson.

With Ayaou in charge, Robert's progress mastering Chinese accelerated. Ayaou and Shao-mei pounced on his Ningpo accent. The penalty was to wash the dishes when they caught him. Keeping strictly to this schedule and routine helped minimize any pitfalls that might open at his feet when Shao-mei had a mood swing. The only times he felt as if he were walking on broken eggshells was at bedtime and in the mornings before he went to the consulate.

After Tee Lee Ping left, Shao-mei, Ayaou and Robert ate the evening meal. Then his lesson with the girls started. They were ardent students. They picked up the written language faster than he was learning it. If this kept up, they would catch up to him before a year had gone by.

While he was teaching, there were giggles and strange hand motions between the girls. During snack time they'd chat, telling each other what had happened in the morning market to rumors about an Imperial theft taking place inside The Forbidden City.

Although they were fascinated with what the neighboring concubines had been wearing in their hair, the girls never spent a penny on their clothing or ornaments. Even after Robert told them they were allowed to do so on special occasions, they didn't think they deserved it.

Eventually when the tutoring ended, which meant bedtime, gloom settled inside the house like thick smoke. It made the long nights colder. Ayaou was no longer a willing bed warmer. She'd turned to ice.

Shao-mei's beautiful, bright eyes had grown dark circles under them. She looked tortured. She'd be happy one moment and sour the next. She blamed herself for everything—the dinner was too salty, or the tea wasn't hot enough. She looked nervous and unwilling to go to her room when bedtime came. Ayaou silently held her sister's hand for a long time before parting for the night. This scene caused Robert's stomach to twist into knots making for another difficult night getting to sleep.

Ayaou went to Shao-mei's room. The sisters whispered into the night. Robert read his Chinese books as he waited for Ayaou. Some mornings he awoke to find her side of the bed empty.

He feared going into Shao-mei's room to see if Ayaou were there. The truth was that Robert feared seeing his beauties, the loves of his heart, in the same bed. He knew his weakness. The warning signs were his dreams. They were filled with him having intercourse with Ayaou and Shao-mei at the same time. While he was inside one of the girls, the other massaged his back and played with his testicles. Then they switched positions before he ejaculated. All the while the sisters urged him not to shoot all his seeds so both would know pleasure and fulfillment.

Sometimes Robert stood at the head of the stairs and listened to them through the door. Shao-mei's tone told him she was holding back a tempest of jealousy and despair.

Shao-mei said one night, "You know what will happen if Robert doesn't come to me. One day he will be short of money. He'll find a reason to sell me. Is that what you want, sister?"

"I'm not going to fall into one of your silly traps," Ayaou replied. "Go to sleep or I'll leave."

As time slipped by, his sense of imbalance turned into depression. At night, his desire sometimes went wild. It was impossible to shut his mind off. The loss of sleep was wearing him down. He honestly didn't know how much longer he could go on like this. Something had to change.

Robert was beginning to hate himself. He was tempted to give up both Ayaou and Shao-mei and move into the consulate or possibly quit his job to become a missionary. As he sat on the idea, he realized he couldn't live without them. Where would they go if he set them free? It was painful for him to consider they might end up as prostitutes, or their father might sell them to the highest bidder again. Besides, Ayaou still belonged to Ward. Letting go of Ayaou meant she might be returned to him. The concept of freedom in China for a woman was almost nonexistent. Women were considered property by almost everyone.

He finished reading *The Dream of the Red Chamber.* Reading the one hundred and twenty chapters spread out over the three volumes had been tedious. Tee Lee Ping spent hours with Robert discussing the meanings between the lines.

"Are you saying that the novel is an extended metaphor?" Robert asked at one point.

"Of course," his teacher replied. "I will have you read the story of *Nu Wa Mending the Sky*. Then you will see how Lin Daiyu is an incarnation and how that creates an alliance between stone and wood."

The look of confusion on Robert's face must have been obvious.

"Yes, I see," Tee Lee Ping said. "You will have to read *Nu Wa Mending the Sky* to understand."

His explanations helped Robert see the Chinese way of thinking. The culture was built with much complexity and sophistication. An ordinary conversation concealed hidden meanings that could be the key to either break or mend a relationship. The tragedy in the story came from misunderstandings and false assumptions. To Chinese intellectuals talking in circles was the way to exhibit the richness of the mind. Any impatient listener was thought uncultured. To understand you also had to be a scholar of Chinese mythology and folklore. Then you could start making the connections. Robert saw that he had much to read and learn.

"Mr. Hart," Master Tee Lee Ping said one day after a challenging discussion. Robert kept getting the characters confused. After all, there were more than four hundred named characters in the book. "Be patient and you will reach your goal. Reading *The Dream of the Red Chamber* and understanding it is the one sure way to know China."

Reading Chinese literature should have satisfied him, for he was a lover of books, but Robert yearned to read in his language. He struggled with the Chinese characters. He thought in English and had to translate every character. At times, he yawned and found his thoughts straying. To get relief, he took breaks and read books in English. Eventually, he forced himself back to the task he was committed to, which was master Chinese and understand how the people thought.

Robert wanted to read about all the cultures of the world and know what was happening in every part of the British Empire. Whenever he got a copy of the *London Times* or another English language newspaper, he devoured them. He recalled fondly the bookshops and libraries of Belfast where he'd spent so much time. Books were the doors and windows to the world. One learned so much from reading.

It was expensive on his salary ordering books from home. When he could afford to purchase one or two without causing a financial burden to his girls, he sent a request and the money to his family.

He'd never stopped writing home, but he was careful what he allowed his family to know about his life. He never mentioned Ayaou or Shao-mei. Many times he crafted fictions in his letters that made his life look like something it wasn't. He also did not forget that someone else like Ward might be reading what he was writing. It was frustrating to realize that someone might be spying on him. It was even worse that he could do nothing about it. He could stop writing the letters. He could instruct his family and friends to stop, but that was unthinkable—those letters were his only contact with home.

As he was finishing *The Dream of the Red Chamber*, several novels arrived from Ireland. One was Charlotte Mary Yonge's *The Heir of Redclyffe*. Robert was a fan of her writing. He read the book in record time and identified with the character of Guy Morville, who had a dark side to his nature that he struggled to control as Robert struggled to control his.

Both *The Dream of the Red Chamber* and Mary Yonge's book made a deep emotional impact on him, since they focused on decadence and the tragedy born of it. Like Guy, Robert struggled to do what was right. Guy was not a villain, and Robert could see he wasn't either.

He hated Guy's cousin, Philip Edmonstone, when he drove Guy to his death by his sanctimonious righteousness. Robert saw similarities between Philip and the missionaries across the river. After all, they had condemned Hollister for having Me-ta-tae. Had those missionaries damaged Hollister as Phillip damaged Guy? It wasn't right to treat others as if you were morally superior to them. All humans had flaws. All faced temptations.

There was also the character of Xue Baochai in *The Dream of the Red Chamber,* who appeared to fill a similar role to that of Philip Edmonstone. Where Philip drove Guy to his death, the scheming of Baochai and other family members indirectly drove Taiyu to her death. Robert wondered if there was anyone capable of driving him to his death.

Shao-mei started to gain weight and wear loose clothing to hide it. Because of her depression, she must have been binge eating when Robert wasn't home. This explained why her stomach was always upset. Her flat chest also vanished, as her breasts developed.

In early December Robert took the girls to see the opera *The Dream of the Red Chamber,* which only covered a portion of the book. His teacher, Master Ping, accompanied them. They shared a box with a Chinese banker Robert had done business with at the Consulate. The banker pointed out the actress who was playing Urjia. He said Peach, the actress's real name, had recently become his fifth concubine. Robert saw by the shine in the banker's eyes that he was proud of her. Robert asked. "How do you manage your relationship with your concubines?"

The banker looked at Robert and laughed. "I've never discussed this topic before. The number of wives a man has in China is a sign of his status—of how successful he is. The concubines are his property. There's no relationship to it." He paused and studied Robert, who was the only foreigner in the audience. Everyone was speaking Chinese. Robert found it amazing that he understood what they were saying.

"I see that you're a man seeking answers." The banker's eyes darted toward Shao-mei and Ayaou, who were sitting with Tee Lee Ping in the other chairs in the shared box.

"I'd like to invite you for an evening meal at my home sometime this week," the banker said. "You'll see how I run my house." He smiled slyly.

They agreed on the Saturday coming up.

During the entire play, Shao-mei and Ayaou sat spellbound. They laughed when the characters flirted by singing poems to one another and wept when the female protagonist, Taiyu, died of heartbreak.

The costumes fascinated Robert. Master Ping said the design of the costumes came from the Ming Dynasty. The embroidery and headdresses were intricate in design. The way the actors painted their faces helped show what kind of character the person was. The characters with the redder face paint demonstrated courage and loyalty above all else while those with the blacker face paint were more impulsive. Blue face paint said the character was cruel but white indicated wickedness. On the other hand, if only the nose was white, it let the audience know this character would impart humor to the plot.

The screeching falsetto of the singers, the loud clacking of the clappers and the noisy banging of drums and cymbals were all shocking. At the same time, the over dramatic nature of the opera kept Robert sitting stiff and erect in his seat lest he miss something. There was never a dull moment.

One brief instant in the opera stood out in his mind. It was the scene where a man named Chah-Lian married three women. The first wife was jealous of the third wife. Although she was instrumental in luring the poor girl into the house to take credit for being a good wife and a dutiful daughter-in-law, the second wife tried her best to stay out of the trouble by flattering the first wife and playing blind and mute.

There were fights among the women, and the third wife was murdered. Chah-Lian, the master, was left out of the criticism. Everyone was to blame but him. The Chinese audience, including Master Ping, cursed the first wife and cheered when she was found guilty and punished.

Robert didn't believe anyone was to blame but the man. He was selfish and irresponsible, but this was too easily said from a foreign point of view. Robert had lived here long enough to *wet his shoes* as the Chinese saying went *when you walked on the beach*. He knew better.

The idea of being with more than one woman didn't sound as bad as it had a few months earlier. After all, he was in China—not Ireland or England with its stifling morality. There was an old saying, *When in Rome, do as the Romans do.* Well, Robert was in China.

On Saturday evening Robert hurried to the banker's house. He went alone, because he did not want his girls to hear the questions he was going to ask. Before dinner, the banker took him on a tour of his home. It was huge. There were courtyards, gardens and many rooms with separate little pavilions inside the walled estate.

"Every one of my wives has a room," the banker said. "Some of them are friends, and some of them hate one another. How they feel is not my concern. What is important is my relationship with each of them individually."

They went into Peach's room. The banker introduced her to Robert, who told her he had enjoyed her performance. The banker went to Peach's closet and showed off all the garments he'd bought for her.

"She loves clothes," he said. "It's my pleasure to make her happy. She is the most beautiful woman in the world to me. Chinese women are trained since youth to know their positions in the family. It is not their concern to learn how many more wives a man is going to get. Their duty is to encourage him and help him get decent ones, so the family can expand. This is good for everyone. The more sons a man has, the more power he has. Same thing applies from the Emperor to a coolie—it is the way of China."

They left Peach's room and walked through one of the gardens back into the main part of the house. "You see, if I make my concubines happy, they make me happy. When my friends and business associates see a house full of happy wives, they see me as a man they can trust, because I am capable of creating harmony. This is the key to success in every kind of business on earth.

"Nothing is wasted in this house. When I have daughters, I arrange good marriages with the sons of my business associates. That will enlarge the family clan. After all, in China whom can you trust except family? How can a man cheat me when his wife is my daughter?"

He stopped and faced Robert. Behind the banker a forty-foot stand of bamboo, growing in a rectangular planter, was swaying with the gentle evening breeze. "May I ask if those two Chinese women I saw with you are your concubines?"

"Yes, they are," Robert replied.

"You haven't gained harmony?"

Robert shook his head and didn't bother to hide his distress.

"Things will change when the younger concubine has a child. I wish for you that it will be a boy. I have five daughters and six sons."

Robert couldn't tell him that Shao-mei was still a virgin. He wondered why it was important for the younger concubine to conceive first. That was the opposite of what Robert was learning about Chinese culture.

"In life," the banker said, "it's best to seek a place where the weather is acceptable and the food is good. In other words, being hard on oneself is not true wisdom. Do you agree?"

In a month the banker rid himself of Peach, his beautiful, expensive actress. It shocked Robert when he learned the banker had thrown her out of his house. Not once while Robert was with him had there been a hint that he was unhappy with her. After all, he'd heaped praise on her.

Robert asked Master Ping about this during one of the Chinese lessons. "Hmm," his teacher replied, after Robert described the evening at the banker's house. "He told you she was the most beautiful woman in the world. That's enough by itself to show that the harmony he was talking about did not exist. Remember all the expensive clothes he showed off. This woman was costing him a lot of money. I'm sure his other concubines and wives were jealous. It is obvious that she managed to get him to marry her with lies and deceit. What she was really after was his wealth. If he had loved her, he would have told you something like she was the ugliest of his wives. He would have made sure she heard him too. That way he would make her happy.

"A concubine that loves her man loves to hear him say that. It means the love between them allows him to say whatever he wants. Praise can be a warning sign that not all is well. Modesty is a virtue in China. That is because Confucius taught us to be modest. If the banker loved his wife, he would have been modest in his statements. He wasn't.

"Also, he couldn't admit to anyone that she took advantage of him—that he had trusted her. He would lose face. A businessman cannot afford to lose face or others will not trust his judgment. They will take their money elsewhere."

"So I should tell Ayaou and Shao-mei they are ugly."

"Robert—" Master Ping said, shocked. "You don't understand what I'm saying. Listen more carefully. You do not tell your concubines they are ugly. When you have guests over for dinner, you tell your guests that they are ugly. You make sure Ayaou and Shao-mei hear you say it. If you praise them in front of others, they will have reason to worry."

"I don't know if I can do that," Robert said.

"Then it is better you don't say anything about them. They will forgive you, Robert, if you do not insult them. After all, they know you are a foreigner."

Chapter 17

That night Robert couldn't sleep until he made the decision to act more like a Chinese man. If he were going to live with two Chinese women that he loved, he'd make an effort to behave properly. He rolled over and shook Ayaou's shoulder. "Ayaou," he said in a whisper. He left the bed to fumble in the dark and light the lantern.

"What's the matter?" Ayaou asked drowsily.

"I've been a fool," he said. "I want you to go out today and buy me some Chinese clothing. When I get home from the consulate, I'm going to wear those clothes and become a Chinese man. I'll still be English at the consulate. However, from this day forward I am going to live two lives. You can expect changes that'll be easier for both you and Shao-mei to live with."

Ayaou squinted at Robert with one raised eyebrow. "That's why you woke me in the middle of the night?" There was doubt in her voice.

"Also have a warm bath ready. I want to be clean for tonight."

When Robert arrived home that evening, the Chinese clothing hung on an inside hook near the front door. The girls bought two outfits, a blue robe made of cotton lined with satin, and the other made of silver colored silk with a gray trim running along the edges. Both fit perfectly.

"This is marvelous, Ayaou. You have a natural sense of measurement."

"It wasn't me," she said. "It was Shao-mei. She is the one who studied you and guessed what size would fit. If you must show gratitude for how well these robes fit, tell Shao-mei."

He remembered that she'd been observing him closely for days. Her searching eyes and bold stare had made him feel uneasy at times. It was as if she'd been undressing him with her eyes. Robert turned to Shao-mei. "You are wonderful," he said.

Shao-mei remained quiet and smiled with her lips zipped. She was sitting on the edge of the couch with her back ramrod straight. Robert knew she was pleased by the way her eyes glowed.

"Time for my bath," he said. The large wooden tub was in the kitchen half-full of steaming water that Shao-mei and Ayaou had heated. Robert did something he'd never done before—he stripped in front of them and left his clothing in a pile on the floor. The girls were startled. Shao-mei flushed— her cheeks turning the color of a peony. Robert wanted to laugh but managed to keep a sober look on his face.

He started to walk naked toward the kitchen. He stopped in the doorway and faced the girls. They were standing together in the middle of the room staring at him as if he had turned green and sprouted horns. "Move!" he said. "What are you waiting for? Get the soap and a washcloth."

Robert pointed at his English clothing on the floor. "Ayaou, take my clothes and wash them immediately. Then hang them on the balcony to dry. Shao-mei, get over here and scrub my back with soap."

Ayaou and Shao-mei looked at each other. They were probably thinking he'd gone crazy. Shao-mei pretended to be indifferent and walked carefully past Robert as if he were a breakable object. She went into the kitchen where she picked up the soap and held it out to Ayaou, who hadn't moved.

"I told you to wash me. Not Ayaou."

Shao-mei stood frozen with an open mouth and a stunned look. Robert smiled and stepped into the tub of water and sunk into it. The displaced water climbed toward the edge of the tub and covered most of his chest. He gasped. It was hot, blazing hot. He had asked for warm, not boiling. He would have to show them what warm meant. His body turned the color of a lobster. He started to sweat. After he adjusted to the scorching water, he said, "Didn't I tell you to scrub my back?"

Still flushed, Shao-mei willed herself to walk forward. Once she was close enough, Robert pulled her closer. He took her hand that was holding the soap and placed it on his neck.

After she applied the soap, she began to scrub—her stiff, timid fingers barely touching his skin.

"Have you heard of a fable called *Mr. Yip, the Dragon Man*?" Robert asked.

"Yes, I have." Shao-mei's voice was small like a mosquito.

"Tell me about it."

"Now?"

"Yes, now. I want you to keep me entertained while you scrub me."

The soap slipped from her fingers. She bent to retrieve it. Her awkwardness thrilled Robert. He felt sinful and stimulated at the same time. Disregarding his will, Robert's member began to grow. As he now saw it, his duty was to bring happiness to both of his concubines so harmony moved into this house and stayed. The banker had made sense. If it were important for Shao-mei to get pregnant first, he'd work hard to see that it happened.

"I am waiting," Robert said. He closed his eyes, so she'd have a free moment to adjust whatever she needed to adjust. "And there is more to wash than just my back. I want you to start on the front now."

She started scrubbing his shoulders and then his chest. She had to lean over as she worked lower. He couldn't see her face. "Shao-mei," he said.

She looked up. Her face was less than an inch from his. He leaned forward and placed his lips on hers. The moment their lips touched, she dropped the soap again. She tried to jerk away. Robert put a wet hand behind her neck and held her in place. At first, her lips were stiff. Then they relaxed. She almost lost her balance and fell into the tub. He helped steady her.

"Is something wrong, Shao-mei?" Robert asked.

"I stopped breathing," she said, "and everything became fuzzy."

Robert tried not to laugh. There was a noise at the door. Shao-mei turned. Ayaou's shadow was visible on the floor. Robert saw Shao-mei's lips forming soundless words. "Get out of here. I'll manage." Ayaou's shadow vanished.

Shao-mei put both hands in the water searching for the soap. His heart beat faster. When her fingers touched him, he held his breath. He was so aroused that his member was sticking out of the water pointed toward the ceiling like a chimney. He considered taking her hand and guide her to it. He managed to resist the urge. He had already planned the night and intended to stick with it. It was a strange feeling to pretend that nothing unusual was happening.

Shao-mei carefully continued to soap and rinse him. When she reached his member, Robert wanted to know what was on her mind. She looked solemn as if wiping the dust around a candlestick on an altar. She couldn't hide her curiosity.

"Story." He reminded her.

She jerked. "Oh, yes. Well, Mr. Yip loved dragons." She cleared her throat. "Although he never saw any dragons, he prayed for the Emperor of Heaven to send one to visit his house. And one day a dragon was sent. Mr. Yip was on his way home, and he saw a giant tail as thick as the chimney come out of his window." She stopped. Her face flushed. Her hands went still.

"Was Mr. Yip happy? Was that what he wanted?"

"No." Shao-mei blinked as if to wake herself. "He was terrified."

"Is that why the story was used to describe people who didn't know what they were talking about?"

"That, Master," Shao-mei took hold of the towel, "is right."

"Were you Mrs. Yip?" He stood so she could dry him. Now his member was visible in all its aroused glory. She stared at it. He saw her gulp for air then her eyes darted away like a rabbit running for cover.

Embarrassed but happy, she said, "Then you are the dragon."

They laughed.

"You do have a tail, Master. It is as thick as the chimney wrapping around the house and me and my sister."

Robert heard Ayaou's laughter from the other room.

A knocking at the door signaled the arrival of Master Ping. Ayaou let him into the sitting room. Shao-mei and Robert remained in the kitchen. She helped Robert dry off and dress in his new silk Chinese robe.

As Robert entered the room, the teacher's shrewd eyes took in the change of clothing. What he saw caused his busy eyebrows to dance. The lesson was conducted as usual, and Master Ping was pleased. He was obviously struck by the desire to ask Robert questions but didn't.

Robert showed him to the door at the end of the session. "Master Ping, thank you for *The Dream of the Red Chambe*r. As you can see, I've applied your teaching and am a changed man."

Master Ping moved his lips as if to make a remark. Then he changed his mind when he saw both Ayaou and Shao-mei come out to say goodbye. They bowed endlessly to him. He left looking puzzled. Twice as he went down the street, he glanced back. Robert smiled and waved.

They returned to the sitting room where Robert became the teacher. Shao-mei appeared brighter and more animated than she had been for months.

Later that night, after Ayaou slipped under the blanket, Robert said. "Ayaou, I'm going to spend the night with Shao-mei. Tomorrow I'll be with you." He quickly kissed her and left the bed. He felt her staring at him.

"What?" he said. He felt as if he were defending himself against a possible accusation. He avoided her eyes.

"You forgot your robe," she said.

"I won't need it tonight." He was bent in one direction and wasn't about to stop. He didn't trust his British upbringing. It might return and spoil everything.

"But you will be cold, and there is no heat in the house."

Without speaking, he took the robe from its hook and slipped it over his shoulders. He walked from the room in his bare feet and crossed to Shao-mei's door where he stopped with one hand on the handle.

The devil is devious, he thought. He can trick people into giving up their souls. Then Robert grew angry. He cursed Ireland and the church. Spending the night with Shao-mei was something he wanted. Didn't he have free will? He had decided, but he couldn't bring himself to open that door. His heart was pounding as if it were going to burst. He was having trouble breathing.

He attempted tricking himself to relax and accept the gift that waited on the other side. To overcome his resistance, Robert fantasized what it was going to be like. While the cold claimed his feet and started spreading up his legs, he closed his eyes and imagined what was going to take place after he stepped through that door.

Her lantern gave off a feeble light. She had the blanket drawn to her chin. She stared at him with big, wide-open eyes. She reminded him of a disturbed sparrow during its quiet time.

Shivering and with goose bumps racing across his back and down his legs, Robert slipped under the blankets onto the narrow bed. He pulls her warm, naked body into his arms.

She received him silently. He felt her stiffen when his cold skin touched her.

Robert flashed back to his first time with Ayaou in Ward's cellar. This was going to be different. There'd be no furtiveness or fear at work here.

"It's your job to warm me," he said. He struggled to contain his lusty excitement. He knew the longer he spent before culmination, the better it would be.

She made no response. She reached across him to turn off the lantern.

"No." He stopped her. Pulling her hand under the covers, he said, "I want to see you. I want you to touch me."

"But—I might be afraid," she replied in a seductive voice that aroused him more.

His fantasy was working. Robert's member was growing.

"Of what?" he asked.

"You. What you have on your body. The hair. Ayaou said it is like a grassland."

"What else did Ayaou tell you?"

"She said it wouldn't hurt."

"Do you believe her?"

She nodded.

"You're a brave girl," he said.

"You're laughing at me. You already think I'm not as good as Ayaou."

"Forget Ayaou. There are only two in this room."

"Does that mean you really want to be with me?"

He pulled her closer. Their bodies touched.

Robert was aroused. Soon he'd have the strength to go through that door and claim his prize.

She wiggled her naked, smooth body as close as she could. The sensation of touching her sent sweet chills to his core.

Robert reached with one hand under the robe and took hold of his member. It throbbed. His fingers curled around it. He stroked it. His breathing quickened. The blood rushed out of his head. He leaned against the door. His legs trembled as the strength drained out of them. His mind dissolved into a puddle of warm honey.

She mumbled strange noises. After a while, she told him she was speaking English and was saying, 'I love you.' He told her in Chinese that he loved her, and he meant it for the truth was that he loved both his concubines.

He begged her to change back to Chinese. "Let me make you happy tonight, Shao-mei."

Her face glowed. She said, "I miss my sister. Could Ayaou join us?"

"No!" He pulled the blankets over them. "I'm not ready for that, and I don't know if I ever will be."

Her hands moved down the length of his body—exploring, while he explored her.

Then Robert lost control. Gasping for air, he slid down to sit on the floor. He'd excited himself to the point that he'd had an orgasm. His member, which he was still holding, had turned flaccid. He held up his hand and examined it. His fingers were sticky. This cannot be happening, he thought. He groaned and rested his head against the wall.

He concentrated on naked images of Shao-mei to get the mood back. It was no good. He yanked at his member to excite it. That didn't work. His Irish side was marching Christian armies into his brain to do battle with his Chinese desires.

With a sinking heart, he looked down the dark well that was the stairway and decided to get dressed and take a walk. He had failed. His upbringing was too powerful. He couldn't overcome his British breeding. He couldn't love his two women in all the ways that word implied. He wiped his slimy hand on the robe. He might as well be going down that stairway straight to hell.

As Robert took the first step down the stairs, a grunting, retching noise came from Shao-mei's room. He turned and rushed into her room. She was on her knees hanging over her chamber pot throwing up. At first, Robert thought it was because she was disgusted with him. She knew about his fantasy and orgasm in the hall.

Seeing him, she jumped to her feet. She was naked. Slime was hanging from her mouth. It wasn't the vomit that caught his eyes. It was the changing shape of her body. He hadn't seen her naked since the day Patridge sold her to him.

How could he have been so stupid? As a boy, he'd been around his mother when she'd been pregnant. The Chinese banker had seen right away, but Robert hadn't understood. The headaches, the moodiness, and the nausea all made sense.

"Who did this to you?" Robert said, feeling a rush of jealousy and anger. Had she gone out and slept with another man because of him? If he had done his duty as she would have expected from a Chinese master, this wouldn't have happened.

Sweat beaded her forehead. Her eyes glazed over. She burst into tears and swayed on her feet. Robert made sure the door was closed and took her into his arms. Her skin was clammy and cold. He led her to the bed and made her get under the covers. He sat beside her.

"Have you told Ayaou?" he asked.

She pulled the blanket up to her eyes and shook her head saying no. Her tears started to flood. She sobbed and trembled. Without taking off his robe, Robert crawled under the covers and held her. She shivered violently inside his arms. "I'm sorry, child," he said, believing he was somehow responsible for what had happened.

It took several minutes for her to calm down. Robert took her face between his hands and turned it toward him. "Who is he?"

She stared at him without saying a word. Fear filled her eyes.

"I'm not going to hurt you. If I had been the master you expected, this wouldn't have happened. Tell me who he is. Did you meet him in the market?"

She shook her head but still did not speak. She attempted to turn from him. He wouldn't let her. Robert held her face firmly between his hands. She had to look at him. "I am your master," he said. "You have to tell me."

"He said he'd hurt us." Her voice was small, almost a squeak. She looked fragile as if she were one of those thin bone China dishes.

"If you love him, I will arrange for him to live with us. You will be his wife," Robert said. "He'll have no reasons to make threats and fear me."

Her expression twisted into something else, something horrible. "I hate him!" She spit out.

Then Robert understood. "You were raped?" Rage smashed into him like a tsunami. "Tell me who did it? If you don't, I will beat it out of you and kill him. If I have to, I'll get Ayaou to pry the name from your lips." The sound of his voice was frightening.

She tried to move away from him, but the bed was too small. She didn't answer. Her expression said everything.

"It was Patridge!" Robert cursed. "That bastard didn't keep his word!" Then he was elated because it meant the devil's contract had been broken. Laughter welled up inside his throat mingled with anger. He was free. He broke out laughing. It was a wicked sound. It looked like he wouldn't be corrupting Chinese with opium anymore.

She was calm now. The wild look in her eyes had faded. She shook her head and Robert knew. "It wasn't Patridge," he said. "It was Payne Hollister." The fear rushed back into her face telling him the truth. His laughter died a reluctant death but the anger remained.

"What did he tell you?"

"He said it was his revenge." She squeaked. "And if I told anyone, even Patridge, he would come back and hurt me and kill Ayaou and you."

An ax blade twisted inside Robert's stomach. It was because of Me-ta-tae. He had caused this with his uncontrolled lust. It was his fault. He was the monster. "I'm a bloody fool, a damned bloody fool." He said it with such acid that Shao-mei started to cry.

Robert couldn't bear to look at her. His temples throbbed. His head hurt. He had to relax and think, but there was nothing he could do but feel helpless. Hollister had sailed to England in his sloop. He was thousands of miles away on his yearlong journey. Robert hoped the ocean swallowed him before he made it home. After all, his sloop was small.

"Listen to me," Robert said, as he had an idea. He forced himself to look into her eyes. This had to work. "You will tell Ayaou the baby is ours. No one has to know that it belongs to Hollister. We will raise it together. You will always belong to me. I will never sell you.

"Tonight I am going to sleep with you, but we cannot have intercourse since you are pregnant. If we did, it might cause a miscarriage. If you had a miscarriage, there would be danger that you might die. I've heard of so many women dying in childbirth that it frightens me. The younger the mother, the more risk and danger there is. I don't want to lose you, Shao-mei."

"You don't want to lose me?" she said. She stopped sobbing and hiccupped. She looked innocent and harmless with wide-open eyes.

This caused his heart to feel as if it were swelling in his chest. His member stiffened with desire. He didn't want this intrusion now. Why couldn't this incessant ache leave him alone? He found some relief at the consulate when he was working, but even that wasn't assured. "Yes, I don't want to lose you." His voice was shaking. He looked at his hands. They were trembling.

"But why? If I died, you would still have Ayaou. Isn't that what you have wanted all along?"

"I have been confused. In my country, living with two women would make me a bad man. Everyone would condemn me as a degenerate. That would injure my father deeply, because he believes strongly that such behavior is wrong. I love my father. I don't want to hurt him."

"Then if I died that would solve your problems. So why not use me? I will die for you if it will make your life easier. Take me." And her hands reached for Robert like a greedy, hungry child wanting candy.

"No, Shao-mei." He pushed her away. She looked hurt. "If you died, my heart would break. Recently, I have come to desire you and love you as much as I love Ayaou. I never realized that a man could love two women equally."

She slipped her arms around him and pulled herself against him until her naked body was against his. "Then why not make love to me? You must desire me. I know my body burns for you."

"I want to," he said.

"How do I know that you are not lying to make me feel better?"

"I am sure that Ayaou explained to you what this means," he replied, and guided one of her hands to his member. She gasped when she felt it.

"It is so big," she said in wonder and pulled the covers back to stare. "It has become a giant." She grasped it and squeezed. "It is cute. It looks like a little man who needs my help, because he has no arms." She leaned down and kissed it.

Robert groaned. "Stop, Shao-mei. I am going to explode. I could lose control."

"I don't care," she said. "Maybe the danger is if you fill me with your seeds. Maybe you would make me pregnant again. The babies would fight inside me. When you are ready to shoot and give me your seeds, you could pull out. That way there would be no danger."

"No, Shao-mei. I don't want to risk it."

"Are you sure there would be danger to the child and to me? How do you know this? I want you to touch me and to make me your woman. Hollister laughed at me and said I wasn't enough of a woman for him. He said that I had the body of a child. That it disgusted him. He said my breasts were like smashed mushrooms. Because of what he told me, I believed the reason you haven't taken me was because I was ugly."

"That's not true. You are beautiful. Your breasts are works of art. I have trouble not staring at them. And your legs are perfect. They are smooth and long, and whenever you are not looking, I admire them. The reason I fear for your safety and the baby's safety is because my mother had twelve children. The family doctor lectured my father on the dangers of having intercourse with her while she was pregnant. Tomorrow you still have to tell your sister that we were intimate anyway."

"But why? Why should we not tell her the truth? I don't understand."

"Because, it is important she thinks the baby is from me. If we don't make love tonight, I cannot be the father."

"Oh." She grew quiet and thoughtful.

"Listen carefully. I'm going to tell you what to say so she believes that it happened—that we made love. Then I will start coming to your room regularly. We will sleep together but cannot be intimate. Do you understand?"

Her eyes were bigger than Robert had ever seen them. They were stained red too. She nodded. The tears had dried on her cheeks. "After the baby is born," she said, "you will still come to my bed. Then you will take me and show me the pleasures Ayaou told me about?"

"Yes, of course," he replied, and hoped that he'd be able to overcome his culture's morality by then. If he could not have these two women and have peace of mind at the same time, Robert didn't know what he was going to do.

Hollister must have taken her in late September and now it was December. She was more than three months pregnant. Robert hated the man for what he had done. "Wait for four weeks. Then we will tell Ayaou you are pregnant. Now I want you to repeat what you are going to say to Ayaou, so she will believe that we were intimate. I do not want mistakes."

Shao-mei smiled and cuddled against him. He kissed the top of her head.

"*Wu Hei Nee,*" she said in the same tone of adoration she had used before. That was when Robert knew he was cured. The moral anguish had vanished. He would have no problem performing when the time came after the child was born. The guilt that had influenced him for so long did not control him any longer. It was gone. He was ready to love the sisters equally.

Robert listened to the sound of her voice as she repeated his instructions. He continued to hold her even after she had fallen asleep. He imagined what her lips would feel like when he kissed her and what her body would feel like when his hands were free to explore without the restraints he had brought with him from Ireland.

The innocent child inside her didn't deserve to grow up treated like an outcast. Robert resolved to do whatever it took to make sure that never happened. He worried that he wouldn't be the father this child deserved. Somehow his knowledge that the child wasn't his might spoil everything. He might resent it, because its father was Hollister.

No, that would never happen. He was strong enough to make sure it wouldn't. An innocent child was not going to suffer because of his weaknesses. Robert would turn to God for strength and work hard to make sure there was always enough to make life comfortable for his family. Instead of working ten and twelve hour days, he'd work sixteen to twenty hours. If possible, he would give up sleep. His love for these two Chinese boat girls was so strong that he was willing to do almost anything to make their lives better and safer.

There was one person Robert felt safe enough to trust this secret with. He pulled Guan-jiah aside the next day and told him what had happened. His servant surprised him with his reply. "You are learning, Master. If the child grows up thinking it is a bastard that would ruin your life. There would be no pleasure."

"But—" Robert started to say.

Guan-jiah held up a hand to stop him. "In China we know how to eat and enjoy life. To do anything else is uncivilized. Most Westerners know nothing about enjoying life. Most never do what you are doing—to accept this child as yours and to hide the truth. To do anything else would be a horrible *loss of face* and a disaster.

"If it were common knowledge that this child was a bastard, there would be no enjoying life in your household. Your concubines would lament and walk about with sorrowful faces, because the outside world knew the truth. Gloom, sorrow and anger would smother all three of you. Shao-mei might even hang herself. The child would grow up hating everyone and become a criminal.

"I admire what you have decided to do, and your secret is safe with me. The pleasures of life are merely matters of the senses—food, drink, your house, the garden, your family and your friendships count. That is what life is about. You are demonstrating wisdom."

Guan-jiah pulled on one of his Buddha like earlobes. His face took on a thoughtful expression. "When the child is born, I will always be willing to help. If you have decided to adopt this child, I will do the same. I can be its adopted uncle." He smiled.

Robert opened and closed his mouth. He couldn't think of a response. Guan-jiah was happy that Shao-mei was going to have this child. What Robert saw as a tragedy, Guan-jiah saw as an opportunity. Robert remembered that his servant was a eunuch. He could never have children of his own. How could he blame Guan-jiah for wanting to be this child's uncle?

To remind himself how fragile life was he touched the pocket where he kept the anonymous letter—the one that accused him of being a thief and using his two girls as prostitutes. Maybe it was a good idea to have Guan-jiah as the adopted uncle.

Chapter 18

Shao-mei was still sleeping when Robert opened his eyes to a dark room. He heard Ayaou downstairs making breakfast with more than the usual noise. There was no clock. Since the heavy window covers kept out the light, he had no idea what time it was.

It took a moment to overrule the desire to stay under the friendly blankets with his second concubine. Her smooth skin was warm like toast from the oven. When he felt his member sprouting, he groaned, slid into the bone-chilling cold, put on the robe and walked across the hall to the bedroom he shared with Ayaou.

While slipping on his trousers, Robert felt Ayaou's frigid hand on his bare shoulder. He jumped at the shock of her icy touch. Twisting around, he found her examining him with shrewd eyes like a naturalist examines a specimen. Robert wanted to learn how last night had affected Ayaou's emotions. He remembered all the misery and jealousy between the wives and concubines in *The Dream of the Red Chamber*. He was afraid the same thing was going to happen inside his house.

It didn't matter that Ayaou had urged him to cross that hall and spend the night with her younger sister. It didn't matter that nothing physical happened with Shao-mei. The important thing was how Ayaou felt. If misery and jealousy were stirring inside her, the harmony he desired could vanish like fog under a hot sun.

Her hair looked different—more stylish and sensual. She'd spent time clipping it up and leaving a few strands before the ears, which accented her high cheekbones and leaf shaped eyes. It stirred his desire.

"Shao-mei had fun last night," she said.

It was obvious Ayaou was struggling to keep her voice calm. There was something in the tone that caused Robert to shiver. It was wild and unpredictable. It frightened him. He didn't want them competing for his affections. He didn't want them to hurt each other. It wasn't fair. He'd conquered his moral guilt only to discover that jealousy might take its place to ruin his life.

Robert wanted to laugh but his ability to see the humor had evaporated. The irony was absurd. He was a man who had achieved most men's fantasies. He had never dreamed of living like this. He had two women he loved that loved him back, and he was worried.

"What are you thinking?" he asked, afraid of her answer.

She turned away so he couldn't see her eyes. "It's cold this morning," she replied.

Robert took her chin and turned her face to his. The look in her eyes revealed her emotions—she didn't like sharing him with her sister. Jealousy was stirring. She didn't know what it was going to do to her, and he wondered if there was anything he could do to stop it. Maybe if he showed more interest in her that would help.

"Did you sleep well?" he asked, and shivering from the cold that was soaking into his bones, he reached for a shirt and pulled it on.

"I didn't sleep," she said.

"Why?"

"I don't know."

"Is that why you were cooking so early?"

"I suppose so."

"Look at you," he said in a lighthearted tone, attempting to kill the threatening mood. "Your apron is loose."

"Tighten it for me." A smile tugged at the corners of her mouth. She turned around and lifted the apron.

"Christ! You haven't anything on underneath!"

"I was in a hurry to cook. I have to go so the potatoes don't burn."

Robert followed as she went downstairs to her wok knowing he'd do nothing but allow her to lead. She wanted to discover if he'd lost interest in her. Once in the kitchen, he took the wok away from her and put it on the sideboard. He held her in his arms and opened the apron. He kissed her slender neck and the tops of her naked breasts and nipples.

Backing up, he sat on a bench and pulled her onto his lap. Her legs wrapped around his waist. She threw her head back. They made love.

Their passion quickly peaked with simultaneous orgasms. Robert wanted more, but she erased the moment by slipping from him and returning to the stove to take hold of the wok's handle. Robert was stupefied.

"You'd better leave for work, or you'll be late." She smiled, stood on her toes and leaned over the counter to reach for a jar of spice on a high shelf. As she stretched further, the apron rode up above her waist. Her naked buttocks protruded at a jaunty angle. The invitation was irresistible. With the frustrating night Robert had just spent with Shao-mei's knees and elbows poking him, he stood, took two steps forward and reached around Ayaou to cup her naked breasts in the palms of his hands.

"I haven't had enough," he said.

"Go to work." Laughing, she hopped away. "You have leaked enough of your essence today. Anymore and it will shorten your longevity. You are my happiness and I want you to live a long life. I can tell by the size and swelling of your sun-instrument, that you are about to shoot again."

She had no idea. "What if I don't want to go?" he said. "What if I go to the bedroom and relax? That way you can join me in a few minutes. I want you for breakfast, lunch and dinner. I want to forget about work."

She struggled to hide her smile and shoved a rice cake into his hand. "Here's breakfast. Get out of here and go to work. One of us will bring you more food later."

Alarmed, he said, "Don't ask for me. Ask for Guan-jiah. Give him the food." He didn't want Dr. Winchester or his wife to know about Ayaou or Shao-mei.

She shoved his coat into his hands and pushed him out the door. As he walked from the house, Robert hoped he'd derailed the mood that was sprouting inside her like a noisy, rebellious child. At the same time, he worried that Shao-mei would forget what he'd instructed her to say and mess it up, so Ayaou wouldn't believe her.

What a predicament! On the other hand, he had his passionate Ayaou back.

He considered praying to God and ask Him to make sure Ayaou was satisfied that Robert had not lost interest in her.

He wanted the sisters to continue to get along. On second thought, a prayer would not be a good idea. God might not approve and make things worse. Instead, Robert could ask a Chinese god for help. He chuckled at his private joke. That was the way the Chinese thought. The idea was to join as many religions as possible. If one god didn't work, maybe another would. He'd learned that from both Ayaou and Guan-jiah.

Before going to the consulate, he took a walk along the waterfront and studied the ships at anchor. One of Patridge's opium clippers from India sat in the anchorage. Robert had been expecting it for days. Patridge had supplied him with a list of potential arrival dates. Robert hired a sampan and went aboard the clipper.

"Captain," he said, once they were alone in his cabin, "do you have the altered manifest."

The ship's captain went to a desk in a corner and found the papers. He handed them to Robert, who gave him the paper that proved his cargo had been cleared by the consulate in Ningpo. The tax paid was less than what it should have been. The Chinese had been cheated again.

"It says that we are delivering bales of wool and cotton up river," the captain said.

"Anyone who is knowledgeable with China would see through that right away," Robert said. "Next time make sure the manifest shows products the Chinese might want—not cotton and wool. The Chinese wouldn't buy any. For one thing, it costs too much. Besides, the Chinese have a source. They also have silk."

"That's too bad," the captain replied. "In India we have been making a large profit since we forced them to stop making cloth and buy what the mills produce in England. It has become a profitable monopoly. Imagine how much we could make in China if we could do the same. However, we've already fought two wars with China just to get them to accept the opium trade. More wars might destroy the country and the markets for our goods. By the way, where do I find the boat people to unload my cargo?"

Robert turned to the chart table and leaned over the map. "Here," he said, and tapped the spot. "About one hundred miles up the Yangtze." Robert didn't approve of what he was doing for Patridge. He'd made a deal, and he was determined to keep his word. He kept reminding himself that his two girls were worth it, but at times he had doubts.

"I heard one of our ships had trouble with the Taipings near Canton," the captain said. "Has Captain Patridge found out who is selling information to the Taipings about our opium shipments? Do I have to worry?"

"It would be wise to play it safe," Robert replied, "and keep your crew on alert until you sail back into the sea. So far, none of the arrangements I have made with any of the shipments of opium have run into trouble. The reason for that is Patridge makes sure no one else sees those instructions but me before I turn them over to his captains. Patridge is a cautious man, and for the last few months since I have been working with him, we have had few problems along the Yangtze. Now, if you don't mind, I'll take my leave."

On his way to the consulate from the anchorage, Robert ran into William Martin, the American Presbyterian minister—the only minister living inside Ningpo. The rest lived across the river near the Presbyterian chapel.

"I haven't seen you at any sermons for weeks, Robert," the minister said, as he fell into step beside him.

"I was away from Ningpo." How long was this encounter going to last? Since returning to Ningpo, he'd gone out of his way to avoid any of the missionaries and their families.

"I heard you were spending time with Captain Patridge, but that was several weeks ago. I do not think I need caution you to be careful whom you allow into your life. Captain Patridge has a reputation and has been linked with others who are even more unsavory." Robert wasn't comfortable with the way William Martin was looking at him.

A rush of memories inundated Robert—his drinking and womanizing in Belfast, Me-ta-tae, Willow, the fight against the Taipings to recover the opium, the danger from Ward, buying Shao-mei, and the night he spent in a cellar with Ayaou. He had a strong urge to confess everything to this man of God but rejected the idea as fast as it appeared. If he confided in this American Presbyterian minister, he'd be admitting his sins and have to do something about them. He was unwilling to give up Ayaou. Besides, Martin was a Presbyterian and Robert was a Wesleyan.

Martin's voice pulled him out of his musings. Robert focused on the minister's words.

"You know I'm the only minister who lives in Ningpo. I have developed close friendships with many Chinese. You were seen attending Chinese operas with two, young Chinese women. Are these young ladies Christians, and when do we meet them? They must be recent acquaintances. We miss you, Robert. Come to church this Sunday and bring them with you. If they are not Christians, help us convert them, so they will have a more rewarding life. As a Christian, it is your duty."

Had Hollister converted Me-ta-tae before he'd sold her into a life of prostitution? It would be ironic if he had.

Robert had considered introducing Christianity to his two concubines but that would threaten the life he was living with them. He knew that it was out of selfishness that he didn't want Christianity near his girls.

Thanks to his father, Robert believed strongly in Christ. However, this tug of war between the Christian denominations was making a mess of the world. All you had to do was look at the suffering caused by the thirteenth century inquisition and all the Crusades to the Holy Land to fight Islam. Many had suffered and died.

What right did anyone have to tell Robert how to live? Only God had that right, and God did not meddle—only those who considered themselves devoutly religious did that. He questioned some of the methods used to convert unbelievers. Anger and resentment started to grow as if it were a vengeful beast. He knew that he had to suffocate it less it take control of his mouth. A true Christian never allowed himself to react out of anger or to judge others lest he be judged.

"How's your wife?" Robert asked, and forced his voice to remain calm. He refused to allow his turmoil and anger to vent itself.

"She hasn't been feeling well. She may be returning to America soon. I worry about her. But there's nothing more I can do but trust in God." William Martin sighed.

"Certainly." They strode the streets side-by-side in silence for a few blocks before Robert spoke again. "I appreciated your lending me *The Middle Kingdom* and the other books. I find the Chinese mind fascinating. By the way, will you miss your wife?"

"My wife and I are faithful Christians as you well know, and after ten years of marriage, I still look forward to spending time with her. God gave us a gift in the covenant of marriage."

"Did He?" Robert said. Marriage! That idea hadn't occurred to him. But if he married Ayaou, she would have to convert to Christianity. There would be witnesses. No, he couldn't allow that. Besides, what about Shao-mei?

Robert stopped walking and faced Martin. He hadn't wanted to explain himself to this man but felt the urge to do so now. "Since you value the love of your wife so highly, you'll understand what I'm going to tell you. I have found a love more valuable than all the wealth one could dream of. It enriches my soul and brings me closer to God. I don't know how to describe the feeling. It's beyond—my comprehension."

William Martin studied Robert's face looking for hidden meanings. "You're a happy man. It's a true blessing."

Robert imagined from the way that the minister was stabbing his eyes at him, Martin was trying to see what Robert was thinking behind his mask.

"Remember that you have the souls of these two women in your hands, Robert. You are a Christian. It is your duty to deliver them to Christ, so he can save them. He died on the cross for our sins. Don't let that go to waste. May God go with you, but remember that sometimes the paradise you think you're living in is hell in disguise."

His words chilled Robert, but he managed to stay calm. "Thank you for the advice, Martin. I hope you haven't been spreading gossip about me. I remember how the other ministers talked behind Payne Hollister's back about Me-ta-tae. Now I must be on my way to the consulate."

William Martin's eyes flashed. "I was never part of that gossip," he snapped. "I don't approve of that. I thought you knew me better. Besides, Hollister is no longer with that woman. He has corrected his ways."

"Hasn't he gone back to England?" Robert asked.

Martin looked surprised. "He hasn't gone home to England. He's in Hong Kong."

The news that Hollister was still in China shocked him. Robert didn't know what to do. He thought of sailing to Hong Kong to have it out with the man, but that was a stupid idea. "What about your wife?" he asked. "Women gossip. It's in their nature, and husbands confide in their wives."

"Well, I—." Martin sputtered, looking indignant and guilty at the same time.

210

"I thought so." He turned his back on the minister and walked away. Before he entered the consulate, he looked back. "Martin," he said, "you are a good man. I have always liked you. I'm sorry if I upset you in any way."

Robert did not wait for a reply. He went to his desk but couldn't focus on the work. He no longer cared what the missionaries might say about him living in Godlessness with savages. He cared what God thought. He didn't want to believe that He would condemn him for loving two women that loved him back.

It wasn't like he was a man who was unfaithful to his wife and had a secret lover hidden in another town. He was not one of those men he'd heard about that had secret families such as sailors with wives and children in several ports. And Ayaou and Shao-mei were not savages. They belonged to a complex civilization and culture that had established philosophies and religions more peaceful in nature than Christianity.

Besides, Abraham, the biblical father of the Hebrew people, had more than one woman. So did the Israelite Kings David and Solomon. The Bible said nothing about polygamy being wrong. Robert had made sure of that by studying the Bible before allowing himself to walk across that hall to Shao-mei's bedroom.

He wondered how things had grown so confusing. At the beginning with Adam and Eve there had been one rule—don't eat the apple from the forbidden tree. Once that had been broken, it took several thousand years for God to give Moses the Ten Commandments. Then hundreds of years after Jesus Christ was crucified, the Roman Emperor Constantine made the Catholic Church the religion of his empire. Since then, Christianity's rules had turned into an endless, growing field of weeds. Robert found it confusing, and it certainly wasn't helping his situation with Ayaou and Shao-mei.

Chapter 19

Robert didn't know that every time Payne Hollister had raped Shao-mei, he smoked one of Patridge's Egyptian cigarettes and blew smoke in her face. Whenever she smelled tobacco, she wanted to vomit.

It was a blustery, rainy January day, and the sky was a solid mass of dark, threatening clouds. When Robert arrived home from the consulate, his concubines undressed him inside the front door to get his wet clothes off. Shao-mei sniffed, wrinkled her nose and held the garments at arm's length. "These stink like Captain Patridge's house?" she said. "I do not like that."

"I smoke the same cigarettes Patridge smokes," Robert said. "If that bothers you, take my suit upstairs and hang it in the hall by the open balcony door. That way it will air out and dry. " She left holding his clothes in front of her as if she were holding a skunk. Her face twisted into an expression of absolute disgust and revulsion.

Ayaou's eyes were alive with an energy Robert hadn't seen before. The house was full of garlic and ginger smells telling him that a special meal was waiting. He detected the subtle scent of lemon grass too.

While Ayaou dressed Robert in the Chinese robe, her hands explored his legs and caressed his genitals until his member started to grow. She smiled and ran her hands across his stomach and around to his backside where she pinched him.

He wiggled. "Stop that, Ayaou. You're tickling me."

She laughed, and said, "Our father told us not to expect much pleasure from any man. He never described a man like you."

212

Shao-mei must have been more convincing than Robert had instructed her to be. What kind of stories had she told Ayaou? A knock on the door signaled Tee Lee Ping's arrival. Shao-mei returned from upstairs and ushered him in. The teacher slipped out of his wet shoes and took the slippers Shao-mei offered.

"Master," Ayaou said to Ping, "we have cooked a humble meal and would be honored for you to share it with us before the lesson."

Tee Lee Ping stopped and looked at Robert. His shaggy eyebrows bounced up and down twice and came to rest in a straight line. "Nice quality robe," he said. Robert saw by the look in his teacher's eyes that he wanted to know what was going on but was too courteous to ask.

"Wearing this robe is part of my learning about how Chinese men think and act," Robert said.

"I didn't know becoming Chinese could be so easy," Tee Lee Ping replied.

"You are attempting to be ironic," Robert said. "That is not exactly what I meant."

"No, I'm serious. If I bought a suit of foreign clothes like those that you wear, maybe foreigners would treat me differently and with more respect. Isn't that why you have now adopted the way I dress, so you can be treated better by the Chinese?"

Robert flushed. He didn't want to tell his teacher the reason. The robe was part of his plan to change his behavior. It was because of his desire to have two Chinese women as his lovers instead of one. "Why are you interested in how a British man behaves?" he asked.

"Because Britain is a most powerful nation. I have studied the French, the Germans, the Russians, the Japanese and the Americans. None of these foreign nations controls such a vast empire as your Queen Victoria. A dream of mine is one day to travel to your country and live there for a time, so I can learn what makes the British more powerful than my nation and the others. That is why I learned English and teach the Americans and British how to speak Chinese."

Robert sobered. Master Ping was serious. He examined his teacher and saw that Ping was an inch or two shorter than his five foot eight inches. "You won't find my type of clothes in China. They have to be ordered from England. I'll give you one of mine. With a little alteration, which my girls can do, it should fit. That way you can experiment and see if you are treated differently."

"How could I accept such a gift?" Ping protested. "It's too much."

"The answer is simple. Compared to my first teacher, you are excellent at what you do. When Ayaou selected you to be my teacher, she made the right choice. I cannot allow you to decline my offer. If you do, it will be a *loss of face* for me."

"That is most gracious of you," Ping replied, and made a small bow to Robert.

The two men sat at the table while Ayaou and Shao-mei served. The meal was anything but humble. The variety amazed Robert. There was a chicken and the meat was cut. Sitting beside it was a large bowl of long noodles. There was a huge fish with its head and tail still attached. Another serving dish held sweet steamed cakes. There was a platter of dumplings with another plate holding peeled oranges and tangerines. It was more than the girls had cooked before. The usual meal was two dishes with rice.

"Ayaou," Robert said, "why so much food? We will be stuffed like elephants if we eat this."

Master Ping held up a hand. "Allow me to explain." His eyes became animated and glowed as if he had discovered a treasure. "Let us turn this meal into an excellent lesson in what it is like to be Chinese. Tonight is a special occasion for your concubines. The Chinese love to eat, and food plays an important role in our culture. All the food on this table has symbolic meanings and is usually served during one festival or another." He paused and looked around the table examining each dish as if he were judging a contest.

"These are all lucky foods," he continued. "Serving that entire chicken cut like it is symbolizes wholeness and prosperity. The longevity noodles symbolize a long life. Just don't cut them while you are eating. If you cut them, it will spoil everything and having a long life will not be assured."

Master Ping pointed at the fish. "That symbolizes both a good beginning and ending for the year. It is customary for the fish to be served on the night of the Lunar New Year. This must be a special day as your concubines are marking this day as a beginning of a new year for your household."

He stopped when he noticed Robert's face turning red again. His mouth opened in surprise as if some of his unasked questions about why Robert had decided to wear Chinese clothing had been answered. Then he cleared his throat, regained his composure and pointed at the plate of peeled tangerines and oranges. "The words for that sound the same as the words for luck and wealth and serving both has the same meaning. It is like asking that your future be filled with luck and wealth."

"What about the steamed cakes?" Robert asked, while he struggled to control his embarrassment. The meal the girls had cooked turned his teacher into a mind reader, but he wasn't judgmental. If Ping had been British, Robert would have been shamed.

"Oh, the steamed sweet cakes have many levels of meaning. The sweet rich flavor symbolizes a sweet life. You know, like much love and tenderness in the home."

Robert lost control and blushed again, but Tee Lee Ping chose to ignore this, which Robert appreciated. "The layers of the steamed cakes symbolize rising abundance. The round shape means a family reunion—in your case possibly the formation of a new family. Maybe one of your concubines will become pregnant soon."

Robert avoided glancing at Shao-mei lest he give away her condition.

They started to eat. Halfway through the meal, Master Ping said, "I would not be surprised if there is a final dish that hasn't been served yet."

"And what would that be?" Robert asked.

"Eight Precious Pudding," Master Ping said. "Eight is a lucky number, and the Chinese word for eight sounds like the word for fortune."

He was right. It was rice pudding filled with lotus seeds, Chinese red dates, cherries, candied fruits and red bean paste. By the time they finished eating, Robert was stuffed to the bursting point and had trouble breathing.

Afterwards, they moved to the study room. "Let us start something new to add to our lessons," Robert said. "Since you wish to learn more about my culture, I will tell you something equal to what you taught me about Chinese food."

Tee Lee Ping scooted forward on his chair in anticipation. "My ears are eager," he said.

"I'm going to tell you about the language of the flowers," Robert said. "After our lesson ends tonight, remind me to lend you a copy of a book by an English author named Charles Dickens." Robert explained that in Britain, unlike China, the moral values supported sexual repression. To get beyond this so you could speak what was in your heart without being judged immoral, the language of flowers had been born. If you wanted a member of the opposite gender to know how you felt, you sent a flower arrangement. They would answer you with another flower arrangement. No words would be spoken or written.

"I believe I have an example that will clarify what I mean. If you passionately love a woman and want her to know, you send an arrangement made from orange and red flowers. If she didn't love you, she would send back an arrangement of betony, marjoram, southernwood, and spiderwort."

"You've never given us flowers," Shao-mei said, sounding disappointed.

"Shao-mei," Ayaou said, shocked. "You should not talk to our master like that." When Robert glanced at her, he saw that her eyes also had disappointment in them.

A moment of uneasy silence settled around the table. Then Master Ping rescued Robert. "So," he said, "in Britain flowers are symbolic and full of meaning but food is only food?"

"Yes, you could say that," Robert replied. He focused on his teacher. "You will understand more after you read Charles Dickens. My country is a land of contradictions. On one hand there is this strict set of moral codes on how you are to live your life. We cannot call a leg a leg. Instead, if we are in mixed company with both men and women, we call a leg a limb like a branch on a tree. At the same time, prostitution exists along with child labor." Robert saw by the confused expression on Master Ping's face he was having trouble understanding.

"Imagine a man wearing the most expensive suit of clothes," Robert said in an attempt to clarify his meaning. "They are clean, pressed and made from the best cloth. However, beneath the clothing he has never bathed. His flesh is rotting."

The confusion left Ping's eyes. He said, "I see. So Britain adorns itself with fancy coverings to hide the rot at its core."

Robert nodded agreement. "Most Western cultures do that," he said.

"China is no different," Master Ping replied.

The lesson turned to the latest Chinese book Robert was reading. He pulled out some drills in Chinese that Tee Lee Ping corrected. His teacher circled those that were wrong and wrote the correct versions beneath, which Robert accepted with grace. Having his mistakes corrected was the best way for him to learn how to write Chinese properly.

Ayaou hovered about watching. Shao-mei sat in a corner knitting a sweater. "In the future you should add a variety of stories for Robert to read, Master Ping," Ayaou said. "Why don't you introduce Robert to stories such as *The Western Chamber?*"

Tee Lee Ping looked sober and thoughtful but didn't say anything.

"Are you willing to teach me *The Western Chamber?*" Robert asked, curious about the story. If Ayaou had mentioned it, there must be something that she wanted him to learn. Robert's request earned a bright smile from Ayaou.

"That will not be a problem," Tee Lee Ping replied. "I planned to introduce it soon anyway. I promise to bring a copy to our next lesson."

Tee Lee Ping stayed for two more hours. After he left, Ayaou and Shao-mei told Robert they couldn't wait any longer for their lesson. Robert had promised to teach them the meaning of a Chinese poem called *The Cheerless Tone*. The girls had already gone over the poem several times. They sat on either side of him. He was aware of their presence through the desirable heat of their bodies. It was distracting, but he managed to stay focused. They followed his finger as it moved from Chinese character to character. Robert took pleasure in the silky sound of their voices.

"Like molten gold appears the setting sun;
Evening clouds like blocks of jade pieced into one.
Where is the one close and dear to my heart,
From whom, without mental pain, I could not part?"

Robert closed the book when they finished reading.

"It's a love poem," Ayaou said. "I'm convinced of it."

"And why is that?" he asked.

"Every line," she replied. "In the first line he describes the sun like molten gold and gold is precious like love. In the

217

second line he mentioned jade. It is also precious. And the third and fourth lines are so obvious."

"Ayaou is correct," Shao-mei said. "What else could it be?"

"What is the poet saying in the third line?" Robert asked. "Look again."

Ayaou bent over the book and took a moment to find the right page. Shao-mei moved closer, and her head hovered next to Ayaou's as they studied the lines. "The poet is wondering where his lover is," Ayaou said in a hushed tone. "Something horrible happened."

"Oh, it is so sad," Shao-mei said. "The poet has lost his lover. My heart aches for him. If I were a man, I would learn to become a poet. My heart echoes with the verses. Women should write poems as men do."

"That poem," Robert said, "was written by a woman named Li Qingzhao more than seven hundred years ago."

That left their mouths hanging open. "Tell us more, Robert. Did she write more poems? If so, read them. Did she lose her lover? What happened to her?" He read the entire collection of Li Qingzhao's poems to them.

With the book back on the shelf, they moved to the kitchen. The girls brewed tea and carefully washed, sliced and peeled the skins from apples. While they sipped tea and ate, Robert listened to the girls tell him about their day. Ayaou was happy with the price she'd paid for the fish. If Robert had been alone, his living costs would have been higher. With the girls doing all the shopping and negotiating, he was putting money aside and had enough to order books from England. He enjoyed keeping up with what was going on in the British Empire and the world.

Since Robert had started eating what his girls cooked, the digestion problems he'd suffered with since arriving in China had vanished. It wasn't that he had been sick. It's just that his stomach had ached and burned after he ate. The cure had started when the girls had stewed a pot of Shan-tung red dates. They insisted he drink a large bowl of the broth and eat the dates twice a day. They told him it was good for digestion. Who was he to argue? It worked.

Shao-mei yawned. A moment later, she said goodnight. She appeared exhausted and went up the stairs lifting each foot as if it were an anvil. Before she disappeared at the top, she looked back. There was a smile for Robert. It was flirtatious. Ayaou saw it and a chilly fog clouded her eyes.

Ayaou quickly cleaned up the table before they went upstairs. In the bedroom, she came to sit on his lap. She put both arms around him and kissed him passionately. She eagerly stuck her tongue between his lips. She was not attempting to hide her intent. He had been with Shao-mei the previous night.

Robert, on other hand, wasn't in the mood for passion. Though several days had gone by, he was still distracted by the conversation with William Martin, the American Presbyterian minister and was having trouble becoming aroused. His member was a limp noodle.

"On the other side of the clouds there is a full moon tonight," Ayaou said. "It's when the wolves mate." She took his ear lobe between her teeth and nibbled on it. "The female wolf howls into the wilderness until her chosen mate comes. Do you want me to howl for you, Robert?"

Ayaou curled her fingers around his flaccid member. It flopped about like a worm. "Tonight I wanted you to relax," she said, "but not that much." She stopped what she was doing and peered at it. "What's wrong with your sun instrument?" Her voice took on an almost scratchy sound. "You want to be with Shao-mei. You are tired of me."

"That's not it, Ayaou. Be patient. I'm just as upset as you are that it doesn't want to work. Something happened earlier in the week that still bothers me. Try harder, Ayaou. Don't give up."

"I know what will work," she said, and a determined look came into her eyes. She moved so her back was cradled against his chest. This revealed to him that she knew what aroused him the most. His hands explored her body. From this position he touched places he couldn't reach when he was on top of her. His eyes devoured her shoulders, her arms, and the long curving line of her backbone down to her buttocks. He was getting excited and could not slow down—not to mention hold back.

Once she felt his swollen member between her thighs, she moved away from him and faced Robert with her legs folded beneath her.

"What are you doing, Ayaou? I'm ready. I don't want to take any chances that my mood will change. Get back here."

A teasing smile creased her lips. "You are not allowed to become exhausted for you may lose your essence as a result. You must make sure that you peak no more than three times a week. It's the Emperor's recipe for longevity."

"I'm tired of hearing this, Ayaou. How am I supposed to control myself?" He reached for her.

She pushed him away. "Do what the Emperor does," she said. "Every time you feel like you're going to let go, pull back. Wait for the tide to ebb and then ride it again. This is the way to achieve the balance of Yin and Yang. You must take time to absorb my juices—the Yin element, while I absorb your Yang element."

The Chinese believed that if a man enjoyed the sexual pleasure of many women without ejaculation, it extended his longevity. It was a wonderful idea, but Robert didn't believe it. He absolutely hated the idea, since Ayaou was always urging him to pull out early.

She pushed Robert onto his back and guided herself onto him until he was inside her. "I love the feel of you," she whispered. "I want to make it last all night."

If he were a wolf, he'd cry to the moon and howl to the wilderness. Robert was so excited he was quivering. He pushed her off and pulled out. "Get on all fours," he said, and she complied. Robert moved behind her and took hold of her shoulders. She rested her face on her folded arms. This accented her shoulder blades and the long curve of her back. "Sorry about your longevity plan, Ayaou." He took her and in a few strokes had his orgasm.

After it was over, Robert rolled onto his back. He was sweaty and exhausted. Ayaou was gasping for air. The sound of rain was still pounding down outside the window.

"I can't move," she said. "I can't even open my eyes. I do not have the strength. I thought I was going to explode. Is this what it is like to be on a ship in a typhoon?"

Robert decided the next time he saw William Martin, he would thank him but wouldn't tell him why. In time, William and Robert would become lifelong friends. Martin would leave the ministry and work for Robert after he was Inspector General of Chinese Maritime Customs. That's when Robert discovered Martin was an *Old Testament* man. William told Robert that his spiritual beliefs were strict and unbending like a Puritan, but Robert's study of Confucianism and Buddhism and his wide acquaintances with men of many nations and diverse religions had made him into a broad-minded and tolerant man. He never told Martin his tolerance started with Ayaou and Shao-mei.

Nothing in his life had prepared him for anything as intense as the love he felt for his two girls. Every experience with women before Ayaou had been only physical and always left him mentally exhausted from guilt. He had not known what love was. He was sure that a man and woman couldn't reach such highs unless they were in love with each other—not just infatuated or full of lust.

After that, night—even when he was at the consulate or on a ship in the anchorage—a moment didn't pass that he did not think about Ayaou and Shao-mei. He could be at his desk in the consulate imagining Shao-mei singing while Ayaou danced, or he'd see them bent over the wok in the kitchen. It was all sensual and arousing, particularly on rainy days when they slid their lovely bare feet into wooden sandals. They carried colorful umbrellas and walked out the door into the wet world.

The girls took Robert to visit their relatives and friends during the Chinese New Year. It started on the first day of the first lunar month in late January and ran into early February. Tee Lee Ping didn't have confidence in Ayaou and Shao-mei to know the exact significance of the festival, so learning this became a part of the lesson before the festival.

Master Ping said, "The Spring Festival is the most important festival for the Chinese people. Wherever they are in the world, families will come together and celebrate. This festival originated about three thousand years ago during the Shang Dynasty. People sacrificed to the gods and their ancestors to close out the old year and start a new one. There are even special foods to eat during the festival like *laba* porridge."

"Wait," Robert said. "I don't know what this *laba* porridge is. I've never heard of it."

Master Ping looked surprised. He glanced at Ayaou with disapproval. Then he turned back to Robert. "It is made with glutinous rice, millet, seeds of Job's tears, jujube berries, lotus seeds, beans, longan and gingko. Do not hesitate to stop me and ask questions if you get confused."

He jabbed a finger at Robert. "Fireworks are most important, because the noise they make drives away evil spirits. That's why during the Spring Festival, you will hear firecrackers all the time.

"People clean everything to get ready for the festival. They want to start the New Year right. It is a new beginning.

"All the door panels in people's houses will have paper pasted on them. On these rice papers will be Spring Festival couplets highlighting Chinese calligraphy with black characters on red paper. In addition, pictures of the god of doors and wealth will be on the front door of every house to ward off evil spirits and welcome peace and abundance."

That wasn't the end of the lecture. Master Ping went into detail about everything people did. It didn't help that Robert stopped him and asked questions when he did not understand something. The amount of information was overwhelming. Robert didn't know how he could remember it all.

It wasn't enough that he had to remember what Tee Lee Ping had instructed him about the festival. After his teacher left, Ayaou and Shao-mei kept him up half the night teaching him how to behave around their relatives and friends.

"Robert," Ayaou said, "when you are with Chinese people be humble. Never brag as if you are better than they are. Many problems between foreigners and the Chinese are because of such behavior. It is a sure way to insult the Chinese and make enemies."

A few days later Robert was introduced to this big society with countless aunts and uncles, cousins and nephews. They lived in a village of boats in the river. Many remembered Robert from when he'd come to save them from the Taipings back in July of 1855.

After this first encounter, Ayaou was so pleased with his behavior that he gained a longer lesson from her. She didn't wait until the next day. They returned home after midnight, and she launched right into the lecture. She was supported by Shao-mei.

"You were wonderful, Robert. Shao-mei and I are proud of you, but there is more you must learn."

"I don't understand. Are you unhappy with me? Did I do something wrong?"

"No, Robert," Shao-mei said. She was sitting on his other side on the bench in the study room. "You were careful to behave exactly like Ayaou told you to. Anything you did wrong was not your fault. That is why we decided we must teach you more."

Robert stifled a yawn. He'd worked a full day at the consulate and wanted to sleep, but he also saw this as an opportunity to learn. He was determined to stay awake and pay attention. "I'm ready," he said. "Please continue. I am grateful that you are willing to give up your sleep to teach me."

"He's getting good, Ayaou," Shao-mei said.

"Yes," Ayaou replied. She leaned over and looked into his eyes. "He looks like he means it too."

"Get started, Ayaou," he said, losing patience.

"I'm ready," Ayaou said. She took a deep breath and started. "When in a conversation, try to get the Chinese to do the talking. We noticed that you talked a bit too much after dinner but not that much.

"If you are talking to a Chinese mother, show interest in the education of her son or sons. Chinese mothers will talk about little else but the son's education. Be interested in what they say even if it makes no sense and is boring. At the same time, do not make it look like you are trying to dig into their personal lives. Most of what they tell you will not be exactly the truth but what they want you to hear about them and their families."

Shao-mei interrupted. He had to swivel his head to see her. "That's not clear enough, Ayaou. He looks confused. His eyes look like glass. Your words are bouncing off him. He is not learning what he should. Let me explain. The Chinese do not like to dump their bad news on others who are not part of the family. That means do not tell anyone your problems. Problems are like shit and no one wants to hear them. Welcome what you are told as if it is the truth even if you do not believe it. Never question their honesty. When a mother tells you her son is doing horrible in school, he is probably the best student. She does not want to look like she is boasting." She took a breath.

Ayaou took advantage of the pause, and he turned to her. "If they want to make you the center of attention, tell them it makes you uncomfortable. Say you do not deserve it. When you are a dinner guest, never take the best crab or the most food. If we have a Chinese guest to dinner, after we have finished eating, you wash the bowls and let Shao-mei and I brag about you our way. Remember that usually we mean the opposite of what comes out of our mouths and other Chinese will understand."

"And never be the last one eating," Shao-mei said taking over. "If you are offered the best seat at the table and there are not enough chairs, take your bowl and chopsticks and stand in a corner and eat away from the others no matter what your rank or position. If you are told that one of the dishes of food tastes terrible, eat it anyway and say it is the best thing you have ever tasted no matter what it is like."

"If you act like this," Ayaou said, and he had to swivel his head to see her, "you will make friends among the Chinese, who will admire you." She started to open her mouth to continue, but Shao-mei interrupted.

"No, Ayaou. You are putting too much on his plate. Let him sleep on our words. In the morning, we will test him to see what he remembers." Robert wanted to hug her. A moment later, he was stumbling off to bed.

With advice from Ayaou and Shao-mei, he balanced people on opposite sides of the political spectrum and remained friends with both. One of his girls was always in hearing distance. They watched over him like mother ducks, and he was their only duckling. If he made a mistake in the Chinese etiquette they were teaching him, he faced a lecture when they returned home. If he made no mistakes, then Ayaou rewarded him with wild sex the next morning before he went to the consulate. It was great motivation for not making mistakes.

Even with this level of scrutiny from his girls, he enjoyed the Chinese people he was meeting. What he was learning also put the books he'd been reading into perspective. As the fifteen days of traditional celebration went by, he went often enough to be accepted. People started to share their opinions freely with him. He made friends.

In the evenings, when the weather was agreeable, which meant it wasn't raining, the girls went outside into the courtyard behind the house and practiced their dances. Robert loved the sensuous way their bodies moved. He never grew tired of watching them. Ayaou was the one who couldn't pass a day without moving her arms or kicking up her feet. She dragged Shao-mei outside taking her away from a book of

---

poems. She wasn't as quick as Ayaou, but she had no less of an ambition than Ayaou when it came to winning Robert's affections.

Eventually, as planned, Shao-mei revealed to Ayaou she was pregnant, and Ayaou received the news in silence. She forced herself to look pleased, but how could she be? Chinese tradition said the first concubine to conceive a boy child became number one. Robert was sure that Ayaou didn't want to be second to her younger sister. It was why he hoped Shao-mei delivered a girl.

He came home early one day to find Shao-mei alone. He sat in the study room. She came to sit on his lap urging him to rest his hand on her growing pregnancy.

"Can you feel our baby moving?" she asked.

She demanded love like a child demands candy. He had mixed feelings. After all, the child was not his, but he was determined to be a good stepfather anyway. Besides, if he took Guan-jiah up on the offer to make him the adopted uncle, the child would have two fathers. Guan-jiah would probably spoil the child rotten.

"What are you doing, Shao-mei?" It was an explosion from Ayaou as if a storm has appeared in the house without warning. She stood in the doorway holding a basket of fresh fruit and vegetables. She dropped the food on the floor sending produce everywhere and walked halfway into the room. Robert saw lightning and thunder in her eyes. The unwelcome visitor he'd sensed hiding in the shadows had arrived jealousy had walked on stage.

Shao-mei jumped off Robert's lap like a startled cat.

"Why are you sitting on his lap?" Accused the older sister. "Today's my day!"

"He loves me too," Shao-mei said.

"I'm the number one concubine. Don't you cross me!"

"But you were not here!"

"Would you like me to steal your food when you're not home?"

"I wasn't stealing, and he's no food."

"If you let me see you steal him again, I'll lock you up."

"Bully!" Shao-mei shot back.

"Don't make me hit you."

"Bully!"

"Try me again!"

"Enough!" Robert roared. He moved between them. "I love both of you. There's no reason for this. Stop this horrid behavior now." He was trembling, and his fiery demeanor appeared to quiet them. They stared at him with startled eyes. He immediately regretted his angry tone but refused to let them know. He hated losing his temper.

That was when he noticed the bruises on Ayaou's arm. "How did you get those?" he asked, thinking the girls had been fighting.

"A foreign sailor tried to grab me on my way to the market," she said.

"What?" He was alarmed. "Tell me what happened. Did you know him?"

She shook her head. "I never saw him before. He stepped from an alley as if he had been waiting for me. When he grabbed my arm and tried to drag me into the alley, I kicked him in his sun instrument. While he was on the ground grunting like a pig, I ran away. He must have thought I was a prostitute."

"Were you near the river?"

"No. I took my usual route to the market."

"I don't want you to go alone next time," he said. "You will take Shao-mei with you. You will both carry sturdy walking sticks."

A strange look came over Ayaou's face.

"What is it?" he asked.

"He knew me. I just remembered. Before he stepped out of the alley, he called my name. When I stopped, he jumped on me."

"How did he know your name?" He was sure it was one of Ward's men sent to kidnap her. There could be no other explanation. He shuddered, and his hand went to the pocket where he kept the accusation letter—the one Dr. Winchester had given him. It was folded in a small, tight square. He took it out of the pocket. Every time he felt threatened, he rubbed it between the index finger and thumb of his right hand. The paper was starting to wear thin. Where he rubbed it, the paper was smudged. It was a habit he was unaware of. He never opened it.

"I do not know," she said. "I never saw him before. You make it sound like it was my fault."

226

"No," he said. "It's not your fault. I don't know why it happened, and I don't like it. Never take the same way to the market again. I don't want either of you out of the house alone. Close all the shutters and keep the door locked when I am gone. Never go at the same time or on the same day each week."

"He was just a foreign devil," Shao-mei said. "I have had them come to me and ask me how much it cost. One foreign devil offered me ten yuan if I would do it in an alley with him. I walked away as fast as I could. That is why I never go near the river."

"That you had to be subjected to such horrid behavior is bad enough by itself, Shao-mei," he said, "but this man knew Ayaou's name, and she didn't go near the river. In the future, if you cannot go together, you must tell me. I'll have Guan-jiah or members of his family come to the house and escort you."

A knock at the door signaled Tee Lee Ping's arrival.

Chapter 20

The next morning, the girls continued to fight. "Robert," Ayaou said, "why are you eating Shao-mei's lotus soup and not drinking the tea I brewed?"

He wanted to say he couldn't do two things at the same time. Ayaou snatched up the bowl of soup and hurried to the chamber pot in the corner where she emptied it. "Since Shao-mei made the soup, it is a poor quality and could make you sick. Drink the ginseng tea. It will give you the energy of a lion."

"That's not fair, sister," Shao-mei said. "You know nothing is wrong with the soup, because you taught me how to make it." Then Shao-mei grabbed the cup of tea from Robert's hand. "The tea will give you a stomachache, Robert." Shao-mei spilled the tea on the floor.

"Clean that up!" Ayaou said.

"It will dry on its own." Shao-mei replied.

"Robert will slip on the puddle and fall. It will be your fault, sister."

Shao-mei glared at Ayaou then turned to Robert. "Did you like the soup or the tea better?"

"My stomach hurts, and it wasn't caused by the soup or tea," he said, standing to leave.

"You haven't eaten yet," Ayaou said.

"You dumped the lotus soup," he replied. "I was eating that." He pointed at Shao-mei. "And she spilled my tea. I'll find something to eat at the consulate."

"See, Ayaou," Shao-mei said, "you are going to cause Robert to become big like Mrs. Winchester. Her food is horrible. She eats enough for five Chinese."

228

He stopped at the door and looked back. They were still in the kitchen glaring at each other. "Don't cook dinner for me tonight," he said. "I'm working late. I'll get something to eat from a street vender."

"No, I'll bring dinner," Ayaou said. "If you eat from a vender, you could get sick. It costs too much anyway."

"Don't bother, Ayaou," Shao-mei said. "He won't like what you cook for him. I'll take him his evening meal."

He opened the door. "Robert," Ayaou said. "Why are you wearing that sweater Shao-mei knitted? You have never worn it to work before. You should know that the yarn is of the poorest quality. It will not keep you warm. Dr. Winchester and his wife will think you are poor. They will pity you."

"That's not true!" Shao-mei stamped a foot.

"I was distracted," he said. He slipped the sweater off and took his jacket from its hook by the door.

"See, he hates your sweater," Ayaou said. "Tell her what you think about it, Robert."

With one foot outside, he stopped and took a slow breath. "I refuse to take part in this argument. This fighting over who I favor or love the most is not my problem. The truth is that I love you equally."

"But, Robert, the lotus soup was horrible," Ayaou said. "You know it was. Tell us whose cooking you like best."

"I will not!" he said. "You are competing, because you're both jealous. You must make peace and solve this constant bickering that is causing me to lose sleep at night."

"It's all her fault," Shao-mei said. "If she hadn't poured the soup I cooked for you into the chamber pot, you would have had something to eat before going to work."

Robert stared at Shao-mei's huge belly. No, he thought, it wasn't Ayaou's fault. It was his. Ayaou was jealous because of the baby growing inside Shao-mei. She was worried it might threaten her position in the family. She didn't know the baby wasn't his. He was tempted to tell her the truth to end this fighting. He considered the consequences and realized if he did that, she would never let Shao-mei hear the end of it. Ayaou would also make the baby's life miserable.

"I don't want to hear any more of this," he said. "Fight when I'm not home if you must. When I come through that door each evening, I want peace and harmony in this house until I leave the next morning. Do you understand? If you don't do as I say, I will do something both of you will regret."

Ayaou's face turned pale. "What would you do, Robert? Would you sell us to be prostitutes? Would you send Shao-mei back to Captain Patridge and me to General Ward? Is that what you would do?"

"The only way you will discover the answer to those questions is if you don't stop this arguing," he said.

Shao-mei collapsed on one of the stools next to the kitchen table. The angry expression on her face had been replaced with worry.

He understood that his position was to ride a horse knowing that bending either way would cause him to fall. At the beginning, his neutrality had worked. The girls managed to solve the conflicts between themselves. They'd come out of each clash as best friends, sisters and lovers, so he hoped they would solve this problem and keep him out of it.

He put on his jacket and fled. It was bone-chilling cold outside, but at least it wasn't raining. The sky was free of clouds and had a greenish blue cast to it.

This jealousy between his girls was getting out of control. There was a tug of war inside him because of it. One part of Robert was pleased that these two beautiful women loved him so much they were willing to fight over him. His other side, the mental voice that gave him Christian advice, said it was wrong to want two women—that it was his duty to stop.

The girls were Chinese and were influenced by Buddhist and Confucius thoughts. Because of that, he almost excused them for their behavior, but he couldn't excuse himself for his part in what was going on. He was sure that a Chinese master would have defused this in no time. Robert felt inadequate.

Turning a corner, he saw William Martin down the street and managed to duck into an alley to avoid him. He chuckled at the irony of it. He was not only running from his lovers, but he was also avoiding his friends.

Then he remembered what businesses were on that narrow, short street close to the river. Foreign sailors came here to find liquor and whores. He peeked and saw Martin standing in front of the entrance to a notorious house of prostitution talking to someone out of sight in the shadows of a recessed doorway. Was William preaching the word of God to a prostitute in an attempt to save her soul?

Then Martin took what looked like a coin of the realm from a pocket and handed it to the person he was talking to. A woman stepped out of the shadows. She was slender with sharp angles in the bone structure of her face. Her shiny black hair reached her knees. She took the Presbyterian minister by the hand and took him to the stairway leading to the second level where Robert knew the prostitutes had intercourse with the men who paid them.

What is Martin doing? Robert thought. An urge to rush down the street and drag his friend from the prostitute entered his mind. Then he shook his head. *"Judge not, that ye be not judged,"* he said, quoting *Matthew 7:1.* How could Robert save Martin when he couldn't save himself?

He realized there was a difference. Robert loved his girls. They were not whores. He was sure Martin did not love this prostitute. The reason his friend was doing this was obvious. Martin's wife had returned to America because of her illness. He was a man lonely for a woman.

Once Martin was out of sight, Robert continued to the consulate. He buried himself in work, but his problems at home refused to leave him alone.

He had followed the Chinese banker's advice—the man he had visited after they had gone to see *The Dream of the Red Chamber.* Since Robert was having doubts about the tactics he was using to deal with his lovers, he decided to ask Guan-jiah for advice. After all, his servant was Chinese and might have a better suggestion.

"I have given this much thought, Master," Guan-jiah said.

"You mean about my situation with Ayaou and Shao-mei?"

"Yes, Master, since you told me about the child Shao-mei carries. If you remember, you agreed I could be the child's adopted uncle. That means I have a responsibility too. If the child is to grow without damage, there must be harmony in your house, and I have noticed your nervous condition."

"What about the banker's advice? Am I approaching it wrong?"

"I disagree with his advice, Master. He is wealthy. His women come from prosperous families. He doesn't understand your situation."

"And you do?"

"I believe that I am the only one who understands, and because of your trust and kindness, I feel as if I am part of your family—an extension like a toe on one foot. I know that you carry a burden because you love your concubines. I know your people would condemn you for your actions if they discovered how you are living and that bothers you. However, you should put this into perspective. You are not doing anything original, so there is nothing to be distressed about. Our emperors have been doing this for thousands of years. More than two thousand years ago, our first emperor, Ch'ing-shi-huang-ti, slept with six concubines each night."

"The fact that your first emperor slept with six girls does not fix my problems with Ayaou and Shao-mei," Robert said. "Talking about what my people would think of me is not going to do it either."

"Master," Guan-jiah said, "the problem has nothing to do with your girls. It has to do with the extreme beliefs in the afterlife by Christians. We Chinese, on the other hand, worship common sense and dislike all unproven theories and all conduct that exceeds accepted moral behavior."

Robert's mouth dropped open. He hadn't expected this opinion from his servant. He forced his mouth to close and erased the shock from his face. "Guan-jiah," he said, "where do you find all the time to dwell on things like this?"

His servant started walking across the consulate kitchen. "Would you like a cup of tea, Master? It is best to discuss common sense over a cup of tea." He went to the consulate stove, picked up the teapot, and poured two cups of tea. He carried them to the table. He set one lukewarm cup in front of Robert.

"Emperor T'ang—over a thousand years ago—said he always listened to two contradictory extremes of counsel over the same issue before deciding," Guan-jiah said, "and he usually took about half the advice from each side to find a middle ground. Since you have already listened to the banker, you should consider me the other extreme. That is why we Chinese call our country the *Middle Kingdom*. Like Emperor T'ang, we seek the middle ground to keep a balance." He took a sip and made a face. "No disrespect, Master, but Mrs. Winchester cannot brew tea." He put the cup down as if it had been poisoned.

Robert sipped and discovered Guan-jiah was right. This tea was bitterly strong. Mrs. Winchester must have used twice as many tealeaves and brewed it too long.

"If you are seeking advice, Master, I counsel that you find the middle ground, which means you cannot lean too far toward your Christian morals, and you cannot act like Emperor Ch'ing-shi-huang-ti and sleep with your concubines at the same time."

"How do I do that? How do I balance Confucianism with Christianity?"

"Think of it this way, Master. Christians live to be accepted into their heaven after death. Everything they do is aimed toward that goal. However, Confucianism is a religion of common sense based on our earthly senses and desires. If you consider man's nature, no man should marry but most men do, so Confucianism advises marriage. It would be nice if all men were equal, but they are not. There are emperors, princes, and generals, and there are workers, followers, and warriors. It is because of this that Confucianism teaches authority and obedience. It is the foundation for *piety*. It is why the father has so much authority. Men and women should not be different, but they are. Confucianism teaches that the sexes are different, and we live in a man's world."

"My religion believes that women are equal to men," Robert said.

"Does that mean you can bear children, Master?"

"You should have been a teacher, Guan-jiah, instead of a servant. How does this solve my problems? You're talking about common sense, and I am dealing with two girls fighting over me. Jealousy does not react to common sense."

"Ah yes, sex." Guan-jiah's eyes glowed with an energy Robert hadn't seen before. The servant went to the stove, poured out the tea and started a new pot. "We cannot drink this, Master. I will brew a fresh pot. I have some chrysanthemum tea more suited to conversation."

Once they had two fresh cups of tea, the conversation continued, but Guan-jiah did the talking. "Buddhism and, from what I've learned, Christianity," he said, "say sex leads to sin. Confucius, on the other hand, says sex is a perfectly normal function, because it is connected with the continuation of the family and the human species."

Robert lifted the lid on his cup and steam billowed out. It smelled marvelous. It was aromatic, sweet, and spicy at the same time. He saw nutmeg seeds floating with the chrysanthemum flowers and shavings from vanilla beans. There were other things he couldn't identify. Maybe that was why Guan-jiah felt this tea was more suitable to a conversation.

"Your solution, Master, is to get both of your concubines pregnant. When Ayaou is also pregnant, she will have no reason to be jealous of Shao-mei. As the adopted uncle, I am willing to go to the herbalist and purchase herbs you will put in Shao-mei's tea and soup, so the baby will be born a girl. Girls are worthless, so this will solve that problem. Then I will go to the herbalist to buy what will help Ayaou get pregnant and have a boy child."

At home, Robert caught himself enjoying the look of concentration on Shao-mei's face as she wrote a new Chinese poem. When she wrote every symbol correct, he rewarded her with ticklish kisses on her neck behind an ear. The sound of her laughter brought joy to his soul. He also loved to watch Ayaou wash her hair and comb it for what felt like hours. When that was happening, he'd catch a look in Shao-mei's eyes. He knew that she was studying him to see what pleased him.

Sure enough, the next day he'd find her doing the same as Ayaou had done—washing her hair and taking forever to comb it out while casting sly glances at him. He made an effort not to disappoint her and watched.

One night Ayaou stopped in the middle of their lovemaking. "Before we finish satisfying your sun instrument, I want you to make a promise."

"What is it?" he said.

"I want you to promise to sleep with Shao-mei once a week. I want to punish her for being too possessive of you."

"What!" he said. This was absurd. It was beyond absurd. "How can you ask me this? I want this to be a house of happiness. That cannot happen if I make such a promise. Shao-mei will be unhappy. I'm not going to stop my current practice of sleeping with you one night and Shao-mei the next." He didn't tell her that when he was with Shao-mei nothing happened beyond cuddling. Robert still hadn't had intercourse with Shao-mei. He was determined not to until the child was born.

"Robert, what other choice have you? If you do not punish Shao-mei, she is going to become more possessive. I see how she looks at you. You are blind."

"This house is like a bucket of milk turning sour. If this is the price to have intercourse with you, we will not make love again." He rolled away from her and pretended to go to sleep.

Ayaou had been knocked into a shocked silence, and the atmosphere in the room turned frigid. Robert had never turned away from her before—not like this. A moment passed. Then she said, "I am sorry, Robert. Please do not punish me like this. I will not be able to sleep unless your hands come to touch me, and your sun instrument shines with pleasure. I will not make this kind of demand again."

Robert suppressed his bitter and victorious smile. He rolled over and reached for her. He had taken Guan-jiah's advice and was spiking their tea and soup with herbs designed to ensure Shao-mei of a girl child and to get Ayaou pregnant with a male child. He hoped it worked.

"I can't wait for your advice to work, Guan-jiah. After Ayaou gets pregnant, we have to wait nine months until she delivers. I'm desperate. There is no way to know how long it will take before she conceives."

"Master," he said, "if you are in a hurry to create harmony in your house, may I suggest that you set up rules as Chinese masters do?"

"And what would those be?" Robert asked, wary of the answer.

"I will write them and give them to you later in the day," he said. "Now is not the time to talk." He cast a glance toward the door that led to the next room where Mrs. Winchester was. "You are getting behind in your paperwork. I know how much that bothers you." Guan-jiah left.

That evening, after Robert finished work, Guan-jiah handed him a leather whip and the sheet of suggested rules. Most of the rules made sense like the one about who spoke the first harsh words that started a fight received the punishment. The punishment was to use the whip and tear the flesh off their lovely backs until they become a mass of scars and scabs. Robert couldn't bear the thought of beating them.

"Why the whip?" he asked. "I can't use that."

"There's no other way to make a horse behave, Master. My father has a whip. All the married men I know have whips or sticks to beat their women, but they seldom use them. All it usually takes is once. If that does not work, you can always hang one with a silk rope. That is what the Emperor does in the Forbidden City to a concubine that does not behave. I heard that one concubine had her arms and legs removed. She was the most beautiful woman in China. It was because of her beauty that she thought it gave her power over the Emperor. They say he cried when she was punished. Her torso was put into a large vase, so her head protruded from the top. The other concubines are made to walk through that room where the limbless concubine is kept alive in that vase as an example.

"Master, if you do not use the whip when you ride your concubines, it will be like riding a horse that goes where it wants instead of where you want it to go. After all, a woman's role is to be ridden, but the outcome is better than just being transported from one place to another."

"Outcome?" Robert replied, shocked at Guan-jiah's explicit images.

His servant looked at him oddly. "Master, the outcome is sons, many sons to carry on the family name. A horse cannot give you that—your concubines or wives can. And if you have girl children, you can arrange marriages with families who will improve your life." He smiled proudly. "Why do you think I suggested the herbs?"

Robert was confused. He wasn't sure when Guan-jiah was talking about women and when he was talking about horses. They seemed to be the same thing to his servant.

When Robert arrived home that evening, he hid the sheet of rules and the whip under the bed he shared with Ayaou. No one cleaned under the beds. The whip and list of rules sunk into a thick layer of dust.

That night he slept with Ayaou. While they were making love, he thought of that whip under the bed and imagined using it on her while he rode her. He saw himself strapping a saddle to her lovely back and making her carry him to work.

When they finished making love, Robert said, "I'm not taking sides between you and Shao-mei. I want to make that clear, Ayaou. I'm not going to allow jealousy to destroy what we have."

Instead of cuddling and throwing her legs on top of his—which was her habit after they had intercourse—she snorted with a derisive sound and rolled over with her back toward him.

Her desirable back, the one he loved looking at, was suddenly not so lovely. Maybe Guan-jiah was right, and a few well-placed scars would solve this problem. He imagined her back with scabs and red scars crisscrossing it. It wouldn't look so desirable and lovely anymore once it was blemished. She might be like a horse to a Chinese man, but she wasn't to Robert. He decided to leave the whip where it was. There was enough anger in the house already.

The next night when he went to Shao-mei's room, she made the same demand Ayaou made. She said that Robert should punish Ayaou by sleeping with her once a week.

He wanted to know who was feeding such ideas to his girls, so he asked.

Shao-mei replied, "You paid for me first, Robert. That makes me the number one concubine. Ayaou should be punished. When she stops arguing, I will stop. After all, I am only defending myself."

"I didn't ask for that. I wanted to know who you are talking to."

"I haven't talked to anyone. What I am saying is common sense."

To make things worse, despite his warnings that having intercourse might damage the baby or risk her having a miscarriage, she started seducing him. She was loud about it too. She turned so the length of her naked back was exposed to him and moved toward him. When her buttocks rubbed against his crotch, Robert's member stood at attention like the little mercenary it was. He was afraid he wasn't strong enough to resist.

When Robert managed not to engage in intercourse, she turned and brushed her lips across the tip of his erection. Fighting his desire to take her, Robert sat and pushed her head from his member. "Stop, Shao-mei."

She refused to listen. Instead, she went down and wrapped her lips around its tip. She tickled his member with her tongue. Robert felt his resolve and his sense of reason vanishing. The little wild beast stiffened into a solid root. "Shao-mei, please. We have a problem to solve." She sucked harder. He found it impossible to think.

She came up for air, and said, "You do not need anybody else. See, though I am heavy with a child, I can still make you happy. You want me. Your sun instrument tells me so." She went down and took it into her mouth again.

"Shao-mei, no." He struggled to stay in control, but he knew he wouldn't last much longer. "Shao-mei, we must talk."

"Talk as much as you want," she said. "Nobody is stopping you." She continued sucking.

Robert was overwhelmed with desire, but he resisted. "I am not a carrot," he said. With a mighty effort of will, he managed to push her away. He put on the robe and tossed a blanket over her. With all the dignity he could muster, he said, "I must tell you, Shao-mei, I don't like what you're doing. I'll deal with you later!" His voice didn't sound convincing. "It's wrong of you to risk your health and the health of the baby like this. It just is."

His erection was protruding from the robe. She laughed then stood and let her blanket slip to the floor. Turning, she threw one naked hip out at an angle. She stood on tiptoe and stuck her buttocks toward him. She arched her back and looked over her shoulder. She licked her tongue along her lips in an invitation that was too bold to mistake. "Look what you are walking away from," she said. "Do you want to do that?"

Robert retreated to the larger bedroom. He found Ayaou quietly sobbing. He climbed into bed next to her and pulled her toward him. "Let's talk, Ayaou."

Her hands went all over him. She saw his erection and anger flared in her eyes. "Fine," she said, "but I must talk my way." She pressed her mouth on his. He tried to push her away, but she was like a leech. "Fight me off if that is what you want," she said, "but I will not stop until I bring you to the pleasure cliff and make you jump."

She pulled over his left hand to touch the wetness between her thighs. His mind tipped off balance and lust took over. He thrust his member into her with such force their bellies slapped against each other.

Ayaou groaned and twisted her body beneath his. Robert couldn't do anything but dance to her rhythm. When he closed his eyes, he saw Shao-mei as if she were the one he was having intercourse with—not Ayaou. It was exhilarating. Guan-jiah was right about one thing. A woman was like a good horse, because, when a man had the right mount, he never wanted to get off.

Robert awoke to the sound of screams from downstairs. He threw on a robe and ran. The study to the left of the stairs was empty. He saw the first victim on the floor in there.

"No," he said, and stumbled into the room. The first victim had been a gift, a silk bag for his ink-stone. Shao-mei had made it. Ayaou must have cut it up with a pair of scissors. He'd loved that bag. Shao-mei had embroidered a pair of lovebirds on it. She'd said that the larger bird was Robert. She was the other one. They were going to build a nest together and fill it with little baby birds. Robert went down on his knees and gathered the scraps.

"You will pay for it." Shao-mei yelled from the kitchen. "Ayaou, I swear that I will not let you get away with this."

"I have warned you several times," Ayaou replied. The tone of her voice was unkind. "This is the last warning, before I tell Robert to sell you."

He froze with the scraps of the destroyed silk ink stone bag clutched in his hands. His stared at the doorway leading to the kitchen. He thought of the whip upstairs. Guan-jiah was right. The whip and the pain it would deliver was his only choice, but he couldn't make himself go up those stairs to get it.

The Angry voices in the kitchen continued. "Do not think you are the only one with power. I have power too. I will make him sell you before you make him sell me. Do not forget that I am the one that carries his child. I am younger and prettier than you are. I have dimples that he is wild about. Every time I smile, he sees my dimples and he forgets you."

Shao-mei's voice escalated into a scream. There was the sound of a blow that came from a fist hitting flesh. Robert ran into the kitchen to see the sisters scratching at each other. Ayaou threw herself on Shao-mei. She wrapped both her arms around Shao-mei and lifted her off the ground. She squeezed and Shao-mei's face started to turn purple.

"The baby!" he said. "No!" He took hold of Ayaou's arms and pried them from Shao-mei. The younger sister lost her balance and stumbled back. He forced his way between them.

Ayaou attempted another blow. Tufts of hair floated in the air. Shao-mei, in her blind fury, scratched Robert's face and blood started to ooze from the wound.

After a few more blows from both sisters to Robert's body, both girls stumbled back. They were stunned they had hurt him. He put a hand up to stop the bleeding and looked from one sister to the other. Shao-mei's blouse was torn. Ayaou's face was also scratched.

"Robert, you must sell Shao-mei!" Ayaou said, breaking the paralyzing spell that had invaded the room. "She has gone mad! I was wrong to let her in. She is ungrateful. This is how she repays my kindness. With her claws! She does not belong in this house. She belongs to Captain Patridge and deserves to be treated like a prostitute. Sell her! It is too late for her to cry sorry, because I will not hear her. Let her go, Robert!"

"See her, Robert!" Shao-mei said—her voice filled with desperation. "Ayaou has turned evil! She has wished me sickness, and she has wished me death. She wants this child to die in my womb. She does not care that I am your concubine too. If you let her stay, she will bring you bad luck?"

No longer could Robert stand this. Anger rushed in and drove rational thought out of his head. "No!" he said in a harsh voice, and he was angry. The girls had never seen him this volcanic before. He took hold of Ayaou and forced her to sit on one side of the kitchen table. When he let go of her arms, dark spots showed where he had grabbed her. He looked sternly at Shao-mei and pointed at the stool on the other side of the table. His eyebrows had become storm clouds. His lips were thin blades. Ayaou and Shao-mei expected lightning and thunder to appear from his head.

After Shao-mei sat, she hid her face in her hands. Robert wanted the look in his eyes to frighten her; that she'd seen something like it before from an executioner before a beheading. He was sure she wanted him to stop staring at her but feared saying anything.

"Do not move," he said in a firm, demanding tone. Then he hurried upstairs to dress in his usual work clothes. After he finished getting ready for work, he reached under the bed for Guan-jiah's whip. When he reached the kitchen, he found the girls still sitting where he'd put them. They looked meek and shrunken. Robert unfurled the whip and cracked it in the air above the girls' heads. They jumped—their startled expressions full of fear and uncertainty.

"Damn it to hell!" Robert said. "I'm going to sell both of you! I'm going to sell you today, now! Pack up your things. I'll send someone to get you. I never want to see either of you again!" He opened the front door and slammed it behind him. During the walk to the consulate, his temper subsided. He felt shame for losing control.

When Robert reached the consulate, Guan-jiah noticed the stricken look on his face. He also saw the bleeding scratch on his cheek. He made Robert sit and used a damp cloth to wash away the blood and clean the cut.

"I wanted to kill them," Robert said, his voice a dull monotone. He stared across the room with dazed eyes. "I'm afraid I'm going to hurt them, Guan-jiah. I'm sleeping with my pistol under my pillow. It's loaded. I wake at every sound worried that Ward is coming. I hear things in my sleep, but when I wake, there is only silence. I also see things that are never there when I look closer. I'm losing my mind." He'd taken out the folded accusation letter and was rubbing it between his thumb and index finger.

Guan-jiah went to the table and started to grind some pepper into a fine powder. His expression was a neutral one. There was no way to tell what he was thinking. When he returned to where Robert was sitting, he spoke softly in a soothing voice. "It is all right, Master. Your anger is gone. I am sure that you have not killed them. You are here now in the consulate and there is no reason to worry." Guan jiah carefully applied the pepper powder to the cut. The bleeding stopped.

"What is going on here?" Dr. Winchester asked, as he walked into the room.

"My master cut himself while shaving this morning," Guan-jiah said. "I insisted on cleaning the wound since it would not stop bleeding."

Dr. Winchester leaned in close to examine what Guan-jiah had put on Robert's face. "What is that stuff?" he asked.

"It is pepper," Guan-jiah said. "It will stop the bleeding and protect him from an infection."

"Pepper?" Dr. Winchester said. "Nonsense."

"I trust him," Robert said. "If he says it will work, I'm sure it will."

With a skeptical look on his face, Dr. Winchester examined Robert's cheek. "Good Lord, it works. I cannot believe what I'm seeing. The pepper has formed a scab over the cut. I've never seen bleeding from a cut stop that quickly." He pointed at a spot where the blood was still oozing. "You missed that."

Guan-jiah carefully placed a pinch of pepper there.

Dr. Winchester squinted to see better. "Amazing," he said. "I see the blood stopping as if you had built a barrier to keep it from flowing. You are a good man, Guan-jiah. Next time I cut myself shaving, I'll try it." He left the room mumbling to himself.

"Bury yourself in your work, Master," Guan-jiah said. He leaned in close like a conspirator. "I know that you are uncomfortable talking about your concubines when other foreigners might hear. We can leave the consulate and talk before you return home tonight."

Robert watched Guan-jiah leave the room to attend to his chores. He worried that he was allowing the eunuch to get too close, too familiar. After all, he was just a servant, and he wasn't a Christian. The trouble was, Robert didn't have anyone else to turn to. He started work.

Chapter 21

Robert didn't know that reading Edgar Allen Poe was about to save his life.

In an attempt to find peace of mind, he tried to sleep at the consulate, but his thoughts were filled with the girls. Since he couldn't sleep, he searched among his books and found a collection of John Donne's poems.

Hoping it would lull him to sleep, he started to read. His plan didn't work. When he reached *Love's Alchemy*, he thought it fit his situation.

> *'Ah, what a trifle is a heart,*
> *If once into love's hands it come!*
> *All other griefs allow a part*
> *To other griefs, and ask themselves but some;*
> *They come to us, but us love draws;*
> *He swallows us and never chaws;*
> *By him, as by chained shot, whole ranks to die;*
> *He is the tyrant pike, our hearts the fry.'*

After finishing the poem, Robert felt as if it were his Cilice. He had known a devout Catholic at college in Belfast. The man wore a Cilice, a shirt woven from goat hair that was itchy and uncomfortable. He said he wore it to help him resist the temptations of the flesh.

Robert's heart felt as if it had been burned. He wanted the girls to understand. They had to learn to rely on each other's strengths to survive and to depend on each other's love and kindness. He refused to treat them like his property, because he believed in their good nature and wisdom. He believed that a whip never created true peace.

Robert considered confiding to William Martin, the minister. He wanted someone else to talk to besides Guan-jiah. He had talked to Martin about the meaning of hypocrisy once. The two men agreed that a sinner could not judge others for the same sin, and he had watched Martin pay a prostitute.

However, he was still reluctant to talk to Martin about his problems. Depressed, he put aside John Donne's *Love's Alchemy* and picked up Edgar Allen Poe. He started to read from *The Raven*.

'Once upon a midnight dreary, while I pondered, weak and weary—'

Robert stopped reading. That would not do. He turned to another page and started to read from *The Tell-Tale Heart*.

'TRUE!—nervous—very, very dreadfully nervous I had been and am, but why will you say that I am mad—'

He slammed the book shut and shuddered. He did not like his dark mood and decided to leave the consulate. With literature like this, he'd stay awake imagining the worst. He wanted to go home.

When he stepped outside the consulate gate, it was late. A thick, menacing fog had smothered the city filling the streets with a flood of mist that converted the buildings into threatening beasts, which reminded him of Poe's stories.

His awareness of his surroundings magnified as he walked away from the safety of the consulate. He held his hand out in front of him. It vanished in the fog. It wasn't until his fingers were inches from his nose that they were visible again. It was as if he were living inside one of Poe's stories.

He was sure that Ward had sent the assailant that tried to club him outside his house. There had been a fog then too. What about that sailor who attempted grabbing Ayaou? A night like this was perfect for a thug to attack without warning.

Robert struggled to put his paranoia to rest. Then he heard what sounded like someone following him. When he listened carefully, he discovered the noise was all around him. It must have been an echo created by the fog and the buildings crowding the narrow, crooked street. The place had become an echo chamber.

He'd never noticed it before. The streets had always been crowded with people when he'd been on his way home. His hand slipped into his coat pocket seeking comfort from the walnut grip of the Colt revolver. He was glad he had the pistol.

He walked faster. The sound he thought was an echo stayed at the old pace for a few beats. Then it sped up to match his footsteps. Alarmed, he stopped and put his back against a wall and held his breath. The footsteps continued for several more beats. Then they stopped and left a dreadful silence in their wake. A pit full of fear opened inside Robert threatening to spin him into a panic. His heart started to pound. His legs trembled and demanded that he run. He took several calming breaths and stood fast. He pulled the revolver from his coat pocket and slowly, quietly cocked the hammer.

The stranger took several halting steps then stopped. It was almost impossible to judge distance. A long moment went by without a sound.

Then a man's voice said, "Curse it!"

Robert jerked from the shock of the man's proximity. He was afraid of being discovered. The stranger was close. If he took one-step forward, he'd bump into the man.

"Where did that bugger go?" The voice had a British cockney accent.

The pounding of Robert's heart accelerated. He started to sweat. He opened his mouth to challenge the man. Then he thought better of it. Speaking would give away his location. Retreat was the better choice. He had walked this way for months. He knew there was a narrow, side street close by.

He knelt and silently slipped his boots off. Then he slid along the wall in his stocking feet until something sharp stabbed the bottom of his left foot. He almost cried out in pain but forced his lips to stay sealed. It stung. He took another step. The sharp object was left behind. It must have been a pebble with an edge to it. When he reached the narrow alley he was looking for, he breathed easier.

"Bert," the first voice called, "has that bloke reached you yet?"

"He mucking vanished, Nick. Maybe the place he lives is closer to the consulate than we thought."

Robert shivered. These two men had set a trap to snare him.

"No, he always walks more than halfway through Ningpo when he's going home. If we knew where he lived, we'd break in and take him like we was paid to and have him pressed into that King's ship. If you didn't keep losing him in the crowd, we'd know where he lived. Don't forget we get paid five pounds once we deliver his carcass. All we have to do is whack him on the head and take him to that naval officer we were told to contact. It is easy money. Better than picking pockets."

"These crooked streets are confusing, and I didn't lose him alone," the man to Robert's left said. "You're a bloody mucking fool. You've followed him before and lost him."

Anger rushed in like a riptide and replaced Robert's fear. Someone was willing to pay these scoundrels to press him into the Royal Navy. If they had succeeded, he would have opened his eyes inside the hull of that British frigate that had dropped anchor in the river six days earlier. It was scheduled to sail for the Pacific coast of North America in the morning. He was tempted to confront these rascals. After all, he had the pistol. If they wanted a fight, he'd give it to them.

He shook his head.

No, that was a foolish thought. Two against one in this fog was not a good idea. Robert started moving again. He had an urge to hurry. Ignoring the temptation, he continued to take slow steps. Then a puddle soaked his socks. The puddle smelled of urine. His stomach churned.

He had to find a different route to his front door. It sounded as if these thugs didn't know where he lived. He wondered who hired them. It had to be Ward. Who else could it be?

Once he was near the house, he hesitated and listened for the longest time. What if they said they didn't know where he lived to fool him? They could be waiting. The silence in the street was like the inside of a coffin. It was so quiet, Robert was sure he'd hear someone breathing twenty feet away.

"Thank you, Edgar," he said in a whisper. If it hadn't been for the mood Edgar Allan Poe's *The Raven* and the *Tell Tale Heart* had put him in, he would have walked into their trap. Then he smiled. He should also thank the evil spirits the Chinese kept out of their cities with the maze of narrow streets.

246

He tried the door and found it wasn't locked. That was wrong. It should be locked all the time. All the fear and caution he had felt walking home rushed back. He leveled the revolver and pushed the door open. The door banged against the inside wall. He leaped into the room.

His girls screamed and jumped off the bottom step of the stairs where they'd been sitting side-by-side holding hands. They were staring at the Colt and not him.

"Do not kill us," Shao-mei said. "Give us a chance to talk to our master first. Did he pay you to get rid of—" Her eyes came up, and she saw Robert's face. He eased the hammer to its safe position and stuffed the weapon into his pocket. He closed the door and locked it. Once they realized who had stepped through the door, they rushed into his arms.

"You frightened us, Robert," Shao-mei said. Tears were running down her cheeks.

"Yes, we thought it was someone coming to murder us or take us to be slaves and prostitutes for foreign devils," Ayaou said.

"Then why did you leave the door unlocked?" he asked.

"We just came in," Ayaou said.

"What do you mean? I told both of you not to leave the house."

"You told us not to go out alone. We did not. We waited all day for you to send someone to get us. Then the fog came. There were noises outside the downstairs windows as if someone was trying to get inside."

"Yes, Robert," Shao-mei said. "Murderers and rapists were coming for us. We were sure you sent them to punish us."

"How did you reach that conclusion from noises at the window?"

"We talked about it after you left," Ayaou said, "and decided that your anger would result in the worst punishment."

"Which was murder and rape," Shao-mei said, "so we went outside to hide in the fog."

"What? Have you lost your common sense? You went outside to be safe from someone trying to break into the house to rape and kill you. That's absurd."

"No it is not, Robert," Shao-mei said. "The floor upstairs kept making noises as if someone were walking around. We decided it was not safe, because there was no fog to hide in.

We went out but could not lock the door. No one was inside to bar it."

"Give us another chance, Robert," Ayaou said. "We agree to behave."

"Yes, Robert," Shao-mei said. "We were crazy. It won't happen again." They buried their faces in his coat.

"If you felt safer out in the fog, why did you come back inside?"

"I realized that if we were attacked outside and carried away," Ayaou's said, "you would not know what happened to us."

"Yes, Robert," Shao-mei said. "We agreed that you loved us too much to send someone to hurt us, so we came back inside. We were upset and forgot to lock the door."

He shook his head and held their trembling bodies. He wanted to live the rest of his life like this. Robert had never had even one-woman love him as these two did.

Robert's mother was a carefree person. She could laugh at almost anything. She allowed him to grow wild in his ways, but she never told him she loved him or hugged him. All he could remember of his father was the time each day the family spent studying scripture.

Father sat with his back straight like a pole. The closest that his father ever demonstrated love was the day Robert left for China. His father gave him fifty gold sovereigns. Robert was starved for the love his girls had an abundance of. He couldn't stay away from it.

The next morning he stayed home waiting for the fog to burn off. He didn't go to the consulate until the British frigate was scheduled to sail. Then he went to the river and checked that it was gone. If he'd been pressed into that British man-of-war, his life would've been turned into a hellish ordeal. What would have happened to his girls with him gone?

He confided in Guan-jiah.

"It wouldn't be good for that child to lose its father before it is born," Guan-jiah replied.

"Yes, Guan-jiah, how could you be an uncle without me?" Robert said. They laughed.

After that, the eunuch routinely met him in the mornings on the way to the consulate. He also walked with Robert to his house each evening. For the next few weeks they never took the same route to the consulate in the mornings or on the way back to the house at night.

Before spring arrived, the house had become a garden of harmony. Shao-mei was huge with child—by Robert's estimate, she was at least six months pregnant if not seven. A few weeks remained before the baby was due.

Special days lodged in his memory and doubled as lessons in Chinese culture. One example was a day Robert arrived home early to hear Ayaou scolding Shao-mei. They didn't hear him come in. He stood still and listened thinking they were arguing.

"You have put too much wood in the stove," Ayaou said. "The fire is too hot. You are going to ruin the dinner."

The stove was made of brick and stood out from the wall. Shao-mei fed wood to the flames from behind while Ayaou cooked.

"What are you talking about?" Shao-mei replied. "If I do not keep the fire going, you could not cook."

Small, meaningless scenes like this endeared the girls to him. If those men had hijacked him, this moment would have been lost.

He arrived home another day to find the girls had been painting. A river cascaded down the length of the chimney and one side of the stove. It wasn't the greatest art, but it was recognizable. Ayaou had stocked the river with bright-orange trout. There was a waterfall with one trout attempting to fling itself into the pond at the top. Those trout were the ugliest malformed fish he'd ever seen, but he was not going to tell his girls that.

"Why fish?" he asked. "I mean it's beautiful and brings this kitchen to life, but why not birds and clouds or trees?"

"Because *Yu*, fish, when spoken, sounds similar to another word that means *to always have enough in life*," Ayaou said. "It will bring us luck—we will never go hungry or be without shelter."

Robert was regularly learning something new about the Chinese culture. His girls were teaching him, and they didn't know it. He cherished any knowledge that came his way, however insignificant. Every time he learned something, he came closer to unwrapping the veil from this culture that was so unlike his.

On the eve of the Lantern Festival, he returned home from the consulate to find Ayaou decorating the front door of the house.

"What is the significance of this?" he asked, knowing that everything the girls did had some sort of meaning to improve life or offer protection. He turned and looked down the street. For the first time, he noticed lanterns of all shapes and sizes hanging from the trees and buildings.

With a look of silent concentration, Ayaou finished fastening on the door a canvas picture of an old fat man leaning on a walking stick. He had multiple chins, a hunchback and a big bump on his head. He held a leash with a young deer tied to the end.

When she finished, she stepped back to examine it. She pointed at the ugly old man. "This is *Shou,* the god of longevity. On the other side is *Kwan-yin*, the goddess of mercy."

The goddess of mercy was a beautiful woman with long flowing hair. She was sitting on a lily pad. Her calm look reminded Robert of the Virgin Mary except *Kwan-yin* was Chinese.

"Look above the door and you will see the Chinese symbols for *Kwan-yin, Fu, Lu,* and *Shou. Fu* means happiness and *Lu* means success." She turned a beaming smile toward Robert.

"Did you paint those words above the door?"

She laughed. "No, Robert. I could never do calligraphy like that. I am still clumsy with a brush. I bought them."

It was easy to believe. This artwork was of a higher quality than the paintings in the kitchen. Robert didn't believe in these superstitions. However, unlike most of his brethren, he was tolerant of them, because it taught him about the Chinese and how they thought.

Robert would always be a Christian, but unlike so many others from Europe and America, he refused to condemn the Chinese for the way they were. He never attempted to convert them into Christianity or rob them like the opium merchants were doing. To him it was all hypocrisy.

On one hand, the Europeans and British were shoving Christianity's message of brotherly love down the Chinese collective throat with the barrel of a rifle. At the same time foreign merchants, mostly British, were selling opium to the populace. No wonder the Chinese were resisting. The Chinese had believed and lived this way for several thousand years. Did anyone have the right to force them to change against their will?

Robert never told his girls any of his true feelings about their superstitions. If it made them happy, he didn't want to be a spoiler. It didn't matter. No one ever visited except Chinese friends and relatives of the sisters.

A few days later Shao-mei hung nine red lanterns in the room where they studied.

"Do we need this many?" Robert asked.

"Oh, Robert," Ayaou replied. "This is simple. I am surprised you do not know the significance of these nine lanterns." Ayaou talked to him as if he were a child. He didn't mind. He liked it. "The Imperial lucky number is nine, which means to develop everything to its potential without over spilling. That is why the Forbidden City has nine hundred and ninety-nine buildings inside its walls. Only the Emperor can get that close to heaven. The rest of us have to be satisfied with the number nine."

"Why not eight or ten or eight hundred or a thousand?" he asked.

"Because ten is too much," she said. "Only God can do a ten. Nine means to be humble and acknowledge God as perfect."

Shao-mei handed Robert a necklace and asked him to put it on. He held it close to his eyes. The beads looked familiar. There were nine on the string. They turned out to be olive pits.

"This will protect you, Robert," Shao-mei said "We spent hours sanding off the pointed ends of the pits and then drilling holes in them with little needles. Look," she held up a hand, "see where I grew a callus from all the rubbing. I poked myself more than once with the needle."

Robert reached for the hand and pulled it to his lips. He kissed the callus. This little dull looking, nothing necklace was full of love from Ayaou and Shao-mei.

"Not only that," Ayaou said, "wear it so you will have peace."

Robert saw that they wore olive pit necklaces too. He took the necklace, slipped it over his head and settled it around his neck.

Eventually, Ayaou added red colored woodcarvings to the walls just inside the front door. The images were characters in various calligraphy styles. Robert recognized them immediately. No one had to explain the significance. They represented the six relationships and the mandate of heaven—the basis of all social connections between people in China. They were all variations of *xiao,* or piety. This time he understood and asked no questions. Living with his girls was teaching him more about the Chinese culture than any number of books or teachers could.

Robert pulled the girls into his arms. He stood there and studied the carvings. "Do you like it?" They asked as if they were one voice.

With a serious expression on his face, he stood for a moment in silence and stared at the carvings a bit longer as if he might not approve of them. He sensed the girls fidgeting nervously. They cast looks of inquiry at him and at each other.

"Yes," he finally said, and smiled. "I like this. It's the right touch to greet me when I come home. It shows what kind of family we are and the harmony that fills our house."

He managed to convince himself that life would go on like this without end. He forgot Ward and relaxed his vigilance against an assault. The accusing note—the one he had a habit of rubbing with his thumb and index finger—was forgotten too. The note was turned to pulp when he didn't remove it from the pocket, and the shirt was washed. He stopped thinking of his family back in Ireland and even erased the Christian missionaries from his thoughts.

It was fortunate that Guan-jiah had not forgotten. His servant arrived every morning and accompanied him to work. The eunuch carried a sturdy walking stick that doubled as a club. Guan-jiah said nothing and became doubly alert to make up for Robert's lack of vigilance. He saw that his master was happy, and he realized happiness was fleeting. He decided not to remind Robert of the dangers. There was no need to spoil things.

There were performances throughout the city on the day of the Lantern Festival. Robert watched the dragon lantern dance, a lion dance, and a land boat dance. He saw men walking on stilts and beating drums. At night, he walked the streets with his girls. They read the riddles that were written on the lanterns. They guessed the answers; then knocked on the doors to ask the owners of the houses if they were right.

They ate a feast that started with small dumpling balls made of glutinous rice flour with rose petals, sesame, bean paste, jujube paste, walnut meat, and dried fruit. Robert couldn't identify some fillings. The dumplings tasted sweet, and he liked the texture in his mouth. He realized that in the West quantity counted and taste and texture took second place. It wasn't like that in China.

When Robert asked Master Ping about the dumplings, his teacher replied, "The name for the dumplings sounds the same as the Chinese word that means reunion. People eat them for harmony and happiness in the family." Master Ping wrote the Chinese symbols for both words on a piece of rice paper and showed Robert what they looked like. He pronounced them. He then had Robert pronounce them until he was proficient. The difference between the words was a slight variation in tone.

"There, you have just added two more words to your knowledge of Chinese," his teacher said, looking pleased.

Each day was a lucky day and a celebration. He was convinced he'd become something more than just a foreign devil. To most men from both the West and East, women were for pleasure and to be breeding machines—each culture just went about it differently. On the other hand, he had transcended both cultures.

Instead of using his girls like objects, he treated them as individuals. They still read together each night and discussed poems. When plays came to Ningpo, they went. Robert and the girls grew closer.

Years later, Robert bought the house in Ningpo. He had the front door dismantled and the stove crated up with the woodcarvings and the lanterns. He kept all these items in storage behind his mansion in Peking. On lonely nights, and there were many, he'd take a pot of tea and go into the storage room and sit next to that stove. He'd smoke an Egyptian cigarette and remember.

Chapter 22

Bugs were everywhere, and the hotter it got the more they resembled a horde of blood sucking barbarians. The winter of 1856 was history and spring was flourishing. By the time summer arrived, the bugs would be in the food. If Robert left his mouth open, they ended in there too. The heat and humidity increased the sewer stench making it undesirable to breathe the putrid air through his nose.

The previous summer, before he had stayed with Patridge, he awoke in the night gasping for air as if his lungs had filled with hot, smelly water, and he was drowning.

As temperatures and humidity soared, he washed often. In Ireland, his family bathed once a month during the winter and twice in the summer. They had a large wooden tub. Every other Saturday the entire family carried buckets from the spring into the house where the water was heated and the tub half filled. The oldest bathed first. By the time Robert's turn came, the water had turned gray and there was a grease line where the water's surface met the tub's wood. Robert wasn't the youngest. Number twelve bathed last.

Since coming to China, he had taken up the habit of bathing with a damp cloth. Though he had a large tub, he didn't want the girls to work that hard heating the water. Instead, he used a bucket wide enough to fit his feet and a tin cup to pour lukewarm water onto his naked body. Then he soaped and rinsed.

"I have watched you do this before, Robert," Ayaou said from the kitchen doorway. "I kept my mouth shut, because I thought this is what you wanted. You should just go to the bathhouse. It costs the price of three eggs, and the water is clean and hot."

Robert stood with his feet crimped in the bucket and water running down his naked skin. A mosquito landed on the back of his right hand. He swatted it away. "Bathhouse?" he said, bewildered. "Where is this place?"

"It's on the next street behind the teahouse."

"I'm going to try it," he replied. "What is it like? There are no bathhouses where I grew up."

"How can that be?" she said. "England is a powerful empire. You must be wrong."

"No, I'm not. In England before 1800 the church outlawed bathing as a mortal sin."

Ayaou's mouth dropped open. "And I thought the English were sensible people since they had so much power. I am disappointed, Robert. This means the English are not as civilized as the Chinese. If your God's church said bathing was a sin, the British made a bad choice in the God they worship."

"Being clean has nothing to do with being powerful or what god is worshiped," Robert replied. When he picked up the pitcher of rinse water and poured it over his head, he gasped from the cold hitting his warm skin. "Hand me that towel, Ayaou."

While drying himself, he said, "Queen Elizabeth bathed maybe three times in her life, and in 1588 her navy defeated the Spanish Armada, which established England as the dominant sea power in the world."

"England must be a smelly place," she said. "If you have to stink to be powerful, maybe the Chinese should stop bathing too."

"Your logic defies explanation," he replied. He was rewarded with a blank look.

"Logic?" she asked. "What does that mean?"

On Saturday Ayaou led him to the public bath behind the teahouse. The tiger stove that heated the water for tea also heated water for the bathhouse. They just opened the water taps and let the water poor into the grated traps. From there the water ran through a pipe under the floor toward the baths.

After a long conversation, Ayaou paid the attendant guarding the entrance to the public baths. She had assured him Robert spoke fluent Mandarin and was not like other foreigners. The man tested Robert and was satisfied when he answered several questions. He was allowed in.

That first experience started as a shock. Back home in Ireland when he bathed, he went alone into a small room off the kitchen and stepped into the bathtub everyone else used. He dried himself and dressed before leaving.

When Robert stepped through the door at the back of the teahouse after Ayaou deserted him, he entered a short hall with both men and women coming and going. He joined the line going in on one side of the hall while clean men and women went the other way to the teahouse. He had no idea what to expect. He was the only foreigner. Almost everyone stared at him as if he had just arrived from the moon or maybe Mars.

The hall turned and went down a staircase descending into a room below ground. When the line reached the bottom, the hall branched at the foot of the stairs. Robert relaxed when the women went to the left and the men turned right. He eventually walked through a door into a steamy room with twenty to thirty naked men of all ages. There was a large pool in the center and several big wooden soaking tubs against the walls. Most of the men were in the pool.

A burly, older woman with the arms of a wrestler and stumps for legs stepped forward, demanded that Robert take off his clothes, and hand them to her. "I will see they are brushed clean and sprayed with a jasmine scent to make them fresh," she said. He stared at her waiting hand. She looked like a witch with frizzy, dry hair protruding in all directions. He didn't want to undress in front of her.

"After you take your clothes off, you will get in the number three wooden hot tub and join the two men already there."

For an instant, he was tempted to leave. All he had to do was turn and run. He'd never taken his clothes off in front of a group before and never in front of a woman except for Ayaou and Shao-mei. The only other time anyone had seen him naked was when he was a baby. All his seductions in college had been at night in dark rooms. Usually he'd been half drunk.

He had no desire to be in this room full of strangers, but what would Ayaou say if he left without taking a bath? He was sure if he came back sweaty and dirty, she'd scold him for being stupid and accuse him of cowardice. He thought of what she'd said about the English being a dirty, smelly people. He had to prove her wrong.

Robert pressed his lips together in a rigid, straight line and pulled off his clothing as fast as possible. He stared straight ahead at the wall avoiding the woman attendant's eyes and the eyes of everyone else, who must have been staring at him as they had in the hall. The skin beneath his clothing hadn't seen the sun for most of his life and was a pale, slug white. Only his hands, face and neck were tanned. He must have been a disgusting, sickly sight.

Once naked, he hurried to get in the tub and gasped when he sunk into the steaming water. He was sure it was going to scorch the skin off his bones. With his body below the surface of the dark water, Robert investigated.

On the far side of the room beyond the pool were tables. When a man left the pool, he went to a table and crawled on top where a male or female attendant used a rough towel wrapped tightly around one hand to scrape all the skin clean. Then the massage started, which looked more like a beating. Since he'd never had one before, he did not know what a massage was like.

What was going on in the common pool fascinated him the most. The pool was more like a small community. All he had to do was focus to hear each conversation. On one side of the pool several old men were arguing about the best types of fighting insects. Across from them two younger men were playing a board game of some kind while others watched or waited for their turn to play. A few slept with their heads propped on the side of the pool. Most surprising of all was the singing. Two of the men were singing songs in an unfamiliar peasant dialect.

Then an ancient looking man, stooped, no hair, facial skin sagging as if it were already falling off the bones, was moving toward the pool from one of the wooden hot tubs. He was so close to the end of life, he couldn't lift his feet. He had to slide them along inch by inch on trembling legs. He wasn't alone.

On one side was probably his middle-aged son, who already had gray hair at his temples. On the old man's other side was a young boy about ten, probably his grandson. The father and son were gently helping the grandfather toward the pool, so he could take the next step in his bath. This was a part of the Chinese culture unlike anything Robert had encountered before. It not only cleansed the body, but it helped cleanse the soul too. It made life more bearable.

The look of love and affection on the grandchild's face as he looked up at his grandfather put a lump in Robert's throat and tears in his eyes. He dipped his head under the hot water to wash the evidence of his emotions away before anyone noticed.

Robert was hooked and resolved to get over his embarrassment. If he hadn't walked through that door and forced himself to strip naked in front of the female attendant—something no one would have done back home—he would never have discovered this precious jewel of life.

It never stopped impressing Robert how much dirt and dead skin those attendants at the massage tables scraped off him each Saturday. Before going to the baths, he must have carried several pounds of the filth with him.

Once he was used to being clean, it was difficult to be dirty again.

It became a ritual that every Saturday he went early to bathe, be scraped clean and pummeled on the massage table until he ached.

After his bath, he spent time in the teahouse taking part in the traditional Chinese *lao-jen ch'a*, the old man's tea ceremony and was introduced to the game of *Weiqi*, known in English as Go. The first time he sat at a table where the game was played, he watched. The second time, he asked questions. One of the men playing was a poet and the other a watercolor artist.

"This game is not for ordinary people," the poet said. "It is complicated. You must have a strong mind to survive."

"Would you like to learn the game?" the artist asked.

"Tell me about the game's history. Then I want to learn," Robert replied.

"It is believed that the game was created by Emperor Yao more than two thousand years ago to help his son Dan Zho learn how to think."

"Others say the game was created as early as four thousand years ago during the Shang Dynasty," the poet said. "No one knows the truth. *Weiqi* is a game where the two players start out equal. It is based on Confucianism, which stresses the rule of Golden Mean that people should not go to extremes. You will learn this game teaches you that if you want to take something from others, you first need to give up something of your own." Although Robert lost many games of

Weiqi, eventually he started to improve and win. He even bought a set and taught his girls to play.

In time, he shared tables with scholars, artists, and workers. He joined in the discussions, which ranged from Imperial politics to which governor was cheating the Emperor the most to who had the best prices for fish that day. His favorite discussions were those that centered on Chinese literature.

The tea boy took care of all the tables, and he never moved from his spot. He filled everyone's cups from a teapot that had a three-foot spout. The spout waved above everyone. The boy managed to fill the cups with boiling water without spilling a drop or burning anyone. At first, having a stream of boiling water appear from above made Robert nervous, but he got used to it.

Against one wall was the person-tall tiger stove. It was made of brick but shaped and painted like a tiger. Near the front were the *tiger's eyes* that were two faucets where containers were filled with boiled water to be carried home. The containers were placed on the tiger's mouth, which was a deck. Inside the tiger's jaws he saw the flames, which looked like bright-orange tongues. At the far end of the stove, a man was feeding coal to the fire.

"Ayaou," Robert asked one Saturday morning before he left for his weekly bath, "why do they spend so much effort and fuel to boil the water people buy?"

She looked surprised. "Do they boil drinking water in England?" she asked, a suspicious look in her eyes.

"No. We just take it from the nearest well, creek or river. We only heat it to cook food like soup or to boil tea. The water we drink at home comes from a spring near our house."

"Smelly and stupid too," she retorted. "Don't the English know if you don't boil the water, you will get the running sickness?"

"Running sickness?" he asked.

"Yes, if you drink water that is not boiled, you will be running to the chamber pot to empty yourself. You will wither up and die."

"But what does boiling water have to do with that?"

She stared at him as if he'd lost his mind. "The Chinese have done it forever," she said. "No one drinks cold water. If it is not hot, you do not drink it or you stand a chance of getting sick. The boiling cleanses the water so you will not get sick."

Robert was baffled. How did boiling the water keep you from getting sick?

She huffed and threw her arms into the air. "You foreign devils are hopeless, Robert. Trust me. Do not drink water that has not been boiled and do not take the word of anyone telling you a glass of cold water was boiled. Now get on your way to the teahouse and get your bath. You stink. You must have been eating that yellow colored stuff you call cow cheese. This week you smell sour."

She was right. Mrs. Winchester had received a shipment of her favorite cheese, Port-du-Salut, produced by Trappist monks in the Brittany region of France. Her husband had a friend at the monastery that shipped them a crate each year. The cheese came in thick cylinders nine or ten inches in diameter with an orange rind and a pale-yellow middle. Robert had snacked on it all week at the consulate.

As he walked to the teahouse, he tried to smell what she smelled but couldn't. How could eating cheese make him sour?

Tea was an indispensable part of life in China. A Chinese saying identified the seven basic daily necessities as fuel, rice, oil, salt, soy sauce, vinegar and tea. China was where the custom of tea drinking started. It was here that he was introduced to his favorite green tea, *Lung-ching*, Dragon Well.

It was in teahouses that Robert gained knowledge of politics and everyday life in China. Gossip about the Imperial government in Peking was also a favorite topic.

"Did you hear about the thefts from the Forbidden City?" an old toothless man said. Robert was one of six at the table that day. He'd finished his bath and was enjoying several cups of tea in a relaxing atmosphere of friendship.

"I heard about a theft a few weeks back," a middle-aged butcher replied. "They said it was a mystery. A priceless jade hairpin vanished from the Empress Tzu Tsi's palace as if it had been an ice cube and melted away. No one could figure out what happened. If that is what you are talking about, I have heard it."

"No," the toothless man said. "That is old news. That was the first theft. Now there has been a second. The first theft is not worth talking about anymore. This time, they say it was a clock, a gift from the czar of Russia. It was there on the wall in the morning and gone in the afternoon. The Forbidden City's Bannermen closed all the gates. The eunuchs searched every building inside the vermilion walls before the gates were opened again. Nothing was found. Not a clue. Imagine that this happened inside the Forbidden City where eyeballs have eyeballs. If there is a thief inside the Forbidden City, it must be a ghost."

"Ghost, hah," the butcher said. "Nonsense. That hairpin was more valuable than a clock. The hairpin had a string of pearls hanging from it. A thing that tells time is worth nothing. Who cares what time it is? When the sun is up, it is daylight, and when the sun is out of the sky, it is night. We work until our work is done no matter if it is light or dark."

"Not this clock," the toothless man said, not to be outdone. "They say this clock had diamonds and rubies for numbers. The even numbers were diamonds and the odd were rubies."

"Whoever this thief is, he will get caught and lose his head," a silk merchant said. "It has to be one of the eunuchs— a stupid one who will not get a chance to enjoy the wealth gained. You cannot spend money when your head is not attached to your neck. Who else lives inside the Forbidden City other than thousands of concubines and the Emperor? The soldiers guarding the city never pass beyond the second gate."

"It would take a band of thieves to pull this off. One eunuch working alone could not do it."

The rumors about thefts taking place inside the Forbidden City and speculations about who was doing it continued. Every few weeks there was a fresh theft. Each item taken was always worth a small fortune. Sometimes months slipped by before a new theft took place. Robert was sure the rumors inflated the values of the pieces taken, but to a common Chinese anything inside the Forbidden City was priceless—including the chamber pots. "Did you know that when the Emperor takes a shit, he has a dozen eunuchs waiting to wipe his ass? The thief is probably one of those eunuchs. How would you like to spend your life cleaning the Emperor's ass?"

On another day, one of his teahouse friends, a man who earned his living making fresh tofu juice from soybeans each morning, invited Robert to take an empty seat at his table.

After he sat, the tofu juice merchant said, "Don't look, Robert, but there is a man sitting at another table in the corner behind you who has been staring at you. I have noticed this strange behavior from the same man before. When you arrive on Saturdays, he is always waiting as if he is expecting you. He sits at the same table with his back against the wall. Before you arrived, he was staring into his teacup. After you arrived, his eyes glued on you."

Robert's desire for tea fled, and his stomach felt as if it were shriveling into a prune. "Is this man Chinese?" he asked.

"No, he looks like he could be a Japanese sailor. He also looks as if he has other foreign blood in his body. He is big like a foreign devil, and his eyes are not right. The look on his face is like that of a man waiting for something to happen. It is strange. I thought I should mention it."

"I thank you for your concern," Robert said. This stranger sounded like the man he'd seen skulking outside his house in the dark that time he'd opened the bedroom window to breathe fresh air. He remembered the mugger with the club. He also thought of the man who attempted grabbing Ayaou, and the two men who had hunted him in the fog to press him into a British naval ship. Was this the beginning of another attempt to ruin his life?

He was sure Ward was behind this too. He believed that Ward was the common thread to the threats against his girls and to him. He had to be careful. Only a crazy man goes to such extremes for such a small thing, and by all accounts, Ward was a lunatic. His reputation as a ruthless mercenary was growing.

On the other hand, Ward had many women to take care of his needs. Why waste so much effort to reclaim Ayaou? Why not just demand that Robert pay the five hundred pounds instead?

It took a strong effort not to turn and stare. By the time Robert was ready to leave, the stranger was gone. After that, whenever Robert entered the teahouse, he always managed a casual glance to see if he could spot this person. According to his friends, the stranger never appeared in the teahouse again. As time went by, this bothered Robert more than if the man had been there. What if this stranger had been a spy sent by Ward to gather information on Robert and Ayaou?

He didn't tell Ayaou or Shao-mei about the strange man from the teahouse. He didn't want to scare them. He just reminded them to keep the window shutters closed and the door locked.

It wasn't enough that he worried about strangers coming to ruin his life. Now Ayaou and Shao-mei were exhausted from the daily war with the growing heat leading toward summer.

In the mornings when he awoke, there was a large wet spot on the bamboo mat from his sweat. The girls looked like dehydrated plants. They sat and frantically waved hand fans to generate a breeze. It didn't help. He urged them to rest and put off scrubbing the floors and laundry for cooler days.

He said they could eat out more often, so they didn't have to cook. The sisters refused to cut any of the chores. They hated the idea of a dirty house, soiled clothing and the cost of eating out.

Robert told Guan-jiah about the teahouse stranger. "I want to move to a safer place," he said. "I'm worried for my concubines. I can't protect them when I'm working. Where can we hide?"

"It is wise to be cautious, Master," Guan-jiah replied. "I suggest you talk to a third cousin of mine who owns property outside the city. Maybe you could rent something from him."

Not wanting to alarm the sisters with the truth, Robert told them he wanted to move to an isolated, out-of-the-way place away from the city where the air was cool and fresh. "The city walls cut off the breeze," he said. "It will be better outside."

"That is true," Shao-mei agreed. "We never lived in a city before. It is difficult to get used to the crowds and the smells. It would be good for us and our child to get away."

Robert made plans and Ayaou arranged a reasonable rate from an Uncle. The old man owned a sampan, and he would take Robert house hunting. This uncle's name was Bark.

Uncle Bark was an old toothless man with skin the color of dried leather. His face looked as if it had been shrunk to fit against the bones of his skull. He looked like a shriveled apple. He had to be over seventy, yet his body was stringy muscle. His energy to keep working no matter what the circumstances or temperature impressed Robert. Uncle Bark eventually played a crucial part in keeping Robert alive.

Guan-jiah's cousin guided Uncle Bark and Robert upriver to an abandoned cottage inland from the river beside a creek. The cousin was the opposite of Guan-jiah. Where Guan-jiah was slender, the cousin was short and round. Guan-jiah had Buddha ears, but the cousin's ears were small like dry flat prunes. The cousin's eyes were black beads set close on either side of a thin nose. He looked like a thief, and that made it difficult for Robert to trust him.

The cottage was surrounded by shade trees. It sat on a knoll a dozen feet above the creek about a half-mile from the river. Uncle Bark tied his sampan onto a half rotting dock. They followed a weed-choked path up the slope to the cottage. The glass was gone from the windows. The outside boards had turned gray. Robert saw dry rot. The front door was missing. Piles of dry leaves crunched under his feet as he walked from room to room. Spider webs were everywhere.

The stove in the kitchen had been stolen. The sitting room was large, and it opened to a garden courtyard filled with weeds. Birds had built nests inside the chimney. There was one bedroom and a musty smelling root cellar. There was no sewer stench. That was a blessing. There were almost no bugs or mosquitoes, and it offered privacy from spies.

He walked outside and studied the wreck. Maybe Ningpo wasn't that bad. Maybe the danger he dreaded was imagined.

Maybe Ward had forgotten about Ayaou.

A breeze rustled the trees and blew toward the creek. This welcome breath of nature drove the few mosquitoes away. The temperature cooled immediately. Compared to the hot, stuffy air in Ningpo, this was a slice of paradise. He remembered the miracle Ayaou and Shao-mei had created with the Ningpo house. He was sure the girls could do it again with this place.

"Who lived here before it was abandoned?" Robert asked.

"A foreign missionary named W. M. Lowrie," Guan-jiah's cousin replied.

Robert was speechless for a moment. This was where pirates had killed Lowrie in 1847. This cottage had been abandoned for almost ten years. "Name a price," Robert said.

"Ten yuan a month."

"Too high!" he replied. "I have to travel almost three miles by sampan to reach Ningpo."

"But Ningpo is down river," the cousin responded. "It takes no work to drift in a boat."

"That is correct, but it takes time to travel from here to Ningpo. When I return in the evenings after a hard day of work, it is not easy to row up river."

"But you don't have to do the rowing," the cousin said. "This old man will do all the work. You can sleep and be rested and fresh for your concubines."

Robert pointed at the cottage. "Does that price include a roof, paint, replacement for any rotting wood, doors, windows, and a thorough cleaning?"

"You clean; you repair," the cousin replied.

"Three yuan a month," Robert said.

"Three yuan is robbery! Seven yuan!" Guan-jiah's cousin raised his voice as if in the market. This man was nothing like Guan-jiah. Robert wished Guan-jiah had been here to bargain with this uncouth third cousin of his. He despised the thief already.

Robert turned to the house and pushed against one of the sideboards where he saw the dry rot was bad. His hand almost went through the wall. "Four yuan," he said.

"Six." The cousin shot back.

"Five, and that is my final offer."

The cousin looked embarrassed as Robert pulled his hand out of the hole. The deal was made, but Robert had to make all the repairs.

The next day was a Sunday, and he had Uncle Bark row them to the cottage.

"This is our summer home," Robert said, presenting the view.

Ayaou noisily sucked in her breath then took Shao-mei and Uncle Bark on a silent inspection.

"What are you paying?" Ayaou asked, once the tour finished.

After Robert proudly told her the amount, she said, "You have been robbed. I should have been the one to negotiate the price. Even Guan-jiah would have done better. We should pay no more than three yuan a month. No, I am wrong. Two yuan a month. The man that owns this place is a bandit. Although the woods, bushes and wild plants are lovely, if we do not live here, no one is going to live here. If we are to fix it, he should pay us." She stamped her foot.

Shao-mei said, "Sister, if you are going to explode, I am leaving. I do not want to be a victim of your storm cloud when

265

it bursts." She waddled away to check the creek. Robert wanted to go with her and find a place to hide.

Shao-mei was so huge she looked like a ripe melon ready to burst. Robert hoped the child would be later instead of early or on time. He wanted Ayaou to think the baby was his instead of born from a rape.

Ayaou demanded she be in charge of all repairs. "Because you are a foreigner, people will charge you the highest prices and use the poorest materials," she said.

He planned to have her to take charge anyway.

Two weeks later Robert moved his family into the cottage. In England, the amount of work done to the house would have taken months and cost a fortune. The Chinese workers Ayaou hired were industrious. They swarmed over the ruin of a house like ants and transformed it.

The first morning after moving in and walking down the weed free path to the waiting sampan, Robert handed a loaded revolver to Ayaou. "I want to know you're safe."

"You take it," she said. "There are pirates on the river. I have the shotgun."

Robert pulled another pistol from his jacket pocket. "Not to worry," he said. "I have a weapon."

He sat in the sampan looking at the freshly painted cottage where Ayaou and Shao-mei stood waving. Sunlight winked from the newly installed windows. Gray smoke drifted lazily above the house from the stovepipe. Uncle Bark pushed away from the dock. The sampan drifted out of sight of this safe sanctuary that was so much better than the crowded, menacing, stinking streets of Ningpo. The house was hidden. It wasn't visible from the river. Who could menace them here?

Chapter 23

In the mornings, he spent from nine until noon at the consulate with Master Ping. Knowing that Christianity influenced his culture, he decided to learn about Taoism and Buddhism. They started with the *Dao De Jing* with plans to move onto the *Tao Te Ching* later.

Since Master Ping was not a serious devotee of Taoism or Buddhism but only a shallow dabbler of these ideologies, Robert didn't worry that his teacher would attempt to seduce him away from Christianity. However, Robert was committed to study this spiritual path even if it wasn't his choice. To him it meant opening another door to understand China better.

During the first lesson on Taoism, the *Dao De Jing* was open on the table between them. Robert stared at the beginning lines.

The way, which can be uttered, is not the eternal Way.
The name, which can be named, is not the eternal Name.

"It makes little sense to me, Master," he said.

"That is because to grasp the meaning of the *Way* you must understand how to balance yin and yang. To do that you must understand what emptiness means in relation to your life. It cannot be put into words." Master Ping tapped his chest. "The meaning of the *Way* must be found in here." Then he tapped his skull. "And in here. That is how I understand it. You must learn how to bend with the wind and to allow the river to flow around you when you are standing in the current. The world and all the people live in the river's current. To survive, you must allow it to flow around you, because you cannot change it."

Soon Robert was to be sorely tested, and the Tao entered his life in unexpected ways to keep him sane. Uncle Bark would also play an important role in that lesson.

In the afternoons and late into the evenings, Robert worked as an interpreter for foreign ship captains that didn't speak Chinese. He was fluent in Mandarin and was picking up other Chinese dialects like the one from Ningpo and another from Shanghai. He was also learning Cantonese, which he couldn't speak clearly but understood.

This traveling back and forth on the river was a big bother. Guan-jiah did the shopping in Ningpo, and Robert carried the products to the cottage in Uncle Bark's sampan. He hated the time lost with his girls and looked forward to the end of summer and autumn when he planned moving back to the Ningpo house for the winter.

With Ayaou and Shao-mei, he had discovered unspoiled happiness. Simple things became glorious to treasure like eating a bowl of bland rice porridge with pieces of yam in it or some vegetable he'd never tasted before.

A meal didn't have to be a feast of delicacies to be enjoyed when the girls cooked. Life was close to ideal—at least what Robert saw as ideal at the time. He never imagined that the simple things he once took for granted were splendid when colored with love, which he gorged on daily.

"What is this?" he asked one evening. He leaned over his plate examining the thick stems and dainty leaves of the wok steamed greens Ayaou had cooked with oil, garlic and ginger for one of the dinner dishes.

"Weeds," she said. "The peasants eat them. Because they eat them, they are stronger and have more vitality than people who live in the city. We are now eating peasant food. A peasant can work from before sunrise to well after sundown and still have energy for bedroom activities."

Robert tasted one of the strands. It was crunchy and delicate at the same time. It rather tasted like broccoli, which he had never liked. This was better.

"Eat it, Robert," Shao-mei urged. "It will make your legs like tree trunks, and your sun instrument will grow stronger roots."

"Be quiet, Shao-mei. He has too much already." Ayaou reached for Robert's plate. "You won't like it, Robert. It's better if you don't eat it."

He slapped her hand away. He stuffed another stalk of the dark green leafy vegetable into his mouth and chewed. "I like it," he said. He sat up straight with his back stiff like a board. He opened his eyes wide and smacked his lips. "I can feel it working already. We won't get any sleep tonight."

The girls laughed—a light, carefree sound, which reminded Robert of the Lancashire Handbell Ringers.

Sometimes Robert sensed the undercurrent of jealousy still lurking behind the girls' eyes, but there was never a serious argument in the cottage—at least while he was there. Squabbles were expected but not raging arguments.

The girls greeted him each day when he returned home. This was why he loved sunsets more than mornings. Like a peacock, the sun spread its colored feathers along the horizon in a blaze of fading brilliance. In the shadowy dusk, the girls stood waiting near the water. The moment they saw the sampan or heard Uncle Bark's oar in the water, they'd start cheering. Every return was a surprise and every departure heartache. In the mornings, Uncle Bark rowed down river into the rising sun. Robert hated that glaring, hot orb blinding him when it filled the sky in front of the boat and bounced harsh light off the water.

In the evenings from where he sat in the sampan, Robert saw their silky silhouettes jumping in excitement like puppies greeting a master when he returned home after a long day. It must have been lonely spending so much time at the cottage with no one near. To fill their time, the girls had planted a flourishing garden filled with vegetables and flowers.

When he stepped out of the boat, the girls moved to either side of him. Shao-mei took his left arm and Ayaou his right. Just the touch of their warm skin chased away the flagging energies brought on by the long day at the consulate and the trip upriver.

"Robert," Shao-mei said one evening, "we have a surprise for you. We have worked all week on a new dance we saw once in a Peking opera and have combined it with something else. We had to alter one of your robes to be more in character."

"Yes," Ayaou said, "there is a role for you to play, but we must paint your face first."

"What colors?" he asked. He knew the colors of his face paint revealed what kind of character he was to play.

"Today we are going to paint you blue and white," Shao-mei replied. When Robert studied her expression, he saw there was a mischievous look in her eyes. Ayaou was better at hiding her feelings. Shao-mei was like glass.

Blue and white meant he was to be cruel and wicked. Robert wondered if there would be a twist added, so he could act out of character. Maybe he would get to spank one of them. That would be interesting. They hadn't done anything like that before.

"And what color is your face going to be painted?" he asked.

"Black," Ayaou said with enthusiasm. Black meant she was going to be impulsive. Just thinking of the possibilities excited him.

"My nose is going to be white," Shao-mei said. "I insisted." That meant she was going to be full of laughter and be the fun of the little family comedy—for he was sure it would be more comedy than drama. The girls were usually too lighthearted for anything serious or dark.

"That's all you are going to paint," he said, "just your nose?"

"No, silly," she replied. "My face will be black like Ayaou's face, but I will have a touch of white. I want to be wicked too."

"And what are we performing tonight?" he asked.

"Something Ayaou discovered by Tuan Cheng Shih, who lived during the Tang Dynasty," Shao-mei said.

"Be quiet, sister," Ayaou said. "That is supposed to be a surprise."

Robert had studied Tuan Shih's *Miscellaneous Record of You Yang* with Master Ping. He took a wild guess what they were going to enact. "Does this little comic drama of yours have a girl who loses her parents and is deprived of her rightful place in life by evil relatives?" he asked. He thought of the Brothers Grimm and their collection of stories that included Cinderella. He knew the first Cinderella story had originated in China—not Germany. The Chinese version had been published a thousand years before the Grimm brothers had been born.

270

"You will have to wait to find out," Ayaou said. She turned to Shao-mei. "Close your mouth sister. It is about to spill the surprise."

He knew what they were doing wouldn't be the same as the Chinese Cinderella. Ayaou always altered the stories so the result turned into an orgy after they went to bed. She planned these rare comedy dramas when it was her night to sleep with him. Shao-mei didn't have Ayaou's wild, inventive imagination.

What they planned turned out to be a riot of laughter. It kept Robert up late. This made going to the consulate the next morning more difficult. He endured the next day's exhaustion just to spend an hour or two with his girls in a room full of fun.

Every morning was the opposite of his evenings. When he left, they accompanied him to the boat in a gloomy silence. Before he climbed into the sampan, they took turns hugging and kissing him as if he were going to float out of sight and never return.

"Do not fall in the water, Robert," Shao-mei said. "We do not want you to be swallowed by a giant carp."

"Silly, sister," Ayaou said. "There is no carp large enough to swallow Robert. All he has to do is roll over on his back and float to Ningpo."

"Then the eels will bite him in the ass," Shao-mei replied. "I do not want to see his smooth ass full of puncture wounds. Stay in the sampan, Robert. Do not go swimming. It is more fun to eat fried eels than have them eat you."

English was never spoken at home, and Robert did not intend to teach Ayaou or Shao-mei his language. He didn't want either of them to learn anything about his culture, its religions, its customs, its philosophies, or its beliefs. He wanted to immerse himself in their world, the Chinese world—this Confucius, Taoist place where he'd finally found some peace of mind.

He knew the truth and realized he'd fled to China, not to escape his sins as he'd originally thought, but to find a different world. He had found exactly that in these two girls.

Most evenings after the language lessons, Robert played his violin while Ayaou danced and Shao-mei played the *pee pah*, which she preferred over dancing anyway.

"Tell us a story about growing up in Ireland," Shao-mei asked one night.

"It's no comparison to China," he replied.

"How can that be?" Shao-mei said. "If it is where you were born, it must be a wonderful place." She looked at Robert with doubt as if she suspected he wasn't being honest.

"We don't have time to waste talking about Ireland. It's on the other side of the world. We live in China, so we read Chinese stories, not Irish."

"I agree with Robert," Ayaou said. "It stinks there. They do not take baths. It is a horrible, smelly place populated by crazy people who want nothing but power over others."

Shao-mei pouted and didn't bring the subject up again.

He was selfish wanting to keep them the way they were. He didn't feel they needed anything. They were naturally beautiful, kind and hardworking. What could his culture offer them? They might walk away from him once they learned to read a Bible and listened to a Christian missionary.

To keep them occupied he guided them in adapting songs so the two musical instruments worked together in harmony. The girls taught him Chinese songs, which they sang together. His favorite was a humorous song called *Sour Grapes*. The girls fell on the floor laughing every time he sang it.

With the love of two women, his longevity was assured. He thanked God every day for bringing them into his life. If this was living in sin, he wanted to sin to stay alive. He couldn't imagine living any other way. He had discovered his true God in China. This God showed him that what was natural and universal prevailed.

It was in early May when Shao-mei made her announcement. She came to Robert with both hands spread across her swollen belly. "The baby is going to come soon," she said.

"Are you sure? Has your water broken?"

She stared at him with an odd expression of disbelief on her face. "How can you break water?" she asked.

Robert explained.

She shook her head. "No, there has been no broken water."

"So, you have labor pains."

"He kicks me all the time."

Robert told her what labor pains were. She shook her head again. "Then how do you know?" he asked.

272

"I had a dream that told me we were going to have a boy any day. The doctor said so. Do not tell Ayaou. I want it to be a surprise."

"Was the doctor in your dreams too?" he asked.

She nodded. Her eyes glowed. She waddled away leaving him speechless. After that, he couldn't concentrate. It wasn't easy seeing himself as the father of another man's child—a man he did not like. Shao-mei also expected him to mate with her soon after the baby was born. That was another dilemma Robert had to deal with that he hated to admit he was looking forward to.

Originally, Robert worried because the pregnancy was taking so long. Before leaving Ningpo for the summer cottage, he'd taken Shao-mei to a Chinese doctor. The man held her wrist, felt her pulse and said everything was fine. She was fit as a buffalo. The baby would be healthy too.

Robert couldn't understand how feeling a pulse told the doctor so much. In China, they practiced medicine differently from Britain and Europe. The Chinese had been practicing it for thousands of years, so it had to work.

He made a mental note to have Master Ping teach him something about Chinese medicine. He wanted to understand. There must be a text he could read.

"First you wanted to learn about Chinese customs. Then you wanted to learn about Chinese women. Now you want to learn about Chinese medicine," Tee Lee Ping said. He took a deep breath and sighed. "You are a hungry man. I have never had a student like you."

"I have a voracious appetite."

"I have discovered that." Ping's shoulders drooped. He looked tired. "Where do you want to start?" he asked. "I will do my best."

"At the beginning."

Ping was quiet for a moment. "That means we have to go back before China had a written language to the time of the Yellow Emperor, Huang-ti, about twenty-seven hundred years before your Jesus Christ was born. It has been said that Huang-ti invented traditional Chinese medicine." Ping looked thoughtful and stared at the ceiling.

When he looked down, he said, "You could read Li Shizhen's book, the *Ben Cao Gang Mu*. However, that is a lot to study. He lived three hundred years ago and is considered the greatest physician and pharmacologist in China. There is a famous British man of science who sailed the world to study animals and nature. I heard he referred to Li's book and that he quoted Li in what he wrote."

"Charles Darwin," Robert said. Darwin had published a book in 1839 titled *Journal and Remarks* about his voyage on the *HMS Beagle*. Robert had read it.

"Charles Darwin," Master Ping said. "Yes, I believe that is the name."

"Charles Darwin's voyage of discovery lasted almost five years," Robert said. "He had enough time to read this *Ben Cao Gang Mu*."

"We could spend years on that book. I have seen it, but I have not read it. It is more for men of medicine like this Charles Darwin than for students of literature like us. Li Shizhen spent twenty-seven years writing the *Ben Cao Gang Mu*."

"Wait," Robert said. His mind was spinning. Did he want to do this and abandon the poems and literature he loved to read and discuss? Wasn't it enough of a struggle to understand Taoism and Buddhism? If he added medicine to the soup, that could all be left behind.

"Maybe you could explain to me the difference between the way my people practice medicine and the way the Chinese do. That should quench my thirst."

"I hope so," Ping said. "I understand foreign medicine is designed to fix a person after he is broken, but Chinese medicine focuses on how a person should live his life so he avoids getting sick. To do this you must balance your life by eating good food, exercising in moderation and having a balanced attitude. This is the foundation of health in China. Most foreigners do none of these things. They eat anything, which means bad food. They consume too much alcohol. They do not exercise, and when the body breaks, they run to a doctor and say fix me." He tilted his head at an angle and looked at Robert with expectation.

"What about an example? I don't understand what you mean by eating right."

"Hmm, you want an example." Tee Lee Ping rubbed his chin in thought. His thick, bushy eyebrows lowered and almost covered his eyes. "Ah yes, I have one. Adapting to the seasons is the foundation of good health and healthy aging. Maybe you have noticed as the seasons change, what your concubines put on the table also changes. In the spring and summer, there should be more fruit or vegetables. In the fall and winter, you should see more grain than fruits and vegetables."

"Yes, I've noticed that. Anything else?"

"Where foreign doctors sometimes let blood out of a person when he is sick, Chinese doctors practice *Gua-Sha*, which means they scrape an area of skin near where the suffering takes place. They do this to stimulate the circulation of the blood in that area believing that stimulating the blood will lead to healing. Chinese doctors do not drain blood out of the body as foreign doctors do."

Master Ping threw up his arms and looked frustrated. Robert had never seen him like this before. "I'm sorry," Master Ping said. "I am not a doctor. I teach people how to read and speak Mandarin. I teach Chinese literature. If you want to know more about Chinese medicine, I suggest you read Li Shizhen's book, but do it on your time. I do not feel it would benefit your education regarding the Chinese language or its literature or its people."

That was the end of his education about the difference between Chinese and Western medicine. The next day, they were back to studying Taoism.

To avoid thinking about what fatherhood would do to his life, Robert buried himself deeper in the language lessons and the work at the British consulate. He added hours to his workday and returned home later in the evenings. Most days, when Uncle Bark tied his sampan to the rebuilt dock below the cottage, it was dark as tar out, and Robert expected to hear a baby crying.

He knew the importance the Chinese gave to the birth of a son. If the baby was a boy, he was sure Ayaou would be happy, crushed and threatened at the same time. He felt as if he were sitting on a powder keg, and the fuse was burning slowly toward an explosion.

He decided to start making love to Ayaou more often in the hope she'd get pregnant. The herbs Guan-jiah had found for him to feed Ayaou hadn't worked their magic yet. He prayed that Shao-mei was wrong, and her baby would be a girl. This would help keep harmony in the house. If Guan-jiah was right, it should be a girl. Robert had fed her double doses of the herbs for the last few weeks to insure it.

He worried about providing for two children. He also didn't want to think about how his family in Ireland was going to react when they learned he had a family.

His womanizing and drinking at college was tame compared to having children with two Chinese women. With a sinking feeling in the center of his stomach, he realized he already knew the answer. It would break their hearts. His family would turn their backs on him.

As long as he was with Shao-mei and Ayaou, he could never return home. This truth thrust him into a depression that he managed to hide from his concubines. Another deadline was looming. After the child was born, Shao-mei expected to have intercourse with him. There was going to be an increased risk of more babies. What was he to do? Maybe he should become a eunuch. Guan-jiah knew what to do.

It was late on a Tuesday afternoon, and Robert was working at his desk in the consulate.

"Bob," Captain Patridge said, as he walked into the room.

Robert was surprised to see the captain. It would be three weeks before another scheduled shipment was to pass through Ningpo, and a few months remained until the end of their one-year agreement. Robert was looking forward to that day.

What could be important enough to bring Patridge from his summer home on Zhoushan Island? They shook hands and Robert offered tea, which Patridge declined. He took a newspaper from his back pocket and spread it on Robert's desk.

"I was in Shanghai on business, and I saw this." Tapping an article on the front page of the *North China Herald*, he said, "Take a look."

When Robert saw the subject of the story, his throat constricted. The mercenary general, Fredrick Townsend Ward, was back.

"I knew Ward had returned before the *Herald* wrote about it," Patridge said. "It wasn't until I talked to him that I realized I had to warn you."

A tomb opened inside Robert as if death were approaching. His fear of losing Ayaou to Ward had finally turned into reality.

She had no idea that Ward still owned her. He dreaded the day she found out. He should have told her. She trusted him and keeping this a secret was a betrayal of that trust.

Patridge reached up and drew a line with a finger through one side of his face down toward his mouth. "As well as a dreadful scar here, Ward lost some of his teeth and part of his tongue. His behavior has turned rancid, and Boss Takee is having trouble controlling him." Patridge paused. The expression in his eyes turned to pity. "I'll stop now if you want me to," he said. "You may not want to hear what I have to say next."

"You might as well tell me everything," Robert replied.

Patridge took a long breath then said, "Ward made some powerful accusations against you. He said you stole Ayaou from him, and that a horse thief should be hanged."

"That's a lie!" Anger pushed out the fear. He hated liars. "We had an agreement. I was to pay him the five hundred pounds. She was to be mine. I never had a chance to pay him. He disappeared after he was wounded at Tsingpu. Didn't you tell him I borrowed the money from you? The fact that I did is proof that Ward and I had an agreement."

"That's a large amount to pay for a concubine," Patridge said. "Who'd believe it? Not that I don't." He hastened to add. "But you should reconsider and return Ayaou to him. There are thousands of girls you can buy for less. Besides, you have Shao-mei. Isn't she enough to satisfy you?"

"I'll go to Shanghai and convince Ward," Robert said. His anger made him deaf. He wasn't listening to Patridge. "He can't hold it against me that circumstances robbed us of our chance to complete the transaction."

"It wouldn't be safe for you to confront him. Ward has more scars than we can see. He acted crazy before his defeat. Now he's a raving lunatic. He slaughters his enemies like pinching mosquitoes. He takes wild risks on the battlefield."

"Maybe he is the one behind the two attacks on me and the one on Ayaou," Robert said.

Patridge looked stunned. "What are you saying? What attacks?"

"A man tried to hit me with a club outside my house one morning. The next incident was when a man tried to grab Ayaou when she was out shopping. She didn't recognize him, but he knew her name. The last assault was by two men that attempted pressing me into a British naval ship bound for the Americas. I escaped in the fog."

Patridge put a hand on Robert's arm, "Why didn't you tell me this happened? You are an asset for my company. We would have done something to protect you. It's not easy to recruit people with your skills in your position."

"How will you protect me against Ward?"

"When did the first incident take place?" Patridge asked.

Robert told him.

"I don't think Ward orchestrated any of this," the captain said. "When the first encounter happened outside your house, he was delirious with a fever fighting for his life. He was in no shape to be plotting against you. Ward would not have you pressed into a naval ship to serve before the mast. If he wanted to make you suffer, he would do something worse. He would want to inflict the pain himself. He doesn't pay someone else to do his dirty work. He does it himself."

"What about his second-in-command, Henry Burgevine? I had a run in with him before he took a shipment of coolies to California. He wasn't happy with me. He could have arranged it."

"That's a possibility," Patridge replied, "but I believe those encounters were coincidences. You are imagining things, Robert. You were in the wrong place at the wrong time."

Robert shook his head. "No, I'm not imagining things. I overheard the men who tried to kidnap me. There was a thick fog. I was standing close to them, but they couldn't see me. I heard enough. Someone paid them to press me into that British man-of-war. Someone wants to ruin my life."

Patridge was quiet for a moment, before he said, "Have you made any other enemies. Have you run up gambling debts?"

Robert laughed. "I do not gamble. I work and go home to my girls. Other than my Chinese language teacher, there is no one else in my life. I don't even go to church anymore."

"I believe what happened to you and Ayaou were not related. Maybe Henry Burgevine was behind the one attempt to press you into the British navy. I will not accept that Ward was connected to any of them. Life can be like that, Robert. People are mugged and kidnapped daily. It can happen to anyone. Your current problem is with Ward. He wants Ayaou back. His ego won't let him forget. Let's solve this problem, and make it go away. Send her to him."

"I won't send her back," Robert said. "I'll seek help. I'll go to Governor Sir John Bowring in Hong Kong. I'll enlist his support. Then I'll confront Ward with the backing of the British navy. I'll pay him the five hundred pounds. He will back off. He won't want the governor angry with him. After all, I do work for the British, and Ward is an American. I talked to Bowring about Ward once, and the governor was not impressed with the man."

"Let me update you," Patridge said. "Ward was wanted for some crime he committed. He was arrested and put in the brig of a warship called the *Chesapeake*. He escaped and managed to make a deal with Admiral Hope. I've no idea how he did it, but he did."

Robert started to speak. He was determined to see the British governor in Hong Kong. He refused to give up Ayaou.

Patridge held up a hand. "Let me finish, Robert. There's more. Ward raised another army of five thousand men and all his officers are American soldiers of fortune. Burgevine also returned from California and resumed his position as second-in-command."

"I'll go to Shanghai and challenge him to a duel," Robert said.

"Don't talk nonsense. He will have you killed. Then he will take both Ayaou and Shao-mei. Their lives will be unbearable, and where will you be?" he asked, then answered the question. "I'll tell you where you'll be. You will be dead and no use to me." His face turned red.

Robert was struck speechless as he watched Patridge sit and take a few calming breaths. "Listen," Patridge said, "I don't want to lose you. My company has increased its profits kindly because of your efforts to help smuggle goods into the country. You've made connections with the Chinese I could never have made. You're gaining a reputation as a man whose word can be trusted. If no one learns you are working for me, you are going to gain rank quickly while working for the British consulate. The higher you go, the more valuable you will be. We will pay you twice as much. That's four times what you are paid to work for the British."

"When the time comes," Robert said, "nothing will stop me from ending our agreement." Feeling desperation clawing at him, he said, "Why, I'll offer Ward twice the amount we agreed to."

"There isn't a woman in China worth a thousand British pounds. Come on, Hart!That's more than six thousand yuan!"

"I've no choice."

Patridge stood and placed a hand on Robert's shoulder. "Bob, in the last month with naval support from Admiral Hope, Ward took the Taiping city of Kaochiao. The Imperials gave Chinese citizenship to Ward and a third-rank mandarin's button. He's no longer just a mercenary general. The Chinese gave him the military rank of a colonel in the Imperial army. His army has been named the Ever Victorious Army. Ward has finally delivered where the Chinese generals couldn't."

"You believe I have no power to fight him."

"Exactly my point."

"Thank you for your concern, Captain, but my mind remains set."

"You're still going," Patridge said. "You're a fool! You have disappointed me. I'm sure your friends will feel the same."

"I have no friends in China," he replied, and mentally corrected himself when he thought of William Martin, the American missionary in Ningpo, and William Lay in Shanghai. Too bad he couldn't count on Horatio Lay as a friend.

Yes, those two men were his friends. He believed that he could count on them if he needed help. There was also Guan-jiah. The eunuch's loyalty was a blessing.

"That's not true," Patridge said. "I'm your friend. I want what's best for you."

Robert didn't trust Patridge but decided to use him anyway. The captain had given him another reason to keep his private life to himself. He believed Patridge wouldn't be here if he didn't think it benefited his pocket, so he said, "Then I need your support as a friend."

Patridge nodded. "I'll do my best. I'll keep Ward off your back if you agree to extend our arrangement for two years."

Two more years. Robert hated the idea but what choice did he have? "How do you intend to control Ward?" he asked. "If a thousand pounds isn't enough to pay this bastard, what is? You just told me that Boss Takee is having trouble with him too."

"Boss Takee is losing his position in Shanghai," Patridge replied. "I will deal with Ward. Leave it to me. Do we extend our business arrangement beyond the first year?"

If he didn't say yes, he stood a chance of losing Ayaou, Shao-mei and his life to Ward. On the other hand, how could he trust Patridge, who was using this situation with Ward to imprison Robert's soul? The answer was that he couldn't trust the man, but he had no choice. "How long will you be in Ningpo?" he asked.

"Until tomorrow, when my ship returns to the Lookong receiving station. We're picking up a cargo of rice. The price is high in Canton again."

"I'll have an answer for you tomorrow morning before you leave. Which ship?"

"I'll show you," Patridge said. He led the way to the riverbank and indicated a brig sitting in the anchorage. It was flying a British flag.

Robert already knew he had to accept, but he couldn't bring himself to do it then.

At two in the morning the next day, a noise woke Robert from a sound sleep. He listened carefully to identify it. It sounded like a stomach in distress. The grumbling was unmistakable. He listened to his stomach. It was quiet. He was careful not to wake Ayaou when he listened to her. It wasn't her either. Shao-mei slept in the living room, so it couldn't be her. Her small bed was in a far corner.

He heard the sound again. It must be her, but how could he hear her stomach when she was so far away? The bedroom door was also closed. He went to the open window and stood next to it with his back flat against the wall. He listened for the night sounds. There was no breeze. The crickets were silent. That worried him. He depended on the insects as his first warning. He heard a frog, but it wasn't close to the cottage.

Then he heard what sounded like someone standing outside the window. The sound was similar to a person shifting weight from foot to foot. His heart beat faster.

He didn't want to disturb Ayaou. What if he were imagining this? It had happened before. Episodes similar to this had started a few weeks after the battle with the Taipings. The first happened soon after the attempt from the lone assailant in the fog—the thug that tried to hit him with a club. Sometimes weeks went by and nothing happened before another nightmare arrived like a demon from hell. This was the first time at the cottage. He was disappointed. He had hoped the demons had stayed in Ningpo.

He returned to the bed and sat. He glanced toward the closed door to the bedroom that led to the living room. There was the shadowy figure of a man standing there. The body shape looked like Ward. Robert's heart started to pound. He fumbled for his pistol on the floor next to his side of the bed. He never felt safe without it. He always kept it close.

He cocked the pistol. He wanted to pull the trigger, but he didn't. What if the dark figure standing there was Shao-mei walking in her sleep? When he stood and walked toward the shadowy silhouette, it vanished. Then he stood in the middle of the room listening to the pounding of his heart and the rapid sound of his breathing.

"Are you all right?" Ayaou said from the bed.

"Yes," he replied, and held the pistol against his chest so she couldn't see it. He didn't want to scare her. "I have to use the chamber pot. Go back to sleep." He heard her sigh.

When he was sure she was sleeping, he went outside and searched around the house but found nothing. Before he went back inside, he looked toward Uncle Bark's sampan. Uncle Bark was sitting in the sampan watching him. His hair was a mess. He looked like he had been having a bad dream too. Robert waved and went into the cottage.

Uncle Bark had heard Robert leave the cottage. It didn't take much to wake Uncle Bark. He hadn't slept through a night for decades. The slightest sound that was out of place could wake him. There had been too much violence and death in his life.

He had watched Robert come outside with the pistol in his hand. Once Robert was back inside the cottage, Uncle Bark put down the machete he was holding. He listened to the night sounds until he was satisfied that everything was as it should be.

Chapter 24

June 12 would be branded in Robert's memory until death.

He had a lot on his mind while Uncle Bark rowed the sampan upriver toward the cottage. The Chinese Imperial officials were nervous because a Taiping army was in the countryside near Ningpo and Robert should have been nervous too.

Instead, he yawned and checked his pocket watch. An hour remained until sunset and he was anxious to see his girls. Due to the rocking motion of the sampan, he felt as if he were a baby in a cradle being lulled to sleep. He closed his eyes.

The week had crawled since Captain Patridge's disagreeable visit. The business relationship continued with one change—when Ward was no longer a threat, it ended. Robert had insisted though Patridge might be motivated to keep Ward stirred up about Ayaou.

Shao-mei, on the other hand, was overdue. Nine months and a few weeks had slipped by since Payne Hollister had raped her. Robert was worried though she wasn't. She trusted the Chinese doctor and felt everything was perfectly safe.

"What are we going to name our child, Robert?" she said a few days earlier. The tone of her voice and the expression on her face convinced him she believed he was the father and the rape never took place. She had deliberately forgotten it.

Robert was impressed with how the mind, like clay, was so malleable. Maybe what she believed wasn't such a bad thing. He decided not to correct her. Why bring back pain? "Wait until the child is born," he replied, "Then we will all select a name?"

"I want to call him *Juan Qu*," she said, with a faraway look in her eyes. "I am sure he will look like his father." She reached up and ran her fingers through Robert's hair. "He will have curly hair like you." She wanted to name the child Curly because of his hair.

He ignored his brooding thoughts and admired the old man moving the boat effortlessly up river as if he were decades younger. Robert had offered to help, but Uncle Bark ignored him. He hoped he had the same stamina when he was in his seventies.

Uncle Bark's sole belongings were the clothes on his back, the sampan, a machete and a long, thin knife for cleaning fish. He had watched the old man eat several times and doubted he'd ever eaten enough to fill his stomach. Ayaou tried to get him to eat more. He refused by ignoring her. Robert would have starved on that much food.

The old man seldom spoke in the mornings. However, on the trips upriver, he poured out rich and sometimes bizarre snapshots of his life that never connected. The stories had no beginnings or endings. They were about one tragedy after another as if they were a continuous series of fierce storms. Listening to Uncle Bark, Robert learned much of what was going on in the common people's lives in China, and how they coped with tragic situations.

One story that stood out was the time Uncle Bark's family was starving, and he had no more daughters to sell. To curb their hunger they ate clay, grass and weeds. There was a drought and there wasn't much grass or weeds to be found except near the river. "It's as if the fish in the river sensed our hunger," Uncle Bark said, "and went into hiding."

The old man never did say what happened to his family. The one time he asked, Uncle Bark fell silent. Robert assumed he'd lost his family and the pain was too much. He didn't ask again.

Usually Uncle Bark joined them for the evening meal inside the cottage. After eating, he returned to his boat. On the trips up-and-down river, Robert sat out of the sun under the sampan's shelter while the old man stood on a plank in the stern under the relentless glare of the sun and rocked the boat with his oar like paddle.

In the mornings, there was always a package of food wrapped in paper for Uncle Bark. Robert suspected that was what Ayaou paid him. He'd do little more than fish during the day but was always waiting to take Robert home. He liked Uncle Bark. There was an indescribable internal peace the old man carried with him. It was as if he had gathered all the pain from his life and tossed it into the river so the current carried it away. He reminded Robert of a Taoist, or at least what he understood a devotee of Taoism to be like. Uncle Bark had been born on a boat. He would probably die on one.

Robert's Chinese lessons with Master Tee Lee Ping had moved on from the *Dao Dee Jing* to the *Tao Te Ching*, which had eighty-one chapters and used about five thousand Chinese characters. Since Robert only knew a few hundred characters, the lessons had slowed to a painful pace. He was forced to expand his written Chinese vocabulary and was determined to succeed.

That morning, he had paused in front of the mirror to straighten his bow tie and felt unhappy with his curly thicket of hair, which made him look like a wild beast. He envied the Chinese their straight hair and wished there were a way to iron out his curls.

"What is wrong?" Ayaou asked, as she came into the room.

"My hair," he said. "The barbers don't know how to cut it."

"Barbers?"

"They don't cut it the way I want. It's either too short, or they leave too many curls."

"Robert, your hair is fine. Just leave it alone."

"I agree," Shao-mei said. Robert's eyes went to her stomach. She was huge—more than huge, gigantic. The baby could arrive any minute. Maybe she carried twins. However, the Chinese doctor said there was only one, and it was going to be big because of Robert's dragon seed. How could the doctor know all that by just holding her wrist? The man could be wrong.

"I dream about having curly hair." Shao-mei fluffed up her straight hair and twisted the long strands into curls. "If I could trade with you, I would." When she let go, her hair fell like a sheet. "Our baby boy will have curly hair like yours. Everyone will be jealous."

It was probably true the baby would be born with curls, because Payne Hollister had more curls than Robert. "Get the scissors, Shao-mei," Ayaou said. "I will fix his hair." Shao-mei ran off and came back with scissors.

"Have you ever-cut hair before?" he asked.

"As the oldest daughter, I cut everyone's hair in the family." She pulled over a stool and had him sit on it. He lost sight of himself in the mirror. Shao-mei stood on the tips of her toes and walked around him getting excited. Ayaou started cutting and large clumps of hair fell on his shoulders, lap and floor. He wondered when she was going to finish and had visions of ending up bald.

"Oh my, Ayaou," Shao-mei's voice went low. "Are you sure of this? I can see the scalp in places."

"What?" Robert jerked upright

Ayaou pushed him down. "Sit still. I almost cut your ear off."

"No! I'm going back to the barber!"

"If you keep frowning like that," Ayaou said, "you are going to age and have lines like rivers on your forehead."

"Oh, Ayaou, look what you've done to the back of his head!" Shao-mei said, making a hissing sound.

"Stop teasing him, Shao-mei. Do you see what you are doing? He is puffing up like a pigeon and ruffling his feathers." After a few more cuts, Ayaou brushed the hair from his shoulders and stepped back. "Done. You look wonderful."

When Ayaou went to the kitchen to get the broom, Shao-mei whispered, "Did you know that every Lunar New Year, our Aunt Grass bought each of us a moon cake filled with sweet red beans? Well, if we did not eat fast enough, Ayaou snatched them from us and gobbled them down. She got away with it the first year. After that, we learned to eat faster. Our younger sister, Lan, never learned. She wanted to make her cake last. She hid it under some clothing and daily took one small bite. Ayaou kept hunting for the hiding place if she knew there was some left." Shao-mei smiled causing her dimples to go deeper?"See what I mean. You should not have trusted her."

He went to the mirror and saw a Chinese man. Ayaou had thinned his hair so much the curls had disappeared. When Ayaou came back and wanted his comment, he said it was innovative. He didn't tell her he was unhappy with it.

"What does innovative mean?" she asked.

"It's a great haircut." He lied.

When Robert went outside to get into Uncle Bark's sampan, the old man looked at his head and grunted. "Good haircut," he said. "You will be cooler on hot days. Put your hat on. You do not want the sun to burn your scalp."

Robert's chin was resting against his chest when he awoke. He jerked his head and wiped drool from his mouth. He'd fallen asleep. He was working too many hours and not getting enough rest. The first thing he saw when his vision cleared was Uncle Bark working the sampan's oar propelling the craft upriver toward the cottage. Robert had been dreaming about the haircut from that morning. He smiled. This time his dream had been pleasant.

"What do you think of this, Uncle Bark?" he asked. He launched into one of the *Tao's* six passages. *"The Valley Spirit never dies. It is named the Mysterious Female. And the doorway of the Mysterious Female is the base from which Heaven and Earth sprang. It is there within us all the while; draw upon it as you will, it never runs dry."*

The sampan was turning off the river and into the creek leading to the cottage. Uncle Bark stared at Robert. He saw that the old man was thinking about his reply. Just as he opened his mouth to speak, something unusual caught Robert's attention. He saw smoke billowing into the sky about where the cottage was situated. Alarmed, he left the shelter and stood.

Uncle Bark followed Robert's gaze and noticed too. He started to row harder. There was the sound of a shotgun blast.

"Hurry!" Robert said. Grabbing a long pole from the bottom of the boat, he thrust it into the shallow creek and pushed to speed the sampan along. His mouth had gone dry. He was sure the smoke was coming from the cottage. "Oh my God!" he said.

Robert put down the pole and checked the loads in his pistol. When the sampan came into sight of the dock, there was a long flat-bottomed boat already there with two men in it. The boat looked like it was full of loot from the cottage. The two men had their backs to the sampan and didn't see it.

He heard Uncle Bark mumble a word that sounded like pirates. Then the sampan rammed into the creek bank where it stuck in the mud. The old man grabbed his machete and leaped ashore.

Robert saw movement behind the thick bushes and trees. He lifted the pistol and aimed at the two in the flat-bottomed boat. One of the pirates turned and revealed a heavily pockmarked face. When he saw Robert, the man's eyes widened in shock. He grabbed for a musket. Robert was faster and fired a shot into his chest. The pirate flipped into the water.

The second pirate jumped out of the boat and ran toward the cottage yelling warnings. Uncle Bark stepped from behind a tree and used his machete to split the man's head as if it were a melon. The body stumbled forward a few more steps before sprawling face down.

Reloading the pistol, Robert advanced on the cottage.

Three men broke from behind the burning building and charged. Uncle Bark took off running to meet them. Robert stopped, took careful aim and shot one man in the face. Uncle Bark collided with the second man, who must have been fifty years younger than him. Uncle Bark's arms were like corded hemp. He slapped the other man's sword aside and cut him across the middle disemboweling him. The third man turned and fled. Robert fired a hasty shot at his back but missed. An eye blink later, the man was out of sight.

Uncle Bark and Robert arrived at the cottage. It was engulfed in roaring flames. The old man grunted and pointed at the pistol. Robert reloaded while the old man stood watch with the machete and his eight-inch fish knife.

A scream sounded up creek. Both Uncle Bark and Robert ran toward the sound. The old man moved ahead of Robert in a burst of speed. His arm whipped back and forward in a blur. The fish knife left his hand. Then he ran between two trees and leaped out of sight like a wild deer.

Robert had to force his way through the thick brush and stumbled on a man trashing about. Uncle Bark's eight-inch fish knife was protruding from his throat. The pointed end of the blade was showing through the back of the man's neck. The pirate's eyes were bulging and blood bubbled from his mouth.

Robert reached down, grabbed the knife and pulled it from the dying man's throat. For good measure, he twisted the blade on its way out. The man waved his arms and lifted his head off the ground. Robert placed a foot on the man's chest and held him down. With a sucking sound, the blade popped free.

When Robert caught up with Uncle Bark, the old man was standing over Ayaou's prone body. The old man was holding off four men with his machete. Robert took up a position and fired. The brains of the first man he shot splashed into the face of the man behind him. The other three ran off. Robert stopped beside Uncle Bark and handed him the bloody knife.

"Ayaou!" Robert got down on his knees. He pulled her into his arms. She felt like a rag doll. There was no sign of blood. She looked pale. He put his ear to her chest and felt relief when he heard her heart.

"Ayaou," he said. "Where's Shao-mei?"

"Come, Robert, the fight is not over," Uncle Bark said. "The pirates might come back. Reload that weapon and bring Ayaou with us. Let us move!" He ran off.

Robert's hands shook as he reloaded the pistol. He took hold of Ayaou again. She opened her eyes. They were empty as if someone had poured the life out of her. Her lips moved, but Robert couldn't understand her. He leaned down and put his ear next to her mouth. "Go find Shao-mei," she said. He jerked upright at the sound of a shot from the direction of the creek. Then someone was screaming. Uncle Bark only had the machete and the dagger.

Pulling Ayaou to her feet, Robert attempted to follow Uncle Bark. She held onto his arm and was like an anchor. Letting go, she took a few steps in the opposite direction. He turned to follow and saw her bend and pick up the shotgun. It had been hidden in the brush. "Go find my sister!" she said, and fumbled in her pocket and brought out a handful of shotgun shells.

"I can't leave you here."

"I have this." She shook the shotgun. Before he left, he made sure she had reloaded.

When Robert found Uncle Bark, the old man was battling a giant who stood a foot taller than him and weighed a good two hundred pounds more. The man was pounding at Uncle Bark's machete with a cutlass. He was driving Uncle Bark to his knees.

Robert ran up behind Uncle Bark and shot the pirate in the chest. The giant staggered back with blood pumping out of his chest like a geyser. Robert fired two more shots into his heart. The giant collapsed to his knees, swayed back and forth and fell like a tree.

"The others are escaping." Uncle Bark wiped his forehead with the back of a hand. His thin shirt was soaked in sweat and blood. It was plastered to his skin.

Ayaou appeared from the creek. She was walking like a drunk. Robert caught her and took the shotgun. He handed it to Uncle Bark. "Can you use this?" he asked.

The old man nodded. With Ayaou leaning against Robert, they walked toward the cottage.

Fear of what he might find curdled Robert's thoughts. As the cottage appeared, he stopped and said, "Keep Ayaou here." Uncle Bark nodded. The old man's head swiveled around taking in everything as he searched for danger. The barrel of the shotgun pointed where his eyes looked.

With every step Robert took toward the cottage, his legs and arms grew heavier. Tongues of flame danced from the windows, and the heat beat at him. If Shao-mei was in there, he thought, it was too late. Keeping a safe distance from the fire, he circled behind the cottage. His steps faltered when he saw Shao-mei.

A violent shiver went through him. A cry of agony stuck in his throat. He stumbled forward three more steps and stood over her with the air sealed in his lungs. He had to struggle to keep breathing. His knees gave. He collapsed next to her. A sob escaped.

She was on her back with her belly slit open. His sweet Shao-mei and the child he wished had never happened were both dead. The guilt he felt doubled him over. He rested his face against her cheek. She was still warm.

Ayaou came with Uncle Bark supporting her. When she saw Shao-mei, she screamed, broke free and stumbled to her sister's side.

All the signs looked like Shao-mei had been raped repeatedly before she'd been murdered. The markings in the leaves made it obvious she'd put up a fight.

He heard the sound of insane laughter from the direction of the creek. Leaping up, he ran. Uncle Bark followed. When Robert reached the water, he saw the flat-bottomed boat drifting toward the river with several men in it. The laughter was coming from the man standing in the boat's stern. He was dressed in bright-red pantaloons. A dark forest of hair covered his bare chest.

When Robert recognized him, blood rushed to his head bringing rage with it. Reason fled and hate drove him into the water. He plowed after the boat. Once he closed the gap, he saw the hole in Ward's face. The mercenary looked into Robert's eyes. Ward's teeth flashed and his tongue snaked in and out of the wound like a fat, mangled, blood sausage.

"She was always mine, Hart," the grotesquely scarred face said.

Robert's gut felt as if he had swallowed ground glass. My God, Ward believed he had killed Ayaou. The bastard had killed the wrong girl.

"I've collected what belonged to me!" Ward laughed as if he were insane. "I fucked her good! She was juicy—a hot bitch! This is what you get when you steal from me! The reason I'm letting you live is so you will pay for the rest of your life for cheating me of the virginity that was rightfully mine."

Robert raised his weapon and started firing. Tears blinded his vision. His arm shook so hard he couldn't aim. His shots went wild. He still managed to hit one of the men, who fell from the boat to float face down in the water. Another man raised a musket and aimed it at Robert. Ward shoved the barrel down. It fired into the creek. Ward cursed, and said, "I don't want him dead. I want him to burn in hell with me."

The shotgun blasted from behind Robert as Uncle Bark fired both barrels. They were wasted shots. Ward's boat was out of range. Robert continued to wade into the creek until the water was to his chin. He kept cocking the pistol and pulling the trigger on empty chambers. Then Uncle Bark's arms came from behind and wrapped around him. Robert thrashed about screaming. He wanted to go after Ward and rip his heart out. With an effort, Uncle Bark dragged him back to shore.

Ward's boat drifted out of sight, but his insane laugh stayed behind lingering in the hot air. Robert hated himself for missing the monster.

He tried to break loose and run into the creek again, but two pairs of arms held him now. Ayaou had joined Uncle Bark in restraining him. He continued to yell until his throat was raw.

They were back in Ningpo before midnight. Shao-mei had been wrapped tightly in a fishing net from Uncle Bark's boat. They carried her through the gloomy, shrouded streets inside that net. They went straight to the Ningpo house and put her on a table in the center of the room where Robert had taught her poetry.

"I must clean my sister and dress her properly," Ayaou said. "She would not want to be seen like this." She started to unwrap Shao-mei from the net. There was no emotion in her eyes. She was in shock as he was.

"No," Robert said. "Uncle Bark, take Ayaou upstairs."

Ayaou struggled. "I have to do my duty."

"It can wait until morning," Uncle Bark said.

"Her body will be hard by morning. It will be difficult to dress her. She might break."

"Morning is close. It will be all right." Uncle Bark guided Ayaou upstairs. She went without protest.

After he was alone, Robert pulled the net from Shao-mei's body. Uncle Bark had wrapped a blanket around her ripped and torn torso to hold her together. The baby was still inside her under that blanket. Robert didn't want to know what gender it was so he left the blanket where it was. Guan-jiah would ask, but that didn't matter. He didn't know if he could tell his servant what had happened. He'd ask Uncle Bark to do it.

He pulled over a stool and sat next to her. He looked into her glassy, open-eyed stare. He expected her to turn and look at him, but she didn't. He closed her eyelids and caressed the side of her face. The second he touched her, he jerked his hand back. Her flesh was stiff and cold and felt as if it were rubber. There was no life. She was gone. He had not allowed himself to believe it was true until that moment.

"I'm sorry," he said, and the sound caught in his throat. He leaned down and rested his face on her chest. "I loved you. I never told you. I should have." He would never hear her laugh or sing or recite poetry again. He couldn't stand it. He avoided looking at her face and took off his jacket to cover it.

He stood beside the table and stared at the shrouded body, and said, "I don't want to say goodbye." Then he fled into the kitchen where he stayed until sunrise. He was afraid that if Ward found out Ayaou was still alive, he would return to finish what he started.

It was morning when Ayaou sewed Shao-mei's wound shut. She washed her and dressed her sister in white for the last time.

Two days later neighbors and relatives came to mourn. Ayaou's father, Chou Luk, was one. He took the news as if it were his fate. He remained outside the room. He didn't want to see Shao-mei.

"She was a sunny girl," Chou Luk said. "A good daughter."

Lan came. Captain Patridge allowed the younger sister to attend the funeral. Lan and Ayaou held each other—their faces swollen from crying. Their pain added to Robert's guilt. Ayaou might never blame him, but he couldn't hide from himself. On top of the guilt was a hatred of Ward so intense he sometimes discovered himself unconsciously grinding his teeth. He didn't know who he loathed more—himself for failing to protect her or Ward for his demonic cruelty. Ward deserved the name others had labeled him. He was the devil's soldier.

Chapter 25

"It would be wise to buy the services of a Buddhist temple," Uncle Bark said. "The monks will take care of Shao-mei's spirit, so she enters the next life properly. I will also accompany a monk back to the cottage to escort her soul home." His words penetrated Robert's depression. He agreed and managed to send a written note to the consulate telling Dr. Winchester he was taking a few days off work. He didn't explain.

The burial ceremony for Shao-mei lasted several hours. The family and relatives burned incense, paper money and paper food for Shao-mei to take to the next life. Robert felt like an outsider and stood in the shadows behind everyone.

Uncle Bark came with a bundle of lit incense sticks. He handed them to Robert, and took him by the hand as if he were a child and led him through the others to the front of the newly piled dirt mound where Shao-mei sat out of sight under the concrete covered earth in a granite armchair.

Guan-jiah stood on the other side of the burial mound with the river a hundred yards or so behind him. His face was puffy, his eyes red, his shoulders sagging, and his lips turned down in sadness. The eunuch was the only one who burned paper clothes, food and furniture for the unborn baby. The child would not travel to the next life with nothing.

Uncle Bark and Chou Luk had argued with Robert that the added expense of the burial wasn't necessary and was reserved for the wealthy or the nobility. He didn't care. He wanted Shao-mei to have what an armchair burial provided—a sense of wealth, comfort and dignity. He paid for it from the five hundred pounds he'd kept to pay Ward. The cemetery was below Ningpo near the river. She was sitting in the granite armchair facing east toward the sunrise.

Robert squatted beside the grave—his vision blurred from tears.

"You may say anything you wish as you place the incense on her grave," Uncle Bark said in a soothing voice.

What could he say? That she died for Ayaou. He'd failed to protect her and failed again to get her killer? Why was he here instead of hunting for Ward?

"Speak to her," Uncle Bark said. "Put aside your anger. You will feel better—to go on living is harder. She loved you. She will be at peace when she hears your words. You will have another chance to speak to her when we return in a few years to dig up her bones and have her second burial."

Robert stared at the grave feeling numb. The sun sunk into the earth as night arrived on silent feet.

The grieving crowd started to leave. With Uncle Bark guiding Ayaou, she walked slowly away like a sick old woman. Robert resolved to never let her know the truth about the child Shao-mei had carried to her grave. It was better that way. Knowing the child didn't belong to him would only add to her grief, which was heavy enough.

What was left of the sun was erased, and a fog stretched fingers toward the graves. The temperature cooled and dew wet his hair. A flock of blackbirds, like angels of death, flew by. The contours of the distant hills looked as if they were part of a canvas for a smeared Chinese brush painting.

He imagined Shao-mei calling to Ayaou from the grave.

The last time he slept with Shao-mei, she complained he was torturing her by making her wait for pleasure until after the baby was born. She'd pretended to be angry. She swore to torture him and to gain Ayaou's help. She was more into playing than anything else. After all, she was barely sixteen, and all she had ever known from a man had been the rape. He regretted that he hadn't given her the physical affections she had craved.

He had no idea what the Chinese said to their dead and decided to recite a poem he had taught her. She had liked it so much she'd memorized it.

"Like molten gold appears the setting sun
Clouds at evening like jade-blocks pieced into one

Where is the one close and dear to my heart from whom
Without mental pain, I cannot part?"

That evening Robert burned his Chinese robes. It would be two weeks before he returned to the consulate, and he revealed none of his pain to the others except Guan-jiah, who suffered an equal amount of agony. After all, he was going to be the child's adopted uncle.

Guan-jiah's third cousin arrived at the consulate a few days later demanding money for the loss of the cottage. Before Robert had a chance to reply, Guan-jiah rushed into the room, grabbed his cousin by the ear and dragged him into the courtyard. The cousin shrieked in pain. Robert heard most of the argument, and it only added to his confusion.

"Your master burned the cottage. He killed his concubine in a fit of rage," the cousin said.

"That is not true!" Guan-jiah replied. "My master is a good man. He is kind. He would never do that. He cares about people. He even treats me as an equal instead of a slave."

The cousin snorted a loud nasal sound. "Hah, you don't know your master. Another foreign devil told me your master is a thief."

"Who told you that?" Guan-jiah said. "My master has a right to defend himself against such accusations. They are lies. What is this foreign devil's name?"

"You are blind," the cousin replied. "Your master caught his concubine having sex with another man. He killed her in a fit of rage."

"You will tell me who this man is that accused my master of theft and murder," Guan-jiah said.

Robert couldn't move from his desk. The shock of hearing the cousin's accusations had frozen him in place. Part of him wanted to join Guan-jiah in discovering the identity of this foreigner. Maybe this man without a name was Ward's agent sent to destroy Robert's reputation. If so, Ward wasn't done with him yet. He felt fear slice through him. Had Ward discovered he'd killed the wrong woman? Was he plotting to come for Ayaou?

"I do not know who this foreign devil is," the cousin said. "He came to me and told me these things. He said he couldn't afford to let anyone know who he was. He said if he did, your master would send an assassin to have him killed. Your master must pay for burning the cottage."

Guan-jiah gasped. "He will do no such thing. You are the one who must worry about assassination, and I will be the assassin if you spread such gossip about my master. You will embarrass our family with such talk. It will be a great loss of face."

The cousin started to argue. Then Robert heard what sounded like someone being slapped or slugged. There was a cry of pain from the cousin, and the clatter of shoes on pavement leaving the consulate. Robert never heard from the cousin again.

Guan-jiah's defense added to Robert's growing respect for him. Through his actions, he taught Robert about the honesty of the Chinese peasant. Until then, Robert thought honesty and integrity rare in China. When he realized that Guan-jiah's honesty and loyalty had been born out of a mixture of Taoist and Confucian upbringing, which had a moral code similar to Christianity's, he knew there were tens of millions like his servant. Most thieves in China were in the Imperial government or were merchants dealing with foreigners like Patridge.

Days passed, and he was never alone. Either Guan-jiah or Uncle Bark stayed in the house keeping an eye on him.

The mental pain caused by Shao-mei's death was so excruciating that he attempted forgetting she'd lived, but she was everywhere. Every time he arrived home, she was inside the entry waiting for him with that dimpled smile—her thin arms stretched wide inviting him to hug her. He stumbled forward to hold her. When her ghostly apparition vanished, his mental anguish returned as an ache he couldn't escape.

Uncle Bark guided Robert in setting up a lotus seat altar on one of the smaller tables. They put the altar in a corner facing east. On it sat a block of wood with Shao-mei's name carved into it. Flowers, candles, incense, food and drink were displayed around the block of wood and replenished on a regular basis. A monk arrived every seven days and performed rituals Robert couldn't watch. Uncle Bark attended, while Robert hid upstairs in the dark, covered his ears and cried.

He considered moving out of the Ningpo house and finding somewhere else to live.

Sometimes life is like living in the middle of a freezing blizzard. The noise keeps you from thinking clearly. The white blinds you. The cold numbs you. To escape, you think of nothing but death. You just want to go to sleep and never wake.

Robert sat at the kitchen table staring at the loaded pistol waiting between his hands. He imagined himself surrounded by noise along with the white and the cold that made you so brittle you might shatter. He was desperate to escape the daily nightmares filled with Ward's demon laugh.

Uncle Bark moved from where he was watching near the stove. He took two steps to the table and slid the pistol out of Robert's reach.

"I have lost five women and twenty-two children in my life," he said. "I have been wealthy and poor. I have outlived all but one son. He lives in southeast China in Macao. Starvation, storms, disease, war, bandits, and the Tapings each took a little here and a little there. Now, I have only my memories. Those memories are my rock in the raging river. Although I never talk to those I loved, I cling to my memories of them. I do not run away from them and deny they ever lived. You still have a woman. You must live for her. Ayaou has almost left her mind. She is going to be a living dead thing if you do not go to her. You must find your rock, cling to it, and let the river of life flow around you. Ayaou cannot be that rock for you. I cannot either. You must be that rock."

"I'm going to collect Ward's head. Then I'll come back for Ayaou," Robert said.

"He will kill you if you do," Uncle Bark said. "He wants you to go after him."

Robert tried to think, but his brain was still trapped in that blizzard.

"Wait for an opportunity to surface," Uncle Bark said. "Then you will get what you want. Even if years or decades must pass, it is the Chinese way. Now I want you to go to Ayaou. I want you both to return to this life and let Shao-mei rest."

He didn't know anything else he could do, so he listened to the old man. His body was all-ice as he went up the stairs and into the bedroom seeking comfort and warmth by crawling onto the bed beside Ayaou. They stayed that way without food or water until Uncle Bark brought summer fruit cut into small pieces with a container of boiled water and demanded they eat and drink. Robert took the food, but Ayaou didn't move or open her eyes. It was as if she were waiting for death to claim her.

For what felt like hours, she didn't respond to any of his words. Her spirit was chasing Shao-mei. Eventually he went to the kitchen, lit a fire in the stove and cooked rice porridge and yams—Ayaou's favorite food. He took it to her, begged her to eat, but she ignored him.

Guan-jiah arrived. He stood along the wall in the shadows beside Uncle Bark and watched.

Then she spoke in a lifeless tone. "I cannot look at you, Robert, because Shao-mei can no longer look at you. It was always this time of the day when she hurried me to the stream. She wanted to be the first to greet you."

The tears in her eyes overflowed. "I was jealous of her and wanted her gone, so I could have you to myself. It was my curse that killed her!"

"Ayaou!" he said, unable to control the anger. "It was Ward who killed Shao-mei! Not you!"

"I know," she replied. "But Ward was in my body. I went to Mr. Yin-Yang, and he confirmed that it was true."

"You're crazy, Ayaou!" He almost yelled the words. "Mr. Yin-Yang is a fortuneteller." His anger embarrassed him, and he fought it wanting to be calm and at peace. Uncle Bark was right. He had to be a rock—no, a boulder. A boulder would survive in the blizzard. A rock might get buried but not a boulder, and there would be room for Ayaou to hang on too. During the last year, he'd almost forgotten that he had fallen in love with her first, and she was still alive.

"No, I m not crazy," she said. "There have been indications everywhere. Remember when I cut Shao-mei's embroidered lovebirds to pieces? Mr. Yin-Yang said it was a sign that Shao-mei would die a violent death." She wailed, and then said, "Oh, Shao-mei, how could I do that to you? Oh, Shao-mei—"

Ward had not just taken the life of one of his concubine's—he'd taken both of them. If Robert made the mercenary die once, it would not be enough to pay for what he had done. When the opportunity Uncle Bark mentioned presented itself, he wanted to make sure the bastard paid dearly. To do that, he had to take charge of his life and leave the suffering behind. After all, he had to stay alive to collect that debt, and he didn't want to do it without Ayaou beside him. He had to revive her will to live. There had to be a way. Then he knew how.

He gathered her into his arms and held her wanting to take the burden of grief from her. He was now a mighty boulder. He was not going to be swept away by floods or buried in snow. "If you don't eat, I will die with you," he said. "Shao-mei will not like that."

She stirred in his arms and brushed stray strands of hair from her eyes. She sighed, and he held out a piece of yam for her to eat. She took it, chewed, and swallowed. He offered water. She drank.

"That yam tastes exactly the way Shao-mei liked them," she said. "Did you cook it?"

"Yes," he said. "I cooked it for a long time at a low temperature."

"I could tell. It melted in my mouth, and it was sweet. How did you know what to do?"

"Shao-mei told me last night."

"That is impossible. Shao-mei's gone."

"No, she's not," he replied. "She will always be with us. We played a game of *Weiqi*. She cheated as she always does."

"You knew she cheated and did not stop her?" Ayaou said.

"She wouldn't play with me again if she lost, so I let her."

Ayaou stared into his eyes searching for the truth. "Is her spirit here?"

"Yes."

"I miss her laugh. Spirits cannot laugh."

"She can," Robert said. "She's laughing now. She's happy we are still alive and together. Listen carefully and you will hear her."

Silence wrapped its silky cocoon around them, and she listened. After a moment, her eyes widened. "Robert, you are right. She said she still hates massaging cabbages. She wanted you to know."

"I remember," he said. "The first time I met her, she told me about learning how to give massages by practicing on cabbages."

"Her cabbages were like my carrots," Ayaou said. "What else did she say?"

He started to tell her.

Uncle Bark nodded. "They will be all right," he said.

"Yes," Guan-jiah replied. "It is time for us to go." Guan-jiah and Uncle Bark left the room.

Years later, the scene of Ayaou cutting his hair and Shao-mei running around having fun teasing him often visited him in his dreams. When it happened, Robert didn't want to wake. In sleep, he was in a true paradise. He awoke weeping and smiling at the same time and was glad to be bald in his later years because no one cut his hair the way Ayaou did. It was, he realized, exactly what he had wanted.

Several years passed before a chance presented itself for Robert to seek revenge against Ward. He met another man, a Han Chinese, who *lost face* because of Ward's lies and accusations. Robert and this high-ranking Han Chinese official formed an alliance. What they could not do alone, they achieved together.

During the waiting, Robert often had an odd feeling every time he glanced in the mirror. The shape of his wrinkles started to change. The *fish-tails* gradually turned into *cactus*— anger and misery formed a wild bush between his eyebrows. He started to age visibly. He felt his vitality slowly draining from his body threatening to leave him empty.

He might have been a boulder, but his moods darkened. He developed a habit of using a black, porcelain, hand sized spittoon with a hunting tiger painted on its side. Every time he got upset, he would cough and spit. It was his way to keep the anger from boiling out.

This irritated Ayaou, but she did not complain. She knew what Shao-mei would have said. "Let him be, Ayaou. He has to spit out his bitterness." She followed her younger sister's advice.

Two: Chapter 26
1857

God could not be blamed for Shao-mei's rape and murder. Instead, Robert blamed himself. The guilt felt as if he were eating ground glass. He should have protected her.

Ningpo had changed since he arrived in 1854. Crime and corruption had collapsed Chinese Maritime Customs, a service established in 1685. Mobs looted its treasury in Shanghai, and Wu Chien-chang, the Chinese official in charge, had gone into hiding.

Without the money Customs collected from foreign imports, the Imperial government was in danger of collapsing. Meanwhile, the Taiping Rebellion, already in its twelfth year, was threatening to sweep away the Ch'ing Empire and millions had already died.

Sir Rutherford Alcock, the British consul in Shanghai had stepped in and was struggling to create a temporary inspectorate of customs in order to fulfill Britain's obligations under the treaty system, a product of the Opium Wars, and help the Ch'ing Dynasty survive.

Western merchants wanted China with its vast population to stay an open market where they could sell opium without restrictions. On the other hand, the Taipings led by Hong Xiuquan, a man claiming to be Jesus Christ's younger brother, wanted to bring down the dynasty and force all foreigners out of China.

Robert had no idea that these horrible events were about to place him on the world's stage where he was going to make a difference.

It was dark when Robert reached home where he placed his back to the door and studied the street. The house was located off a narrow, crooked alley that seldom had foot traffic. Two people were in sight. One was an old bent woman hobbling along in obvious pain—the other a middle-aged man with dark bags under his eyes.

He watched the man until he was gone. Once the street was empty, he knocked on the door. A moment dragged by before he heard the scratching sound he was waiting for. He knew the spot Ayaou would be scratching. In reply, he scratched back. He heard the locking bar being lifted from its brackets. The door swung open.

He stepped into gloom, closed the door and locked it by dropping the bar into its four brackets. Ayaou stood in the shadows beside an inked wall hanging that was two feet wide and five feet long.

There was the same dreadful look in her eyes he'd seen daily since Shao-mei's death. He could see that the woman he loved was close to death too, and he didn't know how to save her.

There were Chinese symbols on the watercolor behind Ayaou that said *he sheng* and *ning jin*, *harmony* and *tranquility*. The words were printed on colorless rice paper. The calligraphy was in black ink with a thin red border like a sliver of blood running around the perimeter three inches from the edge. There were several red ink stamps in the lower right-hand corner showing the name of the artist, but they looked more like clots of blood.

Shao-mei and Ayaou bought that wall hanging. The sisters had bought all the art in the house. It hurt to look at it. The words on that wall hanging were all lies.

He frowned. For an instant, he wanted to tear the calligraphy from the wall and shred it. On the other hand, he knew if he destroyed it, Ayaou would feel as if he were attacking her. She believed Shao-mei's ghost lived inside that paper and every other object the girls had bought and carried into this rented house.

On Ayaou's left, the steep, worn stairs with the narrow steps were swallowed by darkness at the top. Shao-mei's empty, closet sized bedroom was up there across the hall from where he slept with Ayaou. Every time h e looked at that door, he wanted to nail it shut so her ghost could not escape.

He stood an arm's length from Ayaou. There were no words of greeting. He reached inside a coat pocket and took out a new Colt revolver. Her eyes shifted to the weapon. He held it in both hands and offered it to her as if it were a dozen roses.

"Ayaou," he said in fluent Mandarin. "I bought this weapon to replace the one destroyed in the fire. You must promise you will never leave the house without it."

She reached for the pistol and took it. The four and a half-pound weight pulled her hand down to her side until the nine-inch barrel pointed at the floor.

"Do you remember how many times you can shoot before you have to reload?" he asked.

"Five," she said in a dull voice.

"Hide the pistol in your clothes, or if you have to, get a basket and cover it with a rag. In fact, you cannot go out unless Guan-jiah or I are with you. Do you understand?"

She nodded. She was still wearing white, the Chinese color worn to mourn the death of a family member or close friend. Her dark hair was pulled back and tied into a tight knot on top of her head. She had a slender neck, small ears and high cheekbones.

Compared to her, he seemed tall. He was five foot eight to her five foot two. "You know why we must do this?" he said.

"If Ward discovers he killed the wrong sister, he will return to finish the job."

He took her in his arms and held her. She pressed her ear against his chest where his heart was beating. "At least I can hear that you are alive," she said. "Sometimes I cannot hear my own heart."

A knot gathered in his throat. His eyes filled with tears, but he blinked them away. He didn't want her to see the fear and worry that had built a nest inside his head.

Robert gasped and woke with a start. It took a moment for the wild beating of his heart to subside as his eyes searched the dark bedroom for intruders. He reached under his pillow and touched the pistol to make sure it was there.

His fears were like cancerous growths eating him. Was the front door strong enough to withstand an assault? Then he remembered that Guan-jiah had reinforced the front door. The eunuch had screwed iron straps to the inside surface. Once the bar was placed in the four brackets, the door was almost invincible.

It would be difficult if not impossible for anyone to break in. He wasn't sure if he had checked the door to see if it was locked before coming upstairs. On the other hand, he knew it was his habit to check before going to bed. However, what if he forgot?

He thought of the rope ladder next. He slipped from under the thick blankets. When his bare feet touched the frozen floorboards, he sucked in his breath but was careful not to wake Ayaou. He stood naked in the dark and listened to her breathing until he was sure she still slept. Then he checked to see if the rope ladder was where he had left it below the one window in the bedroom.

Soon after Shao-mei's funeral, he'd bought this rope ladder from a British ship. If Ward or another assassin set fire to the house as they had done to the cottage, he planned to use that rope ladder to escape from the upstairs bedroom into the alley.

He knelt and reached under the bed. Once his fingers touched the double-barreled shotgun, he relaxed. With that weapon, he could blast anyone in the alley before climbing to safety

He picked up a pocket watch from the side table and moved to the window where moonlight helped him see that it was one in the morning.

Two or three times a night, he awoke at the same times. He checked the pistol under his pillow first; the rope ladder second and then the shotgun. Sometimes he went downstairs to inspect the front door and the window shutters though he had done that before going to bed.

That next morning, he and Ayaou sat on the benches at the kitchen table with the uneven top. They ate rice porridge from chipped, white ceramic bowls. The only sound was the crackling fire from the stove.

"In my prayers," he said, his voice hollow as if it belonged to a stranger. "I keep asking God to explain why Shao-mei suffered so horribly before she died. God doesn't answer. I know He has more important things to do than to explain why a sixteen year old died such a horrible death and took her unborn child with her." He cursed himself. He regretted speaking his thoughts. He should have kept his mouth shut.

"It was Ward's revenge," Ayaou replied. She was nineteen, his age when he arrived in China more than three years earlier, yet she looked old beyond her years. She had been sixteen when he met her in that battle with the Tapings. She had been so beautiful and full of life. That's why he fell in love with her. Now she was a shadow of her former self with no expression on her face. It was as if she was carved from sandstone, and he feared she might crumble and he'd lose her.

"You forced him to sell me to you," she said. "You pointed a pistol at him and offered him no choice. He wanted to keep me, even if it meant throwing me to his men then feeding me to the dogs. That would have been better. At least, Shao-mei would be alive and happy with you."

"Don't think that way, Ayaou." He wanted to say something cheerful, but he couldn't. It was impossible to get nice things to come out of his mouth.

"I'm afraid Ward isn't finished with us yet," he said. He and Ayaou had become lifeless puppets without strings to guide them. He didn't know what to do except get up each morning and let his legs carry him to the consulate.

"If Ward learns you are alive, he will return and murder you too." The words leaked out. He couldn't stop them. He didn't tell her there was nothing he could do to protect her. After all, Ward commanded an army of mercenaries. In addition, due to the battles Ward's army had won, the Ch'ing Dynasty had granted Ward Chinese citizenship. Robert, on the other hand, was nobody. "You have to be careful, Ayaou. For your safety, you have to do as I say."

When she didn't respond, he said, "Ayaou?"

She held her rice bowl in both hands with her mouth hanging open as she stared with empty eyes at nothing.

Seeking answers, Robert turned to God and attended William Martin's sermons on the Sabbath. William, an American Presbyterian minister, the only minister living inside the Chinese city of Ningpo, was the one foreigner he trusted not to judge him. He did not want anything to do with the

306

other ministers that lived across the river near the Presbyterian chapel. They were hypocrites. He knew he was being harsh in his judgment, but he didn't care.

However, William crossed the river at least once a week to visit the other ministers, who gossiped. They would eventually talk about him as they had talked about Hollister and his concubine, Me-ta-tae. William would hear their opinions. They would call Ayaou a whore as they did to Me-ta-tae.

Neither Me-ta-tae nor Ayaou were whores. In China, a concubine was not a whore. In China, a concubine was a second-class wife and had no power over her life or future. A concubine, like most women in China, was property to be bought and sold.

The truth was as complicated as China—something most foreigners didn't want to learn and probably couldn't understand if they tried.

Master Ping, Robert's Mandarin language teacher, said it best. "The foreigners want to force China to become a Christian nation. That is impossible. China is a nation influenced by Laozi and Confucius, a way of life older than Christianity by a thousand years.

"Most Chinese will ignore the missionaries as if they were invisible—yet be polite to them when face to face. How can you force someone to believe anything when he dissolves once you let him go?

"If forced, a Chinese man will agree to almost anything. Then he will go about his business as if he'd said nothing. He will follow Taoism's path and become the rock in the stream that lets the water flow by without struggling against it. By doing nothing, nothing is left undone. Meanwhile he will live by Confucius's belief of a well-ordered society by being true to the five great relationships. There is no room for your Christ in China. To the Chinese, evil sprouts where the five great relationships do not exist, and everyone outside of the Middle Kingdom is considered a barbarian."

He wanted to share his feelings with someone else besides Guan-jiah, his Chinese servant. He wasn't sure William was the right choice, but there was no one else he could trust. William was one of the few foreigners that cared about the Chinese and their culture. It worried him that William might think less of him if he discovered the truth about Ayaou and Shao-mei.

He knew the risk he was taking by attending William's services. During one conversation while Shao-mei was alive, William asked if he was going to convert the girls to Christianity. Although Robert was a Christian, he didn't want to change his girls. He wanted them to stay the way they were.

He felt as if a monster had moved inside his head. It had always been a struggle for Robert to hide his feelings. If William looked, he'd see the truth. William had the ability to look into another person's eyes and see the pain. There would be questions. To combat this, Robert was learning how to turn his face into a mask but he wasn't ready yet. Since Shao-mei's death, he had practiced using a mirror.

Until he achieved the ability to hide his feelings, he made sure to arrive every Sabbath shortly after William started his sermon. He sat at the rear of the room near the door. When the sermon ended, he left. Sitting on that bench at the back and listening to the sermons worked like a drug to soothe his nerves.

The American started with a prayer to God asking Him to make sure he didn't lead his Chinese flock astray. William didn't tell them what to think or what to do as most foreigners did. He taught them to think and find a compromise between their ancient beliefs and Christianity; to fold one inside the other. When dealing with the Chinese, it was the best choice.

It wasn't easy for Robert to avoid a man he considered a friend.

Chapter 27

The weather conspired with Ward to make life miserable for Robert and Ayaou. The winter of 1858 was the coldest since he'd arrived in China.

Guan-jiah, his Chinese servant, insisted on doing the shopping so Ayaou stayed inside the house alone most of the time. Each day Guan-jiah brought in frost bitten cabbages that were withered and looked rotten. The potatoes were loaded with ice crystals and tasted like pork liver.

Robert was in a surly mood, and others went out of their way to avoid him. He spent hours concocting far-fetched schemes on how he was going to exact revenge for Shao-mei's death.

He bought another revolver for Guan-jiah and took the eunuch into the countryside daily for target practice. On those days, for her protection, Ayaou visited boat people she had known all her life.

They found a place to practice without witnesses. There, away from the city, among the trees and rice paddies, Robert's servant learned to shoot.

At first, Guan-jiah's hands shook. When he squeezed the trigger, he closed his eyes and jumped at the sound of the boom. "I'm going deaf, Master," he said.

"Then take cotton and plug your ears," he replied.

"What about my eyes, Master? How do I keep them open?"

"We'll work on it. If you learn, I'll add five yuan a month to your pay." He stood behind his servant and reached around him putting his hands over Guan-jiah's to steady the shaking.

"Put your index finger on the trigger and squeeze," he said. "Do not jerk the trigger, or you will miss the target."

Since he was behind Guan-jiah, he couldn't help but observe the eunuch's shaved skull. A tail of hair called a queue grew out of the back of the eunuch's head and hung halfway down his back. He was a bony, short man with a turned-up nose and eyes set far apart.

After helping Guan-jiah fire his first five shots, he stepped back to observe and was aware of his servant's graceful, feminine posture and movements. Since Guan-jiah had voluntarily castrated himself at a young age to apply for a job inside the Forbidden City, he was no longer a man. He was a *lao-gong*, a eunuch. If he grew his hair long and dressed like a woman, he could easily pass for one. He was sure that men would find Guan-jiah attractive as a woman. As it was, he looked homely in his drab colored, baggy peasant clothing.

It was a tragic blow when Guan-jiah did not get the first job he applied for as a *tai-jian*, a court or palace eunuch. Robert realized his servant was not alone. He'd heard that as many as fifty-thousand boys castrated themselves each year to be eligible to apply for the few positions available in the Emperor's palace. Many that were not accepted killed themselves.

Guan-jiah, on the other hand, decided to live. He respected his servant for the burden he had taken to feed his siblings, his parents, his grandparents, his uncles and aunts, and cousins.

It took days to get Guan-jiah to keep his eyes open and calm enough to hit the target. The target was only twenty yards away, but it might as well have been a mile. The eunuch learned and hit the target on average four out of every six shots. They went through two hundred rounds before Robert was satisfied.

He suspected he was being followed. When Robert turned to catch the person, the phantom melted like fog. He questioned his sanity. He suspected he was imagining things—that Shao-mei's death had made him paranoid. On the other hand, he felt he couldn't take the chance that he was wrong.

One evening on his way home, he confronted a man that looked like a Japanese sailor. The man had been walking behind him for three blocks by the time Robert decided to confront him.

He turned and pointed a finger at the sailor's face. "Why are you following me? Trying to discover where I live, huh?" Robert's other hand was in his jacket pocket holding the Colt revolver.

The man was taller than he was, but Robert's intensity and anger caused the man to step back. The sailor looked around at the Chinese on the street as if he were seeking help against a lunatic.

None of the Chinese paid the slightest attention to this dramatic scene in their midst. Robert knew why—what happened between foreigners or strangers was none of their business. Why should they care if two barbarians killed each other?

"Leave me alone," the sailor said. He took another step back.

Robert pursued him. "You have been spying on me. Admit it."

The sailor ran. Although Robert felt satisfaction at chasing the man off, he worried that next time the spy would be sneakier and harder to detect. At least, he had proved he was ready if something unexpected happened.

When he opened the front door one morning, it resisted as if the hinge pins had swollen. He examined the door and discovered scratches and dents on the outside surface as if someone had been attempting to force the door with a metal pry bar.

He sucked in a breath—shocked. Without thinking, his right hand slipped into the jacket pocket where he kept the Colt revolver. He stared at every face in the street and looked at the rooftops expecting to see someone watching. A wave of dizziness swept over him. He had to lean against the wall to keep his balance.

He wanted to yell, *I am here, you bastards! Come get me!* His house had been violated. The woman he loved had been threatened. He felt helpless, useless.

"Master, what is wrong?" It was Guan-jiah. Since the attempt to hijack Robert into a British warship months earlier, before Shao-mei had been murdered, the eunuch arrived every morning and accompanied him to the consulate. He came with a sturdy walking stick—a gnarly, knobby thing that doubled as a bludgeon.

Robert pointed at the door's hinges. "They came to get her." He continued to babble as the eunuch guided him inside. Then the servant went back out.

Robert sat on the nearest stool. He pulled the Colt out of his pocket and stared at it. When Guan-jiah returned, the eunuch slipped the bar into its brackets securing the door.

"Master," Guan-jiah said. "Why do you hold that thing? It is dangerous." He took the revolver out of Robert's hand and put the weapon on a small table next to the door.

"I have to be ready."

"It was only a thief, Master. Do you think the men that murdered Shao-mei and her child would have given up because they could not force their way into the house if they knew you were inside?"

Robert shrugged. "What am I going to do? I feel helpless. I couldn't protect Shao-mei. She is dead because of me. How can I protect Ayaou?"

"Master, I will hire a craftsman to repair the door. The man will make it stronger. I will see to that." Guan-jiah knelt and looked into Robert's eyes. "What happened is something to feel pleased about. The door held. You and Ayaou are safe. Your efforts to protect your concubine worked."

"That's true," he replied, and sat straighter. "Make sure the new hinge pins are twice as strong as the ruined ones. The thieves will come better prepared next time. We must be ready. This house must be strong enough to withstand an army."

"Do not worry, Master. When the workers are finished, the hinge pins in this door will be the sturdiest in Ningpo."

At the consulate, Robert often slipped into a trance and stared at the wall. He thought about the three men he had angered since coming to China. There was General Frederick Townsend Ward, the American mercenary. If he hadn't forced the general at gunpoint to sell Ayaou to him, Shao-mei would still be alive.

"Master," Guan-jiah said.

Caught-off guard, Robert jerked.

The eunuch put a tray on the desk. There was a steaming teapot and a cup with a lid. "This tea will help calm your nerves." Guan-jiah took a step back, folded his hands together and nodded.

312

Robert lifted the lid on the cup. Steam escaped. "How do you know that I need something to calm down? What's in this?" he asked. "It smells familiar."

"That would be the chrysanthemums. I have added orchids, jasmine, black tea, green tea and some peppermint. It is a blend I developed. I suggest you allow me to bring you some each morning."

"Good idea."

Guan-jiah left. Robert took a sip then put the cup down and placed the lid on. He returned to his paperwork. It didn't take long before his mind drifted to the other two men.

The second was Unwyn Fiske, someone Robert angered during a battle with the Taipings. He wished there was some way he could erase the hate Unwyn felt for him. He still didn't understand why the man blamed him for wanting to save those boat people from the rebels.

He had no idea what Captain Patridge had done to Unwyn. He dreaded finding out. Had Unwyn lost his job because of Robert's complaints? If so, where was Unwyn? Did he want revenge?

He picked up the tea and lifted the lid. He buried his nose in the aromatic scent. The heat and fragrance of the ingredients acted as a balm. Guan-jiah had been right.

If Captain Patridge hadn't invited him to spend his holiday at the captain's summerhouse on Zhoushan Island during the summer of 1855, Robert would have never met Ayaou. It hadn't helped that Captain Patridge was the principal agent for the largest British opium merchant in China.

It didn't take long to fall in love with Ayaou. However, love came with a price. He had to help the captain smuggle opium into parts of China where it was outlawed. For doing this, Patridge had promised to protect him and Ayaou from Ward.

That hadn't worked.

He shook his head to snap out of the trance. He checked to see if anyone had noticed. Dr. Winchester, the consul in Ningpo, was in another room busy with a British merchant making sure the man didn't avoid paying the legal duty for his goods. The other two assistants were out, probably on ships checking manifests.

Good, he didn't want anyone to discover there were moments when he stopped working. How would he explain that he was struggling to figure out a way to keep the woman he loved alive? They didn't know he had a concubine. Ayaou was his greatest secret. If his parents and friends in Ireland discovered he'd bought a woman, they'd never forgive him.

The third man he angered was Payne Hollister, the British consul in Ningpo when Robert arrived at his first duty station in 1854. They worked together for a few months before Hollister quit.

Robert considered it his fault that Hollister held a grudge against him. After all, he had seduced Me-ta-tae, Hollister's concubine. Months later, to get even, Hollister raped Shao-mei making her pregnant.

He slipped a hand inside his vest and rubbed an ache growing in his gut. It was a constant burning born with Shao-mei's death. It was growing as if it had a life of its own.

After the attempted break in, his ability to sleep deteriorated. He awoke several times a night and saw Ward's face. The mercenary's eyes glowed in the dark. His teeth flashed and his tongue, like a fat mangled blood sausage, snaked in and out of that open wound in the side of his face.

"She was always mine, Hart," Ward said.

When he heard Ward's demonic laugh, Robert broke out in a cold sweat. "No!" He yelled, waking Ayaou.

"What is it?" she asked.

"Nothing. Go back to sleep."

"You have soaked the sheets." She touched him. "You are covered in sweat. You will get sick if you do not dry off."

"Leave me alone." He left the bedroom to search the house for intruders. He carried the revolver with the hammer cocked. He looked like a pale wraith floating naked from room to room through the darkness—one phantom chasing another.

"I think we should move," he said a week later. They were in the parlor, the room where the three of them had once read and discussed poems together. The laughter that once filled this room had died with Shao-mei. Now the house was a tomb for two dead people. He remembered Guan-jiah saying that a poet had killed himself in this house leaving evil spirits behind.

Scrolls with Chinese calligraphy hung from the walls. There was a bench with a table and some chairs. Against one wall was the altar for Shao-mei's spirit. He stared at one vase sitting on the altar. It held the ashes from his Chinese robes, the robes Shao-mei bought for him. They had been a perfect fit. One had been linen and the other silk. After Shao-mei's death, he burned the robes and swore he would never wear Chinese clothing again.

While staring at Shao-mei's shrine, he finished dressing. He put on his silk waistcoat and over that a long frock coat. He buttoned only the top button of the coat. He picked up the brown Derby felt hat from the table in front of the bench. Ayaou ran a brush through his unruly hair. His hairline was starting to recede. He imagined that if this kept up, he'd be bald soon.

She brushed the hair back. It was thick and curly along the neckline. "It is a pity you have to cover this lovely hair with a hat," she said. "Shao-mei loved your hair. I think you want to move because this house is haunted by her."

"Yes." He lied. Robert didn't want to scare her with his paranoid speculations that someone was hunting them. Captain Patridge had been right when he said Ward wouldn't hire someone else to do his dirty work. Ward did it himself, like the day he murdered Shao-mei thinking she was Ayaou.

"When I brush your hair, I think it helps you relax," Ayaou said. "I am going to brush it before we go to bed tonight and see."

Maybe the person who tried to break into the house was a common thief. Even if that were true, he couldn't risk it. The man could also be an assassin. What if it wasn't Ward, but it was Unwyn Fiske or Payne Hollister or Henry Burgevine, Ward's second-in-command? Robert had not forgotten the argument he had with Burgevine on that ship bound for California with a load of coolies.

He stopped Ayaou from brushing his hair. "That's enough," he said. "I heard Shao-mei coming up the stairs last night. That's why I left the room." He compounded the fiction. "Last week, I heard her crying and went to see. When I opened the door to her room, I saw her on the bed. She was expecting me. She looked at me with those large eyes and smiled. I saw her dimples. She was crying and tears ran down her cheeks. She had her favorite blanket tucked under her chin, and she reached out a hand for me."

Ayaou seemed to shrink, so he pulled her against him. Her body felt frail. He wanted to protect her. He sent prayers to God every night asking for help.

"One morning I found you in her bed," Ayaou said. "You were cold and curled on the blanket. When you awoke, your eyes were empty like an abandoned well. I was afraid she had taken your spirit."

Ayaou had her face pressed against his chest. He rested his chin on top of her head. "I remember," he said. "You held me for a long time, and I came back."

"Once when I was cooking the evening meal—" Ayaou's voice cracked. "I heard her scolding me—like she did from behind the stove. She said I was demanding too much to keep the fire at a perfect heat." He felt Ayaou tremble. His insides burned and ached. Then in a muffled voice, Ayaou continued. "She is lonely without us, Robert. If we leave, she will follow us. She might get lost in the city. We cannot escape the love she has for us that keeps her ghost here."

Tears filled his eyes. He hated when that happened. Tears were not for men. He blinked them away without touching his face and buried his misery.

He realized it didn't matter if they moved. Whoever was out there was waiting for the right moment. Moving was not a guarantee of safety. After all, Ward had found the cottage in the countryside where Robert had taken the girls to hide them.

No, they wouldn't move. They would stay in the Ningpo house. There would be no running and hiding. Not anymore. If fate were to come for them, he would face it and die beside Ayaou. They'd fight together as they had the day they met.

When he arrived home later than usual that evening, he stood outside the door afraid to knock. He hadn't been this late since Shao-mei's death. What if something had happened?

He kept a hand in his pocket on the grip of the loaded pistol and examined every shadow. He leaned against the door and it creaked.

A scratching came from the other side. That was a relief—a sign she was okay. She must have been sitting by the door for hours. He scratched back and heard her remove the locking bar.

As the door opened, Ayaou stepped from the darkness and threw herself at him. He saw the feral hunger in her eyes and

316

took the bar out of her hands and dropped it into its brackets. No one would damage this door. He had done everything possible to turn the small house into a fortress.

Their eyes locked together in lust. His coat came off, and the revolver in the pocket hit the floor with a solid thump. He fumbled at his canvas suspenders. Removing his shirt, a button popped. It rolled across the floor making little tinkling noises. He clawed at his pants to remove them. Ayaou became his mirror image as she stripped. He pulled her naked body against his and pushed into her—not tenderly like before Shao-mei's death, but like a beast devouring its prey. That was the first time they'd made love since Shao-mei's death.

Finished, they lay exhausted and sweaty on the floor. He gathered the scattered clothing and covered their bodies against the cold.

"My breathing is the only sound I hear during the day," Ayaou said. "This house is like a tomb when you are not here."

"Don't you have enough books to read? Do you want me to buy more?"

"Although I love the books since you taught me to read, they cannot replace Shao-mei."

His heart ached. He pulled her close and smelled the warm ocean scent in her hair.

After that cold January day and for the next several weeks, this was the pattern of their lives. They made love with fierceness and desperation. They did it on the floor, on the stairs and on the kitchen table. Sometimes, Ayaou pressed her trembling body against him. She put her face into the space between his chin and collarbone. Without warning, she convulsed with sobs as she relived the nightmare of her sister's death.

Robert didn't have that luxury. He had to stay strong. He had to keep the tears locked away. It wasn't easy.

Chapter 28

Ayaou and Robert started to live again in March. His Chinese language teacher triggered the change. He started working the schedule he had used with Master Tee Lee Ping over the summer. To keep the guilt brought on by Shao-mei's death from eating him, he worked harder to understand the Chinese.

He learned how to talk in circles and never hit the center of any message he was trying to give. Communication in China was an indirect art form that flew in circles and never landed. In the West, it was more like shooting a bullet into the center of a target. The better he became at getting his meaning across indirectly, the easier it was for the Chinese to accept him.

"I am marrying," Tee Lee Ping said at the end of one session late in the evening. They were at Robert's house in the first-floor sitting room. Ping handed him a bag of candy. "You are invited to my wedding in two weeks. If you want to bring Ayaou, that is fine with me."

At first, he found it strange that the Chinese didn't invite people as a couple but only through the man of the house. Then he learned that since most affluent Chinese men had more than one concubine or wife, and no one knew which concubine or wife the man might bring, trouble was avoided by leaving the decision to the man.

He'd seen men come by themselves. Bringing one concubine or wife could cause jealousy from the others, which Robert now understood thanks to the battle for his love that had once raged between Shao-mei and Ayaou.

"How long have you been engaged?" he asked. "You've never mentioned it before." Though he knew Master Ping's private life was none of his business, he was curious. The man had been his teacher for more than a year.

"I just turned twenty-six. I have been engaged for thirteen years."

"That was a long engagement, Master Ping," he said, and poured red wine into his teacher's glass to congratulate him. "Why so long?"

"Well, I did not have sufficient money to fix a good home for the woman that will be my wife," Ping replied. "My friends and family have given me gifts. They were worried that the engagement might fall apart."

"Did you worry?"

"Terribly. My parents-in-law wanted specific things for their daughter. I finally gained their permission with heaven's help. In China, the girl listens to her parents more than her lover or husband. She suffers but does not rebel."

After his teacher left, he asked Ayaou to purchase gifts before the wedding. Two days later, she bought a pair of hens.

He frowned. "What kind of gift is this?"

"It is the Chinese style. These are egg-bearing hens—the best gift one can give."

On the day of the wedding, it rained. The narrow streets were awash with streams of water cleansing the city of its filth and its sins. The wedding and the rain also washed away some of the mental anguish Robert and Ayaou had suffered with since Shao-mei's death.

Ayaou rented a sedan chair. They arrived with the hens in baskets decorated with red ribbons. Tee Lee Ping met them at the entrance to his parents' house wearing a knee-length blue silk gown with a giant red silk flower tied with a ribbon across his chest. He led them to a hall inside the house. Ping was pleased with the gifts and thanked Robert repeatedly. The other guests had brought ducks, fish, marinated pig heads and thighs. He was happy with Ayaou's choice.

The walls of the hall were gaily decorated with pictures and scrolls. The ceiling supported an army of red lanterns. Every chair and table was covered with red paper painted with the symbols of love and harmony. The people crowding the room were dressed in their best.

On one side of the hall, a band played a song of greeting every time a new guest arrived. Robert approached Tee Lee Ping's parents and older relatives and did what Ayaou had instructed. He clasped his hands, brought them to his chin and bowed deeply. A little startled, they returned the bow.

One old man, probably in his nineties, half-blind, who Robert assumed had never seen a foreigner in his life, pointed at him, and said, "What is wrong with his hair? So yellow! Tell him to eat more black sesame seeds, so he can get his color back."

Robert found humor in the old man's statement that eating black sesame seeds changed hair color. Ayaou was dressed in a peach-colored, satin Chinese robe. The other women wore similar robes but in different colors with different patterns. He had on a black, English suit with a cravat. Two pocket watches with fobs were displayed hanging from his front waistcoat pockets.

Ayaou was a bit concerned about the locals response to him since he was considered a barbarian. Her worries were soon put to rest. Everyone was polite. Some greeted him with questions about his health. Ayaou had told him that the state of his health was no one's concern. It was only a formality—a way to say hello. That's why his answers were not specific. He also discovered that his weekly visits and conversations at the bath and teahouse helped.

A shout caught everyone's attention. "The flower chair has arrived."

The chair was brought into the reception room where water from the rain dripped onto the floor. The four men carrying the chair set it down and removed the poles. Next, they removed the patchwork quilt of ornamental wood that made up the door. Two bridesmaids stood on either side of the opening.

A slight figure dressed in a beautiful bright-red dress stepped out of the chair. The bride's head was covered with a piece of red cloth and her face was hidden beneath it. Taking small steps, she was guided into the hall. She had the smallest feet Robert had seen on a woman. Since most of his time was spent with men, he had never seen a woman with bound feet before. None of the women among the boat people had bound feet, and Ayaou and Shao-mei had regular sized feet.

"It is customary to wait five hours." Ayaou whispered. "You should thank Master Ping for telling you to come right before the bride arrived."

The servants replaced the candles on the tables with larger candles. On the sides of each candle, good wishes were carved into the wax. Each candle had a different scent symbolizing separate elements and aspects of life. One scent was particularly strong. Robert started to wheeze and his eyes itched. He discovered that candle had opium mixed in the wax. He moved to the far side of the room. It took a few minutes before he recovered.

The elaborate ceremony went on. Nobody seemed to care about time. Finally, the *Bye Tiendee*, begging for heaven's blessing, began. Ayaou watched with interest when the couple started what Robert called the endless 'pecking'. They bowed to the altars, the spirits of their ancestors five generations back, to great-uncles and aunts, to grandparents, and to both sets of parents. He felt sorry for their poor necks going up and down.

Ayaou hid behind the crowd while they watched. When he attempted to put an arm around her, she moved away from him as if she didn't want anyone to know they were together. She smiled carefully to people who greeted her. Robert remembered that belonging to him caused her to lose face to other Chinese. Understanding her behavior didn't stop him from resenting it. At the same time, he felt as if he were a hypocrite.

There was envy in Ayaou's eyes. Although she did not express it, he knew she would have loved to have the same ceremony for herself. On the other hand, she knew that she'd never get the respect Tee Lee Ping and his bride received. She belonged to Robert, a foreigner. She was an outcast in her community. The Chinese had unspoken moral rules running like veins through the body of their society. Master Ping had invited Robert, not out of respect for Ayaou but for his student. To the Chinese, Ayaou had no status—she did not exist and was as good as dead.

Robert could offer Ayaou no comfort. If he married her, he'd be considered decadent to the Western community. The missionaries, except William Martin, would sentence him to hell and eternal damnation. They would say he'd gone native—that the heathens had enticed him away from the one true God.

He knew that William would attempt to convince him to convert Ayaou to Christianity. William had tried once before, but Robert had ignored him. He had his reasons for not wanting Ayaou to become a Christian.

Besides, his family belonged to a Methodist religion founded by John Wesley, who preached that women were equal to men and not chattel.

Robert had been avoiding this. He wanted to be accepted by his people. He believed that if he married Ayaou, his career in the British consular service would become frozen. He'd never advance. It was expected that he marry a woman from Ireland.

Before they departed, Robert wished the bride and groom great luck and plenty of children. Tee Lee Ping accepted the wish and again thanked him for the hens.

The rain had let up, so he dismissed the sedan chair. He checked his coat pocket to make sure the revolver was there. "Do you have your weapon?" he asked.

Ayaou lifted the cloth bag she had brought with her so he could see the revolver. He nodded. "Good," he said. "Be alert." They walked down the narrow street toward their house. She was unusually quiet. He thought she was worried like he was. He hated living in fear—not knowing when another blow was coming.

He tried to get her to talk. "They certainly had to wait a long time to be married. The poor bugger had to save his money for thirteen years to put that on in proper style. It must be horribly expensive."

Ayaou did not respond. She appeared deep in thought.

Until that night, their lovemaking had been frantic as if they might not live another hour. Once home, Ayaou was tender. While they were making love, he smelled the sun and the ocean in her hair—something he cherished.

"I fear the future," Ayaou said.

He knew what she meant, but what could he say? One part of him wanted to make a marriage proposal right then, but his other half, the British half, said no.

He slipped his arms around her. She nestled against him. "No matter what happens," he said, "you must know that I love you." He felt a twinge of guilt. Sleep wasn't going to come easy.

One evening soon after the wedding, he arrived home to find Ayaou's father waiting in the downstairs sitting room. He hadn't seen the old man since Shao-mei's funeral.

By the expression on Ayaou's face, he knew her father's reason for being there was not good.

He greeted Chou Luk properly, and they made small talk for an hour. He learned that Chou Luk had been busy moving opium inland for Captain Patridge.

Ayaou served tea. Then she sat on the far side of the room with her arms folded across her chest. She avoided eye contact with Robert. Something was wrong, but he couldn't guess what it was. His stomach churned.

Finally, he couldn't take the Chinese way of beating around the bush any longer. He leaned toward Chou Luk and asked, as only a foreigner could without causing insult or embarrassment, "What has brought you here?"

"A family matter. I have discovered that both Ayaou and Captain Patridge have been lying to me."

"I'm sorry," Robert said. "I am not sure I understand."

The old man avoided looking at him. Instead, he took a sip from his teacup. His eyes remained downcast. A moment later, he said, "Until last month, I had not been in Shanghai for a long time. When I was there recently, I had business with Boss Takee. Ward was there."

Robert's stomach tightened like a hangman's noose during an execution. He thought he might vomit. He avoided looking at Ayaou. "Tell me what he said." His voice was strained. It felt as if a bucket of ice water had been dumped on his head.

"He told me you took Ayaou from him without paying for her. He said you insulted his patience, which led him to kill Shao-mei by mistake. He knows he killed the wrong sister. He still wants Ayaou."

"Ward lied," Robert said. The anger swelled like a giant balloon. He struggled to control the explosion. With an effort, he calmly explained what happened. "I borrowed the money from Captain Patridge. I went to Shanghai to pay, but Ward had been seriously wounded in battle. He wasn't there. I couldn't find him. Eventually, I discovered he'd gone to the countryside to mend. I am still willing to pay." Robert knew he couldn't pay. He'd spent too much on Shao-mei's funeral. Most of the money was gone.

He wanted to know how Ward found out that he had killed the wrong sister. Who told him? Maybe Ward had spies in Ningpo watching. That thought scared him. He looked at the front door making sure the locking bar was in place. Maybe someone would come for her tonight. Maybe he should take Ayaou and find a place to hide. But where? Maybe they could flee to the Yellow Mountains in Anhui Province. He had read the poem by Li Bai, the great Tang poet.

Thousands of feet high towers the Yellow Mountains
With its thirty-two magnificent peaks,
Blooming like golden lotus flowers,
Amidst red crags and rock columns.

He'd seen watercolors for this breathtaking area of China. Maybe one of the Buddhist monasteries hidden in those mountains would let them stay. He frowned—too many maybes. He hated maybes.

He wondered if Captain Patridge was behind it all. Was he keeping Ward stirred up over Ayaou so Robert would stay bound to him? After all, it was to Patridge's benefit that he continued to use his position with the British consulate in Ningpo to help smuggle opium into China. Patridge had also asked him to keep the duties low for the legal cargoes. Due to his efforts, the captain was making a fortune for his employer and himself.

"Ward is crazy." Chou Luk folded his hands, and they disappeared inside his long, wide sleeves. "I want no trouble with him."

"What did you tell him?" he asked, afraid of the answer.

Chou Luk leaned forward. The skin around his eyes crinkled causing his eyes to look like they were shrinking. "Ward believes Ayaou is still his property. If—" The stony expression on Robert's face stopped him.

It took all his discipline to stay seated. He wanted to strangle Chou Luk. However, it would have been wrong to kill the messenger. Besides, Ayaou wouldn't like it. He almost laughed at the irony. "Ayaou is not leaving!" he said.

"I do not want to see Ayaou go with Ward either." Tears filled the old man's eyes. "He killed Shao-mei. He will have no trouble killing Ayaou. The problem is that he is after me now. He wants me to give him Ayaou, or I will lose my life. I told him to allow me some time to find her. I lied. I did not tell him where she was. Think of a plan quick."

Ayaou left her chair and went to the kitchen. Robert knew she was angry. He never told her she still belonged to Ward. At this point, there was nothing he could do to keep her from getting hurt. He feared losing her. He couldn't survive another blow like the loss of Shao-mei.

"If you believe he means to kill you," he said, you must take your family to Macao, find Uncle Bark's son, and stay with him on his junk Do you have money for passage?"

"Not enough."

"I'll help."

"What about you and Ayaou?" Chou Luk asked. "He knows where you are."

"I'll deal with it," he said. He didn't know what he was going to do if Ward came with a bunch of cutthroats. He didn't have the money to pay for protection. If he wanted protection, he'd have to ask Captain Patridge for help. He was sure the opium merchant would say yes.

Patridge wanted his oath that he would serve for decades. But Robert did not believe the opium trade was a good thing. It was a poison of the worst kind.

Ayaou came to bed after she settled Chou Luk in for the night. She had her back to Robert. He put a hand on her shoulder. She shrugged it off. "Please tell me what's on your mind," he said, and managed to keep his voice from sounding as if he were begging.

"You believed that if I did not know the truth, I would be better off. But, Robert, you were wrong. Being kept in the dark has always frustrated me more than anything. That is why I constantly seek a fortuneteller's advice. Since Shao-mei's death, my life is filled with chaos. Even you, my closest one, keep secrets from me."

"I did what I felt was best. Turn around, Ayaou, please. I want to talk to your face."

She turned. He saw the tears and pulled her into his arms. Her body was stiff like a limb from an old tree. "I am your woman, Robert. You bought my body, not my heart. It was me who offered my heart."

"Yes and that is priceless. I only hope to be worthy. But—" He felt a bitter taste in his mouth that he couldn't explain—not to Ayaou or to himself.

Ayaou leaned over him and stared into his eyes. Her long, black hair tickled his face. He felt her warm breath against his skin. The way she was looking at him made him nervous.

"I dug a hole in the yard and buried an ugly stone with dog shit," she said. "It is to keep Ward from reaching us. Mr. Yin-Yang gave me instructions. He predicted we would be safe for now. But there was something else he said that bothers me."

"What is it?" He moved out from under her and sat. He was disgusted with himself for falling into this superstitious trap. On the other hand, he wanted to hear what the fortuneteller had said.

"I do not want to believe it," she said. "Mr. Yin-Yang said that I might be doing something unwise. I might be trying to fetch the moon's reflection in the water with a bamboo basket. Mr. Yin-Yang believes that my safety rests in your heart. I kind of know what he meant, but—"

She didn't finish. He dreaded what he thought she meant. Could he measure up? Was his love strong enough? He wasn't sure.

Chapter 29

He was going to Canton—to war. He was going to be in the thick of it.

Thinking that death might be waiting in Canton pushed Ward's threat from his mind, and Canton was a thousand miles south of Ningpo and Shanghai.

This all came about in March 1858. He had been advanced in rank to become a second assistant, and his annual pay increased to five hundred pounds.

There was another reason he was pleased. Transferring to Canton meant an end to his business relationship with Captain Patridge. It felt good knowing he would no longer help Patridge cheat the Chinese while smuggling opium into China. All he had to do was stay alive.

"Robert," Master Ping said during their last lesson, "to truly understand China, you must know that China is not one culture but many."

He was going to miss his language teacher. They had become friends. During the winter, the lessons had moved to the kitchen table closer to the tiger stove. The parlor was deserted. Since Shao-mei's shrine was in there, he didn't miss that room.

He brewed the chrysanthemum tea Guan-jiah had given him. He wanted this last lesson with Master Ping to be two friends saying goodbye.

"To understand what I am talking about," Ping said, "I recommend that you study poems written during the fourth, fifth and sixth centuries during the time northern China fell under the control of the invading Tartars. Southern China stayed under Chinese rule as a separate nation. The poetry of the south focused on love, while the poetry of the north focused on the spear or the sword."

"It's too bad that the Cantonese aren't writing about love today," Robert said. He took the kettle and poured hot water over the dried flowers, spices and berries in each cup. When the cups were full, he capped them to steep. He then placed the cups on a tray and carried them to the kitchen table. There was a bowl of dried red dates on the tray too.

Master Ping took his cup, lifted the lid and inhaled. His frog like features relaxed. His eyelids closed halfway. Then he said, "The focus of these poems demonstrates why China has never been ruled by a southerner and that most if not all of the generals of China's armies have always been from the north where life is harder."

Robert's mind kept drifting. What was Canton going to be like? Since Qin-shi-huang-di, the First Emperor, had unified China two hundred years before Christ, the Cantonese had wanted to be a nation again, separate from the rest.

"The invading Tartars came from the north and so did the Mongols. The Ch'ing Dynasty that rules China today also came from beyond the wall." Ping took his cup, lifted the lid and made loud sucking sounds as he sipped tea.

Since the Arrow Incident near Canton in 1856, the British and French had been at war with the Ch'ing Dynasty. The Dynasty was being forced to fight two wars—one with the Taipings and the other with the British and French. The British and French were also fighting the Taipings. That made the British and French allies with the Dynasty. It was confusing.

"Master Ping, I doubt if I will find another teacher as sensitive to my needs as you have been. I've learned much under your guidance. I honestly don't know what I will do without you."

The British were demanding that China be opened to British merchants. They wanted the opium trade legalized and foreign imports to be exempt from internal transit duties. There were more demands, but the one about opium bothered Robert the most. There were times he was embarrassed to be working for the British.

Ping put his cup down, folded his hands together, and nodded. "I thank you for the praise," he said. "However, you no longer need a teacher. You are now skilled enough in both the written and spoken language of China to learn on your own. The only thing left is to see that China is not one culture and one nation but many. Since you are going to Canton, you will see this firsthand. People in the south are not like those from the north. You will experience what I mean by living with them."

"I don't understand," Robert said. "What is it that I have to look for?" He wondered if he had the time—if it would be safe to try.

Master Ping took a handful of the dried dates and started eating them. At first, he was careful to make sure there were no pits. Then he started to chew with enthusiasm.

"How has China survived being conquered so many times and stayed one nation?" Robert asked. "When barbarians conquered the Roman Empire, everything fell apart. It took centuries to rebuild and instead of one empire, many nations argue and fight each other. War follows war."

"Maybe that explains why China is so weak," Master Ping replied. "For centuries, no nation threatened China. We were too powerful. The answer to your question may be in the power of piety. In Europe and Britain, individuality is the focus. In China, the family is the center of all things. I believe that is the reason China survived. The family unit has always been too strong to allow a collapse like what happened to your Roman Empire." He sipped tea and ate more dates. "Emperors and dynasties come and go but piety remains as the anchor that keeps China from sinking.

"China is like a house, and the family instead of the individual is the foundation. One wall may be built of stone, another of wood and a third of hay. The front of the house may be glass. Because of the family foundation, the house stays together and refuses to collapse. Every family member does his duty and keeps his wall standing."

Robert thought of Guan-jiah and his family. Once, they had land and prospered in the silk trade. Due to the Taiping rebellion, they had lost it all and fled to the safety of Ningpo to start over. His servant made a great sacrifice when he castrated himself and applied for a job inside the Forbidden City to help his family. He didn't think anyone in the West would have suffered like that. He knew he would not have gone that far to help his family.

Before leaving Ningpo, Ayaou and Robert had a heartbreaking separation.

"Ayaou, can't you understand? This is my job. This is how I earn the money that pays for everything we have—even the food we eat."

She sat with her back to him. Every time he walked around to look into her eyes, she turned away. It was tearing him up to see her face twisting itself into a dishrag of misery.

"You are going to leave me as Shao-mei did," Ayaou said. "I have heard talk of Canton and the fighting. It is safer here. Everyone is a stranger there. Tell them you do not want the job in Canton. Stay in Ningpo. If you love me, you will leave this job with the British consulate, and we will go live in a cave. You can work the fields so we have rice and yams. I will sew and cook and keep the cave clean."

"I'm not going to abandon you, and I am not going to live in a cave."

"Then you do not love me as you keep saying. You are a liar."

"I told you that after I settle in Canton, I will send for you and Guan-jiah."

"Guan-jiah!" She spit the eunuch's name out as if it was the pit from a rotten fruit. "I do not want to live with strangers."

"Who else is there to live with? Your father has taken his family and gone to Macao to live with Uncle Bark and his son. They had to go so Ward wouldn't hunt them down. There's no one here for you to live with but my servant and his family. We're lucky they are willing to take you in."

"Ha," she said. "You are paying them. I will be an orphan. I do not believe I will ever hear your voice or feel your touch again. I am destined to sleep alone on a bed of dry rice. I will become a virgin again. I will shrivel and blow away with the next monsoon."

"Stop, Ayaou! I can't take this. No more complaints. I should take Guan-jiah's advice and beat you."

She stared at him. With the backs of her hands, she wiped away her tears. "You will really beat me?" It was as if he had poured hope into her.

"Yes, I will," he replied, not sure where this was going.

"Then you do love me." She threw herself into his arms. "Only a man who is willing to beat his concubine will keep her.

The man who does not care will ignore her like she was a shoe with a hole in it." She pushed away and stepped out of reach. Her eyes narrowed into slits. "You just said that to give me hope. Guan-jiah instructed you to threaten me, so I would feel better."

"No—a thousand times no!" It was frustrating. He didn't know what was coming next.

"So, why are you not hitting me?" She put her hands on her hips. "You are lying."

Robert couldn't believe it. She wanted him to hit her. He stepped forward and pushed her shoulder. She rocked back on her feet. Her face dissolved into misery. Tears flowed. "I knew you did not love me." She wailed. "That was not a blow. That was a breath of dead air. Our love has drowned in the river."

Robert grabbed her and sat on the bed. He pulled her onto his lap and turned her so her back faced him. With an open palm, he spanked her as hard as he could. He kept at it until she cried from the pain.

He shoved her off his lap. She hit the floor with a thud. She rolled over and stared at him. Her mouth was hanging open.

"How much love does that add up to?" he said. "Tell me, was that enough to convince you I am going to send for you—that we will be together in Canton?"

She rubbed her bottom. "I do not know if I will be able to sit for a week. It will hurt to walk. I am going to have to hobble around like someone with bound feet."

"It hurts doesn't it?"

She nodded. There were no more tears. Her eyes were wide and unblinking. She looked stunned.

"Good, if you complain again about my going away and vanishing and not loving you, I'll beat you until you are covered in black and blue bruises. If that's what it takes to get you to see that I'm telling you the truth, I'll do it."

"Robert, I do not speak Cantonese and most Cantonese do not speak Mandarin or any of the northern dialects. I am going to be nobody in Canton—a person no one will hear or see or talk to. I will be a lonely ghost."

"You have nothing to worry about. Our love is strong like the love between Niu Lang and Zhi Nu." He was referring to a romantic allegory that had been in China for almost two thousand years since the Chin Dynasty. "You know what I'm talking about. We've read the *Fairy of the Magpie Bridge* and talked about it."

"Yes, I know that poem," she said, and recited it. "In the middle of the lovely clouds above the heavenly river crosses the weaving maiden. A night of being together again crossing the sky of autumn exceeds joy on earth. Moments of tender love and dreams. So sad to leave the magpie bridge."

"Do you remember who wrote it?" he asked.

"Yes," she said, "Qin Guan during the Sung Dynasty." Tears escaped from her eyes. Her chest heaved. "I do not have a magical cowhide that will carry me to you." She stopped to catch her breath between sobs. "And even if I did, the Queen of Heaven would draw a line across the sky to keep us apart. We could only meet once a year on the seventh day of the seventh lunar month."

"We aren't Niu Lang and Zhi Nu, Ayaou. We are both mortals. Zhi Nu was a fairy and you are not a fairy. You are human. The Queen of Heaven will not keep us apart. I only mentioned the poem because the love Niu Lang and Zhi Nu have for each other equals ours. It is eternal."

"I still cannot speak Cantonese. That will be the line separating us. You will forget your Mandarin."

"Not true, Ayaou. I will not forget Mandarin. We will speak it daily. I also taught you to read and write."

"But I cannot go shopping. No one will understand me."

"Guan-jiah assures me he can make himself understood in Cantonese and understands more than he can speak. When you shop, Guan-jiah will go with you. Besides, I don't want you out of the house alone. Everything will be okay. You have family in Macao less than a hundred miles from Canton. I'm sure that Chou-luk will come to visit when the fighting subsides."

Robert was letting go of the Ningpo house. The furniture would go into storage. When he sent for Guan-jiah and Ayaou, the furniture would come with them. He felt that Ayaou would be safe living with Guan-jiah's family. Guan-jiah understood Ayaou's importance to Robert. He was the only one he trusted with Ayaou's welfare and safety.

If Ward had spies watching, he hoped they would follow him to Canton. That way, they wouldn't notice where Ayaou went.

Guan-jiah said, "I will die, Master, before anyone touches one hair on her head." He threw himself to the ground and started knocking his head against the stones. Robert lifted him to his feet before he hurt himself but not before he'd bruised his forehead.

"What have I told you about doing that, Guan-jiah? Never again."

"I am sorry, Master. I am an acorn, and China is the oak."

The voyage south from Ningpo to Hong Kong covered nine hundred miles. Robert sailed aboard the *Prospero*. He stayed in Hong Kong for a few days where he met a young, attractive American.

"My name is Patricia," she said. He could tell she was an American by her colonial accent. She'd surprised him by being the first to speak. Most proper British women would have waited for the man to start the conversation and then would have replied only under proper circumstances. That meant a chaperon had to be there along with her parent's approval.

A moment of silence stretched between them until he realized she was waiting for him to respond. "My name is Hart, Robert Hart," he said.

"Are you Irish?" she said. "I can tell by your accent. I've always loved the Irish. My grandfather came to America from Ireland." She cocked her head at an angle and smiled. It was a cute gesture, and his body responded. This weakness embarrassed him. He hoped she wouldn't notice.

"How long have you been in China? What do you do? It's exciting, isn't it?" She had a smooth cream-colored complexion. Her lips were full and inviting. She had shiny, straw colored hair. Her eyes were sky blue. He was tempted to touch her hair to see if it was as soft as it looked.

"I've been here four years," he replied. "I work for the British consulate as an interpreter." He felt his neck heating under the tight, white collar. Good god, he was turning red. He hated when that happened.

Her eyes grew wide. "You speak Chinese," she said. "How fantastic!" For an instant, he thought she was going to jump up and down like a child. "I hoped that you wouldn't be another boring merchant who can think of only one thing—money."

He almost laughed. She had flashing eyes. He couldn't help but notice that she also had an ample bosom. His desire was heating toward the boiling point. This was how it had always started in college.

"I hate to be so forward, Robert," she said, "but I'm on my way to Singapore in a few days to visit my father. He works there. I have no friends here and no one to dine with." She touched his wrist with her fingertips. Her touch lingered too long. His breath became shorter, faster. He struggled to stay in control. "After we eat, you could go shopping with me. Your Chinese will come in handy."

She was attractive. He was taken by her. He was ready to accept her invitation to dine. Then he remembered Ayaou. Before falling in love with Ayaou, he would not have hesitated but his world had changed. He had not realized how much until this moment. A voice screamed inside his head telling him to accept and take her to dinner and shopping. Afterwards, anything might happen. His imagination went exploring—his hands touching her naked body and her responding.

"I'm sorry, Ma'am, but as lovely and fetching as you are, I'm not free to dine with a single woman. You see, I have a wife, and I love her."

You are a liar. Ayaou is not your wife, the inner voice said. She is your concubine. The Chinese will not condemn you if you take this woman.

If I did cheat, he replied, it would hurt Ayaou.

That doesn't matter, the voice replied. Ayaou is a piece of furniture that you own. How can property complain?

The disappointment in the Patricia's eyes didn't help.

He regretted not accepting her offer, and sleep eluded him that night. While he had been attending college in Belfast, his goal had been to get the girls in bed as quickly as possible. That eventually got him in trouble with his father and was the reason he was in China. Not only had he embarrassed his family, but he had caught syphilis too.

Since he'd had intercourse with so many young women in Belfast, he wasn't sure who gave it to him. After arriving in China, the same weakness drove him to have sex with Me-ta-tae. That resulted in Payne Hollister becoming his enemy. He

334

didn't know what was worse—having syphilis or another man hating him.

He should have been glad he had rejected the American girl. Instead, he was confused. The only way to evict the image of Patricia and shut off the voice inside his head was to masturbate. Then he slept.

Soon he would be in Canton and have other problems to deal with like staying alive.

Chapter 30

On his third day in Hong Kong, an ensign came to Robert's room in the consulate with a summons from the captain of the *Forrester*, a British gunboat.

"We're sailing immediately, sir," the ensign said. "The captain sent me to fetch you. We must hurry."

He hadn't expected to leave on such short notice and didn't have time to wait for his luggage. It had to be left behind to be shipped by chop, a licensed cargo boat for transporting goods between local ports.

Fog rolled in and it rained destroying his chance to see the countryside along the river during the trip. Canton was eighty miles inland along the Pearl River, the third longest in China after the Yangtze and the Yellow.

Arriving off Canton, the *Forrester* drifted to its anchorage passing one of the floating villages dotting the wide river. The different sized sampans had been tied together to form a dingy, ramshackle village of houseboats with rounded, turtle like tops. Small children were fastened to ropes to keep them from falling into the river. A rooster preened its rusty colored feathers. Chickens walked about the decks pecking at whatever was edible.

Ayaou and Shao-mei had come from this culture, which is why he asked Tee Lee Ping about the boat people.

"A myth explains it," Ping had replied. "Several thousand years ago, a clan of Chinese boat people wronged an emperor. Because of this, they were banned forever from owning land or living on it. Many boat people are born and die on their boats without walking on land."

He was overwhelmed with emotion and missed Ayaou horribly as if a vital part of his body had been left behind. They had been together three years without a separation.

He soon learned that Canton was an armed camp filled with British and French troops. James Bruce, the Eighth Earl of Elgin and the Twelfth Earl of Kincardine, was the British High Commissioner. At one time, Bruce had been the Governor General of Canada and the viceroy of India.

But the man responsible for Canton, with a population of a million, was Harry Parkes, who was part of the three man allied commission appointed to govern the city due to hostilities with local rebels and an element of the imperial government led by Chinese Commissioner Yeh.

The Chinese Commissioner had put a thirty-dollar bounty on the head of each Englishmen. Robert had heard that Yeh was a stubborn man, loyal to Peking.

He was quartered with army officers in a large building converted into a military barracks. The building was in a part of the city taken over by British and French forces.

The small room was on the second floor. It was the size of a closet with a narrow bunk and dresser. The one window had a glass pane missing. There was no closet. After washing his face and hands, he left for his first meeting with Commissioner Parkes.

It didn't take long to reach the headquarters building. When he entered Parkes's office, the commissioner was seated behind a massive teak desk. Parkes came around the desk and shook Robert's hand. "Great to meet you, Hart," Parkes said with a voice that promised unlimited energy. Parkes was a man of middle height, olive fair complexion, light-yellow hair and soft, sandy whiskers.

Robert handed Parkes a letter. "From your wife, sir," he said.

Parkes put the letter on his desk without opening it. "I miss her. It is unfortunate that she must live in Hong Kong, but it's too dangerous here."

Hearing this caused Robert to question if it were wise to have Ayaou join him. But she was not foreign and she wasn't his wife.

"I've heard you can read their minds," Parkes said, "and know what a Chinese man is thinking before he opens his mouth. I speak Chinese, but I seem to put my foot in my mouth every time I deal with these buggers. I'm counting on you to do the talking and help get this mess straightened out."

"I'm flattered, commissioner, but it isn't true. I don't read minds. I learned how the Chinese think."

"Capital," Parkes said. "It's a rare man that knows when to shut up and listen. I'm not one. Have you heard the rumor that I am not an easy man to work for? I'm sure you have."

"I haven't been here long enough to hear anything, and I don't take rumors seriously. I never have. I let actions speak for themselves—not words."

"Well, I don't agree with that rumor," Parkes said. "I demand that my people do their jobs. That sometimes means going without sleep and working long hours. It also means taking risks."

Parkes slapped Robert on the back and guided him toward the door. "Before you settle into your quarters, I have a job for you. I need an interpreter who knows how to change my words so the Chinese aren't insulted. I will also get a chance to see if what they say about you is true. Since I speak Chinese, I may learn something."

A mounted squad of military police waited outside the building. Parkes swung into his saddle and indicated another horse. "Mount up, Hart."

"What do you want me to do?" he asked, not wanting to rush into something he knew nothing about.

Everyone was mounted and the column started to move.

"I can see you are the cautious type," Parkes replied. His horse tossed its head and pranced about. "We'll talk on the move." Parkes left.

Robert mounted and had to hurry to catch the squad. The clatter of the horses warned the Chinese to move out of the way, and the streets emptied as if by magic.

"A new Chinese viceroy, Huang Tsung-han, is expected in Canton soon," Parkes said. "The problem is that the current viceroy wants to leave the city to greet him before he gets here and that won't do. What do you suggest?"

Robert thought fast. "Commissioner, if he doesn't go, the Imperials in Peking will accuse him of a lack of courtesy. The emperor is considered the same as a god. If he commands, the Chinese obey. The first of Confucius's Five Great Relationships is between ruler and subject and the emperor is the viceroy's master."

"Stupid cultural habits," Parkes said. Robert didn't know how to respond. "Well, that can't be all you have to say. Spit it out."

"The viceroy will lose face if he doesn't do what he's told. The emperor will see it as an insult. Violating the first relationship demonstrates a lack of loyalty. He might have to kill himself or lose his head to make up for it."

"And how are you going to get around that obstacle?" Parkes asked.

"Allow me to use this time while we are on our way to the viceroy to think of what to say." He was frantic to be understood by the viceroy and had to think of a way to resolve this problem. He hated the thought that a man might die because of Parkes's ignorance.

Parkes stared at Robert under lowered eyebrows that looked more like storm clouds, before he said, "Yes, I understand. Good. In addition, my dear chap, you should know he isn't expecting us. This is a surprise visit. I was afraid if he knew we were coming, he'd leave earlier than planned."

Robert was about to say the Chinese didn't like surprises. Then the squad made a sharp turn in to a wider avenue with more people crowding it. Before he could say a word, the squad of armed military police increased the pace to a gallop. Parkes's mount shot forward in a burst of speed leaving Robert behind. The Chinese people scattered like chickens chased by a fox. It was a challenge to keep up since he didn't ride horses often.

When the column reached the viceroy's house, Parkes gave orders. The military police spread out setting up a cordon around the building.

"Come on, Hart. I need you. Remember, you do not have to say exactly what I tell you. Just get what I mean across in a way that will not insult the man. I don't want another crisis."

Two flustered servants ushered Parkes and Robert into the viceroy's presence as he was slipping into his ceremonial robes. "Hello, dear chap," Parkes said.

Robert interpreted it into something more honorable than 'dear chap'.

"Tell him we've heard he's anxious to go meet the new viceroy that's replacing him. I understand it is his duty, but we don't want him to leave Canton. If he leaves, there are those who sympathize with the Taipings that want to cause riots. If he stays, there won't be riots."

Parkes not only spoke fast, but he gestured with his arms and hands to emphasize his words. He looked like a windmill. "We also understand that he'll lose face if he doesn't meet the new viceroy. We are going to solve that by keeping him here under guard. That way he can blame everything on me and tell his superiors I prevented him from fulfilling his duty."

It was Robert's first challenge in Canton. He was sure there would be others. He changed what Parkes wanted him to say into Chinese so the viceroy would not feel insulted.

He planned to bribe the man but not make it look like a bribe. The minute he saw the viceroy, he guessed his weakness. The man was fat. There weren't many fat Chinese. Knowing how much the Chinese loved food, Robert felt confident of a solution. The Chinese accepted food as they accepted sex. This man looked like he enjoyed food more than the average Chinese did.

First, Robert introduced himself and nodded. Then he started a conversation. "I have become addicted to eating crabs," he said. "How do you feel about crabs?"

Parkes's eyebrows bounced and a look of consternation flooded the commissioner's face. Robert was glad that Parkes kept his mouth shut. Otherwise, his scheme might have fallen apart.

"I'm a slave to crabs," the viceroy said.

"Why?" Robert knew there was a shortage of crabs in Canton. He also knew they could be found in Hong Kong or Macao and shipped overnight on a British gunboat.

"I'm addicted to the fragrance, the flavor and the color."

"What about bamboo shoots?" he asked. "I understand the rebels have made it difficult to get fresh bamboo-shoots into the city and local supplies are running low."

The viceroy's expression saddened in a dramatic fashion. Robert knew the man was guessing what was going on and was playing his part. "I haven't had young bamboo shoots for weeks."

Robert was elated. He was sure that the viceroy was going to cooperate. He was also sure the viceroy was getting the food he wanted and was paying a premium for it. Food on the black market was expensive.

"I have a solution. I'm sure that you can eat as well as the emperor in Peking and probably better." The French were in the city, and he'd heard an officer in the British barracks talking about one of the French colonels who was a fantastic cook.

The viceroy looked curious. Robert had caught his interest and free food was going to be the bribe.

"Commissioner Parkes wants you to stay in Canton until your replacement arrives. He is willing to provide the freshest crabs, the tenderest bamboo shoots and any other foods that are available you have missed because of the rebels and the difficulties with trade."

Parkes's eyebrows lifted in surprise and stayed that way. Robert guessed he was struggling to control himself from speaking or possibly burst out laughing. Either action would kill the negotiation and embarrass the viceroy. He was nervous that Parkes was going to mess everything up. Parkes started to open his mouth.

Robert switched to English. "I don't wish to sound rude but drastic circumstances call for drastic words. Keep it shut, commissioner, or this mess you wanted to avoid will materialize." Parkes's face turned scarlet and his cheeks puffed up.

Robert turned to the viceroy. "Commissioner Parkes says he knows a famous French cook who can create miracles and cause you to groan in pleasure after every meal. He wants to do this because if you leave, trade will become disrupted. The rebels will take advantage of your absence and cause trouble.

"Many fathers in Canton will go without food. Their sons will die of starvation. Grandfathers will die of thirst. Many may lose their heads and never enjoy the taste of crabs or the sensation that young bamboo shoots give to your teeth while you are chewing them." He paused to let the words sink in hoping the viceroy would recognize the hidden meanings.

"Of course," Robert said, "it is your decision. If you have to leave because the emperor ordered it, we understand." This time Robert did not glance to see how Parkes was reacting. He could imagine the man swelling up like a pidgin in distress.

Deciding to add icing to the cake, he said, "I know this Frenchman has stood beside the greatest Chinese cook in Hong Kong and taken lessons from him." It was a lie. "He knows the secrets from the Emperor's kitchen in the

Forbidden City. In other words, if you leave before your replacement arrives, you will eat poorly all the way to Peking. There will be no food to be had on the journey. You will have to eat rice and grass the entire trip." Robert paused to create some drama and lifted his eyebrows as if he were asking an unspoken question.

"Oh the other hand," he said, "if you stay, we will make sure you have a supply of your favorite foods to go with you when you leave on your safe journey north."

A distressed look filled the viceroy's face. Robert knew he was struggling. He held his breath waiting for the reply. The silence lasted too long.

"You are worried the emperor may be angry when you do not arrive on time," Robert said, afraid he was going to fail. If he didn't succeed, he could find himself out of a job or demoted.

"You may even be worried that the rebels may strike and harm you or your family. But there is no reason to worry. Commissioner Parkes has agreed to take full responsibility for your tardiness. I will draft a letter the commissioner will sign that absolves you of all blame. It will be written in Mandarin so there will be no problems interpreting it. If you stay, you will eat better than the emperor will.

"It would help convince the emperor, if you made a formal request that Commissioner Parkes leave his military police here to watch over your house. That way, if the emperor asks, you could say you had no choice, because you weren't allowed to leave. We can help stage the entire affair so no one will know you are eating your way to heaven."

They returned to the headquarters. Robert was invited to dinner along with two assistants, both taller than he was. During dinner, Parkes talked the most.

"I liked what you did at the viceroy's, Hart," Parkes said. "You accomplished a near miracle. If anyone else had been with me, it would have probably instigated another crisis. You're as good as they say, a real mind reader." He stopped and a stern look came into his face. He sat straight and cleared his throat as if ready to pass sentence on a criminal.

"I apologize for my rudeness, commissioner," Robert said, anticipating what might be coming.

Parkes shook his head. He smiled. "You are a mind reader, young man. From now on, I expect you to be ready at a moment's notice to accompany me anytime I need another miracle. By the way, who is this French cook you were talking about?"

"I have no idea."

One of the other men at the table choked on his food. His face flushed dark. He took a glass of wine and drank half.

"Be careful, Lockwood," Parkes said. "I don't want you to die on me."

Lockwood waved a hand and managed to clear his throat and breathe. He drank more wine and turned his head aside to cough.

"I heard that one of the French colonels loves to cook," Robert said. "I took a chance. I'm sure you can discover who the man is and arrange for him to show off his skills. It will be easy to have crabs and the best-quality bamboo shoots shipped from Hong Kong or Macao and anything else the Frenchman requests. Besides, since the viceroy agreed, he will not want to lose face. Even if the food doesn't measure up, he will act as if it does. He will say anything to save face. No one on his staff will disagree because of piety and the Five Great Relationships."

"You are amazing, Hart. Won't it ruin your reputation among the Chinese if the food is bad?"

"Not really. The viceroy will keep his mouth shut. He will not want anyone to discover that I fooled him. If I helped him save face, he will never forget. He will even owe me a debt."

"Explain these confusing Confucian relationships to me."

"The Chinese have lived with them for twenty-five-hundred years, sir. That's when Confucius spent his life preaching the moral code that is China's bedrock." Robert went into detail.

When he finished, Parkes looked around the table at the others. "I've never heard anything like it. Hart, you are amazing."

Robert stared at his food, sipped wine and avoided the eyes studying him. He remembered the times Ayaou or Shao-mei or Guan-jiah had lectured him on why he had to behave in certain ways toward the Chinese. He felt a twisting pain in his gut. He missed Ayaou. He missed his servant, and he still felt grief at Shao-mei's loss.

He managed to keep his expression neutral. No one was going to discover what he was thinking. He also hated it when others felt sorry for him. Besides, he didn't want anyone to know about his life with Ayaou. They would not understand.

Parkes complements were appreciated, but Robert didn't let the praise go to his head. "This Frenchman might be a horrible cook," he said. "That doesn't matter. My goal was to allow the viceroy to say yes instead of being forced into doing what you wanted. He knew what would happen if he didn't agree. He saved face by accepting the offer. To his staff, it will look like he accepted a culinary bribe. Even if the food is bad, he will tell everyone he went to heaven eating this Frenchman's cooking. Of course, it would help if this French colonel is a good cook."

After the meal, Parkes offered everyone a cigar. Robert did not feel like smoking. The other two men at the table also declined.

Parkes, on the other hand, lighted the cigar and started to fill the room with thick smoke. He puffed with the same energy he seemed to apply to every task. Parkes appeared to have enough energy for several, and up until meeting Parkes, Robert considered himself a hard worker. Now, he was exhausted. He hadn't slept since leaving Hong Kong the previous morning.

Parkes puffed away while continuing to talk. Without warning, he stopped talking in the middle of a sentence. The muscles in his face relaxed. His eyes were still open but looked vacant. The cigar fell from his lips.

One of the others took the cigar and snuffed the ember before placing it in an empty bowl. Parkes's head slumped forward until his chin rested on his chest. He had fallen asleep.

"It's okay to go, Hart," Lockwood said. "He won't expect you to stay. He will be awake and working at midnight. We can be sure of that. However, he doesn't expect any of us to keep the same hours."

Robert reached his room at midnight to discover a breeze blowing into the room because of the missing pane of glass. The room felt like a locker filled with blocks of ice.

He would have to get that window fixed. He had one wool blanket. It didn't take long to learn one blanket was not enough. He would have piled his clothing on top of the blanket but the rest of his clothing might not arrive for days. He didn't bother to undress when he covered himself with the blanket. His nose and toes felt frozen. He listened to the sentries and struggled to get warm by curling into a ball.

A sentry yelled, "Who goes there?"

"A friend," came the reply

"Advance, friend, and give the parole," the sentry said.

"England," came the reply.

"Pass, friend, and all's well."

Since Robert couldn't sleep, he thought about Ayaou. Sleeping without her didn't feel right. He started to shiver. He worried that he might freeze and never see her again.

That night a British sailor was murdered and his body found on the beach the next morning. Everyone was talking about it when Robert arrived at the officers' mess for breakfast.

Parkes was a hurricane of activity. He seemed to have a second sense for trouble. They were always rushing from one place to another. It was impossible for Robert to find time to search for a house.

Parkes praised him every time he soothed ruffled Chinese sensibilities. That didn't help Robert's frustration. He wanted to find a house and send for Ayaou and Guan-jiah. He wanted his adopted family back. He wanted to be warm again. He did manage to find two more blankets although they didn't help much.

When he brought up the subject about a house, Parkes said, "No, you will be safer with the British officers. I've had other hot-blooded, young men want to live in the city where they are free to keep the company of local women, but with the danger from the rebels and the imperials, I won't hear of it."

How could he tell Parkes that he wanted to send for his Chinese concubine? After all, Parkes wasn't impressed with the Chinese people and their culture. He had seen Parkes act arrogant and obnoxious in front of the Chinese. Parkes and others like him created new challenges to solve on a daily basis from their transparent attitudes and blunt behavior.

They were riding to a meeting with another Chinese official when they saw several lovely Chinese women. Because one looked like Ayaou, Robert stared.

Parkes made a thumb down gesture. "I saw you admiring that lady," he said. "There is nothing to see. Their bodies are childlike and their breasts small. How could an Englishman want such a woman in his bed? It would be like having intercourse with a child."

He worried about what Parkes might think if he knew those characteristics were precisely what excited him. He couldn't stand large breasts, big bottoms and thick thighs. Ayaou was exactly what he wanted.

His main job, besides helping Parkes keep a delicate balance in the city and the surrounding countryside, was to work as interpreter for the Anglo-French commission. The commission's job was to assist the Chinese governor in maintaining order and to take notice of legal cases where foreigners were concerned. The commission consisted of Colonel Thomas Holloway, Captain F. Martineau des Chavez, and Parkes.

On Tuesday, he left the protection of Canton with Parkes and six armed men. As they rode through one of the city gates into the countryside, Parkes said, "This is the northeast gate where Captain Bate was killed reconnoitering the walls after the capture of Lin's Fort. A bloody mess."

Bate had died when a combined allied military force of British and French soldiers took the city from the Imperial Chinese army. Hostilities had not ceased. The rebels and elements of the imperial army continued to resist and make life difficult. Canton was a dangerous place. It was worse outside the city's walls.

He wrote a letter to Ayaou and sent money. In the note, he told her to have Guan-jiah pack and purchase passage for Canton. He could not wait to be reunited. He hoped he wasn't making a mistake.

A few days later, Robert questioned why he'd done that. He'd been selfish. He knew the answer—there was a deep, dull ache inside that wouldn't go away. Only Ayaou could dispel that ache.

He would have Ayaou and Guan-jiah find a house close to his military quarters. He'd slip out in the night and spend a few hours with her before returning to the cold, unfriendly bed at the commission. The broken window had not been fixed.

One Friday afternoon, Robert left the city with Captain Pym, the commander of a hundred-man police force armed with swords and revolvers. They rode to a house outside the city walls where spies said rebels were hiding concealed weapons.

When the hundred-man column arrived, there were no people in the street. It was almost as if they had been expected. Robert felt exposed. Had they ridden into a trap? He hoped he would survive to spend another night with Ayaou.

"I don't like this," Pym said. He turned the horses over to a few men and put his back against a wall to study the rooftops. Everyone looked nervous. That didn't help how Robert felt. Pym ordered some men to climb on the roofs to keep watch. He directed most of his force to fan out and set up a perimeter. They quickly searched and secured the empty houses on both sides of the street.

"We're spread too thin," Robert said.

"I agree," Pym replied. "We should have come with twice as many men. I don't like this."

Robert felt as if hidden eyes were watching but every time he looked, nobody was there. He hoped the others would not see his nervousness.

The house they'd come to inspect was locked. After Pym's men broke in, they searched and found no weapons. They shoved furniture aside, broke table legs with their roughness and pounded on tiles, cracking some, looking for hollow spaces below the floor.

Once the search was finished, Robert followed Pym outside.

The captain spread his legs wide and put his hands on his hips. He stared at the rooftops where his men were on guard. "It makes my back crawl," he said. "If the cowards are going to attack, I wished they'd get it over with. I hate this waiting."

Robert knew exactly how he felt. It was a relief to return to the city. Later, they discovered the street had been abandoned for weeks.

Chapter 31

On the last day in May, three armed British soldiers escorted a Chinese boy into the commission. The soldiers did not look friendly, and the boy's eyes were filled with fear.

"He was asking to see you, Mr. Hart," one of the soldiers said. "We were going to knock him upside the head if he didn't leave, but he insisted."

"That's okay. You may go."

The soldiers didn't move.

Robert knelt and spoke in Cantonese. "Did someone send a message?" The boy nodded. It was obvious he was too scared to talk.

The guards glared at the boy. Robert said, "This boy weighs less than forty pounds. Do you insult me by insinuating I cannot defend myself against a child? Go."

They left.

Parkes wasn't around, and Robert knew no one in the room spoke the language. "What is the message?" he asked. His heart was pounding and he held his breath. The boy handed him a folded note. It was from Ayaou. Robert's hand trembled. She was in Canton. It took an effort to keep his voice calm and his features composed. His legs and feet wanted to run—to find her. Instead, he forced himself to breathe.

He took a yuan out of his pocket and held it for the boy to see. A common Chinese laborer had to work a sixteen-hour day to earn two or three yuan. The boy couldn't take his eyes off the coin. He reached for the money.

"Not so fast," Robert said, and held the money out of reach. "Show me where the boat is first."

The boy guided him to the river and pointed at a junk anchored a hundred yards from shore. Robert put the coin in the boy's palm, and the child stared at it as if it were a precious jewel. Then he popped it in his mouth. With the coin safely hidden, he looked to see if anyone had noticed.

"Kui loh, Kui loh, Kui loh." Robert stared at a group of adolescent boys on the other side of the street. They had called him a foreign devil. He was the only Westerner on the street and considering the state of affairs in Canton, he'd just put himself into a dangerous, life threatening situation. He remembered the murdered British sailor.

He glanced at the spot where the messenger boy had stood and discovered he was gone.

The pistol was not in Robert's pocket. A ball of fear blossomed inside his gut. Ayaou's letter had so excited him that he hadn't thought to get his revolver and bring it with him. What a stupid thing to do?

With his stomach churning, he walked toward the river. He was not going to show his fear by running. His back felt as if it were crawling with wasps. He examined all the beached sampans and was careful to pick a boat person. He hoped that a boat person would not be connected to the rebels because of their low status.

He heard a noise and looked over his shoulder. The boys were picking up rocks. Robert slipped his hand into a pocket and lifted that corner of his jacket as if a weapon were there and his finger the barrel. He put a menacing look on his face and took two steps toward the gang. The five adolescents looked from his face to the pocket as if a pistol were inside. They dropped their rocks and ran.

Robert stepped into the sampan.

He knew Ayaou when he saw her. She was standing near the junk's stern in the shadow of one of the masts. It was the way she tilted her head and her posture, which was tattooed in his memory. The only difference was that she was dressed like everyone else in the baggy, threadbare rags of a boat person. It was smart that she had not dressed in the clothing he'd bought her in Ningpo.

"Go around to the other side," he said, afraid someone onshore might notice that a foreign devil had gone aboard this junk. The sampan moved around to the far side and bumped against the larger boat's hull. He was so nervous he almost fell in the water when he missed the knotted rope tossed down.

His legs were shaky and weak from anticipation. He managed to take hold of the rope and climb. Tempted to look down, he closed his eyes instead, reached for the next knot in the rope, and pulled himself toward the deck.

"Master." It was Guan-jiah's voice. Robert opened his eyes. The eunuch's smiling face hung above him. The servant took his hand and pulled him aboard. Robert shrugged off a desire to throw his arms around the eunuch. Another man, looking like a younger Uncle Bark, stood next to Guan-jiah.

"This is Cousin Weed, Uncle Bark's only surviving son," Guan-jiah said.

Robert nodded to Weed, who nodded back. "How is your father's health?" Robert asked.

"He is well. He's waiting to see you."

Robert forced an iron band around his heart in an effort to be polite. He was trying to see Ayaou without looking obvious. She wasn't where he'd first spotted her from the sampan.

No matter how eager he was to be with her, he felt it only proper to see Uncle Bark first and pay his respects. After all, the old man had been instrumental in helping Robert survive his darkest hours.

He was ushered into a large cabin at the stern of the junk where Uncle Bark waited. He still looked like the old toothless man Robert had first met in Ningpo. Bark's skin was the color of dried leather and looked as if it had shrunk to fit against the bones of his skull making his head look like a shriveled apple. He was close to eighty, yet Robert knew this old man was strong. He remembered how easily Bark had killed men half his age during the fight that saved Ayaou's life.

Guan-jiah had already steeped the chrysanthemum tea. The cabin was filled with the flowery scent. There was also a bowl of Shan-tung red dates. "Sit," Uncle Bark said. He held out a hand to guide Robert to the floor mat in the center of the cabin. A serving tray with the tea and dates sat between them.

Robert reached for the teapot. Uncle Bark said, "Allow me." The old man poured the tea into two cups without spilling a drop. His hands looked like dried roots but did not tremble.

"I see you are in good health," Robert said.

"Early in the morning when I open my eyes, I stare at the stars before the sun chases them from the sky and feel as I did when I was a young man. Then I move, and the stiffness reminds me how long I have been eating bitterness." He shrugged and studied Robert's face with shrewd eyes. "How have you been?"

"My days are busy. The rebels make life challenging. I do not have much time to think."

"But when you try to sleep, you feel an emptiness," Uncle Bark said. "Do you remember when you were sitting at your kitchen table in Ningpo with the loaded pistol between your hands?"

"Yes, it was after Shao-mei's funeral. It was a dark moment and you took the pistol away before I made a horrible mistake. I was desperate. Ward's laughter haunted me."

"And what did I say?"

"You told me about the five women and twenty-two children you lost during your life. You said that Ayaou was going to be a living, dead thing if I didn't go to her. I had to be the rock she could cling to while the river of life flowed around us."

Uncle Bark nodded. "I often think of Shao-mei's burial ceremony. Do you remember what I said about the incense I gave you?"

"That I could say anything I wished."

"I left before I could hear your words. What did you say?"

Robert recited the poem he had taught Shao-mei the one she had memorized. "Like molten gold appears the setting sun. Clouds at evening like jade-blocks pieced into one. Where is the one close and dear to my heart from whom without mental pain, I cannot part?" He felt a twinge of agony but managed to keep it from showing. Why was Uncle Bark dredging up memoires Robert wanted to bury?

The old man studied him. "You have recovered better than Ayaou. She has been deeply wounded as the land after a typhoon uproots trees and blows houses away. It takes a great effort to rebuild. For Ayaou to heal, you must be the manure and water that her roots need. It is the only way. She fears the future."

"I still love her," Robert said. "How could she doubt that?"

"When you were working at the consulate, Shao-mei and Ayaou were inseparable. For Ayaou to heal she must find a

351

balance where she is yin and you are yang like a pair of Mandarin love ducks. She will recover knowing you are always there."

"She has doubts?"

"When you left for Canton, she was not ready for the separation. Be patient. When her tongue tests you, remember the good times before Ward murdered Shao-mei. It is the only way that the darkness might be pushed back and for her light to shine again." Uncle Bark waved a hand. "Go to her. We can sip tea another time."

Instead of speaking, Robert grasped Uncle Bark's hand in a warm embrace. He didn't trust his tongue to say what he was thinking. He blushed and cursed himself for this sign of weakness.

Once he was outside, Guan-jiah said, "Go down that ladder, Master." The eunuch indicated a rectangular, black hole in the deck. "Ayaou is waiting."

He hurried to the hole and remembered the first time he had been intimate with Ayaou. He'd dropped into a similar opening not knowing what to expect. This time he didn't feel the same misgivings. In his rush, he half slipped on the ladder and almost ended in a pile at the bottom. It was gloomy and musty like Ward's cellar the first time he'd been with her. He squinted to see.

Then he saw her and stepped forward. He couldn't describe how it felt holding her again. His throat swelled with emotion. His eyes watered. He could have missed this moment if he'd been killed on shore. He did not want to let go. He smelled the warm, ocean scent clinging to her hair, and Uncle Bark's warning was forgotten—for now.

"Let us go to our house," she said. There were tears in her eyes.

He heard the hunger in her raspy voice. His heart beat faster with anticipation. "There is no house," he said. "I didn't have time. The situation here is dangerous. After I leave, send Guan-jiah to find a house. Even with all the English and French soldiers in Canton, the wives of Westerners are staying in Hong Kong or Macao. People are killed daily. Many have fled."

"I see," she said. The following silence indicated she wasn't pleased.

"Once we have a suitable place, I'll come in the night," he said. "I will have to leave in the morning before sunrise. Until it is safer, that is how we will meet. Tell Guan-jiah to send the same boy with the location of the house."

"Poetry cannot take your place in my heart," she said, and stared into his eyes as if she were trying to read words there. She brushed his hand aside and pressed against him. He felt the rise and fall of her breasts, and her heart was beating fast like his.

"It sounds like you have been missing me, Ayaou." His eyes had adjusted to the darkness. He lifted her chin to see her face and kissed away the tears.

"I do one thing when I miss you too much," she said.

"What's that?" he asked. He loved listening to her silky voice. It reminded him of the evenings he'd spent teaching her and Shao-mei to read.

"I read books. I still have trouble believing I can read. Books are blocks between us. Every time I remove one, I am one-step closer to you. See, it is true. I am here."

"How did you get here so fast?" he asked.

"This junk belongs to Cousin Weed," she replied. "When I received your letter, I went to Uncle Bark for advice and discovered his son had delivered a cargo to Shanghai and was returning to Macao. We sailed with him."

The sensuous way her lips moved as she talked captivated him. He did not want to go ashore and return to his empty, cold bed.

"Would you like to stay tonight?" she asked. "I have been practicing on eggplants, so I would not forget how you like to be kissed."

"Eggplants?" He felt like laughing but looked serious instead. "The first time we were together, you told me your father made you practice on carrots."

"Carrots are hard," she replied. "Boiled eggplant is soft like your lips." He had a hard time imagining that his lips felt like eggplant. It was not a flattering image.

She took his hand and led him to a lower deck where the headspace was restricted. He had to walk bent over, and he wasn't a tall man. His thoughts were lost in a bedlam of emotions. He worried that if he didn't return quickly to the commission his absence would be noticed. What would Parkes say if he knew about Ayaou? The first voice in his head said to leave before he was missed. A second voice said to stay—it won.

The smell of mildew and rot was strong. Bales of cargo crowded the space. She pulled him between the bales, pushed past a burlap curtain and into a narrow space filled with quilted pads and blankets. It reminded him of their first time together in the root cellar under Ward's house.

Thinking of Ward reminded him that while the mercenary lived, he was a threat to Robert's happiness and Ayaou's safety. Canton might not be a safe place for Ayaou, but it was a long way from Ward, which brought Robert some comfort. The further they were from the Devil Soldier, the safer he felt.

She took both his hands in hers and pulled him down beside her. Their lips fed on each other. "This is much better than eggplant," she said.

"That's nice," he replied.

"Be quiet," she said.

It was a night to remember. They didn't sleep.

Robert went ashore before dawn and made his way through the dark streets back to the commission. He hated leaving the junk. Ayaou's scent clung to his clothes. As much as he wanted to keep her smell as a reminder of their night together, he didn't want anyone else to discover it and guess where he'd been.

In his room, he washed his upper torso, arms and face. He changed clothing. The cramped space seemed colder and lonelier than before.

At the commission, it was hard to focus on his work. His concentration dissolved every time someone entered the room. When the messenger boy wasn't there, his heart sank and the hours dragged. He could barely contain himself.

Guan-jiah's note arrived late in the afternoon when a soldier escorted the same boy to Robert. The note said Guan-jiah found a small house hidden in a spider-web of streets. When darkness fell, the boy guided him there. Before he knocked, Robert gave the boy another yuan. The boy smiled and popped it in his mouth before he ran off.

The house was nothing like the one in Ningpo. It was old and smelled of oil, garlic and hot peppercorns. Over the years, the odor of cooking had soaked into the boards. The place crawled with cockroaches and other vermin. There were rat and mice droppings everywhere. During the night, he heard them inside the walls.

"Make sure this place gets a thorough scrubbing." He told Guan-jiah the next morning before he returned to the barracks. It wasn't the kind of place he wanted to spend with the woman he loved.

But he had no choice. Anything more luxurious might gain the attention of the wrong people. Even a place like this was preferable to death or being discovered by Parkes.

Dressed in a Chinese disguise, he hid his face under a cone shaped, woven bamboo hat with a large brim and made his way to the house each night. It was the same type of disguise he'd used to avoid capture from the Taipings after that horrible battle where he almost died.

Under the robe, his sweaty hands held the revolver while his eyes searched the shadows. Every suspicious sound he heard caused him to leap around inside his skin. Each morning when the roosters crowed, he made his way back to the commission before sunrise.

Many Cantonese hated him because he was not Chinese. If he were discovered, they would take their time tearing his arms and legs out of their sockets. He would suffer a long and horrible death before they cut his head off and threw it in the river. The Chinese believed if you were not buried whole, your soul would be lost forever.

As much as he disliked sleeping alone at the commission, it was more comfortable than the bedroom he shared with Ayaou in that house. Guan-jiah could not find a suitable bed, so Ayaou and Robert slept and made love on old rice mats rolled out flat on the creaking, hardwood floor.

It didn't take long to discover that the mats were infested with lice. Robert took daily baths and thought he was going to scrub his skin off to get rid of them. Guan-jiah and Ayaou worked hard to clean the place, but it seemed a losing battle. Every time they cleaned the floor of droppings, the creatures returned in the dark.

One night, a rat woke him. It was sitting on his chest licking the salt from his skin. He screamed. The rat leaped off. Robert grabbed his pistol and almost fired a round before it escaped into a hole in the wall he hadn't noticed.

"Master, what is it?" Guan-jiah rushed into the room half-naked. He held his Colt revolver in one hand and a machete in the other. His eyes had a wild, dangerous look to them.

The eunuch kept his head shaved except for his queue. Robert was sure if his servant had hair, it would have been sticking in all directions. "Rats!" he said. "You have to rid this house of them, Guan-jiah."

"Master, since so many people have left the city, the rats have no one to hunt them down and keep their population in control."

"Find a way!"

Chapter 32

It rained for two weeks. His quarters were damp, both at the commission and at the house where he spent his nights with Ayaou.

To clean the house, Guan-jiah used boiled water with a vinegar-garlic solution to scrape the floors and wash the clothing. Robert didn't know what was worse, the smell or the lice and rats.

The evening meal was always the same: a variety of beans, coarse bread, spinach and peas. "What happened to pork and beef?" he asked. "Is food so scarce that you can only find this?"

"No, Robert," Ayaou replied. "With this food, the lice won't like the way you taste. They will stay away."

He stared at the half-empty plate, sighed and continued eating. He was getting tired of the same food every night but wasn't going to argue. It wasn't worth it. Besides, maybe she was right.

Guan-jiah scoured the city and found sleeping mats that were lice free. The traps he set out and bated with a peanut paste caught scores of rats and mice. Before the month's end, the rats and lice were gone.

"Guan-jiah," he asked, "what's wrong with your hands?" His servant's hands looked bright red and raw. Scabs were forming.

Guan-jiah hid his hands behind his back. "Nothing, Master."

"I told him not to keep the lice killing solution so hot," Ayaou said. "I thought he was going to cook his hands."

"Let me see your hands." Guan-jiah stuck them out. "We have to do something," Robert said. "I'll see if I can find an ointment."

Ayaou started to do little things for him that Shao-mei had done when she was alive. One thing that Ayaou did was to sew a bag for his ink stone to replace the one she had destroyed during an argument with Shao-mei. It was an exact duplicate. Robert didn't know what to make of it. He didn't tell her it brought back the memories—the grief.

One night, Ayaou insisted they read together as they once did with Shao-mei. She wanted to read the poems that Shao-mei loved. He should have seen these changes in her behavior as warning signs, but the grief he was struggling to hide and the events taking place in and around the city were conspiring to keep him from seeing what was going on in the mind of his lover.

Early the next morning, Robert stumbled back to his quarters in the barracks and struggled to stay awake and do his job.

Around sunrise on May 30, shortly after he slipped back into his quarters at the commission, a large band of armed Chinese rebels attacked two policemen on duty at the city's southwest gate. One of the policemen was cut in several places on the head but managed to escape. The left hand of the other policeman was almost severed from his arm.

"I heard that a Chinese shopkeeper saved the second policeman by leading him across roofs and over the city wall," a British infantry lieutenant told Robert.

That same evening, instead of going to Ayaou, he rode with Captain Pym and his police through the western suburbs. A spy of Pym's said that rebels, known as the Canton Braves, were planning another raid similar to the one against the southwest gate. The troop rode for hours through the streets and outside the city walls as a show of force. It must have worked. There were no large assaults against the city that night—only skirmishes.

He didn't reach Ayaou until well after midnight. She answered the door when he knocked and threw herself in his arms. "I was afraid something happened to you, Robert," she said, trembling. "We heard the shooting." When he tilted her head back to see her face, he noticed the worry lines growing around her eyes.

"You can't sit here for hours like this. You will get sick." He'd been blind these last few weeks. She was losing weight. "You aren't eating," he said.

"How can I eat? You could be killed."

That night, their lovemaking was frantic.

On July 3, an hour before noon, a band of Taiping rebels attacked four French sailors who shouldn't have been outside the city walls. Three of the sailors escaped. Pym's police found the headless body of the fourth sailor in a stream. They never found the head.

"The French commander must make sure his troops do as they are told." Parkes face was swollen and his eyes red as he walked back and forth from one side of his office to the other. Robert and several officers stood in silence listening to his anger.

Parkes's lips curled into a sneer and twitched. "Orders were posted that all troops were to stay inside their compounds. It isn't safe to be wandering around alone. It also isn't safe for the Chinese that are friendly with us." He stopped and slammed a fist into a palm. "There must be no exceptions! Any soldiers that disobey must spend time in the brig."

Robert feared for Ayaou's safety. How could he protect her when he wasn't at the house? But Guan-jiah was there with a revolver and the eunuch knew how to use it. However, Robert didn't know if his servant would fight and that worried him.

That night, he was impotent. Ayaou did her best to arouse him. However, no matter how much he wanted to make love, he couldn't make it happen. His mind was filled with worry for her.

Ayaou sounded desperate when she said, "You do not find me attractive any more. You want to forget me." She looked forlorn.

"That's not true, Ayaou. It's the fighting. When we aren't together, all I do is think about your safety. It consumes me."

"What is there to worry about? I am only a woman. If I die, you can replace me. If you die, my life is over." She started to cry and he held her until she fell asleep.

When she did, she was curled against him with her legs twined with his. Her head was on his chest. He wanted to roll onto his side because his back ached but was afraid to wake her. Guan-jiah had told him she couldn't sleep when he wasn't there.

He listened to every noise inside and outside the house. He fell asleep hours later only to wake drenched in sweat with the blanket twisted between and around his legs.

Ayaou was still sleeping but had moved to the far side of the mat with her knees against her chest and her arms around her legs.

He'd had a terrible dream where Shao-mei was dressed as a French sailor and was being chased by Taipings. They caught her and beheaded her. In the nightmare, Guan-jiah brought Shao-mei's head to him so he could bury it. Guan-jiah couldn't find her body, and when Robert looked at the face on that severed head, it wasn't Shao-mei. It was Ayaou.

He couldn't tell if Ayaou was breathing. Then he was afraid it wasn't her. His heart started to pound. To make sure this was Ayaou, he propped himself on an elbow and put his face inches from hers trying to make out her features in the dark.

He admonished himself for thinking crazy. Who else could be on the sleeping mat with him?

That didn't stop him from wanting to know if she were still alive. He stuck one of his fingers in his mouth to moisten it and placed it under her nose to feel the cool touch of her breath.

With caution, he straightened the blanket and spread it evenly over both of them. She still didn't move. Her body was warm and the room was chilly. He slid closer to her. She responded by throwing a leg across his and pressing against him. He held his breath afraid she'd wake. His member stood at attention, and he wanted to make love.

Then there was a sharp noise like someone trying to pry a shuttered window open. Robert untangled himself from Ayaou's arms and legs and slipped naked from the blankets into the cold. He took an eight-inch knife and his revolver from the floor next to the sleeping mat. He stopped in the doorway and looked longingly at Ayaou. He wanted to stay, but it was his duty to protect the woman he loved. He'd failed once. He wasn't going to fail again. He would die first.

Like a pale ghost, he slipped silently downstairs until he saw the shadowy shape of a man standing by the front door. Robert lifted the cocked pistol and started to squeeze the trigger when he heard a similar click from the shadow. He shivered in dread expecting a round to tear through him.

"Master, is that you?" Guan-jiah said, just as Robert was going to squeeze the trigger.

"Guan-jiah." He relaxed and let the heavy Colt drop to his side until the barrel pointed at the floor. His neck was stiff, and he rotated his head in circles to relax it. "Did you find anything?" Good Lord, he'd almost shot his servant.

"Nothing, Master." There was a click as Guan-jiah released his weapon's hammer.

"I don't think I can sleep after this." Robert glanced longingly at the stairs and shivered. The cold was soaking through his skin.

"Master, you are going to be sick standing here naked." Guan-jiah hurried away and returned with a blanket that he draped over Robert's shoulders.

"Brew a pot of that famous chrysanthemum tea of yours, Guan-jiah."If we aren't going to sleep, we might as well find something to do." He pulled the blanket tight around his body.

"The tea will warm us," his servant replied, and hurried to the kitchen to add twigs to the glowing embers inside the belly of the ceramic stove.

When it was time for Robert to leave, they were still sitting around the table drinking tea and eating dried Shan-tung red dates from a bowl. The only sound was the crunch of the dates between their teeth.

It was nerve-racking as he made his way through the city to the commission that morning. He'd dallied too long and missed the cover of darkness. Maybe Ayaou should return to Ningpo.

No, that wasn't a good idea. In Ningpo, she would be too close to Ward. She should go to Macao and live with Cousin Weed on his junk along with her father and Uncle Bark. If Ayaou did that, life would be easier for both of them, and Robert could stop skulking about in the early morning darkness expecting to lose his head.

A few days later, Robert heard that the Yamen, the Bureau of Foreign Affairs for China, had sent armed English and French soldiers to the street where the French sailor had been taken. Under the Yamen's orders, they shot fifty Chinese at random that lived or worked near the site.

He was with Parkes when he heard the news "This is crazy! This kind of action will stir up more sentiment for the rebels. Aren't things bad enough as they are? The ones who killed the French sailor are gone. Why should innocent people suffer for someone else's deed? This is going to make things worse."

"Calm down, Robert," Parkes said. "It's their country, and the imperials know how to handle their people. Besides, the French were screaming for blood so the Chinese gave it to them."

"The Manchu overreacted. We should have stopped this."

Parkes shook his head. "I'm disappointed. This doesn't sound like you at all. I thought you believed in letting the Chinese make their own decisions."

"This is not a productive conversation," Robert said. "Besides, I have work to do." He went to his desk unconcerned if Parkes was angry with him for his abrupt departure.

It was a waste of time and effort trying to educate people like Parkes about China. They didn't listen. He had almost mentioned how the foreign powers like Britain had been dictating policy to China for years while forcing China to swallow opium. The Chinese government did not have a choice. When they refused to cooperate, the result was war.

It was like a robber holding a gun to the victim's head, but at the same time helping the victim stay in business by supporting ruthless tactics that harmed innocent people. It made no sense.

That night, he visited Ayaou again. His feelings and fears leaked out of him against his wishes. He was worried more than ever for her safety.

"What if you or Guan-jiah had been in that part of city when the fifty innocent victims had been randomly rounded up and shot?" he said. "There wasn't even a trial. You could be dead."

"You miss the point, Robert," she replied. "The imperial government knows that such an action makes a statement.

When the people see the caged heads of those fifty Chinese hanging above the city's gates, they will know they have to take the government's orders seriously. The Longhaired Bandits will not gain the support they have been getting. The people will think twice before they offer again. I thought you understood China better than that."

To make matters worse, Parkes discovered he had been going out every night. "Why have you been sneaking away from your quarters like a common thief?" Parkes asked.

Robert stood before Parkes desk and avoided the commissioner's eyes. He felt like a student called in front of the headmaster for a prank he'd committed. His face heated. His breakfast curdled in his stomach, and he wanted to vomit.

"Come on, Hart, speak."

He didn't want to tell Parkes he'd been sneaking away to be with his Chinese concubine. What would Parkes think? Robert continued to stare at the floor and resented the fact that he felt this way.

"Hart, if you don't tell me, I'll have to order you to be confined to your quarters. When you were recommended to me, there were rumors saying you were unreliable. I heard you were a liar and a coward and couldn't be trusted."

Robert's head jerked up as hot anger flooded his face. "Who's spreading such lies?" He immediately regretted the tone in his voice.

"Does it matter?"

"Yes, it does." His voice was firm, not as angry.

"Tell me where you have been going, and I'll give you a name." Parkes pounded the surface of his desk with a closed fist. "Damn it, Hart, you are a good man. I don't want to believe what I've heard."

"It's a woman," he said, and the words tasted bitter. "I've been going out to spend my nights with a Chinese woman. Please don't tell anyone." His face burned with embarrassment.

"What's wrong with you? Men need women and women are easy to find here. If you want a woman, why are you sneaking around about it?"

"I didn't want anyone to know. It's personal."

"I see. Well, if you have to go out to be lusty with a whore, you will have a corporal and five men accompany you. Of course, the corporal will report to me, so I will know where you are going and whom you are seeing. I don't like my men sneaking around. It would be better if we just brought the whore here."

"Who was spreading lies about me?" Robert asked.

Parkes blinked. "Yes, I did say I'd trade information. Don't do anything rash. I've never met the man. They told me he works out of Hong Kong and Macao and has three small sloops. He is an opium merchant. A small one—nothing big."

"His name, sir."

"Let's see." Looking uncomfortable, Parkes stared at the ceiling. Robert felt as if he had taken control of the moment. "Payne Hollister. Yes, that was the name."

Hearing Hollister's name was like a heavy blow between the shoulder blades. Hollister was still in China! The man hadn't returned to England after all. "You said he was an opium merchant?"

"That's what I was told, and the reason why I didn't take what I heard seriously. Do you know this man?"

Good Lord, if Hollister was spreading vile lies in an attempt to ruin Robert's life, the man still harbored a grudge for what happened with Me-ta-tae. If that was true, maybe Hollister was behind the attacks on Ayaou and Robert in Ningpo. It was bad enough that he had Ward to worry about in Northern China. Now he had to worry about Hollister in the South.

"I asked a question," Parkes said.

"I worked with Hollister in Ningpo before he quit the consular service. I thought he returned to England."

"If he is generating gossip like this, he must dislike you. If something happened between you two, I don't want to know about it. That's not my concern." Parkes came around the desk. "Robert," he said, "you have proven that you are an honest, courageous, hardworking man—someone I depend on. Forget about this Hollister fellow. His type always comes to a bad end anyway.

"And stop whoring around. If you want a woman, we can have one brought here to take care of your needs. If you don't like that, then you are going to have to give up women until Canton is safe." Parkes looked tired when he shook his head. "We all have our vices. I just thought better of you. Whores!" He said the last word as if it were something repulsive.

"Ayaou is not a whore," Robert replied, as the blood rushed to his head again. "She's my concubine." He stopped talking—shocked at his admission.

"I trust you will keep this conversation private," he said, then held his breath.

Parkes nodded. "I will keep your secret," he said.

It was as if a weight had been lifted from his shoulders. "When I bought her, she was a virgin. We have been together for three years. I can't go see her with an escort. An escort will draw attention to where I am going and the rebels will mark her and my servant for death. I trust you will keep this conversation private."

Parkes did not look surprised.

"Have you had someone watching me?" Robert asked.

"Of course. You were sneaking around like a common thief. Once I discovered what you were up to, I wanted to know if I could trust you. It didn't take long for my man to discover you were seeing a woman. Until now, we didn't know whom that Chinese man was that was staying with her. We thought it might be possible you were being blackmailed by someone to reveal information about our operations."

"You didn't have to spy on me," he said. "All you had to do was ask. I would have told you what I was doing."

"Robert," Parkes said, "these are difficult times. Even I must do without my wife and family. I miss her, but she is safer in Hong Kong. If you care for this woman, why is she still here? Send her to Hong Kong or Macau with your servant."

"It looks like I have no choice."

"Precisely. You are too valuable to end up dead. Take this as a direct order. You are forbidden to leave the compound unless you are with an armed guard. We cannot trust anyone but our people at this point. Send this woman and your servant away."

Robert started to open his mouth.

Parkes shook his head and looked as if he were disappointed. "No one will hear from my lips what we talked about, Robert. I'm not the sort for gossip or rumors. You should know that by now."

Robert brooded the rest of the day trying to figure out how he was going to get word to Guan-jiah and Ayaou. He hoped that a lull in the fighting would provide an opportunity.

Regrettably, it turned out that Robert was correct about the shooting of the fifty innocent Chinese. Attacks against the city started coming day and night. The streets became extremely dangerous. After several days of confinement in the barracks and fear for Ayaou's safety, he decided to risk sneaking out.

After making his decision, he didn't want to give his plans away by appearing suspicious. Anyone could be watching.

"Robert," a British captain asked, "is something bothering you? Lately, you act as if you have a lot on your mind. Did something happen with your family?" Robert knew the officer was talking about Ireland. They had played chess and shared stories of their growing up. His name was Kenton, and he'd spent most of his youth in boarding schools. His parents were important people. His father was in parliament and owned large estates.

"It's nothing, Kent. A tooth hurts when I chew. I don't want anyone here to touch it. What am I to do? "

"I understand," Kenton replied. "I don't trust the battalion surgeon either. I have heard some grisly stories about him ripping out teeth when the job didn't need to be done. If you can hold off, I suggest a trip to Hong Kong to take care of it."

"That's exactly what I was thinking. How about a game of chess?" Robert thought this would throw any suspicion off him if others saw them in the common room playing a game. He planned to slip away later that night.

To avoid the sentries and other spying eyes, Robert climbed onto the roof of the large building where he was quartered. He then jumped to the next building. It was risky but the Chinese style of the city lent itself to this kind of stealth.

Most of the streets were narrow twisting alleys and the tiled roofs hung over the streets and were close together. He knew that the haphazard design was intentional. The Chinese believed in spirits and ghosts who were only capable of walking in straight lines. That was why the Chinese had built the city with a maze of twisting streets—to keep ghosts from getting into the city.

The first time he jumped from one roof to another, he thought he was going to fall two stories to his death. Running on the brittle, smooth tiles and leaping out into empty space toward the other roof put a scare into him. He landed on the other side and managed to keep from sliding off. However, a few loose tiles clattered to the street below. He held his breath and waited to be discovered. When nothing happened, he moved on.

While he scurried like a monkey across the city's roofs, there were heavy rockets being fired into the city. From his high vantage point, he watched as arcs of fire and sparks revealed the trails the missiles followed as they dropped inside the city walls setting off a bright flash, then the rumble of an explosion. Dancing spots of light impaired his vision and made him feel helpless. When that happened, he stopped until his night vision returned.

After an hour, he thought God might be on his side and that was why no one had seen him. He was sure that if a British or French patrol spotted him leaping from building to building, he'd be shot like a squirrel in a tree.

"Halt, I say," a voice said from a narrow street Robert had just crossed by leaping from roof to roof. He dropped to the tiles and did not move. His heart hammered like a drum. The air was cold, but he started sweating.

"What is it, Fairfax? Were you seeing Chinese ghosts again?"

"No, I saw something up there between those buildings. It was suspicious like."

The sentries fell quiet. Robert knew they were waiting for him to move or make a noise. He hugged the roof wanting to become part of it. He could smell the fear in his sweat.

"There's nothing there, Fairfax. You're seeing things again."

"It was one of those Chinese spirits, Wetherby. I know it was."

"You're daft. Let's finish our rounds. We'll be relieved soon. You can report your suspicions then. If you do, the lieutenant will probably order us to go on the roofs and risk breaking bones searching about. If I was you, I'd keep my mouth shut."

"I don't know."

"Next time you see one of those ghosts of yours, shoot it, Fairfax. Then we'll find out if it has flesh and bones or is just your imagination."

Robert tensed as he listened to their voices fade. Once he was sure they were gone, he crawled over the rooftop and down the other side. His legs were so shaky he was afraid to walk.

He started to doubt his ability to reach Ayaou. Next time, the sentries might shoot.

Chapter 33

When he reached the house, Robert lay on a roof across the street and studied the area to make sure none of Parkes's people was watching.

He was getting good at this skulking about and almost chuckled but bit his lower lip to keep his mouth sealed. When Shao-mei had been alive, there had been attempts on all three of them. He had to be careful.

Thinking about Ayaou and Shao-mei sobered him. He closed his eyes, rested his face against the cool roof tiles, and remembered the time Ayaou had cut his hair and Shao-mei had teased him. He could still hear the hissing sound Shao-mei made before she said, "Oh, Ayaou, look what you have done to the back of his head!"

Tears filled his eyes, but he smiled from the memory. That haircut had been a precious moment he didn't want to forget.

He was not going to risk climbing down while in this mood, so he stayed on the roof longer as he struggled with the sorrow.

Once calm, he found a way off the roof to the street. Dear God, he thought, I hope you understand how much I miss Shao-mei. I know it was a sin to live with and want two women, but you know I never used her in that way.

Taking a calming breath, he dashed across the street and discovered the door to the house locked. He knocked and listened to the silence hoping to hear Ayaou's answering scratch.

He jumped as rockets hit the city sending blast waves through the crooked streets with an invisible force. The ground trembled, and he cursed himself for being a fool. He gritted his teeth and knocked again.

Maybe he should return to the barracks. What if Guan-jiah and Ayaou were dead?

Then he heard a scratching from the other side of the door, and it matched the code used in Ningpo after Shao-mei's death. He scratched back and Ayaou's muffled voice cried out in surprise. As he waited for the door to be unlocked, he expected a squad of British Marines to come and arrest him.

What if the person on the other side wasn't her? What if this was a trap? He attempted seeing through the darkness engulfing the street. Everyone was smarter than he was. He was a fool taking a chance like this. He lifted his revolver and pointed the weapon at the door.

When it opened, he saw Ayaou. Pushing past her, he locked the door behind him and leaned over with hands braced against knees to laugh until tears streamed down his face.

Once he was calm, he studied her and saw the dark circles under her eyes. She had grown thinner. Then he saw Guan-jiah standing in a corner holding a revolver. As usual, Guan-jiah's hand was shaking.

"We were about to go and look for you," she said, and then started to cry. "We thought you were dead."

Robert looked at Guan-jiah, who had eyes the size of gold sovereigns. "It is true, Master. You have not been here for days. We thought you were dead. I did not know what to do. We were running out of rice, which is all the food we have left."

"I'm alive today," Robert said, "but I can't make promises for tomorrow."

"I will go to my room. If you want tea later, I will have it ready." Guan-jiah slipped the pistol into a wide sleeve and left.

He watched his servant disappear into the cupboard-sized space where he slept. Once Guan-jiah was gone, he turned to Ayaou. "Never leave the house, Ayaou." He cupped her chin in a hand. "You stay here and let me find you. Promise. Guan-jiah will find food without your help."

She nodded obediently, but Robert had doubts. He wasn't sure the message telegraphing itself from her eyes agreed with what he wanted her to do.

"Guan-jiah, did you hear what I said?" He aimed the words toward his servant's room. "That goes for you too. I know you can hear me. You have the ears of a bat. Don't go out for anything but food and water and make sure Ayaou stays inside. Only go out during the day. Most of the attacks take place at night. Also, stay away from the city's walls and gates. That's where the fighting takes place. I don't want either of you getting shot or beheaded."

"Yes, Master," Guan-jiah's muffled voice replied.

Just the thought of the risks the eunuch was taking caused Robert's throat to thicken with emotion. He valued his servant's loyalty. Guan-jiah didn't have to stay. He could quit and go home to the safety and comfort of his family.

"Come, Robert," Ayaou said, her impatience evident. She took his hand and pulled him toward their room. The house felt deserted as if no one lived there. The rooms were empty of furniture. The floors and walls, however much Guan-jiah or Ayaou had scrubbed them, still looked filthy. It wasn't where he wanted to spend a night with the woman he loved.

Once in their room, his greedy hands explored every inch of her body. Her hunger was as strong as his was. They made frantic love, but it ended too quickly.

Afterwards, he heard a creaking sound in the hallway as if someone had stepped on a loose board. Robert disliked the lack of privacy in this house. The bedroom door couldn't be locked, and the gaps between the door's planks made it possible for a spy to watch and remain unseen.

Guan-jiah was up to his skulking again watching and listening to them making love.

"When you are not with me," she said, in a voice devoid of energy, "my dreams are always about you dead. I fear sleep." Her exhaustion was visible, her skin wasn't as radiant as it had been, and stress lines were growing from her eyes like spider webs.

He couldn't tell her he was living in the same state of fear. He dreaded speaking, because his voice might betray him. To compensate, he pulled her close and held her. Such contact had aroused him when they lived in Ningpo. Now it did nothing. The desire that had driven Robert since first meeting Ayaou had fled, and he hated its absence. Life had become uncertain. They couldn't even be sure of the next moment.

Near midnight, an explosion, much larger than the rockets, shook the house and woke them. Robert held Ayaou's trembling body and listened to the sounds of bugles and drums calling the British and French troops to assemble.

"I have to go," he said. He tried to get off the mat, but Ayaou wouldn't let go. "Ayaou, I'm needed." He managed to pry her off and started to pull his clothes on.

Ayaou walked to him on her knees and wrapped her arms around his legs to hold on. "Do not go," she said. "Do not leave me again."

"I can't stay, Ayaou. The commissioner needs me." He tried to pry her arms from his legs so he could finish dressing, but she hung onto him. He moved toward the door dragging her with him.

"No!" She wailed. "You will die!"

He didn't know what to do. He stared at the top of her head but couldn't see her face. She was pressed into the space between his knees. Her arms were stubborn ropes.

"Do you want me to go with you, Master?" Guan-jiah came into the bedroom. "I have my pistol. I will fight." The eunuch was fully dressed.

"No, stay and look after Ayaou. Keep her safe." He gestured at her. "Guan-jiah, remove her. I can't walk like this."

Guan-jiah managed to pry her off. Then she rolled into the shape of a ball, placed her forehead on the floor and sobbed with great gulping sounds. The eunuch kept a reassuring hand on her shoulder.

The guilt Robert felt was terrible. "If something happens to me, take care of her? I am counting on you, Guan-jiah. I have no one else I can trust."

The eunuch stared at the floor and didn't reply.

"Guan-jiah," he said, "you are like a brother. I depend on you."

"Stay, you will be safer here," Ayaou said. Her face was flushed and wet with tears. Guan-jiah seemed to notice that she was naked. He started to leave.

"Guan-jiah, stay with her. She's in no shape to be alone, and I have to go."

"Master, she has no clothes on."

"Guan-jiah, you've seen naked women before. What's the difference? Besides, she can put clothes on. Did you hear me, Ayaou? Get dressed. This isn't acceptable."

Guan-jiah found clothes and attempted to dress her but she did not cooperate. She kept her arms wrapped around her knees and rocked back and forth.

"This is impossible, Master."

"Nothing is impossible. She will settle down. Get a blanket around her. Keep her warm."

Guan-jiah found a blanket. Then he did something Robert had never seen before. He wrapped his arms around her as if she were a child and started to hum. Ayaou turned and pressed her face against the eunuch's chest. Her arms went around his neck. Guan-jiah rocked her and patted her back while he hummed. Her sobs subsided.

Robert hesitated. He was glad his servant wasn't a real man. He couldn't make himself open the door, so he knelt on one knee in front of Ayaou. "I have to go," he said in as gentle a voice as he could muster. "It's my duty. To stay here would brand me as a coward in my colleagues' eyes. I can't live with that. Besides, Commissioner Parkes knows about this house and has forbidden me to come here. If I'm not in my quarters, he'll send soldiers to find me."

"What about your duty to your child?" Her tears had stopped, her face was puffy and a defiant look had appeared in her bloodshot eyes.

Guan-jiah's head snapped up, and his eyes fastened on Robert. "The mistress carries a child?" he said. "I did not know that, Master, or I would have told you."

He saw a gleam of hope in the eunuch's eyes. Robert almost groaned. His servant was thinking he was going to have a second chance to become an adopted uncle again. "Maybe we didn't hear her right," he said. "What did you say, Ayaou?"

"What do you expect after having planted your dragon-seeds in me so many times? I have to carry it for a while before we find a way to get rid of it."

"Get rid of him!" Blood rushed into his head along with anger. "What are you talking about?" He signaled Guan-jiah. "Get a robe on her!"

The eunuch rummaged in the standing closet. When he returned, he had a satin robe and draped it over her.

"Get up," Robert said. She stood and let the robe hang open revealing her nudity.

"You don't look pregnant."

She barked a laugh. "You want to be blind. What does it matter what you believe? I am not your wife." She waved her arms and the robe slid off.

"Guan-jiah," he said.

"Master, she isn't cooperating." Ayaou walked about the room as the servant chased her attempting to put the robe on.

Her face was twisted and ugly. She stopped, placed fists on her hips and leaned toward him. "I am not even your concubine. I still belong to Ward. I do not want to be shamed."

Why does she keep throwing this at me? Then he remembered Uncle Bark's words of advice and fought his anger.

Guan-jiah managed to get the robe on her, and he struggled to tie the cord. She lifted her arms and the robe slid off. Guan-jiah looked embarrassed as he pulled the robe around her again. She ignored him and focused her fire on Robert. This time the robe stayed. Guan-jiah looked relieved.

Robert ignored the furious look on her face. "What's important is that he is our child," he said. His anger struggled to break free, but he managed to keep his voice calm. "How long have you known?"

"What does it matter when it started to grow?" she said. "It is a foreign devil's seed. This creature will be condemned in China. When they see it on the streets, they will spit on it."

"How long?" Maybe the child belonged to another man. The anger was winning. He closed his eyes and thought of Uncle Bark's words. *"When her tongue tests you, remember the good times before Ward murdered Shao-mei."*

"April!" she replied. "I knew in April!"

"I want him, Ayaou. This child is mine, and he belongs to God. We have no right to take his life. I'll think of a way. Now I have to go. The Taipings could be invading the city. Every man is needed." He hurried to the front door.

She followed with Guan-jiah close on her heels. The robe started to slip from her shoulders again, since it was too large for her. It was one of Robert's. Guan-jiah pulled the robe back up.

"I do not believe in your silly, filthy God," she said.

He stepped outside the house and looked back. "Don't talk about God like that," he said. The anger locked inside felt like fists pounding to escape. "Don't let her out of the house, Guan-jiah. Keep her safe."

Guan-jiah had a look in his eyes that Robert recognized. He was thinking of the baby that had died with Shao-mei when she had been murdered.

Dear God, spare me, he thought. "Yes, Guan-jiah," he said. "I know what you want. You can be the adopted uncle. Heaven knows the child will need someone to watch over him—someone I can depend on when I'm not here. Someone who will love him as I will."

Guan-jiah smiled. "Mistress Ayaou, we must get inside. You could get sick standing here half-dressed. We must think of the child."

"Close the door," Robert said.

The look on Ayaou's face changed from anger to one of loss and her face dissolved into pain. That was the last thing Robert saw before the door closed.

Ayaou's expression followed him down the street. He shouldn't have left, but he didn't have a choice. War was calling. He thought about the time Ayaou had saved his life after Ward's defeat at Sungkiang when he had been wounded and Ayaou managed to hide him in an abandoned farmer's hut where he had recovered. She could have left him and saved herself. Instead, she risked her life.

He knew that behind her angry words, she still loved him. Then he stumbled when a bright flash lit the sky followed by the rumble of another explosion. The ground trembled. Robert started to run.

Back at the commission, Robert asked the first officer he met what had happened.

"Rebels blew up the northwest corner of the city wall and got inside," the officer replied. "They managed to occupy two city blocks, but we beat them back."

The man's face was smudged with gunpowder. His eyes pulsed with excitement. "The royal engineers are repairing the breech as we talk."

A little after two in the afternoon, Robert was walking from Colonel Walsh's quarters toward his when a rocket hit the ground in front of him sending sparks in every direction. Some of the sparks hit his face burning him and he leaped from the heat. Thank goodness the rocket didn't explode. If it had, he would have been blown to pieces.

There wouldn't have been anything left to bury if that had happened. Ayaou would have been crushed into insanity and their unborn child would've grown-up without a father and treated as an outcast. Then he remembered the look in Guan-jiah's eyes.

No, the child wouldn't grow up without a father. He would have his adopted uncle, who couldn't have children of his own.

If anything happened to him, Guan-jiah would raise the child if Ayaou didn't want it. And even if she kept the baby, Robert was sure Guan-jiah would stay close. The child would not go without love. He was sure Guan-jiah had enough for a dozen children. It was a relief that he had someone like Guan-jiah to depend on.

He stared at the rocket sticking out of the ground. Half of it was buried in the dirt. The shock drained the strength out of his legs. He leaned against the nearest wall to keep from collapsing.

Men came running. "Good god," a colonel said. Several soldiers attempted lifting the rocket.

"What are you doing?" the colonel said. "It might explode. It could have a delayed fuse."

Everyone ran. Robert managed to get his legs moving and followed. Once he was inside peering around a sturdy doorframe at the rocket, he thought, Ayaou could've been a widow without ever having been a wife.

He resolved to write his last will and testament and leave what little money he had to Guan-jiah, who could use it to care for Ayaou and the child.

The thought of dying without making provisions for the woman he loved and the child she carried horrified him. The next time he talked to Guan-jiah, he would tell his servant what he wanted done if he was killed.

The Western forces poured out of the city a few hours later and counterattacked. British and French gunboats in the river pounded the rebel positions. The shelling killed hundreds. Soon after the shelling and the counterattack, the rebel forces retreated north. English and French scouts followed and reported that the rebels numbered several thousand.

Robert joined Parkes as he attended endless funerals while Chinese bands played music in the background. The Chinese seemed to celebrate every funeral as if it were a birth and not a death.

However, he'd seen enough death and stopped attending the funerals. With Ayaou and the baby in his thoughts, he

376

decided to risk his life and see her one more time before he sent her to Macau. Now that she was pregnant, there was no way she was going to stay in Canton.

Chapter 34

Robert had crossed the roofs risking life and limb a second time. Inside the house, he led Ayaou to the bedroom. As stark as this worn-out house was, the bedroom was the closest to being a home of sorts. The other rooms made him feel uncomfortable as if they were designed to be coffins.

"Guan-jiah, I want you too."

"Master?" Guan-jiah looked shocked as if he were going to be asked to join them on the sleeping mat and take part in the lovemaking.

"Don't worry," Robert said, stifling his laughter while keeping his face composed. "I only want to talk. You're both going to Macao tomorrow." Robert held out twenty pounds. "Take the money." It was more than one-hundred-twenty yuan.

"I am not leaving without you," Ayaou said.

"You have no choice!" Anger flooded his face, and his voice roared. "Do not be difficult now! This is not the time or place!"

She talked louder. "I have never been to Macao. I do not know what the place is like. I might get lost there. You might not find me. My father told me it happened to a concubine that belonged to Captain Patridge. He forgot about her!"

Swallowing the anger, he said, "You have nothing to worry about." He caressed the side of her face. "Guan-jiah will look after you and stay in touch with me."

"You want to get rid of me, because I carry your child."

He threw up his hands in frustration. "What am I going to do with you?" No matter what he said or did, he couldn't convince Ayaou that he wasn't going to abandon her. "I curse your father for the poison he planted in your head. I curse the fortuneteller who has filled your mind with nonsense."

"Do not talk about my father like that. If my father told me to leave you, I would."

Guan-jiah moved between them.

"Leave the room," Robert said.

Hurt appeared on the eunuch's face, but he didn't move. Guan-jiah was a gentle man. Robert doubted he'd hurt a fly. "It's okay. You may leave."

The eunuch's words came in a rush with nervous gulps of air between phrases. "No, Master, I have never seen you this angry—you might hit her—she deserves it—but you said I was the child's adopted uncle."

Guan-jiah shifted his gaze to his feet then his words came slower. "It is my duty to protect him. I have to protect him. You know that I would help you beat her if it weren't for him. Beat me instead."

Robert's anger evaporated. Guan-jiah was willing to die to protect the unborn child. The look in his eyes said so. Robert pitied any Taiping that came near Ayaou in her condition for it was obvious Guan-jiah would fight to the death.

Ayaou had dropped to the sleeping mat and was staring at the floor with a lost look. She rubbed dirt off her feet.

"You went outside against my orders!" His heart leaped into his throat.

"You do not own me. Ward does," she replied.

Without thinking, he raised a hand as if to slap her. Guan-jiah grabbed his wrist. "No, Master, you cannot hit her. You are letting her words stir evil. Do not damage the child. I promise to beat her after the child is born."

Robert stepped back. "You're going to Macao where you and our child will be safe," he said. "Guan-jiah, if you have to, stuff her in a burlap sack and carry her there."

She dropped to her back and stared at the ceiling—her face a mask of pain and defeat.

"She'll calm down," Robert said. "Let's go in the other room and brew a pot of tea so we may plan how you two are going to leave the city safely. Have you ever been to Macao?"

"No, Master."

Chapter 35

For the next few months, Robert buried himself with work in an attempt to avoid thinking about Ayaou. He wanted desperately to stabilize the situation with the Chinese, so he could be with her again. To achieve this, he glued himself to Parkes, and they went everywhere together as battles raged in and around Canton.

The world turned to black and white with occasional violent flashes from the British and French cannons and rebel rockets. Without Ayaou, there was no color in his life. Even the food lost flavor. He couldn't tell the difference between a sip of water and sweet plum pudding.

He thought about Payne Hollister often. Determined to deal with him, he contacted people in Hong Kong. They found an address. He wrote a letter.

"Hollister, I read your lies. I find it amazing that you still hold a grudge after all these years.

"Yes, I admit that something happened with Me-ta-tae. Something I regret. It happened once and was over in moments.

"If forcible intercourse with Shao-mei wasn't enough to satisfy your anger and you still want revenge, I'm willing to offer you satisfaction. Your choice, swords or pistols? Name the time and place. I will be there. That is, unless you are a coward."

To prepare himself, he improved his sword skills by practicing with a British major. They worked for hours most evenings until Robert was drenched with sweat. He didn't

Lloyd Lofthouse

worry about his skill with a pistol. He'd always been a good shot. Even as a child, he'd been a better shot than his father had.

His motivation ran deeper than he wanted to admit. Every time he practiced, he imagined what it would feel like to kill Hollister and make him suffer as Shao-mei had.

Weeks went by and there was no reply from Hollister. Robert had no way to know if the letter had reached him. One good thing came of it—writing that letter and sending it put the episode concerning Me-ta-tae behind him. Confronting his guilt regarding the seduction of Me-at-tae and his willingness to die to atone for it helped him shed that sin.

He continued to practice with the sword. After all, Hollister might appear any day.

A court-martial commenced for three Royal marines. Robert acted as the interpreter for the Chinese witnesses. Seventeen charges had been brought against these men— charges for assault, attempted rape, robbery and murder. During their questioning, it became apparent that they believed they could do anything they wanted to the locals.

The affair disgusted him, but he kept his opinions to himself since most British and French didn't feel the way he did.

The punishment for the criminals was light compared to the crimes they had committed. Their victims could have included Ayaou or Guan-jiah. Those soldiers should have been shot. Instead, they were reduced in rank, spent thirty days in the stockade and then sent back to duty. The message said a Chinese life was worthless.

He hated the fact that his parting with Ayaou had been bitter. To compensate, he wrote letters to her on a daily basis. It felt as if he were bleeding his misery onto the paper.

China did not have a proper postal system, and it wasn't easy finding a way to mail his letters and have them delivered. As impossible as the idea seemed, he swore if an opportunity presented itself in the future, he would do what he could to remedy that situation and create a Chinese postal system.

He dreaded going to bed because all he did was think about her, and he often saw her dead like Shao-mei. To avoid

381

the nightmares, he stayed late in the mess playing chess or joining conversations with British army officers.

When alone, he struggled to read by lantern light in his small cubbyhole of a room, but thoughts of Ayaou kept intruding. He often had to read the same pages several times.

The attacks against the city continued. Noise from rockets, rifle fire or cannons was a constant companion.

He had to do something to ease his loneliness. Slowly, he made friends among the military officers. He also made friends with a few of Canton's Imperial Chinese officials he met as part of his job. When invited to eat at their houses, he felt more at home than he did in his quarters.

A British gunboat brought the first letter from Macau. He was disappointed when he discovered it was from Guan-jiah— not Ayaou.

> "Master," Guan-jiah wrote, "Ayaou believes you will abandon her. She has seen other foreigners do this to their concubines. To protect herself, she is busy tearing her passion and love for you out of her heart and head as if they were strands of gray hair. She is attempting to murder her feelings with poisonous words and thoughts.
>
> "I know how much you love your concubine. It would be a tragedy if she stays in Macau. It is time to risk our lives and have us return to Canton. Even if we die, it would be better than the changes Ayaou is going through."

Robert thought Guan-jiah was wrong. Ayaou could never believe he'd abandon her. He had risked his life to take her from Ward, and she had risked her life to save him from the Taipings.

> "Master," Guan-jiah wrote in another letter, "You do not understand that it is only natural for Ayaou to fall back on her family and their Chinese ways to survive. Believe me when I say that the fear of being abandoned has never left her and is growing stronger."

He threw that letter away believing Guan-jiah was filling his mind with delusional thoughts. Robert had not forgotten Guan-jiah's opinions of boat people.

Family was important to the Chinese, and the eunuch had no family in Macau. He'd been away from Ningpo too long. He probably wasn't getting along with Ayaou's family.

He'd had a conversation about this topic with Guan-jiah years before. "My great-grandmother was from the boat people," his servant had said. "Great-grandfather was Han Chinese. He was a village farmer, who only owned one acre and couldn't afford a better woman.

"My grandmother was trouble like all boat people," Guan-jiah had said. "My great-grandfather was fortunate when she died in childbirth without giving him the curse of a daughter." It was regrettable that Guan-jiah harbored a bias against these boat people.

It amazed him that the Chinese, with all the different languages and dialects, managed to make the culture work.

He saw the irony in the fact that Europe had imported its problems to China disturbing what had once been a peaceful kingdom. The Taipings were converted Christians led by a false prophet. Having them in China was like setting fire to brush soaked in oil.

Although Robert had no way to have his letters carried to Macao where Ayaou's family lived, Guan-jiah sent news through the British consular mailbags out of Hong Kong. It couldn't be easy for the eunuch to make this happen.

In one letter, Guan-jiah suggested that Robert write to Ayaou care of the Hong Kong consulate. He followed his servant's advice. When she didn't respond, he started to have doubts. What if Guan-jiah's warnings were true? He dashed off another letter to Guan-jiah asking why Ayaou hadn't replied.

Guan-jiah wrote back that he had tried to get Ayaou to write. She wouldn't listen. It was as if she were mute.

"Master," Guan-jiah wrote, "since we have been in Macao, Ayaou found Mr. Yin-Yang's replacement, a Mr. Sua-min, another fortune teller. He has become the guru of her spiritual life.

"Ayaou is convinced you are the moon's reflection in the water that Mr. Yin-Yang predicted, and that she will never truly have you. Mr. Sua-min told Ayaou to get as much money as she can from you while you are still part of her life.

"Mr. Sua-min is a thief. I believe he will take the money you send her for his services.

"Master, if she asks for money, do not give it."

Robert believed Ayaou would never cheat him even for a fortuneteller, and he ignored Guan-jiah's advice. He was sure that the love Ayaou felt for him was too strong for anything like that to happen. Whatever she was going through, it wouldn't last.

He spent sleepless nights fantasizing that things would return to the way they had been in Ningpo during the best of times. Life would be as it had been when Shao-mei was alive. They would laugh over Chinese ink paintings, poetry, music and haircuts. He followed Uncle Bark's advice and only thought about the good times they had together.

In July, Ayaou sent one of her cousins to Canton. The fifteen-year-old girl's name was Fooyen. The note she handed Robert asked for one hundred yuan.

"Why so much?" he said.

"The money is for the family," Fooyen replied. "The junk needs repairs. It is old and leaks. We have borrowed enough that we will never be able to pay back in this life. The moneylenders will not give us more. If the junk sinks, we will all die. It is where we live. It is how we make our living."

He gave the girl a hundred and twenty-five-yuan, more than Ayaou wanted. He also trusted Fooyen to deliver the letters he'd written that he hadn't sent.

Fooyen became their messenger, and he kept up a correspondence with Ayaou for the next few months. Her only replies were when she asked for money, and he sent it.

It was through Fooyen that Robert learned how to find Ayaou in Macao.

In December 1858, Robert went to Parkes and requested ten days leave. Since the rebel activity had subsided, the commissioner granted the request. He sailed on one of the British gunboats to Hong Kong where he transferred to another ship and arrived in Macao's crescent shaped bay late in the afternoon.

Macao was a Portuguese colony and the wooded hills were crowded with houses that were light blue and pink and yellow. The architectural style was that of Southern Europe. The Portuguese had first settled here in 1557, almost three hundred years before Hong Kong became a British Crown Colony.

The hulls of the junks crowding the harbor were painted red. Other junks sailed into the bay with the sunlight gleaming off tan and beige matted sails. It was difficult to believe that war with the Taipings and other rebels was raging throughout most of China.

Piles and baskets full of fish crowded the dock where he went ashore. More fish were spread to dry on the junks' roofs. Rusty colored fishing nets had been hung from tall masts to dry in the afternoon sun.

A coolie offered him a ride for a small price. He climbed into the rickshaw and off they went down Praia Grande Avenue, which was shaded by banyan trees. Turbaned East Indian police directed traffic.

When he found Cousin Weed's junk, he had to cross three other boats to reach it. The first familiar face he saw belonged to Guan-jiah. He went up to his servant and took hold of his hands. "It's good to see you, my friend," Robert said.

Guan-jiah looked embarrassed and pleased at the same time.

The distance the Chinese put between servants and masters unsettled Robert. Since he'd never had servants before coming to China, this was something he had trouble getting used to. To him, Guan-jiah was his equal and shouldn't be calling him master. He had trouble seeing himself as the master of any person.

Robert had been raised a Wesleyan. His father was a pastor and taught his twelve children that all men and women were equal. It also bothered him that Ayaou thought of herself as the property of a man.

He didn't think about it often but when he did, it was with pangs of guilt. For that reason, he never mentioned Ayaou to friends and family in the letters he wrote to Northern Ireland. They'd never understand.

He doubted Ayaou would be treated as an equal. He suspected that the beliefs of his family did not include people outside their own race. Over time, Mary and his mother might accept Ayaou, but he didn't want to take the chance that they would hurt her feelings. He loved her too much to subject her to that form of cruelty.

"Chou Luk is here," Guan-jiah said. "Master, it would please Ayaou if you greeted him first. It is only proper."

Every time he talked to Chou Luk, he only heard bad news. "Where is the old man?" Guan-jiah bobbed his head and led the way. They found the Chou Luk sitting aft in the shade with two young girls cooling him with large handheld fans.

He tried not to stare. Chou Luk had aged and gained weight. A lot of his hair had fallen out and what remained looked greasy and stringy. The flesh on his face sagged and the mole on his chin looked larger. The bags under his eyes seemed filled with black ink.

"Ah," the old man said. "My son-in-law has come to pay his respect."

Robert almost said, I am not your son-in-law, but he managed to keep his mouth shut and his face expressionless.

Chou Luk made no effort to rise. The old man's puffy eyes were half closed. From the length of his whiskers, it looked like he hadn't shaved in days. His body had a rancid, sour odor. Robert wanted to ask if he bathed, but he knew this to be unacceptable and rude. Piety forbids criticizing elders. To do so, would only earn Ayaou's anger. He didn't want that. He wanted his stay to be pleasant.

He recognized one of the girls. She'd been with the old man when Robert had fallen in love with Ayaou. Although he knew she had to be at least fifteen, she looked younger. He wondered who the other girl was. He didn't think she was one of Ayaou's sisters. He'd never seen her before.

"I see you are well cared for," Robert said, after nodding his head slightly. He didn't offer his hand. He didn't want to give this old man too much respect.

Chou Luk gestured with his hands. "My wives," he said. "I bought another wife a few months ago since the first one

386

hasn't given me a son." Chou Luk spit on the deck and scowled. "Only two daughters—clean that up, girl," he said to the first wife. "Daughters are useless. All they do is eat and cost money. I was going to stuff them in a sack filled with rocks and toss them in the river, but she cried and begged. She said if I got rid of them, I wouldn't have them to help feed and clean me when I can't leave my bed any longer."

Robert hid the revulsion he felt. He knew that in China women had little or no value. Instead, he said, "Your business must have been profitable to be able to acquire a second wife." The thought of these two young girls with this old man sickened him.

"No, business has been bad. Ayaou gave me the money. She said two wives would take care of me better than one and provide double happiness and double the chance of a son to carry on the family name."

After the greetings, Guan-jiah led Robert forward, away from Chou-Luk. "Where did he get the money to buy the second girl?" he asked. He suspected the truth and feared he was right.

"Ayaou took it from the money you sent."

Blood rushed to his head. God, forgive me, he thought. Light headed, he grabbed the railing to keep from losing his balance.

"And the rest?" His stomach felt as if it were full of snails, shells and all. He feared the answer. What if she had given it to the fortuneteller?

"It went to Cousin Weed. He used it on repairs for the junk. I made sure of that, Master."

"Thank you, Guan-jiah." He felt like he was going to lose his breakfast. It sickened him to think that some of his money had been used to buy Chou Luk another young girl. The girls were no beauties, but what a horrible fate. He wondered what would happen to them after Chou Luk died. Would Cousin Weed take care of them or sell them to someone else?

His reunion with Ayaou was strained from the start. She'd given birth two months earlier, and Robert was relieved to learn that she had gone through the delivery without difficulty since he'd worried she might die during childbirth.

He had not forgotten about the child—a memory that only magnified his guilt. Since he was not married to Ayaou, he was betraying everything he'd been taught as a Christian.

The baby was a girl with dark skin and fluffy brown hair. Although still beautiful, Ayaou looked tired. "Robert," she said, "it needs a name."

"She's two months old and doesn't have a name yet?" He couldn't take his eyes off the child. "I don't understand."

"You are the father," she said. "You name it."

He did not want to give the baby a name. If he named her, he was accepting responsibility for her. He stared at the child and hated himself. He was starting to think too much like a Chinese man.

Although he admired much about Chinese culture, that was one aspect he refused to adopt. "I'll name her Anna," he said. He decided Anna should have his last name. He didn't want her to hear the word 'bastard' during her life. "Her name will be Anna Hart."

"If you hadn't come, I would have named it after Uncle Bark."

"You're not serious," he said. Could she have been that cruel? He didn't want to believe it.

"Is Uncle Bark here?" he asked.

"Uncle Bark is dead," she said.

Later, Robert asked Guan-jiah. "Is it true that Uncle Bark is gone?"

"Yes, Master. He died like a ripe fruit dropping from a tree. It was peaceful and natural, a good death."

Losing Uncle Bark reminded him of his own mortality and that life could end any time. He'd miss Uncle Bark and would never forget him. If it hadn't been for that old man, Robert would already be dead. He would have killed himself or Ward would have done it.

Bark Hart, he thought. It was a good name but not for his daughter. He looked at the timbers above his head. I am sorry, Uncle Bark. I'm sure you would understand that it would not be fair to Anna.

It didn't take long for Anna to capture his heart. He forgot about his discomfort at giving the child his last name. Happy moments arrived when he held her and looked into her chubby face. He marveled at how tiny every part of her was. It thrilled him when she wrapped her hand around one of his fingers and held on.

He swore that he would never abandon the child God gave him.

He trembled and a slight chill raced along the surface of his skin. Startled, he sucked in a breath and listened for something in the silence.

Surely, God was sending him a message. If that is what it was, he had to be a good father.

Robert worked alongside everyone else wanting to impress Ayaou.

"I protest," cousin Weed said. "I cannot have a guest working as if he were a peasant."

Robert detected approval in his eyes. Cousin Weed looked like a younger Uncle Bark with the same features and leather skin.

"I insist," Robert replied. "It is my duty to share the work, and Chou Luk called me his son-in-law. Surely, I must earn the right to be part of this family."

Cousin Weed put Robert to work pumping water out of the bilge or moving cargo on and off the junk. Ayaou did sweaty, backbreaking work alongside him with Anna strapped to her chest.

Cousin Weed's junk had two large sails made of bamboo. Because the bamboo was so strong, there weren't many ropes. The boat's design reminded Robert of the interior structure of bamboo with multiple compartments separated by hatches and ladders. The stern was horseshoe-shaped. The bottom was flat with no keel.

Meals consisted of fish, seaweed and rice, while toasted watermelon seeds were always available as a snack. Years later, he remembered the sound of Ayaou cracking the seeds as she squatted on the deck beside him.

When they worked together, he often took a strand of hair that had fallen into her eyes and tucked it behind an ear. In the past, she smiled when he did that. This time there was no response. She kept right on working as if nothing had happened.

His heart shriveled.

When the ten days ended, he had no choice but to return to Canton. "I should be going with you," she said.

"It's too dangerous," he replied. "We have Anna to think about now. Macao is a safer place for her. Most of China is dangerous what with the Taipings, bandits and the smaller rebellions here and there."

"I should be sharing the risk with you." The spark he missed was back in her eyes, and he regretted leaving. She said, "Cousin Weed's wife will take care of Anna. Have you forgotten that I fought beside you against the Longhaired Bandits and saved your life?"

"My answer is still no," he said, and walked away as he had in Canton. He felt her eyes staring at his back, and his stomach twisted itself into a painful knot as if he had eaten spoiled salt pork.

He wanted to hold her and tell her she could come with him, but his legs refused to cooperate. He kept walking until he was off the boat and ashore. He regretted that he hadn't spent enough time alone with her.

The last thing he saw was Guan-jiah standing aft watching him. His servant held Anna in his arms. He took her little hand and made it wave goodbye. When Ayaou did not appear, a stab of deep pain and regret twisted his guts.

Guan-jiah was doing his job being a father to his child. The eunuch was more of a man than he was.

Thinking like that was dangerous. As the man of the family, he had to earn the money. His job was in Canton, a place too dangerous for the woman and child he loved.

Back in Canton, there were many sleepless nights where he thought of the Ayaou he'd known and loved in Ningpo. He lay awake on the narrow bunk in his cramped quarters while the sounds of rockets and rifle fire crackled in the distance. He dreamed of returning to Ningpo and the time when he had been teaching Shao-mei and Ayaou how to read.

Why couldn't life be like that all the time? he thought. The buzz-saw snore of the major in the next cubbyhole vibrated the wall between them and Robert covered his ears.

He remembered how Ayaou had helped guide his Chinese teacher, Master Ping, in the language lessons. He recalled with fondness the discussions late into the night that he had with the girls about the meanings buried in the books and poems they read together.

What he missed most was the sound of Ayaou's voice—of her singing in the morning when she cooked.

He wondered if he would live to see Ayaou and Anna again. He wrapped the pillow around his head to cover his ears. He couldn't even be miserable. The major's snoring intruded on his suffering.

Chapter 36

A few months before Robert went to Canton, Master Tee Lee Ping taught him about China's dynasties. They met at the house in Ningpo where the lessons took place.

"My mind is famished," Robert said.

Tee Lee Ping arranged his robe and sat on the bench in the parlor. "You are not talking about food." His nose wrinkled. He sniffed. The crackle of oil popping and the scent of ginger and garlic came from the kitchen.

"No."

"However, I am," Ping replied. "Your concubine is a great cook. I love simple food soaked with flavor."

Robert smiled. "That's why she's cooking. I'm going to squeeze you dry tonight. I want to deviate from our regular literature and language lesson. I want to know about China's dynasties."

"So, once again, I must go beyond improving your perfect pronunciation of Mandarin."

"Yes."

"Good, I will earn the meal Ayaou is cooking." He smacked his lips.

"I'm counting on it."

"The first dynasty started with the Yellow Emperor thousands of years before the birth of your Jesus Christ," Ping said. "No one knows if the Yellow Emperor really existed, because we have no writing from that time. Only myths."

"And how many dynasties were there if we count the Yellow Emperor?"

"More than twenty."

"It sounds as if I'm not going to get my money's worth. Should I tell Ayaou to stop cooking?"

"Of course not." Ping stuck his squashed nose in the air and sniffed. "My mouth is watering. We should move to the kitchen and eat while we talk."

"Only if you tell me about the Ch'ing Dynasty."

"Such a curious student."

"And knowledge is the food I crave. I am willing to trade Ayaou's cooking for that."

Ping laughed. "I will help, but it is getting late. If I do not eat soon, I must be on my way. My wife will have dinner ready. She cooks for the family now." He sighed. His bushy eyebrows lowered making his frog-like face look sad. "Alas, my wife needs cooking lessons. It seems her mother never taught her. She shrivels the vegetables and the rice is like eating pebbles. My mother criticizes her, but it does no good."

"Bring your wife next time," Ayaou said. She stood in the kitchen doorway holding a wooden cooking utensil. "While you two talk, I will teach her tricks that will make your mother happy."

"A good idea," Ping said. "What you are cooking smells delightful."

"Master Ping, tell me as much as you can about the Ch'ing Dynasty, and we will fill your belly before you leave." Robert led the way to the kitchen.

They played this game often. He acted curious and begged for knowledge, and Ping, with a sparkle in his eyes, said it was getting late while being pleased he had such a curious student. Of course, stuffing him with Ayaou's cooking helped.

"The first Manchu emperor sat on the Dragon throne in 1644. However, the Manchu are not Han Chinese. They are horse people from north of the Great Wall. They came to power by accident. It is amazing they have ruled so long. They can be brutal even when unnecessary." He stopped talking to fill his mouth.

"How did this Manchu accident happen?"

Ping swallowed and patted his lips dry. "They conquered China with cleverness. An opportunity presented itself and Prince Dorgon, the Manchu regent, plucked the moment as if it were a ripe peach."

"Details," Robert said.

Ayaou placed a platter of steamed buns filled with a sweat bean paste on the table. Ping took one between his chopsticks and held it in front of his mouth. "It is a long story," he said.

"After the last Ming emperor hung himself, two Chinese generals named Wu and Li met in battle with their armies to see who would sit on the Dragon throne. General Wu made a mistake by seeking help from the Manchu."

Ping tore off half the bun with his teeth and sucked at the beans paste that filled the hollow space inside. "Robert, you are a lucky man," he said, as he finished the steamed bun.

"Don't forget, I'm trading Ayaou's food to learn about the Ch'ing Dynasty."

"Of course." Ping popped a ribbon of seaweed into his mouth. There were three types of tofu on the table. He selected a piece of each. "Dorgon, the commander of the Manchu army, waited until the armies of Li and Wu were battered senseless. When the earth was soaked with Han blood, Dorgon's army slaughtered the survivors.

"When Dorgon arrived in Peking, he claimed the throne for his six-year-old Khan, and Shunzhi became emperor of China instead of just the Manchu people."

Ayaou set a bowl on the table filled with fresh green beans she had stir fried with peanut oil, ginger and garlic. Master Ping used his chopsticks to pick one. "So fresh. So crunchy. So much flavor." He rolled his eyes as he chewed. His chopsticks flashed back and forth from the bowl to his wide mouth.

"You can't leave me hanging like this," Robert said. "I want to know the rest."

Ayaou poured Master Ping a cup of jasmine tea. He drank half. "The Manchu hold power for three reasons. The first is the fighting skills and brutality of the eight Manchu banner armies, which maintain the harmony in China."

A steamed fish arrived, head and all. Ping used his chopsticks to peel back the skin and selected pieces of the white meat that the chopsticks plucked from the bones.

"The second reason is that the Manchu leaders adopted Han ways.

"The third is that Taoism and Confucianism influences the way the Han Chinese think. Because of that, the Manchu are allowed to rule China."

Master Ping leaned back in his chair, patted his swollen belly and belched. He looked contented. "I am stuffed," he said. "Ayaou, you are trying to make me into a fat man." He stifled a yawn.

"It is getting late. I must be on my way." He walked to the front door where he stopped, and said, "The Manchu fear the Han will depose the Ch'ing Dynasty. That is the reason so few Han hold important positions in the government and army.

"The Ch'ing often hires foreigners to run important parts of the government and to command elements of the imperial army as General Ward does near Shanghai. If you stay in China, you will see for yourself. The Manchu may even offer you a position."

"Does the Dynasty pay more than I earn as an interpreter for the British Consulate?"

Ping's bushy eyebrows danced. "Robert, I have heard that foreigners working for China are well rewarded. I do not know how much. Are you planning to work for the Dynasty?"

"It was a thought."

"The emperor would be lucky to have you. You understand the Chinese and do not judge them like most foreigners. You do not want to exploit China or convert the Chinese to become Christians. I appreciate the fact that you have always treated me as an equal. No other Westerner has done that."

Months later, Robert was not surprised when he was approached by Heng-ch'i, the Hoppo for Canton, along with Imperial Governor General Lao Ch'ung-kuang.

They offered him a position as the new Deputy Commissioner of Customs for Canton, the same job Horatio Lay held in Shanghai.

He'd met Horatio in 1854, and the man had recently left the British consulate in Shanghai to go to work for the Manchu Dynasty.

If Robert accepted the position, his pay would leap from five hundred to fifteen hundred pounds a year—a three-hundred percent increase.

On May 29, 1859, he turned in his resignation to the British Consul in Canton.

Horatio Lay, who Robert had not seen for several years, came south to help set up the new Custom's house in Canton. Horatio stayed into 1860 before returning to Shanghai.

It didn't take long for Robert to be reminded that Horatio still held a low opinion of the Chinese.

"Has Patridge been to see you?" Horatio asked. They were going over manifests and computing the duties that were to be paid to the Chinese by the foreign ships anchored in the river.

"I haven't talked to Patridge for months," Robert replied.

"Well," Horatio said, "don't be surprised if the scoundrel walks into your office in an attempt to buy you off so his ships won't have to pay duties." His brows lowered, and he started to storm about the crowded office knocking papers to floor. Robert knelt to retrieve them. It seemed that Horatio's temper hadn't changed either.

"He had the audacity to offer me a bribe," Horatio said. "I sent him packing after I gave him a piece of my mind. The gall of that man to treat me like a thief he could buy."

Robert was still gathering papers from the floor. He avoided eye contact with his superior, thinking of the services he had provided for Patridge while still living in Ningpo. Should he tell Horatio? What would Horatio think if he found out about the money Patridge had paid him to do exactly what Horatio was angry about?

"This goes no further," Horatio said. "What I have to tell you stays between us. Agreed?"

"What stays between us?" Robert asked.

"Do you agree?"

He was reluctant to agree to something he knew nothing about. What if Horatio was going to confess to murdering someone? On the other hand, he might learn something. He remembered the advice the Governor of Hong Kong, Sir John Bowring, had given him soon after he arrived in China.

"Take everything that happens and learn from it," Sir Bowring had said. "In the end you will be a better, stronger person. Don't shy away from understanding things even if you disagree with them." That advice had served Robert well so far.

He overruled his sense of caution, and asked, "What is it?"

"Only if you agree that what I tell you does not leave this room."

It irritated him to be thrust into a situation like this.

"Look at me. I want to see the sincerity in your eyes."

Robert realized he was not being given a choice. If he refused, Horatio would never trust him.

The mask he had worked hard to perfect slid into place. He looked into Horatio's eyes confident his expression would hide his true feelings. "I agree."

"Good," Horatio said. "I've heard you can be trusted. While I was working with the British Consulate in Shanghai, Patridge bribed me to help with his shipments. However, the situation in China has changed. The last treaty between Britain and China forced the emperor to create a uniform Imperial Customs Service throughout the empire. The provincial governors will no longer be allowed to collect taxes for imported goods and keep the money. Those duties will go to the imperial treasury. Do you know the reason for that?"

"So China has more money to modernize."

"You are so naïve." Horatio shook his head.

Feeling resentment, Robert maintained his neutral expression. He had forgotten how Horatio treated others as if they were all schoolboys. He had disliked Horatio from the day they had first met in Shanghai in 1854.

"Robert, China still owes Britain, France and the United States reparations for losing the first Opium War. When the Treaty of Nanking was signed in 1842, China had to open five treaty ports for trade; pay an indemnity of six million for the opium destroyed by Commissioner Lin; three million for debts owed to British traders by Canton merchants, and another twelve million to England for the cost of the war. Two years later, France and the United states made similar demands.

"Without a steady source of revenue, the emperor has no way to pay back those reparations." Horatio laughed, then said, "I always find it amusing that Britain and France started the war, but the Chinese have to pay because they lost.

"The emperor is lucky. Britain and France could have conquered China and divided it between them. and I believe it would have been better if they had."

Horatio's smile vanished. "Before that, everyone working for the British consulate service was in the pay of someone like Patridge, but times have changed. If we allow the opium merchants to cheat the Chinese, the British, French and the United States governments will not be paid. Our loyalty must be to Britain first. There is enough theft among Chinese officials as it is. If the Ch'ing Dynasty is to survive and keep China stable so the opium trade flourishes, they need a steady source of revenue and that is our job. Do you understand?"

Robert stood with the papers he had gathered from the floor. "Yes, Horatio. I had the same thoughts myself. No more taking bribes."

"Exactly." Horatio switched from English to Mandarin. "I thought you and I might have similar opinions. Knowing you were in Patridge's pay, I wanted to sound you out to see if you had changed your ways."

Robert's composure slipped for an instant. Horatio had been testing him.

"I have been hearing good things from the Chinese about you, and Harry Parkes has nothing but good to say."

He put a hand on Robert's shoulder as if they were old friends. Robert had an urge to shrug the hand off but didn't. "Be careful, Robert. There are those who will trample you to climb to the top. You and I are on our way and if you are loyal to me, I will do right by you. One day, you will be assisting me in running China for Britain. When that time comes, the Ch'ing Dynasty will do our bidding as we see fit."

Robert replied in flawless Mandarin. "You have nothing to worry about, Horatio. We have both seen the last of Patridge's money. I will not disappoint you."

He didn't tell Horatio that when he accepted this job, his loyalties switched to the Ch'ing Dynasty. He refused to work for two masters. Horatio would learn that one day, but now wasn't the time to let him discover Robert's true feelings. He had to establish himself first.

The truth was that he wanted Britain and China to be friends. He admired the Chinese that much.

"My, my," Horatio said. "You are as good as they say you are with this barbaric language. I remember when you first arrived in China and could not say one proper word in Mandarin. Now your accent is flawless and better than mine is. If I closed my eyes, I would think I was talking to someone from the imperial court.

"Robert, mark my words, before we leave China we will be rich, powerful men. Our names will be in the history books."

Robert couldn't imagine how that was going to happen.

Chapter 37

The rebels attacking Canton had been defeated.

After Horatio Lay returned to Shanghai, Robert wrote a letter to Ayaou in Macau. He had difficulty forming the Chinese characters, because his hand trembled as he wrote it. For that reason, he kept the note brief.

"Ayaou," he wrote, "it's time to come home. I miss you. You are always in my thoughts. Bring Guan-jiah too."

It was difficult to stop from pouring his feelings into the letter. In the last line, he told Ayaou to bring Fooyen, as she would make a good nanny for Anna. He sent five hundred yuan for Ayaou to give to her cousins to help repair the junk.

A week later, his boat-girl was back.

She stood before him in the bedroom looking like the slender girl he'd first met during that battle with the Taipings years earlier. He'd forgotten the ocean scent of her hair, and it made him dizzy. "I've missed your beauty," he said, "and your smell."

"You are a crazy man," she replied. "I am no beauty. My face is not round and pale like a full moon. You have forgotten how large my feet are. I have high cheekbones and dark skin. In China, this means I am ugly."

"But I'm not Chinese. I see beauty from a different standard. You are everything I want in a woman." He pulled her close feeling the familiar curve of her spine—something he'd dreamed of daily. His starved hands slipped under her clothing to explore the smooth warmth of her body.

They made love for hours like drunken sailors who had been without rum too long.

The next morning, Ayaou was fascinated when he took her on a tour of the new house he had bought. He started with the front entrance. The house was long and deep. Three large rooms were on the ground floor. Between each room was an open garden courtyard. The previous owners had abandoned the house and never returned, and the plants had died.

The kitchen was behind the third garden. Behind the kitchen was another courtyard where the servants hung the laundry. A twelve-foot-high wall surrounded the house. A gate at the front opened to the street.

"This house would hold all the boat people from my village," she said, her voice filled with awe. She twisted one way then another, as if she were painting the images into her memory. "We might be able to drag our boats here from the river and keep them safe from floods."

"How many people are in your village?" he asked, afraid of the answer.

"Do you remember the people you saved from the Longhaired Bandits the first time we met?" she replied. "Double that."

The thought of his house filled with so many people sent a violent shiver through him. He imagined chickens and roosters running wild and there would be droppings everywhere. Babies would be toddling about without diapers. The floor would never be the same. He shook off the images and guided her through the last of the downstairs rooms.

The servants' quarters were behind the last courtyard, and covered walkways ran along both sides of the house to the back. Two stairways led to the second level. One set of stairs came from the kitchen and the other from the walkway to the right of the third hall. Each stairway was outfitted with a two-inch thick wood hatch that could be dropped in place and locked to close off the upper floor.

The family sitting room on the second floor was at the front of the house, with the main bedroom in the back. There were six bedrooms. As nanny, Fooyen would be sleeping in Anna's room. Robert had turned one bedroom into an office and another into a library.

"I feel like a princess," Ayaou said. "I do not deserve this."

The tone of her voice told him she was thrilled, and that was enough to fill him with pride. "You are wrong," he said. "We both deserve this. You can have a hot bath anytime you want without going to a bathhouse or heating the water. The servants will do the work for you."

"A true luxury," she said. "One I will never get used to."

He told her that he would have a party in two weeks. He'd invited the governor general, the Hoppo of Canton, members of the Yamen, the Tartar general, military officers, Parkes and the other members of the commission, and all the foreign consuls in Canton. "I'm going to show you off. You are worth more than gold."

"Do not be silly," she replied. "If you turned me into gold, I will be stiff and cold in bed. Having this celebration is the right thing for your career. In China, personal connections are a true treasure. I suggest providing good food, because China is an eating culture. A party without different types of food will be bad so make sure to order delicacies such as stewed bear paws, deep-fried snakes, marinated sparrows and duck feet."

His stomach lurched at the thought of marinated sparrows. He'd seen a street vendor selling fried sparrows with the beaks and feathers still on. "Ayaou, half my guests will be Westerners. They will not eat such things. If I put a feathered sparrow on a Frenchman or Briton's plate, they will be offended. They might get sick."

"But what about the Chinese guests?" she asked. "You do not want to disappoint them, do you?"

"Leave the menu to Guan-jiah and the cooks," he said. "They know what to do. Cooking isn't your responsibility any longer. What we are going to do is buy you the best silk gown for this occasion. I want you to look like a Manchu princess."

"Impossible," she replied. "I am not a Manchu."

He ignored her. After all, she was smiling when she said it.

He started to have doubts about her joining the dinner party. He wasn't sure how the others would react. He hadn't forgotten how the missionaries in Ningpo had talked behind Hollister's back about Me-ta-tae.

At the same time, he didn't want to act as if he were embarrassed about her either. Just having these thoughts bothered him. It took an effort to keep his features composed so she would not guess his thoughts.

"Do not forget," she said, "I am not a princess."

"Nevertheless," he replied, "you will be dressed like one."

The party was planned for a Saturday evening during a full moon.

After he had accepted the job with the Imperial government, he promoted Guan-jiah. Instead of being the only servant, Guan-jiah managed more than a dozen. Robert didn't want to leave the courtyards full of dead plants, so he also made Guan-jiah responsible for landscaping the gardens.

When Guan-jiah finished the first courtyard, he called Robert to see it. "What do you think, Master?"

"I'm speechless." He was amazed and didn't know what to say. It was early evening and a half-moon was glowing in the sky. He stood in the garden's center and felt as if he were in the mountains surrounded by a forest.

"How did you do it?" he asked.

"Do what, Master?"

"Design this space so it feels ten times larger than it is. I can see the moon and the stars. I like that. These trees and plants don't block the view."

"My plan would have failed if the trees were thick enough to cover the beauty of the night sky." Guan-jiah pointed at the open space that revealed the moon. "I made sure not to fill that part of the sky."

Robert studied the pile of boulders. They looked as if they were leaning against the side of a mountain. There had been a fountain there. Now there was a waterfall with a brook flowing through the boulders. Behind the boulders was a tall stand of bamboo that hid the house. Other, smaller trees were planted among the climbing pile of boulders and the scene looked as if it had been plucked from the wilderness. In fact, it felt as if the house didn't exist. "Who did you learn this from?" he asked, as the garden calmed him.

"From Li Liwen," Guan-jiah replied. "He lived during the seventeenth century, and Shen Fu, who lived at the end of the eighteenth century. Liwen said, 'First, we look at the hills in the painting; then we look at the painting in the hills.'"

"Look at the rockery." Guan-jiah pointed at the pile of boulders. How could anyone call them a pile when they looked like the forces of nature put them there? Many were larger than a man was. Robert wondered how the Chinese workers managed to get them in here.

"If you look around, Master, nowhere will you find a straight line. When you reach the center of the garden, you are surrounded by nature as if you were in the mountains. To the

Chinese, the mountains and rivers are alive. We can see the dragon's back along the winding ridges of the mountains, and the dragon's tail where the mountains merge into the plains or the sea.

"My goal was to capture that essence, so you can surround yourself with tranquility. Shen Fu said, 'show the large in the small and the small in the large, provide for the real in the unreal and for the unreal in the real,' and that is what I attempted to do.

"Of course, I am no master, and we still have to train the trees to get the right look. That will take time. To make sure you wouldn't see any walls, I had creepers planted. I am sorry to say that in the daylight you can still see some of the house but at night it is what I imagined."

"You have created magic, Guan-jiah. You never fail to amaze."

"I dreamed that one-day I would do something like this for my family. Since this garden was completed, I have carried Anna here daily, so she is not separated from nature. I want her to appreciate the small things in life by learning how to grow flowers."

Robert imagined Guan-jiah in the garden with Anna. The image filled his eyes with tears. He turned so the eunuch couldn't see. He spent so many hours at work that he didn't have much time left for his family.

"What you have done is a miracle," he said, careful to keep the emotion out of his voice. "This garden suggests a wild place. It is as if you tamed nature. Thank you, Guan-jiah. I will be proud to show this to my guests."

"It is regrettable that I cannot finish the other courtyards before the party."

"You have done enough, my friend."

Guan-jiah blushed. He cleared his throat. "Master, it is Ayaou."

"What do you mean?" Robert was alarmed. Was something wrong with his lover? Maybe she was pregnant again.

"Master, she is a boat person. She will not know how to act."

"Nonsense." He was relieved that it wasn't serious. "All she has to do is show up and wear the gown that is being made for her. Instruct her to sit, eat and look lovely. That shouldn't be difficult. I don't want to hear anymore about this. Just do your job, Guan-jiah. After all, you are the house manager.

"Does that mean I manage the concubines too?"

"Of course," Robert said, "but don't let them know." He didn't bother to say that Ayaou would be his only concubine.

Chapter 38

As Robert walked through the main rooms on the ground floor, he watched the servants decorate the house and prepare food. "Guan-jiah," he said, "I haven't seen any musicians. Where is the opera troupe?" He felt nervous. It was the afternoon of the day before his first dinner party. He had planned carefully, but worried that something would go wrong, as if the house might catch fire. He wanted the evening to be perfect.

"Mistress Ayaou cancelled them, Master," Guan-jiah replied.

"Why?"

"Ayaou said she was going to perform for the guests."

"No!" His stomach did a flip-flop and his face went numb. He couldn't think. He had to shake his head to get his mind working. "Guan-jiah, find any available entertainment and get them here within the hour. Pay double if needed."

He fought panic as he hurried upstairs to find Ayaou standing in front of a tall dressing mirror. Stopping in the doorway, he struggled to compose himself. He didn't want to say anything until the words coming out of his mouth were not controlled by anger. When he felt he was ready, he walked into the room.

White powder caked Ayaou's face. Her mouth looked like a giant cherry. Her eyes met his in the mirror. He forced a smile to hide his true emotions and stared at his image in the mirror thinking he looked like a buffoon.

She continued to slip into the same dance clothes she'd worn that time at Ward's house in Shanghai. Since her hips were wider now, she struggled with the silk pants getting them on. His breath caught in his throat. Watching her dress was like stepping back to that time several years earlier when she had been on the auction block for sale to the highest bidder.

His world had been different then, and he'd been easily fooled.

She glanced over her shoulder. Her eyes were alive with excitement. "Give me a moment, and I will be done," she said, turning back to the mirror.

If she performed tonight, the Western women would be scandalized, and their men would have difficulty keeping their tongues in their mouths. He was sure they'd treat Ayaou like a whore. There was a strong chance some of his male guests would offer to buy a night with her.

"Ayaou," he said, "what are you planning to do? Why aren't you putting on that silk gown we bought, the one similar to what the Imperial concubines wear for a formal audience inside the Forbidden City?"

"I am dressing like this to entertain your guests. After I sing and dance, I will come upstairs and change into the gown. Lend me a hand, Robert. I am having trouble getting dressed."

Guan-jiah had been right. Growing up as a boat girl had not provided Ayaou with opportunities to see how the wealthy and powerful lived or entertained. She came from peasant stock, trained to be a concubine, to please the man who bought her. She didn't know any other way.

What could he do? He didn't want to see her hurt and decided to take a drastic step. There wasn't time for anything else.

He picked up a handkerchief and handed it to her. "Wipe that powder off your face and change into the gown, or you'll have to stay here in the bedroom during the party. That outfit doesn't fit anymore. You'll look ridiculous."

"Am I the hostess?" she asked, looking confused. "Am I to make everyone happy? What is wrong with dressing like this? You loved it the first time you saw me wearing it. You even told me so when we made love in Ward's cellar. I know I am taller and heavier but not by that much. I can fit."

"Some other time, Ayaou."

"Why not this time?"

"Well, many of my guests are—" He tried to choose the right words. He was entering a pool of lice and had no idea how Ayaou was going to react. "They are not Chinese," he said.

"That is why it is a good idea to offer them something truly Chinese."

"You don't understand. Westerners are judgmental. They wouldn't appreciate—"

She cut him off. "I am sure they would like my dancing. You enjoyed it. Remember? It was what made you fall in love with me. It is why you were willing to pay a fortune for me to be your concubine."

He didn't want to tell her that at Ward's the intent had been for her to look like a high-class, desirable whore to drive the price higher. She had been meat for sale.

Her expression soured telling him that she had guessed his thoughts. Backing away, she held a hand out to ward him off. She looked devastated. Her lips trembled. "You are ashamed of me."

"No," he said. What she said was true but also not true. He was ashamed of the woman she had been raised to be, but he wasn't ashamed of her. Not counting Guan-jiah, she was one of the most sensible people he knew. The truth was that he needed time to think.

Maybe she was right. Maybe he had been attracted by her dancing and the scanty outfit. Maybe it was also her lack of sophistication. While growing up in Ireland, his family had smothered him with proper behavior. Yes, that was it. The wild streak he'd seen in her had attracted him. On the other hand, maybe it was her courage in battle when they had fought the Taipings side by side. He'd never known a woman with so much courage.

She said, "I thought you loved me—that I did not have to pretend to be someone I am not. I thought I was blessed with a master like no other master in China." Her eyes filled with tears.

"Give me time to explain, Ayaou." He fumbled for words. "Don't you understand that none of the people at this party would approve if I allowed you to show yourself like this? That is why we bought that silk gown, so you'd look imperial."

"What do I look like dressed like this?"

"I won't say it, Ayaou." He was losing control. That wasn't what he had wanted to say. He hated letting those words escape.

The color in her face drained away and the warmth fled from her voice. "So, I am only a whore to you."

"Ayaou, don't."

"I always suspected. There is no doubt about it now." Her arms wrapped around her shoulders as if she were cold. Her features collapsed into agony.

"I love you." He felt helpless, and a void opened inside his guts. He put his hands on her bare shoulders knowing that what she'd said was partly true. Touching her excited him. He realized that he'd wanted a woman who acted more like a whore, but he wanted her to be a virgin too.

His member stirred inside his pants. He was tempted to throw her down and take her.

She pushed him away and started to take off her costume. "I have been a fool. When it comes to the heart, you are no different than Captain Patridge."

"That isn't fair, Ayaou. I would never treat you like he would." He couldn't help but stare as she stripped nude.

Then he knew the truth. Out of selfishness, he'd wanted someone who wouldn't hold back when it came to passion. What he didn't want was a stiff, upper crust British woman, the kind that would be like a tub of ice in bed. Ayaou was exactly right for him.

She opened a drawer, took out her boat rags, put them on and then went to a corner of the room, squatted on her heels and stared at the floor.

This was frustrating. He bit his lower lip and wished he could sweep all the words he'd said back into his mouth and start over again. The trouble was, even if he could, he still didn't know how to deal with this situation.

Ayaou started to cry.

This increased his sense of helplessness and his guts twisted into knots followed by a headache. How could he tell her that he loved the wild abandon that was the sluttish part of her—the girl that tossed and turned during orgasms as if she were having an out of body experience?

"Ayaou, please listen." He knelt in front of her and took her cold hands in his. She yanked her hands back and hid them under her armpits.

"I will not listen to your lies," she said. "You say you love me but part of you always rejected me. I can tell sometimes that you are in a battle with yourself. The bags of your culture are heavier than Cousin Weed's junk. I understand that now, because I have experienced the same thing."

He rocked back on his heels as if she had slapped him. "How so?" he asked, afraid of the answer. He had hoped she had recovered from the trauma of Shao-mei's death. He should have listened more carefully to Uncle Bark's warning.

"Some of my relatives warned me that your hair is yellow because you are evil natured and unhealthy. They even asked if I ever saw puss oozing from under your armpits. Their views did not influence me, and I am not ashamed of you."

"I know that, Ayaou. I want to be the same, but—"

"You have been trying. I can see that. I also know that you are afraid of what your family and Irish friends will say and think. You believe that your future depends on their tongues. It was okay when you were an interpreter. Now, you are too big to risk slander. Your reputation is your ladder to China's top. That is why you came to China—to become rich and powerful like Patridge and General Ward?"

"That is not true, Ayaou." His words sounded hollow as if they were lies. He felt as if he were on shaky ground. Part of what she was saying was correct, but he had also come to China to run away from a culture that condemned him for his nature, something she'd never done—until now. He avoided her eyes.

"Go ahead and keep lying," she said.

"I am not lying. We will always be together. What happened to that sweet, innocent girl I fell in love with, the one willing to die beside me?" He reached out to touch her face. She jerked out of reach. His fingers tingled and the pain inside his head increased. His eyes started to ache.

"Do not touch me," she said. "My father was right. It was wrong for me to learn to read. That is why I can see who you really are. I have learned from the books I have been reading. I know why people act the way they do."

"What you are thinking is wrong," he said.

"The truth is that you do not want anybody to know that I am the mother of your child, or that you have a bastard. Am I wrong?"

The shock of her words caused his heart to race. His hands went behind his back where he twisted his fingers together. He stared at her in horror and didn't want to answer.

"You hope that no one will ask you about me," she said. Her words felt like hammer blows. "You expect me to walk around your party like a ghost. At night, you sneak me into your bed and we steal love like thieves, and bang, one day you will tell me that you have found yourself a proper wife from your people, and here, Ayaou, is some money, and I am discarded."

She broke down sobbing. "Mr. Sua-min read it in my palm and consulted Ba-Gua, the evidence of my fate. He said that I would not be able to fight it."

"That's preposterous. I promise I will never marry anyone else but you." He wiped at her streaming tears with a handkerchief. "You will be the only woman in my life. I am asking you to give me time to work things out. My friends, who are coming to this party, have certain expectations of me. I can't force my views on them overnight, can I?"

"Create as many excuses as you want. Do not expect me to believe them." She pushed past him and left the corner to sit on the bed. She wouldn't look at him.

Someone in the room's doorway cleared his throat. Robert looked and discovered it was Guan-jiah. "What is it?" he asked in a sharp tone that he regretted immediately. He hated losing control.

"Master, the guests are arriving."

"I'll be right down." His voice sounded calm now, but his thoughts were in turmoil. His insides were going crazy flopping around like a fish out of water. He didn't hear Guan-jiah say 'Yes, Master', so he looked and saw the man making odd eye-gestures and pointing his chin toward the hallway as if he had something private to say.

Feeling numb, he went into the hallway with the eunuch. "What is it?"

"The mistress is getting rebellious." Guan-jiah whispered into his ear. "It is the Chinese way to beat such a woman into submission. Master, you must crush her rebel spirit to get her to listen to you."

"I know what you are telling him, Guan-jiah." Ayaou's voice was high, screeching. "I will make you pay."

Robert glanced over his shoulder at her. Her face had twisted into a mask of anger. He looked back. "No, Guan-jiah, I cannot do that. She and I have shared too much together."

"I see." Guan-jiah paused, stared at the floor and fingered his chin. Then his eyes lit up. "Why don't you let me beat her for you, Master?"

"You can't be serious." He studied Guan-jiah's face and saw that the eunuch meant it. Robert shook his head. "No one touches her!"

"Yes, Master." Guan-jiah face emptied of emotion. He nodded. "Master, I caution—"

Robert held up a hand. "No, I don't want to hear anymore nonsense. I've had enough."

They both looked toward the room to make sure Ayaou hadn't heard. She wasn't watching. She had rolled over and buried her face in the pillow.

"What should I tell the mistress?" Guan-jiah asked.

"Tell her to refresh herself; help her dress in the proper gown and send her down to join me. Don't let her leave the room if she won't do as she's told."

"Yes, Master."

He hurried to greet his guests. Everyone came with gifts as a way to congratulate him for his move up.

The band was loud and cheerful. The food and wine fabulously presented. The guests enjoyed the opera performance. The exotic costumes, makeup, acrobats and marshal-artists fascinated everyone.

However, Robert kept glancing at the doorway Ayaou had to use to enter the room. He pretended that he was happy, but inside he was in turmoil. He wanted her to be there beside him, but at the same time was afraid that she would show up.

Laughing along with the guests, he emptied several glasses of hard liquor. He ate some bear paw and deer meat but didn't pay attention to the taste. He knew he was guilty of some of what Ayaou had accused him of, but he truly loved her.

Half-drunk, he switched from whisky to wine and started to tell stories about himself to his new friends. With his tongue loosened from the alcohol, he started to boast. He knew it was wrong, but he couldn't stop. At one point, Guan-jiah whispered in his ear. "Master, you should stop drinking so much."

"Leave me alone, Guan-jiah. Go back to Ayaou and keep her locked in the bedroom where she belongs." His words were slurred. He didn't care how they sounded. He walked away from his house manager and joined three men smoking cigars.

"What was on your mind when you first arrived in China?" a colonel asked. He was from one of the British regiments stationed in Canton. During the rebel activity, Robert had played several games of chess with this colonel, but he couldn't remember the man's name.

The colonel studied him with wise eyes as if he were reading Robert's mind.

"In 1854, when I first arrived in Hong Kong," Robert replied, "I was a nineteen-year-old, wide-eyed and adventurous youngster. I had dreams of castles, titles and wealth." He stopped and struggled to focus on the colonel's face. The man had a thick, waxed mustache that stuck out on either side of his nose. The ends turned upward in a twist. His sideburns were thick and shaggy and came down to his jaw line. He was in his dress uniform and there were many medals pinned to it.

Robert shook his head trying to clear it. "Colonel, did you come here thinking of such things too?"

The colonel took the glass of wine from Robert's hand. "Tea would be better," he said. The officer signaled a servant and spoke to him in Mandarin. A pot of tea materialized. The colonel guided Robert away from the others and sat beside him on a couch. Another couple approached. The colonel looked sternly at them. Then Guan-jiah appeared and talked to them. They walked away.

"Tell me about yourself, colonel. I'm tired of talking about me. I sound like a fool."

"Nonsense," the colonel replied. "When the pressure gets to be too much, a man has to let go. You have accepted a position with great authority and responsibility, and you are only twenty-four. It takes time to learn. With age comes wisdom."

The colonel nodded. "Drink your tea. Now that your life has become like a serious game of chess, you must pick the right time and place to let go. This is not that time and place. The way you were talking reminds me of men back from battle trying to drown in liquor." They both sipped tea, and there was a moment of silence.

"I've been away from home for two decades," the colonel said. "I spent most of that time in India and came to China recently. I must admit that I thought of such things like you mentioned." He waved a hand toward the cigar smokers. "But I was barely a lieutenant when I arrived in India. Now I'm a colonel and unless I accomplish something incredible, I'll probably retire as a brigadier general in another ten to fifteen years."

"I understand how you feel," Robert replied. He took a moment to empty the cup of tea and hold it out for a servant to refill. The second cup was bitter, stronger. He saw Guan-jiah across the room watching.

"Good," the colonel said, "keep drinking. That tea will clear your head and allow you to regain control. It isn't wise to lose control in front of the troops, and some of the men here with their wives work for you."

"You are a wise man, colonel. At first, when I was struggling to learn Mandarin, I doubted myself. Now, here I am on the threshold of achieving even bigger goals, and I still doubt myself. I thought I would grow out of that."

"Men never escape doubt," the colonel said. "With time and age, one learns how to deal with it."

"When I first arrived," Robert said. "I didn't plan to stay long. Now, it looks like I must. England will never offer me what China has offered and will continue to offer." He stopped to drink more tea and focus his eyes. The room was still blurry around the edges.

"What about you, colonel. If the Chinese offered you one of their armies, would you take it?"

"I wouldn't consider it. My regiment is my family, and I go where my orders send me."

"I'm envious. You have an entire regiment for a family."

"What about you, Hart? Is your family in Britain?"

"I have two families," he replied. "One is near Belfast. The other is invisible and my heart aches because of them." He glanced one last time at the empty doorway Ayaou had not walked through and realized how much he missed her.

After all, Ayaou, Anna and Guan-jiah were his Chinese family. He now thought of his house manager as more than just a servant. He wondered what his life would have been like in China without them.

Chapter 39

The situation between China and the foreign powers worsened. Emperor Hsien Feng took his family and the imperial court and fled beyond the Great Wall abandoning Peking and the Summer Palace.

Robert's knowledge of the history behind the current political crises was limited. He had learned much in Ningpo from his teacher, Tee Lee Ping, but not enough. Determined to discover what was going on, he started asking his Chinese friends questions. What he heard shocked him.

British merchants had bullied the Chinese for decades over opium smuggling and some British merchants had served as British counselor officers.

Since many of these merchants were smuggling opium into China, that was a conflict of interest. Some had manipulated the situation causing the current Allied invasion of Northern China. Their goal, to remove all restrictions on the opium trade and increase profits.

"Guan-jiah," he asked, "why can't the British merchants be satisfied with what they were earning from the opium trade the way it was?" It was early morning and still dark. They were alone in the kitchen sipping tea before he left for work. Even the cook wasn't up.

"Master, the answer is simple, the Ch'ing Dynasty levied taxes that were so high that the drug was restricted to a few wealthy Chinese. It was impossible for the foreign merchants to make fortunes from such a small number."

"They should have been satisfied with what they had."

"Greed holds great power over men," Guan-jiah replied. "The merchants saw a huge, potential market among the poor.

They want to sell opium at a lower price to reach more people, so they bypass the imperial taxes by smuggling the drug into China. That's why Ayaou's family is involved in the opium trade. The foreign merchants hire poor people to carry the drugs upriver to reach more peasants.

"It has become so bad that even eunuchs in the emperor's household are addicted. Did you know that when Emperor Tao Kuang closed China to the opium trade, a letter was sent to Britain's Queen Victoria seeking her help to save the Chinese people?"

"No, I didn't." He'd learned from Tee Lee Ping that Tao Kuang had been the current emperor's father. He died in 1850, shortly before the Taiping Rebellion.

"Queen Victoria did not respond," Guan-jiah said. "Her answer arrived when the French and British declared war on China."

Robert had trouble sleeping that night and thought of his father, a Wesleyan minister, who had raised his children to act morally. Now that Robert worked for China, he felt it was his duty to help end the opium trade. There had to be a way, so he could atone for what he had done for Patridge.

For some reason he could not fathom, he thought of Horatio Lay, who had also been paid to help smuggle opium into China when he worked for the British consulate. However, thinking of Horatio and his arrogance made Robert feel worse.

"The Emperor appointed Lin Zexu to end the opium problem," Guan-jiah said, during tea the next morning. "Lin demanded that British subjects in China turn over all opium to him. He destroyed three million pounds of it, which led to Britain invading with a large army from India in 1840. The Opium War ended with a treaty in 1843, which opened China to limited opium trade."

"Guan-jiah, I want to see what opium has done to China. Do you know a family that uses it?"

"No, but I will find one."

Several days later, Guan-jiah took him to visit a Chinese family where everyone had been addicted to the drug. The house was dark and had a sour smell that came from unwashed bodies. The stench was so bad that Robert had to cover his mouth with a wet cloth scented with jasmine.

"I paid fifty yuan for them to let us into their house," Guan-jiah said. He lighted a candle. The meager light revealed that the house was filthy. They moved from room to room. Robert saw an army of cockroaches and a few rats. He gasped and staggered back in horror when he discovered that the seven family members had no lips. Before the tour was over, he realized that there were no young children.

Once they were outside breathing fresh air, Guan-jiah said, "Lin discovered that the only way to stop people from smoking opium was to cut their lips off. That way they could not close their lips around the stem of the opium pipe and suck."

"I didn't see any children. In every Chinese house I've visited, there have always been children. Why not here?" He was afraid of the answer.

"They sold them to buy more opium," Guan-jiah replied.

Robert swallowed the bile that rushed into his throat and stiffened his resolve to learn more. He could not turn his back on this tragedy. Because he had helped smuggle opium into China when he worked in Ningpo, he felt responsible. There had to be something he could do. But what?

That night, he sat in the bathtub twice as long and scrubbed his skin with a bristle brush until his flesh glowed pink. Near the end of his bath, he recalled some advice Uncle Bart gave soon after Shao-mei had been murdered.

"Wait for an opportunity to surface," Uncle Bart had said. "Then you will get what you want. Even if years or decades must pass, it is the Chinese way."

The next day, before work, Guan-jiah continued the lesson. "After the Opium War in 1842, the emperor was forced to sign a treaty allowing the foreign devils to open five treaty ports to trade."

"I know that much," Robert said. "And now, the American, French and British are demanding that the treaty from the Opium War be renegotiated.

He was aware that a combined English and French expeditionary force was marching on Peking to force the emperor to ratify the new treaty, which would open more of China to Christian missionaries and opium and explained why the emperor had fled beyond the Great Wall into Mongolia.

The fact that Britain and France were linking opium and Christianity in the same treaty upset Robert. How could any true Christian be part of such a horrible thing? No wonder a Chinese Christian convert had started the Taiping rebellion and wanted to rid China of opium too.

He felt helpless. If the emperor could not stop the opium trade due to smuggling and the military superiority of Britain and France, what could Robert do from Canton?

Two days later, he was ready to learn more. "How many Chinese lost their lips like that family?"

"Thousands," Guan-jiah replied. "Commissioner Lin was desperate to stop the spread of opium addiction. The emperor was concerned. Since the family is China's foundation, if enough families are ruined, China is doomed. The culture will collapse."

He couldn't sleep that night. Every time he closed his eyes, he saw the grotesque, lipless faces of that Chinese family. Before morning, he vowed to do whatever he could to end or restrict the opium trade in China.

On a Saturday in February, he was busy at work when Guan-jiah came to the custom's building to report that Chow Luk had arrived unexpectedly. Ayaou wanted him home as soon as possible. Worried, he put his paperwork away. Another tragedy must have struck Ayaou's family. That usually meant it was going to cost money.

Before he left the office, he took his pistol from a desk drawer and slipped it into his jacket pocket. No matter what his sympathies were regarding China and the opium trade, he still looked like a man with a big nose and the wrong color skin.

There were Chinese, especially among the Christian Taiping rebels that hated everything foreign because of the opium trade. No wonder so many Chinese called foreigners devils, he thought. After he reached the house, he had to be patient and listen to Chou Luk while he talked in circles before discovering the reason for the visit.

"Cousin Weed was taken by the Longhaired Bandits," Chou Luk finally said. "They are holding him for ransom. If they are not paid by the end of this month, they will behead him."

Robert did not ask the expected question. How much was this going to cost him? It was easy to guess what was coming. Ayaou and her family saw him as a river of silver taels that could solve their financial problems. After all, he was already paying for the crucial repairs to the family junk.

Ayaou cleared her throat. She was staring at him with her lips pressed tight and her eyes looked glassy. The pressure he felt stirred up a nest of resentful hornets inside his head. The Taipings were sure to ask for a huge ransom, which might be more than he could pay. At the same time, he did not see how he could borrow the money without going to Captain Patridge, which he refused to do. He would not help smuggle more opium into China, not after witnessing the horror of that family without lips.

"The Longhaired Bandits demand five thousand yuan to release Weed," Chow Luk said. "I have come to borrow the money."

Knowing the Chinese as well as he did, he was sure that Chow Luk had been waiting for him to offer first. A son-in-law with resources was expected to do that without question. By not making the offer without being asked, he was not showing proper respect to Ayaou's father.

Robert fought back the harsh words that climbed his throat. He cast a sideways glance at Ayaou—afraid that she would guess what he was thinking. She was sitting in a chair staring at the floor with her hands folded on her lap.

Her head came up. She saw him watching her. The look in her face changed, and her eyes started to give dangerous flashes of light. He frowned and looked away. If she had used a softer approach instead of looking so judgmental, he might have tried to reason with her and Chou Luk.

"I don't have that kind of money," he replied, controlling both his voice and the expression on his face. How could he tell Chow Luk and Ayaou that he could not help because of the opium trade? He would not save one man while destroying the lives of thousands. He knew Ayaou and Chou Luk would never understand his reasoning. A banker he'd known in Ningpo had once offered advice that explained everything. The banker had said, "After all, in China whom can you trust except family?" That translated into family comes first and was more important than a bunch of strangers.

"Ayaou told me that you have an account in Hong Kong," Chou Luk said, and his eyes darted to Ayaou for support. She made an aggressive noise in her throat that said she was angry.

This stiffened Robert's resolve not to yield. Despite his earlier desire to stay calm, he became upset and the angry hornets spewed from his mouth. "The household expenses are great," he said, trying to infer that his money was none of Chou Luk's business. "I have other financial obligations. My family in Ireland also needs my support. I send money to them regularly, which means I don't have that much on hand."

Why couldn't he say what the real reason was? He knew the answer immediately. Chou Luk and his family had been involved in the opium trade for decades. They would not understand Robert's moral dilemma. In fact, far too many Chinese were involved in the opium trade and saw nothing wrong.

"You are a man of growing influence," Chou Luk said. "I heard that your pay increased by one thousand pounds a year? In China, that makes you a very wealthy man. Certainly, you can go to the moneylenders."

Robert placed his elbows on his knees and leaned toward Chow Luk in a menacing gesture. His hands curled into fists, and his eyebrows lowered into storm clouds. "I won't borrow!" he said. He cast a dark glance at Ayaou. He felt his upper lip curl into a sneer. He focused his attention back on her father. She should not have told Chou Luk how much he earned. It was none of the old man's business.

Chou Luk leaned away from him. Robert sensed that Ayaou had leaped to her feet. He refused to look at her. She was probably shooting flames and smoke from her eyes.

"How did Cousin Weed get himself into this mess?" he asked. His voice sounded frigid. He knew that he should avoid this subject, but he could not help himself. "Was he smuggling opium up the Pearl River? Did the Tapings catch him doing that?"

Chow Luk's eyes darted away from Robert. "It does not matter what Cousin Weed did," he said. "What counts is that a member of our family can no longer support his wives and children. Ayaou said it is your duty to help."

So, it was opium, he thought. "What about the junk? Did the Taipings get that too?"

"The junk is having its hull scraped," Chow Luk replied. "Weed took a smaller boat."

"Of course," Robert said. "I should have remembered. After all, I am paying for that." His voice sounded shrill.

Then his anger dissipated like a lanced blister so the fluid drains out. How could he blame Ayaou's family for taking part in the opium trade? They weren't the only Chinese involved. There was a lot of poverty in China and smuggling opium was a way to survive. The merchants kept the lion's share. They paid the Chinese barely enough to feed themselves. It wasn't fair but the world was not a fair place.

In a much calmer voice, he said, "I liked his father, Uncle Bark, and I like Cousin Weed too. I wish I had the money, but I do not. I am sorry. I cannot help."

With guilt nibbling at his heels, he avoided eye contact with Ayaou and retreated from the room. To the Chinese, family came first, but he'd been raised to live within his means. His father was a frugal man who avoided the moneylenders and had always managed to save even with the expenses that came from raising twelve children.

The opium trade was the primary reason Robert could not help. If Robert produced the ransom, he would be just as guilty as the rest of the smugglers.

He found Anna downstairs with Fooyen. He picked his daughter up, and she threw her arms around his neck, which became a bit of sunlight driving the storm clouds away—at least for the moment.

He had a thought. What if Anna grew up to become addicted to opium? What if she had her lips sliced off too? That horrified him, and he held her tighter. "I love you," he said, and she drooled on him.

He didn't want Ayaou angry with him, but what could he do? He was not responsible for this situation. The opium trade was. Seeking tranquility, he took Anna into Guan-jiah's garden and stood listening to the water cascading down the boulders and to the wind rustling the trees and the bamboo.

That night, after Chou Luk left, Ayaou displayed her unhappiness by sleeping in another bedroom.

In the morning, feeling empty and tired from a night where he didn't sleep, Robert left the house while it was still dark and went to work.

Hours later, Captain Patridge arrived unannounced and walked into the middle of Robert's ugly mood. Considering what he had learned about the opium trade, Patridge wasn't a welcome sight. For a moment, he was tempted to shoot the merchant.

"What are you doing here?" he asked, suspecting that he was not going to like the answer. Was it possible that Chou Luk had gone to Patridge? If so, like a leech, Patridge had smelled blood. Over the years, Robert had discovered that Ayaou was right about this man. Money was all Patridge was interested in.

"Business!" Patridge replied, in his usual no nonsense way.

Living and working among the Chinese had made Robert more accustomed to talking in circles. He didn't like Patridge's directness. He had to calm down and walking usually accomplished that. He suggested they take a walk. Besides, if he decided to shoot the man, he didn't want witnesses.

"Whatever happened to Unwyn?" Robert asked, not wanting to talk about Patridge's business.

"Why should you care about a bastard like him?" Patridge replied. "You had a disagreeable incident with him during that fight with the Taipings. I've heard that Unwyn is making a name for himself as a smuggler and a thief. I would forget about him if I were you. He's nothing but trouble."

"I was curious."

They walked on in silence.

After a few blocks, Captain Patridge said, "I heard that Ayaou's family needs money. The Tapings are holding a cousin hostage and demanding ransom. Since you are in a position to increase my profits, I can help. We need your assistance to ship opium inland. We will pay you handsomely."

He had guessed right. Ayaou and Chou Luk had contacted Patridge. He realized that if he hadn't learned the history behind the opium trade from Guan-jiah, he might have agreed. He took out his black porcelain, hand sized spittoon with a hunting tiger on its side and spit into it.

"With the unrest in China because of the Taiping rebellion and a war starting with Britain and France, it is getting increasingly difficult to do business here," Patridge said.

Robert stopped walking. It was all he could do to keep his anger from appearing on his face. "As far as I'm concerned, any business I had with you was terminated the day I stopped working for the British."

Patridge opened his mouth.

"I don't want to hear what you have to say," Robert said, "You wasted your time coming to Canton." He wanted to say something more acerbic but controlled his tongue. He realized that news of this would reach Ayaou and Chou Luk. They would apply more pressure. He refused to help free Cousin Weed by allowing more opium into China. The faces of that lipless Chinese family flooded his thoughts and sickened him.

"Well—" Patridge said. His face had turned red and started to swell. He sputtered as if he had been insulted. "You have not paid the debt you owe, and we want to negotiate an extension. As an assistant commissioner in China's customs service, you are more valuable now that the emperor is being so stubborn. We will pay more than we paid before."

"Our business is ended, Captain Patridge. If you feel I owe you money, send me an accounting."

"It isn't going to be that easy," Patridge replied. "We signed a contract. You have taken bribes for years."

Robert hated losing control. As his temper started to reach the boiling point, he forced himself to look calm. Patridge would not see or hear the anger he felt. He slipped a hand into the pocket where he kept his pistol. He should shoot this devil for the crimes he had committed. Maybe doing that would save a few Chinese families from the ravages of opium. He was sorely tempted to squeeze the trigger.

"If it hadn't been for that distasteful business with Ward over Ayaou," he said, "our business relationship would never have taken place. If you want to report our transactions to the British consulate, that is up to you. I doubt that anyone will listen since most of them are also involved.

"However, it wouldn't matter even if they listened to you. My current employer is the emperor, and he does not want opium in China. His interests are mine.

"Why don't you approach Horatio Lay in Shanghai and see if he will cooperate? After all, I am only Deputy Commissioner of Customs in Canton. Lay is Inspector General, and he would be more valuable than I am. He outranks me."

He already knew what had happened between Horatio and Patridge, but he wanted to discover how Patridge would respond. He forced his hand to relax and pulled it from the pocket where he kept the loaded pistol. He was not going to add murder to his sins.

"It was easier dealing with both of you when you worked for the British and were poorly paid. Lay's answer was the same as yours. But your situation is different because of General Ward and the threat he poses to Ayaou."

"This meeting is over," Robert said. What he wanted to do was take Patridge by the throat and choke him. "I intend to have no business with merchants who import opium into China. I will hire only men who will support the emperor's policies. Good day, sir." Turning his back on Patridge, he started to walk away.

"You can't leave that easily," Patridge said with a menacing tone.

Robert spun around and jabbed a finger at him. "You mentioned Ward's name," he said, "so I'll mention one. Shao-mei! I counted on you to keep Ward away from my girls. Where was that protection when he murdered her?" He glared.

Patridge avoided eye contact.

"Don't bother me again, Captain Patridge."

Chapter 40

Work ended well after dark, and he walked the short distance home hoping Ayaou's mood had changed for the better. If Patridge or an assassin appeared, he was ready and kept a hand on the pistol in his jacket pocket.

He now considered Patridge a threat to his safety and the safety of his family. But as a highly placed offical in the imperial government, he had ways to protect himself and his family that he didn't have when he had been a British interpeter in Ningpo. If Patridge aimed Ward in his direction, Robert would use his growing ties to the Manchu rulers of China to deal with the mercenary.

He reached home and entered the front hall where Guan-jiah waited with a sober look on his face, which did not bode well.

"Where's Anna?" Robert asked. She and Fooyen were usually waiting in the front hall or first courtyard. Guan-jiah handed Robert a note written in Chinese. "What's wrong?" he asked.

"Master," Guan-jiah said in a strained voice, "I suggest you read the note."

"What do you mean? Have you already read it?"

Guan-jiah nodded. With a sinking feeling in the pit of his stomach, he opened the note.

"I am asking you to release me as your concubine." Ayaou's shaky handwriting revealed her emotional state. She must have been crying. He brought the paper closer to his eyes. It looked as if there were stains from teardrops. "You have insulted my father. I am going back to Macao and taking Anna and Fooyen with me."

His face went numb, and his fingers tingled. He dropped into a chair—still staring at the note, but not seeing it. Everything blurred.

He understood the Chinese way of thinking perfectly, but he seemed an illiterate when it came to comprehending what Ayaou expected and how she would react when he didn't comply. He crumpled the note and shoved it in a pocket. If it hadn't been for the opium trade, this would never have happened.

The Manchu officials he worked with respected him and considered him a man of courtesy. When he felt a Westerner was mistreating a Chinese, he negotiated a proper settlement between them, so the Chinese official would not be taken advantage of, while also saving the man's reputation. He thought he was good at communicating.

However, his brain was stuck in a thick fog when it came to dealing with his family, which meant Ayaou and by extension, her father and everyone connected to them by blood.

He recalled the words of the banker in Ningpo who said that family were the only ones you could trust. It was obvious that Ayaou and her father thought of him in the same way. In a world full of madness, he was considered trustworthy to her Chinese family.

"Is there anything I can do, Master?"

"No, Guan-jiah." His servant didn't move, so he looked. The concern etched in Guan-jiah's face told Robert that the eunuch felt his pain. "You're thinking I should have let you beat her, aren't you?" he said.

Guan-jiah eyes widened with a startled look. "Of course not, Master. I would never think that you were wrong about anything."

How ironically Chinese. He felt his lips curve into a smile and laughed. He should not be reacting like this. Instead, he should be screaming in frustration. "It doesn't matter what you were thinking, Guan-jiah. You were probably right. I was pigheaded as usual. Since you are the house manager, I am sure you have more important things to do. I will suffer alone. Go." He flapped a hand in a dismissive gesture.

Guan-jiah backed from the room.

Robert didn't know what hurt worse, Ayaou's letter or the pity in Guan-jiah's eyes. He went to a sideboard and filled a glass with several ounces of brandy then swallowed the liquor in one gulp.

That was a mistake.

The brandy went down his throat like a live moray eel burning all the way and hit his empty stomach as if it were an exploding bomb. The blast went straight to his head lifting him onto his toes. He staggered and grabbed the table to keep from losing his balance. The shock of the brandy had driven the breath from him, and he struggled to breathe while the house swayed around him.

Once he regained his sense of balance, he poured the glass tumbler to the brim and lifted it to his mouth. Wanting to dive in, he stared at the amber liquid then remembered he had turned to liquor once before in Belfast. The pressure from his studies at the university coupled with a powerful lust for women had taken control of his life. Going from pub to pub, he had stayed drunk for weeks and lost track of the easy women he'd seduced.

After his family discovered his lascivious nature, guilt drove him to abandon his goals to earn a master's degree and become a pastor like his father. Instead, he found a job with the British government and fled to China.

He couldn't stand the thought of living without Ayaou or Anna. Liquor had not solved his problems in Belfast. It wouldn't now. His head was already filling with an alcoholic fog, so he carefully poured the brandy back into the bottle.

Knowing the eunuch would be close by watching over him, he said, "Guan-jiah." He words were slow and slurred. "Bring me something to eat." He went to his desk and waited for the food. He would eat before he wrote a reply to Ayaou and send it to Macau. He didn't want the liquor to do his writing for him.

He hated being manipulated, but what was he to do? If Uncle Bark had still been alive, he could have turned to him for a dose of wisdom. He imagined the old man's voice. "This is one of those times you must not resist. Bend with the wind. Let it flow around you. What is more important, the money or Ayaou? The tree that resists, breaks."

Guan-jiah came with food, but Robert wasn't hungry so he forced the food down without tasting it. With a full stomach, the anger subsided. He pushed aside the empty plate and picked up a pen. "Grind me some fresh ink, Guan-jiah," he said.

"Ayaou, I do not have five thousand Chinese yuan. I suggest that your father negotiate with the Taipings to extend the date they have given us to raise the ransom.

"If I am to help free Cousin Weed, your family must stop smuggling opium. Since I deal with merchants and imperial officials daily, I will use my influence to make sure Cousin Weed will always have a legal cargo that is not opium.

"My Chinese associates in the merchant trade will help, but I will owe them favors in the future. That way, your family will survive without being part of the opium trade. I cannot help free Cousin Weed any other way.

"If your father can negotiate a smaller amount as a token of our intent, we may gain time to raise the rest. In addition, I cannot be expected to produce the entire amount. The family must put in their share.

"I continue to love you. In the future, when events of this nature take place, I would appreciate it if we could work it out between us before you run off. It does not help when we let anger rule our actions."

The food helped him resist the urge to add a few choice phrases to the letter that would have caused more trouble with Ayaou. Finished, he sealed the envelope with hot wax and handed it to Guan-jiah. "I want you to go to Macao and hand this to Mistress Ayaou yourself," he said. "I don't trust anyone else."

Ayaou was too much a part of his life to let her slip away. He realized that he was hopelessly in love with this boat girl, even her explosive, unpredictable side. It was as if she were the spice that made dull food taste delicious.

On the other hand, she was a practical person who never wasted money frivolously. He appreciated that. He had learned a lot from his girls when they had lived in Ningpo before Shao-mei was murdered by Ward and he missed those days.

Ayaou's reply came a few weeks later. She wanted to know how much he'd contribute. He surprised himself when he burst out laughing. The old Robert would have gone into a rage.

It took a few months to contribute three thousand yuan. The effort was enough to keep Cousin Weed from losing his head. To earn more, he worked extra hours translating Chinese documents for the British consulate.

Then an unexpected incident took place.

The imperial army captured Harry Parkes while he was under the protection of a white flag. Robert couldn't blame the Chinese for what they had done. After all, Parkes was one of the men behind the Second Opium War.

In 1860, to force the emperor to make the opium trade legal in all of China, Parkes had supported the looting and destruction of the Summer Palace known by the Chinese as the *Yuan Ming Yuan*, located several miles outside Peking.

Before the destruction and looting by the combined British and French forces, the emperor had fled inland to Jehol, the imperial hunting grounds on the other side of the Great Wall. He had taken his family and the court, numbering in the thousands, with him.

Robert did not understand what was so special about a palace surrounded by gardens.

Guan-jiah explained. "All Chinese consider the destruction of the Gardens of Perfect Brightness as humiliating and a great loss of face."

"Why? They are only gardens. Can't they be replanted?"

"The *Yuan Ming Yuan* is much more than a garden, Master. I have heard that the place is one of the great wonders of the world with gardens, palaces, pavilions, lakes and streams surrounded by walls. People that worked there have said the beauty steals your breath and that the place is a slice of heaven. The gardens and palaces are part of China's history and culture. The construction started in the twelfth century. During the eighteenth and nineteenth century, the Qianlong emperor expanded them."

The next day, James Bruce, the Eighth Earl of Elgin and the British High Commissioner to China, surprised Robert with a visit. He had never met the man before.

"Mr. Hart," the earl said, after being ushered into his office by a stunned clerk, "I've heard a lot about you."

It wasn't proper to stay behind his desk, so he stepped forward to greet the earl. "I'm flattered that you came to see me, Sir Bruce. You should have summoned me. I would have come." They shook hands.

"No," Bruce replied. "I felt discretion was the better choice. I did not want anyone knowing what I was doing. That is why I came in person. We need your help."

"My help!" he replied, confused. "What can I do for the Crown? I no longer work for the British."

He thought the earl's visit had to do with Harry Parkes. The allies needed someone to approach the Chinese—someone the Chinese trusted, someone who could bridge the gap and negotiate a deal that would allow the Chinese to save face, and keep the second Opium War from expanding out of control.

The way he saw it, this war was not a profitable venture. It disrupted trade. The allies wanted it over, but they also wanted results, which meant more opium flooding into China. The recent visit by Captain Patridge told him as much. It seemed that the opium merchants were the tail wagging the dog.

"You are wrong, Hart. You can do the Crown a valuable service. We would like you to talk sense into the Chinese government. They must release Harry Parkes. If they do not, the Crown is going to send a larger army to punish the Chinese for this transgression. They should have never violated our white flag."

"The white flag has nothing to do with it," Robert said. "The Chinese are not happy that foreign powers are dictating policy to them. Every time they are forced to do something against their will, it is a loss of face for the emperor. To the Chinese, that is unforgivable. The emperor does not want opium sold to his people, and he wants to say which ports are open for trade. Britain, France, Japan, Russia, America and the other foreign powers are not allowing that." He watched the earl's response, and it was exactly what he expected.

Bruce looked surprised. "It doesn't matter what this emperor thinks," he said. "Britain's interests come first."

Robert kept a sober face. "What would Britain do if it were China dictating to Queen Victoria and parliament how to trade and do business in England?"

"That is not the situation, and it is not relevant. We want you to have the Chinese release Parkes." The earl looked flustered.

Robert did not smile and would not back down even for an earl. "What opium is doing to the Chinese may not be important to Britain, but it is to the emperor and he is my employer. I do not see how I can be of service to the Crown in this matter."

"You can intercede and explain to them the errors of their ways. They are like disobedient children and must be spanked. Tell them what a white flag means. Tell them the consequences if they don't free Parkes."

He turned his back on Bruce and stared at the stack of papers waiting for his attention. It was a rude gesture to make in front of such an influential man, but he did it anyway. It wasn't easy dealing with people like the earl, who thought the world revolved around him. When he turned back, he saw that the earl's face had swollen and turned red.

"Sir Bruce, if you start making demands of the Chinese with that attitude, it will only worsen the situation. Then, unfortunately, more Chinese will suffer and die. Who knows, the emperor may even make peace with the Taipings. Then there will be two armies to deal with. After all, the enemy of my enemy is my friend. Is that what you want?"

"Is that even possible?" Bruce said. "What have you heard?" He looked concerned. The idea of the Taipings ending their rebellion against the Manchu and freeing millions of soldiers from both sides of the conflict was something to take seriously.

"Rumors," he said. It was a lie, but it might come in handy for future negotiations. There was no way the Ch'ing Dynasty would work with the Taipings. To the Dynasty, the Taipings were Longhaired Bandits. "Sir Bruce, I don't work for the Crown. I do not have to take orders from anyone in the British Empire. What I will do is tell you the truth."

The earl's face turned a darker shade. Robert watched as he struggled to maintain a semblance of control. "What if we hired you as a consultant and a go between?" Bruce asked.

"That would work." He named a price for his services and the earl agreed.

Robert hid his excitement. He now had enough money to free Cousin Weed from the Tapings. How ironic that the money would come from the British because of the Second Opium War. "But only on one condition," he said.

"I'm not used to others dictating to me," Bruce said. "This is outrageous."

"I agree. I ask you to please remember that I am an employee of the Chinese imperial government and forgive my unacceptable behavior. I have seen what opium does to the Chinese. I don't approve."

"What happens to the Chinese is not important," the earl replied. "Your opinion is also unimportant. Trade with China, any kind of trade, benefits England. That is important."

Robert smiled. "I understand," he said. "Don't forget. You need me. I don't need you. I want you to know that my loyalties are split between two governments. If you want me to handle this, I will do it for the price we agreed to. At the same time, I will not allow any interference. No one will tell me what to do."

The earl was quiet for a moment as he studied Robert's face. "Agreed," Bruce said.

"Good. I want the British government to stay out of this until I free Parkes. If anyone interferes, I cannot guarantee success. What the British government does after Parkes is free is none of my business. After all, I count Harry Parkes as a friend. I don't want to see him lose his head either."

They sealed the bargain by shaking hands. "I can see why Parkes spoke so highly of you. I hope you know what you are doing."

"You will not be disappointed," he said.

Robert talked to the Chinese governor of Canton and convinced him that killing Parkes would cause more destruction. With the governor's help, Harry Parkes was released three weeks later. But twenty of his men were beheaded. To avenge this act, the allies conducted a series of reprisals killing thousands of Chinese.

"It's wrong," he told Guan-jiah. "This war should never have happened. The Chinese had every right to board that ship in 1856. The crew was pirates and opium smugglers."

"Master, that does not matter. The *Arrow* was British registered. The Dynasty should have ignored it. Arresting the crew only gave the British and French an excuse to make war and expand the opium trade."

A few weeks later, Robert discovered that Sir Bruce was the one who ordered the destruction of the emperor's Summer Palace.

"I'm ashamed of being British," he said. "The destruction of the Summer Palace was an uncivilized act of barbarism. If I had known that Sir Bruce was behind it, I would have never cooperated with him."

Guan-jiah looked confused. "Master, the imperial troops are no better. They have destroyed entire villages that supported the Longhaired Bandits and killed everyone. There is no justice in war. The only way is to end war, which will never happen due to man's nature."

In October of 1860, Prince Kung, Emperor Hsien Feng's brother, and the Board of Rites in Peking ratified the Treaty of Tientsin. As the *cultural-go-between*, Robert worked nonstop to bring understanding to both sides.

It was frustrating to see the Chinese being victimized by the British and French, and he was ashamed of his own people.

"The demands that the British and French are making is one-sided," Robert said, "It is wrong."

"It is best to flow with the river's current, Master. As evil as the opium trade is, the Imperial Dynasty should not have resisted. It would be unwise to protest."

Robert realized Guan-jiah was right. "Don't worry," he said. "I will guard my tongue around the British and French."

"Do not trust the Chinese either," the eunuch said. "Loose lips are capable of spreading a plague."

Working on the treaty was challenging. Robert felt trapped between fundamental cultural differences and his values. He still remembered the time he'd been searching for Ward in Shanghai and ended in one of Boss Takee's opium dens. China would be better off without the drug, yet here he was helping the trade expand.

The final treaty favored the British opium merchants and the opium trade was legalized, the collie trade grew, and the British merchants were exempt from paying internal transit duties for their imports. The Dynasty had to pay two million silver taels to the British merchants for the opium confiscated and burned early in the war, and another two million taels

432

went to the British and French governments for the cost of the war.

"I will not be silent if this happens again," Robert said. "If there is another unjust war as this one was, I will speak my mind. I will not stand by and watch China be raped and robbed."

"Master, one voice is easily lost in the crowd's noise. I have learned that all wounds may heal, and only those who feel like victims suffer. The dead feel nothing."

The days were long, and he often finished working late at night. As was his habit, he walked home alone but kept a hand on his revolver in a jacket pocket. On a dark and empty street, just a block from his house, he sensed a movement to his left.

The moment he saw the knife in the man's hand, he felt a rush of energy. Everything around him slowed while he moved at lightning speed. He brought out the revolver and fired a round into the assailant. He fired a second shot for good measure.

There was a grunt of surprise. The man staggered back with a stunned look on his face.

When he was on his back and appeared not to be a threat, Robert stood over him. When he saw the knife was still in the man's hand, he kicked the blade away and looked around to make sure they were alone. Once he was satisfied there were no other threats, he knelt and examined the man, who was dressed like a common sailor.

"Who sent you?" he said. Obviously, the man was not going to live long. Blood gushed from both wounds.

The assailant laughed. "You're a marked man, governor," he said in a dry cockney accent, which marked him as a man of the docks from Plymouth or London. He coughed and blood bubbled from his mouth. "You made the wrong man angry."

Was Patridge behind this? That made sense. After all, Robert had spurned the captain's offer, and Patridge had many sailors working for him in the opium trade.

"I never expected it to turn out this way," the man said. "I thought I would finish the job as I've done before and collect the rest of my pay and be done with it." He coughed and blood bubbled from his mouth.

Robert searched the man's pockets. The assailant tried to fend him off but was too weak. He found a hundred-pound Bank of England note. "Is this what Patridge paid you?" he said. "I'd think I was worth more than that."

"Who is Patridge?" the man asked. Then he coughed and sprayed blood on Robert's jacket. "There would have been more when I finished the job," the assassin said.

When he discovered the other pockets were empty, Robert slapped the man's face. "Tell me who paid you to do this? Was it the same man who was after me in Ningpo? Was it General Ward? Was it Hollister?

"Don't know them," the man said, as he wheezed and spit up more blood.

Robert looked around. None of the local Chinese had come out of the surrounding houses at the sound of the shots. That was not unusual. If a small child were being swept away by a river and drowning, most Chinese would continue about their business as if no one was screaming for help a few yards away. The child would surely die.

He focused his attention back on the assassin to discover the man's mouth hung open and his eyes looked empty. Robert listened for a heartbeat and found none. The man was dead.

His hands started to shake, and he searched the clothes again for any evidence that might tell him who had sent the man to kill him. When he found nothing, he left the body and hurried home feeling ill as if he were going to throw up.

After that day, he never traveled the streets without guards. Next time there was an attempt on his life he might not be so fortunate. It bothered him that he didn't know who his enemy was and might be anyone even the Taipings.

His only clue was the one hundred-pound note and the fact that the man was British. It didn't make sense that a Chinese would pay a foreigner to kill him. If the Chinese had sent an assassin, Robert would have suffered a horrible and painful death from poisoning. He was sure of that.

Chapter 41

One morning in March 1861, Robert was at work when a dispatch arrived. After opening it, he gasped, and said, "Good Lord!"

Gerard, one of the clerks, a Frenchman at a nearby desk, said, "What is it, Monsieur Hart? You look as if you saw a ghost."

Robert's hand trembled and the paper fluttered.

"Is it about your family in Ireland?" Gerard asked, staring at the shaking hand.

"No. Horatio Lay was walking down a major Shanghai street without guards when a riot broke out around him and an unidentified assailant attacked him with a knife. Horatio was stabbed in the back and several times in his abdomen."

"Are you talking about the inspector general in Shanghai?" Gerard asked, as if he didn't believe what he was hearing.

"Yes." Robert held out the dispatch. "Read for yourself."

"It says Monsieur Lay is fortunate to have survived," the clerk said, and his face turned pale. "Two Germans armed with pistols saw Monsieur Lay go down, and they fired shots to scare off the Chinese mob. Then they carried him to the nearest consulate where he was provided with immediate medical care."

Gerard handed the dispatch back. "Monsieur Hart, this is a most horrible tragedy. You may be called to Shanghai to manage Customs until the inspector general recovers. Pardon me for being outspoken, but Monsieur Lay doesn't have your diplomatic skills. He is too abrupt with the Chinese and does not show them the proper respect and courtesy. I don't like speaking ill of someone who just came so close to death, but it is true."

"I appreciate your words." He was pleased at the loyalty Gerard demonstrated, but he was careful not to smile thinking it would be inappropriate to agree even though he did. "We must get back to work."

Gerard returned to his desk. Robert reread the words at the end of the dispatch. 'He was fortunate to still be alive'. What had happened to Horatio could happen to any foreigner. He looked from the dispatch to Gerard. The Frenchman was going over numbers in a ledger. He made the right decision hiring Gerard. More than a dozen had applied for the position, but Gerard, besides having the skills needed, had been the only applicant who felt as Robert did about China.

Most of the interviews ended quickly. However, he had spent more than an hour with Gerard talking about Taoism and Confucianism and how both influenced the culture. The others applicants had expressed no interest.

In fact, Robert made it a point to reject anyone that thought like Horatio Lay or people like Parkes or Sir Bruce.

"Monsieur Hart," Gerard had said during the interview, "I've read Confucius in the original Chinese and was impressed at what he said about the 'first of all virtues'."

"Go on." Robert already knew about the positive and negative aspects of Confucius and his teachings, but he wanted to hear what Gerard had to say.

"Confucius said that the reason for filial piety is not because it is to be seen in the home and not everyday life. The central idea behind filial piety was so man respects all those who are fathers in the world, and younger brothers should respect all those who are older brothers."

"And what did Confucius mean?"

"That those who love their parents dare not show hatred to others and that those who respect their parents dare not show rudeness to others." Gerard's green eyes were full of light. "After I read Confucius, I felt ashamed, because I have often taken my father and my three older brothers for granted. I vowed I would never do so again."

"Do you see a similarity between filial piety and the Fifth Commandment: 'Honor thy father and thy mother: that thy days may be long'?" Robert asked.

"Yes, it seems Confucius agreed with God about honoring parents. Do you think that Confucius knew about the Ten Commandments?"

"The possibility exists. After all, Moses led the Israelites out of slavery in Egypt between thirteen and sixteen hundred years before Jesus Christ was born, and Confucius lived about five hundred years before Jesus. It would be safe to say that a thousand years would be sufficient time for knowledge of the Ten Commandments to reach China."

That interview had taken place months ago.

He was still staring at Gerard, who was engrossed in his work. Robert closed his eyes and rubbed them. He had been getting only a few hours sleep at night, and his eyes were dry and itched. There was much to be done and never enough time.

The dispatch about the assault on Horatio was folded and filed. He was pleased with his Frenchman, because Gerard was honest, loyal and hardworking. Best of all, he had an inquisitive mind and respected other cultures.

Robert felt guilt. After all, Lay was older than he was. To Confucius, it didn't matter that Horatio was someone Robert did not respect or like. Robert had to show respect no matter what. He was not allowed to be rude. He understood what Confucius meant. On the other hand, he was not Chinese.

When he thought about Horatio in mixed company with the Chinese, he saw a clumsy vulture blundering among peacocks. For that and other reasons, Robert could not always be courteous, as Confucius had taught— to forgive and look the other way as if nothing had happened.

He had been in China long enough to see that as one of the flaws of Chinese culture. It automatically allowed unworthy people to gain positions of respect and power just because they were older.

Horatio saw China through a different lens. What Gerard had said about Lay was true. Horatio did not have a grasp of the Chinese mind or their culture. He spoke Mandarin fluently but saw China as another outlet for the British Empire to expand its power and add to the profits of its merchants.

What baffled Robert was why the Dynasty trusted Horatio. After all, Horatio did not believe that the Manchu or the Han should rule China. He felt Britain should be in charge as they were in India.

The only explanation was that Horatio had learned to keep his opinions to himself, at least around the Manchu royalty.

After the news got out, the subject of most conversations in Canton's foreign community focused on Horatio Lay's assault. Robert avoided getting involved, but he heard what others had to say.

"I dread taking a walk even with a pistol," one merchant said. "Who can be trusted in China besides our kind?"

"I've had similar thoughts," his companion replied. "What if China's population suddenly goes over to the Taipings and defeats the Manchu? If the Ch'ing Dynasty falls, we will be sitting on a mountain of gunpowder ready to explode. It wouldn't take long for the natives to be at our throats."

"From now on, if one of them gets too close, I'm going to give that Chinaman a thrashing he won't forget," the first merchant said.

That kind of talk worried Robert. If the foreign merchants and diplomats continued to treat the Chinese without respect, it would be like lighting the fuse to that pile of gunpowder. He saw that his job as a 'cultural-go-between' was going to become more of a challenge.

Chapter 42

A request to attend a private meeting with Lao Ch'ung-kuang, the governor-general of Canton, arrived a few weeks after Horatio had been wounded. Robert went to the governor's palace and met Lao in his private office next to the formal audience hall. The office was twice as wide as it was deep. To the left sat a desk.

Twenty feet to the right by glass doors that opened on a courtyard sat a table, couch and chairs. The table was on a Persian carpet, and on the table was a wide, oval brass bowl holding fresh fruit. There was also a steaming teapot and two cups. The couch had its back against the wall near the glass doors while the chairs and table were closer to the center of the room.

The rosewood furniture was intricately carved with flowers and birds. Lao offered one of the chairs next to the table and a servant poured tea.

Obviously, this meeting wasn't formal and Robert relaxed. Court ritual added hours to a meeting and he dreaded that.

They drank tea and talked about local issues first.

"Prince Kung sent word that I should present you with an invitation," Lao said, when he finally broached the subject of the summons. "I am sure you heard that Horatio Lay is returning to England to recover from his knife wounds. Because of this, Prince Kung wants you to go to Peking and meet with him and his grand-board members. If you agree, you will become acting inspector general for Customs in Shanghai until Horatio Lay returns."

Robert's first reaction was doubt. He was only twenty-six. Was he ready? He wasn't sure that he could do the job. What if he failed and made a fool of himself? Then he remembered that

Lay was only three years older. "Why have I been selected?" he asked. "There must be any number of men who could do this job, men older and wiser than I am."

Lao waved a hand as if to erase Robert's words. "Your reputation as a man who can fix things has spread. I told Prince Kung that you were the only suitable candidate. In fact, I would like to see you replace Horatio Lay and have considered suggesting this to the Emperor."

He was surprised to hear that the Chinese thought so highly of his abilities. He didn't know what to say, and his face turned hot. "Thank you," he said, "but I cannot take Horatio's job from him while he is recovering from wounds gained serving China. It would be improper."

"You do honor to your family," Lao said. "Your father would be proud. Prince Kung will understand if you accept the position in Shanghai until Horatio Lay returns. If you decline, I will let Prince Kung know that you would prefer to stay in Canton."

"It is true that I'm reluctant to leave. My job in Canton is not finished. Who will replace me?"

"The head is more important than a toe. You must go. The Emperor is aware that you are the only foreigner working hard to keep China from being eaten by Britain and France."

"That cannot be the true," Robert replied. "There must be others."

Lao shook his head. "At first, we thought you would hire only English. When you did not, we were confused. We watched you hire men from every nation, even Han Chinese. That clever thinking won our approval."

"The Dynasty trusts me with a great responsibility. I will go to Peking."

"Of course, if given a choice, I would prefer that you stay in Canton. Now that you have accepted the offer, Hung-chi, as inspector general of Canton, will have to do the work until your return."

He hesitated for Hung-chi would destroy everything Robert had built. Lao stood and with hands clasped behind his back walked back and forth.

Robert started to stand.

"Sit. No need to get up. My thinking is clearer when I am on my feet. A bad habit. Eat something." He waved at the fruit. "I picked them this morning in my garden."

Robert poured tea into his cup and examined the fruit. He selected a white peach and bit into it. His mouth was flooded with juicy sweetness, and he had to put a cupped hand under his chin to catch the juice. Then a servant handed him a warm, damp cloth.

"When I told Hung-chi, he protested and urged me to keep you here. That confused me. He has only complained about you before."

Hung-chi was a thief. He was taking bribes from just about everyone. He had even tried to bribe Robert. Instead, Robert had instituted polices that made it difficult for Hung-chi to get money illegally and if he became the inspector general in Shanghai, he would outrank Hung-chi.

"Hung-chi is overwhelmed with all the challenges he faces," Robert said. "If you will accept my recommendation, I will assign an assistant, a man I have trained, to replace me while I'm gone. You can trust that he will do the job adequately. His honesty is above reproach."

Lao stopped pacing and stared at Robert. "What I find disturbing is that Peking sent the message to Hung-chi first. When you did not respond, Peking asked me to talk to you. Did you get that message?"

"No."

"When I asked Huang-chi why he never gave the invitation to you, he said he never received it. I know that is not true. Do you know why Hung-chi did this?"

"I have no idea." He lied. "The only explanation I can think of is that he is overwhelmed with problems from the English and French."

Lao studied Robert's face looking for answers. He had just insinuated that Hung-chi was incompetent and was sure that Lao thought there was more to it than that.

"Anyone you recommend to replace you will be accepted," Lao said, returning to his chair. He signaled for more hot tea. A servant came with a fresh pot.

"It wouldn't hurt if you kept a closer eye on Hung-chi." Robert was skirting close to the edge. It was not wise to be direct. It was acceptable to reach the truth in a roundabout way, even if it meant using small lies. His hands were cold and damp from stress. He wanted to dry them but needed to look calm. If he appeared nervous, Lao might distrust what he said.

Lao's eyes narrowed. "Why? Is there something that I should know?" He formed a tent with his fingers and hid most of his face behind it.

"What I mean," Robert replied, "is to have your people stand by in case the English or French become too difficult to deal with. Many of their merchants have been coming to Hung-chi asking for advice. It has been difficult for him. I am sure if you discover why Hung-chi is having these difficulties and solve that problem for him, you will gain face. You might consider placing a trusted servant in Hung-chi's home and another in his office."

Lao's eyebrows shot up. He took a long breath and relaxed by sipping tea. Then he nodded. "I see," he said. He leaned toward Robert, as if they were coconspirators. His eyes gleamed. "So, who is this man you are recommending to take your place and be a thorn in Hung-chi's side?"

Robert resisted the urge to laugh. Lao knew more than he was letting on. He probably already had spies watching Hung-chi. "My replacement is a Frenchman named Gerard. He speaks Chinese fluently and understands the meaning of filial piety. He has studied Confucius and is fearless. No one will intimidate him. You can trust him as much as you trust me."

"Really," Lao said. "Then we will rely on him. I did not think there could be two foreigners like you in China."

With the unexpected promotion came higher pay, and Robert requested an advance on his salary. Once the silver taels arrived, he sent enough money with Guan-jiah to Chou Luk in Macao.

"Once Cousin Weed is free, bring Ayaou back," he said.

Guan-jiah nodded and hurried off.

The day Guan-jiah returned from Macao, Robert met him inside the mansion's front entrance. "Good news, Master."

"If it isn't about cousin Weed, I don't want to hear it," Robert replied and tried to see around the eunuch. The double doors were almost closed and only a sliver of sky was visible revealing that it was going to be dark soon.

A huge grin split Guan-jiah's face. "Chou Luk managed to meet the ransom demands." The eunuch pushed the double doors wide and stepped aside revealing Ayaou and Anna holding hands. Fooyen stood behind them, but Robert couldn't see Ayaou's face since it was hidden in the shadows.

"Ba, Ba," Anna said. She yanked her little hand free and ran to him.

He squatted and braced himself as the two-year-old leaped into his arms. He was amazed. When Ayaou had left, Anna had been unsteady on her feet. Now she was running. He imagined she must be getting into everything, and she had called him daddy. "She talks," he said.

His eyes watered from emotion. "Have you any other words in that mouth?" He held her at arm's length and examined her. She squirmed and giggled. He ticked her and she laughed louder.

"She knows a few words," Fooyen said, as she came into the room.

"Take Anna upstairs. I want to be alone with Ayaou." He gave Guan-jiah a look, and the eunuch said, "Pardon me, Master, but I must make sure the servants have kept the house clean." He hurried away.

Ayaou stared at the floor avoiding eye contact. He, on the other hand, could not take his eyes off her. He felt angry and wanted to tell her. Instead, he walked around her, as if he were on an inspection tour and liked what he saw. He sensed that her eyes were trying to follow him.

"I apologize for running away," she said. Her voice was soft and difficult to hear.

"What did you say?" he asked.

"What you did to save Cousin Weed is worth more than money to me," she replied.

He stopped in front of her and lifted her chin to see her face. Her eyes were swimming in tears. Her lower lip trembled. He felt a pain in his chest, and he wanted to take her in his arms to comfort her. He resisted the urge. It wasn't time yet.

"I was a fool to leave. What you did is proof of your love for me," she said. The tears started to overflow and run down her cheeks. "Your respect for my father and family shows that you value me. I no longer think that I am a property you bought. And your love is no longer just words of passion. I am unworthy."

"Enough," he said. "I was also a fool." He pulled her into his arms. They kissed. Her lips were warm and soft.

Later that evening, alone in his study, he remembered something that Patridge had said years ago.

"Chou Luk should have waited. Though you don't have the wealth Ward has, you're a dependable man. It probably has not crossed Chou Luk's mind that we think differently from the Chinese. He sold three of his daughters to men he believes are going to help take care of him. You think that I will. He'll get no help from Ward either."

The captain had underestimated the sisters. Robert was sure that whoever their masters were, Chou Luk's daughters would find a way to get help for their father and family, even if they had to steal.

Thinking about Patridge raised a thought that he hadn't considered before. Patridge had asked both Horatio and him to continue accepting bribes and help smuggle opium into China. Both had refused.

Then that British sailor attacked Robert. Next, Horatio was knifed in Shanghai. The coincidence was difficult to ignore.

On the other hand, the weapons in both attacks had been knives. That was odd. Knives did not sound like Patridge. He was sure that if Patridge sent assassins, they would use a large caliber pistol, rifle or shotgun.

Patridge's motive was strong enough. If he got rid of the two men that stood in his way and replaced them with people to do his bidding, he would reap greater profits. Robert would have to be more careful to avoid Horatio's fate. At least Horatio was getting out of the country until his health returned. As much as he disliked the man, Robert did not wish death on him.

On the last night before he left for Peking, he waited until Anna went to sleep before going to the bedroom he shared with Ayaou. He sat beside her on their bed and took her hands in his. He explained what his journey was about and how important it was to his career.

"I need your help, Ayaou," he said.

"How can I help if you are in Peking, and I am here? After all, it is my duty as your concubine to bring you to the pleasure cliff and help you jump off so we both soar among the clouds. My body is your way to relax, to reach ecstasy and find harmony. Take me with you if that is what you want. I will do all that I can to insure your longevity."

444

"That is tempting," he said, "but I must go alone, and I will miss our intimacies. I will also have trouble sleeping soundly." He paused for a moment then said, "I hate being without you."

Her eyes darted away from his. "I suggest that you find another concubine in Peking to keep your bed warm. It is only fitting for a man of your stature."

"No," he said. "That isn't what I meant. I want more from you than just your body."

"I do not understand." She cocked her head to one side and looked at him with curiosity. "What else have I to offer?"

He liked the way she looked when she did that and was tempted to kiss her. "I want you to support me outside of bed too. You will spend time in the teahouses talking to others and listening. I require an unspoiled perspective of what the Chinese people are saying.

"Listen to the conversations among your family members regarding politics and the common people's concerns. Write to me and tell me what you are learning. This will be of great value to me. I want you to be my eyes and ears. You can start by telling me what you already know."

Robert and Ayaou talked late into the night about many things. What she already knew turned out to be priceless. Before that night ended, she helped him understand why the Taipings had gained support from the peasants.

"Not only do the foreigners want to drug us by selling opium," Ayaou said, "but they also want to take our souls by making us believe in their religion and their God. What if we did the same to you and went into your country uninvited and opened up businesses in your backyards? What if we forced your people to follow the teachings of Confucius or become Buddhists?"

"I have thought about that," he said. "That's why I never expect the Chinese to believe what I believe or to think like me. Instead, I find a middle ground."

"Robert, you must be careful in Peking. The people cannot tell you from the other foreign devils that burned our Emperor's palaces. They will not know that you are there to help. You are my happiness. I do not want anything to happen to you." She rested her head on his shoulder.

A lump grew in his throat. He let go of her hands and put an arm around her. "You have nothing to worry about," he replied. "I have an armed escort, and I will be careful." He kissed her neck. "I will miss your lips."

Looking serious, Ayaou pushed away. "Do you know that Emperor Hsien Feng is very sick?" she asked. "The rumors say that he is dying in Jehol."

"Yes, I have heard." It was amazing how fast news and opinions traveled in China. "I have also heard that Prince Kung will take over the imperial business if the emperor dies. Even though the title of emperor will go to Hsien Feng's six-year-old son, Kung will be the true ruler behind the dragon throne. He is the one I will be working with in Peking."

Ayaou's mouth dropped open in astonishment. "Robert, is that true?"

He nodded. "Prince Kung understands that to succeed, China must learn to deal with the foreign powers sensibly. He has established an organization called the Tsungli Yamen (Office in Charge of Affairs of All Nations) to administer foreign affairs."

Overwhelmed by excitement, Ayaou leaped off the bed and took several calming breaths, before she said, "People spend fortunes to buy favors and gifts just to meet the powerful royals. But you do not have that kind of money. You have just spent your next year's salary on Cousin Weed. How can you possibly buy your way in? How did you get Prince Kung to hire you?"

"My understanding of the Chinese, which I learned from you and Shao-mei, has turned in to a gift for him to use." He didn't bother to hide his elation.

"In fact, I'm more than a gift. Prince Kung needs me. I am going to be his bridge between Britain and China. I will be worthy of his trust. I want to see China thrive, so smart girls like you can go to school. One day, your family will not have to live on a junk. There will be no beheadings, because no one will have to steal to eat and no need for rebels like the Taipings to make war."

A sober look crossed Ayaou's face. She moved closer. "Hold me," she said. "Robert, you are not like the Chinese, and you are not like the English or French either. You are unusual. No one in China is like you."

That wasn't true of course. There were others, and he was recruiting them. Finding them, on the other hand, was like discovering one hidden flower getting ready to bloom in an acre of waist high weeds.

A splendid smile that resembled Shao-mei's blossomed on her face except Ayaou didn't have dimples. "To me it sounds like a dream, Robert. I will pray for the wind in Peking to be favorable for you."

"I welcome your prayers," he said, "but my trip to the Forbidden City may not be smooth since my boss Hung-chi has been doing everything he can to stop me from leaving."

The intimate look in her eyes turned to concern. "That is understandable," she said. "Hung-chi is worried, because you know too much about his corruption. He is afraid that once Prince Kung and you get together, he will be exposed."

He was shocked. "How did you learn that?" He hadn't said one word about Hung-chi's corruption to anyone but Gerard, not even Guan-jiah knew.

"Everyone in the teahouses in Canton is talking about it," she replied.

"How do you know what they are saying?" he asked. "You don't speak Cantonese. Where did the people learn this?"

"I learned Cantonese while I lived in Macao. Guan-jiah and I found an old woman to teach us." She nodded and shoved him in a playful way. "Silly, people know about Hung-chi, because the Manchu hires the Han to be their servants. The Han hear everything."

"You are amazing. If the common man knows that Hung-chi is a crook, why don't the imperials know?"

"Canton is a long way from Peking," Ayaou said, "and the Manchu do not listen to the Han."

"But the Han make up ninety percent of the population. The Manchu should listen."

She shook her head. "Robert, even if the Manchu listened, people fear talking to them. It is easy to lose your head in China. Besides, the Manchu do not trust the Han."

"So, Hung-chi has nothing to worry about," he said. That was a depressing thought.

"You are wrong, Robert. Hung-chi should be worried. You are a man of honesty and Hung-chi is a leech who thrives on bribery. Everyone in Canton knows where his money comes from, but no one dares to expose him. Everyone fears him. On the other hand, he dreads you. I have heard people say this."

"My job is clear. I must convince Prince Kung of the importance of getting rid of these leeches from his government."

"I do not think Prince Kung wants to hear you tell him how to run his business. Let me tell you what the scholars say in the teahouses. Prince Kung should stop his soldiers from deserting their posts by paying them on time. He has to gain back the army's loyalty. The other is to trade for medicines with the foreigners. There is too much sickness in China."

That made sense. The bottom line was money. Prince Kung needed it urgently to rebuild the nation. Robert would provide the Dynasty with tons of silver taels through taxes on imported and exported goods. First, he had to reorganize Customs to be more efficient and weed out the corruption.

As inspector general, he could hire and fire whom he wanted. He could get rid of people like Hung-chi. He couldn't wait to leave for Peking.

Yet, he feared the coming depression. He might be helping China, but he'd be away from Ayaou. In the last few months, there had been enough of that. Now, just when they were together again, he had to leave, and he had no idea how long he'd be gone.

"I should talk to Hung-chi before I go and convince him to stop stealing or else."

Ayaou's eyes widened in fear. "No!" She placed a hand on his arm. "Robert, he does not know what you will do. He is only afraid of what you might do. If he knew what you were planning, he would have you assassinated."

"Then I will keep my thoughts reserved for Peking." Ayaou was right. A confrontation like the one he had just proposed with Hung-chi was very Western. It would be a mistake.

If he were to be successful in China, he had to keep Taoism and Confucianism in mind. He had to plan his battles around the teachings of those two philosophers. He had to learn how to bend while working to help build a better China. It would take patience. He would also apply some of what he had learned from studying Sun Tzu's *The Art of War*.

Dawn leaked through the shutters that covered the windows. A spring rain had soaked the fields penetrating the earth and waking the seeds. When he opened his eyes, he discovered Ayaou's head resting on his chest. Her dark hair

448

spread out like a fan, and he smelled her ocean scent. Why couldn't every morning be like this?

She rolled over and looked at him.

They kissed, touched and made love. She whispered that if there was a next life, she wanted to be born as his concubine again.

"Robert," she said, "You have become a great man, and I am your bed warmer. I will not pressure you again to make me your wife or accuse you of only thinking of me as a whore. I know my place. I will always be standing in the shadows out of sight but in reach. I will understand when you bring a proper wife home."

"There will never be anyone but you," he whispered. They made love again.

Chapter 43

It was late spring in 1861 when Robert reached China's capital city. As his imperial escort rode into sight of Peking, he couldn't help but stare. The walls were forty feet high and on each corner were ten-story watchtowers with windows where archers could shoot at invaders. A sixty-foot tunnel with gates at either end led through the wall.

His escort was a troop of Manchu bannermen, and their yellow uniforms and flags signified the banner to which they belonged. His Ningpo teacher, Tee Lee Ping, had taught him that eight banners made up the Manchu army, three upper banners and five lower banners. In addition, there were eight Mongol banner armies and another eight Chinese banner armies. The three upper Manchu banners answered only to the emperor.

Inside the walls, people stopped and stared at the foreign devil riding with a troop of the emperor's bodyguard. Thousands of eyes examined him tearing his clothes off in their imaginations to see his naked, white skin. He'd never had this kind of attention before, and it made him uncomfortable.

Did these people consider him another parasite that had come to suck the emperor's blood as so many others had done before? Would they hate him and throw rocks? Had he made a mistake accepting the temporary position of inspector general? Would he end up like Horatio Lay?

He was surprised to discover that instead of twisted narrow streets as in Canton and Ningpo, Peking had wide avenues lined with shops and gray windowless houses.

At times, there were long stretches of red plastered walls with decorated tiles capping them. The troop rode alongside an open sewer that ran down the center of the wide avenue. When he first saw it, Robert expected it to stink, but the stench of human waste wasn't as intense as in Ningpo. He did not have to cover his mouth and nose with a damp, scented cloth.

In the distance, he saw China's heart, the rose-colored walls of the Forbidden City. He was nervous and excited at the same time. It occurred to him that instead of arriving like a conqueror as the invading allied army recently had, he was here as a friend. How ironic, he thought.

His attention was caught by a long line of camels on the opposite side of the avenue on their way out of the city. On their backs, between the twin humps, were trade goods going to far-flung provinces. His imagination sent them into the Gobi Desert and along the ancient Silk Road to Persia.

Tee Lee Ping had said that Peking had been China's capital for nearly five centuries. Yong-Le, an emperor of the Ming Dynasty, had built the Forbidden City, and it took two hundred thousand laborers thirteen years from 1389 to 1402 to complete the work.

Peking was a city built in the style of Chinese boxes that enclosed communities called hutongs. The Forbidden City was the emperor's palace, which covered hundreds of acres surrounded by a wide moat. Inside its walls, capable of housing thousands of concubines, eunuchs and imperial guards, was where the emperor was supposed to live.

However, he knew Emperor Hsien Feng was still in Jehol, more than a hundred miles from Peking on the other side of the Great Wall.

Now that he was actually in Peking, what impressed him most was the confidence in the city's architecture. Utterly self-inspired, different from anything he had seen in China so far. It made him wonder who had planned and built the city.

On the way in, he'd seen the hills in the distance covered with a green velvet gown of trees and bushes in full summer foliage. He'd strained to see the Summer Palace that the allied forces had destroyed the previous year, but saw nothing. The distance was too great for the naked eye to bridge.

He wondered how far the Summer Palace was from the Forbidden City. His curiosity was urging him to explore. He hoped he would have time but doubted it. He had not come to Peking for pleasure.

A troop of men riding shaggy ponies cantered by headed in the same direction as Robert's slower moving escort. They were all crossbowman dressed in jointed bamboo armor. Soon, they were out of sight.

He felt as if he had traveled to the Middle Ages, a thousand years in the past. Until now, he had not realized how much the Chinese empire was like a huge medieval kingdom. No wonder the battles between the allied army and the banner armies had resulted in China losing. From what he had discovered, it had been a slaughter. Tens of thousands of Chinese troops had died with only a few casualties among the allies. How could men armed like this stand against a modern army with cannons and rifles?

Robert's fears that he might be assaulted were put to rest when he arrived at his assigned quarters. Guards were posted outside the house. He didn't know whether he should consider them his jailers or his protectors.

He knew that the Manchu were distrustful. Considering all the troubles and wars foreign nations had imported to China in recent decades, he couldn't blame them. In their position, he would feel the same.

The weather was dry and hot. The wind blew from the Inner Mongolian deserts and in half-a-day, Robert's desk was covered with a film of dust. He wrote daily to Ayaou and worried that the letters wouldn't reach her. The mail service in China was unreliable. Maybe he would get a chance to fix that one day if he stayed long enough.

Ayaou had never been to Peking, so he described everything he'd seen in detail. He asked about Anna. He wanted to know if his baby girl had added any new words to her vocabulary besides daddy.

After he finished the letter, he worked on the reports he would present to Prince Kung with recommendations to improve China's financial situation.

Most foreigners in his position would have lost patience as the days slipped by waiting for an audience. He, on the other hand, knew to ignore such feelings to achieve his goals. Besides, to the Chinese, he was a barbarian. His first challenge was to prove he wasn't.

After several days, he had a meeting with Minister Wenhsiang at the Tsungli Yamen in a walled compound near the

Forbidden City. The minister was Prince Kung's right-hand man, but it still disappointed Robert that he wasn't meeting Prince Kung first.

Wen-hsiang was a small, bony man that looked like a peasant from the countryside, and he was dressed in blue, silk robes. Robert's bow was a bit deeper than Wen-hsiang's to indicate that he knew the minister's rank and importance in the imperial government. He was careful not to stare.

Wen-hsiang looked surprised. Few foreigners knew how to address a man of the minister's rank properly. Robert realized that first impressions were extremely important. Once the greetings were completed, he turned and gave directions to the servants carrying his five suitcases.

"What is this?" Wen-hsiang said. His tone sounded distrustful. The servants lined the suitcases in front of the minister's desk as instructed then scurried from the office.

Robert struggled to hide his nervousness. His hands were clammy. His insides churned. However, he looked calm and confident.

Wen-hsiang examined the worn leather suitcases. His eyes shifted to Robert. "Did you bring your clothing with you?" he asked. "Are you planning to live at the Tsungli Yamen? We do not have bedrooms here. Only offices."

He suspects I am an idiot, he thought, and knew he had only one chance to prove he was not like the other foreigners. If he bungled this meeting, it would be almost impossible to gain trust in the future.

Besides, if the minister had dealt with Horatio Lay, he had a right to be suspicious. Robert was sure that Lay had insulted the Chinese at every turn without even knowing he was doing it. Lay spoke the language fluently, but like so many others, he knew nothing about the Chinese people.

Without saying a word, Robert picked up the first suitcase, put it on the minister's desk and opened it. It was full of papers and notebooks.

"What I have here, Minister, are my records from Canton going back more than a year showing how much revenue has been coming in from customs and how much the imperial treasury should expect. I've also worked on projections for each of China's trading ports."

Wen-hsiang stared at the notebooks and papers. Then he looked at Robert, who forced a smile to hide his frayed nerves.

He opened the first notebook and pointed at a row of numbers. "This shows the duties we collected in Canton over a period of one-week back in May of 1859. Here, at the bottom of each page, is the subtotal that was destined for the emperor's treasury. It is unfortunate that I have no control over these silver taels reaching Peking."

Wen-hsiang leaned over the notebooks and hissed in astonishment. "That much just from Canton!" he said. "That amount did not reach us."

"That's because no one is keeping proper records anywhere but Canton and now Shanghai. I have discovered that the imperial bucket has many holes in it. If you give me the authority, I will patch those holes."

"Hmm," the minister said, "let me see more." He fingered his chin. They literally rolled up their sleeves and spent the day going-over the numbers, first for Canton then Shanghai.

"After I arrived in Shanghai, I set things right," Robert said. "My clerks went through the documents for the last year and recorded the figures in new ledgers, which I have in another suitcase. I replaced half the staff to get the job done the way I wanted."

The minister asked many questions and Robert had trouble understanding him at times. Wen-hsiang's Mandarin was mixed with imperial usages, which Robert hadn't learned yet. He would have to hire another tutor to strengthen that area of his Chinese language skills. Because there were so many languages and dialects in China, that would always be a challenge. He was determined to do his best.

Before the first meeting ended, he succeeded at proving to Wen-hsiang that he was not Horatio Lay and was not a fool. It was dark by the time they finished and closed the suitcases.

He asked, "Would you have your servants carry these outside where my bodyguards are waiting? I want to take these ledgers back to my quarters. Tomorrow, we will go over my projections for the other ports."

"You will not have to return to that house," Wen-hsiang said. "You will stay at the Tsungli Yamen."

Robert worried that he would be sleeping on top of a desk or the floor. He remembered the time he'd stayed at Guan-jiah's house and slept on a thin rice mat on a hard floor. "Forgive me for my ignorance," he said, "but I thought there was no place to sleep here."

"The guesthouse is across the street. It would be better if you stayed there. That way you would not have to travel far to reach the Tsungli Yamen. After today, I can see that we have much to discuss."

"Maybe I should leave my papers in your office," he said.

Wen-hsiang looked alarmed. "No, it is best they stay with you. Even with thousands of bannermen watching over the Forbidden City and the Tsungli Yamen, things have a way of vanishing. These papers are valuable, and we cannot risk losing them. We have never known how much money was being raised in the provinces before."

"I heard some time ago that thefts were taking place inside the Forbidden City," Robert said. "I thought they were rumors."

"They are not rumors and the thefts have not stopped. Several eunuchs have already lost their heads and more will probably tumble. Occasionally, something valuable that belongs to the emperor or one of the empresses manages to sprout wings and vanish."

Wen-hsiang indicated the suitcases. "I would hate to see these papers disappear. They may not look valuable inside those worn suitcases, but those numbers will breathe new life into the Dynasty. Keep those papers away from prying eyes. Knowing how much revenue is going to be flowing into the imperial treasury might give a thief the idea to try something big."

"If there is anything I could do to help, I am more than willing," Robert said.

Wen-hsiang became silent. He glanced at the suitcases, then at Robert. "I am sure that a man of your talent might actually be able to do just that."

"Might I suggest something?" Robert felt elated and wanted to jump up and down and shout. Instead, he maintained his composure. He had succeeded. He'd gained the minister's trust.

He had learned enough about the Chinese thought process to know that because of the lack of scientific study in China, the ability to analyze a situation was sometimes missing.

To the Chinese, telling a head eunuch to make sure nothing vanished then punishing him when something was taken meant punishing the one in charge. The reality was that it was difficult to stay awake twenty-four hours a day. Even the head eunuch had to visit the chamber pot and sleep. If Robert could do anything to stop the loss of an innocent life, he wanted to try.

"I am curious," Wen-hsiang replied. "How could you offer help when you have never been inside the Forbidden City?"

"With analytical logic." He pointed at the suitcases. "The same thinking I used to create the system I've put into place in Canton and Shanghai."

"Then, by all means, speak."

"Send spies into the city and have them discover who buys stolen goods like valuable jewelry. I would hazard a guess that most of the pieces taken were special and recognizable. I think a skilled jeweler would be needed to take each stolen piece apart and make something new."

"Amazing idea," the minister said. "I will suggest it to Prince Kung. I am sure he will send thousands of bannermen, eunuchs and servants into the city to ask questions."

"No, not that way," Robert replied, alarmed. It took an effort, but he managed to control the sudden flutter of panic that burst like a bomb inside his heart. He didn't want to be misunderstood.

"I'll write up a detailed proposal tonight with step-by-step directions on how the search should be conducted." His plan did not include the Manchu or anyone living in the Forbidden City. They would have to recruit waifs from the Han majority— someone like a Chinese Oliver Twist or David Copperfield would blend in and not arouse suspicions.

Those Han waifs would learn what to say and would not warn anyone they were part of an investigation for the emperor. It would be a challenge, but one Robert was sure he could make work.

Wen-hsiang said. "I will be eager to see what you produce."

Robert felt confident that he had proved himself. He found Wen-hsiang a capable man. The minister now had a better idea about the taxes the imperial government should expect to earn from customs.

It wasn't going to be that easy. He would have to travel to every treaty port and interview each employee. In the end, he would probably fire many and replace them with people like Gerard, the Frenchman he had left in charge in Canton.

The first thing he did after he moved into his new quarters was to write another letter to Ayaou, which he sent off with a courier the next morning.

"My nights in Peking are lonely and cold without you," he wrote. "I miss seeing our daughter's bright eyes. I hope she is not getting into too much mischief, and that Fooyen and you are getting enough sleep.

"I hate to tell you this, but I'm going to be staying in Peking for some time. I have no idea when I will be returning to Canton. I miss you and Anna horribly like a wilting flower deprived of water."

Chapter 44

After several meetings with Wen-hsiang, Robert waited ten days before an audience was arranged with Prince Kung.

Kung greeted him with great respect at his palace, The Garden of Discerning, in a hutong near the drum tower not far from the Forbidden City. A high wall surrounded the palace and garden. The audience hall was close to the gate. Kung's family and the servants lived in the other buildings clustered nearby.

Behind those buildings was one of the most beautiful gardens Robert had seen in China. Kung took him on a tour and stopped by a shadowy pond encircled by towering elms.

"This pond is shaped like a bat," Kung said. "The leaning trees protect the carp so hawks won't take them. This is where I come to find tranquility."

Kung didn't seem to remember he had rejected Robert six years earlier when Captain Patridge arranged an ill-fated interview in Shanghai. If Kung had forgotten that meeting, it was easy to understand why. Robert had failed miserably to show any understanding of Chinese history and literature, and his ignorance had been embarrassing.

He had not forgotten the first question Kung asked, "Do you know the difference between the verses of the Tang Dynasty and Sung Dynasty and the style of ruling between Han-ti, the Emperor of the Han Dynasty and Nurhachi, my ancestor, the founding Emperor of the Ch'ing Dynasty?"

Robert could not answer.

"This one does not grasp the complexities of Mandarin or Chinese history enough to serve us," Kung said, before dismissing them.

Prince Kung's parting words had fueled Robert's appetite for everything Chinese. He hated being ignorant.

This time, he was confident with his answers. An hour into the meeting, the subject changed to foreign policy, trade, customs, taxation and finance.

"My questions are like a child's," Kung said. "It is embarrassing that I know so little." He asked to be enlightened.

Robert found it ironic that this time he had answers to questions the prince didn't know. His Mandarin carried him through explaining to Prince Kung the most difficult concepts about Western economy and culture, and the conversation went well after dark.

That night, he slept for three hours before he was up writing the proposals Prince Kung had requested. Before leaving for the Yamen, he made time to write a brief reply to the first letter he'd received from Ayaou.

Anna was still not sleeping through the night, and Ayaou and Fooyen were losing sleep trying to see what they could do to settle the child down. Anna had unlimited energy and was into everything. She demanded attention at all hours. If she didn't get her way, she threw terrible tantrums. Once, Anna threw a book Ayaou was reading into a full chamber pot.

Growing up with eleven siblings and being the oldest had taught Robert about babies, so he wrote, "You must deny Anna's endless energy and curiosity when it is time for her to sleep. Make her go to bed. Let her cry herself out. Eventually, she will start to sleep through the night."

On June 6, he arrived early at the Yamen and found Prince Kung alone, and he was in a terrible mood.

Kung revealed the cause of his distress when he pointed at a large map of China that was pinned to a wall. With a stick, he tapped an area north of Manchuria. "We just lost a war to the Russians. They have robbed this entire region from the Dynasty. This is terrible news for China, and the emperor's health will suffer.

"These wars are draining our treasury. We never start them. When they end in tragedy for China, the foreigners find more excuses to gnaw on our bones and demand that we pay for wars they started. Soon, we will not be able to buy rice to feed ourselves. Their greed is endless."

"Once I have Customs working properly," Robert said, wanting to comfort Kung, "you will have enough money to pay these debts. I understand things are difficult and the treasury is almost empty, but I assure you that the money problems will soon be eased."

"And what can we do about the Germans?" Prince Kung asked. He stuffed his hands inside his loose sleeves and turned away from the map. "At present, I am negotiating a treaty with them, and they are being impossible. The French must feel they have not taken enough from China, because they are helping the Germans join in the robbery!" He threw up his arms in exasperation.

"I believe I may offer the beginning of a solution that in time will solve these problems." He knew that the ideas he was going to propose went beyond his responsibility as inspector general. Ayaou had warned him not to be so bold. However, he felt he had no choice and stepped closer to the map and studied it.

When he saw Kansu province in the center of China west of the Great Wall, he remembered an American merchant he'd met in 1854, soon after arriving in China. The man had looked like Ichabod Crane, a character from *The Legend of Sleepy Hollow*. Ichabod had mentioned that Kansu was east of Shanghai when in reality Kansu was to the west. Until today, Robert hadn't thought of that conversation.

Now, he saw Ichabod as an example of how ignorant most foreigners were of China. At the time, Robert hadn't noticed the error because he too had been ignorant of Kansu's location. He was proud that was no longer true.

He told this story to Prince Kung.

"It is a sad truth that most foreign devils only come to China to steal from us or cheat us. They do not spend the time to learn about our people and culture. They sail in and sell their opium, buy Chinese women, defile them and leave the women with ruined lives. Unfortunately, the foreign generals are not as ignorant. They know where to send their troops."

The conversation went from that topic to buying modern weapons to solving the domestic problems caused by the Taiping rebels, to building railroads, installing a telegraph service, funding a navy, establishing a postal system, opening Western idea based schools across the empire and how parents should raise their children in the strict British tradition.

It was a long day.

"Write up these proposals we talked about," Prince Kung said. "I want you to present them to key members of the imperial cabinet tomorrow."

The next day, he had a meeting with Prince Kung, Wen-hsiang, and Kuei-liang, the prince's father-in-law. At first, they seemed overwhelmed and confused with his ideas, but they listened.

Robert was patient and took time to explain until they understood. He was excited to be speaking with the true rulers of China since the emperor listened to these men. He told them what Ayaou had said about modern foreign medicines.

"There is a lot of sickness in China," he said, "that can be dealt with if we buy modern medicines from countries like Britain and France." He also mentioned that to buy loyalty, they should pay the imperial troops on time.

"How do you know that the imperial troops are not being paid?" Kuei-liang asked. "We have sent enough silver to satisfy their hunger."

"If someone farts inside the Forbidden City," Robert replied, "within days it is being talked about in tea houses as far away as Canton. Loose lips spread the news that the imperial bucket has leaks."

All three looked stunned. "We must discover who is stealing the money that was supposed to pay our troops," Kung said.

"Yes, and the thieves must lose their heads," Wen-hsiang replied.

Robert did not realize how much Prince Kung trusted him until the day he was criticized by one of the conservative, hard-liners, who was also a senior adviser for the emperor.

"Prince Kung," the conservative said, "you are too free with your words around this foreign devil. You should not discuss sensitive state secrets while he is in the room."

Robert tried not to make it look too obvious that he was straining to hear and interpret every word the conservative minister said. For as fluent as he had become in Mandarin, he still thought in English. Before he could understand anything said in Chinese, he had to translate it into English first.

He wondered what the conservative would have thought if he knew Robert was sitting there going over the proposed treaties being negotiated with the Germans. He was taking notes and thinking of ways to offer acceptable counterproposals that would lessen the impact on China.

To his surprise, Prince Kung reacted out of character and laughed in the conservative's face. Later, Robert realized that by laughing in the man's face, Kung had gained face in the eyes of the others in the room, as if he had taken some from the other man and added it to himself.

"Are you talking about 'Our Hart'," Prince Kung replied. That was the day Robert became known as 'our Hart', and he was flattered.

Kung indicated Robert. "This foreign devil is sitting at a desk behind you. He understands every word you say. He speaks better Mandarin than you do. He even knows where Kansu is."

Robert tried to melt into the desktop and become invisible. He felt his face burning. He hated being the center of attention, but no one was looking at him. It was as if each man in the room had become isolated. In fact, no one was looking at anyone except Prince Kung, who was staring at the conservative.

The conservative, clearly feeling insulted, cleared his throat in disgust and started to leave the room. Prince Kung waved a hand in dismissal.

"I do not care if you think of him as a foreign devil or even a long haired bandit," Kung said. Robert was sure the conservative was still listening. "That is because I am a rebel in the imperial parliament. I am used to people shooting arrows at me. Besides, this foreign devil is worth a dozen ministers. At least he is trying to help us with our problems instead of demanding that we continue to fight losing wars." The conservative minister was gone by the time Kung finished.

"Have your servant taste your food before you eat anything, Robert," Kung said.

He was alarmed. Kung had stepped out of bounds by insulting the man. The prince must dislike him, Robert thought, to risk being poisoned. "What about my servant?" he asked. "He might die."

Kung shrugged. "They know it is their job."

Everyone else kept working as if nothing had happened.

A few days later, he arrived early at the Yamen and found Prince Kung already there going over Robert's proposals for the treaty with Germany.

Without warning, Kung reached out and lifted the front corner of Robert's suit jacket. "How is this made?" he asked. "I am interested in the pockets. Imagine all the things I could put in these pockets if I had them sewn into my robes?"

"Let me show you," he said, taking off his jacket and handing it to Kung.

The prince examined the stitching around the inside of the pocket that held it in place. "I have never worn clothing like yours. It must feel different," he said.

When several others entered the room, Kung handed the jacket back. Robert was sure that if they hadn't arrived, Prince Kung would have asked him to undress, so he could try the suit on.

That night he wrote a letter to Ayaou and told her everything. He ended the letter with, "It's very early in the morning, and I haven't had a chance to sleep. When I wake, my first thoughts are always of you and Anna. I have not heard from you in days. I wonder if you did what I suggested about Anna crying during the night.

"I am eager to know if it worked, and if you are getting more sleep. One of us has to get adequate rest. I think about sleep a lot lately, since I am not doing much of it. If I am fortunate, I'll manage to sleep an hour or two before I return to the Yamen."

In one private conversation, Prince Kung and Robert agreed that there were no Chinese officials in the government that the emperor could trust. It didn't matter if the official was Manchu or Han since corruption was everywhere.

The conversation moved to talk of hiring foreigners to run China's customs offices. He assured the prince that he would be careful to select individuals who were ethical and had the same moral values he had. "I will do all that I can to find honest Chinese to work for customs too," he said.

"That is good," Kung replied. "With you entering China's service, we have nothing to worry about."

Robert was stunned. What if he couldn't live up to Prince Kung's expectations?

Chapter 45

On June 12, Robert faced fear with a cold, chilling sense of helplessness and a brush with death that was too close.

It happened because he was feeling lonely for the old days in Ningpo when he went to festivals with Ayaou and Shao-mei, which is why he went for a ride to the market to watch locals performing The Lion Dance.

Without warning, the crowd turned on him. The Chinese called him 'bloodsucker, bastard of a yellow-hair-ghost and devil that deserved to be sentenced to the lingering death'. They spit at him and threw rocks.

It was madness.

He had made a mistake by going without his pistol and bodyguards. He barely avoided being hit by the rocks and was fortunate to be on a horse. Without the horse, he would have never escaped to the nearby British Consulate.

Inside the consulate, he waited for his racing heart to grow calm. One of the British consular officials brought a small glass of brandy, and Robert gulped it without tasting. He'd eaten a large breakfast, so the alcohol did not hit hard.

It was his fault. He was a fool to let his guard down. It was not safe for anyone not wearing a Chinese face to be out alone. He remembered Shao-mei. She had been killed because he had relaxed his guard, and he still felt responsible for her death. When would he learn?

"Another brandy, please," he said.

He hadn't known such fear before. Even the fight with Taipings in fifty-five did not compare. He had not felt helpless then. Afraid yes, but not helpless, because he had been armed and ready. This time he had been surprised. The tsunami of hate from so many Chinese had been overwhelming.

In the letter he wrote to Ayaou that night, he did not mention the rock-throwing incident. He did not want to worry her. After all, she had warned him to be careful.

The next day at breakfast with Prince Kung and Wen-hsiang, Robert talked about his experience in the marketplace and expressed resentment.

"We are sorry for your bad experience," Wen-hsiang said, "but you have survived. Prince Kung has good news that will make up for what you suffered."

"I sent your proposals to the emperor in Jehol," Prince Kung said. "Even in his delicate health, he read them. His majesty instructed us to make prints and share them with the court, and his majesty wants to put your ideas to work."

Robert's narrow escape with death was shoved aside by a flush of pride. To think that he, a young man who had once been a low-ranking interpreter for the British consulate, had gained the attention of an emperor. He was tempted to pinch himself to see if he were dreaming.

That evening, he wrote to Ayaou knowing she would be proud. He wished Shao-mei had lived to see this day. It was a pity, because the sisters had played an important part in his understanding the Chinese culture.

Thinking about Shao-mei reminded him that he still had unfinished business with General Ward, the man who murdered her. His resolve for revenge against the Devil Soldier had sprouted deep roots. He would not be careless again.

Soon, he hoped, his position in China would offer an opportunity to exact revenge against the mercenary. Uncle Bark had said to wait until the time was right, and Robert believed that day was close. He took out the black, porcelain, hand-sized spittoon with the hunting tiger painted on its side, opened the lid and spit into it.

In early July, he traveled seventy miles to the coast and Tientsin, where he stayed for two months interviewing and hiring people. He wrote to Ayaou telling her that after he finished in Tientsin, he'd be traveling for the rest of the year setting up new offices in China's major ports.

Since he wanted to build a network of people he could depend on as if they were an extended family, he did not trust anyone else to do the job. Loyalty, courage, honesty and trust were his watchwords. All he would have to do was find a few hundred more like Guan-jiah and Gerard. A daunting task, he was sure, but one he was determined to make work.

Borrowing a page from Horatio Lay, he set his trap at the beginning of each interview. "The Chinese are like children," he said to the applicant. "Since they are simpleminded and not Christians, how do you plan to deal with them?"

Only those that countered that they did not feel the Chinese were simpleminded had a chance for a job with Customs.

Those that made it beyond the first test then had to explain how the Chinese culture differed from foreign nations and go into detail about the best approach to take when dealing with the Chinese. When he interviewed a Chinese applicant, he took a different approach and focused on Confucius's five great relationships to see how important they were to the man.

He was looking for sensitive diplomats that not only demonstrated an ability to handle the Chinese without insulting them but also knew ways to calm ruffled feathers when a person like Horatio Lay or a Harry Parkes upset Chinese officials.

His plans changed after the Manchu emperor died. In late August 1861, he returned to Peking where he first heard the news. The emperor had been thirty and his death was a shock reminding Robert how unpredictable life was. After all, the emperor had only been four years older than Robert, and the narrow escape in June from the rock-throwing mob was still on his mind.

What if one of those rocks had hit him in the head and knocked him off the horse?

With the emperor's death, the Chinese people were more resentful of foreign interference, and it wasn't wise to be out on the streets even with other Westerners. Several bannermen escorted him everywhere he went.

Not sure what the next day might bring, he decided to move his family closer. He wrote to Ayaou instructing her and Guan-jiah to relocate to Shanghai, where he planned to join them in the fall. His instructions were detailed about the house he wanted.

"The house must be one to match my status," he wrote. "It must be equal to or surpass the house in Canton. Since we have a growing family, there will be more servants. I want room for the children to exercise their curiosity. Guan-jiah will know what that means. He must use his skills to make sure the gardens are big places in small spaces."

Prince Kung and Robert met soon after the emperor's death. Their meeting took place in one of the garden pavilions behind Kung's palace. Unsweetened, strong green tea was served.

"Since my brother died, a power struggle has blossomed with Prime Minister Su Shun," Prince Kung said.

"Are you alone in this fight?" Robert asked. What he knew about the prime minister concerned him. If Kung failed, Robert's goals to help modernize China would die. Su Shun's Iron Hats wanted to keep China frozen in time. To make this happen, they were willing to plunge China into a war that could kill millions.

"No, I have formed a coalition." Kung looked exhausted. Robert had never seen the prince this tired. It was as if he were carrying the weight of China on his back.

"I have no idea how this will turn out," Kung said. He wilted a bit more, as if the burden were increasing with each perceived threat.

"I'm not worried," Robert replied, wanting to offer encouragement. "Even though I've never met the prime minister, I have heard enough to know that his arrogance and ego will destroy him. On the other hand, you are a pragmatic, quick thinker. You will be ready when he stumbles."

"I hope you are right. If I lose, your head could join mine on the ground inside the Forbidden City. The Iron Hats resent you. In addition, the foreign legations do not have the military strength in Peking to protect them, not in the short term. They will be slaughtered."

"Surely, the Iron Hats are not that stupid."

"But they are. The Iron Hats are determined to drive the foreign powers from China. They have talked about moving the capital back to Xian, where it will be easier to fight battles they can win."

"That might work," Robert replied. "After all, Xian is more than six hundred miles from the ocean while Peking is only seventy. The allied supply lines would be long, and their armies could easily be cut off."

"I know, but how many Chinese will die fighting that war? If the British and French occupy Peking again, they will destroy the Forbidden City as they did the Summer Palace last year. I might fail, so I suggest you leave Peking. You will be safer in Shanghai."

"I'm not worried. You will not lose, so I will stay. If Su Shun wins, the real danger is to China. For Su Shun, like the rest of the Iron Hats, refuses to see China as weak and backward in the ways of war. He is blind to the fact that Britain and France have modern weapons, while Chinese armies fight like they have for centuries with crossbows, swords and spears."

Prince Kung snorted. "You have more confidence than I do," he said.

"When you win, I want to be where I can help. China's armies need to modernize to equal the armies of Britain and Europe. If I leave, how am I to do that?" He finished his tea and a servant refilled the cup. The tea was bitter, which seemed appropriate.

Prince Kung smiled. "You amaze me, Robert. No one else believes we can beat the Iron Hats. Why do you care so much about China? After all, China is not your land."

Robert sipped his tea. A breeze rattled the bamboo outside the latticed window. "It is because the Chinese honor poets and artists above generals, merchants and politicians," he said. "I have not seen that in my country."

Prince Kung put his teacup down and studied Robert for a long moment. "Interesting," he said, "and I thought that was our weakness. We need talented generals, not more poets."

"China has good generals," Robert replied. "I've been to General Yue Fei's tomb in Hangzhou, and I saw people honoring his memory."

"General Yue Fei died more than seven hundred years ago. We have no Yue Fei today."

"I disagree. Su Shun is like those ministers that betrayed Yue Fei with their lies. My confidence is in you. I believe you are cleverer than Su Shun. What about the Empress Dowagers, Tzu Hsi and Tsu An? You didn't mention them."

"They are still in Jehol. I have tried to communicate with them, but Su Shun has blocked every attempt."

"You need the empresses to be part of your coalition. Be bold. Go yourself. Demand to see your brother's coffin. You have a right to pay respect to your brother. Take advantage of that."

"Interesting," Kung said. "Go on."

"Su Shun will be off balance because of your unexpected appearance. That is when you should enlist the empresses to join your side. From what I have heard, Su Shun has no respect for them. I have no doubts that they will join you in this struggle. By now, they have had a chance to see Su Shun at his worst, and realize that if he comes to power, they are doomed."

Prince Kung walked to a latticed window to stare at the ponds and trees. Birds chirped. "I have thought the same," Kung said, "but until you suggested what I should do to get close to them, I didn't know how to go about it. I will leave for Jehol soon. Thank you, my friend."

Prince Kung left in September.

Robert wished that he could have done more to help. It bothered him that he was in no position to do so. What worried him more was that although the women were empresses of the highest rank, they were still women, and women in China were nothing but bed warmers to most men. He had even heard Prince Kung belittle the empresses.

Although women had little value in China, Robert understood the power of the Chinese mother in a family and in the home. The two empresses were considered the mothers of Tung Chih, the six-year-old son of the dead emperor, and as such, when their son sat on the Dragon Throne, they could wield great power in the Forbidden City and China.

He hoped that at least one of the empresses would be intelligent enough to see the same thing. The longer he spent in Peking, the more he learned, and one thing he had discovered was that Hzu Hsi, the birth mother of Tung Chih, was a clever woman.

On November 1, a coup d'état was attempted while Emperor Hsien Feng's coffin was being carried to Peking for burial. An assassin hired by Su Shun tried to murder the Dowager Empress Tzu Hsi.

"With help from my brothers, several Han mandarins and with General Jung Lu commanding the emperor's upper three banners, I outwitted Su Shun and arrested him and his men," Prince Kung said.

This meeting took place in The Garden of Moonlit Fertility, where they sipped more green tea. It was early night and a hint of daylight remained. The trees surrounding the ponds and streams swayed from the wind. Crickets filled the air with sound.

Prince Kung never told Robert all the facts, but he felt a great relief for his friend, who saw things as he did.

"We are fortunate, Hart," Prince Kung said the next time they met. "Before I had Su Shun arrested, he had already placed an order to close the Tsungli Yamen. He would have stopped all negotiations with the foreign powers and attempted to drive them from China by force."

"Then we are blessed. If you had lost, and Su Shun waged his war as planned, China would have been divided between England, France, Germany, Japan and Russia, and they would have chewed her to the bone."

"But we wouldn't have been here to see it," Kung replied.

The Empress Dowagers issued an edict on November 8, which decreed that Su Shun would receive the worst punishment possible for his high crimes, a lingering death known as the Death of a Thousand Cuts.

"On his deathbed, my brother named the empresses coregents until the boy emperor comes of age," Prince Kung said.

This time Robert met Kung in Beihai Park, which was closer to his palace. Beihai, which translated to North Sea, had been built between 916 and 1125.

They were walking beside the lake near the Nine Dragon Screen, a towering stand-alone wall with colorful tiled dragons on both sides.

"I did not discover this until I arrived unannounced in Jehol demanding to see my brother's body and pay my last respects," Kung said. "The empresses were clever. They managed to be in the coffin room with me. After we talked, it was obvious Su Shun was planning to get rid of them. They said he had ignored the emperor's dying request that the empresses be coregents.

"Since my brother's death, Su Shun was making all the decisions without consulting them. He cut the empresses off from the court and put them under a form of house arrest."

Robert and Prince Kung reached the footbridge on the far side of the lake from the Nine Dragon Screen. The bridge led to the Jade Flowery Islet in the middle of the lake. Once across, they climbed the stairs toward the White Dagoba. "Did you know that before this Tibetan dagoba was built in 1651, Kublai Khan had his palace here?"

"I heard he met Marco Polo in that palace," Robert replied.

Kung stopped. He signaled the servants and guards to take a few steps back. Robert and Kung looked toward the Five Dragon Pavilions lined along the far shore of the lake.

"If it hadn't been for your suggestion that I go to Jehol, Su Shun would have succeeded," Prince Kung said. "You are truly 'Our Hart'." Kung put a hand on Robert's arm and squeezed affectionately as only a friend or relative would do.

He didn't know what to say. He was overwhelmed with emotion and tears filled his eyes. He blinked them away knowing then that he would probably be the only Westerner Prince Kung would ever trust.

"You should also know that Minister Wen-hsiang followed your directions about the thefts inside the Forbidden City. He took special care recruiting the young boys that will search the city. He is very hopeful."

In the end, Su Shun was beheaded in public in Peking's vegetable market on Greengrocer Street. The public notification of the date for his execution was posted everywhere.

Out of curiosity, Robert went to watch. Knowing a Chinese merchant who lived there, he took precautions. The bottom floor was a warehouse, and the top floor was where the merchant lived with his family.

He'd met the merchant in a bath and teahouse near the Yamen. Their conversations led to several invitations for dinner. Not wanting to risk being stoned again, Robert arrived early. The day of the execution was a bright, sunny day, and crowds stuffed the streets.

"Many of these people camped here last night to secure the best viewing spots," the merchant said. "They are acting as if this were a festival. Look at the street venders selling treats."

Robert peered in safety from behind a latticed, second-floor window and saw children sitting in the trees, on walls and roofs. When the cart that caged Su Shun like a beast rolled past, people spit at him. Even from the window, Robert saw Su Shun's face dripping with saliva.

He had seen the same thing near General Yue Fei's tomb. There were four-life sized, kneeling iron statues with hands tied behind their backs inside a fenced area. These statues represented the ministers that lied and turned the emperor against the general. People visited daily and spit on those statues to insult men dead seven centuries.

The platform where the executioner waited was within sight. It took the executioner one stroke and Su Shun's head was off, but it did not roll away. Robert watched in horror as the head swung back and forth attached to the body by a thin strip of skin at the front of the neck. He lost his appetite and trembled. If Su Shun had won, that could be him or Prince Kung down there.

"They say that Su Shun's family bribed the executioner with enough money to insure that the head and body were still connected by a strip of skin," the merchant said.

"But why?" Robert asked. "You would think they would need that money now that he's dead."

"It is considered bad luck in the next life if you arrive missing any parts and one of the most important is the head."

As he watched the body being carried away, he recalled that Su Shun had been one breath away from being the guardian of the young emperor and the regent of China. Prince Kung had said that if he had succeeded in assassinating Empress Tzu Hsi, he would have eventually set himself on the Dragon Throne as the emperor.

With the removal of Su Shun, Prince Kung, in a partnership with the two empresses, was the power behind the child emperor.

Robert believed that it was his responsibility to produce a reliable, steady source of income for the Dynasty, so China would not only survive but also modernize and prosper.

Even with Su Shun and his Iron Hats out of the picture, it wasn't going to be easy making the changes. He had a vague idea how he could make that happen but knew it might take decades.

Chapter 46

After Su Shun's execution, Robert drafted his proposal to solve the Dynasty's money problems. He hoped Prince Kung and his cabinet would accept them. With a six-year-old emperor, most of the power belonged to Kung then the dowager empresses.

Robert slept only when he was too tired to think. Often, he would nod off holding the pen to wake and find a blot of dried ink obliterating what he had written. He wished Guan-jiah had been there to grind the ink so the eunuch would be there to take the pen when Robert fell asleep.

The floor became littered with discarded drafts. After he finished the English version, he translated that into Chinese. It was difficult. Keeping in mind the Chinese way of thinking, every sentence had to be a masterpiece.

This caused headaches, and his stomach churned. He gripped the pen so hard at times his hand ached. He couldn't afford to make one mistake with the Chinese characters. Every stroke had to be exact.

He imagined Ayaou saying, "It will not be easy, Robert. There will be resistance everywhere you go. The imperials are cut off from reality inside the walls of the Forbidden City. They do not know what is going on in China. Everything they hear is filtered like tea through a sieve."

She was right, and his proposals might be rejected. After all, his ideas would upset the way things had been done for centuries. Even with the Iron Hats dead or stripped of their power, there were still conservative governors in the provinces that Shu Shun had appointed in the name of the emperor.

China's government was decentralized. The provincial governors ruled as if they were kings and had their own armies

474

and tax collectors. To rule a province, all a governor had to do was pay the emperor a set rent. Any provincial taxes collected beyond that amount, the governor kept.

If Robert's plan was accepted, it meant the governors were going to lose a source of revenue. The silver and gold from foreign duties was going to pour into The Forbidden City's treasury instead of to the provincial governors. Although the domestic trade was left untouched, the governors would not be happy with this.

Before the end of October, Robert completed *The Regulations of Trade throughout the Ports of the Yangtze River.* He proposed that all foreign merchants entering inland China by water pay a tax in Shanghai first. The regulations also insisted that the merchants pay half the tax before leaving China with their goods.

He planned to have his employees implement the same standards in every treaty port. As it stood now, each port operated under different rules depending on the local governor and the influence of the Chinese and foreign merchants.

If the governors and merchants knew what he was up to, they would stop at nothing to discredit him and remove him from his position as Acting Inspector General. There might even attempt to have him assassinated.

The day Robert turned the proposed regulations over to Prince Kung was a day he could not focus on work. He tried, but the idea that he might hear 'no' haunted him.

The imperial cabinet knew about the power of the merchants, both foreign and domestic, and some imperial ministers were probably in the pay of people like Patridge.

In addition, it was possible that the provincial governors would refuse to cooperate. There would be pressure to keep things the same. After all, many had become rich and powerful because of the old system. Upsetting the proverbial apple cart would ruffle feathers. The more he thought about it, the more he believed he was going to fail.

Days went by as Robert waited. It would have been easier if Ayaou had been with him. When he was under stress, she calmed him. Her methods were amazing. If sex wouldn't do it, she'd get him to discuss poetry or drag him to a play. Once, she had given him a lesson on ink painting then declared he had no talent.

Highly agitated and not to be undone when his proposal was rejected as he expected, he started drafting another plan.

The door to his office creaked and drifted open. That was odd. His men always knocked. Thinking the worst, Robert pulled open the drawer where he kept his pistol and rested a hand on it.

Prince Kung stepped the room. Robert took his hand from the drawer and closed it while trying to read the expression on Kung's face, but true to form, the prince gave nothing away.

With a sinking feeling, he noticed that the prince's hands were empty. What had happened to the Regulations of Trade? Had it been burned or worse? He shuddered, thinking of all the work he had put into drafting that proposal.

He nodded and Prince Kung mirrored him. Servants arrived with tea and sliced fruit with the skin removed. Robert and Kung settled into chairs to drink and make small talk while Robert fought the hive of curious bees swarming inside his head.

Finally, an hour later, the moment of reckoning arrived. He felt it in the air as the topic they had been discussing drifted to a conclusion. This had to be how a man convicted of a capital crime felt before the verdict was announced.

Would it be life or death?

"Robert," Prince Kung said, "your ideas and proposals for regulating trade in China were—" Prince Kung paused to cover his mouth. He coughed politely then sipped tea. "I apologize. The discussion was long and loud. My throat is raw." His eyes shifted to the sliced fruit. He picked up a piece of apple. "This should help."

It was a challenge for Robert to hold his tongue and look calm while Kung chewed the slice of apple. Was the news so bad that even Kung was having trouble delivering it? Robert's stomach filled with dread. How was he going to do his job if he couldn't collect those taxes?

When Kung finished the apple, his eyes were smiling. "Your plans were excellent and practical. My cabinet praised them to the emperor's ministers. The agreement for your proposal was unanimous. We thank you for producing a plan that will go far in saving China."

Had he heard correctly? He sensed that there was more. He imagined the blade coming down.

"Robert, it reads as if a Chinese wrote it. Did you have help?"

Robert took a breath and relaxed. "No. I wrote every word." Despite how excited he was, he would not reveal his emotions. If Kung acted inscrutable so could he.

He wanted to tell the prince that some credit should go to Ayaou and Shao-mei, but he knew Kung would never accept that. Women in China received little or no credit for anything they did. Robert was sure that Kung had consulted with the dowager empresses, but he had not mentioned it.

The truth was that without Ayaou's insights and what he had learned from her and Shao-mei during his early years in Ningpo, Robert would have never come up with language tailor-designed to fit the culture and traditions of China. Until this moment, he hadn't been confident in his written Chinese. This felt as if he had passed an important examination.

A month later, Robert was angry. He had known it wouldn't be easy to change the way import and export taxes were collected in China from foreign merchants. However, he had not expected it to be this difficult and endanger the lives of his people.

The first warning arrived from his agent in Hankow. "Kuan-wen, the governor general, doesn't accept the regulations of trade that you have set up along the Yangtze River," the agent wrote.

"We haven't been able to do anything since we arrived and moved into our offices. We fear being seen on the streets. If it were not for our loyal Chinese servants risking their lives to go out and buy food, we'd starve.

"Kuan-wen has sent proposals to the emperor in an attempt to change the regulations. He has also gained the support of other governors. They have repeatedly rejected our requests to open offices in ports along the river."

Robert decided to confront Kuan-wen himself and went to Prince Kung with the idea.

"That will not be wise," Kung said. "Kuan-wen was appointed by Su Shun."

He knew that Ayaou would have agreed with the prince. "I have no choice," Robert replied. "If the regulations of trade along the Yangtze are going to work, I must have cooperation from the governors."

"You would be risking your life. Send someone else. You do not see any of the imperial princes rushing off to solve these problems. We send generals and armies to do our work."

"I am one of your generals."

Prince Kung's face froze as he stared at Robert for a moment. Then he nodded. "But you do not have an army."

"I will not go unarmed. I will have my pistol."

Kung raised an eyebrow. "I can see that you are determined."

"If I cannot establish the system that you and the council have approved through the name of the emperor, I will not be able to raise the money you expect."

"I see," Kung replied. "Then you will be accompanied by a dozen bannermen. I will have General Jung Lu pick them himself. Their lives will depend on seeing that Our Hart returns still breathing."

In early November, before Robert set out on his journey to the river port of Hankow in Hupeh Province, he had no idea what he was going to face.

"How dangerous can a journey upriver be?" he asked. He was in his office talking to his assistant, Henry. "Surely, you exaggerate. It can't be that dangerous. Since I arrived in China, I have survived pirates, Taipings, assassins, kidnapers, mercenaries, and a rebel rocket that almost hit me in Canton during the Arrow War. I will survive this too. Besides, I'm going to travel from Shanghai by water. That is less risk than going overland."

"I still don't like it, Inspector General," Henry replied. "It will be risky."

"I'm not worried. Why should you be?"

"The Taipings control much of the Yangtze," Henry said. "We can't afford to lose you. Send me instead."

"No, Kuan-wen won't listen to anyone else. We already have agents there. They are afraid for their lives and are in hiding. We are getting nowhere. If there is to be progress, governor Kuan-wen must cooperate. I don't see how he can refuse. After all, I serve the emperor the same as he does. I am the Acting Inspector General of Chinese Maritime Customs. The governor must hear me out."

"Just because you serve the emperor, doesn't mean Kuan-wen does. I believe he serves his interests first."

"No matter. If he proves disloyal to the new emperor, he may lose his head."

"The emperor would have to send an army to replace him. To get there, they would have to fight through the Taipings first, since they are between Hankow and Shanghai."

"I am going anyway. We cannot have progress without risk."

"The price might not be worth it."

"Enough," Robert said. "I'll hear no more protests."

That night, Robert wrote a last will and testament leaving half of his money in the care of Guan-jiah with instructions to support Ayaou and Anna. The other half was to go to his family in Ireland. He was confident that he could depend on Guan-jiah.

"Henry," he said the following morning. "If something happens to me, I trust that I can depend on you to see that my wishes are carried out." He handed the papers to his assistant.

"That will not happen, Inspector General."

"But if it does—"

"I will see that it is done."

It took a week to make the arrangements. Robert used his Chinese friend Wang Dewie to find boats with captains he could depend on. The merchant owned the house off Greengrocer Street where Robert had witnessed Su Shun's execution, and the captain of the first boat was his cousin.

After departing Shanghai, Robert sailed through a zone controlled by the Taipings. While passing Nanking, a large group of rebels, at least a hundred, came alongside and demanded that the boat stop for an inspection.

The captain hid Robert and his guards in a cabin below the waterline. It was stuffy in that oven of a room. Robert handed the captain a purse filled with yuan to help pay a bribe if needed.

If the Taipings discovered him and his bodyguards in that cramped cabin, they would be slaughtered, and the captain could lose his head. There would be no way to defend themselves in that cramped, coffin shaped space. He remembered that time in Ningpo when the Cantonese pirates set fire to that lorcha filled with Portuguese pirates. He slipped his hand into his pocket resolved that if that happened, he'd shoot himself before the fire reached him.

His guards stood between him and the door and all were willing to die. He hoped it wouldn't come to that. The air grew thicker and was difficult to breathe. Robert sweated rivers and his clothing was soaked. He saw that his escort was in the same condition. Nevertheless, they stayed alert with hands on weapons watching the door.

At one point, the Taipings were outside the cabin in the narrow hall. Robert pressed his ear to the bulkhead to hear. With his heart beating like a loud drum, he listened to them talking to the boat's captain.

The Taipings would pay handsomely for Robert's head. He hoped this cousin of merchant Wang could be trusted. He felt sorry for his friend. If he died because of Wang's cousin, the merchant would feel responsible and be riddled with guilt. He might take his life due to the loss of face.

Robert sighed in relief when the voices moved away. An hour later, the boat was underway again. He did not ask for the yuan back. The captain offered, but Robert refused.

"Your family needs this more than I do. Besides, you risked your life for me today."

"It is an honor to serve you, Inspector General. The Longhaired Bandits are not China. They are a plague on all our houses."

Kuan-wen received Robert in the audience hall inside his palace compound. The room was large and voices echoed. The floor was white marble. The structure was wood. The roof was tile. Heavily armed Chinese soldiers in battle armor stood along the walls. It was a show meant to intimidate.

When Robert started to speak in perfect Mandarin, the governor's face showed surprise.

Kuan-wen replied, "If your regulations of trade are implemented along the Yangtze, you will ruin me and every governor in China. We have done business this way for centuries, and you cannot change that."

"I'm not doing this for me or for any of the foreign powers," Robert replied. "I'm doing this for China. The Dynasty needs those duties from trade to survive. You will have to adjust your life accordingly. I have looked at the numbers. You will survive."

The governor dismissed him.

Robert and his bannermen were assigned a small house built against the city's wall. Each day, surrounded by his guards, he went daily to request an audience. The governor refused to meet again.

It was tense when the governor's soldiers came to evict Robert from the city. The confrontation took place in the courtyard in front of the small, dusty house in a corner of the city. After Robert refused to leave, Chinese soldiers on the wall started throwing their trash on the house and pissing on it. The urine stench was strong. The servants that had been there when he arrived fled. Each morning, the twelve bannermen cleaned the mess. Prince Kung had ordered them to stay glued to him. They even watched him shit, which was something Robert didn't enjoy.

Prince Kung had been adamant. "Do not let him out of your sight." Robert knew the price. If he died, these men were to die with him. For a moment, he regretted his decision to confront Kuan-wen.

Several days later, the Chinese soldiers returned. This time Kuan-wen was with them. The governor's men crowded into the small courtyard and surrounded Robert's small troop.

It was an impasse. The pale yellow uniforms of the Manchu bannermen were like an impenetrable shield surrounding him.

Kuan-wen yelled at his general to drive Robert and his guards from the city. "Do what I have ordered or I will have you beheaded?"

The Manchu officer in charge of Robert's guards glanced at him and saw the determination on his face. Then he marched over and stood in front of Robert. Bracing his legs, he rested a hand on the hilt of his sword and glared at the Chinese general as if he were daring him to make the first move. It was a tense moment. Robert knew that the Manchu bannermen had a higher status than the city's Chinese garrison did. However, would it be enough?

The Chinese general demanded that Robert and his guards leave the city.

The Manchu officer did not budge.

The Chinese general glanced at the governor. The look on the general's face said, "What do I do now?"

The governor threatened to have his soldiers attack. Robert feared that this was going to end in a slaughter. The governor would have the bodies tossed into the river and lie about how they died. He'd say it had been a gang of robbers.

Robert had to do something. He pushed his way between his guards and confronted the governor. He lowered his voice so only Kuan-wen could hear. "Do you want this trouble that will threaten the existence of your family? I'm here on the imperial court's behalf to open an office in your city and collect duties from foreign merchants. If you insist on making a problem, I'll have no choice but to report to Prince Kung."

"Prince Kung is not the emperor," the governor replied. "He cannot tell me what to do. The emperor appointed me. He is who I answer to."

"You are correct. Prince Kung does not rule the emperor. However, until Emperor Tung-Chih comes of age, Prince Kung and the Dowager Empresses rule China in Tung-Chih's name."

The expression on Kuan-wen's face froze. "Tung-Chih is not the emperor," he said. His voice faltered. "Emperor Hsien Feng is."

"You haven't heard?" Robert replied, shocked. He then realized the truth. Of course, he hadn't. Kuan-wen's province was nearly cut off from the rest of China by Taiping armies.

"Emperor Hsien Feng is dead," Robert said, "and Prime Minister Su Shun has lost his head."

The muscles in Kuan-wen's face turned to putty. "Emperor Hsien Feng is dead!" he said, "and Su Shun lost his head." He looked dazed.

Robert mentally kicked himself. He knew that Su Shun had appointed Kuan-wen. If he had been aware that Kuan-wen hadn't known of Su Shun's death, this affair might have been concluded days ago. "Yes," he said, "and Hsien Feng's six-year-old son, Tung-Chih, sits on the throne. His regents hold the power."

Kuan-wen deflated like a balloon and appeared to age as Robert watched.

"Open your office," the governor said. He turned and walked away muttering to himself. "I did not know. I did not know."

"And you will not collect duties from the foreign merchants," Robert said to the governor's back. "You understand that, don't you?"

Kuan-wen turned. "I do," he said. Obviously, this man had just lost a lot of face, and having so many of his Chinese soldiers witness his loss made it worse.

Robert's agents came out of hiding, and the office opened that week.

Robert met with little resistance during the remainder of his trip. He took the boat east toward the ocean and changed to a ship to sail along the coast.

A few weeks later, as he rode with his bodyguards into sight of the city walls of Fuzhou, the capital of the Fujian province, a small, slight man dressed in a brilliant blue and green silk robe wearing his official headgear with its tassel and feather stood alone in the open city gate. Robert dismounted and nodded to the governor of Fujian, who nodded deeper to honor Hart.

That was a big change considering that at Su Shun's orders a few years earlier, this governor had refused to open his center gate to receive Britain's ambassador.

By the end of December, Robert established offices in five of China's major ports. In January, he sailed north. During the voyage, he wrote detailed plans to open offices in five more ports.

Robert had traveled thousands of miles and was exhausted. When he stopped in Shanghai for a few days to rest, he stayed at the Imperial Maritime Customs building. It had been built in 1857, and looked like a Chinese temple. He hadn't heard from Guan-jiah or Ayaou for weeks. He wondered when they would be moving to Shanghai and hoped there would be mail waiting when he reached Peking.

A few days later, a pack of English merchants arrived and demanded that Robert see them. He had been expecting something like this and wasn't surprised. "Show them in," he said to his clerk.

"We believe you should grant us favors and special treatment," the spokesperson said. The rest mumbled support as they stood on one side of his desk glaring at him. Robert remained seated. "We will do nothing of the sort," he replied. "My people have been directed to tax everyone the same."

"You cannot do this, Hart." The leader of the group almost shouted. He was a fat man with a red, puffy face, and his stomach strained the buttons on his jacket. As his chest swelled in anger, one of the buttons popped off and rolled across the floor. The more anger that he displayed, the calmer Robert became.

"You are British," the merchant said. "How can you do this to us? We have families to care for. We expect you to cooperate."

Robert replied, "Every merchant from every country that trades in China will be treated the same. That includes merchants from Britain. If you do not like that, I suggest you take your demands to Peking or London."

These fat merchants were not going to be allowed to become wealthier by cheating the Chinese of what little they had left. Compared to the average Chinese, these men would still be wealthy. They just wouldn't get rich as fast. He hated greedy people and resolved not to give an inch.

They departed his office in a huff. "You will hear from us again, Hart. We will ruin you."

It would take months to resolve the fiasco with the English merchants, who banded together and went to court in England to put pressure on Robert to give them special dispensations over other nations.

Robert refused and used every contact he had developed in England to state his case. In the end, he won. The English merchants had to pay like every nation that traded in China. Robert was sure that when these English merchants were in a pub, they would be throwing darts at his effigy.

Robert returned to Peking to endless meetings at the Yamen. A stack of letters from Ayaou waited, but he had no time to read them. He was aware that if it were not for his crushing schedule, he would have felt as lonely as he had in Canton when he had lived there without Ayaou during the Arrow War.

Robert's workdays often ran twenty hours. He slept between midnight and four in the morning and would be in his office before dawn. He was too tired to even dream about Ayaou.

When he wasn't in meetings, he was composing drafts telling the Manchu ministers what he was learning from his agents throughout China. In addition, he had to write follow-up reports when there were changes and revisions.

He was also involved in the details of establishing the piloting service and harbor regulations. These were sensitive issues. He had to hire harbor pilots for each port. For the sake of China's national defense, the imperial government wanted him to hire only Chinese pilots.

It took several frustrating months to learn that none of the Chinese pilots was any good since they hadn't been professionally trained.

"If I hire any of these men and a foreign ship is wrecked, whose face will suffer?" he said to Wen-hsiang, hoping the minister would speak for him inside the Forbidden City, the one place Robert wasn't allowed to visit since it was closed to all foreigners.

"It won't be mine," Robert said. "It will belong to those ministers demanding I hire people that are not qualified. My recommendation that we do not hire these people will be part of the imperial record. I am not going to lose face over this."

It didn't take long before he was allowed to hire foreign pilots.

Only then did he find time to read and spent an evening going through Ayaou letters. Near the end, she said that Guan-jiah was arranging the move to Shanghai. They should be there to greet him when he returned from Peking.

He read the stack again and was pleased to discover that his little girl was sleeping through the night. Ayaou said Anna was getting into everything. She had to be watched all the time to make sure she didn't hurt herself and Fooyen had her hands full. Robert chuckled at the image.

Soon, Anna would be three. He wanted to be home when she celebrated her birthday.

A few weeks later, Robert was on his way to Shanghai, and he had no idea if Ayaou would be there. He had to do something about improving the mail service in China. The challenge was finding the time. There was so much to do.

He fears vanished when he arrived in Shanghai to find Guan-jiah waiting in a sampan to greet him as the ship dropped anchor.

How had the eunuch known?

"Master," Guan-jiah said, "I found a suitable house inside the walled portion of the Chinese city as you instructed."

He wanted to take Guan-jiah in his arms and hug him but didn't. After all, now that he was Inspector General, he had an image to uphold.

Guan-jiah took charge moving the luggage to the new house.

The layout and size of the house was similar to the one in Canton. The difference was in the light since there were many windows. It made the rooms pleasant, especially during sunny days, as Robert would discover. The shadows of trees projected on the floors through the glass made the atmosphere exuberant.

When he stepped inside the house for the first time, Ayaou was sitting on a bench prim and proper with her back held straight as a board. She was dressed in white silk pants and blouse. Her hair had been combed to a high gloss and braded in one long strand down her back. This revealed her pixy ears and long neck, two things he'd always admired and loved to smother with kisses.

Fooyen stood to the side and was holding Anna. Robert took a step toward his daughter. Looking shy, Anna stuck a thumb in her mouth and hid her face against Fooyen's chest.

"I have been gone too long," he said. "She's forgotten who I am." He was disappointed. With a sinking feeling, he realized how much he had loved to hear her call him Ba Ba.

Fooyen brought Anna to Robert, and said, "You cannot forget who your father is." She thrust Anna toward him, but the child twisted away and the thumb stayed in her mouth as she whimpered.

"Give her time to remember you," Ayaou said. "Take Anna to her room." Fooyen took the child and left.

"No one will bother you, Master," Guan-jiah said, before the eunuch hurried deeper into the house.

Robert had been so busy working endless days and nights, he'd forgotten Ayaou's beauty. Tears filled his eyes and he went down on one knee to rest his head on her lap.

Seconds later, her fingers arrived to explore his face and hair. Part of him yearned for their old life in Ningpo when he had been a lowly interpreter for the British.

Her eyes glowed and her body advertised its excitement.

"Show me the bed," he said. Once they were upstairs behind a closed and locked door, he pulled Ayaou into his arms while his hands explored her body and savored the smooth, inviting warmth of her skin.

Ayaou was pregnant before the end of January 1862.

Chapter 47

For most of 1862, Robert was on the move along China's coast and rivers. He felt like a migrating bird when he returned to Peking. Since he traveled on an armed, imperial junk with a large crew, pirates left them alone.

He was so busy that he had only a few minutes each day for letter writing when he managed to jot off brief notes to Ayaou.

"This is horribly lonely work," he said in one midnight letter. "Some nights, I consider quitting so I can come home to stay, but those are foolish thoughts.

"It grieves me that I am missing every achievement Anna makes. I wasn't there when she started to sleep nights. I missed seeing her learn to crawl, walk, and eat on her own. I feel that I am failing as a father.

"Then I think if I quit, who would replace me? Moreover, would that person have China's interests at heart? Whenever I make a decision, I always think of what is best for China. I want you to know that it is through you that I have learned to love your country.

"China is like another concubine, and she's in trouble. I cannot abandon her."

He sealed the letter in an envelope with hot wax then rested his head on his crossed arms and cried. He missed both his families, the one in Ireland and the other in Shanghai. While tears streamed down his cheeks, he started to laugh and that soon turned to hiccups.

It was ironic. Here he was with two loving families. He had eleven brothers and sisters and both of his parents still lived. He had Ayaou and Anna with another child on the way. He had friends in every major coastal and river port in China. He was a rich and important man, yet he was feeling sorry for himself.

That night, Shao-mei visited him in his dreams. In the morning, he had a pounding headache and struggled with depression all day.

Along with his developing skills for solving problems between the foreign powers and China, he was gaining a reputation for keeping secrets.

This reputation started late one afternoon in Peking when Minister Wen-hsiang approached Robert while he was strolling in the Yamen's garden.

They walked together as the minister confided that he had a nephew who was addicted to opium. The minister's first wife and her sister, the boy's mother, were agonizing over it. Wen-hsiang didn't know what to do.

"How old is your nephew?" Robert asked, feeling a twinge of guilt from his years working with Captain Patridge. He hoped he could help Wen-hsiang somehow. Maybe this would be a way to atone for those sins.

"Nineteen. He has two wives and three children. Do you know what we should do to help him?"

Robert found it strange that the minister felt he might know of a solution. On the other hand, it made sense. After all, Westerners were responsible for the addiction. "Send him to an isolated monastery in the Yellow Mountains in Anhui province. That way, he will be as far from opium as possible."

Several weeks later, after another trip along China's coast, Robert was back in Peking working at the Yamen. Wen-hsiang asked, "Did you tell anyone about my nephew?" It was well after dark and everyone else had gone.

"Are you talking about the nephew addicted to opium?"

The minister nodded.

"I told no one," Robert replied.

"It never occurred to me that you would not talk to anyone about it," Wen-hsiang said. "I thought it best to live with the gossip instead of hearing my wife and her sister crying over the boy all the time."

Robert held a thumb and finger to his lips and made as if he were buttoning them. "I hate gossip," he said. "When you sought my advice, I was honored that you saw me as someone you could confide in. How is your nephew?"

"He is hidden away in the Yellow Mountains suffering. I have been told he sweats and screams and vomits and cannot eat. We also hired an acupuncturist to help with the healing process."

They had stopped working. Robert went to the stove where a teapot was simmering. He poured two cups. "Tell whoever is watching your nephew to make sure he doesn't swallow his tongue. They should tie him to the bed, so he does not fall and hurt himself. Recovering from an opium addiction is difficult."

Wen-hsiang accepted the offered tea and sipped. "Be careful, it is hot," he said, and blew on the tea. "There is nothing to worry about. Besides the acupuncturist, there is a trusted doctor, who has several servants keeping watch so my nephew does not come to harm."

"I'm glad to hear that. I'm sure he will be fine." Robert finished the strong, bitter cup of black tea and returned to the report he was working on.

"Your advice on how to catch the Forbidden City thief was also correct," Wen-hsiang said a few minutes later. "We followed your instructions carefully."

Robert was surprised. He had forgotten that incident and had heard nothing for months. He put his pen down. "Did you catch this burglar?" He crossed his arms on the desktop and leaned forward. "I'm interested to hear the outcome."

"One of the child spies found the jewel merchant that was buying the stolen items just as you described. We offered another valuable piece of imperial jewelry as bait. After the jeweler bought that, the children took care that the jeweler would not know they were watching.

"Two nights after the last theft, the jeweler was followed through the streets to a teahouse where he met a foreign devil. Our agents witnessed the sale." Wen-hsiang stopped and peered about as if looking for someone listening to the conversation. There was nothing but deserted desks in the large room. Even the servants had been dismissed.

"Go on," Robert urged. "I'm a captive, eager audience waiting to discover what happened." To think that he had helped catch a thief was exciting.

Wen-hsiang leaned forward until their noses were almost touching. He talked in a conspiratorial tone, which Robert found humorous. "The Empress Tsu Hsi was so impressed with your methods that her spies are being trained to use them."

"I'm flattered," Robert said. "What happened to the thief?"

"It is a long story, and it is late."

"Don't leave me in suspense. My imagination will keep me awake wondering what happened. We still have time. It isn't midnight yet."

Wen-hsiang smiled slyly.

"You old devil," Robert said. "You are playing with me."

Wen-hsiang smiled and shrugged. "It is half the fun of telling a good story. Well, the foreign devil and the Han jeweler were placed in chains. The imperial torturer questioned them and discovered that this foreign devil worked for a British man who was planning the thefts, similar to how you wrote out the directions used to catch them. We also learned the name of a eunuch inside the Forbidden City that was putting the stolen items in hollowed out gourds to float across the Grand Canal."

Robert held up a hand. "So there were five thieves: the bannerman, a young eunuch, the foreign devil, the jeweler and a British man. Was the first foreign devil you caught also British?"

"No, he was Japanese."

"You are sure he was Japanese?" Robert asked, wondering if he was the same man that followed him in 1856, when he still worked for the British in Ningpo.

"Yes." Wen-hsiang nodded. "He lost his Chinese while being tortured, and we had to find someone who understood his barbaric, island tongue. Shall I continue?"

"Go on. Tell me how they used the gourds."

"Retired concubines from previous emperors have these gourds. They carve them to pass the time, and this eunuch borrowed a few." Wen-hsiang looked nervously about.

"Get on with it," Robert said. "No need to keep me waiting. No one is going to hear us talking. The Yamen is guarded by bannermen. Why be so nervous?"

"The Empress Dowager Tsu Hsi does not want anyone to learn about these methods. She has kept the children to use again. She already has spies inside the Forbidden City. With these children, she now has spies outside the walls too. The information they gather might be useful."

"Interesting," Robert said. He doubted whether the children were sophisticated enough to gather the kind of information that would be useful for ruling an empire.

"This stupid eunuch would seal the hole in the gourd with a plug and throw it into the Grand Canal that surrounds The Forbidden City. The bannerman waited on the other side and retrieved the gourd and carried it to the Japanese foreign devil, who then contacted the Han jeweler."

"Confound it," Robert said. "Get to the conclusion. We don't have forever."

Wen-hsiang smiled. "Such impatience is unlike you, Our Hart. It was as you said. The jeweler told us how he took each piece apart and made them into other pieces that could not be recognized. He melted the gold and silver and used them to make new pieces of jewelry."

"And did you catch the mastermind?"

The minister's look of satisfaction dissolved. "Unfortunately, the Japanese thief died before he could tell us who this British man was. We also discovered that the bannerman, the eunuch and the jeweler didn't know his name."

"Did they describe him?"

"Describe him?" Wen-hsiang looked confused.

"What he looked like." Robert said.

"What good would that do? Most foreign devils look the same. Besides, they never saw him. The Japanese thief was the middleman."

"What are you going to do with them?"

"Wet silk handkerchiefs for the eunuch. The bannerman already had his arms and legs removed. He is being kept alive as an example for the others in his troop. He was put in a cage that hangs inside the barracks so his fellows can see and hear his agony. We cut off the jeweler's head and sent it to his family. The rest of his body was sliced into thin pieces and fed to fish."

Robert shuddered at the horrible images. He had been looking forward to eating, but his appetite was gone now. He'd heard about the wet silk handkerchief method that smothered a person slowly. The condemned was tied to a bench and one wet silk handkerchief after another was put on his face until he died of suffocation. Near the end, the victim's body strained and heaved with the effort to suck in enough air to stay alive but eventually it became impossible. Death took hours or even days to arrive.

"Do not share this with anyone?" Wen-hsiang asked.

"Of course not," Robert replied. He didn't see how it could be kept a secret. The horror of the punishment would spread like a fire and be talked about in teahouses as far away as Canton.

Once word got out that Robert kept secrets, it seemed that every Manchu, Han official or high-ranking military officer Robert met had a complaint to make or sensitive questions to ask.

Both the Manchu and the Chinese were taking the name 'Our Hart' seriously. He could have suggested they change 'Our Hart' to 'Father Confessor', but he was sure they would not understand.

Owing to this, the opportunity to get even with Frederick Townsend Ward for the death of Shao-mei appeared. It happened at an imperial party held by one of the princes at his palace in Peking where Robert met the famous Han Chinese General Li Hung-chang. When dinner was served, the general was seated next to him.

While they were eating, he discovered that Li was also an enemy of Ward. During the conversation, Li revealed that he was experiencing a terrible time working with Ward fighting the Taipings.

"Ward's conduct is selfish and careless," Li said. "His actions have cost the lives of many of my men in combat. What is even more difficult to swallow is that Ward goes around telling others that he is not guilty of what I have accused him of and even worse, he has publicly insulted my intelligence.

"I feel trapped because the minister of defense has ordered me to continue working with this barbarian. It is a fight I will never win what with Ward blocking my every step. If I discovered an assassin coming for him, I would not stand in the way."

Robert was thrilled to hear this. Li was saying this out of frustration and anger, but as the Chinese saying goes, 'The speaker had no intent when the listener took the words to his heart'. Robert felt this was a God-given opportunity, and he decided to get involved.

"General," he said. "I want to invite you to dinner at my quarters near the Yamen later this week."

"Agreed. Which day would be best?"

"Let's make it Wednesday."

"I am glad you asked. I have been eager to meet you since I heard that you want to modernize China. I feel the same. China must manufacture steamships and modern weapons to survive. I am interested in hearing your ideas."

"I'm sure there will be much for us to talk about," Robert replied.

After Wednesday's meal, Robert suggested they take a walk in the garden. He didn't want to take any chances they would be heard by the servants or guards. Alone and surrounded by tall stands of swaying bamboo, Robert broached the subject.

"We have something else in common besides wanting to modernize China," he said. "General Ward is also my enemy. He murdered one of my concubines, and I long for justice." To emphasize the seriousness of his statement, he opened the lid of his black porcelain, hand sized spittoon with the hunting tiger on its side and spit in it.

When he closed the lid, he looked into Li Hung-Chang's eyes and smiled. "Would you like a cigarette?" He pulled out a box and offered one.

"Isn't it amazing how one small match can light such big fires? Imagine if I gave you this match and by accident and it somehow burned Ward's house in Shanghai. I am sure such a match would be very expensive. Of course, since I was responsible, I would feel obligated to pay for the damage. It would be hoped that Ward would not be home when the fire started. If Ward was home and died, I would have to pay more since it was my match that started the fire."

The general's eyes went from Robert's face then to the spittoon then to the box of Egyptian gold tipped cigarettes and back again. Without saying a word, Li Hung-Chang took a cigarette. He used the same match to light his cigarette. "That tiger looks fierce," he said, indicating the spittoon.

"That's why I bought it soon after I lost my concubine."

Cigarette smoke obscured the general's face. He said, "I am not surprised that Ward killed your concubine. Such cruelty can be expected of him. If there is anything that I can do to help you gain justice, you have only to speak."

Robert held up the blackened match used to light both cigarettes. "How much do you think it will cost to replace this match so we will have one that works? Of course, I'm sure that it will take many men to light the new match and use it properly."

A price was mentioned. Although it was an outrageous sum, Robert did not raise an eyebrow. He smiled and threw the dead match to the ground and used the toe of his shoe to push it into the dirt.

"Yes, I will be willing to pay that price and a handsome bonus to every soldier involved after the objective is achieved. After all, we are doing this to help China rid itself of a parasite. One more thing, Ward must pay for his burial. We will call it a 'match tax'.

Three months later, one of Li's men came to Robert's house with a box and a note.

The note said, "The messenger is a family member. He can be trusted. General Frederick Ward has honorably given his life for international peace. Enclosed, please find the 'match tax' he paid for the ground he was buried in."

Robert opened the box and saw five intricately carved gold rings set with diamonds, rubies and emeralds. They sat on black velvet. The first time he had seen those rings on Ward's fingers was the day the Devil Solider bought Ayaou. Ward had made sure that everyone saw those rings that night in Shanghai.

Tears filled Robert's eyes and slid down his cheeks. Li's man looked away. The tears weren't from misery but from relief. He remembered Shao-mei's smile with her lovely dimples. "Tell me what happened," he said.

"Ward took off these fancy rings in an attempt to buy back his breath. Shortly before he died, I whispered your name and told him the rings would not buy him his freedom, because they were for the tax he had to pay to be buried. Ward's body was stabbed, his skull cracked and his jaw dismantled. We even pried out his gold teeth while he still lived. It was a masterful job. His soldiers thought he died of battle wounds. There was no suspicion."

Robert handed the box with Ward's rings to the messenger. "Keep these as a bonus," he said. "It is fitting that the man who collected the tax keeps it." The soldier took the box, nodded and left.

Within days, Robert made a trip to Ningpo. On the way, he stopped in Shanghai where he told Ayaou what had happened. She broke down and cried, and he held her through the night. The child she carried was too close to term, so he felt it best that she stay close to her doctor. He took Guan-jiah with him instead.

In Ningpo, they went to visit Shao-mei's grave to let her know that her death had been avenged, but the graveyard no longer existed. There had been a landslide due to heavy rains, and that land was now part of the East China Sea.

Robert was overwhelmed with grief. He stared at the water where her grave had once been. He couldn't believe it was gone. How could he tell Ayaou?

"Master," Guan-jiah said. "I suggest we buy nine floating lanterns and find a local monk to help light the candles. In this way, we will free Shao-mei's spirit from the river."

It was night when the chanting monk had Robert light incense and let the lanterns glide into the river's current. A brisk wind was blowing toward the sea. They stood and watched the red paper lanterns float away with the candle flames glowing through the flimsy paper.

As the lanterns drifted, the flickering flames took on the aspect of a beating heart. Robert held the bunch of incense sticks in his hand while the smoke from the burning tips followed the lanterns like a ghostly fog, and for a moment, he thought he saw Shao-mei's fading image drifting with the wind.

If Ayaou had been there, she would have said that her sister's soul was traveling to meet her. A great weight lifted from Robert's shoulders as a black spirit spread its wings and flew away from him that night.

Chapter 48

Robert was in Peking when the Taiping rebellion, after a lull of several months, erupted, and imperial armies were being defeated one battle after another. The rebels advanced on all fronts until they controlled a third of China.

When he heard that a Taiping army was approaching Shanghai, he worried for his family and had trouble sleeping since his Shanghai home was in the Chinese section of the city, where vicious fighting against the Taipings had taken place in 1854.

With a goal to make Shanghai safe for his family, Robert arranged a private meeting with Prince Kung.

The prince's office reminded him of the Ningpo house he had shared with the sisters. Bamboo grew in a corner ceramic pot the size of a squat, fat Buddhist monk. A breeze blowing through an open window rattled the stems. There were inked wall hangings that invoked longevity, harmony, peace and tranquility.

After small talk over tea and slices of fresh fruit, Robert guided the conversation to the state of affairs. "If the Taipings take Shanghai," he said, "we will see a disruption of duties from customs and the imperial treasury will go dry like a river during a drought. I suggest we ask the British and French for military help."

"How can we ask these countries for help against the Longhaired Bandits?" Kung replied. "After all, they caused this plague. If it had not been for the wars started by England and France over opium, there would have been no Christian missionaries and no rebellion."

Kung left his desk and walked to a map of the Chinese empire that covered an entire wall and indicated the top of the map. "The Russians are attacking from the north and the French from the south while England takes bites out of the Dynasty in Tientsin, Shanghai, Hong Kong and Canton with help from the others. In addition, they demand we pay reparations for the wars they started. The only peaceful province is Tibet, and that is where they may attack next. The British could bring an army from India."

"This is different," Robert said. He was desperate. It was frustrating how the imperials seemed so blind. It was as if they didn't believe there was any real danger to the Dynasty. He suspected that Prince Kung and the other royals thought heaven was on their side. Surrounded by tranquil gardens while writing poetry and creating ink paintings of nature, they were in denial.

"This isn't like the last time the Taipings occupied Shanghai." Robert said, "In 1854, the export, import duties were insignificant because of the old system of corruption and bribes. Today, it is different. Most of the imperial treasury flows through Shanghai. Without those gold and silver taels, it will affect the ability of the Dynasty to continue fighting the Taipings. Trade must not be disrupted. I urge that you act soon."

Prince Kung carried the message to the Dowagers. A few days later, Robert was instructed to contact representatives from England and France and ask for military assistance. This resulted in England and France warning the Taipings to stay away from Shanghai.

However, the warnings were ignored, and the Taiping army continued to advance. Foreign and Imperial forces fought together and drove the Taipings back.

With the situation in the rest of China growing worse, Prince Kung visited Robert at the Tsungli Yamen.

"Your help gaining the support of the British and French against the Longhaired Bandits was much appreciated," Kung said. "The Dowagers want to know if you have any other suggestions to defeat the rebels."

The Tsungli Yamen was crowded with busy Han and Manchu ministers. There had to be a reason Kung was asking this in public. Could it be that Prince Kung and the Dowagers wanted others to know about his contributions without an official proclamation?

Robert resisted the desire to look around and study the reaction. There probably would be nothing to see anyway. In public, the Chinese were experts at hiding their feelings.

Be bold, he thought. With so many listening, it was possible his opinions would be taken seriously.

"First," he said, "I want to point out that since 1644, no Han Chinese has been allowed to command a significant army. There are talented Han generals, but they are being held back. That is hurting the Dynasty."

Robert knew this because he had talked in confidence with several Han Chinese officials. He had also heard conversations at the tea and bathhouse he visited on Saturdays.

"There is a reason the Han do not command powerful armies," Prince Kung replied.

Robert detected discomfort in Kung's eyes and realized he was stepping outside what was considered polite talk.

"If we allow the Han too much power," Kung said, "they might eat the Dynasty. Putting Han generals and ministers in important positions in the government and the military is a risk."

"It is a risk that must be taken," Robert replied. "The Taipings are a greater threat. The recent defeats are evidence that there is not enough talent among the Manchu generals." It was important to keep a serious expression, so Robert did not smile.

He imagined that everyone in the room was mentally gasping in shock. No one else dared to say what he had just said. The only reason he felt confident that he would get away with such impertinence was because he was a foreign devil and the royals called him Our Hart. Even the Dowagers called him that.

"I have heard that General Tseng Kuo-fan is someone the Dynasty can rely on to change the situation," Robert said. "He has a talent for winning battles. From what I've learned, he would not be a threat to the Dynasty. His loyalty is beyond question. I urge you to give General Tseng Kuo-fan a chance. Put him in command of an army that's fighting the Taipings."

He knew that the Manchu called Tseng Kuo-fan *Head Chopper.* Tseng was a Han Chinese officer that had risen in rank as high as the Dynasty would allow. It was time for the Manchu to make an exception. He hoped that the Empress

Dowager Tzu Hsi might be the one who tipped the scales and made that happen.

Although Robert had never met the empress, he had learned enough to suspect that she was levelheaded, unlike many of the hotheaded Manchu living in denial of China's tenuous situation. He suspected she had made the difference in the decision to bring the French and English into the fight against the Taipings around Shanghai.

"This recommendation will be considered," Prince Kung said. "Have you anything else to say?"

Robert noticed the hush. Normally, the Tsungli Yamen was a noisy place with people coming and going. Now, no one was talking or moving. They weren't watching either. Their eyes were glued on the papers they were reading or writing. However, he was sure every ear in the room was focused on his words.

This was Prince Kung's real reason for starting this conversation, Robert thought. He wants the others to hear, so he can sound them out later to see what they think. That is the only plausible reason this discussion is taking place in a public forum.

He raised his voice so everyone heard. It was time to see if he could gain a big win. "China needs a modern navy." Robert remembered the difficult trip up-river to Hankow the previous year. He'd also talked with General Li Hung-chang about this, and Li felt the same.

"The Dynasty needs to control the rivers and coasts. I suggest that I go to Shanghai and work with Governor Xue Huan to see if we can generate enough money to buy a squadron of naval ships from Europe. China cannot stand on its legs if it has to rely on England and France for naval support."

"How can you possibly squeeze more money?" Prince Kung said. "All of China's national, annual income goes to pay for war penalties imposed by foreign powers. The imperial ministers will be reluctant."

"Let me think about that." Robert started to pace. Everyone watched him walking back and forth. Work had been forgotten. Losing the Opium Wars had created this debt for China, Robert thought. Why not use opium to solve the current crises? At least for a short time.

He turned to Kung. "Lift the ban on opium," he said. Someone gasped. Kung started to protest, but Robert held up a hand. "Hear me out. If we do this right, it will stimulate the merchants and boost trade. This will increase revenues. This is our only choice. I know it sounds like we are cutting out part of China's lungs to patch its kidney but our immediate objective is to buy time. The opium trade cannot be stopped anyway. Instead of smugglers getting all the profits, we will get a share through taxation. A sacrifice must be made so China can survive.

"We tried to tax opium," Kung replied. "It did not work."

"The situation is different now. The corruption has been removed. I am confident that my people are ready to make this happen, and I trust them."

"I will take these recommendations to the Dowagers," Kung said.

Robert was sure that the imperial court would be buzzing about this.

Later that night, when the Tsungli Yamen was almost empty, one of the lower-ranked Han ministers told Robert in confidence that the Han respected him for speaking out.

"None of us could do that without risking assassination or getting beheaded. You are the only one who can speak out," the Han minister said. "Forgive me, but even as a foreign devil, you are probably the only man in China the Dynasty will listen to."

That did not mean he would always win, Robert thought. He also realized that he must not let this go to his head.

In a few days, Kung let Robert know that the Dowagers had agreed to his recommendations. General Tseng Kuo-fan was put in charge of the conflict against the Taipings. The general's orders were to start marching toward Nanking, the Taiping capital.

The imperial government appointed Robert to act on China's behalf to purchase a small fleet from England. Robert returned to Shanghai and raised eight hundred thousand taels, enough to purchase a fleet of four medium-sized naval vessels and three smaller ships with equipment and ammunition.

He wrote to Horatio Lay, who was still recovering in London from his knife wounds. He asked Horatio if he would act as China's agent and purchase the ships since he was already there.

Weeks went by before Horatio's reply arrived. Lay suggested that his friend, Captain Sherard Osborn, an officer in Britain's Royal Navy, command the fleet during the voyage from Europe to China.

Robert replied with instructions to proceed.

In September, Robert was in Hong Kong when he learned that Ayaou had given birth to a boy. On his way back to Peking, he stopped in Shanghai and stayed a few days.

He named his son Herbert. That afternoon, he carried the sleeping infant to the garden and was tempted to wake the child so he could show him what Guan-jiah had done to the place. He hoped Herbert would appreciate nature, but he never woke up.

Hours later, he said, "Herbert is quiet compared to Anna when she was this age."

They were in bed and Ayaou was resting her head on his stomach. She snorted. "You are not always here. Even Anna had her quiet times. When you go, Herbert will notice. Then he will wake the house. He knows who the master is."

"Herbert has a lot of dark hair. Have you been feeding him black sesame seeds?"

"No," she said. "I want his hair to be the same color as yours. When he is older, I will feed him golden sesame seeds."

"That won't work."

"Of course it will."

He wanted to laugh. This sounded more like the Ayaou he'd known in Ningpo. "It's not easy leaving," he said. "I'm sick of being alone."

"You are an important man," Ayaou replied. "We are proud of the work you are doing for China. With your rank and pay, you can afford to buy more concubines and have two or three in Peking, so you will not have to sleep alone."

"I know. Prince Kung has hinted the same thing." He shook his head. "That won't happen. I am determined that you will be my only lover. Besides, when I'm in Peking, I'm so busy, I wouldn't have time."

"That might not be wise," she said.

"I want to talk about where Herbert should go to school. Now that I am going to be a rich man, I want him to go to Eton, Harrow or Rugby."

"What do you mean?" she said. "What is Eton?"

"It is a boarding school in Britain where the children of the nobility and the wealthy go to live. Since the fathers are too busy to educate their boys properly, the children are sent to places like Eton."

"A school where Herbert would live?" She sounded worried. "But England is a smelly place. He will be lonely."

"Herbert will manage. Schools like Eton produce gentlemen. It is a luxury I never experienced. I was lucky to attend the Queen's University in Belfast. Our son will have the best education money can buy. When he is old enough, he will live at the school with boys who will one day rule the British Empire, and his best friend could be a member of the royal family."

Robert was back in Peking a week later to discover that a letter had arrived from Horatio detailing what he would do to purchase the fleet. Robert presented the imperial court with the entire list of items, such as cannons, rockets, and the number of foreign captains, operators and technicians that should be recruited. The court did not like the idea of having their navy crewed by foreigners.

Robert wrote to Lay. "There should be no more than fifty foreigners in the fleet, and I want them to train the Chinese.

"Once trained, the Europeans must leave. I do not see a need for the ships to arrive in China with full crews, since the goal is to have a Chinese navy."

The imperial court debated keeping Horatio Lay as China's acting agent in Europe. They had not forgotten Horatio's haughty, superior attitude.

Robert had put his reputation on the line by recommending Horatio for the job. If anything went wrong, it would be his loss of face. He realized that he had to find someone he could trust to act as his agent. Maybe he should find someone he had already hired to work for him in China, and send that man to London.

"Who else can work on our behalf?" Robert asked during a meeting with Prince Kung and the other Manchu ministers.

"Horatio Lay's father was in China for years as a diplomat for Britain. Horatio speaks Mandarin. He is still the inspector general. One day he will be back, and then I will return to Canton. He understands China's needs better than a stranger."

The imperial court approved the recommendation. Robert remembered Horatio's feelings about the Chinese being an inferior race and hoped he had not made a mistake.

He sent Horatio a letter certifying him as the agent for China then asked Prince Kung and the cabinet to consider whom the Chinese admiral was going to be that would work with Osborn.

Robert described the type of men who should be considered to crew the new navy in a report he submitted to the Tsungli Yamen. "The age of those young men must be more than eighteen and less than thirty," he wrote.

"Their jobs would be heavy in labor. I suggest selecting Hunannese as cannon operators, for they are known for their wits and bravery although they are small men.

"I also suggest that you pick Shandongnese for sailors, for they are strong in physiques and have a traditional way of sharing brotherhood and loyalty with men who speak their dialect.

"Last, I suggest that you pick Manchu bannermen for officers and key positions."

Filled with homesickness and a desperate need to see Ayaou, he returned to Shanghai. He had been away too long and was questioning what was more important: power and wealth or family and love. He wanted both. There had to be a way.

They were in bed and Ayaou was beside him on her stomach. There were worry lines on her forehead. While he had been gone, she had slimmed down. They had just attempted making love, but he could not perform.

"What is wrong?" she asked. "You have not had this problem since the fighting in Canton. You are always like a wild stallion. Have you found another woman? Have I lost the beauty you once saw? That would make sense. My family says I am no beauty and you are blind."

"There is no other woman, and you are still the one I dream of when I am alone. My mind is distracted by my job.

"Have you any idea what I have to do in Peking to get anything achieved? It's like swimming in sand. I have trouble sleeping waiting for the imperial turtles to move. I have urged the Manchu princes and the Dowagers to make faster decisions.

"Instead, they go hunting or write poetry or make ink paintings. When news arrived that a Chinese army has been slaughtered by the Taipings, the Dowagers hired an opera troop to perform at the Summer Palace and invited the royalty. They don't understand how important it is to train China's new navy so they are ready when the ships arrive. They do not even call the Taipings rebels. Instead, they call them Longhaired Bandits as if they are insignificant."

Ayaou crawled on top of him and started to rub her naked body against his. "Maybe this will give your thoughts a rest," she said.

Robert laughed. "It seems that you have worked your magic again," he said, and pulled her face to his to smother her with kisses. "I know there was a reason I had to come home." He kissed her neck and licked an ear.

A few months later, Horatio returned to China, and they met at the Shanghai, Imperial Maritime Customs building that faced the Huangpu River.

"You will be pleased to learn that I purchased the fleet," Horatio said. "Eight vessels. The flotilla should be here in a few weeks. I recruited six hundred British navy personnel to be led by Osborn."

"That's not what I directed you to do."

"You have forgotten your position, Robert," Horatio said in a scolding tone. "I am the Inspector General, and you work for me. There will be no need to find a Chinese admiral and illiterate Chinese peasants to fill out the crews. The Chinese are incapable of taking care of themselves, and owing to their childlike nature, they would never take to the discipline needed to create a sound navy."

"But, Horatio, this is not what Prince Kung and the Empress Dowagers expected."

Horatio held up a hand to stop him. "I also spent more than the budget you sent. I took out a loan for two-hundred-and-seventy-thousand taels in China's name to purchase the navy I felt China should have. After all, as Inspector General of

Customs, I will have control of the navy and the emperor will have to go through me to issue orders to Osborn."

"What have you done, Horatio?" Robert mind stopped working. He wanted to scream—to hit the man or break something. He felt hot and suddenly cold. A feeling of helplessness swept over him, and his face went numb. The rage in his chest was like a hurricane ready to wreak havoc. "I gave my word to the Dynasty," he said, and thought, I trusted the wrong man. I handed China to a jackal.

"It isn't that bad," Horatio replied. "We have faced worse. It will not take the Manchu long to know who rules China. God is on our side and everything will work out."

"Let me see that contract you signed with Osborn." Robert held out a hand.

Horatio rummaged on the desk and found it. "Here, I'm sure you will be impressed."

As Robert read the contract, a pain started to radiate from his chest, his stomach burned and his fingers tingled. The key elements were horrible. The worst parts were four and five.

Robert's voice trembled. "It says that it is understood that Osborn will have the right to refuse any form of an order, decree or edict that comes without your validation. It is also understood that you have the right to refuse any order, decree or edict from the imperial court that does not make sense to you."

"Precisely," Horatio said. "The Chinese are incapable of ruling themselves, so I have solved that problem."

Robert's vision blurred and he had trouble breathing. He had an urge to kill Horatio. His fingers curled. He imagined grabbing Horatio's neck and choking him. The Chinese imperial government had paid for the fleet, but this contract made Horatio the owner. The man was worse than a pirate was.

With an effort, he gained control over his emotions. "Horatio, there is no way that Prince Kung or the Dynasty will accept what you have done. Your blind ambition has undone both of us, because it is unrealistic that you can take control of China's modern navy. I am advising you to reconsider your actions for the sake of our positions in the customs service, and more importantly the future of British influence over China. Cancel the contract with Osborn and return to the original plan that was endorsed by both Dowagers and Prince Kung as regents for the young emperor."

"Calm down, Hart. I will not comply with such nonsense. I am the Inspector General of Imperial Chinese Customs. That is not your job. Do not forget that you were acting for me. The purchase contract stays as I wrote it, and Osborn will be the admiral of China's navy. Be advised, I am also writing a letter telling Prince Kung of this. He must know his place.

"When I resume my post as Inspector General, my goal is to control China's national revenue, and with Osborn in command of China's navy no one will stand in my way. I have seen with clarity what must be done, as God is my witness. With money and weapons at my command, I see myself as a minister for Britain ruling China. In the end, China will be converted to Christianity at my direction. These heathens will have no choice."

Robert realized that Horatio had no idea what he had done. The Chinese people would not sit still and allow their culture to be taken over by someone like him. There would be more rebellions. China would be torn into a hundred small countries. There would be great suffering and deaths. If the Chinese become Christians, it had to be their decision to convert and that might take centuries.

Horatio smiled. "I will also request a palace from Prince Kung. It must be equal to a cathedral where I will conduct services for the Church of England."

Robert was sure that someone high in the British government or someone in the Church of England had fueled this insanity. He had no idea if there was anything he could do to avoid this tragedy. The unexpectedness of it all had left him numb. He had to find time to think, and he couldn't do it here with this idiot watching him.

Chapter 49

Soon after Horatio arrived in Peking, Robert visited him. Since he had recovered from the shock of what Horatio had done, he was ready to deal with the Osborn issue.

He discovered that Horatio had been assigned a small house in the Chinese City near the Lock Hospital some distance from the Tsungli Yamen. Peking was divided into two cities, the Tartar City where the Forbidden City had been built and the Chinese City. Although one wall surrounded Peking, another wall divided the two sections.

Once inside the house, he saw that the furniture and floors were covered with a film of dust. Obviously, no one had cleaned the house before Lay's arrival.

The house had a small courtyard filled with dead bamboo and the garden walls extended twenty feet toward the sky making the courtyard feel as if it were the bottom of a dry well. It was depressing place.

Robert suspected that having Horatio stay in this house was meant as a slap in the face, and he wondered if Horatio realized that the Manchu were not pleased with him. Probably not. Just because Horatio spoke Mandarin, didn't mean he understood the culture.

They were alone in the front chamber, which only had a few chairs and a hardwood table. The walls were empty of art, and the room had a low, oppressive ceiling.

"Listen," Robert said. His voice bounced off the walls as if he were inside a metal drum. That stopped him, and he looked around. Odd, he thought. It took an effort to focus. It must have been irritating to live there

"China is not India," he said. "The imperial court is upset with your actions. You must reword Osborn's agreement. You were not a free agent acting on your behalf, but that is exactly what you did."

Horatio frowned. "There is no need to get angry. Once I explain, you will understand. I am doing this for God and Britain. God willing, this is the only way the Chinese can be saved. If I control the emperor, I control China. In this way, I will open every corner of China to Christian missionaries and to British influence. Between us, we will civilize these heathens."

The first thing Robert thought of was the opium that would follow or precede the Christians as they spread through China. "You are wrong," he said, keeping his voice under control, although he didn't feel calm. It would have been easy to yell at and then hit Horatio with a fist.

Instead, he said, "You will achieve the opposite if you attempt to force our God down the Chinese throat. That is wrong thinking. After China is healthy economically, there will be opportunities to achieve what you want by other means. It will take patience and maybe centuries to accomplish and there is no guarantee of success."

"What do you mean by 'our God'?" Horatio replied. "He is everyone's God and these heathens must learn that. There is only one true God."

"Did you hear what I said?"

Horatio waved a hand in dismissal. "This is an opportunity that I will not miss. I do not want to discuss anything else. You are a Christian. How can you challenge me? Matthew tells us to 'Go ye therefore, and teach all nations, baptizing them in the name of the Father, and of the Son, and of the Holy Ghost'."

"Why are you quoting from scripture?" Robert was stunned. Horatio's knife wounds may have healed, but his mind was damaged.

"The Lord created this opportunity and sent me to China to serve Him. It was the Lord's doing that I became the inspector general for the emperor of China."

Robert watched the blood rush into Horatio's face like a bush exploding into flames and thought of Jeremiah's words in the Bible. 'Behold, I am against the prophets, saith the Lord, that use their tongues, and say, He saith.'

He considered using that Bible quote, but realized it might be ignored. If anything, Horatio would become more heated in his religious zeal. He would reply with other passages from the Bible to defend himself. No, nothing would move Horatio from his path. He was committed. To fix this problem, Robert had to be cautious in what he quoted from the Bible and how he said it.

"It is our duty," Horatio said. "How am I going to do that unless I rule China through the child emperor? If it weren't for God's intervention, I would have been murdered when I was stabbed in Shanghai."

It would have been better if you had died, Robert thought. This fiasco wouldn't have happened.

"God was testing my faith like He tested Abraham by ordering him to sacrifice his son Isaac." Horatio's voice sounded as if he were pleading. "I was Isaac, and as my blood soaked into the earth, God spoke to me." He talked louder, and Robert saw tears running down his face. "I was allowed to live, because I promised to serve Him." Saliva flew from his mouth, as he shouted. "My purpose is to give China to God!"

Robert lowered his voice to a soothing tone. "And that is why you want to give China's navy to British officers?"

He knew that the Chinese didn't need saving—not Horatio's kind of salvation anyway. When Robert first arrived in China, he held similar opinions like most Christians that the Chinese were heathens.

As time passed and he learned about the culture, Robert knew that the Chinese had a strict moral code, which had its roots in Confucius's teachings about piety. Of course, there were flaws behind the mixed Confucius Taoist influence, but the shortcomings weren't any worse than those found in Christian doctrine were.

"You can't force the Chinese to believe in God out of the end of a cannon or rifle, Horatio," Robert said, as if he were talking to a child. "It also says in the Bible that 'Those that are busy minding other people's business probably do not have any worthwhile business of their own. Instead of being quiet, they're busy causing great disturbances among their neighbors.'

"Horatio, if you force the Chinese to believe in God, they will only believe what you want because they fear you. What you propose is no different from what the Spanish did during the Inquisition. Are you going to bring that horror to China? Isn't it bad enough that Hong Xiuquan, a converted Chinese

510

Christian, has caused so much suffering and death with his Taiping rebellion?"

Doubt appeared in Horatio's face. Robert dared not reveal what he was thinking. Instead, he forced his face and body to look concerned and caring. He wanted to pour water on that burning bush in Horatio's eyes, so he led Horatio back to the topic of China's navy. "Without the imperial court's permission," he said, "you can't bring the fleet to China."

After that, it wasn't long before Horatio agreed to renegotiate the written agreement he had forged with Osborn.

Robert thanked his father for making him memorize the Bible and all the lessons to understand what scripture meant. Without that knowledge, he was convinced he would not have succeeded against Horatio's religious fervor.

Every time Horatio quoted from scripture, Robert's mind had raced to think of the proper quote to counter him. It was like crossing a lake on thin, brittle ice. One wrong step and he would have plunged into the depths and lost.

A few days later, Horatio met with Prince Kung's representatives. Robert had persuaded Kung to let General Tseng Kuo-fan, a levelheaded dogged Chinese, and Li Hung-chang talk to Horatio. The suggestion was another move to convince the Dynasty that the Han Chinese could get the job done and be trusted.

The negotiations lasted a month. In the end, Horatio reluctantly agreed to discard his original thirteen item agreement with Osborn and establish a new one.

A Manchu commander, Cai Kuo-Hsiang, was assigned to be the admiral of the fleet with Osborn as his assistant. The new agreement stipulated that the fleet would be under the control of the governor of the province where any fighting was to take place. Horatio would have no say.

As Robert was getting ready to return to Shanghai, he received a report from the Yamen that Osborn had arrived in China and was refusing to take orders from a local governor.

He realized that this would be seen as an insult to the Dynasty, and that Prince Kung and the ministers would turn to him for help. Depressed, lonely and angry, he wrote Ayaou telling her that he would not be home as planned.

In June 1863, to add further injury to the insult and loss of face, Osborn sailed from Shanghai to Tientsin without orders. Leaving the flotilla anchored in the Bohai Gulf, he traveled overland to Peking to challenge the imperial court insisting that the original thirteen-item agreement be honored.

Robert was there when the confrontation took place with Prince Kung and the other ministers from the Tsungli Yamen. General Tseng Kuo-fan and Li Hung-chang were also there.

Osborn, with several of his officers, entered the Tsungli Yamen's main audience chamber. The ministers stood along the walls beside the armed guards and watched.

Osborn was a tall imposing athletic looking man. He was dressed in his full dress uniform with a chest full of medals. His face was clean-shaven and his hair cut short. He did not nod or show any sign of respect. Instead, he marched across the room and stopped in front of Prince Kung, who was seated in an intricately carved rosewood chair.

Several bannermen guards stepped forward from their positions against the walls. Kung lifted a hand and stopped them, and they stepped back. The prince stared at Osborn without expression with eyes that were cold, dark stones.

Without waiting, Osborn said, "The only man I will take orders from will be Horatio Lay. That's the only way I will allow the ships I command to be part of the Chinese navy."

Robert felt his face flush hot. He wanted to slap Osborn or better yet cut out the man's tongue. This insult could lead to another war with Britain and the other foreign powers. It could fuel the Manchu conservatives to sound the battle cry that died when Su Shun was beheaded. Millions of lives were at stake. What a fool Osborn was.

After Prince Kung heard the interpretation, he didn't say a word. Robert could tell he was angry by a slight tightening around the eyes. The tension in the room was like the silence before an earthquake.

General Tseng Kuo-fan's battle armor rattled as he threw himself on the floor in front of Prince Kung. He kowtowed several times and requested approval to have Osborn beheaded. "I will do it myself," he said, "so we don't have to wait for the executioner."

Tseng Kuo-fan was not known as the 'Head Chopper' for nothing. Robert had heard that in battles against the Taipings, he was ruthless and took no prisoners. Those who were captured lost their heads.

From the look in Prince Kung's eyes, Robert guessed that he was about to agree. It was time to intercede. As much as he regretted what he was about to do, he saw no other choice.

He knew that violence was not going to solve this problem. The British officer had to leave Peking alive and in good health. Robert was thinking furiously how he was going to save the Dynasty's face. It wasn't going to be easy.

If Osborn had talked to the Queen of England like this, he would have ended in the Tower of London and possibly hanged for sedition. If he had been defiant to a superior officer in the British navy, he could have been keelhauled and his carcass hung from the yardarm of the flagship of the fleet, but this was taking place in China and there was a double standard involved.

Robert stepped forward. "I agree with General Tseng Kuo-fan," he said. "But if a farmer chops off the toe of an eight hundred-pound sleeping bear, which has already destroyed half his crop, what will happen to the farmer?"

"Horatio told me about you, Hart," Osborn said. "I don't speak Chinese, so I don't know what you are saying. However, from what I learned, I suspect you are telling them not to listen to me. I will have none of that. Your loyalty should be to Britain, not China. I want you to make these heathens understand that if they do not do as I demand, Britain will spank them as they have never been spanked before."

Blood surge into Robert's head, and he turned to confront Osborn. "You fool," he said in English. "I'm trying to keep that head on your shoulders. You have no idea what mess you have stirred by your arrogance."

"I refuse to hear such talk," Osborn replied. "You are a traitor if you support these little yellow men."

Robert took a calming breath. It was all he could do to maintain control. "You are in Peking with a handful of men. Thousands of Manchu bannermen that guard the emperor are stationed near the Tsungli Yamen. Even the guards stationed around this building number in the hundreds. Do you think your officers will be able to fight their way out once your head hits the floor?"

"They wouldn't dare," Osborn said. "I am an officer in the royal navy."

"You are wrong. Harry Parkes made a similar mistake and almost lost his head. I know, because I negotiated the deal that saved his life, but the twenty men with him still died."

"You can't speak to me like that," Osborn said. His face was bloated with anger.

"Shut your mouth, Osborn, and let me save that foolish ass of yours from a certain death. God knows I shouldn't."

"You fool!" Osborn replied.

Without warning, he hit Osborn on the jaw as hard as he could. He hit him again on the nose and a third time in the gut. The naval officer staggered back and went to his knees with blood gushing from a split lip and nose.

The other British officers stepped forward, and the armed bannermen moved away from the walls. The room was a powder keg ready to explode.

Robert put a foot against Osborn's chest and shoved. The British naval officer sprawled on the floor unconscious. He then held up a hand to stop the other British officers. "Listen to me," he said. "This idiot was going to get you all killed. Take him and leave. Do it now!"

When they hesitated, Robert pointed a finger at the door and in a commanding voice said, "Consider that my rank in China is equal to a general. Osborn is only a ship's captain. I outrank him. Get him out of here, and do it now! Osborn has just insulted China's emperor. What would you do if a foreigner barged into Buckingham palace and insulted the queen by making such demands?"

The British officers looked at the stern faces of the Manchu guards around the perimeter of the room as if gauging their chances. Then they studied General Tseng Kuo-fan, who had moved to stand beside Robert. The Chinese general looked as if he could chew iron, and he had a wicked looking sword hanging from his belt.

The British officers hurried forward, picked Osborn off the floor then carried him from the room.

Robert turned to Prince Kung. He now knew what had to be done to save the emperor's face. "I have been honored to have the support of great men like General Tseng Kuo-fan to purchase a modern navy for China," he said, "but I must now request that you cancel the purchase of the fleet and send it back to Europe. It is the only way to let the world know that

China will not swallow insults from people like Osborn or Horatio Lay."

Robert lowered his voice. "I stand with General Tseng Kuo-fan and support his request to behead Osborn. However, if we do, we will have a war with the foreign powers again. Do not forget that China is recovering from the last Opium War, and the Taipings are still a threat. I urge you to consider my words." Robert went down on one knee and bowed his head in submission. General Tseng Kuo-fan joined him.

Tseng Kuo-fan glanced at Robert and said softly so only Robert could hear. "When the nightingale sings, its voice is sweet and true but the bird has the talons of a hawk. You are everything they say you are." He made a slight nod to Robert.

Prince Kung acted immediately and dismissed Osborn and the entire contingent of six hundred British sailors. It wouldn't be until November 1863 that the ships would return to England and it would cost China another three-hundred-seventy-five thousand taels. Some of the money would be regained when China sold the fleet to other European countries.

When all was done, the final cost was one-point-seven-million.

"Ayaou," Robert wrote late that night, "I'm shattered. My misjudgment recommended Horatio to Prince Kung. Until now, the ministers and the Dowagers put their trust in me believing I could handle the most difficult tasks.

"But now I have failed miserably. Although no one in the government has said a word about it being my fault, I accept the guilt. Clearly, I can do nothing to reverse this situation. What I must do is work hard to preserve my honor.

"Besides, thanks to this fiasco and others like it, I've missed being home when our son was born. What have I done to deserve this? When Anna was born, I was also not there when I wanted to be by your side.

"When it is late at night and I'm working at my desk, there aren't any ghosts to see my tears and hear me sob. I miss you and our family. I crave your sweet, sensible voice to set me right as you have done in the past."

Robert sealed the letter and set it aside to send to Shanghai with the next courier. He folded his arms on the desk and rested his head on them. The depression and the loneliness were more than he could take.

What a fool he had been. Life had seemed complex when he had lived in secret with his two concubines in Ningpo. Yet, that time was nothing compared to now. He had been twenty then and all he had to worry about was the safety of Ayaou and Shao-mei. He could see now how silly he had been agonizing over two women being in love with him. He should have welcomed their embraces. Instead, like a fool, he had almost gone crazy.

Now he was twenty-eight, and he felt the weight of an ancient empire on his shoulders. He also worried what was going to happen to China once Horatio Lay resumed his duties as Inspector General.

He thought of Captain Patridge, Parkes, and Sir John Bowring. All had acted to further the interests of Britain and to fill their pockets with Chinese gold and silver leaving China almost bankrupt and a wreck. They were like intestinal parasites destroying the body of the host. He had met few foreigners willing to help China survive.

A pain stabbed deep into his guts, and he rubbed his stomach. He had no idea what he was going to do. Why couldn't he be like his father and sit down daily with Ayaou and the children for supper? Clearly, he would never live the life he had once wanted. With every passing day, the fate of China seemed his responsibility and his alone. Why couldn't this burden belong to someone else?

Robert returned to Shanghai to be with his family expecting that Horatio Lay would soon be sending him back to Canton where he would resume his old post. He almost welcomed the change. At least in Canton, the responsibilities would not be as daunting. There was also the possibility that Horatio would replace him with someone that would do as he was told, and Robert might get his old job in Ningpo back after all.

He wondered how long he would have to wait before the orders arrived sending him south? Should he tell Guan-jiah to start packing for the return trip to Canton? If that happened, at least he would have time to read and discuss Chinese poetry with Ayaou.

On November 29, Robert was surprised when he received word from Prince Kung that Horatio had been officially dismissed by the Yamen from his position. He was no longer inspector general, and Prince Kung wanted Robert to take Horatio's place.

He was ordered to move to Peking and take up residence immediately. Prince Kung had already selected a house for him in the same Hutong where his palace was located. Robert's pay would increase by another eight hundred pounds a year.

He wrote a reply. "Prince Kung, I cannot accept this position for I have failed you. I am responsible for what happened with Horatio and Osborn. I ask that I serve a punishment instead."

It was two in the morning several days later. He had worked late and hoped Ayaou would be sleeping, but she wasn't. Once he was under the blanket, she rolled over and pressed against him and he discovered she was naked.

"Ayaou, I don't feel like making love," he said. "Prince Kung has not responded to my letter. It is all I can think about."

Ayaou would not take no for an answer, so he surrendered. After they finished making love, she wrapped her arms around him.

He ran a hand down one of her long, slender legs and marveled at how smooth she felt compared to his sandpaper skin.

"The prince has not replied for a reason," she said. "Accepting the position of Inspector General is your punishment." He felt her warm breath on his neck as she whispered in his ear. The silky sound of her voice excited him. He shivered. "It is your responsibility to clear up the mess that Horatio and Osborn made? Would you trust anyone else?"

She made sense, which endeared Robert to her even more, but he still had doubts and was racked with regrets. "I'd rather be kissing you," he said. "I have considered quitting. I am sure the British would take me back as an interpreter. No foreigner knows the Chinese as well as I do. They would assign me to one of the consulates. Maybe Ningpo again or we could stay in Shanghai. I would probably be in charge. With luck, maybe even Hong Kong. We would have to give up this house and the servants. We'd still have Guan-jiah though."

"We cannot go back," she said. "Your fate has been decided. You are to serve China. Running away will only make things worse."

"But we would always be together," he said, knowing that he had already lost to her wisdom.

"When China is at war again with the foreign devils, you would feel the blame and our love would suffer."

With regret, Robert saw that there was no turning back to that simpler time in Ningpo. An old ache appeared deep inside where his broken heart from the loss of Shao-mei had gone into hiding. He looked around expecting to see her in the room watching.

"What is it, Robert?" Ayaou asked.

"Nothing." He rolled over and kissed her while his hands became busy.

To Robert's surprise, Osborn came to see him in Shanghai, and the bruises that he had inflicted on Osborn's face in Peking were still visible.

He met the man in his first floor study, a room furnished with a sturdy teak desk and chairs. One wall was lined with shelves filled with books and scrolls, and a Turkish wool carpet covered half the floor, while a latticed window opened on a lush garden filled with trees, flowering plants and a stand of bamboo.

He had Guan-jiah and two large servants stay in the room standing in the shadows near the door.

"Don't accept the position of Inspector General," Osborn said. "If you do, I'll spread word when I return to Britain that you were behind a conspiracy to oust Horatio and take his job. I'll make people believe that you long desired his position and planned his downfall." Osborn's smile was smug. "This is the only way for you to avoid being considered a traitor. I will ruin your reputation."

Robert was furious but hid his emotions behind an inscrutable mask he'd spent years perfecting. He was tempted to have Guan-jiah and the servants beat the man with the stout sticks they held.

"I appreciate your concern," he replied. "However, others have threatened me before and did not succeed. You can be assured that if you hadn't come to see me, I would have resigned before accepting the position."

Robert knew that wasn't true, but he said it anyway. Ayaou had already convinced him he couldn't quit. "Since you have seen fit to come here and threaten me, I have changed my mind, and I thank you for that. By the way, how is your nose?"

Osborn sputtered his indignation. He took a step forward, his face full of purple anger. His fists started to come up, but Guan-jiah and the two servants grabbed Osborn from behind and escorted him from the house.

It was ironic that Osborn had stiffened his resolve. He refused to allow Horatio or anyone like him to use China for their personal benefit. Horatio's younger brother William had been right all those years ago, when he had warned Robert about his brother. If Robert had listened, he would never have recommended Horatio as China's agent in Europe.

He wasn't concerned about the Prime Minister or the Queen believing that he was a traitor. Robert had friends working in the British legation. He knew the governor of Hong Kong. He had helped save the life of Harry Parkes, and had earned respect from James Bruce, the 8th Earl of Elgin.

That night in bed, Robert said, "Ayaou, we should find a cellar like the one in Ward's Shanghai house where we first made love and have a honeymoon."

"What is a honeymoon?"

Robert laughed and kissed her. For some reason, he felt like an adolescent again. He explained.

She sat up. "I have a surprise." She left the bed and started to rummage in the wardrobe. When she turned around, there was a mischievous smile on her face. She had her hands behind her back as if she were hiding something. "Do you know where the root cellar is?"

He nodded.

She said, "Wait five minutes then go there."

"Ayaou, what are you doing?" he asked, as she hurried from the room. "It's late." Since she was gone, his words faded. He had no choice but to get dressed and follow.

A few minutes later in the root cellar, he discovered baskets of yams and bags of rice. Manure clung to the produce. It looked and smelled like his memories of their first sexual encounter.

The low ceiling sloped toward the far end of the cellar where a dim light leaked around a stack of burlap bags filled with rice. The place reminded him of that night. It was like déjà vu. He remembered the rat that had run across his boot. Would there be a rat too?

Smiling, he walked the length of the root cellar and had to get down on all fours to squeeze around the fifty-pound bags of rice and into the narrow space beyond.

Once Robert crawled past the rice, light brushed away the gloom. He saw Ayaou sitting against a wall with her knees pulled to her chest. She looked just like she had eight years ago. She was even dressed in the same dancing clothes. She had lost weight since having Herbert, and the clothes fit. The top of her head was inches from the close ceiling. She turned the lantern to its softest illumination and put the light on top of a small barrel nestled in the corner behind her.

"Welcome to my secret place—this sanctuary of our love. This is where I have been going when I want to be alone and remember."

"I thought you burned those clothes after the way I treated you in Canton."

"How could I do that, Robert Hart?" she said. "After all, I know why you are here."

He didn't know what to say. He shifted around uncomfortably in the tight space until he faced her.

"I believe you are here to make me your concubine," she said.

"I'm not here to cause you unhappiness." He remembered his words from that night, but he wasn't nervous this time. If she wanted to relive their first moments together, he was willing to take that journey with her. "It is too bad your father has to sell you. You must hate it."

"I do not hate it," she replied, shaking her head. "My father hates what he does to feed his family. He has to sell us. He is not the only man in the village who does that. He has to treat us like hens and fish in the market. He cannot afford to be soft hearted."

Instead of seeing tears in her eyes like before, Robert detected a sexual hunger, and he felt the same way. "But he's selling you to a stranger."

"This time my master will not be a stranger." There wasn't any uncertainly in her eyes. She knew what she was doing.

"How much will your price be?"

"I do not know. My father said I am no beauty. My skin is too dark, and I am too thin. My chest is a washboard." She lifted a foot. "My feet were never bound. I do not have a pale moon face, and that is the requirement for selling at a high price to a Chinese man."

Their legs touched and the excitement was more than he could handle. He didn't know how much longer he could play this game.

"There is an empty rice bag in the corner behind you," she said. "Hang it in the opening so the light does not leak out."

He twisted around to do it.

"Do you think that you would like to be my master?" she asked.

Robert reached for one of her hands and held it between both of his. Her flesh was hot. They both knew exactly what they wanted.

"My father will decide soon to which man I will be sold. Can you afford my price?"

He had said 'no' in 1855. This time his answer was different. "Yes, because I am the Inspector General of China's Customs Service. I work for an emperor. No one will beat my price for the woman I want."

"I like that," she said.

"I will never abandon you like you once feared."

"I know that now," she said. "You are a good man. No Chinese man or any other foreign devil would promise that and mean it. I am lucky you found me."

He couldn't wait any longer. The desire was spreading through him like hot lava, and he pulled her closer.

"Hurry," she said, throwing her arms around his neck.

"I'm going to kiss you," he replied.

She leaned away from him. "I am not sure I will like that." She pouted, and her lips looked inviting. "My father had me practice kissing by sucking a carrot."

"A carrot." He wanted to laugh. He remembered this conversation.

"Yes. He said barbarians liked it."

"What did he mean?" He was ready to burst. He hadn't wanted her this bad in years.

"He said the carrot is the barbarian's tongue."

"I see. So, you didn't like it."

"No, my father ruined my appetite for carrots for good."

"That's a pity."

"How are you going to kiss me?"

"I'll show you."

"Do I have to suck?"

"You don't have to do anything."

"That will be nice," she said.

He kissed her nose, her cheeks, her ears and her neck where he lingered. Then he took her face between both hands, held her, and kissed her warm, moist lips. That kiss was nothing like the first time. It was better.

"I want more, Robert Hart. I have always wanted more."

Robert slipped his tongue into her mouth. "Kiss me back," he said.

She became the aggressor, and they peeled off her thin layers of silk together.

When he started to undo the buttons on his shirt, she slapped his hands away. "I will do that," she said, and he watched the hunger in her eyes explode as she unbuttoned his shirt and slipped her hands inside to explore his chest and back.

He groaned, and said, "This is torture. I can't hold myself much longer."

Her laughter sounded like chimes. "So much hair," she said, as she ran her fingers through it. "It no longer feels strange like it did then." She threw herself on top of him pushing him onto his back then pressed her lips against his.

His hands explored her muscular, naked legs and ended on her firm bottom. There wasn't much room, but he managed to pull off his shirt and crawl out of his pants and for an instant, their lips parted.

"Touch me everywhere." Her voice was husky and full of experienced lust. "I like the way it feels when you do that."

They rolled over until she was on the bottom, and their naked bodies mingled. He kissed her breasts and ran his tongue around her nipples, and she tasted salty.

"Now," she said, "make me yours again."

The sexual heat flooded through him. He thrust into her while grunting like a stallion. After she gasped and her body convulsed, he rolled her over and entered her from the rear. He took hold of her hips and pulled her into him. After several deep thrusts, it was over.

Sweaty and exhausted, they slept in each other's arms. This time when he awoke, she was still there and there was a warm quilted blanket covering them against the chill.

The floor creaked above their heads and Robert heard a small voice say," Ba Ba." It was Anna looking for him.

Before Horatio left China, he also came to see Robert. They met alone in the same study.

"I thought I could trust you," Horatio said. "That's why I recommended that you fill my job while I was recovering from the knife wounds. Why did you turn the Dynasty against me?"

"You will never understand," Robert replied. "I didn't sneak in and plot to replace you. Your arrogance did that. You speak excellent Mandarin but you do not understand the Chinese. If I were still in Canton in my old position, things would have turned out worse. Osborn would have lost his head and you might have been executed. There would have been another war more devastating than the two Opium Wars."

Horatio reached in his jacket and pulled out a Bible. "You are not only a traitor, but you are a fool." He opened his Bible to a page marked with a red ribbon. "Paul said that part of our love of brethren includes restoring one who is overtaken in a trespass. You have done me wrong, Hart." He looked at the Bible and read. "Brethren, if a man is overtaken in any trespass, you who are spiritual should restore him in a spirit of gentleness. Look to yourself, lest you too be tempted."

He closed the Bible. "I'm returning to England. I will do so in a spirit of gentleness. I will pray for your soul, so you might walk with God instead of cavorting with these Chinese devils." Horatio left.

Robert realized that Horatio's words and thoughts were examples of how the foreign powers thought and why they were raping China with opium and modern weapons. The people of China deserved better. He resolved to be the man to set things right or die trying. Thinking about the years ahead was exhausting. How many more challenges would there be?

Chapter 50

Now that he was inspector general he had to fix Horatio's mess, and one challenge to overcome was the Yamen's memories of Horatio's bully tactics. Fortunately, Robert understood the virtue of patience.

His first task was to write letters to his commissioners in China's major ports.

"We are all in China's service. Information is important if we are to do our jobs efficiently, which means we must stay on top of national events and politics in every province. I'm directing you to keep an eye and an ear open in your regions. To do that, you must cultivate friendships among the Chinese people."

He remembered his first visit to a tea and bathhouse in Ningpo. At the time, he had only been with Shao-mei and Ayaou for a few months. Ayaou caught him in the kitchen one morning bathing with a small cloth in a large bucket that barely fit his feet.

"I have watched you do this before, Robert," she had said, as she stood in the kitchen doorway. "I kept my mouth shut, because I thought this is what you wanted. Why not go to the bathhouse? It costs the price of three eggs, and the water is clean and hot."

That was the day he discovered China had bathhouses.

Ayaou had guided him there. Then he stood in a long line waiting to get in. The gatekeeper had been a burly, older woman with the arms of a wrestler and stumps for legs. She had demanded that he take off his clothes and hand them to her for cleaning.

It had been quite an experience. It hadn't felt humorous at the time, but now he chuckled at the memories before dipping the pen into the puddle of ink to continue the letter.

"To gather this vital information properly, I suggest you spend time cultivating friendships with the Chinese in local teahouses, which are fountains of information when one is a master in the art of conversation. I also expect that you will find the nearest bathhouse and take a public bath with the Chinese once a week.

"We have all talked about how to do this, so I am confident you will succeed with this task without hesitation.

"Discover what is going on and how people feel about current events and send a report to me once a month. Take care to send these reports with trusted couriers since we do not want this information falling into the wrong hands."

Robert had learned the art of conversation while living with Ayaou and Shao-mei in Ningpo. While hiring his people, he had taught his men the same methods. Soon, he planned to launch a Chinese language school for his foreign employees.

During those long months when he had traveled extensively through China hiring and firing people while setting up offices in all the major trading ports, he had taken each of his people to a teahouse. He had them observe and learn how to talk to the Chinese from the lowest peasant to the wealthiest merchant. The most important skill was to learn how to listen and interpret meaning. The challenge was to ask simple, short questions that resulted in long revealing answers.

It took several months before regular reports started to arrive from his men, and what he discovered was not good. The Dynasty was weak and the provinces troubled.

The problem was that the central government was limited. All of the high provincial officials, who could be removed at any time at the pleasure of the emperor, were appointed from Peking.

However, once appointed, the governors of provinces and cities had the power of kings, which meant that Peking had little control over anything, even taxation. Robert had learned how difficult that was when he had confronted Kuan-wen, the governor-general of Hankow.

Since then, he had learned that the best man wasn't always chosen for a high-ranking position. The Manchu distrusted the Han Chinese and many times when a Han was the best man for the job, he was passed-over for a Manchu, who was usually corrupt, incompetent or both.

Silence was the best advice for a Han to follow when a Manchu official could have him beheaded or assassinated for protesting or criticizing too much. It was safer for a Han Chinese to keep his lips sealed even if his superior was heading blindly for disaster.

Robert, on the other hand, did not hold back. He was honest with Prince Kung and the other ministers at the Tsungli Yamen.

"Robert, you must take care," Prince Kung said. "At times, your criticisms are too sharp. The Iron Hats may have been defeated and their leader Su Shun beheaded, but there are still conservative ministers. All it takes is one to think you speak too loudly. If he wants to silence you, I cannot protect you from a bribed servant and a vial of poison in your rice porridge."

Kung's warning alarmed Robert. After that, he took more care in what he said. Thinking of death also reminded him that he didn't like living alone. Since he was spending more time in Peking than Shanghai, he decided to bring Ayaou and the children to the capital.

He would keep the house in Shanghai and return with his family as circumstances dictated. It was 1863 when Guan-jiah was told to move the family to Peking and Robert was twenty-eight, Guan-jiah twenty-seven and Ayaou twenty-four. Robert had been in China for almost a decade.

Within weeks, Ayaou, Anna, and his son Herbert arrived in Peking. He didn't want to be separated from his Chinese family again.

On the other hand, he knew that his Irish family expected him to find a wife in Ireland, which would make his father and mother happy.

However, no one in Ireland knew Ayaou existed, and he dreaded the day when he told his friends and family about her, which was a topic he had avoided for years.

The thought that they might learn about his private life from a stranger bothered him. When he had been in interpreter working for the British, he had been almost invisible. Now that he was working for the emperor of China in a powerful position, he was standing in the sunshine for everyone to see, and it felt as if he were being examined under a microscope.

If his family discovered that he had offered money to buy Ayaou, his father might disown him. When he had fled Ireland for China to escape the scandal that took place while he was still attending the University of Belfast, he did not imagine that he might make things worse. Compared to Belfast where he had often been drunk and seduced too many women, buying one as if she were a brick to warm a bed would crush his father.

The truth was that for the first time since arriving in China, he felt fulfilled. He knew that he should be the first to tell his father about Ayaou, but he was not ready.

"Guan-jiah," he said one morning before leaving for work, "I don't want other foreign devils to know about Ayaou or the children. I want my family to be safe. They are no one else's business. I'm counting on you to help make that happen."

"I understand, master," the eunuch replied. "If the Longhaired Bandits discovered that you have two children, they could be used as pawns to reach you."

Ayaou had never been to Peking. His boat girl looked as if she had been beached and didn't know what to do. She walked around the house in a daze. Robert imagined she was stupefied, considering that she had lived most of her life with a large family on a small boat with no servants. Now she had two mansions with a different staff in each one.

Her first day in Peking was spent in bed with Robert. The second day he spent some time with Anna and Herbert. Anna was four, and Herbert had taken his first steps and was tottering around the house getting into everything. Poor Fooyen was at her wit's end keeping up with the children.

The house in Shanghai was visible from the street. The one in Peking was in the Tartar City near the emperor's palace and was hidden behind high walls, and there wasn't just one building. He had a building for meeting people. A structure for storage. A main house for his family. Another for guests. Behind the buildings, there was a garden with a teahouse. It was small compared to Prince Kung's estate but large by most standards.

Robert decided to teach Anna the violin. "Ayaou," he said, "I want you to teach her Chinese songs and to play the Pee Pah. I'm also considering getting a piano for her. I want her to play the piano too."

"A piano?" she said. Robert described what a piano was. She'd never seen one.

"I'm replacing our literature discussions that we once shared with Shao-mei with politics."

"Politics?" She looked confused. "I don't understand."

"This is Peking, Ayaou, the capital of an empire, and you are going to be my spy."

"I'm no spy," she said, and he could hardly hear her voice.

He took her by the hand and led her out of their bedroom into the privacy of a garden. He stopped by a carp filled pond.

The first-time Robert had seen Prince Kung's pond he had been fascinated. "These fish bring the owner luck." Kung said.

He had watched as the prince trailed a hand in the water and a monster black and gold carp at least three feet long drifted from the shadowy depths to rub against his fingers.

"This one knows me. If you feed them, Robert, some are smart enough to learn how to eat from your hand. I will send a work crew to your house to build a pond similar to mine, and a few of these carp will be a gift."

Once Ayaou and Robert were seated on a boulder beside the pond, he took her face between his hands. "Are you ready to listen?" he asked.

Comprehension trickled back into her eyes. She nodded but had trouble making eye contact, and he noticed she was having trouble breathing and kept swallowing.

"I am not going to ask you to sneak into the emperor's palace, Ayaou. I want to discover what the common people think about what is going on in China. I want to know what they feel about the Dynasty and the Taipings and the foreigners and opium and anything else you discover."

She looked unsure. "I do not know anything about the emperor and the royals. The emperor is like a god; like the sun, and the center of the earth. How does someone like me understand that?"

"You're going to learn," he said. "Your job is to listen to what people are saying when you are out shopping or having tea. All you have to do is ask the right questions then listen and tell me what you hear."

"I am not sure how I can do that," she said.

"This is important, Ayaou. You were doing something similar for me in Canton. Have you forgotten already? I am a foreign devil. I cannot blend in. Besides, my guards would scare everyone senseless. The royals would never try. However, you can. No one will know you are my lover. The common people on the streets or in the teahouses will talk when you are standing or sitting next to them. Because you are one of them, you are invisible. I know you can do this. You are a lot smarter than you think."

"I thought I was only here to give you children and keep your bed warm at night."

"You are more than a bed warmer," he said. "I thought you knew that already. I trust you. We are a family."

"I cannot—"

"No, Ayaou. I will not accept that answer. You will become my eyes and ears on the streets of Peking as you once were in Canton."

"But they will see that I am a boat person and treat me as if I were not there." Her eyes were large and full of fear. "This is the city of the royals. They rule China. I could be squashed like a bug."

"Precisely," he said. "That is the idea. Not to be squashed but to listen."

From that day on, after Robert got home, he talked with Ayaou about what she'd heard. The more they talked the better listener she became and the dazed expression and the fear vanished. She became more alert and surer of herself. She wanted to please him and went out of her way to shop and gather information. In time, she made an excellent spy.

Robert's job pulled him in all directions. Not only was he to be at Prince Kung's side when summoned to consult on treaties with foreign nations, but he was responsible for handling day-to-day details for his staff. He attended weddings and became a godfather to many children scattered throughout China. He even had to deal with deaths that took place in customs and preside over funerals.

He also handed out justice. When one of his assistant commissioners, A. J. Campbell, had a sexual liaison with another man's wife, a written complaint arrived from Shanghai, and Robert took his family with him when he went to investigate. He left Ayaou and the children at the Shanghai house when he went to confront Campbell at the Imperial Maritime Customs building on the Bund near the Huangpu River.

Campbell was a large Scott with a ruddy complexion. He came from a middle-class merchant family. Like Robert, Campbell had done well at a Queen's college. He had been recruited to work in the British consulate in Canton where Robert met him and later talked him into leaving the British to work for China.

Robert knew the man wanted more out of life than being a clerk. Campbell had ambitions, but how far was he willing to go to achieve them, and some men were never satisfied with the love and companionship of one woman.

Robert knew what that was like. He had faced a similar temptation when Shao-mei had been alive. Before Shao-mei, there had been Me-ta-tae then Willow, one of Patridge's concubines. Those two brief trysts had almost been his undoing. Maybe Campbell had fallen for the same temptation too many times.

"I heard that you had an affair with a colleague's wife," he said.

Campbell's eyes widened. "Who said that?" He saw fear in the man's eyes. Campbell glanced beyond Robert at the two Manchu bannermen standing guard by the door.

"Did you?" Robert asked. Watch the eyes, he thought. They are a window into a man's soul.

Campbell's eyes shifted to the floor. "Of course not, Inspector General. Such behavior is unacceptable. I don't even know who you are talking about."

Robert named the wife and husband. They were both Italians and the husband worked in Campbell's office.

"I didn't sleep with her. Someone must be out to destroy my reputation—to ruin my career."

Robert always made it a point to study the language of the body when he was talking to someone. In this way, he would know when a person was becoming bored or maybe wasn't telling the truth. When Campbell said he had not had an affair with the Italian's wife, his eyes had shifted about as if searching for a place to hide. That was a strong sign that the man was not being honest.

If it turned out that Campbell was lying, he would have to pay for his deceit. Robert couldn't stand the thought of a liar working for him, and he had to find out.

He talked to a few trusted friends and asked them to dig deeper. He then sent Ayaou to talk to Campbell's Chinese servants. "Be discreet, Ayaou. I don't want Campbell to discover that I don't believe him." He managed to have Ayaou show up as another cook to work in Campbell's kitchen.

A few days later, Ayaou reported. "Two of the servants say he was seduced by the Italian's wife, and she has been to the house many times. One servant said she has heard them grunting and moaning like cows in his bedroom."

Other witnesses were found and the evidence said that Campbell had lied. If the man was bold enough to lie to Robert, what else was he willing to do?

He sentenced Campbell to three months imprisonment and a fine of one thousand yuan. After the time was served, he was reduced in rank and moved to another office hundreds of miles from Shanghai. Robert talked to the commissioner of that office and warned him to keep an eye on Campbell. Since he had to keep his people in line, Robert had no choice. If Campbell had been honest, the punishment would not have been as severe.

It bothered Robert each time a rare case of this type surfaced. He'd interviewed everyone in the service and hired men based on his judgment. In Campbell's case, he'd taken a liking to the man. Campbell laughed easily and always had a ready smile that lit his freckled face.

Prince Kung often walked into Robert's office without warning, and this visit was no different as he slipped in unannounced.

"If I had another hundred like you," the prince said, "we could resolve all the problems in China."

Robert, engrossed in a report from Canton, was startled but recovered quickly. "That's a big reputation to live up to," he replied, and realized that he would never let Kung down intentionally.

"My spies have informed me that the Longhaired Bandits have put a price of one-hundred-thousand taels on your head," Kung said.

"How could they know about me?" Robert asked.

"It seems that maybe there is an Englishman who works for them as a spy, and this man told them you were behind the agreement that led to the French and English military joining the Imperial army that led to the Taiping defeat near Shanghai." The prince noticed a new vase sitting on a bookshelf. He walked over and picked it up. It was imperial yellow with blue stallions decorating the sides.

"It was a gift from the Empress Dowager Tzu Hsi," Robert said.

"Better than her ink paintings," the prince replied. He nodded his approval and put the vase back. He looked around and noticed the flowers.

"She sent the flowers too," Robert said.

"She enjoys working in her gardens," the prince said.

"What else did your people learn?"

Kung plopped into a chair in front of the desk. "This Englishman also told the Longhaired Bandits that you were behind buying the modern weapons China is getting from Europe and America. We are trying to discover how he gets his information. He even knew you were responsible for General Tseng Kuo-fan being given the job to defeat the rebels. Hong Xiuquan, the leader of the Longhaired Bandits, is unhappy about that, because Head Chopper is winning battles."

"Could this be the same Englishman that was behind the Forbidden City thefts?"

"That is possible," Kung replied.

"He may know that I was behind stopping the thefts. He may want revenge."

"If so, he is doubly dangerous. This Englishman has convinced the Longhaired Bandits that you need to be assassinated. For that reason, your bodyguard will be increased from a dozen to one hundred bannermen. General Jung Lu has been informed and will select his best men. From now on, your house will be guarded until the Taiping threat is eliminated."

"I'm curious about this man working for the Taipings," Robert said. "Did your people get his name or describe what he looked like?" He had thought that when Ward died he had rid himself of the only man wanting him dead. It seemed he was wrong.

"Is this man large with red hair?" he asked, thinking of Burgevine, Ward's second-in-command. Burgevine had been close friends with the Devil Solider. It would make sense if he were seeking revenge. Had Burgevine somehow found out about his deal with General Li Hung-chang to kill Ward? No, that wasn't possible. Burgevine was not clever enough to make that kind of discovery. He was a brute with low intelligence.

"My spies never saw this Englishman," Prince Kung replied. "He is like a ghost. Robert, cooperate with your guards. I have heard that you tend to walk ahead of them even when you are urged to stay close. China cannot afford to lose you, and I do not want to lose a friend. Stop walking. Use a sedan chair. That is not a suggestion."

There were others that might want to do him harm. He had not forgotten Payne Hollister. Because of Robert's indiscretion in Ningpo with Me-ta-tae, Hollister held a grudge against him and had written that letter to Harry Parkes in Canton in an attempt to ruin his reputation.

Then there was Osborn and Horatio Lay. Both men had reason to seek revenge. In addition, there were the English merchants he had rejected and defeated in a London court for seeking favors.

Good god, Robert thought, it seemed enemies never ceased popping up when one gained rank and power. He thought of himself as a simple, honest, hard worker from Ireland. It had never occurred to him that success included this sort of danger.

After that, he couldn't go anywhere without a squad of bannermen. It was only in the office or inside his home that they didn't follow him, and he started to carry his pistol in a coat pocket again.

He confided in Guan-jiah, who thought it best if Ayaou didn't know of the threat. "Master," Guan-jiah said. "She might get suspicious with all the guards around. What do I say if she asks?"

"You're clever. Think of something."

When he traveled through the streets, half his bodyguards cleared the way while the other half kept his sedan chair surrounded. It was embarrassing that so many eyes were trying to see who hid behind the sedan chair's curtains. He hated being confined in a damned box on legs while four men carried him everywhere.

When he was in Peking on Saturdays, Robert usually worked into the afternoon and returned home early to spend time with his family. Since Anna was turning five, he decided to surprise her. He'd bought a bamboo flute several weeks earlier, and one of his Chinese employees had been teaching him to play a few simple tunes on it.

There were seven holes in the flute. The first hole was between the hole for the mouth and the first finger hole. It was covered with a membrane that produces a kazoo like buzzing that added a rich sound to the notes—one that he thought Anna would delight in. That sound was something he had discovered was unique to Chinese flute playing. He knew the tunes he had learned were not perfect but Anna was only five. He hoped she would be pleased with his musical gift.

Guan-jiah met him at the door and was wringing his hands. "Why do you look so nervous?" Robert asked. "Has something happened?"

"Nothing has happened, Master. It is a surprise. They are waiting upstairs in the piano room."

"Who is waiting?"

"That is part of the surprise. Do not be disappointed, Master. She has been practicing eight to twelve hours a day for months. If she is not perfect, do not criticize her. At times, it was very hard for her and she cried a lot."

"Ayaou has been practicing—what?"

"I cannot say. It is a secret."

Robert raised an eyebrow in exasperation. He patted the jacket pocket where he kept the flute. Well, he had a surprise too. He smiled. Maybe later, he would have time to give Anna the flute after he played a tune for her.

"Remember, Master, act surprised and be happy no matter what happens. Ayaou is worried that you will not be pleased."

Robert sighed and followed the eunuch upstairs to the back bedroom that had been converted into a piano room. When they entered, Robert stopped. Fooyen stood in the shadows on the far side of the room. Herbert, a year old now, was in his pen next to Fooyen. He was holding onto the side with both hands and was drooling.

There was a familiar looking foreign man in the room. He was tall and thin with gray hair, and he wore wire-frame glasses. He fingered his goatee nervously and stepped forward to introduce himself. "I am Kurt Brugman, Mr. Hart." The man's English was thick with a German accent.

"He is the German piano teacher Ayaou hired," Guan-jiah said in Mandarin. "He was the best and was willing to work the hours Ayaou wanted."

"I didn't know."

"That's because it was a secret, Master."

"Mr. Brugman, don't you work at the German consulate? I've seen you there."

The man nodded.

"How were you able to find the time?"

"The ambassador felt it was a good idea because of your position in Peking."

"Please thank the German ambassador for his thoughtfulness." Robert turned to see that Ayaou was dressed in a green-silk gown embroidered with lotus blossoms and bats. Anna, sitting on the piano bench, was wearing a matching gown. Her pixy face was composed, but her eyes looked worried.

"Anna is going to play for you, Mr. Hart," Brugman said. "We have been working hard to be ready for this day." The man started to open his mouth to say something else, but Guan-jiah clapped his hands and guided Robert to a chair against the wall. Brugman went and stood at the corner of the piano where Anna could see him. Ayaou folded her hands on her lap as if she were calm, but Robert detected from her eyes that she was nervous.

He was well aware that the Chinese often showed off their children's talents to others. There was nothing new in that. Even though Confucius regarded morality as the most important subject to learn and practice, he also emphasized what he called the "Six Arts"—ritual, music, archery, chariot riding, calligraphy and computation. They were woven into the fabric of Chinese culture and children often started learning young, so Robert was not surprised to see Anna sitting on the piano ready to play. He wondered what simple song she had learned. Maybe they could play a duet together.

A silence settled over the room. Anna's little hands moved toward the keys then her fingers touched. As she started to play, Robert felt his eyes widen in surprise. It was Chopin's First Piano Concerto. Anna missed a note, and her eyes darted toward Ayaou then back to the piano. A stern look came into Ayaou's eyes. Anna kept playing, but her eyes glistened from tears.

Guan-jiah said Anna had been practicing eight to twelve hours a day. It must have been torture for the five-year old. Robert leaned back. His mouth dropped open and he had to force it to close. The pride he felt at his daughter's accomplishment was like a balloon expanding in his stomach and chest. Anna played for more than fifteen minutes. When she stopped and leaned back, the silence was thick.

Before anyone could speak, Robert leaped to his feet and hurried to sweep Anna from the bench and into his arms. He turned toward Ayaou. "She was perfect," he said. "Perfect!" His eyes filled with tears. "I'm so pleased." He kissed Anna on the cheek, and she threw her arms around his neck. "I love you," he said.

"The concert isn't over," Brugman said in his thick accent. "She learned Beethoven's Piano Concerto No. 5 in E Flat Major too—The Emperor Concerto."

Robert placed Anna back on the bench and sat beside her. "You have made me very proud today, Anna. Please play Beethoven."

"It is my favorite, Ba Ba," she said in English.

"English too!" Robert said.

"A teacher has been coming from the British consulate," Guan-jiah said. "It seems that everyone wants to please you."

Robert decided to save the flute for another day. He watched in pride as Anna's fingers reached for the ivory keys.

Nights were sweeter than ever. During intimacy, Robert found Ayaou's trust had returned.

"I never thought about being called to live in Peking," she said. "My Shanghai fortune-teller, Mr. Sua-min, predicted that the moment you became powerful, you would abandon me."

"You found another fortune teller!" he said. That upset him. "First there was the one in Ningpo and next the one in Macao. They only fill your head with nonsense."

"I have to know what my fate is going to be so I am ready," she replied. "I paid Mr. Sua-min for his words, but I did not let them eat me."

His chest was her pillow. She had become quite talkative recently. Learning to become his eyes and ears in Peking had opened her like a blossoming flower. He didn't know if he liked that. He was used to her being the quiet sort.

The silk sheet slid off revealing her breasts. He couldn't take his eyes off them, so he pulled the sheet back to cover them. He wanted to pay attention to what she was saying. She might test him to make sure he was listening. She had been doing that recently.

"Living in Canton then Shanghai while you were gone was not a pleasant experience," she said. "Every time a messenger came to the house, I expected bad news. Not about you but about me. I loved you and would rather be dead if I could not be with you. I dreaded each day."

She studied his face. "You were not paying attention," she said.

"Yes I was. You thought I might abandon you. You were surprised to come to Peking to live with me. That fortune teller was a liar."

She pinched him.

"Ayaou," he said. "That hurt."

"I did not say Mr. Sua-min was a liar."

"He was wrong wasn't he? Do not pinch me. You know I hate that."

Satisfied that he was listening, Ayaou rambled on. His right arm was pinned under her, and it was going numb. Although he wasn't listening closely to what she was saying, he liked the smooth sound of her voice.

It was better than the silence he'd lived with after taking this job in Peking. He pulled his arm out and stretched it while his fingers tingled with returning circulation.

She shifted her position and threw a leg across both of his. She started to play with the hair on his chest. "I can never get used to this," she said. "Your hair feels so strange. My private grassland." She laughed.

He heard the sound of boots in the courtyard outside the window signaling the changing of the guard. Now that bannermen had been assigned to guard Robert night and day, there were new sounds to get used to.

"I am not sure if we match now that you are truly a powerful man, Robert. I prayed that you would be promoted. When you were, I was happy for your success. On the other hand, it gave me nightmares. I could see matchmakers tempting you with beautiful ladies."

Now seemed a good time to tell her what he'd been considering the last few weeks. He might be powerful, he thought, but together they had made reality of a dream.

Without her, he would be a lonely man and nothing would please him. When she had been in Canton or Shanghai and he'd been elsewhere, Robert had enjoyed the company of friends but when they left, he envied them. They had homes with families waiting. He had only loneliness for a companion.

There was no home for him without Ayaou. Since leaving Canton, his life had been half-empty. Now, his days were full. He ran his fingers down the supple length of her back counting her ribs. She was lean and thin. It was time to make her an honest woman. She had stopped talking and her breathing had slowed.

"Ayaou, are you sleeping?"

"No." By the slurred sound of her voice, she wasn't far from it.

"Before you came to Peking," he said, "I was having terrible dreams. They were always the same where Shao-mei came to fetch you, and the two of you vanished without a trace. That dream kept me awake nights. You wouldn't believe how this bothered me." He was nervous like a schoolboy wanting to talk to the girl he had a crush on.

"I asked my assistant every day to check to see if there were any messages from Guan-jiah," he said. "I couldn't find peace until a dispatch came telling me you were well. I was sick with worry, and that taught me I mustn't wait any longer." His heart started to thud and his hands felt clammy. This was foolish. He'd been with Ayaou for years. They had two children. They were not strangers.

She rolled onto her stomach, propped her head up on one hand and stared at him. "Wait for what?" she asked.

"You know what I'm going to say, don't you?"

She nodded. "You want me to become more than your eyes and ears? I like that job."

Robert gently cupped her face with his hands. "I love looking into your eyes," he said. "I see secrets hidden there." He kissed the tip of her nose then found her lips for a long, passionate kiss. When they parted, he ran his fingers across her face and into her long hair. Touching her was arousing him. "Your bone structure was sculpted by an artist."

"You know that is not true, Robert. I am—"

"Hush," he said, and took a breath to bolster his courage. "I'm proposing a wedding like Tee Lee Ping had but grander. Would you like that? I want to hear you say yes. We can marry in Peking or Shanghai. It doesn't matter where. What's important is that you become my wife."

If he married her, it might be easier to tell his father, since it would be better if she were his wife instead of a concubine.

When her face dropped into a look of despair, his heart went with it. He braced himself for the unpredictable, the unthinkable. How could she say no? Isn't this what she has wanted all along? From the look on her face, he wasn't sure anymore.

Chapter 51

"When we lived in Ningpo, the answer would have been yes," she said, then fell silent and looked away to focus on Prospect Hill, which was visible from the window. It was the highest point in Peking built from dirt removed to create the moat surrounding the Forbidden City. There was a garden with a pavilion at the top. It was outside the main walls and across the moat but still part of the palace complex.

"It was my dream to be your wife," Ayaou said. "Your love made my heart grow tender and kinder, and every time a letter came, I fell deeper in love. I was able to see what I could not see before. I began to understand why you hid our relationship. There are invisible rules and boundaries from both our societies. Crossing means to kill your future with your own hands."

"Ayaou, I don't care."

"Do not be unwise. You are not taking my words seriously. Peking is a class and rank-minded city. Even in the teahouses, like the place you took me to this morning, the nobles get seats that are sunny and bright and they face south while the common customers sit in the back where there is little or no view. Robert, I am not blind. I scc things and they make sense."

"What makes sense?" He dreaded the answer.

"I see how you will throw away what you have built."

"But my reason for everything I've done the last few years was for us. Don't you want to be my wife?"

Tears glistened in her eyes. "Of course," she said, "That is why I have to make sure I do not hurt you."

"You're contradicting yourself." He envisioned a mouth opening beneath him and swallowing him in one gulp.

540

She shook her head. "I cannot explain myself good enough for you."

"What about the wedding?"

She bit her lip and made no answer. Herbert started to cry from the other room and Ayaou got up.

"Let Fooyen take care of him," he said, but she went anyway.

Prince Kung's father-in-law, Kuei-liang, Robert's neighbor, planned a party to celebrate Robert becoming Inspector General. Prince Kung, several of his brothers and people who worked at the Tsungli Yamen planned to attend.

Robert saw an opportunity to repent for what he'd done to Ayaou years earlier in Canton when he wouldn't let her sing and dance for his guests at a dinner party. She had been upset and stayed in her room missing the celebration. This time he wanted her with him and thought she would be pleased.

However, when he told Ayaou that she was going to a party given by a Manchu royal, she panicked.

"Robert," she said, "this is an imperial party?"

"So?"

"I am not fit to go. What do I say when people ask what family I am from?"

"The party is for me, and you're my wife-to-be."

She kept shaking her head. "Please, Robert, do not do what you will regret."

"You," he said, and emphasized this by tapping her on her shoulder with an index finger, "are coming with me. Guan-jiah, bring that dress I bought." His resolve was set in forged iron.

Guan-jiah came through the door and held the dress in front of him. It was a full-length black silk gown with a pattern of red azaleas on it.

"No, Robert, you cannot do this." Her eyes were darting about as if she were looking for a way to escape. "You are crazy to even—no, I will not go."

He grabbed her and forced her to look at him. "Listen, taking you with me to this party is a way to show how proud I am of you. You should feel confident, because you probably know more about the confusing state of Chinese politics than the nobles do. Walls, eunuchs, and corrupt ministers surround them. You would be shocked to discover how much they don't know. Without your knowledge to guide me, I'd be of no use to them."

"But people will make fun of me once they learn where I am from. They might discover that you bought me!"

"Stop it, Ayaou. You are letting yourself panic and have forgotten I never bought you. Now that Ward is dead, you're free. You are truly my partner and should be my wife."

He took hold of her chin. "I'll have you carried over there if I have to. I told Prince Kung I was in love with a Chinese boat girl. He didn't believe me. You must show your face, so he knows the truth."

Ayaou covered her mouth with both hands and started crying.

"Guan-jiah, I'm right aren't I?" he asked, wanting an ally.

A look of panic flooded the eunuch's face. His eyes darted away.

Robert sighed. Obviously, Guan-jiah agreed with Ayaou. It was annoying that they were both against what he wanted. "Thank you, Guan-jiah. You may leave." The eunuch took the gown and retreated.

"Ayaou, you are going," Robert said. "That's the last we will talk about this."

The party wasn't what he thought it would be. Soon after they reached the house, Prince Kung's father-in-law managed to separate Ayaou from him. She was taken away by two concubines to another room. He kept looking around searching for her, and occasionally caught a glimpse of her in a doorway or behind a screen or a large-potted plant.

Robert discovered that Prince Kung had arranged the party to introduce him to highborn, young Manchu women. One by one, these lovely creatures were introduced to him.

A banker in Ningpo once told Robert that you could only trust members of your family, and so it was wise to marry your business associates to your daughters. It made perfect sense, but that didn't mean Robert had to like it.

Then he saw her—a seductive, classical beauty. She was tall with wide shoulders and a graceful neck. Her bone-white face stood in contrast to her black glossy hair, decorated with fresh flowers and glittering, dangling jewels. When she saw that he was admiring her, she smiled and crossed the room.

"I am Nee-Nee," she said. She held her hand out to shake in the Western style. He took hold of her fingertips and his heart started to pound. "My uncle told me about you. He said we must talk."

He guessed she was at least seventeen and tried not to stare at a perfect red dot painted on her lower lip. "Your uncle?" he asked. She had large eyes that wove a spell over him, and he felt dizzy.

"Prince Kung," she said, and laughed.

There was music in her laughter that caused breathing problems. Kung had set him up. Nee-Nee was amazing. Maybe Ayaou was right. Maybe he should have a royal wife and keep her as his concubine.

"I understand you love to read," she said.

He started telling her about the *Fall of the House of Usher* and how it compared to *The Dream of the Red Chamber*. As he babbled on, he imagined undressing Nee-Nee, which confused him, and he forgot what he was saying.

"Chinese novels can be classified into several types," she said, as if she knew what she was talking about. The conversation went from there. Nee-Nee had an educated woman's openness and she said many interesting things about literature and operas.

During the conversation, she reached out and touched his arm. Her fingers lingered before they slid down the back of his hand in an invitation. An electric shock raced through him. Robert had a feeling that Nee-Nee knew she was weaving a spell and succeeding. No woman had affected him like this since that first time with Ayaou.

"There are the novels of adventure like *Outlaws of the March*," she said. "Then there is the historical novel *The Romance of the Three Kingdoms*. Have you read *The Plum in the Golden Vase?*" She smiled an invitation as if she were making promises to him. Then her long eyelashes fluttered, and she glanced away as if she was embarrassed, but he didn't think she was.

Yes, he had read *The Plum in the Golden Vase* and most of it had been pornographic. The novel had shocked the Ming Dynasty so much in the early seventeenth century that the book had been banned at the time.

Her fingers still rested on the back of his hand. When she finished saying the name of the pornographic novel, she ran her fingernails across his skin setting his nerves on fire. This excited him and he couldn't concentrate, which was embarrassing.

It took a glass of hard liquor to drench the flames and calm him down.

As the night wore on and after many had left, Robert managed to break away from Nee-Nee. It wasn't easy.

He found Ayaou, and they went home. There was an early morning appointment at the Tsungli Yamen, and he wanted a few hours of sleep so he would have a clear head for the meeting.

Still dressed in her silk gown, Ayaou sat on the edge of the bed. "The concubines told me what Prince Kung and the ministers are planning for you," she said.

"Let's sleep," he said. "I'm tired." He pulled off his shirt and yawned. His eyes felt as if sand was in them, and he attempted rubbing the irritation away but only made it worse.

"I saw you talking to the princess," she said. "Your eyes were eating her as if she were a feast. She is Prince Kung's niece, and you were flattered. You cannot hide that. The prince wants you to be a member of his family. She was perfect for you, and it would bind you to him."

"Stop, Ayaou, I am not interested."

"I do not believe that," she said. "They will change your mind. Prince Kung picked the best for you, and she was told to capture your heart. I do not see you resisting her since she will make you more connections leading to more wealth and promotions."

"What are you worried about—that you'll lose me? You didn't want our wedding anyway!" He regretted the bitter words but did not apologize.

Without expression, she undressed, slipped under the sheet and slept with her back to him.

In the morning, he went to work early as planned. Before the day ended, Robert was called home, and Guan-jiah was waiting at the gate when he arrived.

The eunuch looked pale and guilty beyond words. "Master, they went shopping this morning. When they were not back by noon, I went to search. I checked the entire market and could not find them."

"Who are you talking about?" he said. "Slow down and make sense."

"Ayaou, the children and Fooyen have vanished," Guan-jiah replied.

Chapter 52

Late in January, a few days after Ayaou's disappearance, Fooyen stumbled into the house. The temperature outside hovered close to freezing, and in the mornings, a crust of frost covered the ground and roofs.

"The Longhaired Bandits have taken Mistress Ayaou and the children," Fooyen said, as she sat in Robert's kitchen shivering despite the blankets heaped about her shoulders and the fire blazing in the stove. Dried mud streaked her tangled hair. Her torn and filthy clothes smelled like dung as if she had crawled through the sewers.

"Do you know where they are?" Robert asked. After hearing the shocking news, he feared that panic, shock, and depression would overwhelm him. Instead, he focused on Fooyen's words as energy rushed through his body.

Slack jawed and with glassy eyes, she shook her head. "Mistress Ayaou did not know we were being followed when we went to shop in the market. A group of Longhaired Bandits came dressed as bannermen shouting 'Death to the barbarians!' They took the Mistress and the children."

"How could the Taipings pretend to be bannermen when they wear their hair long?" he asked.

Fooyen stared at him with a blank face.

Of course, he thought, the Taipings shaved their heads for this subterfuge to succeed. His family could be dead. A cold chill swept through him, and he swayed on his feet, but Guanjiah was there holding him by the arm, steadying him. He felt an oppressive fear stirring in his guts. Then a calm voice inside his head said that losing control would not bring his family back. Until he learned they were dead, he had to stay focused. He closed his eyes and pressed fingers against them to fight the fear.

His mind raced to discover a solution. He examined one choice after another as if they were specimens. It was like living in a high-speed dream, and the world around him was moving in slow motion. He found it odd that he was relieved that Ayaou had not run away like before.

Prince Kung should have assigned guards for Ayaou and the children, but even Robert hadn't considered that. Guan-jiah had mentioned the risk to his family after the Taipings had put a price on his head, but Robert had been a fool and didn't listen.

Fooyen's hand went into a pocket. "Here, Master. They told me to give you this note. I cannot read, so I do not know what it says."

His hands shook as he carefully opened the damp scrap of paper. The Chinese characters were poorly written and difficult to read. No Chinese had written this. The characters were too sloppy. Even the construction of the phrases sounded wrong. He thought of the Englishman Prince Kung said was working for the Taipings and wondered if that man was involved.

"Deliver one hundred thousand taels and pick up your whore and bastards at the port of Ningpo on February fifteenth, or we will behead them in public. You must come alone.

"Do not seek help from the corrupt Manchu. We have eyes and ears everywhere. Nothing will save your family unless you do exactly as told. If you do not, we will kill them sooner and make them suffer horribly before they die."

He closed his eyes and took several calming breaths, before he said, "Guan-jiah, count the silver taels!" The thought of losing Ayaou and the children was threatening to crush him, but he wasn't going to let it. "And come with me to Ningpo. We only have two weeks. We have to act now."

"Master, I suggest you do not go," Guan-jiah said. "I believe it is a trap. The Longhaired Bandits are set on killing you. Remember, they put a price on your head that is the same as the ransom. They want you to pay for your execution."

"Caution be damned," Robert said. He quickly wrote a note explaining what had happened and arranged for a messenger to deliver it to Prince Kung late the next day. "There is no time to waste. Obviously, I can't do as the Taipings demand."

Guan-jiah threw himself on the floor and kowtowed repeatedly. "Master, I will follow you to hell."

"Oh, get up, Guan-jiah," he said, exasperated. "You have to stop doing that." He took the eunuch by the shoulders and pulled him to his feet.

With a gentle expression, he looked into his servant's eyes. "I know I can count on you, Guan-jiah. You have proved that more than once over the years. I still recall that time you were ready to fight alongside Dr. Winchester and me at the Ningpo consulate against those pirates. I value your loyalty as if you were my brother."

Guan-jiah stared at the floor and shuffled his feet. "I am unworthy of your praise, Master." Robert detected a smile of pride tugging the corners of the eunuch's mouth. "How are we going to save the mistress and the children?"

"By doing something the Taipings least expect," he replied. "We are going to give everyone the slip, including the bannermen who are my guards. Even if the Taipings have spies watching, if we move fast enough, we will arrive in Ningpo before any message they could send."

"We are only two, Master. How are we going to defeat a Taiping army?"

"I'll think of a way."

Guan-jiah stared at him as if he had gone mad.

An hour later, Guan-jiah and Robert, looking like peasants wearing rags with dirt smeared faces, managed to avoid the guards and slipped out of Peking unnoticed. Once outside the walls, Guan-jiah bought two horses.

Impulsive thoughts raced through Robert's mind while they rode the eighty miles to the coast and Tientsin. He rejected one far-fetched scheme after another. It was crazy to act impulsively, but he had to do something. If he didn't keep moving, the fear and panic would take control. Then he would be useless. He also knew that if he acted with too much caution, the Taipings would kill Ayaou and the children before the deadline.

If he asked Prince Kung for help, he was sure the prince would shrug it off as futile and let Ayaou and the children die. After all, to Kung and the other Manchu princes and ministers, Ayaou was a worthless Chinese boat girl and the children were bastards. Prince Kung wanted Robert to marry a Manchu princess anyway, and this was a perfect opportunity to achieve that goal.

Halfway to the coast, a possible solution materialized. Just as he'd constructed the plans for China's future, he knew what had to be done to have any chance to save his family.

It was reckless, a total gamble, but the audacity of it might work. With luck, they would have the same results Patridge had all those years ago when he made that daring raid against the Taipings. With overwhelming odds against him, Patridge took back his opium and freed the boat people. Robert planned to do something similar but more dangerous.

By sunset, they were almost to Tientsin and could see the city's ancient walls in the distance. Tientsin was thirty-seven miles up the Peihao River from the ocean and had been opened to world trade in 1860. It now had foreign concessions similar to Shanghai, and because it was a major port, Robert should find a steamship to speed him south. A steamer would be much faster than a junk, which he assumed was what the Taipings were using to spirit Ayaou and the children away.

Ningpo was seven hundred miles by water from Tientsin. He planned to put together a force of trusted men from Tientsin and Shanghai. They would have to come from the customs service since he couldn't trust anyone else.

Modern weapons were stored in Shanghai. He knew what was in the warehouse, and the shipment that should be there now was exactly what he wanted. Without modern weapons, he wouldn't have considered going ahead with his wild scheme, and the weapons Robert had in mind were special.

Once in Tientsin, he gathered a group of his employees in a large back room at the customs house. They were all men he had carefully selected for their courage, loyalty and honesty.

Under the Chinese system of government, Robert was like a king and his kingdom was the customs service. The only higher authority was the emperor of China. Since the emperor was a child, that meant Kung and the Dowagers ruled the empire, three who called Robert 'Our Hart'.

"I have always had a difficult time asking for help," he said, "but since most of you are family men, I think you will understand.

"I know everyone here as if we were members of the same family. I attended one wedding in Tientsin." He looked at

Anwar Cardiff, a wild looking Welshman, but one of the gentlest men he'd ever known.

"Not long ago," he said, "a certain Welshman was pining for his love, so I arranged, without him knowing, for her to come from England to join him. I was even his best man at the wedding. And one of you asked me to be godfather to your last newborn child." He looked at Henry Cooper, who grew up on a farm in Devon, England. "We've worked many long hours together."

Robert struggled to fight back the tears that were sparkling in his eyes. This time when he spoke, his voice cracked as he struggled to maintain control. "The woman I love and my children were kidnapped by Taipings." He had to stop. Taking several breaths, he calmed down.

"I can't count on the Dynasty for help—at least not in the time left before my family will be executed. I need your help in a risky venture to save my family from certain death. If you are willing, please step forward. If you aren't, I will understand."

Everyone stepped forward, which caused a balloon of gratitude to swell inside his chest. The expressions on their faces caused tears to escape from his eyes, and he turned away to hide his face as he struggled to regain control.

These were his men. Among them were Italians, Germans, Americans, and British citizens and even one Chinese, Guan-jiah.

Other Chinese worked here, but he doubted that any had ever handled a weapon. This was China, the land of Confucius and Taoism, which respected scholarship and learning above all else.

The Chinese warriors were either in the army or were bandits and as such were considered below the status of a scholar. Even the wealthiest merchants were not equal to the poorest scholar, and the Chinese who worked in customs were all scholars of some sort—men who spent their free time writing poetry and painting ink on rice paper.

"One more thing," he said, after he wiped the tears from his face. "I must be assured that all of you know how to use firearms and ride horses, as we may have a tough fight. My plans are to arrive and leave by ship but if circumstances warrant, we may have to use horses to escape."

Anwar, his Welshman, chuckled. His gentle voice did not fit his appearance. "No worries there, Sir. I was with the Duke of Cornwall's Light Infantry at Lucknow during the Indian Mutiny, and I'm not the only veteran here." He gestured toward Cooper, a thirty-year-old whose head was bald as the moon. "Cooper was with the 93rd Highlanders in the Crimean War."

"I fought in second Opium War in 1857," Leopold Huber, a German, said. Leopold had a weak chin and a thin nose. "That's what brought me to China, and I decided to stay." Two others nodded to include themselves in that war.

"And I served in the second Maori War in New Zealand with the 14th West Yorkshire regiment in 1860," another man said.

"Every man here can use a musket or shotgun," Cooper said. "We've all hunted wild game, and you'll have a hard time finding better marksmen."

"What about horses?" Robert asked.

"That's like asking if a duck has wings and can float," Anwar said. "None of us grew up in a city like London. We are all country boys. Since Britain has been in so many wars around the world, I doubt you'll find many of us that haven't served somewhere. Fighting is what took us away from home. Then after we saw some of the world, it was difficult to go back because we wanted to see more. You could say we're the adventuresome sort."

This was why Robert had decided to talk to these men. It was gratifying to know he'd judged correctly.

"Guan-jiah," he said, "I dare not risk leaving this building with these men until it's dark in case there are spies watching. However, you will not be noticed, as you are Chinese. I want you to go and find us a suitable, fast ship.

"Once you find one, go aboard and talk to the captain. Introduce yourself. Mention my name. Tell the captain that we have pressing business in Shanghai and Ningpo. Say that I will make it worth his while if he gets underway immediately once we are on board."

"No one will listen to me, Master," Guan-jiah replied. "They will see a skinny Chinese and ignore me."

"That will not happen," Robert said. "I'll write a note. That should work."

The eunuch returned after dark and took them to the *Nanzing*, which was bound for Shanghai with passengers and a cargo of wheat. The *Nanzing,* owned by the British firm of Trautman and Company, was a steamship that worked the coast from Shanghai to the northern ports.

The captain met Robert the moment he stepped on deck. He studied Robert's face and nodded. "Just wanted to make sure you are who the Chinaman said you were. I was suspicious of that note."

They shook hands, and Robert said, "You understand that we have pressing business and must be on our way."

"The Chinaman didn't say much about what that business was."

"But he did tell you what I'm willing to pay?"

The captain nodded.

"Then you know what's important. To earn that money, you must have us in Shanghai then Ningpo as soon as possible."

"Well, the Chinaman—"

"His name is Guan-jiah," Robert said. "How soon before we are underway?"

The captain's eyes went from Robert to the serious faces of the dozen men standing behind him. "We were planning to raise anchor in the morning."

Robert pulled out his pocket watch. "Morning arrives in ten hours. It's eight now. You know who I am, so take what I say seriously. If Trautman and Company wants to continue doing business in China, we will be underway sooner, within the hour. Do we understand each other?"

The captain looked startled then nodded yes.

"When will that departure time be?" Robert asked.

"Tonight before nine."

"Make it faster!"

In thirty minutes, the *Nanzing* was steaming from Tientsin. During the voyage, Robert stood next to the captain in the wheelhouse and watched every junk they passed for any sign that it might be the one carrying Ayaou and his children to their fate.

Of course, he couldn't see inside the junks and to stop and search each boat would have been futile. Still, he had to do something and sleep was not a choice.

The *Nanzing* reached Shanghai in less than three days and unloaded the wheat and the passengers. Robert recruited nine more men from the customs office there.

After he finished, he went to the warehouse where he ordered the Chinese men who worked there to load several heavy crates on a wagon to be delivered to the *Nanzing.*

Once on board ship, with Guan-jiah's help, he went to work cleaning the weapons and loading them. It would have been easier to have someone else do this job, but he didn't want anyone messing with the hardware.

While steaming the hundred miles to Ningpo, he gathered his small army of twenty on the aft deck and stood by the crates that were covered by a canvas tarp. "I understand that most of you are good shots and know how to use muzzle loaders and shotguns, but what I have here is something most of you may never have seen before."

He pulled back the canvas tarp and Guan-jiah stepped forward with a pry bar and used it to remove the top off a wooden crate. Robert reached in and took out one of the revolvers. "This is an 1860, .44 Caliber United States Army Colt Revolver. It weighs two pounds and eleven ounces. It also holds six black powder bullets."

He lifted the revolver and aimed at the waves as the *Nanzing* steamed along. Squeezing the trigger, he fired the first shot. He then cocked the hammer and squeezed the trigger again. After the sixth blast died away, he said, "This weapon has a revolving cylinder. It will fire as fast as you can cock the hammer and pull the trigger. We have enough of these Army Colts so each man has two, and you will have leather cartridge boxes holding fifty .44 caliber bullets for reloading."

"What about holsters?" Anwar asked. "I hope we don't have to shove those beauties under our belts. That barrel looks mighty long."

"Eight inches," Robert replied, and handed Anwar the Colt. He then reached into the crate and brought out a belt with two hip holsters. Leather cartridge boxes filled with bullets were fastened to the belt. He handed that to Anwar, who took it and strapped it to his lean waist before he took a step toward the crate.

"Hold it," Robert said. "I'm not done." Anwar took a step back to stand with his colleagues. He examined the Colt as if it were priceless and then ran his fingers through the unruly mop of curly brown hair that covered his head and smiled.

Guan-jiah pulled back the tarp to reveal a larger, heavier crate. He used the pry bar to open it.

"How fast can you load a musket and fire?" Robert asked.

"If you're good," Cooper said, "maybe two or three times a minute but you have to be fast. And if you panic, you might forget to pull the ramrod out and shoot that. Then you're in trouble."

Robert reached in and took out the first rifle. "This is a lever-action breech-loading Henry repeating rifle. It holds sixteen .44 Caliber bullets." He lifted the weapon to his shoulder, aimed at the ocean and pulled the trigger. After he fired, Robert worked the lever, ejected the spent cartridge and loaded another bullet.

"You can fire up to twenty-eight rounds a minute when used correctly. Before I bought this shipment, I was trained to use this weapon, and I am going to teach you what I learned before we get to Ningpo. You will all be experts on the use of the Henry and the Colt before we arrive."

"Who made these rifles?" Anwar asked. "I've never even heard of anything like this before."

"It was made in the United States to be used in fighting the Confederate Army. You have heard that there is a Civil War going on over there now?"

"I've read about it," Anwar said, and several others nodded. "Those damned Yanks are inventive. No wonder we lost the colonies to them. When do we get started? My hands are itching. Seeing a weapon like that excites me more than if I were with a virgin in a hayloft."

The others laughed.

"Be my guest," Robert said, and handed a Henry repeating rifle to Anwar. "Go ahead, men, the crates are open. You will have fifty rounds for each rifle. Keep that ammunition in the larger leather pouch that will hang around your neck and shoulders. We also have a small crate full of bullets for practice. Those rifles cost the emperor forty-two American dollars each so after this is over, I would like to return them to the rightful owner."

"I am glad the Chinese didn't have these during the last Opium War," Leopold said, as he stepped up to the crate and reached for a Henry repeating rifle. "Oh, this is a beauty." He kissed the barrel.

"Not to worry. I couldn't buy enough of these to outfit an army. There aren't that many in production yet. Only the emperor's personal guards will have them in the Forbidden City."

Robert trained his clerks how to operate the weapons, and they practiced by shooting at driftwood and other floating objects in the water. Since all of them were hunters and many were war veterans, it didn't take long to learn. It sounded as if a war was being fought on the aft deck of the *Nanzing*. A few times, he saw the ship's Captain and some of the crew watching with worried expressions.

He hoped that the little time he had to get his army ready for the coming battle was going to be enough. Then it hit him hard when he realized he could be taking all of these men to their deaths. What if he were fooling himself, and there was nothing he could do to save Ayaou and the children? These loyal men could die for nothing.

Chapter 53

The *Nanzing* was steaming along the crowded Yong River covering the last sixteen miles to Ningpo.

Since the Manchu general had fled with his troops in December, the Taiping army had occupied the city without a fight leaving the battlements in good shape. Taking the city back was not going to be easy, because the walls were made of granite.

A Chinese army was already gathering, and Robert had helped select a capable general, so he knew that in a few months war was returning to Ningpo. This time it was going to be bloody and many would die.

"I'm uneasy taking the *Nanzing* this close to the Taipings," the captain said. "I've heard they have cannons that can reach across the river and shell the Western settlement."

"You have nothing to worry about, captain," Robert replied. "I have it on good authority that the Taipings are cooperating with the foreign merchants so trade will flourish. Ningpo is the only major port the Taipings have. They cannot afford to have it blockaded by British and French warships. If they fired on the missionaries and merchants living across the river or any Western ships like the *Nanzing*, the British and French navies would react. Your ship is safe."

Harry Parkes had told him the two Taiping generals controlling the city had assured Western representatives that trade would continue as usual, and that all foreigners would be respected and protected. It was unfortunate that Ayaou wasn't a foreigner.

"We will cooperate with these blasphemous creatures for now, Robert," Parkes had said during a recent visit to Peking. "British policy is to support the Ch'ing Dynasty in this

556

rebellion, not the pretender, who claims he is the younger brother of Jesus Christ. Ningpo is too important for foreign trade to see the port closed. We know why the Taipings are doing this. Until now, they've had trouble getting their hands on modern weapons. With Ningpo, they now have the access they wanted."

Robert knew things Parkes did not know. The Ch'ing Dynasty was negotiating with Apak, a notorious Cantonese pirate, and that Apak's pirate fleet was going to support the Manchu army when it arrived.

"We don't have a navy," Prince Kung had said. "Without Apak and his fleet, we will only be able to attack by land. We have no choice."

"Apak is a monster," Robert replied. "Innocent people will suffer."

"It is the price the inhabitants of Ningpo must pay for cooperating with the Longhaired Bandits."

Robert thought of the fifty innocent Chinese in Canton that had lost their heads during the Arrow War. The Manchu could be brutal, and he didn't always approve of their methods.

He also had not forgotten what Cantonese pirates had done to Portuguese pirates in Ningpo while he had still worked for the British consulate. Some of the Portuguese had pounded on the locked gate to the British consulate begging for sanctuary. He had wanted to let them in but Dr. Winchester, the acting vice consul, said no. The Portuguese that survived to surrender were put on one of their ships and then that lorcha was set on fire with them in it. Apak had been the leader of the Cantonese pirates.

Once the *Nanzing* was anchored near Ningpo, Guan-jiah went ashore to spy, while Robert stood by the rail and studied the foreign settlement across the river where the Christian missionaries and merchants lived. He had crossed the river many times his first year in China to have dinner on the Sabbath. That had been a lonely year. There had even been a British widow he liked with one leg shorter than the other. Then he had met Ayaou.

A few hours later, Guan-jiah was back.

"I entered the city through one of the water gates," he said. "As hoped, I was not challenged."

"The Taipings are lax and inefficient," Leopold said. His German accent was thicker than usual. "They will be easy to kill."

"Most are just peasants with little or no military training," Robert replied, "but do not underestimate them. What they lack in training is made up for with an intense zeal."

"Once night comes, the water gates will be lowered," Guan-jiah said. "We must be inside before dark." Guan-jiah spread a map of the city on the deck of the ship.

"I found Mistress Ayaou and the children," he said. "They are imprisoned at the Yen-ch'ing temple near the city's south gate." He hesitated as his eyes jerked nervously toward Robert and away. "I saw posters announcing the date of their beheading."

Robert face went numb and a chill invaded his heart.

"Bastards," Anwar said. He lifted his rifle and shook it. "This weapon is the right tool to wreak vengeance on these devils. With this, our numbers will sound like hundreds. They won't know what hit them."

But they will know soon enough, Robert thought. If we lose the element of surprise, even the Henry repeating rifles will not make a difference.

"With these weapons, we will sound like an army," Cooper said. "Without reloading, twenty men can fire hundreds of rounds a minute." His baldhead was covered with a floppy bush hat.

"What date was on the posters?" Robert asked, afraid of the answer. However, he wanted to know.

"February twelfth," Guan-jiah replied. His eyes met Robert's eyes. "I am sorry that I protested before we left Beijing. You were right, Master. If we had come on the fifteenth as the note demanded, the children would have been dead. It was a trap, and Ayaou and the children were the bait."

"Yes," he managed to say. A lump in his throat was strangling his ability to talk clearly. It was as if he were standing on the edge of a cliff in danger of falling. He had doubts and considered moving the assault up several hours. He was afraid the Taipings might close the gates early. The raid had to take place that night, and there wasn't going to be a second chance.

It took all his discipline to suppress the urge to move sooner. Once inside the city, one mistake, one slip and all could be lost—they'd be slaughtered with Ayaou and the children. He could not abandon the original plan. It was their best chance.

"How about these Taipings?" Anwar asked. "How are they armed?"

"Mostly spears and swords," Guan-jiah replied. "Maybe two hundred have ancient muzzle loading muskets, but they probably are not good shots. They do not have enough gunpowder to practice. However, that is changing. The Taiping generals have been buying modern cannons and munitions. The new cannons have been installed on the river wall. More shipments arrive daily, and I discovered that a shipment with several thousand muskets will arrive soon."

"How good is this information?" Anwar asked.

"Most of my family lives in the city, and I picked their brains. My father believes that there are hundreds of Longhaired Bandits with crossbows. They have a few ancient muzzle loading cannons on the walls facing inland. Since the Ch'ing army is expected to attack the city by land, most of the Taiping soldiers are sleeping on the walls. Only a few are watching the river."

"Are you positive that the Inspector General's family is being held in this temple?" Anwar asked.

Robert looked at the wild looking Welshman with gratitude. Anwar seemed to know he was having a difficult time.

"There were only a few guards outside the temple," Guan-jiah replied. "I managed to sneak past them and find the room Mistress Ayaou and the children were in. But I did not see them. Food was taken into that room. When the door opened, I heard a child who sounded like Anna. A woman's voice replied. It was Mistress Ayaou. I am sure of it."

Robert felt relief, and he looked at Anwar. "Thank you," he said. Anwar acknowledged with a nod. "How many Taipings inside the city?" he asked, dreading the answer.

"Thousands," Guan-jiah replied.

He felt a sinking sensation in his stomach, and his mouth turned dry. That was many times the number of Taipings Patridge had confronted in 1855.

"Guan-jiah, did you tell your father to take the family and leave the city?" Robert had told him about Apak and the Cantonese pirates.

"Yes, Master, I did as you said. He promised to leave, and they should be gone by now."

"Captain, wait until we return," Robert said. "I'm counting on the *Nanzing* being here when we are done with our business in the city." When Robert turned away to join his troop by the rail, he didn't like the look he saw in the captain's eyes. He was not sure he could trust the man, but what choice did he have?

With the sun's last rays fading along the western horizon in a swath of washed out yellow with strings of blood running through it, his men, disguised as Chinese peasants, left the *Nanzing* in sampans and glided into the city through the two water gates. Once they were on the lake, the sunlight died, and the evening gloom hid them.

They rowed the length of the lake and went ashore opposite the county school. Since Robert knew Ningpo's streets well, he decided to avoid the main avenues and use side streets to reach the temple.

He gathered his troop in a narrow alley across from the Yen-ch'ing temple. It bothered him that the *Nanzing* was anchored far out in the river on the opposite side of the city. Trying to return to the steamer through the city would increase the odds of failure.

They couldn't use the water gate again, since it was closed for the night, and the newer cannons the Taipings had been buying faced the river. Even in the dark, his band would be easy targets all the way to the steamer.

It would be safer if they attempted making their escape through one of the land gates to a spot along the river far enough from the city to be out of reach of the Taiping cannons.

He gathered his men in a close huddle. "We might not be able to fight our way through the city once the Taipings know we are here. We must act quickly and make our escape through the closest gate before their generals realize that we are a small force."

"We must strike like the cobra and fly like the hawk," Anwar replied. Nervous laughter answered him.

Robert sent Guan-jiah and two men outside the city to purchase horses and hold them near the south gate at the Altar of Agriculture. He was counting on the eunuch to find enough horses.

"Guan-jiah," he said, "if we don't get out of the city, you must take the horses and the two men with you and return to Shanghai and safety."

Guan-jiah's eyes closed until they were narrow slits, and Robert didn't like what the eunuch was probably thinking. "Guan-jiah, you must do as I say. After all, the rest of us might have to take a different route to reach the *Nanzing* if we cannot make it to the south gate. If you do not leave, all three of you might be caught."

Guan-jiah did not say a word. He took his repeating rifle and left, and the other two followed. Robert watched until the night swallowed them. He hoped his servant would survive.

It was a long wait in that dark alley until midnight. He worried that Guan-jiah had been captured and the Taipings were torturing him. He was sure that the eunuch's loyalty to Robert's family would keep him from talking despite the pain. What about the other two? Would they hold up under torture? If the Taipings discovered his plans, the rebels could be setting a trap inside the temple walls.

He checked his pocket watch for the hundredth time while the minute hand inched toward midnight. Finally, it was time.

"Let's go," he said. He was the first out of the alley and heard the others behind him as they ran across the wide street. The guards at the temple's main gate died under a storm of bullets that made the small band sound as if they were an invading army. They must have fired hundreds of rounds crossing that street to reach the temple grounds.

Robert heard voices shouting and yelling in the distance. He held up a hand to stop his band. "I want Leopold and Brent to secure the gate," he said. "Reload before going inside."

A moment later, he led the way toward the locked door that would let them into the temple. They battered the door until it crashed open. Several Taiping guards waited on the other side with crossbows. One managed to get off a shot that wounded Cooper. Then the guards were dead.

"Cooper?" Robert asked.

"It's nothing," Cooper replied. "A flesh wound." He'd lost his bush hat and brushed a hand across his baldhead leaving a smear of blood. "Don't stop on my account. I will keep up."

They hurried down the hall to the door that Guan-jiah had marked on the detailed map. Robert feared that he would open the door and find the room empty—the Taipings could've changed their minds and beheaded his family before the execution date, or maybe they had moved Ayaou and the children to a different location.

Dreading the worst, he pushed the door open and lunged in with his two Colt revolvers ready. A shrill scream halted him. It was Ayaou. Her hair was in disaray and there was a wild look in her eyes. She held a wooden bench above her head and looked as if she were ready to smash him with it.

Anna was holding Herbert and was hiding behind her mother's legs. When Ayaou recognized him, her eyes registered disbelief. She tossed the bench aside and hurled herself across the room into his arms.

He pushed her away. "We don't have time." He thrust one of the revolvers into her hands. "I'm sure you haven't forgotten how to use this." She had fought beside him against the Taipings in 1855 and saved his life.

"Ba, Ba." Anna ran to him, and Robert hoisted her and Herbert into his arms. His eyes filled with tears. His chest was tight and he struggled to breathe. He swallowed hard to help bury his feelings. It wasn't time to rejoice.

"We run," he said. Spinning around, he led the way down the hall, out of the temple and to the gate. As he reached the street, a crossbow bolt buried itself in the wood of the gate a few inches from Anwar's face. Robert and Anwar fired at the same time killing the Taiping who shot at them. The other Taipings turned and ran. Robert's men crowded into the street and started shooting, but there was no one to shoot at. The roar of rifle fire was deafening. Keeping up a steady barrage, they fled down the avenue.

His thinking seemed clear and focused, but everything around him was moving in slow motion. He guessed that they could sustain this rate of fire for about four minutes—not counting the time it would take to reload.

"Hold your fire! Save your ammunition! Shoot only if you see the enemy. To the south gate!" A wild desperation was driving him. "If the gate is closed, we fight our way out!" He realized that they could fail in an attempt to take the gate. That had not occurred to him earlier. He cursed himself. He should have brought explosives to blow the gate open.

The others ran in a pack surrounding Robert's family. The smell of their sweat and the sound of heavy breathing filled the air.

As they hurried down the street, the men reloaded their weapons. Except for distant yelling and a ringing in Robert's ears, it was as if a blanket had been tossed over the city to muffle sound.

Drums started pounding as the Taipings sounded the alert. Panic tugged at his heart. Reinforcments would be sent to the gates and in a few moments they could be trapped inside the city. If they didn't escape soon, there would be no place to hide.

"Shoot sparingly and only when needed," Robert said, loud enough to be heard above the throbbing drums. "We do not have an endless supply of ammunition." He feared that a large troop of Taipings would be guarding the south gate.

To his surprise, they discovered the gate was open, and the two men he had sent with Guan-jiah were there. The half-dozen Taipings who had been guarding the gate were dead—the bodies piled to one side.

"Who thought of this?" he asked, and felt a jolt of fear. "Where's Guan-jaih?"

"Guan-jiah didn't want to just go outside and buy horses," one of the men said, "so we killed these guards and took the gate. The noise you were making at the temple was loud enough so no one heard us. Guan-jiah was worried we might find ourselves outside with the rest of you trapped. Once we took the gate, he went to find the horses. It was his idea that we stay."

"This way!" It was Guan-jaih, who had emerged from the darkness of the tunnel leading through the city wall. He was breathing hard and was drenched in sweat. "My cousins are watching the horses at the Altar of Agriculture. We must hurry."

Robert stepped aside and waved for the others to move, but they hesitated. "What are you waiting for? Go." He followed with his children and Ayaou.

When everyone emerged from the tunnel, he said, "Guan-jiah, you are truely amazing. Without your fast thinking, we could have been trapped inside the city and killed. What did I do to deserve such loyalty and steadfastness? Surely, God guided you to me when I first arrived in Ningpo."

Guan-jiah's reply was classically Confucious in its thinking. "Well, you could thank your God for bringing us together, and you might be correct. But then there is no way to prove that your God actually exists." The eunuch shrugged and led the way across the bridge spanning the moat. Someone shouted from the wall. His troop turned and fired a volley at the battlements, and screams were heard

After everyone was across, Guan-jiah said, "Help me push this wagon to the bridge." The wagon full of dry hay was heavy, and it took half the men to move the wagon, while the other half kept up a withering barrage on the city's wall so the Taipings could not shoot back.

Robert watched in amazement as the eunuch set fire to the hay.

"That hay cost ten yuan," Guan-jiah said. "I could not get the farmer to lower his price."

Robert wanted to laugh but didn't. "Good thinking," he said. "How did you accomplish all that in such a short time?"

"Probably with your ghost God's help," Guan-jiah replied.

Once the fire was blazing, Guan-jiah led the way toward the Alter of Agriculture. "It might be wise to thank your God just in case He does exist," he said. "It is not a good idea to anger a god. Besides, you have been a good master and the money I have earned has helped my family live a better life so I am also thankful that your God brought me to you."

The horses were waiting with Guan-jiah's cousins. The eunuch took his cousins off to one side and gave them money while the troop mounted.

As they started moving, clouds obscured the stars. It was early morning and the air was chilly. The weather reminded Robert of the many times he'd taken walks along this river bank.

Hearing the Taipings swarming inside the city sounding like billions of bees attacking a bear was enough to stir fear in any man. By now, the rebels had to know that Robert's force was small. Soldiers on the wall would have seen and reported, so he led the way around the city in an attempt to reach the river to escape.

The Taipings on the wall started shooting at his troop, but they were out of range of the muskets and crossbows. Then Robert heard the shouting of a large body of men coming from the direction they were headed. When he saw the vanguard in the distance, he knew that there had to be hundreds of rebels in that formation. "We have to turn back." He wheeled his horse. "The way to the river is blocked."

A cannon boomed.

His reaction was to jump from the horse and drag Ayaou and the children to the ground so he could cover them with his body. He expected to get hit by grapeshot or see some of his men blown out of their saddles. Instead, it appeared from the sound of the boom and the bright flash that the ancient cannon must have exploded and taken some of the Taipings on the battlements with it. They were fortunate that the modern cannons faced the river.

How had the Taipings taken a third of China? Were the imperial armies that bad? If so, he knew another reason why China couldn't defend itself against foreign invasions. It meant that the corruption among the Manchu generals was worse than Robert had thought. They must have bribed their way to be put in charge of armies.

While riding north, there was a skirmish with a group of Taipings guarding a roadblock. His troop fired the Colt revolvers as they charged. Once again, surprise and superioirity in weapons won the moment but that could last only as long as they had ammunition.

As they rode past the roadblock and up the dirt road, he didn't see any muskets with the sprawled bodies of the dead Taipings, but there were crossbows.

Robert stopped his troop and listened to the sounds of men chanting and the tramp of many feet. "We're being followed," he said. "Push the horses harder. We have to put distance between us and whoever that is. Hopefully, when we reach the mountains, we will lose them."

"Sounds like there's a thousand of them," Leopold said with his thick German accent.

As the miles slipped beneath the horses' hooves, the sounds of pursuit diminshed.

By midnight, Robert and his troop dismounted and walked the horses. They might have hundreds of miles to go before they would be safe. Without the horses, Robert doubted they would survive.

Once they were away from the rich, agricultural, flatlands around Ningpo, they would be entering hills then mountains. He thought the best chance to escape was to head to

Shanghai. The trouble was, there were Taiping armies between Ningpo and Shanghai. If those armies were alerted, they would be ready and waiting.

Chapter 54

Concerned faces gathered around the map Robert spread on the ground. "We can't go north," he said. "The Taipings will be watching for us to try for Hangzhou Bay, and we cannot go west either, since the Taipings have occupied the city of Hangzhou."

"What are we going to do?" Anwar asked.

"We go southwest until we have bypassed Hangzhou then turn northwest and make for the Yangtze River."

"That's more than two hundred miles," Anwar said. "After we are north of Hangzhou, why not turn east and ride to Shanghai?"

"The Taipings have an army between us and Shanghai. The last report I read before leaving Peking said they were less than fifty miles from the city."

"My god, what are we going to do?" Leopold said. "It doesn't matter what direction we go, there is always a Taiping army in the way." It took Robert a moment to figure out what the German said owing to his accent.

"Calm down, Leo," Anwar said. "Pointing out the obvious isn't going to help." Leopold looked sheepish.

"We move toward Nanking," Robert said.

Everyone looked shocked. Even Guan-jaih. "Sir," Anwar said, "Nanking is the Taiping capital. We would be walking into a viper's nest."

"We have to do the unexpected," Robert said. "Two Ch'ing armies are operating east of Nanking along the Yangtze and Generals Li Hung-chang and Charles Gordon command them."

"What about Lake Tai?" one of the Shanghai men asked. "It's closer than the Yangtze. If we reach the lake, we can take a boat to Shanghai."

"That's another option," Robert replied, "and the Grand Canal meets the lake."

What he did not say was that Li Hung-chang was a friend and when Robert had reached Shanghai, he'd sent a message to Li about the raid on Ningpo to save Ayaou and the children. He had written that if he couldn't escape Ningpo by boat, he would ride overland toward Li's army.

Li Hung-chang was no fool. He was Han Chinese and was an intelligent, capable but ruthless general. If Li expected Robert to come overland, he would move troops south to close the gap.

"It's a gamble," Anwar said.

"I see it as our only choice," Robert said.

"We could head toward Hong Kong," another man said.

"Too far," Robert said. "More than twice the distance. We'd run into bandits, pirates, brigands and rebels. Apak's pirate fleet works the waters between Ningpo and Hong Kong. He has spies along the coast. No, we will make for the Yangtze. Mount. We have to get moving."

They rode through the night. Reaching the top of a hill as dawn arrived, Robert saw a large force of Taipings blocking the road ahead and haulted his troop. Waist high grass grew on both sides of the dirt track they had been following. "Hobble the horses and let them feed," he said, dismounting.

Anwar rummaged in his pack and brought out a tube that was a collapsing telescope. His wild hair looked like a bush that had lost its foliage. "Got it in India," he said, and handed the scope to Robert.

What he saw was depressing. The Taipings blocking the road were armed with muskets. He also saw a man dressed in Western clothing, who seemed to be giving commands. Could that be my phantom Englishman? Robert thought.

He adjusted the telescope attempting to increase the magnification to see the man's face but couldn't. His hands tightened on the tube, and he gritted his teeth in frustration. That man is like a nightmare, he thought.

He was tempted to charge downhill and fight. With the repeating rifles and the Colt revolvers, some of his people might break through and escape.

"What is it, Robert?" Ayaou asked. She had walked up behind him.

Frustrated, he shook his head. "Taipings are blocking the road," he said. "It looks like a foreign devil is leading them."

"Ba Ba," Anna said. Robert glanced at his little girl, who was holding one of Ayaou's hands, and her eyes were swimming in tears. "*Ta men dai,*" she said, meaning, 'They bad?' She pointed at the distant Taipings as a tear slipped from one eye. Robert picked her up, and her little arms went around his neck. He swallowed as a lump appeared in his throat. "I will protect you," he said.

Her arms tightened, and she buried her face against his shoulder. She smelled like warm hay. No, he was not going to charge down there and trust capricious fate. Imagining Ayaou and his children bloody and dead was more than he could deal with. Then he thought of the families of the loyal men who had risked their lives to help save his family. There was no way he was going to fight a pitched battle if it could be avoided.

"Let me look," Ayaou said.

He handed her the scope. Guan-jiah came, and Robert gave Anna to the eunuch. The child accepted the servant immediately. Guan-jiah started to sing to her while he carried her back to where her infant brother was sleeping. Herbert was curled on the ground on a bed of thick grass the eunuch had picked. The infant's knees were tucked tight against his chest. The sun was beating on him, and his hair glowed from the light. A thumb was tucked into one corner of his mouth. He looked fragile, like a snail without a shell.

Robert turned from this vision of innocence and put an arm around Ayaou. He couldn't stop thinking that Herbert might not get a chance to grow up and discover a woman to love.

Ayaou looked through the telescope for a long time before she handed it to Anwar.

"That could be the man who was leading the Longhaired Bandits that kidnapped us in the Peking market," she said. "They were dressed like bannermen, but he was dressed like you and your men. He spoke Mandarin with a bad accent. He was not nice. When Anna cried, he slapped her and told her he would throw her in a fire if she did not stop. He was at the Ningpo temple three days ago. How did he get here so fast?"

"My god, I should have thought of that," Robert said. "That demon guessed right that we would go southwest, so he marched inland through the night to cut us off. He must have driven his men like cattle and taken an easier route. The path we have been following curves around like a snake doubling the distance."

Anwar was staring through the scope. "What I'm looking at is a traitor," he said. "I would love to get my hands on that man."

"You aren't the only one who wants that," Robert said. "Unfortunately, we don't have the luxury. He has at least two hundred men, and they are armed with muskets, which takes away our advantage."

"What now?" Anwar asked.

"Backtrack down this hill and turn north at the first path we find then head for the Grand Canal where we will find boats. The Grand Canal goes to the Yangtze and from there to Peking. Even if we don't run into the Grand Canal, we will eventually find the Yangtze, which we can't miss. Once on the river, we may be able to reach Shangahi. We aren't out of options yet."

Anwar was silent for a moment, then said, "He has a field glass, and he's looking in our direction."

Robert felt a shock race through him then shouted. "Off the hill!" Startled faces turned toward him, then the troop scrambled to get off the hilltop.

While they were riding, Anwar folded his telescope and stored it in his pack. "That rat has several hundred miles to catch us," he said. "I don't like the odds."

"I don't either," Robert replied. "However, unless something better materializes, it's what we're going to do—try to reach the Yangtze and hope we find Li Hung-chang or Charles Gorden. At times, we will have to walk the horses. If we push them, they will start dying on us. Without the horses, we are lost for sure. With the horses, we can cover seventy-five to a hundred miles a day. Without them, only a third of that distance at best.

"That group," he gestured toward the Taipings on the other side of the hill, "is at least two hours from us, and the Taipings from Ningpo may be three or four hours behind us. I don't think they have been stopping to rest as often as we have."

Leopold, the German, joined them. "It sounds like we are in a vise," he said. Anwar glared at him. Leopold squirmed. "Don't look at me like that."

"Then don't talk about how bad our situation is."

Leopold swallowed then turned to Robert. "This Charles Gordon," he said, "was he once an engineering officer in the British army?"

"Yes," Robert replied.

"Then I know of him. He also fought in the Second Opium War against the Ch'ing Dynasty. I find it strange that he is working for them now. He was in charge of blowing up most of the Summer Palace. They say Gordon hated that job but had no choice."

Sixteen hours later, as another night loomed, the horses looked as if they were the walking dead. They had slowed to a crawl hours ago and were dragging their hooves through the dust.

A running man could have caught them at that pace. The horses' heads and tails drooped and the muscles in their legs quivered with each step. Robert's body ached, and he wanted to sleep for a week. It was easy to see by the slumped figures that everyone else was in the same exhausted state.

Anna had gone to sleep in Robert's arms, and Ayaou was struggling to stay on her saddle. Her eyelids looked heavy.

Not far from Robert, Guan-jiah, who carried Herbert, was also struggling to stay awake. His head nodded, fell forward until his chin touched his chest, then he jerked erect and smacked his face several times until his cheeks glowed red from the blows.

The dirt track they followed ran northwest and was climbing higher. For the moment, the Taipings were out of sight, yet Robert knew if he stopped, they would quickly close the gap.

Several times, he'd ridden alone to a hill they had recently crossed and waited. He'd seen the two groups, the one following them from Ningpo and the one with the foreign devil, join forces hours ago. Then he would ride his horse hard to catch up with his troop.

The Taipings numbered at least six hundred. Robert suspected that his men didn't have much ammunition left. Even if every shot killed a Taiping, hundreds would survive.

When they reached the top of another hill, the troop rode into a valley with a small, walled town in the center surrounded by farms. The sun was already slipping below the horizon as another night arrived.

Robert twisted in the saddle to study the road behind them. It was empty as far as he could see. However, there was the hint of a dust cloud in the distance marking where the Taipngs were marching.

It was too dangerous to stop, but they needed rest.

An evening fog was forming in the valley. "Let's ride to that town and get behind a wall," he said. "Dismount and walk the horses. They need a break and walking will do us good."

"What are you thinking, Inspector General?" Anwar asked.

"That we can't go much further without stopping to eat and sleep. The Taipings have to rest too. After all, despite what they believe about their leader being sent to them by God, they are still human."

"That town could become a trap," Anwar said. "There might even be Taipings there."

"I've thought of that. What other choice have we?"

Anwar gestured toward a large grove of trees halfway down the hill and off to the right. "We camp there. It would be better to stay in the open. Those walls don't look that impressive."

"You're right," Robert replied, and led his troop off the road into the trees where they were soon hidden. With Guan-jiah's help, he strung a rope between the trees and tied the horses to it. Anwar and Leopold returned to the road and used branches broken off trees to obscure the tracks that showed them leaving the dirt path.

"Before anyone sleeps, pull as much grass as you can and feed your mounts," Robert said. "We will need them fed and rested in the morning. See if there is water nearby. The horses need water too."

By the time the men were sleeping, it was close to two in the morning. Robert checked Cooper's wound and found that he'd managed to keep it clean and no infection had set in. The crossbow bolt had hit his thigh and tore it open. It was an ugly wound.

"I've lost blood," Cooper said. "All of this riding caused it to open a few times and start bleeding again."

"Let's see if we can find some spider webs in these bushes." Robert had learned that trick from Ayaou. "We'll pack the wound with as many as we can find. That should help slow the bleeding and form a scab."

"I have some pepper in my pack," Guan-jiah said.

"Good, we'll mix the pepper with the spider webs and fill the wound." Robert put a hand on Cooper's bald head. It was cool. "Here, drink." He handed Cooper his tin canteen.

Cooper drank most of the water before handing the canteen back. "Thank you, Inspector General," he said, and closed his eyes. Guan-jiah went looking for spider webs.

So far, Robert had not lost one man. He thanked God for that. He took that as a sign that his life with Ayaou was not cursed and wasn't going to end soon. He was sure they would have many years together. Then he had a shocking thought. The Taipings believed in the same God, and he shivered.

As the hours crawled, the heat of day dissipated and the air chilled. Robert was exhausted but couldn't sleep. He worried about Ayaou, the children, and the men whose lives he was risking.

He walked to the edge of the grove to watch the dirt road. The fog had settled like pools in the bottom of the valley and had obscured the walled town. He looked at the full moon as a breeze rustled the trees with a soothing sound. The damp scent of the earth wrapped around him, and he was tempted to close his eyes. Maybe this was a nightmare, and he would wake up in bed with Ayaou and hear Herbert crying for milk early in the morning before the roosters signaled the coming dawn.

Then he wondered who this Englishman was that was hounding them. Could he somehow be connected to all the problems that went back to that time he had been assaulted in Ningpo? Could it be Hollister? After all, Hollister had tried to discredit him with slander more than once. He was the only man Robert could think of who held a grudge against him.

He heard the crunch of leaves and turned as Ayaou appeared from the mist. It was cold and he could see she was shivering. He pulled her against him to share the warmth, and her nearness infused him with strength.

"You should get some sleep," he said.

"What about you?"

"I can't."

"You are worried?"

Robert nodded. "Besides you and the children, I have these men to consider. Some have families, and they risked their lives when I asked them to."

"And this surprises you?" she said. "You are a great man and great men inspire others."

He blushed, and his face grew hot. "You've been reading too much poetry, Ayaou." She buried her face against his chest. Robert was sure that Ayaou was thinking the same thing he was—that once they were out of this mess, they would never be apart again.

Dawn appeared along the horizon as a slim, icy band of misty light. In an hour, the sun would be following that light into the sky.

"Master!" Guan-jiah came running from the top of the hill. He was breathing hard and pointing behind him. "There's trouble! The Longhaired Bandits!"

"Haven't you slept?" It was obvious that the eunuch hadn't.

"It's a good thing that I didn't," Guan-jiah replied, "or we would all be dead soon. Follow me." He turned and walked to the top of the hill.

Ayaou and Robert followed. Near the top, the eunuch went on his hands and knees and crawled the last few yards on his belly. Ayaou and Robert followed his example.

"Oh, good god," Robert said when he saw hundreds of Taipings climbing the far side of the hill his troop was camped on. Soon, they would be in the valley. It was easy to spot the Western man leading them. "That man must be the devil," he said.

They hurried back to camp. Guan-jiah and Ayaou went to ready the horses. "Get up! Get up!" Robert said, shaking the men awake. "Mount your horses. We have to cross this valley. The Taipings are almost on us. If we are fortunate, the fog will hide us."

Chapter 55

Robert helped Ayaou onto a horse. "Guan-jiah, carry Herbert. I'll take Anna." He turned to the others. "Stay in the trees. It's too risky returning to the road, and the trees will provide cover until we reach the farmland at the bottom of the hill. Once we are in the open, the Taipings may see us and start shooting. That's when we ride like hell is nipping at our heels."

"Thank God the horses are rested," Anwar said.

Robert glanced to where the horses had been tethered and saw the grass surrounding the trees was gone. It looked as if the horses had used their hooves to dig up the roots. He hoped that would be enough to sustain them since there would be no stopping now.

The first horse, foaming at the mouth, died late in the afternoon. Its front legs collapsed with its hindquarters stuck in the air. The entire party stopped and stared as the rider jumped free. With a groan, the quivering horse rolled over and let out a long breath with its eyes rolling in fear. The rider pulled out his revolver and fired one shot to end the animal's suffering.

Robert feared they weren't going to make it. "Double up," he said, and the man climbed behind another rider.

By the time dusk arrived, three horses had gone lame and were set free.

"We have to walk," he said. "If we keep losing horses, we will not survive."

Cooper slipped from his horse and sat by the side of the road, and Robert dismounted and walked back leading his horse. "What are you doing? Can't you see the dust cloud is closer. We have to keep moving."

"Go on without me," Cooper said. His bald head was covered with sweat and his face was the color of pale-yellow parchment. "The least I can do is slow them down and kill as many as possible, but give me more ammunition. I have only twenty rounds left." He pulled out his shirt and exposed his thigh wound, which had scabbed over but was still seeping blood. In fact, the pant leg was soaked in it. "I do not have the energy to go on. See that dead tree over there." He pointed. "I will make my stand behind that."

"If you cannot walk, you will ride a horse. If you don't, we will stay and fight with you until we are all dead. I will leave no man behind. I am your son's godfather and will not tell your wife you died because we abandoned you."

Cooper looked at the others, who had gathered around. He frowned, shook his head and then wearily struggled to stand. Leopold slipped an arm around him. They leaned against each other and started walking.

Like a shepherd, Robert stayed at the rear of his flock driving them forward. If anyone fell behind, he begged them to keep going. If begging didn't work, he shouted, threatened and bullied.

When sunset spread itself in a blaze of autumn colors along the horizon, Anwar said, "The demons are getting closer."

Exhausted faces turned and stared. "Those fiends must be running," one of the men said. "They can't be human."

"Mount," Robert said. "We will ride until the horses drop. Then we will abandon them and walk." The sense of impending doom and defeat was overwhelming. He was determined not to be taken alive. Before shooting himself, he would put a bullet in each of his children and Ayaou.

"I smell water," she said, as if she did not believe her senses. She was standing beside her horse. Then she shouted. "Water! It's water!" Her horse must have smelled the water too, and it started to run. Ayaou grabbed a handfull of mane and leaped on.

Robert mounted and kicked his horse in the ribs urging it to move. If Ayaou was right and that was the Yangtze, there might be boats and a chance to escape.

A bend in the road and the trees obscured the view. Then the shouting of hundreds of men in unison came from beyond the trees, and Robert felt an iciness invade his bowels.

That devil of an Englishman must have somehow managed to get another band of Taipings to block their retreat. He knew how Cooper must have felt when he didn't want to go on and was tempted to give up too. He pulled his horse to a stop and twisted to look behind him.

The Taipings following them came into sight and were close enough so Robert could see the red cloth bands tied around their foreheads. The expressions on their sweaty dirt stained faces was a mixture of exertion, determination and feverish hate.

Robert had one regret. If he died before he could shoot Ayaou and the children, they would suffer horribly at the hands of the rebels. He didn't want that to happen. He turned at the sound of shouting and saw Guan-jiah racing toward the trees and that bend in the road. "Guan-jiah, no!" Robert said, as the eunuch vanished from sight.

Robert felt totally defeated for the first time in his life. "My son." He felt wretched and tears of defeat stung his eyes. Believing that his servant and son were already dead, he took the Colt revolver and pressed the barrel against the back of Anna's little head. He had a responsibility to shoot her, so she wouldn't suffer. Then he would find Ayaou and shoot her before killing himself.

Anwar was yelling for the men to form a British battle square. "We will fight to the last man!" he said. "We will not surrender!" Anwar ran to Ayaou, grabbed her and dragged her off her horse and into the middle of the small square the men were forming. He waved at Robert. "Inspector General, hurry! They are almost on us!"

Although defeat had settled into his guts like a pile of stones, Robert couldn't pull the trigger and kill his little girl. Slipping the weapon into its holster, he lifted Anna and turned her so she faced him. She leaned into him, pressed her face into his shirt and her little arms went around his neck. He was going to follow Guan-jiah and die fighting, and Anna would die with him.

When the Taipings started shooting, Anna would be hit first. He had turned her around so she wouldn't see death coming. He kissed the top of her head. "I love you," he said, as tears filled his eyes. He would never hear her play the piano again. "Hold on tight."

She grabbed the back of his shirt and twisted the fabric with her hands.

The horse leaped forward when he dug his heels into its sides and galloped past Anwar's British military square. Startled faces turned and stared. Robert pulled his Colt and cocked the hammer. Leaning forward, he urged the horse to run faster as the tears blinded him and the world blurred.

His horse pounded around the corner with thick trees closing in on both sides, and then he saw the imperial Manchu banner company in full battle array. He pulled hard on the reins, and the horse skidded to a stop. Frantically wiping the tears from his eyes, he blinked and squinted. He couldn't believe what he was seeing.

Maybe I'm dead, he thought. These were the elite of the Manchu army, and they sat on their warhorses with pride. The yellow color of their uniforms and flags told him they were from one of the upper three banners, which served only the emperor. Robert's bodyguard came from the same banner.

It looked as if it were one of the smaller units, a *niru*, about three-hundred men. Robert slid from his horse, but his legs wouldn't support him. Hugging Anna to his chest, he stumbled two steps toward the Manchu formation. He was dizzy, and the world swirled around him. Losing his balance, he fell to his knees and rolled onto his side. The child squirmed from his grasp and started crying.

"Hold me, Ba Ba! Hold me!" Anna said. Her mouth was twisted into an ugly grimace of fear, and the tears had mingled with the dirt smearing her face. She held her arms out, and he managed to pull her to him.

The wind came from the river rustling the trees and snapping the plain yellow banners. The soldiers opened a path between the columns allowing Robert's dazed men to lead their horses through the Manchu ranks to the rear of the *niru's* formation.

Anwar had dissolved the British square and had followed Robert.

Still sitting in the dirt, Robert turned and saw that the Taipings had halted at the curve in the road less than a hundred yards away and were milling about. The devil of an Englishman walked back and forth haranguing them, and the rebels started forming a battle line. The Manchu then moved forward to form their battle line between Robert and the Taipings.

We are out of the demon's reach, Robert thought, and he started to laugh, then Ayaou was there holding him. He buried his face in Anna's hair and took a deep breath. She smelled of childish sweat and the sun and the sky.

Compared to the Manchu, the Taipings were a band of undisciplined bandits and only a third had muskets. Although the bannermen had been defeated by modern foreign armies in the last two Opium Wars, Robert knew that the Taipings were no match for these seasoned warriors. Besides swords and lances, they had muskets and those weapons were out and ready. He was sure that every man in this *niru* was a crack shot and could hit a target at a hundred yards at a full gallop.

A ragged crackle of musket fire came from the Taipings. A few of the Manchu were hit. Some fell from their saddles. The imperial battle line did not waver.

Robert pulled Ayaou and Anna to the ground covering them with his body. He heard a Manchu officer bark orders. The bannermen lifted their rifles, aimed and fired. The sound was like a solid clap of thunder. They started to reload.

Another ragged volley came from the Taipings. A few more Manchu were hit. Since the bannermen blocked his view, Robert couldn't see how many casualties the rebels were taking.

The Manchu commanding officer, whose rank Robert saw from the markings on the uniform, came and helped him up. Ayaou stood and Anna slipped between them holding her mother and father's hands.

"I am here to deliver Prince Kung's message," the Manchu officer said. "He hoped the rescue would not be too late. General Li Hung-chang was ready when we arrived, and he directed my *niru* to take this road. The armies are looking for you along this side of the Yangtze. I am honored to be the one who found you."

"I am grateful," Robert said. His voice sounded hollow, as if it didn't belong to him. He pulled Ayaou closer, and she rested her head on his shoulder and closed her eyes. He lifted Anna from the ground, and she clung to him.

"Prince Kung ordered General Jung Lu to send the banners to find you and make sure you returned to Peking safely."

"How many banners did he send?" Robert asked, having a difficult time believing he was standing in the middle of China while a battle was brewing talking to this man in Mandarin as if they were old friends. In fact, he knew this officer. "You were with me in Hankow when we confronted Governor General Kuan-wen."

"That is true. I have the privilege of serving you again." The officer dropped to one knee and lowered his head.

"No, don't do that," Robert said, and reached for the officer to get him to stand. "I won't allow anyone to kneel to me. After all, your men saved my family and my friends."

A strange look appeared on the officer's face as if he were seeing one of heaven's creatures. "I was told," he said in a hushed voice, "that if I didn't bring 'Our Hart' back alive, my head might be removed. Inspector General, many thanks for holding on." He signaled his men to get ready.

The Manchu army was divided into eight banners. Half were in Peking. The *niru* was the smallest unit. Five *niru* made up one *jalan* and five *jalan* made up one *gusa* or banner. So, under ideal conditions one full banner, like the plain yellow, had about seven-thousand-five-hundred fighting men.

"Before you go into battle, I have one request," Robert said.

"Your words are my command," the officer replied.

"There is an Englishman in Western clothing with those Taipings. Do all that you can to capture him. It is important that I question him."

The commander of the *niru* effortlessly swung into his saddle. Taking Anna and Ayaou, Robert walked closer to the fight and climbed into a tree so he could see better. Ayaou stayed on the ground and stood behind the tree while peering around it.

The bannermen were dressed in padded war robes and the horses draped with padded battle armor. They charged in a line sending up a boiling cloud of dust. More than a thousand hooves pounded the earth. The *neru* fired another volley. Robert saw hundreds of Taipings fall. Some lay still while others writhed and screamed. It looked like half the rebels were already down.

The bannermen slipped the muskets into the leather holders attached to their saddles and lowered their lances. Every movement was precision and done at blinding speed.

The Taipings fired a ragged volley and several bannermen tumbled from their horses. Then the Manchu warriors slammed into the Taipings like a tsunami hitting a beach.

After the lances had impaled hundreds more, out came the swords. Robert watched as the last of the day's sunlight reflected from the blades as they fell and came up bloody while the yellow banners fluttered and snapped in the breeze. He heard the ring of metal as swords clashed and the dull thuds of horses' hooves pounding flesh.

Robert handed Anna to Ayaou then climbed down. She leaned against him. Guan-jiah arrived to watch the battle with a fierce look on his face. His lips were moving but Robert couldn't hear what the eunuch was saying.

"What is it, Guan-jiah?" he asked.

"I should be out there killing Longhaired Bandits for what they did to the mistress and the children."

Robert suppressed the urge to laugh, because too much killing was going on. This should be a serious moment. No place for levity. He had to show the right attitude as an example for his family and men. He would never have guessed that his gentle servant could be so dangerous looking—this philosopher eunich that lived to be an adopted uncle for his children.

The Taipings, like true zealots, fought to the last man without giving an inch. Near the end, a few formed a circle while the bannermen swirled around them like a tornado slashing with swords. After the battle, the *niru* suffered two dozen casualties and lost a score of men.

One bannerman came riding back, swung off his horse and bowed to Robert. "Inspector General," he said, while staring at the ground, "the commander sent me. We have captured the foreign devil as you requested. What do you want to do with him?"

"Take me to him." He had to do something about all this bowing and scraping. After all, he wasn't the emperor. He wasn't even a prince. He handed Anna to Guan-jiah. The soldier guided him through the carnage of the battlefield where soldiers were busy cutting off rebel heads.

One wounded Taiping struggled to stand. A bannerman walk up behind him, grabbed his hair, jerked his head back and slashed the cutting edge of his sword across the man's throat severing the head. A fountain of blood gushed from the neck stump as the bannerman pushed the body away from him. It hit the dirt with a dull thud. The bannerman tossed the head, and it bounced when it hit the ground.

In the middle of the battlefield a knot of bannermen surrounded the Englishman, who was on his knees. The man's arms were tied behind him and a bannerman was holding his hair forcing him to look at Robert as he approached.

The man's white face was smeared with a mixture of dust and blood. He had a fresh cut on his cheek that was bleeding. "You look familiar," Robert said in Mandarin. "Do I know you?"

The man struggled and when he couldn't break free, he spat at Robert but even that fell short. "You bastard," he said. "You ruined my life."

"How so?" Robert asked. "I honestly don't know you and do not know what you are talking about."

"Captain Patridge dismissed me back in fifty-five after you told him you wouldn't work with me. I had to become an opium smuggler and a common thief to survive."

Robert knew where he'd seen this man before, but he couldn't remember his name. "We were in the same boat during that fight against the Taipings when Patridge recovered the opium. You were angry with me after that meeting in the captain's cabin—before the fight. Patridge said you were the illegitimate son of an earl. I don't recall your name."

"You should," he said.

"Why?"

"I was behind the death of your concubine. I am the one who told Ward where that cottage near Ningpo was and goaded him so he would go after you. I wanted him to kill you, but he only killed that pregnant bitch." He struggled to break free. The two bannermen holding him strained to keep him pinned in place.

He should have been angry. Robert should have killed the man then, but he had a feeling this man was responsible for more than Shao-mei's death. He wanted to know everything. "And you were the one that tried to have me abducted and forced to serve in a Britsh man-of-war headed for the Americas."

"That was Hollister. He didn't have the stomach to have you killed. He just wanted to ruin your life as you did to us. Later, I hired a man to go after you, but that fool failed. You killed him. After that, none of my people could get close."

"I heard Hollister was smuggling opium," Robert said.

"He was until he lost two of our three ships to whores and gambling. I killed the fool and tossed his corpse into the Pacific and let the fish have him."

Robert wasn't surprised.

The man twisted his face into a mask of hate. "Hollister was riddled with syphilis and his brain was rotting. He deserved what he got."

Then Robert remembered. "You are Unwyn Fiske."

Fiske cackled. "So, you haven't forgotten, after all."

"I haven't thought about you for years," Robert said. "Why should I? That battle was one day in my life—a few hours."

Fiske peeled his lips from his teeth and leered. "I have hated you from the moment you opened your mouth and wanted to save those boat people."

"How odd," Robert said. "You didn't speak Chinese then."

"There was nothing in Britian for me. After all, I was dismissed from Jardine and Matheson because of you. My father didn't want me in England reminding him that he had a bastard. China offered opportunities, so I stayed and learned the language. Men were making fortunes. That stopped after they put you in charge of Chinese Maritime Customs. You ruined it." He struggled to break free again.

"You were the Englishman behind the thefts from the Forbidden City."

Fiske's eyes widened. "How did you discover that?"

Robert looked at the Manchu commander. Since Fiske and Robert had been speaking Mandarin, the officer understood every word. Fiske had caused the emperor's upper banners to lose face, because they couldn't stop the thefts. One bannerman had lost his legs and arms and been stuffed in a cage to hang from the barrack's ceiling as a reminder of the banner's embarrassment.

"Guess who helped the Dynasty catch your partners in crime," Robert said.

"You?" What little color was left in Fiske's face drained away.

"Yes. After that failed, like everything else you have done with your life, you went to the Taipings and offered your services to them. Then you talked them into coming after me. When they couldn't get near me, you persuaded them to take my family."

"Don't give yourself credit for everything," Fiske said. "I was being paid by the Taipings before you arrived in China. I was going to be rich and powerful. I was going to show my father."

Robert kept his face composed as if that news had not surprised him. If what Fiske said was true, he was the reason for Jardine and Matheson's lost opium shipments. He was the man Patridge had been looking for. "Now, I understand. You were feeding information to the Taipings about Ward's movements that led to his early defeats?"

"You ruined that too," Fiske said. "I could have become wealthy off Ward's stupidity. I heard rumors that Li Hung-chang was behind Ward's death. You and General Li have become close. I assumed you helped Li get rid of Ward to avenge the death of your bitch."

"Enough," Robert said. He glanced at the Manchu commander. "I am done with him. Do whatever you want."

The officer nodded. Robert walked away.

"Get back here, Hart!" Fiske said.

That was the last time Robert saw him. Fiske was taken to the Forbidden City and died slowly from *chi-lin*, the death of ten thousand cuts. Robert later heard that the pain drove Fiske mad before he died. The first thing the royal torturer did was peel the skin from his face as if it were an orange.

While they were steaming north along China's coast toward Tienstsin and home, Robert and Ayaou went on deck. They stood by the rail. The children were in the cabin sleeping while Guan-jiah watched over them.

Robert had an arm draped across Ayaou's shoulders. He could smell the salt water and sun in her hair. A look of tranquiltiy was on her face.

"While I was in that temple waiting to die," she said, "I reached a place of peace I have never known. I was not afraid. I knew that my beheading was going to take place soon. That you might not be able to save me.

"I had come to my own wisdom," she said. "I understood what nature had long hinted at us to understand through the moon and the river. The river flows day and night and like the moon it never disappears. It does not stay full at all times. But it is always there."

Chapter 56

It was a cold day in February when Robert returned to Peking with his family. On the way back, he stopped in Shanghai then Tientsin where he left the men who had fought beside him, which was a luxury he did not have, and he envied them for it.

It never occurred to him that with power came sacrifice, such as living away from home for weeks and months at a time while his children grew without him. He'd been in China almost ten years. When he first arrived, his dreams had never reached this high, and he questioned if achieving more than he had wanted was a curse.

Unlike the men who worked for him, he had to be satisfied with a few days at home before he was off again dealing with challenges brought on by the turmoil in China. He was still rebuilding the mess he had inherited from Horatio Lay, and he prayed he could turn it in to an efficient organization that one day would run itself like a well-oiled machine giving him more time at home. What a luxury it would be to sit down daily for supper with Ayaou and the children as his father had. They could talk, and he could ask Anna and Herbert what they had done that day.

Soon, he'd be gone on another inspection tour. He couldn't ignore the fact that he had three children, and the most challenging child was the Chinese Maritime Customs service, which he ruled as if he were a king.

Robert both celebrated and regretted making love to Ayaou that night. When he left in the morning, he would be gone for weeks and hating every moment away from his family. He could have had other women, but there was only one he wanted. It was important for him that he be loyal to her.

While they were making love, he heard a creaking sound outside the door and wondered if Guan-jiah was in the hall. The door was locked and there was no crack or hole to spy through. If his loyal servant was out there, all the eunuch could do was listen.

Long after Ayaou had fallen asleep, he stayed awake staring into the darkness comparing his feelings for Ayaou in 1855 to the way he felt now. He had changed. Although he still found her attractive and desirable, he didn't lust after her as he once did.

What he enjoyed more was the companionship and the things they shared. They spent their evenings talking about art, poems and books. Once a week on Sunday afternoon, they walked in one of the city's imperial gardens. They went to operas where he spent more time watching her responses than watching the drama unfold on stage. When he wasn't with her, he missed these moments.

The pain in his guts started to burn again. Not wanting to wake her, he suppressed a groan and pressed against the spot where it hurt.

The next morning before he left, he said, "Guan-jiah, I'm counting on you to write and tell me everything that is happening to Ayaou and the children." Robert handed his house manager a schedule of dates and locations. "When you said you wanted to be the adopted uncle for my children, we didn't realize just what that would mean. You have to take my place when I am not here. Make sure Anna practices the violin and the piano daily. Do not neglect their language lessons. I want them to speak English, French, Mandarin and Cantonese perfectly."

"I will write often," the eunuch replied. "If Anna loses a tooth, you will read about it."

"Thank you." He put a hand on the eunuch's shoulder. "I'm glad you're here, Guan-jiah. With you watching the children, I'm sure they will become fine, upstanding individuals even if their father is absent."

Guan-jiah blushed and stared at the floor. The paper with the list of locations and dates slipped from his fingers and fluttered away like a butterfly. He scrambled after it. "Sorry, Master."

He did not like it when Guan-jiah called him master. He had tried to stop that, but this time he didn't say a word.

In October, Robert ate lunch at his Shanghai house with Major General Brown, the commanding general of the British troops in Hong Kong.

"Have you heard about Charles Gordon?" the general asked.

Robert sipped Spanish sherry. "Yes," he said, putting the glass down. "One of my people mentioned that he fought in the second opium war. He also took command of *The Ever Victorious Army* soon after Ward died at the battle of Tzeki. I've heard he has been defeating the Taipings."

"You do keep up with events, don't you?" General Brown said. "You are as sharp as they say. Gordon is doing an excellent job."

"I don't know much about Gordon beyond what I've heard," Robert said. "I know that he took part in the destruction of the Summer Palace outside Peking. What else was he involved in?"

"He fought under Staveley around Shanghai when they drove the Taipings from the city."

"If Gordon took part in the destruction of the Summer Palace, I wonder how he gained the command of *The Ever Victorious Army*."

General Brown snorted and then laughed. "That is a complicated and ironic story. The Chinese were not happy with Ward's first replacement and the governor of Jiangsu province asked Staveley to appoint a British officer to take command. I don't think the Ch'ing Dynasty knows Gordon blew up most of their precious Summer Palace."

"The Dynasty must have been impressed with how Staveley handled the Taipings outside Shanghai to ask for his advice." Robert picked up a knife and cut into the roast chicken on his plate. He took another sip of sherry.

The general nodded. "Gordon held the rank of major when he took command of that army. He immediately marched his troops forty miles northwest of Shanghai to drive the Taipings from the town of Chansu. He did such an admirable job that he won the respect of his men. Under Ward, they weren't much better than an unruly mob. Gordon trained them and created a disciplined, military force."

Robert signaled a servant to refill the General's wineglass and bring out the plum pudding. When the servant refilled the glasses, the general took another sip. "Excellent sherry," he said.

"I'm glad you approve. I have several cases. Take one when you return to Hong Kong."

"Thank you kindly."

"How has Gordon done since Chansu?" Robert asked.

The General finished chewing a mouthful of chicken. He speared a piece of boiled potato dripping with butter. After he chewed and swallowed, he wiped his mouth. "After Chansu, he captured Kunshan, but it cost his army heavy casualties. He's there now bringing his forces back to strength before joining Li Hung-chang's army to take the city of Soochow from the Taipings."

"Li Hung-chang and I worked together once," Robert said. "I rely on him to verify information I'm gathering from my custom's offices about what's going on in China. He has an excellent spy network."

"Why don't you join me tomorrow? Gordon sent one of his gunboats, the *Firefly*, to bring me to see what he is up to."

"I'd love to see what Gordon has done with this army," Robert said. "I fought under Ward soon after I arrived in China. He made me an officer in command of men."

"You fought in Ward's army?" the General said, surprised. "I didn't know that. How did that go?"

"I only fought in one battle. Ward blundered and it almost cost my life."

"I'm not surprised. Ward made mistakes on the battlefield. He was a man without fear, but he lacked common sense. On the other hand, you will be impressed with Gordon. He has built a fortress at Kunshan. When we sail tomorrow, I want to hear more about your adventures with Ward during the trip."

"I would not call it an adventure. More like a tragedy."

That night rebels boarded the *Firefly* as she lay at her moorings, and the gunboat was burned and sunk. The boat's engineers vanished. The trip to meet Gordon did not take place, and General Brown returned to Hong Kong. Robert's friend, Li Hung-chang and Charles Gordon joined forces in December 1863 to take the city of Soochow.

Another crisis was about to threaten the Ch'ing Dynasty.

Prince Kung called Robert to his palace early in March 1864. The messenger didn't tell Robert the reason except that it was serious.

He knew what such meetings usually meant. *Our Hart* was the man to call when a crisis appeared others could not solve. He assumed that this was another such challenge.

The meeting took place in Kung's garden. It was a fairy tale scene with trees full of birds and ponds stocked with brightly colored carp flashing about under the surface of the reflecting water. It was hard to remember that outside the tall walls surrounding this lush palace there was so much danger and suffering.

"An incident has taken place between Charles Gordon and Li Hung-chang," Kung said. "It could put the Dynasty in a position of risk that may lead to defeat by the Longhaired Bandits."

"What kind of incident?" Robert asked.

"The generals had a disagreement, and Gordon does not trust Li. Gordon took his army and returned to his fortress in the Kunshan heights. The Dynasty wants you to solve this. Li and Gordon must join their armies and continue to defeat the Taipings.

"We estimate the Taiping armies in central China number two million troops. However, they are in disarray. The Dynasty cannot risk letting these armies regroup. We feel that you are the only man capable of bringing Gordon and Li Hung-chang back together before it is too late."

Li Hung-chang wasn't exactly Robert's friend. When Li was in Peking, they often ate a simple breakfast together of rice porridge with yams. They had come to rely on each other and shared information. It was more of a business relationship.

Li was the head of the imperial army called *Huai* from the Northern Yangtze River provinces. The *Huai* was known in China for its toughness. Gordon and Li working together had proved invincible.

The Taipings were retreating, as they had never done. The rebellion had killed millions on both sides. Robert thought it ironic that the leader of the Taipings, Hong Xiuquan, had named his realm the *Kingdom of Heavenly Peace*. "What are the details that caused this distrust?" he asked.

"The fracture between Li and Gordon took place during the battle for the city of Soochow," the prince said. "Weeks went by and they couldn't break through the thick walls. Deciding that another strategy might work better, they agreed to use a secret agent inside the city and sent a message to King Nah, one of the two Taiping leaders. They asked him to organize a coup for money, control of half the city of Soochow and an imperial title.

"The deal was made and ten days later King Nah murdered his partner King Mu. Nah opened the gates and surrendered Soochow to Li and Gordon's combined armies."

"A brilliant move," Robert said. "I don't understand how that caused a problem between Gordon and Li."

"I will explain," Kung replied. "Gordon was responsible for making this deal with King Nah. Before the coup, Gordon had secretly met King Nah and had given him his word that Nah would be safe. However, on the second day of the Soochow occupation, Li ordered King Nah and eight Taiping generals beheaded."

"And Gordon was furious," Robert said, "and believes his personal reputation was damaged. He thinks Li deliberately broke the agreement with King Nah. I am sure Gordon also believes that his word is worthless now, and this will affect his ability to defeat the Taipings."

Kung stared at him. "You understand?"

"Yes. I'm also sure that Gordon is refusing to cooperate with any Chinese generals."

"He said he cannot trust them to honor his promises," the prince replied, "and, the Longhaired Bandits are taking advantage of this situation. Our spies tell us they are gathering their forces to counterattack.

"Robert, we are counting on you to meet with Li and Gordon before it is too late. We must have these armies fighting together again. The imperial council and the Empress Dowagers feel you are the only man who can mend this rift."

This trust was his burden. Although he had never met Gordon, he admired the man's strengths. On the other hand, if Robert accepted this challenge and failed, the fate of an empire and millions more lives were at risk. "When will I leave?" he said.

He was already planning what he was going to say to the two generals and didn't want to consider that he might be making a horrible mistake—that he might fail.

Chapter 57

Before Robert and his bodyguards departed for Tientsin, where a steamship waited to take them to Shanghai, a shipment of books arrived from Ireland. He took two to read. One was *La Capitaine Fracasse* written by the French author Theophile Gautier. The second was also French by Victor Hugo, *Les Miserables*.

It should have been warmer since it was the beginning of spring, but it was bitterly cold. He hated traveling in such weather and had trouble sleeping, so he filled his time by reading.

Gautier's book was a fairy tale where everyone lived happily ever after, but *Les Miserables* shocked him. The main character Jean Valjean, much like him, became a force for good. Jean saved one woman from a life of prostitution as Robert had saved Ayaou from a similar fate. Jean also raised this woman's daughter as his own. In the end, Jean Valjean died but the adopted daughter went on to a happy life with her lover.

As he finished *Les Miserables*, he wondered if he were going to die like Jean Valjean. After all, he was on the way to a battle. If he died, Ayaou's life and the life of his children would become a tragedy.

The solution wasn't one he liked to dwell on. He realized that to protect Ayaou and their children, he would have to marry her no matter how she felt. He could no longer ignore it. Of course, he expected that his parents and friends would not accept Ayaou since she was Chinese and was not a Christian. However, that wasn't important. The children came first.

He didn't want them called bastards behind their backs and sometimes to their faces. Unwyn Fiske's father had sent his illigitimate son to China, because he didn't want anything to do with him. That mistake had resulted in great suffering.

When he finished reading the last book, he decided to write a letter.

"Ayaou," he said, "when I accepted this task from Prince Kung, I was surprised that they still trusted me after my failure selecting Horatio Lay to purchase a modern navy. I should have listened to you when you told me not to be so hard on myself."

He stopped writing and stared out the window remembering the first time he had sailed along this stretch of the Yangtze, which was soon after he'd arrived in China. There had been miles of beautiful scenery. The architecture of the farmhouses had caught his interest and the crops had turned the earth into a patchwork quilt of green shades. He had seen women washing their clothes and dishes in the river. Dogs and chickens had roamed free while children playing flutes rode on the backs of water buffaloes.

Staring at the destruction and desolation as the ship approached Soochow, he remembered something Ayaou had said years ago. "Above there is heaven, below there is Soochow." His vision blurred, and a phantom image of a laughing Shao-mei appeared on the glass. He could see her dimples then an image of Ayaou appeared beside her.

A thick wool blanket of despair that he hadn't felt for weeks and maybe months smothered him as if dark clouds had obscured the sun. He dipped the pen in the black pool of ink and continued writing.

"It breaks my heart to tell you this, but Soochow is no longer heaven. The destruction I see on both sides of the Yangtze is unbearable. I see headless bodies rotting on both shores. I see no living men, women or animals in sight. The once lovely farms are either burnt or abandoned.

"This isn't the first time I've seen the scars of war, but the destruction here is so total that it has struck me mute, and I wish that I were blind. I cannot describe to you how utterly melancholy this has made me. After witnessing such desolation, I am determined more than ever to mend the rift between Li and Gordon. Only when peace and order are restored to China, will these lands thrive again."

Late that afternoon, he arrived in Soochow.

"I am so glad to see you, my friend," Li Hung-chang said, after Robert was ushered into the general's headquarters. Li at six-foot-four towered over his five-foot-eight inches. Li took one of Robert's hands in both of his and shook it for what seemed forever. It wasn't a cold handshake but one expressing warmth.

Li was dressed in a casual Chinese knee-length gown. His headquarters, the mansion of a local man of wealth, had spacious gardens. "Come this way. Tea is ready and you may join me for breakfast. How are your concubine and two children? The girl's name is Anna, am I right? I have daughters, and they are a joy to behold. I was told your son's name is Herbert. After the misfortune with the Longhaired Bandits, I hope your family came out of that trial in good health and high spirits."

"Thank you for asking," Robert replied. "They are happy to be back in Peking. How's your family?"

"Too far away," Li replied. "I haven't seen them for months. All of this fighting against the Longhaired Bandits keeps me from home. Let's drink to the end of this war so we can go home and build a strong China that will withstand the ravages of time."

In Li, Robert felt he had a friend that understood how precious his feelings were for Ayaou—something Prince Kung and the other royals didn't understand. Li had been General 'Head Chopper' Tseng-kuo-fan's apprentice, and was a capable and ruthless Han Chinese. The rulers of China were Manchu, but it was becoming clear to Robert that the future of China belonged to the Han.

After three cups of hot tea and idle conversation, he was ready to work. Before he could start, Li stopped him with an upheld hand. "I know why you are here," he said. "I am glad that Prince Kung sent you."

"Why do you think that?"

"Because Gordon and I are both fans of yours," Li replied. "I also have no problem speaking to you frankly. In my career as a military man, I have had thousands of rebels beheaded. I do not know why Gordon is so upset. I had no intention of harming his reputation."

"I understand that perfectly," Robert said. "That is why there is no reason for what took place between you and

Gordon. Explain to me why you beheaded King Nah and his generals."

"They were dressed in the imperial yellow, a color that only the emperor wears," Li replied. "And they didn't want to give up their ownership of the city."

"The solution should be simple. I have an idea that may heal your relationship with Gordon, but first you must be willing to go on a journey with me."

"If you will be the bridge, I will cross it," Li said. "I trust that you will preserve my reputation and interests while achieving this."

"You have my word. Issue a statement explaining your reasons for the beheadings. In this way, Gordon will see that the beheadings were ordered for something that happened after he gave his word."

"It will be done immediately."

"When you write this statement, make sure it is clear that Gordon had nothing to do with the executions. That you are the only one responsible and make sure there is no confusion that the reason for the beheadings was King Nah disobeyed the imperial dress code and that he was greedy for more land than he was entitled to.

"Also send Gordon silver taels, enough to cover a month's worth of expenses for his army, another twenty thousand taels for his wounded and a report to the emperor crediting Gordon as the main force in attacking Soochow. After that, I will see what I can do to reimburse you for the taels you give to Gordon."

Once immersed in solving the crises, Ayaou and the children became shadows that only visited in the early morning hours. Thoughts of marriage slipped away. He stayed with Li until Gordon had accepted all the gifts then traveled to Gordon's fortress in the Kunshan Heights.

Chapter 58

Robert arrived at Gordon's fortress early in April 1864. On his way from the Yangtze to the Kunshan Heights, he rode through a water-world of lakes, streams and canals. Farms covered the land and lush vegetation and forests blanketed the slopes of the nearby hills.

After leaving the farmlands, his guards approached the fortress on a dirt track that crisscrossed hills blanketed with a thick forest. Then they emerged on a steep hillside stripped of vegetation. The road crossed in front of a moonscape of earthworks holding cannons and a death trap bristling with sharp wooden spikes.

To his great delight, Gordon arranged a military spectacle with his troops to welcome Robert. A tent with the sides rolled up sat near a bluff that plunged hundreds of feet to the shores of a lake. They stood under the canvas in shade and watched the troops march by as they moved in perfectly aligned formations.

He had never met Gordon before, who had gray eyes that had a distant look to them as if he had seen things most men never saw. He wore riding boots and a frock coat. He smoked one cigar after another and carried a small cane. Several young boys attended them, pouring tea, and offering sliced fruit.

Robert stared at the boys and doubted that any were ten years old yet.

"They are orphans," Gordon said. "The Taipings slaughtered their mothers and fathers. I saved these children from death at the hands of the Taipings and adopted them." He snapped the little cane he carried against his baggy pants for emphasis. Robert had heard the troops calling that cane

Gordon's magic wand for victory. He often went into battle with no weapons and carried only the cane.

"I hope you don't expect to have wine with supper," Gordon said. "There is no liquor in this camp, and I sent the opium smokers packing the first week I commanded this rabble."

"That was a wise move," Robert replied, remembering how Ward's army had been drunk when the Taipings attacked from the besieged city of Sungkiang. He almost died that day, but Ayaou saved him. "I heard that the Americans, French and the British didn't want you to have this command. They wanted Ward's second, Burgevine, to take it. I was against that from the start."

"You will be pleased to hear that Burgevine is dead. Drowned, thanks to Li. He said you advised the Dynasty not to place Burgevine in charge of *The Ever Victorious Army*." Gordon snorted as he laughed. "Did you know that the Taipings called these men the Almost Always Beaten Army? They are still sadly wanting, but both men and officers, although ragged and perhaps slightly disreputable, are in capital order and well-disposed as you shall see."

"Putting Burgevine in charge would have been a disaster," Robert said. "Ward earned the sobriquet, the Devil Solider, but he was dangerously intelligent. Some of those battles he lost were because of a spy in the Taiping's pay that he trusted, and Burgevine was not intelligent enough to command an army. Both men were corrupt and worked with Boss Takee and Wu Hsu in Shanghai and were involved in the opium trade, gambling and prostitution."

Gordon nodded while he puffed vigorously on his cigar. "After I was given command of this rabble, I discovered that Burgevine was planning treachery against me. It was a good thing that he and the others were swept away by Li during the Shanghai campaign." Gordon snapped his magic victory wand against his pants again.

He puffed on his cigar, pulled it from his mouth, and said, "We should have met months ago. I understand you were with Major General Brown in October. The affair with the *Firefly* was unfortunate."

"Did you discover what happened to those missing ship's engineers?"

"No. They vanished."

"I understand you were in Peking in sixty."

Gordon's face clouded. "That was another unfortunate incident. I'm an engineer. I regret that I was ordered to destroy the Summer Palace. It isn't something I am proud of. Before we started blowing the buildings up, I spent time walking through the spacious gardens. It was a true wonder."

"Your victories since Chansu show you are making up for what happened at the Summer Palace. The loss of a few buildings outside Peking can never compare to what would happen to China if the Taipings won. Every time you deliver a victory for the Dynasty, it pushes the Taipings a step closer to the edge of a cliff. For that, the Dynasty has already awarded you the rank of Mandarin and a yellow jacket."

"I don't fight for the Dynasty." Gordon's eyes filled with a fury. "I fight for the Chinese people so they will not have to suffer."

Robert was silent for a moment. He admired Gordon for that sentiment. After all, helping the Chinese people was his goal too. "The day will come when you or another general will push these rebels into the abyss where they belong. There is a lot to admire in China. I would hate to see it fall under the control of fanatics and the false prophet that leads them."

"I agree. The Summer Palace was a sight-to-behold, and China still fascinates me. The architecture is different. It's as if the Chinese design buildings with nature in mind unlike Europe where buildings are more like rectangular blocks of wood or stone that demand dominance over nature. I find most buildings in China easy on the eye instead of an insult."

"I have thought that," Robert replied.

As the conversation went on, they discovered many common feelings and opinions about China. Gordon also didn't feel it was right to convert the Chinese to Christianity.

"They have morality and values older than Christianity," Gordon said. "It isn't like they are a bunch of savages feasting off their neighbors' flesh. Why should we foist our form of morality on them?"

"Do you always speak so openly? Not that I disagree."

Gordon looked startled. "Of course not. I don't share these thoughts with everyone. There are prudes in the military like everywhere in British society." He stuck the cigar in his mouth and puffed furiously several times before pulling it out. "Li told me everything he knows about you. I admire the reputation you have built in China. You have developed a trust with the Dynasty that did not exist before. What year were you born?"

"Thirty-five."

"I was born in thirty-three. We are close in age."

"What are your views of the world outside China?" Robert asked, feeling that getting Gordon into a conversation that didn't focus on the problems at hand would soften him later when Robert felt the time was right to bring him and Li together.

"The world is an unstable place and people like us are here to bring peace and prosperity," Gordon replied. "Of course, we can't solve the problems that are out there, but we can do our part to alleviate suffering."

"I understand you were in the Crimea. How realistic was Lord Tennyson's poem *The Charge of the Light Brigade*?"

The cigar went into his mouth and he puffed sending a cloud around his head. "That poem says it all," Gordon replied, and recited from memory, as he waved the cigar around. "*Half a league, half a league, half a league onward, All in the valley of Death rode the six hundred. Forward, the Light Bridge! Charge the Guns—* If I die a similar death, I shall go happy to the next life."

"I admire your success on the battlefield," Robert said. "Li shares my views. Both Li and I see you as a great hero. If you choose to keep Li as an enemy, you'll lose a sincere admirer."

He watched a shadow fill the general's gray eyes. Giving Gordon no time to reflect, he made his voice sound lighthearted. "Is it true that you chased Li to Soochow and tried to kill him when Li came begging for your forgiveness? You know how rumors are."

"Li didn't come to me seeking forgiveness," Gordon said. There was a bitter tone in his voice. He stuck the cigar in his mouth and looked like a furious, fire-breathing beast. Out came the cigar. "He told me that he had every reason to behead King Nah."

"It is possible something was lost in the translation. I have found in Chinese many times the true meaning often is the opposite of the words that are spoken." He went on to help Gordon understand that Li wouldn't risk losing face among the Chinese to satisfy Gordon's pride.

"That makes sense," Gordon said. "After all, the Chinese do not think like us. What is your advice?"

"You must give Li Hung-chang a chance to 'step off the stage' as the Chinese idiom goes."

"You may be right. Li did show modesty by his recent actions. However, I'm not sure it is time to let this dispute dissolve. I'm still angry." He stuck the cigar in his mouth and chewed on the end while he sent up a cloud of smoke. "Did you know that I turned in my resignation to Britain's ambassador to China, and he turned me down?" Gordon hit the tabletop with the side of a fist. The teacups rattled in their saucers. "If I'm to cooperate with Li, what can be done to put pressure on the imperial court to restrict his arrogance?" He put down the cigar, picked up a metal teapot, and drank from the spout.

"Do you understand why the British ambassador turned you down? Everyone in the Western community is afraid that without you, this army will fall apart. I'm sure that was what the ambassador was thinking."

The teapot came down with a crash and the cigar went back into Gordon's mouth. "What about Li's arrogance?" He puffed on the cigar while he talked. "My pride is just as important as his is." There was still an edge to his voice, but Robert thought it wasn't as harsh. Maybe Gordon was softening.

This was going to take longer than he had thought. In fact, it took the rest of the night. Robert educated Gordon on the way a highborn, powerful Chinese man like Li would think. He explained that the behavior Gordon thought was arrogance was just Li's way of saving face, which was normal.

"Do you now understand that when he beheaded those Taiping rebel leaders, it was because they had insulted the emperor? It was his duty to keep the emperor from losing face. If Li allowed the emperor to lose face by King Nah's actions, Li would also lose face. Li is Han Chinese and the Manchu do not trust the Han. Any hint that a Han general or minister might be disloyal is swiftly dealt with."

"How can that be?" Gordon said. "I have difficulty believing the emperor of China would have one of his successful generals beheaded because he let another man wear the emperor's colors and didn't punish him. How absurd!"

"How well do you know the Chinese culture?"

"What does that have to do with fighting a war?"

"Everything. How can you be effective when you don't understand the motivations of the people you are fighting for?"

"Explain these differences, so I will understand."

Robert saw this as a move in the right direction. He smiled. "Who are your favorite artists?"

"Why are you asking me that? What does art have to do with this subject?"

"It has everything to do with it. Humor me."

"I like Rembrandt and Michelangelo," Gordon said. "And of course there are others."

"Why do you admire them?"

"The realism of their work. When I study a Rembrandt, the characters are so real that they look like they could come alive and step from the painting."

"But the Chinese don't paint like that, do they?"

"They paint a lot of silly flowers and trees in ink and watercolor."

"This shows us that flowers and trees are important to the Chinese. To truly understand China, it is wise to understand their art. There are places inside the Chinese soul that only their art can explain. If you want to get behind the unemotional mask of a Chinese man, you must understand what that difference is. Chinese art shows a taste and finesse and an understanding that distinguishes the best products of the human spirit. Chinese art represents calm and harmony, and that calm and harmony comes from the soul of the Chinese artist.

"The Chinese art lover is happy to contemplate a dragonfly, a frog, a grasshopper or a piece of jagged rock. The spirit of western art is more sensual, more passionate, and fuller of the artist's ego, while the spirit of Chinese art is more restrained and in harmony with nature."

Gordon's eyes widened. "Why, that's what I said about Chinese architecture." He gently puffed on his cigar with a thoughtful look on his face.

"The art and the architecture are no different. They are the same."

"I think I'm beginning to see what you mean." Out came the cigar and he waved it about. He spit in the dust, picked up the teapot and drank from the spout again.

"Then you should understand that the differences in art between the West and China parallel the differences in what is important to the Chinese on a personal and family level.

"If the emperor were allowed to lose face, or lose respect because one of his Han generals didn't have enough respect for him to behead someone who insulted the Son of Heaven, the emperor could no longer work with that general or trust him. Hence, the proper action would be to behead the general since by his inaction he also shows disrespect for his ruler."

"If we thought that way in England, many would lose their heads," Gordon said. "It must be dangerous being a general for the emperor. Do they always lose their heads when they don't help the emperor save face?"

"No, some of them get demoted in rank and sent to the outer provinces where they might spend decades before they are called back. That is, if they are fortunate enough to be called back. And that is the reason Li beheaded those Taiping generals and their king.

"Li didn't want to risk losing his head or finish his life in some godforsaken flea-hole of a fortress somewhere on the other side of the Great Wall. He might have been sent to the northwest and Xinjiang to fight Uygur rebels. If Li lost his head, there is a good chance his entire family would earn the same fate."

"All of that to preserve the emperor's face?" Gordon looked astonished, as he stared at Robert with the smoldering cigar in his hand—forgotten.

"Yes," Robert said. "Face is very important in China. Now, will you consider putting England's needs before yours? China needs a friend, and England should be that friend. You and I can make that happen if we work together to mend this wound that exists between you and Li."

"You are right." Gordon's voice was soft with some thoughtfulness to it. He took several gentle puffs from the cigar. "After all, I'm not fighting for myself. Even with the differences and disputes that exist between Britain and China, they've one common enemy, the Taipings."

In Li's name, Robert invited Gordon to Soochow. After Gordon accepted the invitation, Robert went with him.

When they passed through Soochow's gates, Gordon saw posters of Li's statement plastered on the city's walls. People stood about in clusters reading the proclamation as they had been instructed. The proclamations were written in both English and Chinese so Gordon could see what they said.

"If you aren't convinced about Li's sincerity, read that." He stopped his horse indicating that Gordon should read the English version of the proclamation glued to a wall.

Puffing on a cigar, the general dismounted. The Chinese crowd parted for him. Robert watched Gordon carefully while he read the poster. Near the end, he noticed a softening in Gordon's posture. He was also gentler with his cigar. It was good that Li had staged the show as instructed. Robert had written the original copy of the poster in both languages and urged Li to use that version.

"You were right about Li. I shouldn't have been so proud and stubborn." Obviously, Gordon felt his reputation had been restored.

When they reached Li's mansion, he exhibited happiness at seeing Gordon. Before they talked, Li handed Gordon a box of the British officer's favorite cigars. Then the three men had a long talk. They celebrated the renewed harmony and settled down to organize the campaign against the Taipings.

Li told Robert that a letter had come from Ayaou. He took it out of the wide sleeve of his robe and handed it across the table. Robert let Li and Gordon continue the conversation while he opened the letter to discover that Ayaou was pregnant and expecting the baby near the end of the year or early in 1865. She must have conceived right before he left Peking— maybe on that passionate night before his departure.

The two generals had stopped talking and were watching him. "Is there something wrong, Robert?" Gordon asked. "You look like you just saw God."

"I'm going to have another child," he replied.

"Great news," Li said. "May it be a son to carry on your family name."

"This calls for a drink." Gordon slapped Robert on the back. "I happen to have some French brandy."

The three men spent the night drinking jasmine tea and sipping brandy while toasting the fact that Robert was going to have a new addition to his family. Li took out an ink brush, had an aide grind some ink and bring rice paper. He painted Robert a picture of a peach tree with five birds in it.

Gordon commented on the delicacy of the strokes that portrayed the birds and the boldness of the lines that denoted the strength of the branch. That surprised Robert. It seemed that Gordon had a better grasp of Chinese art and what it meant than he had let on.

"This painting should bring you luck, Robert," Gordon said. "It looks like your family stands on a strong foundation. That means one-day your young birds will take wing and leave the nest, like you left Ireland."

"Precisely," Li said.

"Ayaou," Robert wrote in a letter a few days later, "the crisis was resolved. Gordon and Li have mended their differences and are cooperating again to end the Taiping rebellion. Gordon has returned to the Kunshan Heights to lead his Victory Army into battle against the Taipings.

"I stayed with Li to find a decent translator for Gordon. It turns out that the translator they relied on for communications botched the job and created the crisis. I have offered the job to an interpreter I trained. You may remember him. He was the young Englishman named Hobson that I brought to dinner one night. I told you I saw a shadow of myself in him.

"It wasn't as easy as I make it sound. At first, Gordon didn't want to let his old translator go. I had to tell him that his old translator was not good enough and that an inadequate translation might cause more difficulties in the future. Gordon eventually accepted my advice and took Hobson."

In April, Li and Gordon's armies worked together to trap the Taipings in Southern China, while Li's mentor, General 'Head Chopper' Tseng Kuo-fan's army approached the Taiping capital of Nanking from the north.

Satisfied that he had completed his job, Robert arranged to return home. However, while passing Changchow, where both Li and Gordon's armies had gathered to deliver a major blow to the Taipings, he couldn't resist their invitation to witness the battle.

"Without you, this battle would never have taken place," both Li and Gordon said.

Gordon assigned Robert a boat for his personal use and a squad of special men to protect him. That boat followed Gordon's command vessel, and Robert had a clear view of the battle.

A few hours into the attack, Li sent people to fetch him, and he went ashore where Li was waiting. Together, they climbed a hill outside Changchow. From the hilltop, he had a grand view of the battlefield, an image he never forgot.

A tall, imposing medieval wall and a deep but dry moat surrounded Changchow. The defenders had burned all the bridges that spanned the moat. Outside the moat were trenches and wooden palisades to protect the assaulting armies from the defenders on the city walls.

The trenches reminded Robert of the spokes from a wagon wheel with the city as the hub of the wheel. However, it was an unfinished wheel. Some of the spokes and portions of the wheel represented by the wooden palisade were still being built.

Some of Li's troops, several hundred in number, marched in formation toward the trenches, broke into what looked like ribbons as the individual lines went into the trenches to move closer to the city. A cannon fired and rebounded while its crew jumped away, then back to reload. The ball hit the city wall and chunks of granite flew.

A cannon replied from the city and the ball hit the wooden palisade that protected Li's men near the front lines. Splinters flew, a man went down, and he writhed on the ground. It was too far away to hear the wounded man's cries of pain, but Robert easily imagined the man's mortal wound. A cheer sounded from the Taipings on the city's wall.

Robert felt like Lemuel Gulliver in the land of Lilliput from Jonathan Swift's *Gulliver's Travels*. Down in that valley, the Lilliputians, represented by Li and Gordon's ant like armies, were taking the battle to their age-old foes, the Blefuscudans, represented by the flea like figures of the Taiping rebels on the walls of Changchow.

Unlike Gulliver, Robert would not refuse to help, and he would not sail away. This fight in China differed from the feud between Catholics and Protestants. The fate of China was uncertain. The Taipings could not be allowed to win.

He left his perch on the hilltop and joined Li in the army's headquarters. The roar of a battery of cannons firing echoed off the hills.

"Look at the battlefield," Li said, pointing at the map. "It is so dark I can't see to fight. It's as if the map is obscured by fog."

There was nothing dark about it. The inside of the headquarters tent was filled with light, but Robert knew what Li meant. He was saying he didn't know what to do to break the standoff. He was at a loss of how to proceed so they could take Changchow without great loss of life.

Li stepped aside to provide a better view of the map. "If you were to shed light on this battle, it might help me see."

Robert was stunned. Li was asking for his advice! He leaned over the map and studied the situation. Li had eight thousand men moving to tighten the encirclement of the city.

The only weak spot seemed near the city wall where Gordon's army was struggling to break through. Then Robert remembered how Li's men looked like ants marching in thin ant-like lines into their underground nests and saw the solution.

"Contact Gordon and ask him to make a move that will divert the Tapings' attention," Robert said. "While Gordon is doing this, your men will dig a tunnel under the wall."

"You mean for us to enter the city through the tunnel?" Li asked.

"Exactly. At first, this work must be done at night. You will cover some of your trenches with a roof and place dirt on top of that roof. That way, the defenders will not know what your men are doing. Gordon should attack from the other side of the city.

"In fact, you should marshal most of your troops on that side of the city with your artillery so the Taipings will think that is where the assault is coming from. Meanwhile, your men will be on this side of the city digging day and night to tunnel under the moat and wall to get inside."

Both Li and Gordon acted on Robert's suggestion. On May 11, 1864, the tunnel was completed. Gordon's army went underground and took Changchow while Li's army secured Soochow.

When Gordon and Li's armies moved on in early June toward Nanking, Robert returned to Peking with news for Prince Kung that the Taipings' defeat was assured.

He had been in the field for several months with Li and Gordon. His life had gained a new meaning and bringing Gordon and Li together was part of that changing picture. If his destiny was to play an important role in bringing harmony to China, then he was willing to pay the price even if that meant staying away from home months at a time.

At least, he was going home. Li and Gordon were not. They were marching off with their armies toward another battle and all the risk that entailed.

Chapter 59

After reaching Peking, Robert went to the Tsungli Yamen to report to Prince Kung.

"Great news, Robert," Kung said. "With Gordon and Li working together, the Longhaired Bandits are losing battles all across China." He rummaged among the papers on his desk, pulled out one and waved it as if it were a flag.

"This report arrived this morning from General Tseng Kuo-fan." His voice went up an octave. "The Longhaired Bandits are in such a panic because of the defeat at Changchow, they have removed most of their armies from his path to Nanking and shifted the fight to Gordon and Li. The back door has been left open." A rare smile creased his lips.

"Tseng Kuo-fan's army is moving toward the Bandit capital. Do you realize what that means? The Longhaired Bandits have panicked, and Head Chopper is going to deliver a killing blow. This could mean an end to the rebellion."

He threw the report down and jumped to his feet. "I am going to update the situation for the Empress Dowagers and the young emperor. I will request that you be rewarded."

Before Robert could open his mouth to protest that he didn't deserve the praise, Prince Kung hurried to the door where he stopped briefly, and said, "Do not leave, I will be back." Then the prince was gone.

He glanced at the reports scattered across the desk. In one of the reports, Li Hung-chang had praised Robert's contributions—not only for solving the dispute with Gordon, but also for the battle tactics that led to the fall of Changchow. A servant came with tea and preserved fruits.

An hour later, Prince Kung returned to the Tsungli Yamen, and said, "Robert, before the year ends expect several honors and titles from the emperor no foreigner has been granted before. The imperial court also decided to display the silver and gold taels the Maritime Customs Service has contributed toward the cost of this war. This is a great honor and all China will learn of it."

Not all the awards and the highest rank in China could dispel Robert's ache to be home with Ayaou and the children. When he was free, he hurried to his Peking mansion with the recently added eight-acre Inspectorate garden, which was another reward for his work.

Ayaou received him with her big belly looking as if she were carrying a large watermelon. Although she looked exhausted, she seemed in good spirits and in harmony with the world.

That night, he went to sleep thinking about how to tell her that he'd decided to make her his wife. There had to be a way so she wouldn't protest. After all, with what he had accomplished recently, this marriage would not cost him his future. The Ch'ing Dynasty wanted to please him.

In addition, his family and friends would have to deal with the reality that he had achieved great success and had a right to decide whom to marry. Besides, it didn't look like he was going to be leaving China for some time. He doubted that he would ever find success like this elsewhere.

The next morning, he was in the kitchen eating a simple breakfast of rice porridge with yams. The baby had been in a kicking mood, so Ayaou had stayed in bed after a difficult night. "Guan-jiah, I'm going to marry Ayaou, but I want to do it on a lucky day. What do you suggest?"

"I know the best date, Master," Guan-jiah replied. "It is in August during 'Qi Xi', a festival for lovers. This is a most auspicious time to marry and will insure happiness and bring more children to fill this house with endless laughter." The eunuch's eyes sparkled. "I will take care of the details and arrange everything to perfection. That way, you will have beautiful memories to reflect on when you are both old. Anna will play the piano during the ceremony. She practices daily for hours, and this will give her a chance to show off what she has learned."

Unfortunately, Robert's job pulled him back into the Maritime Customs whirlpool. In China, it was easy to accept bribes and every man had a price if it could be found.

Less than a week after returning from Changchow, he was leaving again. With reluctance, he said goodbye to Ayaou and the children. He was tired. He never had enough sleep. Even in Peking, his workdays lasted twenty hours.

"My love," he said, taking her face between his hands, "I have no choice. Customs is like an infant, and I am the father. I have to deal with the growing pains and make sure it learns to walk properly."

"Customs is certainly a large baby," she replied. "Since you have to travel all over China to wipe its ass and see to its feeding, you had better hurry so you can return home." She was smiling when she said this, but she couldn't hide the disappointment in her eyes and voice.

He was tempted to tell her that they were going to be married soon. However, he decided to break the news when he was staying home instead of leaving. He held her for the longest time. "I want to be here with you," he said. "It is lonely on the road, and I think of you often."

At first, when he let go, her arms stayed around him as if she didn't want him to leave. "I am afraid I will never see you again," she said in a trembling voice. Then she released her hold and stepped back.

Tears glittered in her eyes, and her lower lip trembled. He reached out to touch her chin and tilt her face toward him. He marveled at how smooth and warm her skin felt. After he kissed her on the mouth, he kissed her neck and whispered in her ear. "You know that I would never abandon you or the children. You are my life and the reason I have become successful."

She nodded. He turned away, so she couldn't see the weakness and turmoil mirrored in his eyes.

"Guan-jiah," he said, before he left, "pick another festival in case I don't return on time."

"Yes, Master," the eunuch replied. "There is the Moon Festival in September; the Winter Solstice in December, and the Spring Festival in February. I will make plans for all three, so it does not matter when you return. We will be ready."

"Good man."

Events conspired to keep him away longer than planned. When his commissioners or clerks could not resist temptation, his spies fed him information, and he always investigated.

During an interrogation in Shanghai, one clerk told him that he'd been approached by Captain Patridge and could not refuse the bribe. "I beg for clemency, Inspector General. I didn't have a choice. I started to visit the opium dens. I couldn't resist the women. Take pity on me. I have a fiancé in England waiting for me. My father has a weak heart. This scandal will kill him. I'm his only son. I am begging you."

"Silence," Robert said, as he remembered the time he'd taken money from Patridge. He understood why men did such things. The flesh was weak, but he had no choice. He could not go easy on this man or others might stray.

"You will be going to prison for two years," he said, "and everything you own will be confiscated to pay the fines. Since you will be in a Chinese prison, if you survive and convince me that you have learned your lesson, I may allow you to work for me again. You will also write letters to your fiancé and your family explaining what you have done and the punishment you are going to suffer. There will be no lies. Only the truth. If you do not write the letters, you will go to prison for five years."

"No, you cannot do this!" the clerk said. He fell to the ground wailing. As the guards dragged him away, he broke down and sobbed with his head hanging between his shoulders.

Late that night, unable to sleep, Robert questioned if he were a hypocrite. What if the man had been married? What if he had children? Would the punishment have been as harsh? He left the bed to write a letter to Patridge warning him to stay away from his people.

For those caught stealing, the penalties were worse. Such a theft was the same as taking from the Dynasty. He had not forgotten what Li Hung-chang had done to the Taiping leaders for wearing the imperial yellow or what had happened to the bannerman involved in the Forbidden City thefts.

If the crime deserved a harsher punishment, the guilty faced decapitation.

One such incident stuck in Robert's mind for weeks after he handed down a sentence of death. He was in Chungking, thirteen hundred miles inland along the Yangtze, where he gave the final verdict on the lives of several corrupted officers that had worked together to siphon thousands of taels from the treasury. As the lord and master of Chinese Maritime Customs, it was his duty to hand out justice without mercy.

These men in Chungking had been caught because Robert knew how much to expect from each port. When duties from Chungking fell short monthly for more than a year, Robert sent spies to discover what was going on. He even asked Li Hung-chang for help with his spy network. The evidence gathered had been overwhelming.

"Why did you do it?" he asked the Han Chinese man, the ringleader of the theft.

The man twisted his face into a mask of hate. "My family was respectable. They had land, mansions and wealth. That was two hundred years ago when the Manchu invaded China. They taxed us to pay for their wars with the foreign devils that came to rob China. They taxed us to fight the Longhaired Bandits. They taxed us to build their palaces. They taxed us to pay for the elaborate tombs for their false emperors."

The trial took place in the largest room at the customs house in Chungking. The desks were moved to one side leaving a space in the center of the room, and Robert's Manchu bodyguards stood against the walls. Since the entire staff in Chungking had been involved, he had brought replacements and everyone attended.

The prisoner stood in the center of the room with his hands manacled behind his back, and he looked as if he had been tortured during the questioning from Li's spies. His face was swollen and bruised.

"My family lost everything. All we had left until you hired me was one small house. There were twenty-eight of us living in one room with a dirt floor. My grandmother and mother had to cook outside under a shed roof where insects got into the food. Do you know what it is like to have beetles in your rice? Do you know what it is like to go to sleep hungry hearing your children crying?"

"Enough," Robert said. "However much your family suffered, many in China suffered worse fates." He thought of Guan-jiah's sacrifice for his family after they lost their wealth. This man's audacity made him angry. "Millions have died in the wars and rebellions that have plagued China. But your family survived. You have no excuse for what you did. At least you had a life. At least you had a family.

"I expected honesty, morality, and integrity when I hired you," he said. "You were an intelligent man that would have been the commissioner in Chungking one-day. You swore an oath to live by my standards." He shook his head.

"You siphoned ten thousand taels over the last three years to buy your family a big house with acres of land. You are fortunate that I am the one judging you. If this case were in the hands of a Ch'ing Dynasty judge, you would suffer the death of ten thousand cuts or worse, and your entire family would be executed. Since I am the judge, they will live, but we will confiscate the lands you bought with that money. On the other hand, I will be merciful and allow your family to keep the house they lived in when I hired you, the hut with the dirt floor."

"I am going to die?" the man said, his face stiff with shock.

"Decapitation. The money you took was destined for the Dynasty's treasury, which means you robbed the Son of Heaven. I am ashamed. I have lost face because of your actions. I made a mistake when I judged you an honest man, and I trusted you."

"What about the others?"

"They will go to prison for ten years and lose everything they own. If they survive prison, they will be sent to Xinjiang to live among the Uygurs. You, on the other hand, were the leader and must suffer the ultimate price. I might have been lenient and sent you to prison for twenty years, but you are unrepentant."

"You may have the power to have me beheaded," the man replied, twisting his lips into a snarl, "but you will always be a foreign devil working for the Manchu. You are their dog. The day will come when all the devils will be driven from China like autumn leaves torn from trees by a strong wind. The silver taels we took belonged to the Han, not the Manchu, who have raped China repeatedly since stealing the Dragon Throne two centuries ago."

Right before the executioner chopped off the man's head, he yelled a curse at Robert condemning his family to a life of suffering.

Robert shivered as a chill swept through him. When he left Chungking, he carried bitterness with him that tasted like moldy, rotten fruit. When there was a failure like this, he could only blame himself. After all, he'd hired everyone that worked for him.

It was early in December 1864, and he wanted to go home since the baby was due soon. The distance from Chungking down the Yangtze to Shanghai was thirteen hundred miles. From Shanghai to Tientsin was another eight hundred miles through the East China Sea to the Yellow Sea before reaching the Bohai Gulf.

Chapter 60

The courier traveled on a gunboat two-hundred miles down the Yangtze from Nanking. When he arrived in Shanghai, he went straight to the Imperial Maritime Customs house off the Bund with a report from General 'Head Chopper' Tseng Kuo-fan.

"Inspector General," the courier said, "General Li Hung-chang suggested that you be the messenger to carry this news to Peking."

Wondering what kind of report it was that required him to be a messenger, Robert took the report and started to read. What he saw caused him to become short of breath, light headed and dizzy. He had to sit down.

"Is there something wrong, Inspector General?" a clerk asked, looking concerned. Others came from their desks to gather about him.

He waved a hand in dismissal. "No, it's the opposite," he replied, taking slow, steady breaths to regain a sense of calm. "I must leave for Peking immediately to deliver this news to the Dynasty. Nanking, the Taiping capital, has fallen to General Tseng Kuo-fan. Hong Xiuquan, the leader of the rebels, is dead. What is the fastest ship anchored in the river?"

"Glory be to God!" An Italian clerk shouted.

A few days later, he reached Peking. It seemed the news had sprouted wings. A sedan chair waited outside the city gate with an escort of a thousand mounted bannermen, and he was to be carried straight to the Tsungli Yamen.

It appeared that word had spread to every corner of the city, and the sides of the avenue were crowded with thousands of people wanting to see the messenger. The rest of the wide street was empty, which was bizarre. It was as if he were at the center of a silent parade with no band and no cheering while the world held its breath praying the rumors were true.

How could he blame the doubts the people must have been thinking? After all, the Taiping Rebellion had started in 1845, nineteen years ago. Tens of millions had died and entire areas of China had been emptied of life. He'd seen the desolation first hand. Would China ever trust Christians again? After all, Hong Xiuquan, a Christian convert claiming to be the younger brother to Jesus Christ, had almost destroyed an empire and caused the deaths of millions to create his Heavenly Kingdom of great peace.

With the sedan chair in their midst, the only sound was the horses' hooves as the thousand mounted Manchu bannermen escorted Robert along the avenue toward the Forbidden City. When he arrived at the Tsungli Yamen, he was ushered inside where Prince Kung waited.

The prince's face showed no emotion, but his posture was stiff. Robert crossed the crowded, silent room as people stepped aside to make room. He took the report from an inside, jacket pocket and handed it to Prince Kung, who started to read, then relaxed.

After a silent moment, Kung said, "Robert, when I heard the rumors, I dared not allow myself to believe. Now I see the truth." He held up the dispatch and shook it. "Our Hart has carried the word to us that the Longhaired Bandits have been defeated!"

Prince Kung started walking quickly around the room as if he could not contain his energy, and the ministers scrambled to get out of the way before he ran them down.

"This is the report of the century," he said, "and it details the final moments of the rebellion."

He stopped abruptly and brought the papers closer to his eyes. "Listen. I will read some of General Tseng Kuo-fan's report. 'Smoke and flames from the burning buildings filled the city—several hundred female attendants in the palace hanged themselves in the front garden, while the number of rebels that drowned in the city moat exceeded two thousand. We searched the city and in three days killed more than a hundred-thousand men—not one rebel surrendered. Many men and women gathered together and burned themselves in a mass suicide.'"

"Women on fire. How ghastly," Robert said. "A great tragedy."

Prince Kung's eyes were animated when he looked away from the report. This wasn't like Prince Kung. Usually he was a serious, sober minded person who seldom revealed emotion in a crowd. Now he was bubbling like a busy fountain.

"Robert," Kung said, "you are too softhearted. Ha!" He shouted. "Listen to me. Our Hart is softhearted." He laughed. "What does it matter if even ten million set themselves on fire? The threat to the Ch'ing Dynasty has been removed. This is a great day."

Kung plopped down in a chair. After taking a deep breath and composing himself, he calmly said, "Robert, you will come to my palace for an official celebration before the end of week. You must honor us with your presence. The nobles will want to see you, as well as any governors that are in Peking. We must have a grand celebration. There will be fireworks. All of China must celebrate. Now, I must carry this news to the young emperor and the Dowagers."

That night the city boomed and crackled with the sound of firecrackers while rockets soared into the sky to burst and bloom leaving trails of colored sparks behind them.

Prince Kung held the celebration at his palace, but Robert did not enjoy himself. The only positive thing was the new connections he made. At one point, he slipped out of the house and went to the gardens behind Kung's mansion. He spent quiet time strolling among the cranes, parrots and hawks. He watched the gold and black carp darting through the ponds. All the while, he wanted to be home with Ayaou. It took an effort to return to the dinner table.

"A large family is desired," Kung said to the crowded table. Then the prince stared at Robert. "It guarantees that you will have heirs to carry on your family name. What is on your mind, my friend? You look sad. Are you still thinking about those women on fire?"

Robert shook his head. "Nothing is wrong," he said. He noticed many eyes watching him and everyone was smiling. He did not like the attention.

"It is time for you to establish a family," Kung said. "When do you plan to marry?" Servants scurried back and forth between the kitchen and the dining room with fresh platters of food. Everyone was stuffing themselves and there was a lot of chatter.

He wanted to say that he already had a family with two children and another on the way any day now. Before he could say a word, Prince Kung cut him off. "You and I are about the same age. I am thirty-one. I have a wife that is the daughter of Grand Secretary Kuei Liang, and I adore her. Her status makes me look good in my people's eyes. A sense of pure nobility is important in China."

"Indeed, I have been thinking of marriage lately." Robert replied.

"That is good news," Prince Kung said. "There are only two reasons to marry. One is to create an alliance to strengthen your position. The second is to have many sons to carry on the family name. Whom do you have in mind? To tell you the truth, I am interested to be your matchmaker. I only trust a few people, and you are one. Grant me this honor."

"I am thinking of marrying Ayaou, my concubine."

"Please do not be kidding, Robert." Prince Kung looked serious. "Having her as a concubine is one thing. Having her as a wife is another. You can still keep her while you marry with someone of proper status from the Manchu. She will understand. After all, your concubine is Chinese. Do you remember Princess Nee-Nee? She has the blood of Emperor Nurhaci in her body. Do you know who that was? She is from his clan."

"Nurhaci was the first Ch'ing emperor," Robert said. "He founded the Dynasty."

"You have learned. Not like that first time when Captain Patridge brought you to me in Shanghai. You knew so little and your Chinese was clumsy as if you had rocks in your mouth." He pointed a finger at Robert. "I knew then that you were hungry to learn. You were different from the other foreigners. I was right about that too. Well, Nee-Nee is still available. I know from the way you looked at her when you first met that you liked her. What do you say?"

How could Robert explain what love meant to a man who had no idea how important it was? Robert remembered when Shao-mei had said she hated him but meant she loved him. Thinking about her caused his eyes to water. He wanted to disagree but feared hurting the prince's feelings. In fact, he dreaded saying anything, because he might start crying.

"Not Nee-Nee, huh. Then I have another idea," Prince Kung said. "Let me petition her Majesty, the Empress Dowager Tzu Hsi, to be the matchmaker. Your status permits you to enjoy such an honor."

"I'm afraid, Prince Kung, that I only desire sleeping with my concubine, Ayaou."

"That is not a problem. In fact, that is the way to go. How many men in the entire court are sleeping with their noble blooded wives? It is a tradition here for men to lust after their concubines. The young emperor has more than a thousand already, and he is only eight. These women will have to wait before the emperor is old enough to bed them. And his father's wives and concubines, all three thousand, were retired when my brother died. Most were virgins and still are. It will be proper for you to marry a princess while continuing to share the bed with Ayaou.

"Why not get a dozen concubines and sleep with them all? It is not important if your Manchu wife has children for she will be the mother to all your children whoever the birth mother is. It is our way."

What about Ayaou? Robert thought. He struggled to suppress the anger he felt. He couldn't see the children he had with Ayaou being raised by another woman. It was not easy, but he managed to keep his expression composed. He had to keep a level head and not fall prey to emotions. After all, the prince was a product of a culture that had a lot to admire. How could he be angry with Prince Kung? No culture was perfect. All had flaws.

With concern in his eyes, Prince Kung put a hand on Robert's shoulder. "Do not act hastily, my friend. Give this a lot of thought. You have everything to lose and nothing to gain from marrying this boat-girl."

Oh, but he did, Robert thought, trying hard to keep his lips sealed. It would bring great happiness to the woman he loved, and his children would not be bastards in the eyes of the world.

It was after midnight when Robert arrived home. When he walked into the bedroom, Ayaou was reading, but she carefully marked the page and put the book of poems on a side table. He could tell that she was naked under the silk sheet. He'd told her years before that he did not like her sleeping with clothes on.

He sat beside her and took one of her hands between his. "Prince Kung wants me to marry a Manchu princess," he said, fearing the worst. "But what they think doesn't matter, Ayaou." The sheet slipped from her shoulders to gather on her lap revealing her full breasts, and his eyes focused on her nipples.

The words slipped from his tongue. "Marry me, Ayaou. We will have the wedding soon. I want to do it before the baby is born."

She showed no excitement. Instead, her eyes filled with sadness and the muscles in her face sagged. She slipped from under the sheet, put on a shirt and sat beside him. "If you marry me, you will never go beyond the position you now hold as Inspector General. Your future will be frozen. More importantly, you will make Prince Kung and even her majesty, the empress, lose face with your rejection of their offer. They could become your enemies waiting for the right moment to lower the blade on your neck as you did for Ward."

"You are so dramatic, Ayaou. It could never be that bad. I am perfectly happy with my position as Inspector General. My dreams are more than fulfilled, and I have no goals to become anything else. If losing face worries you, I want you to know that I can handle that. Therefore, when I return in a few days from a brief inspection trip to Tientsin, we will marry. Guan-jiah has arranged everything."

Ayaou did not reply, and she was weeping. In silence, tears spilled from her eyes dripping from her chin. A moment later, she said yes. Her voice was so low he had to strain to hear her, and he wasn't sure if her tears were of happiness or from worry.

"Get that shirt off, Ayaou, and get back in bed."

A lazy evening breeze drifted through an open window near the far end of the room. Robert's hands explored the familiar shapes of her body. He did not mind that she was huge with the baby. Touching her excited him. He couldn't recall a moment when he'd been happier. He believed he had finally defeated the moral trappings he'd carried from Ireland.

She whispered. "Robert." She rolled over with a serious look on her face. "Can you see yourself one day in your mansion with a full banquet table and no guests? Will you still tell me that you love me then?"

"Yes. Always." He kissed a favorite spot on her neck below one ear. "I'll keep telling you how much I love you until you get sick of hearing the words, then I will say them some more. Over the last decade, all my adolescent fantasies about love came true, even with the angry times.

"When Shao-mei died," he said, "I thought my ability to love had died with her, but I was wrong. That passion came back to life because of you. Nothing is left for any other woman, not even Princess Nee-Nee and I refuse to marry her."

He stared at her watermelon belly then lifted her chin, kissed the tip of her nose and saw that her eyes were still swimming with tears.

"I wouldn't be who I am today if it weren't for you. We have shared both good and bad. How can I leave you in the shadows? Because of you and Shao-mei, I learned how to think like a Chinese but found love that most Irishmen only dream of. If I had stayed in Ireland, I would have never experienced the passion I have had with you. That has made all the difference, and I do not want to be with another woman."

"I wish Shao-mei were here," Ayaou said. Using the back of one hand, she wiped away the tears. "I would like to share this night with her."

"She has never left us, Ayaou. Death makes no difference. She will always be part of our lives."

That night, they sent up rockets and set off endless firecrackers. They hardly slept.

Chapter 61

In early January 1865, Robert was in the northern port of Tientsin eighty miles from Peking. The city was built on flat, swampy land along the Peihao River thirty-seven miles from the Bohai Gulf. The temperature was a few degrees above freezing, and it was raining. A few degrees lower and the rain would turn to sleet, then snow. The only place to be on a day like this was indoors near a hot stove.

There had been a discrepancy about the number of imports and exports flowing through the city. The time it was taking to solve this problem with the city's governor-general was making Robert nervous. He realized that the baby was due any day, and he wanted to arrive home in time to marry Ayaou before the birth.

The city's governor general was probably keeping some of the revenue. Although Robert doubted it, the discrepancy could have been an honest bookkeeping mistake. The reason didn't matter. If they had to collect some of the import and export taxes from the city's governor-general instead of the merchants, they would.

"Inspector General." said Cooper, the commissioner of the Tientsin Customs House, as he entered the office. A wool knit cap with earflaps covered his baldhead. The wound in his thigh had healed and left a scar.

"Your people did a fine job again, Cooper," Robert said. "I want you to send an unofficial note to the city's governor-general and let him know his people are making mistakes. Use the proper language and remind him how much he owes the treasury. He's often arrogant so gently cause a little loss of face."

"I'm not here to talk about import or export taxes," Cooper said. "Guan-jiah just arrived from Peking and is in the outer room."

"In this weather!" Robert said, then his voice faltered when he saw the serious expression on Cooper's face. "What is it?" He was alarmed. Something must have happened.

"He says he has to speak to you in person. I think you should see him."

His stomach turned queasy, and he worried. Could one of the children have been injured or even worse? Not wanting to wait, he left Cooper's office and walked into the main room where Guan-jiah stood by the half-open door.

The eunuch's robe was soaked and covered in frost. He looked like he was in shock and his gentle features were twisted into knots. Before the door slammed shut cutting off the cold, Robert saw the coach that had brought him. The horses were lathered and looked exhausted.

The eunuch's expression was worse than the time the Taipings took Ayaou and the children. A pit opened inside Robert's stomach. He feared the worst and dreaded what he was about to hear. When Guan-jiah looked like this, it was never good.

"Master—" The moment he saw Robert, Guan-jiah started to cry. "It is Ayaou—it is Ayaou!" He sobbed, and then started to shoot phrases at Robert between gulps of air. "She does not want me to bother you with bad news—she has delivered a boy. She named the baby as you wished. Arthur is very healthy and weighs more than Herbert when he was born—"

Work had stopped. Everyone was watching the eunuch.

Robert became more alarmed because this behavior was totally unlike Guan-jiah, who was always calm, organized and courageous even during the worst of times. "What's wrong?" he asked.

As if shocked back into his senses, Guan-jiah said, "Something broke—" He paused to suck air. "The Mistress lost blood. It is terrible! The bleeding will not stop. Everyone was afraid. The doctor too." His face dissolved into a portrait of agony and the tears streamed.

Darkness descended over Robert's vision as if he were wearing blinders. All he saw was the eunuch. He took three steps, grabbed Guan-jiah by the collar of his wool cape and pulled his servant toward him wanting to squeeze the words out faster.

"Master, Master!" Guan-jiah was trembling. "I am not finished."

Robert let go and stepped back. There was a buzzing in his ears. "Is she alive or dead?" he asked, feeling numb, while struggling to remain calm. He feared the answer, and his heart was pounding in anticipation.

Guan-jiah's trembling stopped. His breathing slowed. "She is dying," he said.

Robert guts felt as if they had turned inside out and he doubled over. His expression must have frightened Guan-jiah, because the eunuch stepped back.

With an effort, Robert straightened. His voice was filled with pain. "Did you go—to the foreign doctor—from the British legation for help as I instructed?" An attack of vertigo threatened his balance. Putting a hand over his mouth, he swayed. Leopold was the first to reach him and put a steadying hand on his shoulder. Anwar, Cooper and the others came to stand on either side.

Guan-jiah wiped his eyes with both sleeves. "That doctor said the Mistress lost too much blood."

Remain calm, Robert thought. Stay in control. It took an effort to hold on. Letting go was a luxury he could not afford. He turned to Cooper, who stood to his right with a face that had turned chalky white.

"I want fourteen horses saddled and ready immediately." His lips felt numb. His voice sounded strained and fragile.

"The rain," Cooper said.

"Damn the rain!" Robert replied. "Just see to it. And wake my guards. Tell them we're leaving for Peking immediately."

Cooper and the others left the room for the stables behind the main building. Robert was the Godfather to Cooper's son.

"Come with me," he said to Guan-jiah. When they arrived at the stables, the horses were being saddled. The dozen troopers from his guard detail were spilling into the place pulling on uniforms. It was obvious they had been sleeping. He counted fifteen horses. "We don't need that many, Cooper."

"You think I'm letting you go cross-country to Peking in this weather without me. You stood by me when I was wounded. Now I will stand by you." Leopold and Anwar came with thick wool jackets piled in their arms.

"Put this on, Inspector General," Anwar said, and he held a full-length winter jacket for Robert. Leopold pulled a navy, wool watch cap over Robert's head and around his ears.

He was overwhelmed and couldn't respond. He had to fight back tears and didn't remember putting the jacket on. He was vaguely aware of the others dressing him while he stood like a statue. Dear God, he thought, please do not take my lover from me.

After the others helped him mount his horse, the gelding reared on its hind legs and pranced nervously as if it sensed his distress. That seemed to wake Robert from the emotions threatening to bury him.

Once he calmed the gelding, they were off at a gallop through the city streets. The horses made a sound like thunder sending a warning to get out of the way. Soon, they were all soaked and the cold penetrated deep as the rain pounded them.

The horses' hooves echoed as they crossed a wooden bridge, then they were racing cross-country toward Peking with the blinding, freezing rain beating against their faces. The bannermen rode in a tight pack behind Robert, Cooper and Guan-jiah.

Wind whipped the rain past his ears. He saw the fleeting images of people scattering to get out of the way. Fields, farmhouses, and trees all blurred past beyond that wet curtain.

The horses were well lathered when they reached the first station where fresh horses were brought out.

The stationmaster protested. "It will be dark soon," he said. "The road is not safe. It will freeze and there are bandits and because of the rain there might be places where the road will be washed out."

Robert glared at him, and said, "Don't be a fool! Bandits will not be out in this."

The station man looked startled. "I understand you are in a great hurry. I just want you to know the dangers."

Guan-jiah handed Robert a revolver, and he put it into a coat pocket. The long wool coat was dripping with water. He squeezed Guan-jiah's shoulder. It was like the old times when they had to watch out for Ward. "Let's get back on the road," he said.

624

"We have to warm up, Inspector General," Cooper said. "We cannot go on until we dry out. Give us half-an-hour, then we will be on our way. It won't do any good if we freeze before we get there."

A half-hour later, they mounted fresh horses. Robert's new mount whinnied and tossed its head. Gaining control, he squeezed his legs against the beast's sides, and they burst from the stable and were in the rain again. The horses' hooves hitting the wet ground sounded like the muffled roar of cannons.

He lost sense of time. Night came and the terrain on either side of the road vanished in the darkness and the unrelenting rain beat on them and still they rode. The cold reached inside with icy fingers and he lost touch with his nose, toes and fingers.

Twice more Cooper took charge and they stopped to crowd around a fire to get warm while new mounts were readied. Cooper, Guan-jiah and the bannermen did all the work at each station.

A colorful kaleidoscope of memories crowded into Robert's brain. He saw Shao-mei and Ayaou going outside in their wooden shoes during the summer holding paper umbrellas over their heads. He jerked when grisly images of Shao-mei's death at Ward's hands pushed the good memories aside. He couldn't remember if Ward was dead or alive.

"Are you okay, Master?" Guan-jiah asked, but Robert didn't hear him. Instead, he heard Ayaou singing. Then the sisters were reciting favorite poems together. Tears blinded him and froze on his eyelashes.

It was as if he was tottering on the edge of hell ready to fall into the endless fires and his girls were reaching for him. *"Don't let us go alone."* Their voices screeched like black crows. *"Come with us, Robert. We love you. We're afraid."*

"You need to eat, Master," Guan-jiah said at one of the stations.

Robert looked around and found himself standing inside stables. He couldn't remember arriving or dismounting. Ice had formed on his clothes and face. As it melted, the water dripped and formed a puddle around his feet. The numb parts of his body started to feel as if someone were jabbing his toes and fingers with needles. Steam came off the horses. He took a shuddering breath and searched for Guan-jiah to discover the eunuch standing beside him. He had no idea where he was.

The bannermen stood around stuffing food in their mouths. Guan-jiah had a bun of steamed bread. He tore off a piece and pushed it against Robert's lips. "Get that out of my face. I'm not hungry," he said. "Are the horses ready?"

"Not yet," Cooper said. "You are going to eat, Inspector General, even if these bannermen have to sit on you while I feed you. Guan-jiah is right. A bit of hot porridge will do you good. It will warm your innards and about now I suspect they need warming."

He glared at Cooper but the man refused to back down, so he ate without tasting a thing.

Once they were in the mud again, Robert leaned forward and wrapped his arms around the horse's neck. The rain and the darkness were so thick that he could not see the ground. He felt the horse's neck heaving beneath him like a boat in a storm, and he treasured the heat radiating from the horse's body. It was as if he were riding the crest of a giant wave that was carrying him toward a rocky shore where he would be smashed into a bloody pulp.

Maybe that was what he wanted—an end to this horrid suffering that came from loving another person as much as he loved Ayaou.

Then dawn broke along the horizon piercing the clouds with a defused light, and they were riding through Peking's open city gates and through that long tunnel beneath the wall. They had arrived, and with his guard detail trailing behind, Robert reached his mansion not far from The Forbidden City.

The servants came running and threw themselves at his feet and knocked their heads on the ground repeatedly. "Don't let them do that, Guan-jiah," he said, and hurried through the house toward the backstairs that would take him to the bedroom he shared with Ayaou on the second floor. A trail of wet, muddy footprints followed him.

In the bedroom, there was a nurse from the British consulate sitting on a stool at the foot of the bed. She stood and stared at Robert as if he were a crazy man. He sensed others in the shadows but ignored them. He hadn't had a haircut in weeks and his long hair was plastered to his face. He'd been waiting to get home and have Ayaou cut it. He loved the way she cut his hair. His drenched clothing clung heavy and limp from his body. His shoes made wet squishy sounds as he walked toward the bed.

Ayaou had her back to him. She was on her side facing the wall. Her long dark hair spread across the pillow like floating seaweed. He knelt by the bed and reached out to touch her. "Ayaou." It was a struggle to keep the urgency out of his voice and make the word sound gentle. He didn't know if she were still alive.

She turned slowly. Her eyes were sunken like two black rocks in wet sand. The brown had fled from her complexion, and she was pale like cold snow. Her colorless lips had peeled and flaked.

She smiled. "You made it." Then she squinted and struggled to sit up but failed. With a wheeze, she dropped back and worry poured into her face. Every word she said took an effort. "You are soaking wet—you will catch your death—Guan-jiah," she struggled to breathe, "see that he changes into something dry—make sure he does it right away."

Trying to control his tears, Robert buried his face in the blankets. Hands plucked at his wet clothing. His jacket came off. Then his pants and his shirt. Someone dried him with a towel. Then they dressed him in dry clothes.

"Do not be sad," Ayaou said weakly. "It is not like I did not get any of you."

He choked not knowing if he were going to cry or laugh then took her hand and climbed on the bed beside her.

"Sir, you shouldn't do that," the nurse said. "She needs rest."

Guan-jiah stopped her, and Cooper stepped forward. They hadn't changed and were still in their wet, half-frozen clothing. Cooper ordered everyone to leave the room and went out last with Guan-jiah. They closed the door leaving Ayaou and Robert alone.

"I held on because I knew you would come." Every word took an effort. "I get to say good-bye—I—trust you with the children. I am sorry, Robert—do not let them grow up in China where they will be abused."

"You're not leaving, Ayaou!" His voice broke on a desperate note.

Looking startled, fear appeared in her voice. "I am—trying not to." Her breath grew thin, and she shivered violently. "Hold me."

He discovered that her body was frail and cold as if life were already leaving to join the winter winds that had chased him to Peking.

"I guess I am going to see Shao-mei tonight." Her voice started to fade. "I can see her waving. I will tell her everything about you. We are going to stay up real late—"

With a smile frozen on her face, the life flew from her eyes, and he could only hear one empty heart beating, his.

Chapter 62
1908

Old Buddha, as many called the Dowager Empress Tzu Hsi, met Robert in The Palace of Benevolent Tranquility for the last time. Other than Robert, she had never met with a Western man before. The audience was private with a few ministers and trusted palace eunuchs present.

He admired the empress and knew she was strong-willed and hot tempered. She was clever too. She had competed against thousands of women for the attention and affections of an emperor. She was the only concubine to give the emperor a son.

In 1861, she'd seen her husband, Emperor Hsien-feng, die, then spent decades struggling against corruption and stifling court etiquette to guide two emperors onto the throne—first her son, whom she watched die, and now a nephew.

"How long have you been in China?" the empress asked.

"Fifty-four years, your Majesty."

She nodded. "You have served China well. The Dynasty has been depending on you for our survival. Our only regret is that we did not take more of your advice. It is amazing that everything you predicted took place as you said it would. If we had listened more closely, we would have avoided many tragedies, and China would be better off today. With all the bad years, the chaos, opium, the Taipings, floods, drought, foreign invasions, your Customs has been the only department that produced a steady revenue."

Robert was dressed in a Chinese ministerial robe. A mandarin square known as a rank badge was on his chest and another on his back. Two embroidered peacocks were displayed on the badge—one walking and one in flight. The peacock was the symbol of a third grade civil official. He was

Inspector General of Chinese Maritime Customs, chief adviser for the emperor, and the Senior Guardian of the Heir Apparent of the Ch'ing Dynasty.

Tzu Hsi put down her teacup. "We were told there was a reason you asked for this private audience." The empress sat on a couch in the center of a raised platform. Her gown of golden-yellow satin was embroidered with pink peonies. Her headdress was made of pearls and jade with flowers on the sides and a phoenix in the center. Over her gown, she wore a cape covered with pearls the size of canary eggs. What she wore was enough to make any man wealthy.

"Yes, your Majesty." It was well known that the empress rewarded loyalty. Robert hoped to take advantage of that. His chair sat close to the platform.

She glanced left and right and the eunuchs and ministers backed out of earshot. She smiled. At seventy-three, she had delicate graceful features, fine skin, slender hands and jewel-encased fingernails. She wore light makeup; her black hair was combed back smoothly.

"I had a concubine once," he said in a low voice. Her name was Ayaou. She—"

"I know this name." The empress nodded. "Prince Kung mentioned her around the time you came to work for us. Was she a boat-girl?"

"Yes, she was."

"What can I do for you?"

"I'd like to see her grave moved to an honorable place to match the titles your Majesty has granted me. And if possible, honor her ancestors as well."

The empress went quiet for a long moment giving him time to reflect. Ayaou was the only woman he ever loved. After she had died in childbirth, he had taken a leave of absence and returned to Ireland with the children.

He found a foster home near Belfast for the children with a good family his father knew. Letting the children go had been painful, but it was what Ayaou had wanted. He had fulfilled her dying wish. Since he worked in China, he never had a chance to see Anna, Herbert or Arthur again. He supported them financially until they reached maturity. The person hurt most was Guan-jiah, who missed the children horribly.

Robert knew the only way he could avoid marrying a Manchu princess was to marry one of his own people. His aunts arranged a marriage in five days. Hester Jane was eighteen and Robert thirty. The marriage took place three months later. She was the daughter of the family doctor. It was a marriage of convenience, and Hester had to be by his side when he returned to China.

He felt a flash of guilt for not loving her. He had tried, but his ability to fall in love with another woman had died with Ayaou. He wondered if he should mention these things to the empress but decided not to.

It was fortunate that over the years, Hester Jane had become his friend and companion. She lost their first child through a miscarriage, and then gave birth to Evey, a daughter, then Edgar, a son. He'd hardly missed her after she left China with their children and returned to London where she had lived for the last thirty-three years.

After Ayaou's death, he devoted himself to making the Maritime Customs Service a success. Hester once said that he loved Customs more than he loved her. There had been no argument. It was true. He had also been behind the building of an efficient postal system and reorganizing China's schools so they could compete with the West.

"I can tell you have been missing this concubine," the empress said, breaking the long silence. "What you are asking says a lot about who you are. I am not surprised."

He nodded—unable to speak, while his heart swelled with mixed feelings. He worried that the expression in his eyes might give him away. He hated others knowing what he was thinking. The empress's next words told him she'd noticed.

"What a fortunate girl," she said. "Even I envy her." Taking her teacup, she sipped. "I will see that it is done."

After the audience, Li Lien-ying, the chief eunuch, who had served the empress for fifty years, walked with Robert to the sedan chair. "You are most fortunate," the eunuch said. "It is seldom that we see the empress show her soft side to anyone, a gift one should treasure."

"I understand," he replied, and climbed into his sedan chair. The bearers lifted it and smoothly carried him from the cloud patterned marble courtyard in front of the Palace of Benevolent Tranquility and out of the Forbidden City.

He had finally found some peace from the pain of Ayaou's loss. He had never forgotten her and memoires of the ten years they had together were always with him.

On the morning of April 13, 1908, Robert left for the train station. He wanted to skip the farewell ceremony. All his friends, employees, and crowds of Chinese people wanted to come and see him off, but he didn't want the pomp. Leaving had become difficult and slipping away quietly was something he desired. He didn't want anyone to see him shed even one tear.

Back in 1859, he'd resolved to help the Chinese to the best of his abilities and had never swerved from that path. What he had achieved hadn't been done just for the glory and the power. He'd fallen in love with the Chinese culture. He could thank Ayaou for that.

Over the years, his rewards had been many. Queen Victoria of Great Britain had knighted him in 1893, along with a grand cross and a baronetcy. More than a dozen countries had honored him. Even the Vatican in 1885 had made him a Commandeur of the Order of Pius IX. Much had happened since he left Ireland in 1854.

His sedan chair reached the train station, and he heard a brass band playing 'Auld Lang Syne'. It was his Chinese band, the one he'd trained, the one that played every Wednesday in Peking at his garden parties in the eight-acre Inspectorate garden. Holding back tears and showing no emotion, he walked slowly past them. He knew that if he stopped, he wouldn't be able to leave.

There was a company of Highlanders with pipers, American Marines, Italian sailors, Dutch Marines, Japanese soldiers and three Chinese detachments of Manchu bannermen from the Forbidden City to honor Robert and see him off.

With help from his cane, he made his way between them while the bands started to play 'Home Sweet Home'. The soldiers saluted.

The train reached the port of Tientsin in the afternoon. What used to take such a long time on foot or horseback now took only a few hours by rail. There'd been no railroads in

China when he first arrived. He was proud that he'd been the one who'd seen that they were built.

Of course, he hadn't been alone. He missed Li Hung-chang and Prince Kung, both gone now. If they hadn't supported his proposals, the Ch'ing Dynasty would never have approved.

He was leaving China with no regrets. He'd fulfilled his life's goals—even the one he held closest to his heart and had shared with only the empress to honor Ayaou's memory.

A Custom's cruiser waited. His trunks, packed with those belongings he'd acquired since the loss of his posessions to the Boxer Rebellion in 1900, were already on board. He never blamed the Boxers for his personal treasures that they looted and destroyed when his mansion was burned to the ground. It was one of those regrettable incidents that were part of history as he was now part of history.

Those few servants he was taking back to England were on the ship with Guan-jiah, who'd been with him since the beginning. So, in essence, he was leaving China as he'd arrived, with only memories and a few possessions.

Eventually, dark smoke spiraled into the sky from the cruiser's smokestacks and the ship steamed toward the Yellow Sea. Robert stood by the rail watching the landmass fade to a blur on the horizon, which brought back images of his first sighting of China.

It was as if he'd opened an old manuscript covered in dust that he had written long ago. In this manuscript was revealed a story that part of him didn't want to revisit while another part wanted to live it over again.

Robert touched a necklace hidden under his shirt. He'd worn it most of his life. There were nine olive pits on the string. Shao-mei had spent hours sanding off the pointed ends of the pits, then drilling holes in them with little needles. She said the necklace would bring him luck. Tears filled his eyes. Poor Shao-mei, he thought. She had never known the love and affection she so deserved. Then he wondered how long he had before he joined the sisters.

Someone draped a cape over his shoulders. "Master," Guan-jiah said, "what have I told you about keeping warm? Even in spring, the sea air can be cool."

###

Printed in Germany
by Amazon Distribution
GmbH, Leipzig